LABYRINTH

LABYRINTH

Kate Mosse

G.P. Putnam's Sons
New York

G. P. PUTNAM'S SONS

Publishers Since 1838

Published by the Penguin Group

Penguin Group (USA) Inc., 375 Hudson Street, New York, New York 10014, USA · Penguin
Group (Canada), 90 Eglinton Avenue East, Suite 700, Toronto, Ontario M4P 2Y3, Canada (a
division of Pearson Penguin Canada Inc.) · Penguin Books Ltd, 80 Strand, London WC2R
0RL, England · Penguin Ireland, 25 St Stephen's Green, Dublin 2, Ireland (a division of
Penguin Books Ltd) · Penguin Group (Australia), 250 Camberwell Road, Camberwell, Victoria
3124, Australia (a division of Pearson Australia Group Pty Ltd) · Penguin Books India Pvt Ltd,
11 Community Centre, Panchsheel Park, New Delhi-110 017, India · Penguin Group (NZ), Cnr
Airborne and Rosedale Roads, Albany, Auckland 1310, New Zealand (a division of Pearson New
Zealand Ltd) · Penguin Books (South Africa) (Pty) Ltd, 24 Sturdee Avenue, Rosebank,
Johannesburg 2196, South Africa

Penguin Books Ltd, Registered Offices:
80 Strand, London WC2R 0RL, England

Copyright © 2005 by Mosse Associates Ltd
First edition: Orion Publishing Group 2005
First American edition: G. P. Putnam's Sons 2006

ISBN 0-399-15344-6

Printed in the United States of America

This is a work of fiction. Names, characters, places, and incidents either are the product of the
author's imagination or are used fictitiously, and, except where stated, any resemblance to actual
persons, living or dead, businesses, companies, events, or locales is entirely coincidental.

While the author has made every effort to provide accurate telephone numbers and Internet
addresses at the time of publication, neither the publisher nor the author assumes any
responsibility for errors, or for changes that occur after publication. Further, the publisher does not
have any control over and does not assume any responsibility for author or third-party websites or
their content.

To Greg, as always, for all things—
past, present and yet to come

To my father, Richard Mosse, a man of integrity—
a modern-day chevalier

And to Leona Nevler, Publisher Extraordinaire,
1926–2005
A great friend to *Labyrinth*—and a
real-life pioneering woman

CONTENTS

ACKNOWLEDGMENTS

Many friends and colleagues have given support, advice and help during the course of the writing of *Labyrinth*. It goes without saying that any mistakes, in either fact or interpretation, are mine and mine alone.

My agent, Mark Lucas, was brilliant throughout and gave not only fantastic editorial feedback but copious yellow stickers! Thanks, too, to everyone else at Lucas Alexander Whitley for their hard work; to everybody at the International Literary Agency, especially Nicki Kennedy, who was patience personified and helped make the process such fun; and to George Lucas at Inlewell Management.

At Orion, I've been very lucky to have worked with Kate Mills, Malcolm Edwards and Susan Lamb; I have been lucky with all my foreign publishers, especially Leona Nevler at G. P. Putnam's Sons and the whole team there.

Both Bob Elliott and Bob Clack, of the Chichester Rifle Club, gave fascinating advice and information about firearms; as did Professor Anthony Moss on medieval warfare.

At the British Library in London, Dr. Michelle Brown, curator of Illuminated Manuscripts, provided invaluable information about medieval manuscripts, parchments and bookmaking in the thirteenth century; Dr. Jonathan Phillips, senior lecturer in Medieval History, Royal Holloway, University of London, very kindly read the typescript and gave excellent advice. I'd also like to thank all those who helped at the Bibliothèque de Toulouse and at the Centre National d'Études Cathares in Carcassonne.

I'd like to thank all those at Orange who have worked with us on the creative reading and writing Web site—www.orangelabyrinth.co.uk—based on the historical research and process of writing *Labyrinth* over the past couple of years.

I'm very grateful to all my friends, too many to name individually, for their tolerance about my longtime obsessions with the Cathars and Grail legends. In Carcassonne, I'd particularly like to thank Yves and Lydia Guyou for their insights into Occitan music and poetry and for introducing me to many of the writers and composers whose work has so inspired me; and Pierre and Chantal Sanchez for their support and friendship over many years. In England, I'd like to mention Jane Gregory, whose enthusiasm way back when was so important; Maria Rejt, for being such a great teacher in the first place; as well as Jon Evans, Lucinda Montefiore, Robert Dye, Sarah Mansell, Tim Bouquet, Ali Perrotto, Malcolm Wills and Robert and Maria Pulley for their support and interest over many bottles of *vin de pays d'Oc*!

Most of all, my thanks go to my family. My mother-in-law, Rosie Turner, not only introduced us to Carcassonne in the first place, but while I was writing provided day-to-day help, practical support and companionship well beyond the call of duty; my love and thanks to my parents, Richard and Barbara Mosse, and to my sisters, Caroline Matthews and Beth Huxley.

Most important, my love and gratitude to my husband, Greg, and our children, Martha and Felix, for their steadfast support and faith. Martha was relentlessly upbeat, positive and encouraging, never doubting that I would finish in the end! Felix not only shared my passion for medieval history, but talked me through the finer points of medieval weapons and siege warfare and made brainy suggestions! I cannot thank either of them enough.

Finally, to Greg. His love and support—not to mention his emotional, intellectual, practical and editorial help and hard work—made all the difference. As they always have done and always will.

HISTORICAL NOTE

In March 1208, Pope Innocent III preached a Crusade against a sect of Christians in the Languedoc. They are now usually known as Cathars. They called themselves *Bons Chrétiens*, Bernard of Clairvaux called them Albigensians and the Inquisitional Registers refer to them as *heretici*. Pope Innocent aimed to drive the Cathars from the Midi and restore the religious authority of the Catholic Church. The northern French barons who joined his Crusade saw an opportunity to acquire land, wealth and trading advantage by subjugating the fiercely independent southern nobility.

Although the principle of crusading had been an important fixture of medieval Christian life since the late eleventh century—and during the Fourth Crusade at the siege of Zara in 1204 Crusaders had turned on fellow Christians—this was the first time a Holy War had been preached against Christians and on European soil. The persecution of the Cathars led directly to the founding of the Inquisition in 1233 under the auspices of the Dominicans, the Black Friars.

Whatever the religious motivations of the Catholic Church and some of the Crusade's temporal leaders—such as Simon de Montfort—the Albigensian Crusade was ultimately a war of occupation and marked a turning point in the history of what is now France. It signified the end of the independence of the south and the destruction of many of its traditions, ideals and way of life.

Like the term *Cathar*, the word *Crusade* was not used in medieval documents. The army was referred to as the Host—or *l'Ost* in Oc. However, since both terms are now in common usage, I've sometimes borrowed them for ease of reference. Further information on the language of the time is provided at the end of this book, along with a glossary.

And ye shall know the truth, and the truth shall make you free.   —Gospel according to John 8:32

L'histoire est un roman qui a été, le roman est une histoire qui aurait pu être.
History is a novel that has been lived, a novel is history that could have been.   —Edmond & Jules de Goncourt

Ten perdu, jhamai se recobro.
Time lost can never be regained.
                    —Medieval Occitan proverb

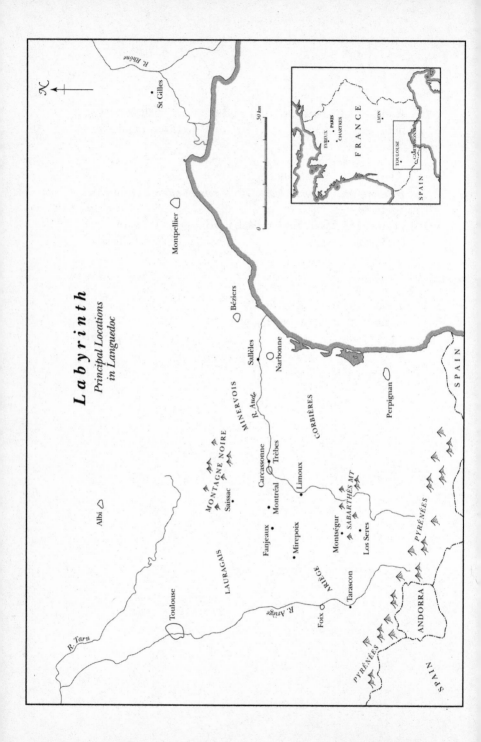

PROLOGUE

I

Pic de Soularac
Sabarthès Mountains
Southwest France

MONDAY, 4 JULY 2005

A single line of blood trickles down the pale underside of her arm, a red seam on a white sleeve.

At first, Alice thinks it's just a fly and takes no notice. Insects are an occupational hazard at a dig, and for some reason there are more flies higher up the mountain where she is working than at the main excavation site lower down. Then a drop of blood splashes onto her bare leg, exploding like a firework in the sky on Guy Fawkes night.

This time she does look and sees that the cut on the inside of her elbow has opened again. It's a deep wound, which doesn't want to heal. She sighs and pushes the plaster and lint dressing tighter against her skin. Then, since there's no one around to see, she licks the red smear from her wrist.

Strands of hair, the color of soft brown sugar, have come loose from under her cap. She tucks them behind her ears and wipes her forehead with her handkerchief, before twisting her ponytail back into a tight knot at the nape of her neck.

Her concentration broken, Alice stands up and stretches her slim legs, lightly tanned by the sun. Dressed in cutoff denim shorts, a tight white sleeveless T-shirt and cap, she looks little more than a teenager. She used to mind. Now, as she gets older, she sees the advantage of looking younger than her years. The only touches of glamour are her delicate silver earrings, in the shape of stars, which glint like sequins.

Alice unscrews the top of her water bottle. It's warm, but she's too thirsty to care and drinks it down in great gulps. Below, the heat haze shimmers above the dented tarmac of the road. Above her, the sky is an endless blue. The cicadas keep up their unrelenting chorus, hidden in the shade of the dry grass.

It's her first time in the Pyrenees, although she feels very much at home. She's been told that in the winter the jagged peaks of the Sabarthès Mountains are covered with snow. In the spring, delicate flowers of pink and mauve and white peep out from their hiding places in the great expanses of rock. In early summer, the pastures are green and speckled with yellow buttercups. But now, the sun has flattened the land into submission, turning the greens to brown. It is a beautiful place, she thinks, yet somehow an inhospitable one. It's a place of secrets, one that has seen too much and concealed too much to be at peace with itself.

In the main camp on the lower slopes, Alice can see her colleagues standing under the big canvas awning. She can just pick out Shelagh in her trademark black outfit. She's surprised they've stopped already. It's early in the day to be taking a break, but then the whole team is a bit demoralized.

It's painstaking and monotonous work for the most part, the digging and scraping, the cataloguing and recording, and so far they've turned up little of significance to justify their efforts. They've come across a few fragments of early medieval pots and bowls, and a couple of late twelfth- or early thirteenth-century arrowheads, but certainly no evidence of the Paleolithic settlement which is the focus of the excavation.

Alice is tempted to go down and join her friends and colleagues and get her dressing sorted out. The cut smarts and her calves are already aching from squatting. The muscles in her shoulders are tense. But she knows that if she stops now, she'll lose her momentum.

Hopefully, her luck's about to change. Earlier, she'd noticed something glinting beneath a large boulder, propped against the side of the mountain, neat and tidy, almost as if it had been placed there by a giant hand. Although she can't make out what the object is, even how big it is, she's been digging all morning and she doesn't think it will be much longer before she can reach it.

She knows she should fetch someone. Or at least tell Shelagh, her best friend, who is the deputy on the dig. Alice is not a trained archeologist, just a volunteer spending some of her summer holiday doing something worthwhile. But it's her last full day on site and she wants to prove herself. If she goes back down to the main camp now and admits she's on to something, everybody will want to be involved, and it will no longer be her discovery.

In the days and weeks to come, Alice will look back to this moment. She will remember the quality of the light, the metallic taste of blood and dust in her mouth, and wonder at how different things might have been had she made the choice to go and not to stay. If she had played by the rules.

She drains the last drop of water from the bottle and tosses it into her rucksack. For the next hour or so, as the sun climbs higher in the sky and the temperature rises, Alice carries on working. The only sounds are the scrape of metal on rock, the whine of insects and the occasional buzz of a light aircraft in the distance. She can feel beads of sweat on her upper lip and between her breasts, but she keeps going until, finally, the gap underneath the boulder is big enough for her to slide in her hand.

Alice kneels down on the ground and leans her cheek and shoulder against the rock for support. Then, with a flutter of excitement, she pushes her fingers deep into the dark, blind earth. Straight away, she knows her instincts are right and that she's got something worth finding. It is smooth and slimy to the touch, metal not stone. Grasping it firmly and telling herself not to expect too much, slowly, slowly she eases the object out into the light. The earth seems to shudder, reluctant to give up its treasure.

The rich, cloying smell of wet soil fills her nose and throat, although she barely notices. She is already lost in the past, captivated by the piece of history she cradles in the palms of her hands. It is a heavy, round buckle, speckled black and green with age and from its long burial. Alice rubs at it with her fingers and smiles as the silver and copper detail starts to reveal itself underneath the dirt. At first glance, it looks to be medieval too, the sort of buckle used to fasten a cloak or robe. She's seen something like it before.

She knows the danger of jumping to conclusions or of being seduced by first impressions, yet she can't resist imagining its owner, long dead now, who might have walked these paths. A stranger whose story she has yet to learn.

The connection is so strong and Alice is so absorbed that she doesn't notice the boulder shifting on its base. Then something, some sixth sense, makes her look up. For a split second, the world seems to hang suspended, out of space, out of time. She is mesmerized by the ancient slab of stone as it sways and tilts, and then gracefully begins to fall toward her.

At the very last moment, the light fractures. The spell is broken. Alice throws herself out of the way, half tumbling, half slithering sideways, just in time to avoid being crushed. The boulder hits the ground with a dull thud, sending up a cloud of pale brown dust, then rolls over and over, as if in slow motion, until it comes to rest farther down the mountain.

Alice clutches desperately at the bushes and scrub to stop herself slipping any farther. For a moment she lies sprawled in the dirt, dizzy and disorientated. As it sinks in how very close she came to being crushed, she turns cold. *Too close for comfort*, she thinks. She takes a deep breath. Waits for the world to stop spinning.

Gradually, the pounding in her head dies away. The sickness in her stomach settles and everything starts to return to normal, enough for her to sit up and take stock. Her knees are grazed and streaked with blood and she's knocked her wrist where she landed awkwardly, still clutching the buckle in her hand to protect it, but basically she's escaped with no more than a few cuts and bruises. *I'm not hurt.*

She gets to her feet and dusts herself down, feeling a total idiot. She can't believe she made such a basic mistake as not securing the boulder. Now Alice looks down to the main campsite below. She's amazed—and relieved—that nobody in the camp seems to have seen or heard anything. She raises her hand, is about to call out to attract someone's attention when she notices that there's a narrow opening visible in the side of the mountain where the boulder had been standing. Like a doorway cut into the rock.

It's said these mountains are riddled with hidden passages and caves, so she's not surprised. And yet, Alice thinks, somehow, she knew the doorway was there, although there's no way of telling from the outside. *Guessed, more like.*

She hesitates. Alice knows she should get somebody to come with her. It is stupid, possibly even dangerous, to go in on her own without any sort of backup. She knows all the things that can go wrong. But she shouldn't have been up here working on her own anyway. Shelagh doesn't know. And besides, something is drawing her in. It feels personal. It's her discovery.

Alice tells herself there's no sense disturbing them all, getting their hopes up, for no reason. If there is anything worth investigating, she'll tell someone then. She won't do anything. She just wants to look.

I'll only be a minute.

She climbs back up. There is a deep depression in the ground at the mouth of the cave, where the stone had stood guard. The damp earth is alive with the frantic writhing of worms and beetles exposed suddenly to the light and heat after so long. Her cap lies on the ground where it fell. Her trowel is there too, just where she left it.

Alice peers into the darkness. The opening is no more than one and one-half meters high and about a meter wide and the edges are irregular and rough. It seems to be natural rather than man-made, although when she runs her fingers up and down the rock, she finds curiously smooth patches where the boulder rested.

Slowly, her eyes become accustomed to the gloom. Velvet black gives way to charcoal gray and she sees that she is looking into a long, narrow tunnel. She feels the short hairs rise on the back of her neck, as if to warn her that there is something lurking in the darkness that would be better left undisturbed. But that's just a childish superstition and she brushes the feeling away. Alice doesn't believe in ghosts or premonitions.

Squeezing the buckle tightly in her hand, like a talisman, she takes a deep breath and steps forward into the passageway. Straight away, the smell of long-hidden, subterranean air envelops her, filling her mouth and throat and lungs. It's cool and damp, not the dry, poisonous gases of a sealed cave she's been warned about, so she guesses there must be some source of fresh air. But, just in case, she rummages in the pockets of her cut-offs until she finds her lighter. She flicks it open and holds it up to the dark, double-checking that there is oxygen. The flame gutters in a breath of wind, but it does not go out.

Feeling nervous and slightly guilty, Alice wraps the buckle in a hand-kerchief and pushes it into her pocket, then cautiously steps forward. The light from the flame is weak, but it illuminates the path immediately in front of her, throwing shadows on the jagged gray walls.

As she moves farther in, she feels the chill air curl around her bare legs and arms like a cat. She is walking downhill. She can feel the ground slop-ing away beneath her feet, uneven and gritty. The scrunch of the stones and gravel is loud in the confined, hushed space. She is aware of the day-light getting fainter and fainter at her back, the farther and deeper she goes.

Abruptly, she does not want to go on. She does not want to be here at all. Yet there is something inevitable about it, something that is drawing her deeper into the belly of the mountain.

After another ten meters the tunnel comes to an end. Alice finds her-self standing at the threshold of a cavernous enclosed chamber. She is standing on a natural stone platform. A couple of shallow, wide steps di-rectly in front of her lead to the main area where the ground has been lev-eled flat and smooth. The cavern is about ten meters long and perhaps five meters wide, clearly fashioned by the hands of men rather than by nature alone. The roof is low and vaulted, like the ceiling of a crypt.

Alice stares, holding the flickering single flame higher and bothered by a curious prickling familiarity that she cannot account for. She is about to descend the steps when she notices there are letters inscribed in the stone at the top. She bends down and tries to read what is written. Only the first three words and the last letter—*N* or *H* maybe—are legible. The others have been eroded or chipped away. Alice rubs at the dirt with her fingers and says the letters out loud. The echo of her voice sounds somehow hos-tile and threatening in the silence.

"*P-A-S A P-A-S . . . Pas a pas.*"

Step by step? Step by step what? A faint memory ripples across the sur-face of her unconscious mind, like a song long forgotten. Then it is gone.

"*Pas a pas,*" she whispers this time, but it means nothing. A prayer? A warning? Without knowing what follows, it makes no sense.

Nervous now, she straightens up and descends the steps, one by one.

Curiosity fights with premonition and she feels the goosebumps on her slim bare arms, from unease or the chill of the cave, she cannot say.

Alice holds the flame high to light her way, careful not to slip or dislodge anything. At the lower level, she pauses. She takes a deep breath and then takes a step into the ebony darkness. She can just make out the back wall of the chamber.

It's hard to be sure at this distance that it isn't just a trick of the light or a shadow cast by the flame, but it looks as if there is a large circular pattern of lines and semicircles painted or carved into the rock. On the floor in front of it there is a stone table, a little over a meter, like an altar.

Fixing her eyes on the symbol on the wall to keep her bearings, Alice edges forward. Now she can see the pattern more clearly. It looks like some sort of labyrinth, although memory tells her that there is something not quite right about it. It's not a true labyrinth. The lines do not lead to the center, as they should. The pattern is wrong. Alice can't account for why she's so sure about this, only that she is right.

Keeping her eyes trained on the labyrinth, she moves closer, closer. Her foot knocks something hard on the ground. There is a faint, hollow thump and the sound of something rolling, as if an object has shifted out of position.

Alice looks down.

Her legs start to tremble. The pale flame in her hand flickers. Shock steals her breath. She is standing at the edge of a shallow grave, a slight depression in the ground, no more than that. In it there are two skeletons, once human, the bones picked clean by time. The blind sockets of one skull stare up at her. The other skull, kicked out of place by her foot, is lying on its side as if turning its gaze away from her.

The bodies have been laid out, side by side, to face the altar, like carvings on a tomb. They are symmetrical and perfectly in line, but there is nothing restful about the grave. No sense of peace. The cheekbones of one skull are crushed, crumpled inwards like a mask of papier mâché. Several of the ribs of the other skeleton are snapped and jut out awkwardly, like the brittle branches of a dead tree.

They cannot harm you. Determined not to give in to the fear, Alice forces herself to crouch down, taking care not to disturb anything else. She runs her eyes over the grave. There is a dagger lying between the bodies, the blade dulled with age, and a few fragments of cloth. Next to it, there is a drawstring leather bag, big enough to hold a small box or a book. Alice frowns. She's sure she's seen something like it before, but the memory refuses to come.

The round, white object wedged between the clawlike fingers of the smaller skeleton is so small that Alice nearly misses it. Without stopping to think if it's the right thing to do, quickly she takes her tweezers out of her pocket. She stretches down and carefully eases it out, then holds it up to the flame, softly blowing the dust away to see better.

It's a small stone ring, plain and unremarkable, with a round, smooth face. It, too, is oddly familiar. Alice looks more closely. There's a pattern scratched on the inside. At first, she thinks it's a seal of some kind. Then, with a jolt, she realizes. She raises her eyes to the markings on the back wall of the chamber, then back to the ring.

The patterns are identical.

Alice is not religious. She does not believe in heaven or hell, in God or the Devil, nor in the creatures that are believed to haunt these mountains. But, for the first time in her life, she is overwhelmed by a sense of being in the presence of something supernatural, something inexplicable, something bigger than her experience or comprehension. She can feel malevolence crawling over her skin, her scalp, the soles of her feet.

Her courage falters. The cave is suddenly cold. Fear catches in her throat, freezing the breath in her lungs. Alice scrambles to her feet. She should not be here in this ancient place. Now, she's desperate to get out of the chamber, away from the evidence of violence and the smell of death, back to the safe, bright sunlight.

But she's too late.

Above her or behind her, she cannot tell where, there are footsteps. The sound bounces around the confined space, ricochets off the rock and stone. Someone is coming.

Alice spins around in alarm, dropping the lighter. The cave is plunged into darkness. She tries to run, but she is disorientated in the dark and cannot find the way out. She stumbles. Her legs go from under her.

She falls. The ring is sent flying back into the pile of bones, where it belongs.

II

Carcassonne
Southwest France

A few miles to the east as the crow flies, in a lost village in the Sabarthès Mountains, a tall, thin man in a pale suit sits alone at a table of dark, highly polished wood.

The ceiling of the room is low and there are large square tiles on the floor the color of red mountain earth, keeping it cool despite the heat outside. The shutter of the single window is closed so it is dark, except for a pool of yellow light cast by a small oil lamp, which stands on the table. Next to the lamp is a glass tumbler filled almost to the brim with a red liquid.

There are several sheets of heavy cream paper strewn across the table, each covered with line after line of neat handwriting in black ink. The room is silent, except for the scratch and draw of the pen and the chink of ice cubes against the side of the glass when he drinks. The subtle scent of alcohol and cherries. The ticking of the clock marks the passage of time as he pauses, reflects, and then writes again.

What we leave behind in this life is the memory of who we were and what we did. An imprint, no more. I have learned much. I have become wise. But have I made a difference? I cannot tell. Pas a pas, se va luènh.

I have watched the green of spring give way to the gold of summer, the copper of autumn give way to the white of winter as I have sat and waited for the fading of the light. Over and over again I have asked myself why? If I had known how it would feel to live with such loneliness, to stand, the sole witness to the endless cycle of birth and life and death, what would I have done? Alaïs, I am burdened by my solitude stretched too thin to bear. I have survived this long life with emptiness in my heart, an emptiness that over the years has spread and spread until it became bigger than my heart itself.

I have striven to keep my promises to you. The one is fulfilled, the other left undone. Until now, left undone. For some time now, I have felt you close. Our time is nearly come again. Everything points to this. Soon the cave will be opened. I feel the truth of this all around me. And the book, safe for so long, will be found also.

The man pauses and reaches for his glass. His eyes are smudged with memory, but the Guignolet is strong and sweet and it revives him.

I have found her. At last. And I wonder, if I place the book in her hands, will it feel familiar? Is the memory of it written in her blood and her bones? Will she remember how the cover shimmers and shifts its color? If she undoes the ties and opens it, careful so as not to damage the dry and brittle vellum, will she remember the words echoing back down the centuries?

I pray that at last, as my long days draw to a close, I will have the chance to put right what once I did ill, that I will at last learn the truth. The truth will set me free.

The man sits back in his chair and puts his hands, speckled brown with age, flat on the table in front of him. The chance to know, after so very long, what happened at the end.

It is all he wants.

III

Chartres
Northern France

Later that same day, over nine hundred kilometers to the north, another man stands in a dimly lit passageway under the streets of Chartres, waiting for the ceremony to begin.

His palms are sweaty, his mouth is dry and he's aware of every nerve, every muscle in his body, even the pulse in the veins at his temples. He feels self-conscious and lightheaded, although whether this is down to nerves and anticipation or the aftereffects of the wine, he can't tell. The unfamiliar white cotton robes hang heavy on his shoulders and the ropes made out of twisted hemp rest awkwardly on his bony hips. He steals a quick glance at the two figures standing in silence on either side of him, but their hoods conceal their faces. He can't tell if they are as edgy as he or if they have been through the ritual many times before. They're dressed the same, except their robes are gold rather than white and they have shoes on their feet. His feet are bare and the flagstones are cold.

High above the hidden network of tunnels, the bells of the great Gothic cathedral begin to chime. He feels the men beside him stiffen. It's the signal they've been waiting for. Immediately, he drops his head and tries to focus on the moment.

"*Je suis prêt*," he mumbles, more to reassure himself than as a statement of fact. Neither of his companions reacts in any way.

As the final reverberation of the bells fades to silence, the acolyte on his left steps forward and, with a stone partially concealed in the palm of his hand, strikes five times on the massive door. From inside comes the answer. "*Dintrar.*" Enter.

The man half-thinks he recognizes the woman's voice, but he has no time to guess from where or from when, because already the door is opening to reveal the chamber that he has waited so long to see.

Keeping step with one another, the three figures walk slowly forward. He's rehearsed this and knows what to expect, knows what is required of him, although he feels a little unsteady on his feet. The room is hot after the chill of the corridor and it is dark. The only light comes from the candles arranged in the alcoves and on the altar itself, setting shadows dancing on the floor.

Adrenaline is coursing through his body, although he feels strangely detached from the proceedings. When the door falls shut behind him, he jumps.

The four senior attendants stand to the north, south, east and west of the chamber. He desperately wants to raise his eyes and take a better look, but he forces himself to keep his head down and his face hidden, as he has been instructed. He can sense the two rows of initiates lining the long sides of the rectangular chamber, six on each side. He can feel the heat of their bodies and hear the rise and fall of their breathing, even though nobody is moving and nobody speaks.

He's memorized the layout from the papers he was given and as he walks toward the sepulchre in the middle of the chamber, he's aware of their eyes on his back. He wonders if he knows any of them. Business colleagues, other people's wives, anybody might be a member. He can't help a faint smile reaching his lips, as he allows himself for a moment to fantasize about the difference his acceptance into the society will make.

He's brought sharply back to the present when he stumbles and nearly falls over the kneeling stone at the base of the sepulchre. The chamber is smaller than he imagined from the plan, more confined and claustrophobic. He had expected the distance between the door and the stone to be greater.

As he kneels down on the stone there is a sharp intake of breath from someone close to him, and he wonders why. His heart starts to beat faster and when he glances down he sees that his knuckles are white. Embarrassed, he clasps his hands together, before remembering and letting his arms drop to his side, where they are supposed to be.

There is a slight dip in the center of the stone, which is hard and cold on his knees through the thin material of his robe. He shuffles slightly, trying to get into an easier position. The discomfort gives him something to focus on and he is grateful for that. He still feels dizzy and he's finding it difficult to concentrate or to recall the order in which things are supposed to happen, even though he's gone over it time and time again in his mind.

A bell begins to ring inside the chamber, a high, thin note; a low chanting accompanies it, soft at first, but quickly growing louder as more voices join in. Fragments of words and phrases reverberate through his head: *montanhas*, mountains; *Noblesa*, nobility; *libres*, books; *graal*, grail . . .

The priestess steps down from the high altar and walks through the chamber. He can just make out the soft shuffle of her feet and imagines how her golden robe will be shimmering and swaying in the flickering light of the candles. This is the moment he has been waiting for.

"*Je suis prêt,*" he repeats under his breath. This time he means it.

The priestess comes to a standstill in front of him. He can smell her perfume, subtle and light under the heady aroma of the incense. He catches his breath as she leans down and takes his hand. Her fingers are cool and manicured and a shot of electricity, almost of desire, shoots up his arm as she presses something small and round into the palm of his hand, then closes his fingers over it. Now he wants—more than anything he's ever wanted in his life—to look at her face. But he keeps his eyes down on the ground, as he has been told to do.

The four senior attendants leave their positions and move to join the priestess. His head is tipped back, gently, and a thick, sweet liquid slides between his lips. It is what he is expecting and he makes no resistance. As the warmth sweeps through his body he holds up his arms and his companions slip a golden mantle over his shoulders. The ritual is familiar to the witnesses and yet he can sense their unease.

Suddenly, he feels as if there is an iron band around his neck, crushing his windpipe. His hands fly up to his throat as he struggles for breath. He tries to call out, but the words won't come. The high thin note of the bell starts to toll once more, steady and persistent, drowning him out. A wave of nausea sweeps through him. He thinks he's going to pass out and clutches the object in his hand for comfort, so hard that his nails split open the soft flesh of his palm. The sharp pain helps him not to fall. He now understands that the hands on his shoulders are not comforting. They are not supporting him, but holding him down. Another wave of nausea overwhelms him and the stone seems to shift and slide beneath him.

Now his eyes are swimming and he cannot focus properly, but he can see that the priestess has a knife, though he has no idea how the silver blade came to be in her hand. He tries to stand, but the drug is too strong and has already taken his strength from him. He no longer has control over his arms or legs.

"*Non!*" he tries to shout, but it is too late.

At first, he thinks he's been punched between the shoulders, nothing more. Then a dull ache starts to seep through his body. Something warm and smooth is trickling slowly down his back.

Without warning, the hands let him go and he falls forward, crumpling like a rag doll as the floor comes up to meet him. He feels no pain as his head hits the ground, which is somehow cool and soothing against his skin. Now, all noise and confusion and fear are fading away. His eyes flicker shut. He is no longer aware of anything other than her voice, which seems to be coming from a long way away.

"Une leçon. Pour tous," she seems to be saying, although that makes no sense.

In his last fractured moments of consciousness, the man accused of giving away secrets, condemned for talking when he should have kept silent, holds the coveted object tight in his hand until his grip on life slips away and the small gray disc, no bigger than a coin, rolls onto the floor.

On one side of it are the letters *NV.* On the other is an engraving of a labyrinth.

IV
Pic de Soularac
Sabarthès Mountains

For a moment, everything is silent.

Then the darkness melts. Alice is no longer in the cave. She is floating in a white, weightless world, transparent and peaceful and silent.

She is free. Safe.

Alice has the sensation of slipping out of time, as if she is falling from one dimension into another. The line between the past and present is fading now in this timeless, endless space.

Then, like a trap door beneath the gallows, Alice feels a sudden jerk, then a drop and she is plummeting down through the open sky, falling, falling down toward the wooded mountainside. The brisk air whistles in her ears as she plunges, faster, harder toward the ground.

The moment of impact never comes. There's no splintering of bone against the slate gray flint and rock. Instead, Alice hits the ground running, stumbling along a steep, rough woodland track between two columns of high trees. They are dense and tall and tower above her so she can't see what lies beyond.

Too fast.

Alice grabs at the branches as if they will slow her, stop this headlong flight toward this unknown place, but her hands go straight through as if she's a ghost or a spirit. Clumps of tiny leaves come away in her hands, like hair from a brush. She cannot feel them, but the sap stains the tips of her fingers green. She puts them up to her face, to breathe in their subtle, sour scent. She cannot smell them either.

Alice has a stitch in her side, but she cannot stop because there is something behind her, getting steadily closer. The path is sloping sharply beneath her feet. She is aware that the crunch of dried root and stone has replaced the soft earth, moss and twigs. Still, there is no sound. No birds singing, no voices calling, nothing but her own ragged breathing. The path twists and coils back on itself, sending her scuttling this way and that, until she rounds the corner and sees the silent wall of flame which blocks the path ahead. A pillar of twisting fire, white and gold and red, folding in on itself, its shape ever shifting.

Instinctively, Alice puts up her hands to shield her face from the fierce heat, although she cannot feel it. She can see faces trapped within the dancing flames, the mouths contorted in silent agony as the fire caresses and burns.

Alice tries to stop. She must stop. Her feet are bleeding and torn, her long skirts wet, slowing her down, but her pursuer is hard at her heels and something beyond her control is driving her on into the fatal embrace of the fire.

She has no choice but to jump, to avoid being consumed by the flames. She spirals up into the air like a wisp of smoke, floating high above the yellows and oranges. The wind seems to carry her up, releasing her from the earth.

Someone is calling her name, a woman's voice, although she pronounces it strangely.

Alaïs.

She is safe. Free.

Then, the familiar clutch of cold fingers on her ankles, shackling her to the ground. No, not fingers, chains. Now Alice realizes she is holding something in her hands, a book, held together with leather ties. She understands that it is this that he wants. What *they* want. It is the loss of this book that makes them angry.

If only she could speak she could perhaps strike a bargain. But her head is empty of words and her mouth incapable of speech. She lashes out, kicks to escape, but she is caught. The iron grip on her legs is too strong. She starts to scream as she is dragged back down into the fire, but there is only silence.

She screams again, feeling her voice struggling deep inside her to be heard. This time, the sound comes rushing back. Alice feels the real world rushing back. Sound, light, smell, touch, the metallic taste of blood in her mouth. Until, for a fraction of a second, she pauses, enveloped suddenly by a translucent cold. It is not the familiar chill of the cave, but something different, intense and bright. Within it, Alice can just make out the fleeting outline of a face, beautiful, indistinct. The same voice is calling her name once more.

Alaïs.

Calling for the last time. It is the voice of a friend. Not someone who means her harm. Alice struggles to open her eyes, knowing that if she could see, she could understand. She cannot. Not quite.

The dream is starting to fade, setting her free.

It's time to wake up. I must wake up.

Now there's another voice in her head, different from the first. The feeling is coming back to her arms and legs, her grazed knees that sting and her scuffed skin that is sore where she fell. She can feel the rough grip on her shoulder, shaking her back to life.

"Alice! Alice, wake up!"

THE CITÉ ON THE HILL

CHAPTER 1

Carcassona

JULHET 1209

Alaïs jolted awake, bolt upright, her eyes wide open. Fear fluttered in her chest, as a bird caught in a net struggles to be free. She pressed her hand against her ribs to still her beating heart.

For a moment, she was neither asleep nor awake, as if some part of her had been left behind in the dream. She felt she was floating, looking down on herself from a great height, like the stone gargoyles that grimaced at passersby from the roof of the cathedral church of Sant-Nasari.

The room came back into focus. She was safe in her own bed, in the Château Comtal. Gradually, her eyes became accustomed to the dark. She was safe from the thin, dark-eyed people who haunted her at night, their sharp fingers clawing and pulling at her. *They cannot reach me now.* The language carved in the stones, more pictures than words, which meant nothing to her, all vanished like wisps of smoke in the autumn air. The fire too had faded, leaving only a memory in her mind.

A premonition? Or a nightmare only?

She had no way of knowing. She was afraid of knowing.

Alaïs reached for the night-curtains, which were hung around the bed, as if by touching something substantial she would feel less transparent and insubstantial herself. The worn cloth, filled with the dust and familiar smells of the castle, was reassuringly coarse between her fingers.

Night after night, the same dream. All through her childhood, when she had woken in terror in the dark, her face white and wet with tears, her father had been at her bedside, watching over her as if she was a son. As each candle burned down and another was lit, he whispered of his adventures in the Holy Land. He told her of the endless seas of the desert, the curve and sweep of the mosques and the call to prayer of the Saracen faithful. He described the aromatic spices, the vivid colors and the peppery taste of the food. The terrible brilliance of the blood-red sun as it set over Jerusalem.

For many years, in those hollow hours between dusk and dawn, as her sister lay sleeping beside her, her father had talked and talked, setting her demons to flight. He had not allowed the black cowls or the Catholic priests to come near, with their superstitions and false symbols.

His words had saved her.

"Guilhem?" she whispered.

Her husband was deeply asleep, his arms flung out claiming ownership of most of the bed. His long dark hair, smelling of smoke and wine and the stables, was fanned across the pillow. Moonlight fell through the open window, the shutter pinned back to let the cool night air into the chamber. In the gathering light, Alaïs could see the shadow of rough growth on his chin. The chain Guilhem wore around his neck shimmered and glinted as he shifted position in his sleep.

Alaïs wanted him to wake and tell her that everything was all right, that she didn't have to be afraid anymore. But he did not stir and it did not occur to her to wake him. Fearless in all other things, she was inexperienced in the ways of marriage and cautious with him still, so she contented herself with running her fingers down his smooth, tanned arms and across his shoulders, firm and broad from the hours spent practicing with sword and quintain for the joust. Alaïs could feel the life moving beneath his skin even as he slept. And when she remembered how they had spent the early part of the night, she blushed, even though there was no one there to see.

Alaïs was overwhelmed by the sensations Guilhem aroused in her. She delighted in the way her heart leaped when she caught unexpected sight of him, the way the ground shifted beneath her feet when he smiled at her. At the same time, she did not like the feeling of powerlessness. She feared love was making her weak, giddy. She did not doubt she loved Guilhem and yet she knew she was keeping a little of herself back.

Alaïs sighed. All she could hope was that, with time, it would become easier.

There was something in the quality of the light, black fading to gray, and the occasional hint of birdsong from the trees in the courtyard, which told her that dawn was not far away. She knew she wouldn't go back to sleep now.

Alaïs slipped out between the curtains and tiptoed across to the wardrobe that stood in the far corner of the chamber. The flagstones were cold under her feet and the rush matting scratched her toes. She opened the lid, removed the lavender bag from the top of the pile, and took out a plain, dark green dress. Shivering a little, she stepped into it, threading her arms into the narrow sleeves. She pulled the material, slightly damp, over her undershift, then fastened the girdle tightly.

Alaïs was seventeen and had been married for six months, but she had not yet acquired the softness and sway of a woman. The dress hung shapelessly on her narrow frame, as if it didn't belong to her. Steadying herself with her hand on the table, she pushed her feet into soft leather slippers and took her favorite red cloak from the back of the chair. Its edges and hem were embroidered with an intricate blue and green pattern of squares and diamonds, interspersed with tiny yellow flowers, which she had designed herself for her wedding day. It had taken her weeks and weeks to sew. All through November and December she had worked at it, her fingers growing sore and stiff with cold as she hurried to have it finished in time.

Alaïs turned her attention to her *panièr*, which stood on the floor beside the wardrobe. She checked her herb pouch and purse were there, together with the strips of cloth for wrapping plants and roots and her tools for digging and cutting. Finally, she fixed her cloak firmly at her neck with a ribbon, slipped her knife into its sheath at her waist, pulled her hood up over her head to cover her long, unbraided hair, then quietly crept across the chamber and out into the deserted corridor. The door closed with a thud behind her.

It was not yet Prime, so there was nobody about in the living quarters. Alaïs walked quickly along the corridor, her cloak swishing softly against the stone floor, heading for the steep and narrow stairs. She stepped over a serving boy slumped asleep against a wall outside the door to the room her sister, Oriane, shared with her husband.

As she descended lower, the sound of voices floated up to meet her from the kitchens in the basement. The servants were already hard at work. Alaïs heard a slap, closely followed by a yell, as an unlucky boy started the day with the cook's heavy hand on the back of his head.

A scullion came staggering toward her, struggling with a massive half-barrel of water he had drawn from the well.

Alaïs smiled. "*Bonjorn.*"

"*Bonjorn,* Dame," he answered cautiously.

"Here," she said, going down the stairs before him to open the door.

"*Mercé,* Dame," he said, a little less timid now. "*Grand mercé.*"

The kitchen was alive with hustle and bustle. Great billows of steam were already rising from the huge *payrola,* the cauldron, hanging on a hook over the open fire. An older servant took the water from the scullion, emptied it into the pot, and then shoved the barrel back at him without saying a word. The boy rolled his eyes at Alaïs as he headed out and back up to the well once more.

Capons, lentils and cabbage in sealed earthenware jars stood waiting to be cooked on the big table in the center of the room, together with pots containing salt mullet, eel and pike. At one end were *fogaça* puddings in cloth bags, goose paté and slabs of salted pork. At the other, trays of raisins, quinces, figs and cherries. A boy of nine or ten was standing with his elbows propped on the table, the scowl on his face making it clear how much he was looking forward to another hot and sweaty day at the turnspit, watching the meat roast. Next to the hearth, the brushwood was burning fiercely inside the dome-shaped bread oven. The first batch of *pan de blat*, wheat bread, was already standing on the table to cool. The smell made Alaïs hungry.

"May I have one of those?"

The cook looked up, furious at the intrusion of a woman into his kitchen. Then he saw who it was and his bad-tempered face creased into a cock-eyed smile revealing a row of rotten teeth.

"Dame Alaïs," he said with delight, wiping his hands on his apron. "*Benvenguda.* What an honor! You've not come to visit us for quite some time. We've missed you."

"Jacques," she said warmly. "I wouldn't want to get in your way."

"In my way, you!" he laughed. "How could you ever be in my way?" As a child, Alaïs had spent a great deal of time in the kitchen, watching and learning, the only girl Jacques had ever allowed across the threshold into his male domain. "Now, Dame Alaïs, what can I get you?"

"Just a little bread, Jacques, some wine too, if you can spare it?"

A frown appeared on his face. Alaïs smiled innocently.

"Forgive me, but you're not going down to the river? Not at this time of day, unaccompanied? A lady of your position . . . it's not even light. I hear things, stories of . . ."

Alaïs laid a hand on his arm. "You are kind to concern yourself, Jacques, and I know you have my best interests at heart, but I will be fine. I give you my word. It's nearly dawn. I know exactly where I'm going. I'll be there and back before anyone even notices I've gone, really."

"Does your father know?"

She put a conspiratorial finger to her lips. "You know what he does not, but please, keep it our secret. I will take great care."

Jacques looked far from convinced, but feeling he'd said as much as he dared, he did not argue. He walked slowly over to the table and wrapped a round loaf in a white linen cloth and ordered a scullion to fetch a jar of wine. Alaïs watched, feeling a tug at her heart. He was moving more slowly these days and he was limping heavily on his left side.

"Is your leg still giving you difficulty?"

"Not much," he lied.

"I can dress it for you later, if you like. It doesn't look as if that cut is healing as it should."

"It's not so bad."

"Did you use the ointment I made for you?" she asked, knowing from the expression on his face that he had not.

Jacques spread his podgy hands in a gesture of surrender. "There is so much to do, Dame—all these extra guests, hundreds once you count the servants, écuyers, grooms, ladies-in-waiting, not to mention the consuls and their families. And so many things are difficult to find these days. Why only yesterday, I sent—"

"That's all very well, Jacques," said Alaïs, "but your leg won't get better on its own. The cut's too deep."

She suddenly realized that the noise level had dropped. She glanced up to see the entire kitchen was eavesdropping on their conversation. The younger boys were propped on their elbows at the table, staring open-mouthed at the sight of their quick-tempered master being told off. And by a woman.

Pretending not to notice, Alaïs dropped her voice.

"Why don't I return later to do it, in return for this?" She patted the loaf. "It can be our second secret, oc? A fair exchange?"

For a moment, she thought she had been overfamiliar and presumed too much. But, after a moment's hesitation, Jacques grinned.

"Ben," she said. Good. "I will come back when the sun is high and see to it. Dins d'abord." Soon.

As Alaïs left the kitchen and climbed back up the stairs, she heard Jacques bellowing at everybody to stop gawping and get back to work, pretending the interruption had never happened. She smiled.

Everything was as it should be.

Alaïs pulled open the heavy door that led into the main courtyard and stepped out into the newborn day.

The leaves of the elm tree that stood in the center of the enclosed courtyard, under which Viscount Trencavel dispensed justice, looked black against the fading night. Its branches were alive with larks and wrens, their voices warbling shrill and clear in the dawn.

Raymond-Roger Trencavel's grandfather had built the Château Comtal, more than a hundred years ago, as the seat from which to rule his expanding territories. His lands stretched from Albi in the north and Narbonne in the south, to Béziers in the east and Carcassonne in the west.

The château was constructed around a large rectangular courtyard and incorporated, on the western side, the remains of an older castle. It was part of the reinforcement of the western section of the fortified walls that enclosed the Cité, a ring of solid stone that towered high above the river Aude and the northern marshlands beyond.

The *donjon,* where the consuls met and significant documents were signed, was in the southwest corner of the courtyard and well guarded. In the dim light, Alaïs could see something propped against the outside wall. She looked harder and realized it was a dog, curled asleep on the ground. A couple of boys, perched like crows on the edge of the goose pen, were trying to wake the animal up by flicking stones at it. In the stillness, she could hear the regular dull thud, thud of their heels banging against the wooden railings.

There were two ways in and out of the Château Comtal. The wide arched West Gate gave directly on to the grassy slopes that led to the walls and was mostly kept closed. The Eastern Gate, small and narrow, was tucked between two high gate towers and led straight into the streets of the *Ciutat,* the Cité, itself.

Communication between the upper and lower floors of the gatehouse towers was only possible by means of wooden ladders and a series of trap doors. As a girl, one of her favorite games was to scramble up and down between the levels with the boys from the kitchen, trying to evade the guards. Alaïs was fast. She always won.

Pulling her cloak tightly about her, she walked briskly across the courtyard. Once the curfew bell had rung, the gates barred for the night and the guard set, nobody was supposed to pass without her father's authorization. Although not a consul, Bertrand Pelletier occupied a unique and favored position in the household. Few dared disobey him.

He had always disliked her habit of slipping out of the Cité in the early morning. These days, he was even more adamant that she should stay within the walls of the château at night. She assumed her husband felt the same, although Guilhem had never said so. But it was only in the stillness and anonymity of the dawn, free from the restrictions and limitations of the household, that Alaïs felt really herself. Nobody's daughter, nobody's sister, nobody's wife. Deep down, she had always believed her father understood. Much as she disliked disobeying him, she did not want to give up these moments of freedom.

Most of the night watch turned a blind eye to her comings and goings. Or, at least they had. Since rumors of war had started to circulate, the garrison had become more cautious. On the surface, life went on much the same and although refugees arrived in the Cité from time to time, their tales of attacks or religious persecution seemed to Alaïs nothing out of the ordinary. Raiders who appeared from nowhere and struck like summer lightning before passing on were facts of existence for any who lived outside the safety of a fortified village or town. The reports seemed no different, neither more nor less, than usual.

Guilhem didn't seem particularly perturbed by the whisperings of a conflict, at least not so far as she could tell. He never talked to her of such things. Oriane, however, claimed that a French army of Crusaders and churchmen was making ready to attack the lands of the Pays d'Oc. Moreover, she said the campaign was supported by the pope and the French king. Alaïs knew from experience that much of what Oriane said was intended only to upset her. Nonetheless her sister often seemed to know things before anybody else in the household and there was no denying the fact that the number of messengers coming in and out of the château was increasing by the day. It was also undeniable that the lines on their father's face were deeper and darker, the hollows of his cheeks more pronounced.

The *sirjans d'arms* on guard at the Eastern Gate were alert, although their eyes were rimmed with red after a long night. Their square silver helmets were pushed high on their heads and their chainmail coats were dull in the pale dawn light. With their shields slung wearily across their shoulders and their swords sheathed, they looked more ready for bed than battle.

As she got closer, Alaïs was relieved to recognize Bérenger. When he identified her, he grinned and he bowed his head.

"*Bonjorn*, Dame Alaïs. You're up and about early."

She smiled. "I couldn't sleep."

"Can't that husband of yours think of something to fill your nights?" said the other with a lewd wink. His face was pockmarked and the nails on his fingers were bitten and bleeding. His breath smelled of stale food and ale.

Alaïs ignored him. "How is your wife, Bérenger?"

"Well, Dame. Quite back to her usual self."

"And your son?"

"Bigger by the day. He'll eat us out of house and hearth if we don't watch out!"

"Clearly following in his father's footsteps!" she said, poking his ample belly.

"That's exactly what my wife says."

"Send her my best wishes, Bérenger, will you?"

"She will be grateful to be remembered, Dame." He paused. "I suppose you want me to let you through?"

"I'm only going out into the *Ciutat*, maybe the river. I won't be long."

"We're not supposed to let anybody through," growled his companion. "Intendant Pelletier's orders."

"Nobody asked you," snapped Bérenger. "It's not that, Dame," he said, dropping his voice. "But you know how things are at present. What if something was to happen to you and it came out that it was I who let you pass, your father would—"

Alaïs put her hand on his arm. "I know, I know," she said softly. "But really there's no need to worry. I can take care of myself. Besides . . ."—Alaïs let her eyes slide sideways to the other guard, who was now picking his nose and wiping his fingers on his sleeve—"what trials I might face at the river could hardly be worse than those you endure here!"

Bérenger laughed. "Promise me you will be careful, è?"

Alaïs nodded, opening her cloak a fraction to show him the hunting knife at her waist. "I will. I give you my word."

There were two doors to negotiate. Bérenger unbolted them in turn, then lifted the heavy beam of oak securing the outer door and pulled it open just wide enough for Alaïs to slip through. Smiling her thanks, she ducked under his arm and stepped out into the world.

CHAPTER 2

Alaïs felt her heart lift as she emerged from the shadows between the gate towers. She was free. For a while at least.

A movable wooden walkway linked the gatehouse to the flat stone bridge that connected the Château Comtal to the streets of Carcassonne. The grass in the dry moat way beneath the bridge was glistening with dew in the shimmering purple light. There was still a moon, although it was fading against the gathering dawn.

Alaïs walked quickly, her cloak leaving swirling patterns in the dust, wanting to avoid questions from the guards on duty on the far side. She was lucky. They were slumbering at their posts and did not see her pass. She hurried over the open ground and ducked into a network of narrow alleyways, heading for a postern by the Tour du Moulin d'Avar, the oldest part of the walls. The gate gave straight onto the vegetable gardens and *faratjals*, the pastures that occupied the land surrounding the Cité and the northern suburb of Sant-Vicens. At this time of day, it was the quickest way down to the river without being seen.

Holding up her skirts, Alaïs picked her way carefully through the evidence of another riotous night in the *taberna Sant Joan dels Evangèlis*. Bruised apples, half-eaten pears, gnawed meat bones and shattered ale pots lay discarded in the dirt. A little farther along, a beggar was huddled asleep in a doorway, his arm resting along the back of a huge, bedraggled old dog. Three men were slumped against the well, grunting and snoring loud enough to drown out the birds.

The sentry on duty at the postern was miserable, coughing and spluttering and wrapped up in his cloak so that only the tip of his nose and his eyebrows were visible. He didn't want to be disturbed. At first he refused to acknowledge her presence. Alaïs dug into her purse and produced a coin. Without even looking at her, he snatched it with a filthy hand, tested it between his teeth, then shot the bolts and opened the postern gate a crack to let her slide through.

The path down to the barbican was steep and rocky. It ran between the two high, protective wooden palisade walls and it was hard to see anything. But Alaïs had taken this route out of the Cité many times, knew every dip and rise of the land, and she climbed down without difficulty. She skirted the foot of the squat, round wooden tower, following the path of the fast-flowing water where it sped, like a mill race, through the barbican.

The brambles scratched sharp at her legs and the thorns snagged her dress. By the time she reached the bottom, the hem of her cloak was a deep crimson and soaking wet from skimming the grass. The tips of her leather slippers were stained dark.

Alaïs felt her spirits soar the moment she stepped out of the shadow of the palisade into the wide, open world. In the distance, a white July mist was hovering above the Montagne Noire. The breaking sky on the horizon was slashed through with pink and purple.

As she stood looking out over the perfect patchwork of fields of barley, corn and wheat and the woodlands that stretched farther than her eye could see, Alaïs felt the presence of the past all around her, embracing her. Spirits, friends and ghosts who held out their hands and whispered of their lives, and shared their secrets with her. They connected her to all those who had stood on this hill before—and all who were yet to stand here—dreaming of what life might hold.

Alaïs had never traveled beyond Viscount Trencavel's lands. She found it hard to picture the gray cities of the north, Paris, Amiens or Chartres, where her mother had been born. They were just names, words with no color or warmth, as harsh as the language, the *langue d'oïl,* they spoke there. But even though she had little to compare it with, she could not believe that anywhere else was as beautiful as the enduring, timeless landscape of Carcassonne.

Alaïs set off down the hill, weaving her way through the scrub and the coarse bushes until she reached the flat marshlands on the southern banks of the river Aude. Her sodden skirts kept twisting themselves around the backs of her legs and she stumbled from time to time. She felt uneasy, she realized, watchful, and was walking faster than usual. It wasn't that Jacques or Bérenger had alarmed her, she told herself. They were always anxious on her behalf. But today she felt isolated and vulnerable.

Her hand moved to the dagger at her waist as she remembered the story of the merchant who claimed to have seen a wolf on the opposite bank, just last week. Everybody thought he was exaggerating. At this time of year, it was probably just a fox or a wild dog. But now that she was out here on her own, the tale seemed more believable. The cold hilt was reassuring.

For a moment, Alaïs was tempted to turn back. *Do not be so cowardly.* She carried on. Once or twice she turned, startled, by noises nearby that turned out to be no more than the flapping of a bird's wing or the slither and splash of a yellow river eel in the shallows.

Gradually, as she followed her familiar path, her nerves melted away. The river Aude was wide and shallow, with several tributaries leading off it, like veins on the back of a hand. A dawn mist shimmered translucent above the surface of the water. During the winter, the river flowed fast and furiously, swollen by the icy streams from the mountains. But it had been a dry summer so the water was low and still. The salt mills barely moved in the current. Secured to the banks by thick ropes, they formed a wooden spine up the center of the river.

It was too early for the flies and mosquitoes that would hover like black clouds over the pools as the heat intensified, so Alaïs took the shortcut over the mud flats. The path was marked by little heaps of white stones to help people from slipping into the treacherous sludge. She followed it carefully until she arrived at the edge of the woods that lay immediately below the western section of the Cité walls.

Her destination was a small, secluded glade, where the best plants grew in the partially shaded shallows. As soon as she reached the shelter of the trees, Alaïs slowed her pace and began to enjoy herself. She pushed aside the tendrils of ivy that overhung her path and breathed in the rich, earthy smell of leaf and moss.

Although there was no sign of human activity, the wood was alive with color and sound. The air was filled with the shriek and twitter of starlings, wrens and linnets. Twigs and leaves crackled and snapped beneath her feet. Rabbits scampered through the undergrowth, their white tails bobbing as they dived for cover among the clusters of yellow, purple and blue summer flowers. High in the spreading branches of the pines, red-coated squirrels cracked the cones' shells apart, sending thin, aromatic needles showering down on the ground below.

Alaïs was shot by the time she arrived at the glade, a small island of land with an open space that led down to the river. With relief, she put down her *panièr*, rubbing the inside of her elbow where the handle had cut into her skin. She removed her heavy cloak and hung it over a low-hanging branch of a white willow, before wiping her face and neck with a handkerchief. She put the wine in the hollow of a tree to keep it cool.

The sheer walls of the Château Comtal loomed high above her. The distinctive tall, thin outline of the Tour Pinte was silhouetted against the pale sky. Alaïs wondered if her father was awake, already sitting with the viscount in his private chambers. Her eyes drifted to the left of the watchtower, seeking out her own window. Was Guilhem still sleeping? Or had he woken to find her gone?

It always amazed her, when she looked up through the green canopy of leaves, that the Cité was so close. Two different worlds thrown into sharp relief. There, in the streets and the corridors of the Château Comtal, all was noise and activity. There was no peace. Down here, in the realm of the creatures of the woods and marshlands, a deep and timeless silence reigned.

It was here that she felt at home.

Alaïs eased off her leather slippers. The grass was deliciously cool between her toes, still wet with early morning dew, and tickled the soles of her feet. In the pleasure of the moment, all thoughts of the Cité and the household were driven from her mind.

She carried her tools down to the water's edge. A clump of angelica was growing in the shallows at the river's edge. Their strong fluted stems looked like a line of toy soldiers standing to attention in the muddy ground. Their bright green leaves—some bigger than her hand—threw a faint shadow over the water.

Nothing was better than angelica for purifying the blood and protecting against infection. Her friend and mentor, Esclarmonde, had drummed it into her how essential it was to gather ingredients for poultices, medicines and remedies wherever and whenever she found them. Even if the Cité was free from infection today, she would say, who could say what tomorrow would bring. Disease or illness could take hold at any time. Like everything Esclarmonde told her, it was good advice.

Rolling up her sleeves, Alaïs slipped the sheath round until the knife was lying flat against her back and wouldn't be in the way. She twisted her hair into a plait to stop it falling over her face as she worked, then tucked the skirts of her dress into her girdle before stepping into the river. The sudden cold on her ankles brought her skin out in goosebumps and made her draw breath.

Alaïs dipped the strips of cloth into the water and laid them out in a row along the bank, then she started to dig at the roots with her trowel. It wasn't long before the first plant came free from the riverbed with a slurp. Dragging it up on to the bank, she used her small ax to cut it into different sections. She wrapped the roots in the cloth and laid them flat at the bottom of the *panièr*, then wrapped the small, yellow-green flowers, with their distinctive peppery aroma, in a separate cloth in her leather pouch. She discarded the leaves and the rest of the stems before going back into the water and starting the process again. Pretty soon, her hands were stained green and her arms smeared with mud.

Once she had harvested all the angelica, Alaïs looked around to see if there was anything else she could make use of. A little farther upstream she spotted comfrey, with its strange, telltale leaves that grew down into the stem itself, and its lopsided clusters of bell-shaped pink and purple flowers. Comfrey, or knitbone as most called it, was good for reducing bruising and helping skin and bone to mend. Postponing her breakfast for just a while longer, Alaïs took her tools and got back to work, only stopping when the *panièr* was full and she had used up every strip of cloth.

Carrying her basket back up the bank, she sat down under the trees and stretched her legs in front of her. Her back, shoulders and fingers were stiff, but she felt pleased with what she'd achieved. She leaned over and took Jacques' jar of wine from the hollow. The stopper came loose with a gentle pop. Alaïs shivered a little as the cool liquid trickled over her tongue and down her throat. Then she unwrapped the fresh bread and tore a large chunk out of it. It tasted of a strange combination of wheat, salt, river water and weed, but she was ravenous. It was as good a meal as she had ever eaten.

The sky was now a pale blue, the color of forget-me-nots. Alaïs knew she must have been gone for some time. But as she watched the golden sunlight dancing on the surface of the water and felt the breath of the wind on her skin, she was reluctant to return to the busy, noisy streets of Carcassonne and the crowded spaces of the household. Telling herself a few moments more couldn't hurt, Alaïs lay back on the grass and closed her eyes.

The sound of a bird screeching overhead woke her.

Alaïs sat up with a start. As she looked up through the quilt of dappled leaves, she couldn't remember where she was. Then everything flooded back.

She scrambled to her feet in a panic. The sun was now high in a sky empty of clouds. She'd been gone too long. By now, she was sure to have been missed.

Rushing to pack her things away as quickly as possible, Alaïs gave her muddy tools a cursory wash in the river and sprinkled water over the strips of linen to keep the cuttings moist. She was about to turn away when her eye was caught by something tangled in the reeds. It looked like a tree stump or a log. Alaïs shielded her eyes from the sun, wondering how she had missed it before.

It was moving too fluidly, too languidly in the current to be something as solid as bark or wood. Alaïs edged closer.

Now, she could see it was a piece of heavy, dark material, puffed up by the water. After a moment's hesitation, her curiosity got the better of her and she ventured back into the water, this time wading beyond the shallows into the deeper water that flowed fast and dark in the center of the river. The farther she went, the colder it got. Alaïs struggled to keep her balance. She dug her toes deep into the squelching mud as the water splashed up against her thin, white thighs and skirts.

Just past the halfway mark, she stopped, her heart pounding and her palms suddenly greasy with fear now she could see more clearly.

"*Payre Sant.*" Holy Father. The words leaped unbidden to her lips.

The body of a man was floating face-down in the water, his cloak billowing out around him. Alaïs swallowed hard. He was wearing a high-collared coat of brown velvet, trimmed with black silk ribbon and edged with gold thread. She could see the glint of a gold chain or bracelet under the water. The man's head was bare, so she could see his hair was curly and black, tinged with flecks of gray. He seemed to be wearing something around his neck, a crimson braid of some sort, a ribbon.

She took a step closer. Her first thought was that he must have lost his footing in the dark, slipped into the river and drowned. She was about to reach out when something about the way his head was lolling in the water stayed her hand. She took a deep breath, transfixed by the bloated corpse. She'd seen a drowned man once before. Swollen and distorted, the sailor's blotched skin had been tinged with blue and purple, like a fading bruise. This was different, wrong.

This man looked as if the life had already left him before he went into the water. His lifeless hands were stretched in front of him, as if he was trying to swim. The left arm drifted toward her, carried by the current. Something bright, something colorful just beneath the surface, caught her eye. There was a lesion, irregular and uneven, like a birthmark, red against the bloated white flesh around where his thumb should have been. She looked at his neck.

Alaïs felt her knees buckle.

Everything started to move in slow motion, lurching and undulating like the surface of a rough sea. The uneven crimson line she had taken for a collar or a ribbon was a savage, deep cut. It ran from behind the man's left ear under his chin, almost severing his head from his body. Tendrils of serrated skin, washed green under the water, trailed out around the gash. Tiny silverfish and leeches, black and swollen, were feasting all along the wound.

For a moment, Alaïs thought her heart had stopped beating. Then shock and fear hit her in equal measure. She spun round and started to run back through the water, sliding, slipping in the mud, instinct telling her to put as much distance as possible between her and the body. Already she was soaking from the waist down. Her dress, swollen and heavy with water, tangled itself around her legs, nearly pulling her under.

The river seemed twice as wide as before, but she kept going, making it to the safety of the bank before nausea overwhelmed her and she was violently sick. Wine, undigested bread, river water.

Half-crawling, half-dragging herself on all fours, she managed to pull herself higher up, before collapsing on the ground in the shadows of the trees. Her head was spinning, her mouth was dry and sour, but she had to get away. Alaïs tried to stand, but her legs felt hollow and wouldn't hold her. Trying not to cry, she wiped her mouth with the back of her shaking hand, then tried to stand again, using the trunk of a tree to support her.

This time, she stayed on her feet. Pulling her cloak from the branch with desperate fingers, Alaïs managed to push her filthy feet into her slippers. Then, abandoning everything else, she started to run back through the woods, as if the Devil himself was at her heels.

The heat hit Alaïs the moment she emerged from the trees into the open marshland. The sun pinched at her cheeks and neck, taunting her. The heat had brought out the biting insects and mosquitoes in swarms above the stagnant pools which flanked the path, as Alaïs stumbled forward, on through the inhospitable landscape.

Her exhausted legs screamed in protest and her breath burned ragged in her throat and chest, but she kept running, running. All she was conscious of was the need to get as far away from the body as possible and to tell her father.

Rather than going back the way she'd come, which might be locked, Alaïs instinctively headed for Sant-Vicens and the Porte de Rodez, which connected the suburb to Carcassonne.

The streets were busy and Alaïs had to push her way through. The hum and buzz of the world coming to life got louder and louder, more intrusive, the closer she came to the entrance into the Cité. Alaïs tried to stop her ears and think only of getting to the gate. Praying her weak legs would not give way, Alaïs pushed her way to the front.

A woman tapped her shoulder.

"Your head, Dame," she said quietly. Her voice was kind, but it seemed to be coming from a long way away.

Realizing that her hair was hanging loose and disheveled, Alaïs quickly threw her cloak over her shoulders and pulled up her hood, with hands that trembled as much from exhaustion as shock. She edged forward, wrapping the material across the front of her dress, hoping to conceal the stains of mud, vomit and green river weed.

Everybody was jostling, barging, shouting. Alaïs thought she was going to faint. She put out her hand and steadied herself against the wall. The guards on duty at the Porte de Rodez were nodding most local people through without question, but stopping vagabonds and beggars, gypsies, Saracens and Jews, demanding to know their business in Carcassonne, and searching their belongings more roughly than necessary until small jugs of ale or coins changed hands and they moved on to the next victim.

They let Alaïs through with barely a glance.

The narrow streets of the Cité were now flooded with hawkers, merchants, livestock, soldiers, farriers, *jongleurs,* wives of the consuls and their servants and preachers. Alaïs kept her head bowed as if she was walking into a biting north wind, not wishing to be recognized.

35

At last, she saw the familiar outline of the Tour du Major, followed by the Tour des Casernes, then the double towers of the Eastern Gate as the Château Comtal came into full view.

Relief caught in her throat. Fierce tears welled up in her eyes. Furious at her weakness, Alaïs bit down on her lip hard, drawing blood. She was ashamed to be so distressed and determined not to humiliate herself farther by crying where her lack of courage might be witnessed.

All she wanted was her father.

CHAPTER 3

Intendant Pelletier was in one of the storerooms in the basements next to the kitchen, having just finished his weekly check of the grain and flour supplies. He was relieved to discover that none of the stock was moldy.

Bertrand Pelletier had served Viscount Trencavel for more than eighteen years. It was early in the cold new year of 1191 that he had been summoned to return to his native Carcassonne, to take up the position of *intendant*—steward—to the nine-year-old Raymond-Roger, heir to the Trencavel dominions. It was a message he had been waiting for and he had come willingly, bringing his pregnant French wife and two-year-old daughter with him. The cold and wet of Chartres had never been to his liking.

What he had found was a boy old beyond his years, grieving for the loss of his parents and struggling to cope with the responsibility thrust on his young shoulders. Pelletier had been with Viscount Trencavel ever since, first within the household of Raymond-Roger's guardian, Bertrand of Saissac, then under the protection of the count of Foix. When Raymond-Roger reached his majority and returned to the Château Comtal to take up his rightful place as viscount of Carcassonne, Béziers and Albi, Pelletier had been at his side.

As steward, Pelletier was responsible for the smooth running of the household. He concerned himself also with administration, justice and the levying of taxes carried out on the viscount's behalf by the consuls who ran the affairs of Carcassonne between them. More significantly, he was the viscount's acknowledged confidant, advisor and friend. His influence was second to none.

The Château Comtal was full of distinguished guests and more were arriving each day. The *seigneurs* of the most important châteaux within the Trencavel lands and their wives, as well as the most valiant, most celebrated *chevaliers* of the Midi. The finest minstrels and troubadours had been invited to the traditional summer joust to celebrate the Feast Day of Sant-Nasari at the end of July. Given the shadow of war that had been hanging over them for a year or more, the viscount was determined that his guests should enjoy themselves and that it would be the most memorable tournament of his rule.

In his turn, Pelletier was determined nothing should be left to chance. He locked the door to the grain store with one of the many heavy keys he carried on a metal hoop around his waist and set off down the corridor.

"The wine store next," he said to his manservant, François. "The last barrel was sour."

Pelletier strode down the corridor, pausing to look on other rooms as they passed. The linen store smelled of lavender and thyme and was empty, as if it was waiting for someone to come and bring it back to life.

"Are those tablecloths washed and ready for table?"

"*Oc, Messire.*"

In the cellar opposite the wine store at the foot of the stairs, men were rolling sides of meat in the salting box. Some cuts were being strung up on the metal hooks that dangled from the ceiling. Others were stored in barrels for another day. In a corner, a man was threading mushrooms, garlic and onions on to strings and hanging them up to dry.

Everybody stopped what they were doing and fell silent when Pelletier walked in. A few of the younger servants got awkwardly to their feet. He said nothing, just gazed around, taking in the whole room with his sharp eyes, before nodding his approval and moving on.

Pelletier was unlocking the door to the wine store when he heard shouting and the sound of running footsteps on the floor above.

"Find out what the matter is," he said irritably. "I can't work with such a disturbance."

"*Messire.*"

François turned and ran quickly up the stairs to investigate.

Pelletier pushed open the heavy door and walked into the cool, dark cellars, breathing in the familiar smell of damp wood and the sour tang of spilled wine and ale. He walked slowly down the aisles until he had located the casks he was looking for. He took an earthenware cup from the tray that stood ready on the table, then loosened the bung. He was careful and slow, so as not to disturb the balance inside the cask.

A sound in the corridor outside made the hairs on the back of his neck stand on end. He put the cup down. Someone was calling his name. Alaïs. Something had happened.

Pelletier crossed the room and threw open the door.

Alaïs came hurtling down the stairs as if a pack of dogs was at her heels, with François hurrying behind.

At the sight of her father's grizzled presence among the casks of wine and ale, she cried out with relief. She threw herself into his arms and buried her tear-stained face in his chest. The familiar, comforting smell of him made her want to cry again.

"What in the name of Sant Foy is going on? What's happened to you? Are you hurt? Tell me."

She could hear the alarm in his voice. She pulled back a little and tried to speak, but the words were trapped in her throat and would not come. "Father, I—"

His eyes were alive with questions as he took in at a glance her disheveled appearance and stained clothes. He looked over her head to François for an explanation.

"I found Dame Alaïs like this, *Messire*."

"And she said nothing about the cause of this . . . the reason for her distress?"

"No, *Messire*. Only that she must be taken to you without delay."

"Very well. Leave us now. I'll call if I need you."

Alaïs heard the door shut. Then she felt the heavy touch of her father's arm around her shoulder. He steered her over to the bench that ran along one side of the cellar and sat her down.

"Come, *Filha*," he said in a softer voice. He reached down and pushed a strand of hair off her face. "This isn't like you. Tell me what has happened."

Alaïs made another attempt to get herself under control, hating the anxiety and concern she was causing him. She rubbed her smeared cheeks with the handkerchief he held out and dabbed her red eyes.

"Drink this," he said, putting a cup of wine into her hands, before sitting down beside her. The ancient wood bowed and creaked under his weight. "François has gone. There's nobody here but us. You must stop this and tell me what has happened to distress you so. Is it Guilhem? Has he done something to upset you? Because if he has, then I give you my word that I will—"

"It's nothing to do with Guilhem, *Paire*," Alaïs said quickly. "It's nothing to do with anybody . . ."

She glanced up at him, then dropped her eyes again, embarrassed, humiliated to sit before him in such a state.

"Then what?" he persisted. "How can I help if you will not tell me what has happened?"

She swallowed hard, feeling guilty and shocked. She didn't know how to start.

Pelletier took her hands in his. "You're trembling, Alaïs." She could hear the concern and affection in his voice, the effort he was making to keep his fear in check. "And look at your clothes," he said, lifting the hem of her dress between his fingers. "Wet. Covered with mud."

Alaïs could see how tired he was, how worried. He was bewildered by her collapse, however hard he tried to hide it. The lines on his forehead were like furrows. How had she failed to notice before that his hair was now flecked with gray at the temples?

"I have not known you be lost for words," he said, trying to coax her out of her silence. "You must tell me what this is about, è."

His expression was so full of love and faith that it pierced her heart. "I fear you will be angry, *Paire*. Indeed, you have every right to be."

His expression sharpened, but he kept his smile in place. "I promise I will not scold you, Alaïs. Now, come. Speak."

"Even if I tell you I went to the river?"

He hesitated, but his voice did not waver. "Not even then."

The soonest spoken, the quickest mended.

Alaïs folded her hands in her lap. "This morning, just before dawn, I went down to the river, to a place I often go to gather plants."

"Alone?"

"Alone, yes," she said, meeting his gaze. "I know I gave you my word, *Paire*, and I ask your forgiveness for my disobedience."

"On foot?" She nodded and waited until he waved her to continue.

"I was there for some time. I saw no one. As I was packing up my things to leave, I noticed what I thought was a bundle of clothes in the water, good quality cloth. In fact—" Alaïs broke off again, feeling the color drain from her face. "In point of fact it was a body. A man, quite old. With dark, curly hair. At first, I thought he had drowned. I couldn't see much. Then I saw his throat had been cut."

His shoulders stiffened. "You didn't touch the body?"

Alaïs shook her head. "No, but—" She dropped her eyes, embarrassed. "The shock of finding him, I'm afraid I lost my head and ran, leaving everything behind. My only thought was that I had to get away and tell you of what I had seen."

He was frowning again. "And you saw no one?"

"Not a soul. It was completely deserted. But once I saw the body, then I started to fear the men who had killed him might still be somewhere close." Her voice wavered. "I imagined I could feel their eyes on me, watching me. Or so I thought."

"So you are not harmed in any way," he said carefully, choosing his words with deliberation. "No one has interfered with you in any way? Hurt you?"

That she understood his meaning was clear from the way her color rose quickly in her cheeks.

"No ill has come to me other than my pride being damaged and . . . the loss of your goodwill."

She watched the relief wash over her father's face. He smiled and, for the first time since the conversation had started, it reached his eyes.

"Well," he said, breathing out slowly. "Overlooking, for the time being, your recklessness, Alaïs, the fact you disobeyed me . . . leaving that aside, you did the right thing by telling me of this." He reached out and took her hands, his giant clasp encompassing her small, thin fingers. His skin felt like tanned leather.

Alaïs smiled, grateful for the reprieve. "I am sorry, *Paire*. I meant to keep my promise, it's just that—"

He waved the apology away. "We will say no more about it. As for the unfortunate man, there's nothing to be done. The thieves will be long gone. They're hardly likely to stay around and risk discovery."

Alaïs frowned. Her father's comments had stirred something that had been lurking beneath the surface of her mind. She closed her eyes. Pictured herself standing in the chill water, transfixed by the body.

"That's the odd thing, father," she said slowly. "I don't think they can have been bandits. They didn't take his surcoat, which was beautiful and looked valuable. And he was still wearing his jewelry. Gold chains around his wrists, rings. Thieves would have stripped the body bare."

"You told me you did not touch the body," he said sharply.

"Nor did I. But I could see his hands under the water, that's all. Jewels. So many rings, father. A gold bracelet made from interlinking chains. Another around his neck. Why would they leave such things?"

Alaïs broke off, as she remembered the man's bloated, ghostly hands reaching out to touch her and, where his thumb should have been, blood and shards of white bone. Her head started to spin. Leaning back against the damp, cold wall, Alaïs made herself concentrate on the hard wood of the bench beneath her and the sour smell of the casks in her nose, until the dizziness faded.

"There was no blood," she added. "An open wound, red like a piece of meat." She swallowed hard. "His thumb was missing, it was—"

"Missing?" he said sharply. "What do you mean, missing?"

Alaïs glanced up in surprise at the shift of tone. "His thumb had been cut off. Sliced from the bone."

"Which hand, Alaïs?" he said. Now there was no hiding the urgency in his voice. "Think. It's important."

"I'm not—"

He hardly seemed to hear. "Which hand?" he insisted.

"His left hand, the left, I'm sure of it. It was the side closest to me. He was facing upstream."

Pelletier strode across the room, bellowing for François, and threw open the door. Alaïs hurled herself to her feet too, shaken by her father's desperate mood and bewildered as to what was going on.

"What is it? Tell me, I beseech you. Why does it matter if it was his left or his right hand?"

"Prepare horses straight away, François. My bay gelding, Dame Alaïs' gray mare and a mount for you."

François' expression was as impassive as ever. "Very good, *Messire*. Are we going far?"

"Only to the river." He gestured him to be gone. "Quick, man. And fetch my sword and a clean cloak for Dame Alaïs. We'll meet you at the well."

As soon as François was out of earshot, Alaïs rushed to her father. He refused to meet her gaze. Instead, he walked back to the casks and, with a shaking hand, poured himself some wine. The thick, red liquid slopped over the side of the earthenware bowl and splashed all over the table, staining the wood.

"*Paire,*" she pleaded. "Tell me what this is about. Why do you have to go to the river? Surely, it cannot be a matter for you. Let François go. I can tell him where."

"You don't understand."

"Then tell me, so I can understand. You can trust me."

"I must see the body for myself. Find out if—"

"Find out what?" Alaïs said quickly.

"No, no," he was saying, shaking his grizzled head from side to side. "This is not for you to . . ." Pelletier's voice trailed off.

"But—"

Pelletier held up his hand, suddenly in control of his emotions again. "No more, Alaïs. You must be guided by me. I would that I could spare you this, but I cannot. I have no choice." He thrust the cup toward her. "Drink this. It will fortify you, give you courage."

"I'm not afraid," she protested, offended he thought her reluctance cowardice. "I do not fear to look on the dead. It was shock that affected me so before." She hesitated. "But I beseech you, *Messire*, to tell me why—"

Pelletier turned on her. "Enough, no more," he shouted.

Alaïs stepped back as if he had struck her.

"Forgive me," he said immediately. "I am not myself." He reached out and touched her cheek. "No man could ask for a more loyal, a more steadfast daughter."

"Then why will you not confide in me?"

He hesitated and, for a moment, Alaïs thought she had persuaded him to speak. Then the same, shuttered look fell down over his face again.

"All you have to do is show me," he said in a hollow voice. "The rest is in my hands."

The bells of Sant-Nasari were ringing for Tierce as they rode out of the West Gate of the Château Comtal.

Her father rode in front, with Alaïs following behind with François. She felt wretched, both guilty that her actions had precipitated this strange change in her father and frustrated that she did not understand.

They picked their way along the narrow, dry dirt track that zigzagged sharply down the hill below the Cité walls, doubling back on itself over and again. When they reached the flat, they broke into a canter.

They followed the course of the river upstream. An unforgiving sun beat down upon their backs as they rode into the marshes. Swarms of midges and black swamp flies hovered above the rivulets and puddles of torpid water. The horses stamped their hooves and switched their tails, in vain trying to stop their thin summer coats being pierced by the myriad biting insects.

Alaïs could see a group of women washing clothes in the shaded shallows on the other bank of the river Aude, standing half in and half out of the water as they beat the material on flat gray stones. There was a monotonous rumble of wheels over the single wooden bridge that linked the marshes and villages of the north to Carcassonne and its suburbs. Others waded across the river at its lowest point, a steady stream of peasants, farmers and merchants. Some were carrying children on their shoulders, some driving herds of goats or mules, all heading for the market in the main square.

They rode in silence. Once they moved from open ground into the shadow of the marsh willows, she found herself drifting away into her own thoughts. Calmed by the familiar motion of her horse beneath her, the singing of the birds and the endless chattering of the cicadas in the reeds, for a while Alaïs almost forgot the purpose of their expedition.

Her apprehension returned when they reached the outskirts of the woods. Falling into single file, they threaded their way through the trees. Her father turned, briefly, and smiled at her. Alaïs was grateful for it. She was nervous now, alert, listening for the slightest sign of trouble. The marsh willows seemed to tower with malice over her head and she imagined eyes in the dark shadows, watching them pass, waiting. Every rustle in the undergrowth, every beat of a bird's wing made her heart race.

Alaïs hardly knew what she had expected, but when they arrived at the glade, everything was quiet and peaceful. Her *panièr* was standing under the trees where she'd left it, the tips of the plants poking out of the strips of linen. She dismounted and handed her reins to François, then walked toward the water. Her tools lay undisturbed, where she'd left them.

Alaïs jumped at the touch of her father's hand on her elbow.

"Show me," he said.

Without a word, she led her father along the bank until she reached the spot. At first, she could see nothing and, for a brief moment, she wondered if it had been a bad dream. But there, floating in the water among the reeds a little farther upstream than before, was the body.

She pointed. "There. By the knitbone."

To her astonishment, rather than summoning François, her father threw off his cloak and waded into the river.

"Stay there," he called over this shoulder.

Alaïs sat down on the bank and drew her knees up to her chin and watched as her father plowed into the shallows, paying no attention to the water splashing up over the tops of his boots. When he reached the body, he stopped and drew his sword. He hesitated for a moment, as if preparing himself for the worst, then, with the tip of the blade, Pelletier carefully lifted the man's left arm up out of the water. The mutilated hand, bloated and blue, lay balanced for a moment, then slithered down the silver flat of the blade toward the hilt, as if alive. Then it slipped back into the river with a dull splash.

He sheathed his sword, bent forward and rolled the corpse over. The body bobbed violently in the water, the head lolling heavily as if it was trying to detach itself from the neck.

Alaïs quickly turned away. She did not want to see the imprint of death on the unknown man's face.

Her father's mood was very different as they rode back toward Carcassonne. He was evidently relieved, as if a weight had been lifted from his shoulders. He exchanged lighthearted remarks with François and, whenever she caught his eye, he smiled affectionately.

Despite her exhaustion and frustration at not understanding the significance of what had taken place, Alaïs was filled with a sense of well-being too. It felt like old times, riding out with her father, when there had been time enough to enjoy each other's company.

As they turned away from the river and headed back up toward the château, her curiosity finally got the better of her. Alaïs plucked up the courage to ask her father the question that had been on the tip of her tongue ever since they set out.

"Did you discover what you needed to know, *Paire?*"

"I did."

Alaïs waited, until it was clear that she would have to draw an explanation out of him word by word.

"It wasn't him, though, was it?"

Her father glanced sharply at her.

She pressed on. "You believed, from my description, that you might know this man? Which is why you wanted to see the body for yourself." Alaïs could tell from the gleam in his eyes that she was right.

"I thought he *might* be known to me," he said in the end. "From my days in Chartres. A man dear to me."

"But he was a Jew."

Pelletier raised his eyebrows. "Yes, indeed."

"A Jew," she repeated. "Yet a friend?"

Silence. Alaïs persisted. "But it wasn't him, this friend?"

This time, Pelletier smiled. "It was not."

"Then who?"

"I don't know."

Alaïs was silent for a moment. She was sure her father had never mentioned such a friend. He was a good man, a tolerant man, but even so, if he had talked of such a friend in Chartres, a Jew, she would have remembered. Knowing well enough there was no point pursuing a subject against her father's wishes, she tried a different approach.

"It wasn't robbery? I was right about that."

Her father seemed happy to answer this. "No. They intended to kill him. The wound was too deep, too deliberate. Besides, they left almost everything of value on the body."

"*Almost* everything?" But Pelletier said nothing. "They could have been interrupted?" she suggested, risking pushing a little farther.

"I think not."

"Or perhaps they were seeking something particular?"

"No more, Alaïs. This is neither the time nor the place."

She opened her mouth, unwilling to let the matter drop, then shut it again. The discussion was clearly over. She would learn nothing more. Far better to wait until he was minded to talk. They rode the rest of the way in silence.

When they were back in sight of the Western Gate, François went on ahead.

"It would be advisable not to mention our expedition this morning to anyone," he said quickly.

"Not even Guilhem?"

"I cannot think your husband would be pleased to learn you had gone unaccompanied to the river," he said dryly. "Rumors spread so quickly. You should rest and try to put the whole unpleasant incident out of your mind."

Alaïs met his gaze with innocent eyes. "Of course. As you wish. I give you my word, *Paire*. I will speak of this to no one but you."

Pelletier hesitated, as if he suspected she was playing a trick on him, then smiled. "You are an obedient daughter, Alaïs. I can trust you, I know."

Despite herself, Alaïs blushed.

CHAPTER 4

From his vantage point on the tavern roof, the boy with the amber eyes and dark blond hair turned to see where the noise was coming from.

A messenger was galloping up through the crowded streets of the Cité from the Porte Narbonnaise, with complete disregard for anybody who got in his way. Men were yelling at him to dismount. Women snatched their children from under the thundering hooves. A couple of unchained dogs jumped up at the horse, barking and snarling and snapping at its hind legs. The rider took no notice.

The horse was sweating badly. Even from this distance, Sajhë could see the lines of white foam on its withers and round its mouth. He veered sharply toward the bridge that led to the Château Comtal.

Sajhë stood up to get a better view, balanced precariously on the sharp edge of the uneven tiles, in time to see Intendant Pelletier on a powerful gray appear between the gate towers, followed by Alaïs, also on horseback. She looked upset, he thought, and wondered what had happened and where they were going. They were not dressed for hunting.

Sajhë liked Alaïs. When she came to visit his grandmother, Esclarmonde, she talked to him, unlike many ladies of the household, who pretended he wasn't there. They were too anxious about the potions and medicines they wanted *menina*, his grandmother, to prepare for them—to reduce a fever, ease a swelling, to bring on childbirth or for affairs of the heart.

But in all the years he'd worshipped Alaïs, Sajhë had never seen her look quite like she had just then. The boy slithered down the tawny tiles to the edge of the roof and lowered himself down, landing with a soft thump and only just avoiding a goat tethered to a lopsided cart.

"Hey! Watch what you're doing," a woman yelled.

"I never touched it," he shouted, darting out of reach of her broom.

The Cité was buzzing with the sights, smells and sounds of market day. Wooden shutters banged against stone in every thoroughfare and alley, as servants and householders opened their windows to the air before the sun became too hot. Coopers watched their apprentices rolling barrels over the cobbles, clattering and bumping and jolting, racing each other to get to the taverns before their rivals. Carts jerked awkwardly over the uneven ground, their wheels creaking and sticking from time to time as they rumbled toward the main square.

Sajhë knew every shortcut in the Cité and he scampered in and out of the jostling arms and legs, dodging between the tapping hooves of sheep and goats, the donkeys and mules laden with goods and baskets, the pigs, lazy and slow, as they plodded their way through the streets. An older boy with an angry expression on his face was herding an unruly gaggle of geese, which honked and pecked at one another and at the bare legs of two little girls standing close by. Sajhë winked at them and tried to make them laugh. He went right up behind the ugliest bird and flapped his arms.

"What do you think you're doing?" shouted the boy. "Get away!"

The girls laughed. Sajhë honked, just as the old, gray goose spun round, stuck its neck out and hissed viciously in his face.

"Serves you right, *pèc*," said the boy. "Fucking idiot."

Sajhë jumped back from the snapping orange beaks. "You should control them better."

"Only babies are scared of geese," the boy sneered, squaring up to Sajhë. "Is the baby frightened of a harmless little goose? *Nenon.*"

"I'm not scared," boasted Sajhë, pointing at the girls, who were now hiding behind their mother's legs. "But they are. You should watch what you're doing."

"And what's it got to do with you, *è?*"

"I'm just saying, you should watch out."

He moved closer, switching his stick at Sajhë's face.

"And who's going to make me? You?"

The boy was a head taller than Sajhë. His skin was a mass of purple bruises and red marks. Sajhë took a step back and held up his hands.

"I said, who's going to make me?" repeated the boy, ready for a fight.

Words would have given way to fists had not an old drunk, who was slumped against the wall, woken up and started yelling at them to clear off and leave him alone. Sajhë took advantage of the diversion to slip away.

The sun was just climbing over the higher roofs of the buildings, flooding sections of the street with slats of bright light and glinting off the horseshoe outside the door of the blacksmith's forge. Sajhë stopped and looked in, feeling the heat from the furnace on his face even from the street.

There was a crowd of men waiting round the forge, as well as several younger *écuyers* with their masters' helmets, shields and hauberks, all of which required attention. He presumed the blacksmith in the château was overwhelmed with too much work.

Sajhë didn't have the blood or the pedigree to be apprenticed, but it didn't stop him dreaming of being a *chevalier* in his own colors. He smiled at one or two of the boys of his own age, but they just stared right through him, as they always did and always would.

Sajhë turned and walked away.

Most of the market traders were regulars and had set up in their usual places. The smell of hot fat filled Sajhë's nose the moment he walked into the square. He loitered at a stall where a man was frying pancakes, turning them on a hot griddle. The smell of thick bean soup and warm *mitadenc* bread, made from half barley and half wheat, stimulated his appetite. He walked past stalls selling buckles and pots, woolen cloths, skins and leather, both local goods and more exotic belts and purses from Córdoba or farther afield even, but he didn't stop. He paused a while by a stall offering knives and scissors for shearing sheep, before moving to the corner of the square where most of the live animals were penned. There were always lots of chickens and capons in wooden cages, sometimes larks and wrens, which fluted and whistled. His favorite were the rabbits, all squashed together in a heap of brown, black and white fur.

Sajhë walked past the stalls selling grain and salt, white meats, ale from casks and wine, until he found himself at a stand selling herbs and exotic spices. In front of the table was a merchant. Sajhë had never seen a man so tall, so black. He was dressed in long, shimmering blue robes, a shining silk turban and red and gold pointed slippers. His skin was darker even than that of the gypsies that traveled from Navarre and Aragon over the mountains. Sajhë guessed he must be a Saracen, although he'd never met one before.

The merchant had laid out his display in the shape of a wheel: greens and yellows, oranges, browns and reds, ocher. At the front were rosemary and parsley, garlic, marigold and lavender, but at the back there were more expensive spices, such as cardamom, nutmeg and saffron. Sajhë didn't recognize any of the others, but he was already looking forward to telling his grandmother what he had seen.

He was about to step forward to get a better look, when the Saracen roared in a voice like thunder. His heavy dark hand grabbed the skinny wrist of a cutpurse who'd tried to steal a coin from the embroidered purse that hung from a twisted red cord around his waist. He cuffed the boy around the head, sending him flying back into a woman standing behind, who started shouting. Straight away a crowd started to gather.

Sajhë slipped away. He didn't want to get caught up in any trouble.

Sajhë wandered out of the square toward the *taberna Sant Joan dels Evangèlis*. Since he had no money with him, at the back of his mind was the idea he could offer to run errands in exchange for a cup of *brout*. Then he heard someone calling his name.

Sajhë turned and saw one of his grandmother's friends, Na Marti, sitting with her husband at their stall, waving to attract his attention. She was a weaver and her husband was a carder. Most weeks they could be found in the same spot, spinning and combing, preparing their wool and threads.

Sajhë waved back. Like Esclarmonde, Na Marti was a follower of the new church. Her husband, Sénher Marti was not a believer, although he had come to Esclarmonde's house with his wife at Pentecost to hear the *Bons Homes* preach.

Na Marti ruffled his hair.

"How are you, young man? You're getting so tall, these days, I hardly recognize you."

"Fine, thank you," he replied, smiling at her, then turned to her husband who was combing wool into skeins ready to sell. "*Bonjorn, Sénher.*"

"And Esclarmonde?" Na Marti continued. "She's keeping well too? Keeping everyone in order as usual?"

He grinned. "She's the same as always."

"*Ben, ben.*" Good.

Sajhë sat himself down cross-legged at her feet and watched the spinning wheel as it turned round and round.

"Na Marti?" he said, after a while. "Why don't you come to pray with us anymore?"

Sénher Marti stopped what he was doing and exchanged a worried glance with his wife.

"Oh, you know how it is," Na Marti replied, avoiding his eye. "We're so busy these days. It's hard to make the journey to Carcassonne as often as we'd like."

She adjusted her bobbin and continued to spin, the rocking of the treadle filling the silence that had fallen between them.

"*Menina* misses you."

"I miss her too, but friends can't always be together."

Sajhë frowned. "But then why—"

Sénher Marti tapped him sharply on the shoulder.

"Do not talk so loudly," he said in a low voice. "This sort of thing is best kept to ourselves."

"What's best kept to ourselves?" he said, puzzled. "I only—"

"We heard, Sajhë," said Sénher Marti, glancing over his shoulder. "The whole market heard. Now, no more about prayer, *é*?"

Confused about what he'd done to make Sénher Marti so angry, Sajhë scrambled to his feet. Na Marti turned on her husband. They seemed to have forgotten all about him.

"You're being too harsh on him, Rogier," she hissed. "He's just a boy."

"And it only takes one person with a loose tongue and we'll be rounded up with the others. We can't afford to take risks. If people think we associate with heretics—"

"Heretic, indeed," she snapped back. "He's only a child!"

"Not the boy. Esclarmonde. It's common knowledge she's one of them. And if it gets out that we go to pray in her house, they'll accuse us of following the *Bons Homes* too and we'll be persecuted."

"So we abandon our friends? Just because of a few scare stories you've heard."

Sénher Marti dropped his voice. "I'm just saying we should be careful. You know what people are saying. That an army is coming to drive the heretics out."

"They've been saying that for years. You are making too much of it. As for the legates, these 'men of God' have been strolling around the countryside for years now, drinking themselves into the grave and nothing's ever come of it. Let the bishops argue it out amongst themselves and leave the rest of us to get on with our lives."

She turned away from her husband. "Take no notice," she said, putting her hand on Sajhe's shoulder. "You've done nothing wrong."

Sajhë looked at his feet, not wanting her to see him cry.

Na Marti continued in an unnaturally bright voice. "Now then, weren't you saying the other day that you wanted to buy a present for Alaïs? Why don't we see what we can find?"

Sajhë nodded. He knew she was trying to reassure him, but he felt muddled and embarrassed.

"I don't have any means to pay," he said.

"Well, don't you worry about that. I'm sure we can overlook that just this once. Now, why don't you take a look." Na Marti ran her fingers over the colorful rows of thread. "What about this? Do you think she'd like it? It's a perfect match for her eyes."

Sajhë fingered the delicate copper-brown thread.

"I'm not sure."

"Well, I think she will. Shall I wrap it for you?"

She turned away to look for a square of cloth to protect the thread. Not wanting to seem ungrateful, Sajhë tried to think of something safe to say. "I saw her earlier."

"Alaïs, yes? How was she? With that sister of hers?"

He pulled a face. "No. But she didn't look very happy all the same."

"Well," said Na Marti, "if she was upset before, then this is just the right time to give her a present. It will cheer her up. Alaïs usually comes to market in the morning, doesn't she? If you keep your eyes open and your wits about you, I'm sure you'll find her."

Glad to be excused from the strained company, Sajhë tucked the package under his tunic and said his goodbyes. After a couple of steps, he turned to wave. The Martis were standing side by side, looking after him, but saying nothing.

The sun was now high in the sky. Sajhë wandered around, asking after Alaïs. No one had seen her.

He was hungry now and had decided he might as well go home, when he suddenly caught sight of Alaïs standing at a stall offering goat's cheese for sale. He broke into a run and crept up on her, throwing his arms around her waist.

"*Bonjorn.*"

Alaïs spun round, rewarding him with a wide smile when she saw who it was.

"Sajhë," she said, ruffling his hair. "You gave me a surprise!"

"I've been looking for you everywhere," he grinned. "Are you all right? I saw you earlier. You looked upset."

"Earlier?"

"You were riding into the château with your father. Just after the messenger."

"Ah, earlier," she said. "Don't worry, I'm fine. I'd just had a tiring morning. How lovely to see your lively face, though." She gave him a kiss on the top of his head, making Sajhë scarlet. He stared furiously at his feet, not wanting her to see. "Anyway, since you're here, help me choose a good cheese."

The smooth round tablets of fresh goat's cheese were laid out in a perfect pattern on a bed of straw pressed tight inside wooden trays. Some looked dry with a yellowish skin. These were stronger flavored and might be a fortnight old. Others, made more recently, glistened wet and soft. Alaïs asked the prices, pointing at this portion and that, asking Sajhë's advice, until at last they had chosen the piece she wanted. She gave him a coin from her purse to hand to the seller, while she pulled out a small polished wooden board on which to carry the cheese.

Sajhë's eyes flared wide with surprise when he glimpsed the pattern on the reverse. Why did Alaïs have it? How? In his confusion, he dropped the coins on the ground. Embarrassed, he dived under the table, playing for time. When he stood up again, to his relief Alaïs appeared not to have noticed anything amiss, so Sajhë put the matter out of his mind. Instead, once the transaction was complete, he plucked up the courage to give Alaïs her present.

"I have something for you," he said shyly, thrusting the package abruptly into her hands.

"How kind," she said. "Is it from Esclarmonde?"

"No, from me."

"What a lovely surprise. May I open it now?"

He nodded, face serious, but eyes sparkling with anticipation as Alaïs carefully unwrapped the parcel.

"Oh, Sajhë, it's beautiful," she said, holding up the shiny, brown thread. "It's absolutely beautiful."

"I didn't steal it," he said quickly. "Na Marti gave it to me. I think she was trying to make it up to me."

The moment the words were out of his mouth, Sajhë regretted them.

"Make up to you for what?" said Alaïs quickly.

Just then, a shout went up. A man close by was pointing up at the sky. A flock of large, black birds was flying low across the Cité, from west to east, in the shape of an arrow. The sun seemed to glance off their sleek, dark feathers, like sparks from an anvil. Somebody close by said it was an omen, although nobody could agree if it was a good one or a bad one.

Sajhë did not believe in such superstitions, but today it made him shiver. Alaïs seemed to feel something too, because she put her arm around his shoulder and pulled him close.

"What's wrong?" he asked.

"*Res*," she said, too quickly. Nothing.

High above them, unconcerned with the human world, the birds continued on their way, until they were no more than a smudge in the sky.

CHAPTER 5

By the time Alaïs had shaken off her faithful shadow and made her way back to the Château Comtal, the midday bells were ringing out from Sant-Nasari.

She was exhausted and tripped several times going up the stairs, which seemed steeper than usual. All she wanted was to lie down in the privacy of her own chamber and rest.

Alaïs was surprised to find her door closed. By now, the servants should have been in and finished their tasks. The curtains around the bed were still drawn. In the half-light, Alaïs saw François had put her *panièr* on the low table beside the hearth as she'd asked him.

She put the cheese board down on the nightstand, then walked to the window to pin back the shutter. It should have been opened well before now to air the chamber. Daylight flooded in, revealing a layer of dust on the furniture and the patches on the bed curtains where the material had grown thin.

Alaïs walked over to the bed and pulled back the curtains.

To her astonishment Guilhem was still lying there, sleeping just as she'd left him before dawn. She gaped in surprise. He looked so perfectly at ease, so fine. Even Oriane, who had little good to say about anyone, admitted Guilhem was one of the finest looking of Viscount Trencavel's *chevaliers*.

Alaïs sat down on the bed next to him and ran her hand over his golden skin. Then, feeling unaccountably bold, she dipped a finger into the soft wet goat's cheese and spread a tiny amount on her husband's lips. Guilhem murmured and stirred beneath the bedclothes. He did not open his eyes, but he smiled languidly and reached out his hand.

Alaïs caught her breath. The air around her seemed to vibrate with expectation and promise as she allowed him to pull her down toward him.

The intimacy of the moment was shattered by the sound of heavy feet in the corridor. Somebody was bellowing Guilhem's name, a familiar voice, distorted by anger. Alaïs sprang up, mortified at the thought of her father witnessing so private a scene between them. Guilhem's eyes snapped open, just as the door was flung open and Pelletier strode into the room, François at his heels.

"You're late, du Mas," he roared, snatching a cloak from the nearest chair and hurling it at his son-in-law's head. "Get up. Everybody else is already in the Great Hall, waiting."

Guilhem scrambled upright. "The hall?"

"Viscount Trencavel summons his *chevaliers,* yet here you lie in bed. Do you think that you can just please yourself?" He was standing over Guilhem. "Well? What have you got to say for yourself?"

Pelletier suddenly noticed his daughter standing at the far side of the bed. His face softened. "Excuse me, *Filha.* I did not see you. Are you feeling better?"

She bowed her head. "Pleasing you, *Messire,* I am quite well."

"Feeling better?" asked Guilhem with confusion. "Are you unwell? Is something wrong?"

"Get up!" Pelletier yelled, switching his attention back to the bed. "You have as much time as it takes me to walk down the stairs and cross the courtyard, du Mas. If you are not in the Great Hall by then, it will be the worse for you!" Without another word, Pelletier spun on his heel and stormed out of the chamber.

In the painful silence that followed his departure, Alaïs felt rooted to the spot with embarrassment, although whether for herself or her husband, she could not tell.

Guilhem exploded. "How dare he burst in here as if he owns me? Who does he think he is?" With a savage kick, he launched the covers to the floor and hurled himself out of bed. "Duty calls," he said sarcastically. "It wouldn't do to keep the great Intendant Pelletier waiting."

Alaïs suspected that anything she said would make Guilhem's temper worse. She wanted to tell him what had happened at the river, at least to take his mind off his own anger, but she had given her father her word she would speak to no one.

Guilhem had already crossed the room and was getting dressed with his back to her. His shoulders were tense as he pulled on his tabard and fastened his belt.

"There may be news . . ." she started to say.

"That's no excuse," he snapped. "I received no word."

"I . . ." Alaïs let her words tail off. *What to say?*

She picked up his cloak from the bed and offered it to him. "Will you be long?" she said softly.

"Since I do not know why I am summoned to Council in the first place, how can I say?" he said, still angry.

All at once, his temper seemed to leave him. His shoulders relaxed and he turned to face her, no longer scowling. "Forgive me, Alaïs. You cannot answer for your father's behavior." He traced the outline of her chin with his hand. "Come. Help me with this."

Guilhem bent forward so Alaïs could reach the fastening more easily. Even so, she had to stand on tiptoe to fasten the round silver and copper brooch at his shoulder.

"*Mercé, mon còr,*" he said when she was done. "Right. Let's find out what this is all about. It's probably nothing of importance."

"As we were riding back into the Cité this morning, a messenger arrived," she said without thinking about it.

Immediately, Alaïs castigated herself. Now he was sure to ask where she'd been so early, and with her father, but his attention was on retrieving his sword from under the bed and he didn't pick up on her words.

Alaïs winced at the harsh sound of the metal as he pushed the blade back into its scabbard. It was a sound that, more than any other, symbolized his departure from her world to the world of men.

As Guilhem turned, his cloak fell against the wooden cheese board that was still balanced precariously on the edge of the table. It fell, tumbling with a clatter to the stone floor.

"It doesn't matter," Alaïs said quickly, not wanting to risk her father's anger by delaying Guilhem any longer. "The servants will do this. You go. Return when you can."

Guilhem smiled and was gone.

When she could no longer hear his tread, Alaïs turned back to the room and looked at the mess. Lumps of white cheese, wet and viscous, were stuck in the straw matting covering the floor. She sighed and bent down to retrieve the board.

It had come to rest on its side propped against the wooden bolster. As she picked it up, her fingers brushed against something on the underside. Alaïs turned it over to look.

A labyrinth had been carved into the polished surface of the dark wood.

"*Meravelhós.* So beautiful," she murmured.

Captivated by the perfect lines of the circles, curving around in ever decreasing circles, Alaïs traced the pattern with her fingers. It was smooth, flawless, a labor of love created with care and precision.

She felt a memory shift at the back of her mind. Alaïs held the board up, sure now that she had seen something like it once before, but the memory was elusive and refused to come out of the dark. She couldn't even remember where the board had come from in the first place. In the end she gave up trying to chase down the thought.

Alaïs summoned her servant, Severine, to clear the room. After that, to keep her mind from what was happening in the Great Hall, she turned her attention to the plants she had harvested from the river at dawn.

The crop already had been left too long. The linen cloths had dried out, the roots were brittle and the leaves had lost most of their moisture. Confident she could salvage something, Alaïs sprinkled water over the *panièr* and set to work.

But all the time she was grinding the roots and sewing the flowers into sachets for air sweeteners, all the time she was preparing the lotion for Jacques' leg, her eyes kept drifting back to the wooden board where it lay mute on the table in front of her, refusing to give up its secrets.

Guilhem ran across the courtyard, his cloak flapping uncomfortably around his knees, cursing his bad luck that today of all days he should be caught out.

It was unusual for *chevaliers* to be included in the Council. The fact that they'd been summoned to the Great Hall, rather than the *donjon*, suggested something serious.

Was Pelletier speaking the truth when he said he'd sent a personal messenger to Guilhem's chamber earlier? He couldn't be sure. What if François had come and found him absent? What would Pelletier have to say about that?

Either way, the end result was the same. He was in trouble.

The heavy door leading to the Great Hall stood open. Guilhem hurried up the steps, taking them two at a time.

As his eyes adjusted to the gloom of the corridor, he saw the distinctive outline of his father-in-law standing outside the entrance to the hall itself. Guilhem took a deep breath and carried on walking, his head down. Pelletier put out his arm, blocking his path.

"Where were you?" he said.

"Forgive me, *Messire*. I did not receive the summons—"

Pelletier's face was a deep, thunderous red. "How dare you be late?" he said in a voice of steel. "Do you think that orders do not apply to you? That you are so celebrated a *chevalier* that you can choose to come and go as you please rather than as your *seigneur* bids you?"

"*Messire*, I swear on my honor that if I had known—"

Pelletier gave a bitter laugh. "Your honor," he said fiercely, jabbing Guilhem in the chest. "Don't play me for a fool, du Mas. I sent my own servant to your rooms to give you the message in person. You had more than enough time to make yourself ready. Yet I have to come and fetch you myself. And, when I do, I find you in bed!"

Guilhem opened his mouth, then shut it again. He could see pools of spittle forming in the corners of Pelletier's mouth and in the gray bristles of his beard.

"Not so full of yourself now, then! What, nothing to say? I am warning you, du Mas, the fact that you are married to my daughter will not prevent me from making an example of you."

"Sire, I did—"

Without warning, Pelletier's fist slammed into his stomach. It was not a hard punch, but it was forceful enough to catch him off balance.

Taken by surprise, Guilhem stumbled back against the wall.

Straight away, Pelletier's massive hand was around his throat, pushing his head back against the stone. Out of the corner of his eye, Guilhem could see the *sirjan* at the door leaning forward to get a better view of what was going on.

"Have I made myself clear?" he spat in Guilhem's face, increasing the pressure again. Guilhem couldn't speak. "I can't hear you, *gojat*," Pelletier said. "Have I made myself clear?"

This time, he managed to choke out the words. "*Oc, Messire.*" Guilhem could feel himself turning puce. The blood was hammering in his head.

"I am warning you, du Mas. I'm watching. I'm waiting. And if you make one wrong step, I will see that you live to regret it. Do we understand one another?"

Guilhem gulped for air. He just managed to nod, scraping his cheek against the rough surface of the wall, when Pelletier gave a last, vicious shove, crunching his ribs against the hard stone, and released him.

Rather than go back into the Great Hall, Pelletier stormed out in the opposite direction into the courtyard.

The moment he'd gone, Guilhem doubled over, coughing and rubbing his throat, taking in great gulps of air like a drowning man. He massaged his neck and wiped the smear of blood from his lip.

Slowly, his breathing returned to normal. Guilhem straightened his clothes. Already his head was filled with the ways in which he would bring Pelletier to account for humiliating him like this. Twice in the space of one day. The insult was too great to be ignored.

Suddenly aware of the steady murmur of voices spilling out of the Great Hall, Guilhem realized he should join his comrades before Pelletier came back and found him still standing outside.

The guard made no attempt to hide his amusement.

"What are you staring at?" Guilhem demanded. "You keep your tongue in your head, do you hear, or it will be the worse for you."

It wasn't an idle threat. The guard immediately dropped his eyes and stood aside to let Guilhem enter.

"That's more like it."

With Pelletier's threats still ringing in his ears, Guilhem slipped into the chamber as unobtrusively as he could. Only his high color and the rapid beating of his heart betrayed anything of what had taken place.

CHAPTER 6

Viscount Raymond-Roger Trencavel stood on a platform at the far end of the Great Hall. He noticed Guilhem du Mas slipping in late at the back, but it was Pelletier he was waiting for.

Trencavel was dressed for diplomacy, not war. His red long-sleeved tunic, with gold trim around the neck and cuffs, reached to his knees. His blue cloak was held at the neck by a large, round gold buckle that caught the light from the sun shining in through the high windows that ran along the top of the southern wall of the chamber. Above his head was a huge shield bearing the Trencavel coat of arms, with two heavy metal pikes forming a diagonal cross behind it. The same ensign appeared on banners, ceremonial clothes and armor. It hung above the portcullis of the moated gateway of the Porte Narbonnaise, both to welcome friends and to remind them of the historic bond between the Trencavel dynasty and its subjects. To the left of the shield was a tapestry of a dancing unicorn, which had hung on the same wall for generations.

On the far side of the platform, set deep into the wall, was a small door that led to the viscount's private living quarters in the Tour Pinte, the watchtower and oldest part of the Château Comtal. The door was shielded by long blue curtains, also embroidered with the three strips of ermine that made up the Trencavel arms. They gave some protection from the bitter draughts that whistled through the Great Hall in winter. Today they were held back with a single, heavy gold twist.

Raymond-Roger Trencavel had spent his early childhood in these rooms, then returned to live within these ancient walls with his wife, Agnès de Montpellier, and his two-year-old son and heir. He knelt in the same tiny chapel as his parents had knelt; he slept in their oak bed, in which he had been born. On summer days like these, he looked out of the same arched windows at dusk and watched the setting sun paint the sky red over the Pays d'Oc.

From a distance, Trencavel appeared calm and untroubled, with his brown hair resting lightly on his shoulders and his hands clasped behind his back. But his face was anxious and his eyes kept darting to the main door.

. . . .

Pelletier was sweating heavily. His clothes were stiff and uncomfortable beneath his arms, clinging to the small of his back. He felt old and unequal to the task ahead of him.

He'd hoped the fresh air would clear his head. It hadn't. He was still angry with himself for losing his temper and allowing his animosity toward his son-in-law to deflect him from the task in hand. He couldn't allow himself the luxury of thinking about it now. He would deal with du Mas later if need be. Now, his place was at the viscount's side.

Simeon was not far from his mind either. Pelletier could still feel the cauterizing fear that had gripped his heart as he rolled the body over in the water. And the relief when the bloated face of a stranger stared, deadeyed, up at him.

The heat inside the Great Hall was overwhelming. More than a hundred men, of church and state, were packed into the hot, airless chamber, which reeked of sweat, anxiety and wine. There was a steady drizzle of restless and uneasy conversation.

The servants standing closest to the door bowed as Pelletier appeared and rushed to bring him wine. Immediately opposite, across the chamber, was a row of high-backed chairs of dark, polished wood, similar to the choir stalls of the cathedral church of Sant-Nasari. In them sat the nobility of the Midi, the *seigneurs* of Mirepoix and Fanjeaux, Coursan and Termenès, Albi and Mazamet. Each had been invited to Carcassonne to celebrate the feast day of Sant-Nasari at the end of July, yet now found himself instead summoned to Council. Pelletier could see the tension in their faces.

He picked his way through the groups of men, the consuls of Carcassonne and leading citizens from the market suburbs of Sant-Vicens and Sant-Miquel, his experienced gaze taking in the room without appearing to do so. Churchmen and a few monks were skulking in the shadows along the northern wall, their faces half-hidden by their robes and their hands folded out of sight inside the capacious sleeves of their black habits.

The *chevaliers* of Carcassonne, Guilhem du Mas now among them, were standing in front of the huge stone fireplace that stretched from floor to ceiling on the opposite side of the chamber. The *escrivan* Jehan Congost, Trencavel's scribe—and the husband of Pelletier's eldest daughter Oriane—was sitting at his high desk at the front of the hall.

Pelletier came to a halt in front of the dais and bowed. A look of relief swept across Viscount Trencavel's face.

"Forgive me, *Messire*."

"No matter, Bertrand," he said, gesturing that Pelletier should join him. "You're here now."

They exchanged a few words, their heads close together so that nobody could overhear them. Then, on Trencavel's word, Pelletier stepped forward.

"My lords," he bellowed. "My lords, pray silence for your *seigneur,* Raymond-Roger Trencavel, Viscount of Carcassona, Besièrs and Albi."

Trencavel stepped into the light, his hands spread wide in a gesture of greeting. The hall fell silent. Nobody moved. Nobody spoke.

"*Benvenguda,* my lords, loyal friends," he said. Welcome. His voice was as true as a bell and as steady, giving the lie to his youth. "*Benvenguda a Carcassona.* Thank you for your patience and for your presence. I am grateful to you all."

Pelletier cast his eye over the sea of faces, trying to gauge the mood of the crowd. He could see curiosity, excitement, self-interest and trepidation, and understood each emotion. Until they knew why they had been summoned and, more significantly, what Trencavel wanted of them, none of them knew how to behave.

"It is my fervent hope," Trencavel continued, "that the tournament and feast will go ahead at the end of this month as planned. However, today we have received information that is so serious and with such far-reaching consequences, that I believe it right to share it with you. For it affects us all.

"For the benefit of those not present at our last Council, let me remind you all of how the situation stands. Frustrated by the failure of his legates and preachers to convert the free people of this land to show obedience to the Church of Rome, at Easter one year ago, His Holiness Pope Innocent III preached a Crusade to rid Christendom of what he called the 'cancer of heresy' spreading unchecked through the lands of the Pays d'Oc.

"The so-called heretics, the *Bons Homes,* were, he claimed, worse than the very Saracens. However, his words, for all their passion and rhetoric, fell on deaf ears. The King of France was unmoved. Support was slow to come.

"The target of his venom was my uncle, Raymond VI, Count of Toulouse. Indeed, it was the intemperate actions of my uncle's men—who were implicated in the murder of the papal legate, Peter de Castelnau—that caused His Holiness to turn his eye on the Pays d'Oc in the first instance. My uncle was indicted on a charge of tolerating the spread of heresy in his lands and—by implication—ours." Trencavel hesitated, then corrected himself. "No, not of tolerating heresy, but of *encouraging* the *Bons Homes* to seek a home within his domains."

A fiercely ascetic-looking monk standing near the front raised his hand, seeking permission to speak.

"Holy brother," said Trencavel swiftly, "if I may beg your patience a while longer. When I have finished what I have to say, then all will have their chance. The time for debate will come."

Scowling, the monk let his arm fall back.

"The line between tolerance and encouragement, my friends, is a fine one," he continued softly. Pelletier nodded to himself, silently applauding Trencavel's astute handling of the situation. "So, whilst I freely acknowledged that my esteemed uncle's reputation for piety is not what it might be—" Trencavel paused, drawing them into the implied criticism, "and whilst I also accept that his behavior is hardly above reproach, it is not for us to judge the rights and wrongs of the matter." He smiled. "Let the priests argue theology and leave the rest of us in peace."

He paused. A shadow fell across his face. Now, there was no light left in his voice.

"This was not the first time the independence and sovereignty of our lands had been threatened by invaders from the north. I did not think anything would come of it. I could not believe that Christian blood would be spilled on Christian soil with the blessing of the Catholic Church.

"My uncle Toulouse did not share my optimism. From the start, he believed the threat of invasion was real. To protect his lands and sovereignty, he offered us an alliance. What I said to him, you will remember: that we, the people of the Pays d'Oc, live in peace with our neighbors, be they *Bons Homes,* Jews, even Saracens. If they uphold our laws, if they respect our ways and our traditions, then they are of our people. That was my answer then." He paused. "And it would be my answer still."

Pelletier nodded his approval at these words, watching as a wave of agreement spread through the Great Hall, sweeping up even the bishops and the priests. Only the same solitary monk, a Dominican from the color of his habit, was unmoved. "We have a different interpretation of tolerance," he muttered in his strong, Spanish accent.

From farther back, another voice rang out.

"*Messire,* forgive me, but all this we know. This is old news. What of now? Why are we called to Council?"

Pelletier recognized the arrogant, lazy tones of the most troublesome of Bérenger de Massabrac's five sons, and would have intervened had he not felt the viscount's hand on his arm.

"Thierry de Massabrac," said Trencavel, his voice deceptively benign, "we are grateful for your question. However, some of us here are less familiar with the complicated path of diplomacy than you."

Several men laughed and Thierry flushed.

"But you are right to ask. I have called you here today because the situation has changed."

Although nobody spoke, the atmosphere within the hall shifted. If the viscount was aware of the tightening of tension, he gave no indication of it, Pelletier was pleased to note, but continued to speak with the same easy confidence and authority.

"This morning we received news that the threat from the northern army is both more significant—and more immediate—than we previously thought. The Host—as this unholy army is calling itself—mustered in Lyon on the feast day of John the Baptist. Our estimate is that as many as twenty thousand *chevaliers* swamped the city, accompanied by who knows how many thousand more sappers, priests, ostlers, carpenters, clerics, farriers. The Host departed Lyon with that white wolf, Arnald-Amalric, the Abbot of Cîteaux, at its head." He paused and looked around the hall. "I know it is a name that will strike like iron in the hearts of many of you." Pelletier saw older statesmen nodding. "With him are the Catholic Archbishops of Reims, Sens and Rouen, as well as the Bishops of Autun, Clermont, Nevers, Bayeux, Chartres and Lisieux. As for the temporal leadership, although King Philip of France has not heeded the call to arms, nor allowed his son to go in his stead, many of the most powerful barons and principalities of the north have done so. Congost, if you please."

At the sound of his name, the *escrivan* ostentatiously put down his quill. His lank hair fell across his face. His skin, white and spongy, was almost translucent from a lifetime spent inside. Congost made great play of reaching down into his large leather bag and pulling out a roll of parchment. It seemed to have a life of its own in his sweaty hands.

"Get on with it, man," Pelletier muttered under his breath.

Congost puffed out his chest and cleared his throat several times, before finally beginning to read.

"Eudes, Duke of Burgundy; Hervé, Count of Nevers; the Count of Saint-Pol; the Count of Auvergne; Pierre d'Auxerre; Hervé de Genève; Guy d'Evreux; Gaucher de Châtillon; Simon de Montfort . . ."

Congost's voice was shrill and expressionless, yet each name seemed to fall like a stone into a dry well, reverberating through the hall. These were powerful enemies, influential barons of the north and east with resources, money and men at their disposal. They were opponents to be feared, not dismissed.

Little by little, the size and nature of the army massing against the south took shape. Even Pelletier, who had read the list for himself, felt dread shiver down his spine.

There was a low, steady rumble in the hall now: surprise, disbelief and anger. Pelletier picked out the Cathar bishop of Carcassonne. He was listening intently, his face expressionless, with several leading Cathar priests—*parfaits*—by his side. Next, his sharp eyes found the pinched, hooded features of Bérenger de Rochefort, the Catholic bishop of Carcassonne, standing on the opposite side of the Great Hall with his arms folded, flanked by priests from the cathedral church of Sant-Nasari and others from Sant-Cernin.

Pelletier was confident that, for the time being at least, de Rochefort would maintain allegiance to Viscount Trencavel rather than to the Pope. But how long would that last? A man with divided loyalties was not to be trusted. He would change sides as surely as the sun rose in the east and set in the west. Not for the first time, Pelletier wondered if it would be wise to dismiss the churchmen now, so that they could hear nothing they might feel obliged to report to their masters.

"We can stand against them, however many," came a shout from the back. "Carcassona is impregnable!" Others started to call out too. "So is Lastours!" Soon there were voices coming from every corner of the Great Hall, echoing off every surface like thunder caught in the gulleys and valleys of the Montagne Noire. "Let them come to the hills," shouted another. "We'll show them what it means to fight."

Raising his hand, Raymond-Roger acknowledged the display of support with a smile.

"My lords, my friends," he said, almost shouting to make himself heard. "Thanks for your courage, for your steadfast loyalty." He paused, waiting for the noise level to fall back. "These men of the north owe no allegiance to us, nor do we owe allegiance to them, except for that which binds all men on this earth under God. However, I did not expect betrayal by one who is bound by all ties of obligation, family and duty to protect our lands and people. I speak of my uncle and liege lord, Raymond, Count of Toulouse."

A hushed silence descended over the assembled company.

"Some weeks ago, I received reports that my uncle had submitted himself to a ritual of such humiliation that it shames me to speak of it. I sought verification of these rumors. They were true. At the great cathedral church of Sant-Gilles, in the presence of the papal legate, the count of Toulouse was received back into the arms of the Catholic Church. He was stripped to the waist and, wearing the cord of a penitent around his neck, he was scourged by the priests as he crawled on his knees to beg forgiveness."

Trencavel paused a moment, to allow his words to sink in.

"Through this vile abasement, he was received back into the arms of the Holy Mother Church." A murmur of contempt spread through the Council. "Yet there is more, my friends. I have no doubt that his ignominious display was intended to prove the strength of his faith and his opposition to the heresy. However, it seems even this was not enough to avert the danger he knew was coming. He has surrendered control of his dominions to the legates of His Holiness the Pope. What I learned today—" He paused. "Today I learned that Raymond, Count of Toulouse, is in Valence, less than a week's march away, with several hundred of his men. He waits only for word to lead the northern invaders across the river at Beaucaire and into our lands." He paused. "He has taken the Crusaders' cross. My lords, he intends to march against us."

Finally, the hall erupted in howls of outrage. "*Silenci*," Pelletier bellowed until his throat was hoarse, vainly trying to restore order to chaos. "Silence. Pray, silence!"

It was an unequal battle, one voice against so many.

The viscount stepped forward to the edge of the dais, positioning himself directly beneath the Trencavel coat of arms. His cheeks were flushed, but the battle light shone in his eyes and defiance and courage radiated from his face. He spread his arms wide, as if to embrace the chamber and all those within it. The gesture hushed all.

"So I stand here before you now, my friends and allies, in the ancient spirit of honor and allegiance that binds each of us to our brothers, to seek your good counsel. We, the men of the Midi, have only two paths left open to us and very little time to choose which to take. The question is this. *Per Carcassona!*" For Carcassonne. "*Per lo Miègjorn.*" For the lands of the Midi. "Must we submit? Or shall we fight?"

As Trencavel sat back in his chair, exhausted by his efforts, the noise levels in the Great Hall billowed around him.

Pelletier could not help himself. He bent forward and put his hand on the young man's shoulder.

"Well spoken, *Messire,*" he said quietly. "Most nobly done, my lord."

CHAPTER 7

For hour upon hour, the debate raged.

Servants scuttled to and fro, fetching baskets of bread and grapes, platters of meat and white cheese, endlessly filling and refilling the great jugs of wine. Nobody ate much, but they did drink, which fired their anger and dimmed their judgment.

The world outside the Château Comtal went on just the same. The bells of the churches marked the devotional hours of the day. The monks sang and the nuns prayed, cocooned within Sant-Nasari. In the streets of Carcassonne, the townspeople went about their business. In the suburbs and dwellings beyond the fortified walls, children played, women worked, merchants and peasants and guildsmen ate and talked and played dice.

Inside the Great Hall, reasoned argument started to give way to insults, recriminations. One faction wanted to stand firm. The other argued in favor of an alliance with the count of Toulouse, arguing that if estimates of the size of the army mustered at Lyon were accurate, then even their combined strength was not sufficient to withstand such an enemy.

Every man could hear the drums of war beating in his head. Some imagined honor and glory on the battlefield, the clash of steel on steel. Others saw blood covering the hills and the plains, an endless stream of the dispossessed and wounded stumbling defeated across the burning land.

Pelletier tirelessly wandered up and down the chamber, looking for signs of dissent or opposition or challenges to the viscount's authority. Nothing he observed gave him real cause for concern. He was confident that his *seigneur* had done enough to bind all to him and that, regardless of individual interests, the lords of the Pays d'Oc would unite behind Viscount Trencavel, whatever decision he reached.

The battle lines were drawn on geographical rather than ideological grounds. Those whose lands were on the more vulnerable plains wanted to put their faith in the power of talk. Those whose dominions lay in the highlands of the Montagne Noire to the north or the mountains of the Sabarthès and the Pyrenees were determined to stand firm against the Host and fight. Pelletier knew that it was with them that Viscount

Trencavel's heart lay. He was cast from the same metal as the mountain lords and shared their fierce independence of spirit.

But Pelletier knew too that Trencavel's head told him that the only chance of keeping his lands intact and protecting his people was to swallow his pride and negotiate.

By late afternoon, the chamber smelled of frustration and arguments gone stale. Pelletier was weary. He was worn out by picking over the bones, by all the fine phrases that turned round and round upon themselves without ever reaching an end. Now, his head was hurting too. He felt stiff and old, too old for this, he thought, as he turned the ring he wore always on his thumb, reddening the callused skin underneath.

It was time to bring matters to a conclusion.

Summoning a servant to bring water, he dipped a square of linen into the pitcher and handed it to the viscount.

"Here, *Messire,*" he said.

Trencavel took the wet cloth gratefully and wiped his forehead and neck.

"Do you think we have allowed them long enough?"

"I believe so, *Messire,*" Pelletier replied.

Trencavel nodded. He was sitting with his hands resting firmly on the carved wooden arms of his chair, looking as calm as he had when he had first taken to his feet and addressed the Council. Many older, more experienced men would have struggled to keep control of such a gathering, Pelletier thought. It was his strength of character that gave him the courage to carry it through.

"It is as we discussed before, *Messire?*"

"It is," Trencavel replied. "Although they are not all of one mind, I think that the minority will follow the wishes of the majority in this . . ." He stopped and for the first time a note of indecision, of regret, colored his words. "But, Bertrand, I wish there was another way."

"I know, *Messire,*" he said quietly. "I feel the same. But, however much it offends us, there is no alternative. Your only hope of protecting your people lies in negotiating a truce with your uncle."

"He might refuse to receive me, Bertrand," he said quietly. "When last we met, I said things I ought not to have said. We parted on bad terms."

Pelletier put his hand on Trencavel's arm. "That's a risk we have to take," he said, although he shared the same concern. "Time has moved on since then. The facts of the matter speak for themselves. If the Host is indeed as great as they say—even if it is half that size—then we have no choice. Within the Cité we will be safe, but your people outside the walls . . . Who will protect them? The count's decision to take the Cross

66

has left us—left *you, Messire*—as the only possible target. The Host will not be disbanded now. It needs an enemy to fight."

Pelletier looked down into Raymond-Roger's troubled face and saw regret and sorrow. He wanted to offer some comfort, say something, anything, but he could not. Any lack of resolve now would be fatal. There could be no weakening, no doubt. More hung on Viscount Trencavel's decision than the young man would ever know.

"You have done everything you can, *Messire*. You must hold firm. You must finish this. The men grow restless."

Trencavel glanced at the coat of arms above him, then back to Pelletier. For a moment, they held one another's gaze.

"Inform Congost," he said.

With a deep sigh of relief, Pelletier walked quickly to where the *escrivan* was sitting at his desk, massaging his stiff fingers. Congost's head shot up, but he said nothing as he picked up his feather and sat poised to record the final decision of the Council.

For the last time, Raymond-Roger Trencavel rose to his feet.

"Before I announce my decision, I must thank you all. Lords of Carcassès, Razès, Albigeois and the dominions beyond. I salute your strength, your fortitude and your loyalty. We have talked for many hours and you have shown great patience and spirit. We have nothing to reproach ourselves with. We are the innocent victims of a war not of our making. Some of you will be disappointed at what I am about to say, others pleased. I pray that we will all find the courage, with God's help and mercy, to stand together."

He drew himself up. "For the good of us all—and for the safety of our people—I will seek an audience with my uncle and liege lord, Raymond, Count of Toulouse. We have no way of knowing what will come of this. It is not even certain my uncle will receive me and time is not on our side. It is therefore important that we keep our intentions hidden. Rumor spreads fast and if something of our purpose reaches the ears of my uncle, it might weaken our bargaining position. Accordingly, preparations for the tournament will continue as planned. My aim is to return well before the feast day, I hope with good news." He paused. "It is my intention to leave tomorrow, at first light, taking with me only a small contingent of *chevaliers* and representatives, with your leave, from the great house of Cabaret, as well as Minerve, Foix, Quillan . . ."

"You have my sword, *Messire*," called one *chevalier*. "And mine," cried another. One by one, men fell to their knees around the hall.

Smiling, Trencavel held up his hand.

"Your courage, your valor, honors us all," he said. "My steward will inform those of you whose services are required. For now, my friends, I bid you grant me leave. I suggest you all return to your quarters to rest. We will meet at dinner."

In the commotion that accompanied Viscount Trencavel's departure from the Great Hall, nobody noticed a single figure in a long blue hooded cloak slide out of the shadows and slip away through the door.

CHAPTER 8

The bell for Vespers had long since fallen silent by the time Pelletier finally emerged from the Tour Pinte.

Feeling every one of his fifty-two years, Pelletier lifted aside the curtain and walked back into the Great Hall. He rubbed his temples with tired hands, trying to ease the persistent, hammering ache in his head.

Viscount Trencavel had spent the time since the end of Council with the strongest of his allies, talking about how best to approach the count of Toulouse. Talking for hour upon hour. One by one, decisions had been taken and messengers had galloped out from the Château Comtal bearing letters not only to Raymond VI, but also to the papal legates, to the abbot of Cîteaux and Trencavel's consuls and viguiers in Béziers. The *chevaliers* who were to accompany the viscount had been informed. In the stables and the smithy, preparations were already in hand and would continue most of the night.

The chamber was filled with a hushed but expectant silence. Because of tomorrow's early departure, instead of the planned banquet there was to be a more informal meal instead. Long trestle tables had been set out, unclothed, in rows running from north to south across the room. Candles flickered dimly in the center of each table. In the high wall sconces, the torches were already burning fiercely, setting the shadows dancing and flickering.

At the far end of the room, servants came in and out, carrying dishes that were more plentiful than ceremonial. Hart, venison, chicken drumsticks with capsicum, earthenware bowls filled with beans and sausage and freshly baked white bread, purple plums stewed in honey, rose-colored wine from the vineyards of the Corbières and pitchers of ale for those with weaker heads.

Pelletier nodded his approval. He was pleased. In his absence, François had deputized well. Everything looked as it should and of a level of courtesy and hospitality Viscount Trencavel's guests had the right to expect.

François was a good servant, despite his unfortunate start in life. His mother had been in the service of Pelletier's French wife, Marguerite, and was hanged for a thief when François was no more than a boy. His father was unknown. When his wife had died nine years ago, Pelletier had taken

69

François on, trained him and given him a position. From time to time, he allowed himself to feel satisfaction at how well François had turned out.

Pelletier walked out into the Cour d'Honneur. The air was cool here and he lingered a while in the doorway. Children were playing around the well, earning a slap on the legs from their nurses when the boisterous games got too rowdy. Older girls strolled arm in arm in the twilight, talking, whispering their secrets to one another.

At first he didn't notice the small, dark-haired boy sitting crossed-legged on the wall by the chapel.

"Messire! Messire!" cried the boy, scrambling to his feet. "I got something for you."

Pelletier took no notice. *"Messire."* The boy persisted, tugging at his sleeve to attract his attention. "Intendant Pelletier, please. Important."

He felt something being pushed into his hand. He looked down to see it was a letter written on heavy cream parchment. His heart lurched. On the outside was his own name, inscribed in a familiar, distinctive hand. Pelletier had persuaded himself he'd never see it again.

Pelletier grabbed the boy by the scruff of the neck. "Where did you get this?" he demanded, shaking him roughly. "Speak." The boy wriggled like a fish on a line, trying to get free. "Tell me. Quick, now."

"A man gave it to me at the gate," the boy whimpered. "Don't hurt me. I've done nothing."

Pelletier shook him harder. "What sort of man?"

"Just a man."

"You'll have to do better than that," he said harshly, his voice rising. "There's a *sol* in it for you if you can tell me what I want to know. Was the man young? Old? Was he a soldier?" He paused. "A Jew?"

Pelletier fired question after question until he'd dragged the facts out of the boy. They didn't amount to much. Pons told him he'd been playing with friends in the moat of the Château Comtal, trying to get across from one side of the bridge to the other without the guards catching them. At dusk, when the light was just beginning to fade, a man had approached them and asked if anybody knew Intendant Pelletier by sight. When Pons said he did, the man had given him a *sol* to deliver the letter. He said it was very important and very urgent.

There was nothing special about the man that marked him out. He was of middle years, neither old nor young. He was not especially dark, nor fair either. His face was unmarked, unblemished by either pox or battle. He hadn't noticed if the man wore a ring, because his hands were concealed underneath his cloak.

Finally satisfied he had learned all he could, Pelletier reached into his purse and gave the boy a coin.

"Here. This is for your trouble. Now, go."

Pons didn't wait to be told a second time. He wriggled out of Pelletier's grasp and ran, as fast as his legs would carry him.

Pelletier headed back inside, holding the letter tight to his chest. He registered no one as he swept through the corridor leading to his chamber.

The door was locked. Cursing his own caution, Pelletier fumbled with the keys, his haste making him clumsy. François had lit the *calèlhs,* the oil lamps, and set his night tray with a jug of wine and two earthenware goblets on the table in the center of the room, as he did every night. The highly polished brass surface of the tray gleamed in the flickering golden light.

Pelletier poured himself a drink to steady his nerves, his head full of dusty images, memories of the Holy Land and the long, red shadows of the desert. Of the three books and the ancient secret contained within their pages.

The coarse wine was sour on his tongue and hit the back of this throat with a sting. He downed it in one, then refilled the goblet. Many times he'd tried to visualize how he would feel at this moment. Yet now it had finally come, he felt numb.

Pelletier sat down, placing the letter on the table between his outstretched hands. He knew what it said. It was the message he'd been both anticipating and dreading for many years, ever since he'd arrived in Carcassonne. In those days, the prosperous and tolerant lands of the Midi had seemed a safe hiding place.

As the seasons rolled one into the next, over time Pelletier's expectations of being called upon diminished. Day-to-day life took over. Thoughts of the books faded from his mind. In the end, he had almost forgotten that he was waiting at all.

More than twenty years had passed since he'd last set eyes upon the author of the letter. Until this moment, he realized, he'd not even known if his teacher and mentor was still alive. It was Harif who had taught him to read in the shade of the olive groves on the hills outside Jerusalem. It was Harif who'd opened his senses to a world more glorious, more magnificent than anything Pelletier had ever known. It was Harif who'd taught him to see that Saracens, Jews and Christians were following but different paths to the one God. And it was Harif who'd revealed to him that beyond all that was known lay a truth far older, more ancient, more absolute than anything the modern world had to offer.

The night of Pelletier's initiation into the *Noublesso de los Seres* was as sharp and clear in his mind as if it was yesterday. The shimmering robes of gold and the bleached white altar cloth, as dazzling as the forts that glinted high on the hills above Aleppo among the cypress trees and orange groves. The smell of the incense, the rise and fall of the voices whispering in the darkness. Illumination.

That night, another lifetime ago, or so it seemed to Pelletier now, was when he had looked into the heart of the labyrinth and made a vow to protect the secret with his life.

He pulled the candle closer. Even without the authenticity of the seal, there could be no doubt that the letter was from Harif. He would recognize his hand anywhere, the distinctive elegance of his letters and the exact proportions of his script.

Pelletier shook his head, trying to dislodge the memories threatening to overwhelm him. He took a deep breath, then slipped his knife under the seal. The wax split open with a soft crack. He smoothed the parchment flat.

The letter was brief. Across the top of the sheet were the symbols Pelletier remembered from the yellow walls of the labyrinth cave in the hills outside the Holy City. Written in the ancient language of Harif's ancestors, they meant nothing except to those initiated into the *Noublesso*.

Pelletier read the words aloud, the familiar sounds reassuring him, before turning to Harif's letter.

Fraire

It is time. Darkness is coming to these lands. There is malice in the air, an evil that will destroy and corrupt all that is good. The texts are no longer safe in the plains of the Pays d'Oc. It is time for the Trilogy to be reunited. Your brother awaits you in Besièrs, your sister in Carcassona. It falls to you to carry the books to a place of greater safety.

72

Make haste. The summer passes to Navarre will be closed by Toussaint, perhaps sooner if the snows come early. I shall expect you by the Feast Day of Sant-Miquel.

Pas a pas, se va luènh.

The chair creaked as Pelletier leaned sharply back. It was no more than he expected. Harif's instructions were clear. He asked no more than Pelletier had once sworn to give. But yet, he felt as if his soul had been sucked out of his body leaving only a hollow space.

The pledge he had given to guard the books had been made willingly, but in the simplicity of youth. Now, at the end of his middle years, it was more complicated. He had fashioned a different life for himself in Carcassonne. He had other allegiances, others he loved and served.

Only now did he realize how completely he'd persuaded himself that the moment of reckoning would not come in his lifetime. That he would never be forced to choose between his loyalty and responsibility to Viscount Trencavel and his obligation to the *Noublesso*.

No man could serve two masters with honor. If he did as Harif commanded, it would mean abandoning the viscount at the hour of his greatest need. Yet every moment he stayed at Raymond-Roger's side, he would be failing in his duty to the *Noublesso*.

Pelletier read the letter again, praying for a solution to present itself. This time, certain words, certain phrases stood out: *"Your brother awaits you in Besièrs."*

Harif could only mean Simeon. But in Béziers? Pelletier lifted the goblet to his lips and drank, tasting nothing. How strange that Simeon had come so forcefully into his mind today, after many years of absence.

A twist of fate? Coincidence? Pelletier believed in neither. Yet how to account for the dread that had swept through him when Alaïs had described the body of the man lying murdered in the waters of the Aude? There was no reason to imagine it would be Simeon, yet he'd been so certain.

And this: *"your sister in Carcassona."*

Puzzled, Pelletier traced a pattern in the light surface of dust on the wooden table with his finger. A labyrinth.

Could Harif have appointed a woman as a guardian? Had she been here in Carcassonne, under his nose, all this time? He shook his head. It could not be.

CHAPTER 9

Alaïs stood at her window, waiting for Guilhem to return. The sky over Carcassonne was a deep, velvet blue, casting a soft mantle over the land. The dry, evening wind from the north, the *Cers,* was blowing gently down from the mountains, rustling the leaves on the trees and the reeds on the banks of the Aude, bringing the promise of fresher air along with it.

There were pinpricks of light shining in Sant-Miquel and Sant-Vicens. The cobbled streets of the Cité itself were alive with people eating and drinking, telling stories and singing songs of love and valor and loss. Around the corner from the main square, the fires of the blacksmith's forge still burned.

Waiting. Always waiting.

Alaïs had rubbed her teeth with herbs to make them whiter and basted a small sachet of forget-me-nots into the neck of her dress for perfume. The chamber was filled with a sweet aroma of burning lavender.

The Council had ended some time ago and Alaïs had expected Guilhem to come or at least to send word to her. Fragments of conversation drifted up from the courtyard below like wisps of smoke. She caught a glimpse of her sister Oriane's husband, Jehan Congost, as he scuttled across the courtyard. She counted seven or eight *chevaliers* of the household and their *écuyers,* rushing purposefully to the forge. Earlier, she'd noticed her father reprimanding a young boy who had been hanging around the chapel.

Of Guilhem there was no sign.

Alaïs sighed, frustrated at having confined herself to her chamber for nothing. She turned back to face the room, wandering randomly from table to chair and back again, her restless fingers looking for something to do. She stopped in front of her loom and stared at the small tapestry she was working on for Dame Agnès, a complicated bestiary of wild creatures and birds with sweeping tails that slithered and clawed their way up a castle wall. Usually, when the weather or her responsibilities in the household kept her confined indoors, Alaïs found solace in such delicate work.

Tonight she couldn't settle to anything. Her needles sat untouched at her frame, the thread Sajhë had given her unopened beside it. The potions she'd prepared earlier from the angelica and comfrey were neatly labeled and stored in rows on a wooden shelf in the coolest and darkest part of the room. She'd picked up and examined the wooden board until she was sick of the sight of it and her fingers sore with tracing the pattern of the labyrinth over and over. Waiting, waiting.

"*Es totjorn lo meteis,*" she murmured. Always the same song.

Alaïs walked over to the glass and peered at her reflection. A small, serious heart-shaped face with intelligent brown eyes and pale cheeks looked back at her, neither plain nor beautiful. Alaïs adjusted the neckline of her dress, as she'd seen other girls do, trying to make it more fashionable. Perhaps if she sewed a piece of lace to . . .

A sharp knock at the door interrupted her thoughts.

Perfin. At last. "I'm here," she called out.

The door opened. The smile slid from her face.

"François. What is it?"

"Intendant Pelletier requests your presence, Dame."

"At this hour?"

François shifted awkwardly from one foot to the other.

"He is waiting on you in his chamber. I think there is some need of haste, Alaïs."

She glanced at him, surprised by his use of her name. She had never known him to make such a mistake before. "Is something the matter?" she asked quickly. "Is my father unwell?"

François hesitated. "He is much . . . preoccupied, Dame. He would be glad of your company presently."

She sighed. "I seem to have been out of step all day."

He looked puzzled. "Dame?"

"Never mind, François. I'm just out of sorts tonight. Of course I will come, if my father wishes it. Shall we go?"

In her room at the opposite end of the living quarters, Oriane was sitting in the center of her bed with her long, shapely legs curled under her.

Her green eyes were half closed, like a cat's. There was a self-satisfied smile on her face as she allowed the comb to be pulled through her tumbling black curls. From time to time, she felt the lightest touch of its bone teeth on her skin, delicate and suggestive.

"This is very . . . soothing," she said.

A man was standing behind her. He was naked to the waist and there was the faintest sheen of sweat between his broad, strong shoulders. "Soothing, Dame?" he said lightly. "That was not quite my intention."

She could feel his warm breath on her neck as he leaned forward to gather the hair from her face, and then laid it in a twist against her back.

"You are very beautiful," he whispered.

He began to massage her shoulders and neck, gently at first, then more firmly. Oriane bowed her head, as his skillful hands traced the outline of her cheekbones, her nose, her chin, as if he was committing her features to memory. From time to time, they slid lower, to the soft, white skin at her throat.

Oriane raised one of his hands to her mouth and licked the ends of his fingers with her tongue. He drew her back against him. She could feel the heat and weight of his body, could feel the proof of how much he wanted her pressing against her back. He turned her round to face him and parted her lips with his fingers, then slowly began to kiss her.

She paid no attention to the sound of footsteps in the corridor outside, until somebody started to bang on the door.

"Oriane!" called a shrill, peevish voice. "Are you there?"

"It's Jehan!" she muttered under her breath, more annoyed than alarmed by the interruption. She opened her eyes. "I thought you said he wouldn't be back yet."

He looked toward the door. "I didn't think he would be. When I left them, it looked as if he would be occupied with the viscount for some time. Is it locked?"

"Of course," she said.

"Won't he think that strange?"

Oriane shrugged. "He knows better than to enter without invitation. Nevertheless, you had better conceal yourself." She gestured to a small alcove behind a tapestry that hung on the far side of the bed. "Don't worry," she smiled, seeing the expression on his face. "I'll get rid of him as quickly as I can."

"And how are you going to do that?"

She put her hands around his neck and pulled him down to her, close enough for him to feel her eyelashes brush against his skin. He stirred against her.

"Oriane?" whined Congost, his voice rising higher every time he spoke. "Open the door this instant!"

"You'll have to wait and see," she murmured, bending to kiss the man's chest and his firm stomach, a little lower. "Now, you must disappear. Even *he* won't remain outside forever."

Once she was sure her lover was safely hidden, Oriane tiptoed over to the door, turned the key in the lock without making a sound, then ran back to the bed and arranged the curtains around her. She was ready to enjoy herself.

"Oriane!"

"Husband," she replied petulantly. "There's no need for all this noise. It *is* open."

Oriane heard fumbling, then the door open and bang shut. Her husband bustled into the room. She heard the clip of metal on wood as he put his candle down on the table.

"Where are you?" he said irritably. "And why is it so dark in here? I am in no mood for games."

Oriane smiled. She stretched back against the pillows, her legs slightly apart and her smooth, bare arms draped above her head. She wanted nothing left to his imagination.

"I'm here, Husband."

"The door was not open when first I tried it," he was saying irritably, as he pulled back the curtains, then fell speechless.

"Well, you can't have been . . . pushing . . . hard enough," she said.

Oriane watched his face turn white, then red as puce. His eyes bulged in his head and his mouth hung open as he gaped at her high, full breasts and her dark nipples, her unbound hair fanned out around her on the pillow like a mass of writhing snakes, the curve of her small waist and soft swell of her stomach, the triangle of wiry, black hair between her thighs.

"What do you think you are doing?" he screeched. "Cover yourself up immediately."

"I was asleep, Husband," she replied. "You woke me."

"I woke you? I *woke* you," he spluttered. "You were sleeping like . . . like this?"

"It is a hot night, Jehan. Can I not be allowed to sleep as I wish, in the privacy of my own chamber?"

"Anyone could have come in and seen you like this. Your sister, your serving woman, Guirande. Anyone!"

Oriane slowly sat up and looked defiantly at him, winding a strand of her hair between her fingers. "Anyone?" she said sarcastically. "I dismissed Guirande," she said coolly. "I had no further need of *her* services."

She could see he desperately wanted to turn away, but could not. Desire and disgust were running in equal measure through his dried-up blood.

"Anyone could have come in," he said again, although less confidently.

"Yes, I suppose that's true. Although nobody has. Except for you, Husband, of course." She smiled. It was the look of an animal about to strike. "And now, since you are here, perhaps you can tell me where you have been?"

"You know where I've been," he snapped. "In Council."

She smiled. "In Council? All this time? The Council broke up well before it was dark."

Congost flushed. "It is not your place to challenge me."

Oriane narrowed her eyes. "By Sant Foy, you're a pompous man, Jehan. 'It's not your place . . .'" The mimicry was perfect and both men winced at the cruelty of it. "Come on, Jehan, tell me where you've been? Discussing *affairs* of state, maybe? Or have you been with a lover perhaps, è Jehan? Do you have a lover hidden away in the château somewhere?"

"How dare you speak to me like that. I—"

"Other husbands tell their wives where they have been. Why not you? Unless, as I say, there is a good reason not to."

Congost was shouting now. "Other husbands should learn to hold their tongues. It's not women's business."

Oriane moved slowly across the bed toward him.

"Not women's business," she said. "Is that so?"

Her voice was low and full of spite. Congost knew she was making sport with him, but did not understand the rules of engagement. He never had.

Oriane shot out her hand and pressed the telltale bulge beneath his tunic. With satisfaction, she saw the panic and surprise in his eyes as she began to move her hand up and down.

"So, Husband," she said contemptuously. "Tell me what you do consider to be the business of women? Love?" She pushed harder. "This? What would you call it, sex?"

Congost sensed a trap, but he was mesmerized by her and didn't know what to say or do. He couldn't stop himself leaning toward her. His wet lips were flapping like a fish's mouth and his eyes screwed tight. He might despise her, but she could still make him want her, just like every other man, ruled by what hung between his legs, for all his reading and writing. She despised him.

Abruptly, she withdrew her hand, having got the reaction she wanted. "Well, Jehan," she said coldly. "If you have nothing you are prepared to tell me, then you might as well go. You are of no use to me here."

Oriane saw something in him snap, as if all the disappointments and frustrations he'd ever suffered in his life were flashing through his mind. Before she knew what was happening, he had hit her, hard enough to send her sprawling back on the bed.

She gasped in surprise.

Congost was motionless, staring down at his hand as if it had nothing to do with him.

"Oriane, I—"

"You are pathetic," she screamed at him. She could taste blood in her mouth. "I told you to go. So go. Get out of my sight!"

For a moment, Oriane thought he was going to try to apologize. But when he raised his eyes, she saw hate, not shame, in them. She breathed a sigh of relief. Things would play out as she had planned.

"You disgust me," he was shouting, backing away from the bed. "You're no better than an animal. No, worse than a beast, for you know what you are doing." He snatched up her blue cloak, which was lying wantonly on the floor, and threw it at her face. "And cover yourself up. I don't want to find you like this when I get back, flaunting yourself like a whore."

When she was sure he had gone, Oriane lay back on the bed and pulled her cloak up over her, a little shaken but exhilarated. For the first time in four years of marriage, the stupid, feeble, weak old man her father had forced her to take as a husband had actually succeeded in surprising her. She had intended to provoke him, certainly, but she'd not expected him to strike her. And so hard. She ran her fingers over her skin, which was still smarting from the blow. He had meant to hurt her. Perhaps there would be a mark? That might be worth something. Then she could show her father what his decision had brought her to.

Oriane brought herself up short with a bitter laugh. She wasn't Alaïs. Only Alaïs mattered to their father, for all his attempts to conceal it. Oriane was too like their mother, in looks and character, for his liking. As if he would care in the slightest if Jehan beat her half to death. He'd assume she deserved it.

For a moment, she allowed the jealousy she kept hidden, from all but Alaïs, to leak out from behind the perfect mask of her beautiful, unreadable face. Her resentment at her lack of power, her lack of influence, her disappointment. What value had her youth and beauty when she was tied to a man with no ambition and no prospects, a man who had never even lifted a sword? It wasn't fair that Alaïs, the younger sister, should have all the things that she wanted and yet was denied. Things that should be hers by right.

Oriane twisted the material between her fingers, as if it was Alaïs' pale skinny arm she was pinching. Plain, spoiled, indulged Alaïs. She squeezed tighter, seeing in her mind's eye a purple bruise spreading across her skin.

"You shouldn't taunt him."

Her lover's voice cut through the silence. She had almost forgotten that he was there.

"Why not?" she said. "It's the only enjoyment I have from him."

He slipped through the curtain and touched her cheek with his fingers. "Did he hurt you? He's left a mark."

She smiled at the concern in his voice. How little he really knew her. He saw only what he wanted to see, an image of the woman he thought she was.

"It's nothing," she replied.

The silver chain at his neck brushed her skin as he bent down to kiss her. She could smell his need to possess her. Oriane shifted position, allowing the blue material to fall away from her like water. She ran her hands over his thighs, the skin pale and soft compared to the golden brown of his back and arms and chest, then raised her eyes higher. She smiled. He had waited long enough.

Oriane leaned forward to take him in her mouth, but he pushed her back on the bed and knelt down beside her.

"So what enjoyment do you wish for from me, my lady?" he said, gently parting her legs. "This?"

She murmured as he bent forward and kissed her. "Or this?"

His mouth crept lower, to her hidden, private space. Oriane held her breath as his tongue played across her skin, biting, licking, teasing.

"Or this, maybe?" She felt his hands, strong and tight around her waist as he pulled her to him. Oriane wrapped her legs around his back.

"Or maybe this is what you really want?" he said, his voice straining with desire as he plunged deep inside her. She groaned with satisfaction, scratching her nails down his back, claiming him.

"So your husband thinks you're a whore, does he," he said. "Let us see if we can prove him right."

CHAPTER 10

Pelletier paced the floor of his chamber, waiting for Alaïs.

It was cooler now, but there was sweat on his broad forehead and his face was flushed. He should be down in the kitchens supervising the servants, making sure everything was in hand. But he was overwhelmed by the significance of the moment. He felt he was standing at a crossroads, paths stretching out in every direction, leading to an uncertain future. Everything that had gone before in his life, and everything that was yet to come, depended on what he decided to do now.

What was taking her so long?

Pelletier tightened his fist around the letter. Already he knew the words off by heart.

He turned away from the window and his eye was caught by something bright, glinting in the dust and shadows behind the door frame. Pelletier bent down and picked it up. It was a heavy silver buckle with copper detail, large enough to be the fastening for a cloak or a robe.

He frowned. It wasn't his.

He held it to a candle to get a better look. There was nothing distinctive about it. He'd seen a hundred just like it for sale in the market. He turned it over in his hands. It was of good enough quality, suggesting someone of comfortable rather than wealthy circumstances.

It couldn't have been here long. François tidied the room each morning and would have noticed if it had been there then. No other servants were allowed in and the room had been locked all day.

Pelletier glanced around, looking for other signs of an intruder. He felt uneasy. Was it his imagination or were the objects on his desk slightly out of place? Had his bed coverings been disarranged? Everything alarmed him tonight.

"*Paire?*"

Alaïs spoke softly, but she startled him all the same. Hastily, he pushed the buckle into his pouch. "Father," she repeated. "You sent for me?"

Pelletier collected himself. "Yes, yes, I did. Come."

"Will there be anything else, *Messire?*" asked François from the doorway.

"No. But wait outside in case I have need of you."

He waited until the door was shut, then beckoned Alaïs to take a seat at the table. He poured her a cup of wine and refilled his own, but did not settle.

"You look tired."

"I am a little."

"What are people saying of the Council, Alaïs?"

"No one knows what to think, *Messire*. There are so many stories. Everyone prays that things are not as bad as they seem. Everyone knows that the viscount rides for Montpelhièr tomorrow, accompanied by a small entourage, to seek audience with his uncle, the count of Toulouse." She raised her head. "Is it true?"

He nodded.

"Yet it is also claimed that the tournament will go ahead."

"Also true. It is the viscount's intention to complete his mission and return home within two weeks. Before the end of July certainly."

"Is the viscount's mission likely to succeed?"

Pelletier did not answer but just continued to pace up and down. His anxiety was spreading to her.

She took a gulp of wine for courage. "Is Guilhem one of the party?"

"Has he not informed you himself?" he said sharply.

"I've not seen him since the Council adjourned," she admitted.

"Where in the name of Sant-Foy is he?" Pelletier demanded.

"Please just tell me yes or no."

"Guilhem du Mas has been chosen, although I have to say that it is against my wishes. The viscount favors him."

"With reason, *Paire*," she said quietly. "He is a skilled *chevalier*."

Pelletier leaned across and poured more wine into her goblet. "Tell me, Alaïs, do you trust him?"

The question caught her off guard, but she answered without hesitation. "Should not all wives trust their husbands?"

"Yes, yes. I would not expect you to answer otherwise," he said dismissively, waving his hand. "But did he ask you what had happened this morning at the river?"

"You commanded me to speak of it to no one," she said. "Naturally, I obeyed you."

"As I trusted you to keep your word," he said. "But, still, you have not quite answered my question. Did Guilhem ask where you'd been?"

"There has not been the opportunity," she said defiantly. "As I told you, I have not seen him."

Pelletier walked over to the window. "Are you scared that war will come?" he said, his back to her.

Alaïs was disconcerted by the abrupt change of subject, but replied without skipping a beat.

"At the thought of it, yes, *Messire*," she replied cautiously. "But surely it won't come to that?"

"No, it might not."

He placed his hands on the window ledge, seemingly lost in his own thoughts and oblivious to her presence. "I know you think my question impertinent, but I asked it for a reason. Look deep into your heart. Weigh your answer carefully. Then, tell me the truth. Do you trust your husband? Do you trust him to protect you, to do right by you?"

Alaïs understood the words that mattered lay unsaid and hidden somewhere beneath the surface, but she feared to answer. She did not want to be disloyal to Guilhem. At the same time, she could not bring herself to lie to her father.

"I know he does not please you, *Messire*," she said steadily, "although I do not know what he has done to offend you—"

"You know perfectly well what he does to offend me," Pelletier said impatiently. "I've told you often enough. However, my personal opinion of du Mas, for good or ill, is neither here nor there. One can dislike a man and yet see his worth. Please, Alaïs. Answer my question. A very great deal depends on it."

Images of Guilhem sleeping. Of his eyes, dark as lodestone, the curve of his lips as he kissed the intimate inside of her wrist. Memories so powerful they made her dizzy.

"I cannot answer," she said eventually.

"Ah," he sighed. "Good. Good. I see."

"With respect, *Paire*, you see nothing," Alaïs flared up. "I have said nothing."

He turned round. "Did you tell Guilhem I had sent for you?"

"As I said, I have not seen him and . . . and it is not right that you should question me in this manner. To make me choose between loyalty to you and to him." Alaïs moved to rise. "So unless there is some reason you require my presence, *Messire*, at this late hour, I beg you give me leave to withdraw."

Pelletier made to calm the situation. "Sit down, sit down. I see I have offended you. Forgive me. It was not my intention."

He held out his hand. After a moment, Alaïs took it.

"I do not mean to speak in riddles. My hesitation is . . . I need to make things clear in my own mind. Tonight I received a message of great significance, Alaïs. I have spent the past few hours trying to decide what to do, weighing the alternatives. Even though I thought I had resolved on one course of action and sent for you, nonetheless doubts remained."

Alaïs met his gaze. "And now?"

"Now my path lies clear before me. Yes. I believe I know what I must do."

The color drained from her face. "So war is coming," she said, her voice suddenly soft.

"I think it inevitable, yes. The signs are not good." He sat down. "We are caught up in events far bigger than we have the power to control, for all our attempts to persuade ourselves otherwise." He hesitated. "But there is something more important than this, Alaïs. And if things go ill for us in Montpelhièr, then it is possible I might never have an opportunity to . . . to tell you the truth."

"What can be more important than the threat of war?"

"Before I speak further, you must give me your word that everything I tell you tonight will remain between us."

"Is this why you asked about Guilhem?"

"In part, yes," he admitted, "although that was not the whole reason. But, first, give me your assurance that nothing I tell you will go outside of these four walls."

"You have my word," she said, without hesitation.

Again, Pelletier sighed, but this time she heard relief not anxiety in his voice. The die was cast. He had made his choice. What remained was determination to see things through whatever the consequences.

She drew closer. The light from the candles danced and flickered in her brown eyes.

"This is a story," he said, "that begins in the ancient lands of Egypt several thousand years ago. This is the true story of the Grail."

Pelletier talked until the oil in the lamps had burned out.

The courtyard below had fallen silent, as the revelers had taken themselves off to sleep. Alaïs was exhausted. Her fingers were white and there were purple shadows, like bruises, beneath her eyes.

Pelletier too had grown old and tired as he talked.

"In answer to your question, you do not have to do anything. Not yet, perhaps not ever. If our petitions tomorrow are successful, it will give me the time and opportunity I need to take the books to safety myself as I am bound to do."

"But if they are not, *Messire*? What if something happens to you?"

Alaïs broke off, fear catching in her throat.

"All may yet be well," he said, but his voice was dead.

"But if it is not?" she insisted, refusing to be soothed. "What if you do not return? How will I know when to act?"

He held her gaze for a moment. Then he searched in his pouch until he'd found a small package of cream-colored cloth.

"If something happens to me, you will receive a token like this."

He laid the package on the table and pushed it toward her.

"Open it."

Alaïs did as she was told, unfolding the material section by section until she had revealed a small disc of pale stone with two letters carved on it. She held it up to the light and read the letters aloud.

"*NS?*"

"For *Noublesso de los Seres.*"

"What is it?"

"A *merel,* a secret token, which is passed between thumb and forefinger. It has another, more important purpose also, although you need not know of it. It will indicate to you if the bearer is to be trusted." Alaïs nodded. "Now turn it over."

Engraved on the other side was a labyrinth, identical to the pattern carved on the back of the wooden board.

Alaïs caught her breath. "I've seen this before."

Pelletier twisted the ring from his thumb and held it out. "It is engraved on the inside," he said. "All guardians wear such a ring."

"No, here, in the château. I bought cheese in the market today and took a board from my room to carry it on. This pattern is engraved on the underside."

"But that's impossible. It cannot be the same."

"I swear it is."

"Where did the board come from?" he demanded. "Think, Alaïs. Did someone give it to you? Was it a gift?"

Alaïs shook her head. "I don't know, I don't know," she said desperately. "All day I've tried to remember, but I can't. The strangest thing was that I was sure I'd seen the pattern somewhere else, even though the board itself was not familiar to me."

"Where is it now?"

"I left it on the table in my chambers," she said. "Why? Do you think it matters?"

"So anyone could have seen it," he said with frustration.

"I suppose so," she replied nervously. "Guilhem, any of the servants, I cannot say."

Alaïs looked down at the ring in her hand and suddenly the pieces fell into place. "You thought the man in the river was Simeon?" she said slowly. "He is another guardian?"

Pelletier nodded. "There was no reason to think it was him, but yet I felt so sure."

"And the other guardians? Do you know where they are?"

He leaned over and closed her fingers over the *merel.* "No more questions, Alaïs. Take good care of this. Keep it safe. And hide the board with the labyrinth where no prying eyes can see it. I will deal with it when I return."

Alaïs rose to her feet. "What of the board?"

Pelletier smiled at her persistence. "I will give it some thought, *Filha*."

"But does its presence here mean someone in the château knows of the existence of the books?"

"No one can know," he said firmly. "If I thought there was any question of it, I would tell you. On my word."

They were brave words, fighting words, but his expression gave them the lie.

"But if—"

"*Basta*," he said softly, raising his arms. "No more."

Alaïs let herself be enveloped in his giant embrace. The familiar smell of him brought tears to her eyes.

"All will be well," he said firmly. "You must be brave. Do only what I have asked of you, no more." He kissed the top of her head. "Come bid us farewell at dawn." Alaïs nodded, not daring to speak.

"*Ben, ben*. Now, make haste. And may God keep you."

Alaïs ran down the dark corridor and out into the courtyard without drawing breath, seeing ghosts and demons in every shadow. Her head was spinning. The old familiar world seemed suddenly a mirror image of its former self, both recognizable and utterly different. The package concealed beneath her dress seemed to be burning a hole in her skin.

Outside the air was cool. Most people had retired for the night, although there were still a few lights shining in the rooms overlooking the Cour d'Honneur. A burst of laughter from the guards at the gatehouse made her jump. For a moment, she imagined she saw a person silhouetted in one of the upper rooms. But then a bat swooped in front of her, drawing her gaze, and when she looked again the window was dark.

She walked faster. Her father's words were spinning around in her head, all the questions she should have asked and had not.

A few more steps and she started to feel a prickling at the back of her neck. She glanced over her shoulder.

"Who's there?"

Nobody answered. She called out again. There was malice in the darkness, she could smell it, feel it. Alaïs walked faster, certain now she was being followed. She could hear the soft shuffle of feet and the sound of heavy breathing.

"Who's there?" she called again.

Without warning, a rough and callused hand, reeking of ale, clamped itself over her mouth. She cried out as she felt a sudden, sharp blow on the back of her head and she fell.

It seemed to take a long time for her to reach the ground. Then there were hands crawling all over her, like rats in a cellar, until they found what they wanted.

"*Aqui es.*" Here it is.

It was the last thing Alaïs heard before the blackness closed over her.

CHAPTER 11
Pic de Soularac
Sabarthès Mountains
Southwest France

"Alice! Alice, can you hear me?"

Her eyes flickered and opened.

The air was chill and damp, like an unheated church. Not floating, but lying on the hard, cold ground.

Where the hell am I? She could feel the dank earth rough and uneven beneath her arms and legs. Alice shifted position. Sharp stones and grit rubbed abrasively against her skin.

No, not a church. A glimmer of memory came back. Walking down a long, dark tunnel into a cave, a stone chamber. Then what? Everything was blurred, frayed around the edges. Alice tried to raise her head. A mistake. Pain exploded at the base of her skull. Nausea sloshed in her stomach, like bilge water at the bottom of a rotting boat.

"Alice? Can you hear me?"

Someone was talking to her. Worried, anxious, a voice she knew.

"Alice? Wake up." She tried to lift her head. This time, the pain wasn't so bad. Slowly, carefully, she raised herself a little.

"Christ," muttered Shelagh, sounding relieved.

She was aware of hands beneath her arms helping her into a sitting position. Everything was gloomy and dark, except for the darting circles of light from the torches. Two torches. Alice narrowed her eyes and recognized Stephen, one of the older members of the team, hovering behind Shelagh, his wire-framed glasses catching in the light.

"Alice, talk to me. Can you hear me?" said Shelagh.

I'm not sure. Maybe.

Alice tried to speak, but her mouth was crooked and no words came out. She tried to nod. The exertion made her head spin. She dropped her head between her knees to stop herself passing out.

With Shelagh on one side and Stephen on the other, she edged herself back until she was sitting on the top of the stone steps, hands on her knees. Everything seemed to be shifting backward and forward, in and out, like a film out of focus.

Shelagh crouched down in front of her, talking, but Alice couldn't make out what she was saying. The sound was distorted, like a record played at the wrong speed. Another wave of nausea hit her as more disconnected memories came flooding back: the noise of the skull as it fell away into the dark; her hand reaching out for the ring; the knowledge that she had disturbed something that slumbered in the deepest recesses of the mountain, something malevolent.

Then nothing.

She was so cold. She could feel goosebumps on her bare arms and legs. Alice knew she couldn't have been unconscious for very long, no more than a few minutes at most. Such an inconsequential measure of time. But it had seemed long enough for her to slip from one world into another.

Alice shivered. Then another memory. Of dreaming the same, familiar dream. First, the sensation of peace and lightness, everything white and clear. Then plummeting down and down through the empty sky and the ground rushing up to meet her. There was no collision, no impact, only the dark green columns of trees looming over her. Then the fire, the roaring wall of red and gold and yellow flames.

She wrapped her bare arms tight around herself. Why had the dream come back? Throughout her childhood, the same dream had haunted her, always the same, never leading anywhere. While her parents slept unawares in their bedroom across the landing, Alice had spent night after night awake in the dark, hands gripping the covers tightly, determined to conquer her demons alone.

But not for years now. It had left her alone for years.

"How about we try to get you on your feet?" Shelagh was saying.

It doesn't mean anything. Once doesn't mean it's going to start all over again.

"Alice," said Shelagh, her voice a little sharper. Impatient. "Do you think you can manage to stand? We need to get you back to camp. Have someone take a look at you."

"I think so," she said at last. Her voice didn't sound like her at all. "My head's not so good."

"You can do it, Alice. Come on, try now."

Alice looked down at her red, swollen wrist. *Shit.* She couldn't quite remember, didn't want to remember. "I'm not sure what happened. This—" She held up her hand. "This happened outside."

Shelagh put her arms around Alice to take her weight. "Okay?"

Alice braced herself and allowed Shelagh to lever her to her feet. Stephen took the other arm. She swayed a little from side to side, trying to get her balance, but after a couple of seconds, the giddiness passed and feeling started to come back to her numb limbs. Carefully Alice started to flex and unflex her fingers, feeling the pull of the raw skin over her knuckles.

"I'm all right. Just give me a minute."

"What possessed you to come in here on your own anyway?"

"I was . . ." Alice broke off, not knowing what to say. It was typical of her to break the rules and end up in trouble. "There's something you need to see. Down there. On the lower level."

Shelagh followed the line of Alice's gaze with her torch. Shadows scuttled up the walls and over the roof of the cave.

"No, not here," said Alice. "Down there."

Shelagh lowered the beam.

"In front of the altar."

"Altar?"

The strong white light cut through the inky blackness of the chamber like a searchlight. For a fraction of a second, the shadow of the altar was silhouetted on the rock wall behind, like the Greek letter *pi* superimposed on the carved labyrinth. Then Shelagh moved her hand, the image vanished and the torch found the grave. The pale bones leaped out at them from the dark.

Straight away, the atmosphere changed. Shelagh gave a sharp intake of breath. Like an automaton, she walked down one, then two, then three steps. She seemed to have forgotten Alice was there.

Stephen made a move to follow.

"No," she snapped. "Stay there."

"I was only—"

"In fact, go find Dr. Brayling. Tell him what we've found. Now," she shouted, when he didn't move. Stephen thrust his torch into Alice's hand and disappeared into the tunnel without a word. She could hear the scrunch of his boots on the gravel, getting fainter and fainter until the sound was eaten up by the darkness.

"You didn't have to shout at him," Alice started to say. Shelagh cut across her.

"Did you touch anything?"

"Not exactly, though—"

"Though what?" Again, the same aggression.

"There were a few things in the grave," Alice added. "I can show you."

"No," Shelagh shouted. "No," a little calmer. "We don't want people tramping around down there."

Alice was about to point out it was too late for that, then stopped. She'd no desire to get close to the skeletons again. The blind sockets, the collapsed bones were imprinted too clearly on her mind.

Shelagh stood over the shallow grave. There was something challenging in the way she swept the beam of light over the bodies, up and down as if she was examining them. It was disrespectful almost. The light caught the dull blade of the knife as Shelagh squatted down beside the skeletons, her back to Alice.

"You say you touched nothing?" she said abruptly, turning to glare over her shoulder. "So how come your tweezers are here?"

Alice flushed. "You interrupted me before I'd had the chance to finish. What I was about to say was I picked up a ring—*with* the tweezers, before you ask—which I dropped when I heard you guys in the tunnel."

"A ring?" Shelagh repeated.

"Maybe it's rolled under something else?"

"Well, I can't see it," she said, suddenly standing up. She strode back to Alice. "Let's get out of here. Your injuries need seeing to."

Alice looked at her in astonishment. The face of a stranger, not a good friend, was looking back at her. Angry, hard, judgmental.

"But don't you want—"

"Jesus, Alice," she said, grabbing her arm. "Haven't you done enough? We've got to go!"

It was very bright after the velvet dark of the cave as they emerged from the shadow of the rock. The sun seemed to explode in Alice's face like a firework in a black November sky.

She shielded her eyes with her hands. She felt utterly disorientated, unable to fix herself in time or space. It was as if the world had stopped while she'd been in the chamber. It was the same familiar landscape, yet it had transformed into something different.

Or am I just seeing it through different eyes?

The shimmering peaks of the Pyrenees in the distance had lost their definition. The trees, the sky, even the mountain itself, were less substantial, less real. Alice felt that if she touched anything it would fall down, like scenery on a film set, revealing the true world concealed behind.

Shelagh said nothing. She was already striding down the mountain, mobile phone clamped to her ear, without bothering to check if Alice was managing all right. Alice hurried to catch her up.

"Shelagh, hang on a minute. Wait." She touched Shelagh's arm. "Look, I'm really sorry. I know I shouldn't have gone in there on my own. I wasn't thinking."

Shelagh didn't acknowledge she was speaking. She didn't even look round, although she snapped her phone shut.

"Slow down. I can't keep up."

"Okay," Shelagh said, spinning round to face her. "I've stopped."

"What's going on here?"

"You tell me. I mean, what precisely do you want me to say? That it's okay? You want me to make you feel better that you fucked up?"

"No, I—"

"Because, you know what, actually it's *not* okay. It was totally and unbelievably fucking stupid to go in there alone. You've contaminated the site and Jesus knows what else. What the fuck were you playing at?"

Alice held up her hands. "Okay, okay, I know. And I really am sorry," she repeated, aware of how inadequate it sounded.

"Do you have any idea of the position you've put me in? *I* vouched for you. *I* persuaded Brayling to let you come. Thanks to you playing Indiana Jones, the police will probably suspend the entire excavation. Brayling will blame me. Everything I've done to get here, to get a place on this dig. The time I've spent . . ." Shelagh broke off and ran her fingers through her cropped, bleached hair.

This isn't fair.

"Look, hang on a minute." Even though she knew Shelagh was well within her rights to be angry, she was way over the top. "You're being unfair. I accept it was stupid to go in—I didn't think it through, and I admit that—but don't you think you're overreacting? Shit, I didn't do it on purpose. Brayling's hardly going to call the police. I didn't really touch anything. No one's hurt."

Shelagh twisted her arm out of Alice's grasp with such force she nearly lost her footing.

"Brayling will call the authorities," Shelagh seethed, "because—as you would know if you bothered to listen to a fucking word I said—permission for the excavation was granted, against the advice of the police, on the understanding that any discovery of human remains would be immediately reported to the Police Judiciaire."

Alice's stomach hit the floor. "I thought it was just red tape. Nobody seemed to take it seriously. Everyone was always joking about it."

"Clearly *you* didn't take it seriously," Shelagh shouted. "The rest of us did, being professionals and having some respect for what we do!"

This makes no sense.

"But why would the police be interested in an archeological dig?"

Shelagh blew up. "Jesus, Alice, you still don't get it, do you? Even now. It doesn't fucking matter *why*. It's just how it is. It's not up to *you* to decide which rules matter and which you're going to ignore."

"I never said—"

"Why do you *always* have to challenge everything? You always think you know better, always want to break the rules, be different."

Alice was shouting now too. "That's completely unfair. I'm not like that and you know it. I just didn't think—"

"That's the point. You never do think, except about yourself. And getting what you want."

"This is crazy, Shelagh. Why would I deliberately try to make things hard for you? Just listen to yourself." Alice took a deep breath, trying to get her temper under control. "Look, I'll own up to Brayling it was my fault but, well it's just that . . . you know I wouldn't go charging in there, on my own, in normal circumstances, except . . ."

She paused again.

"Except what?"

"This is going to sound stupid, but it sort of drew me in. I knew the chamber was there. I can't explain it, I just knew. A feeling. Déjà vu. Like I'd been there before."

"You think this makes it better?" Shelagh said sarcastically. "Jesus, give me a break. You had a *feeling*. That's pathetic."

Alice shook her head. "It was more than that—"

"In any case, what the hell were you doing digging up there in the first place? And on your own? That's just it. Break the rules just for the hell of it."

"No," she said. "It wasn't like that. My partner's not here. I saw something underneath the boulder and, since it's my last day, I just thought I'd do a little more." Her voice tailed off. "I only wanted to find out if it was worth investigating," she said, realizing her mistake too late. "I wasn't intending—"

"You are telling me, on top of everything else, that you actually found something? You fucking found something and didn't bother to share this information with anyone else?"

"I—"

Shelagh held out her hand. "Give it to me."

Alice held her gaze for a moment, then fished in the pocket of her denim cut-offs, pulled out the handkerchief and handed it over. She didn't trust herself to speak.

She watched as Shelagh folded back the white folds of cotton to reveal the brooch inside. Alice couldn't help herself reaching out.

"It is beautiful, isn't it? The way the copper round the edges, here and here, catches the light." She hesitated. "I think it might belong to one of the people inside the cave."

Shelagh looked up. Her mood had undergone another transformation. The anger had gone out of her.

"You have no idea what you have done, Alice. No idea at all." She folded the handkerchief. "I'll take this down."

"I'll—"

"Leave it, Alice. I don't want to talk to you right now. Everything you say just makes it worse."

What the hell was that all about?

Alice stood bewildered as Shelagh walked away. The row had come out of nowhere, extreme even for Shelagh, who was capable of blowing up over the smallest things, then had blown out just as quickly.

Alice lowered herself down on to the nearest rock and rested her throbbing wrist on her knee. Everything ached and she felt utterly drained, but also sick at heart. She knew the excavation was funded privately—rather than attached to a university or institution—so was not subject to the restrictive regulations that hampered many expeditions. As a result, competition to get on the team had been fierce. Shelagh had been working at Mas d'Azil, a few kilometers northwest of Foix when she'd first heard about the excavation in the Sabarthès Mountains. The way she told it, she'd bombarded the director, Dr. Brayling, with letters, e-mails and testimonials until finally, eighteen months ago, she'd worn him down. Even then, Alice had wondered why Shelagh was so obsessed.

Alice looked down the mountain. Shelagh was so far ahead now that she was almost out of sight, her long, lean figure shielded by the scrub and broom on the lower slopes. There was no hope of catching her up even if she wanted to.

Alice sighed. She was running on empty. *Like always.* Doing it alone. *It's better that way.* She was fiercely self-sufficient, preferring not to rely on anybody else. But right now, she wasn't sure she had enough energy left to make it back to camp. The sun was too fierce and her legs too weak. She looked down at the cut on her arm. It had started to bleed again, worse than ever.

Alice looked out over the scorched summer landscape of the Sabarthès Mountains, still in their timeless peace. For a moment, she felt fine. Then all at once she was aware of another sensation, a pricking at the base of her spine. Anticipation, a sense of expectation. Recognition.

It all ends here.

Alice caught her breath. Her heart started to beat faster.

It ends here where it started.

Her head was suddenly filled with whispering, disjointed sounds, like echoes in time. Now the words carved in the stone at the top of the steps came back to her. *Pas a pas.* They went round and round in her head, like a half-remembered nursery rhyme.

That's impossible. You're being stupid.

Shaken, Alice put her hands on her knees and forced herself to stand up. She had to get back to the camp. Heatstroke, dehydration, she had to get out of the sun, get some water inside her.

Taking it slowly, she started to descend, feeling every bump and jolt of the mountain in her legs. She had to get away from the echoing stone, from the spirits that lived there. She didn't know what was happening to her, only that she had to escape.

She walked faster, faster, until she was almost running, stumbling on the stones and jagged flints that stuck up out of the dry earth. But the words were rooted in her mind, repeating loud and clear, like a mantra.

Step by step we make our way. Step by step.

CHAPTER 12

The thermometer was nudging thirty-three degrees Celsius in the shade. It was nearly three o'clock. Alice was sitting under the canvas awning obediently sipping an Orangina that had been pushed into her hands. The warm bubbles fizzed in her throat as the sugar rushed into her bloodstream. There was a strong smell of gabardine, tents and disinfectant.

The cut on the inside of her elbow had been sterilized and the dressing reapplied. A clean white bandage had been wrapped around her wrist, which had swollen to the size of a tennis ball. Her knees and shins were covered in tiny grazes and cuts, dabbed clean with disinfectant.

You brought this on yourself.

She peered at herself in the small mirror that hung from the tent post. A small, heart-shaped face with intelligent brown eyes stared back at her. Beneath the freckles and tanned skin, she was pale. She looked a mess. Her hair was full of dust and there were smears of dried blood down the front of her top.

All she wanted was to go back to her hotel in Foix, toss her filthy clothes in the wash and take a long, cool shower. Then, she'd go down to the square, order a bottle of wine and not move for the rest of the day.

And not think about what happened.

There didn't seem much chance of that.

The police had arrived half an hour ago. In the car park below a line of white and blue official vehicles was lined up next to the more battered Citroëns and Renaults of the archeologists. It was like an invasion.

Alice had assumed they would deal with her first, but apart from confirming that it was she who'd found the skeletons and saying they'd need to interview her in due course, the police had left her alone. No one else had come near. Alice sympathized. All this noise and mess and disruption was down to her. There wasn't much anyone could say. Of Shelagh there'd been no sign.

The presence of the police had changed the character of the camp. There seemed to be dozens of them, all in pale blue shirts and knee-length black boots, with guns at their hips, swarming all over the mountainside like wasps, kicking up the dust and shouting instructions to one another in heavily accented French, too quick for her to follow.

They cordoned off the cave immediately, stretching a strip of plastic tape across the entrance. The noise of their activity carried in the still mountain air. Alice could hear the whir of the autowinding cameras competing with the cicadas.

Voices, carried on the breeze, floated up to her from the car park. Alice turned to see Dr. Brayling walking up the steps, accompanied by Shelagh and the heavily built police officer who appeared to be in charge.

"It's obvious these skeletons cannot possibly be the two people you are looking for," Dr. Brayling was insisting. "These bones are clearly hundreds of years old. When I notified the authorities, I never for a moment entertained the notion this would be the result." He waved his hands around. "Have you any idea of the damage your people are doing? I can assure you, I am far from happy."

Alice scrutinized the inspector, a short, dark, overweight middle-aged man, with more stomach than hair. He was breathless and clearly suffering in the heat. He was clutching a limp handkerchief, with which he wiped his face and neck with little effect. Even from this distance, Alice could see the circles of sweat under his armpits and on the cuffs of his shirt.

"I apologize for the inconvenience, *Monsieur le Directeur*," he said in slow, courteous English. "But since this is a private excavation, I'm sure you can explain the situation to your sponsors."

"The fact we are fortunate enough to be funded by a private individual rather than an institution is neither here nor there. It's the unwarranted suspension of work which is so aggravating, not to mention inconvenient. Our work here is highly important."

"Dr. Brayling," said Noubel, as if they had been having the same conversation for some time, "my hands are tied. We are in the middle of a murder enquiry. You have seen the posters of the two missing persons, *oui*? So, inconvenient or no, until we have proved to our satisfaction that the bones you have found are not those of our missing persons, work will be suspended."

"Don't be a fool, Inspector. There can be no doubt the skeletons are hundreds of years old!"

"You have examined them?"

"Well, no," he blustered. "Not properly, of course not. But it's obvious. Your forensic people will bear me out."

"I'm sure they will, Dr. Brayling but until then . . ." Noubel shrugged. "There is nothing more I can say."

Shelagh stepped in. "We appreciate the position you're in, Inspector, but can you at least give us any idea of when you might be through here?"

"*Bientôt*. Soon. I don't make the rules."

Dr. Brayling threw his hands in the air in frustration. "In which case, I shall be forced to go over your head to someone with authority! This is utterly ridiculous."

"As you wish," replied Noubel. "In the meantime, as well as the lady who found the bodies, I need a list of anyone else who went inside the cave. Once we have concluded our preliminary investigations, we will remove the bodies from the cave, then you and your staff will be free to go."

Alice watched as the scene played itself out.

Brayling stalked off, Shelagh put her hand on the Inspector's arm, then immediately withdrew it. They appeared to be talking. At one point, they turned and looked back toward the car park. Alice followed the line of their gaze, but saw nothing of interest.

Half an hour passed and still no one came near her.

Alice reached into her rucksack—brought down from the mountain by Stephen or Shelagh, she presumed—and pulled out a pencil and her drawing pad. She opened it at the first empty page.

Imagine yourself standing at the entrance, staring into the tunnel.

Alice closed her eyes and saw herself, fingers on either side of the narrow entrance. Smooth. The rock had been surprisingly smooth, as if it had been polished or worn away. A step forward, into the dark.

The ground sloped down.

Alice started to draw, working quickly now she'd fixed the dimensions of the space in her head. Tunnel, opening, chamber. On a second sheet, she drew the lower area, from the steps to the altar and the skeletons halfway between the two. Beside the sketch of the grave, she wrote a list of the objects: the knife, the leather pouch, the fragment of cloth, the ring. The face of the ring had been entirely smooth and flat, surprisingly thick, with a thin groove around the middle. Odd that the engraving was on the underside, where no one could see it. Only the person wearing it would know it was there. A replica in miniature of the labyrinth carved into the wall behind the altar.

Alice leaned back in her chair, somehow reluctant to commit the image to paper. How big? The diameter was nearly two meters maybe? More? How many circuits?

She drew a circle that filled most of the page, then stopped. How many lines? Alice knew she'd recognize the pattern again if she saw it, but since she'd only held the ring for a couple of seconds and seen the carving through the distant darkness it was hard to recall it precisely.

Somewhere in the rambling attic of her mind was the knowledge she needed. History and Latin lessons at school, curled up on the sofa with her parents watching documentaries on the BBC. In her bedroom, a little wooden bookcase with her favorite book on the bottom shelf. An illustrated encyclopedia of ancient myths, its glossy, garish pages grown dog-eared at the edges where she had read it so often.

There was a picture of a labyrinth.

In her mind's eye, Alice turned to the right page.

But it was different. She placed the remembered images side by side, like a spot-the-difference game in a newspaper.

She picked up the pencil and tried again, determined to make some progress. She drew another circle inside the first, trying to connect them together. No good. Her next attempt was no better, nor the one after. She realized it wasn't only a question of how many rings there should be spiraling in toward the center, but more that there was something fundamentally wrong with her design.

Alice kept going, her initial excitement giving way to a dull frustration. The collection of scrunched-up balls of paper around her feet grew larger.

"Madame Tanner?"

Alice jumped, sending the pencil skeetering across the surface of the paper.

"Docteur," she corrected automatically, getting to her feet.

"Je vous demande pardon, Docteur. Je m'appelle Noubel. Police Judiciaire, département de l'Ariège."

Noubel flashed his identification card at her. Alice pretended to read it, at the same time shoveling everything into her rucksack. She didn't want the inspector to see her failed sketches.

"Vous préférez parler en anglais?"

"It would be sensible, yes, thank you."

Inspector Noubel was accompanied by a uniformed officer with alert, darting eyes. He looked barely old enough to be out of school. He was not introduced.

Noubel squeezed himself into another one of the spindly camping chairs. It was a tight fit. His thighs bulged over the canvas seat.

"Et alors, Madame. Your full name, if you please."

"Alice Grace Tanner."

"Date of birth."

"Seven January 1976."

"You are married?"

"Is that relevant?" she snapped.

"For information, Dr. Tanner," he said mildly.

"No," she said. "Not married."

"Your address."

Alice gave him details of the hotel in Foix where she was staying and her home address, spelling out the unfamiliar English names letter by letter.

"It's a long way to come every day from Foix?"

"There wasn't room in the site house, so . . ."

"*Bien*. You are a volunteer, I understand, yes?"

"That's right. Shelagh—Dr. O'Donnell—is one of my oldest friends. We were at university together, before . . ."

Just answer the question. He doesn't need your life story.

"I'm just visiting. Dr. O'Donnell knows this part of France well. When it turned out I'd got business to sort out in Carcassonne, Shelagh suggested I detoured via here for a few days so we could spend some time together. A working holiday."

Noubel scribbled in his pad. "You are not an archeologist?"

Alice shook her head. "But it's common practice to use volunteers, interested amateurs, or archeology students to do some of the basic work apparently."

"How many other volunteers are there?"

She flushed, as if she'd been caught out in a lie. "None actually, not right now. They're all archeologists or students."

Noubel peered at her. "And you're here until?"

"This is my last day. It was anyway . . . even before this."

"And Carcassonne?"

"I have a meeting there on Wednesday morning, then a few days to look around. I fly back to England on Sunday."

"A beautiful city," said Noubel.

"I've never been."

Noubel sighed and wiped his red forehead again with his handkerchief. "And what is the nature of this meeting?"

"I'm not sure exactly. A relative, who's been living in France, left me something in her will." She paused, reluctant to go into it. "I'll know more after I've met with the solicitor on Wednesday."

Noubel made another note. Alice tried to see what he was writing, but couldn't decipher his handwriting upside down. To her relief, he left the subject and moved on.

"So you are a doctor . . ." Noubel left the comment hanging.

"I'm not a medical doctor," she replied, relieved to be on safer ground. "I'm a teacher, I have a Ph.D.—Middle English literature." Noubel looked blank. *"Pas médecin. Pas généraliste,"* she said. *"Je suis universitaire."*

Noubel sighed and made another note.

"Bien. Aux affaires." His tone was no longer conversational. "You were working alone up there. Is that usual practice?"

Immediately, Alice's guard went up. "No," she said slowly, "but since it was my last day, I wanted to keep going, even though my partner wasn't here. I was sure we'd found something."

"Beneath the boulder shielding the entrance? Just for clarity, how is it decided who will dig where?"

"Dr. Brayling and Shelagh—Dr. O'Donnell—have a plan of what they want to accomplish within the time available. They divide the site up accordingly."

"So Dr. Brayling sent you to that area? Or Dr. O'Donnell?"

Instinct. I just knew there was something there.

"Well, no. I moved higher up the mountain because I was certain there was something—" She hesitated. "I couldn't find Dr. O'Donnell to ask her permission . . . so I made an . . . an executive decision."

Noubel frowned. "I see. So, you were working. The boulder came free. It fell. Then what?"

There were genuine gaps in her memory, but Alice did her best. Noubel's English, although formal, was good and he asked straightforward questions.

"That's when I heard something in the tunnel behind me, and I—"

Suddenly the words dried in her throat. Something she'd suppressed in her mind came back to her with a thud, the piercing sensation in her chest, as if . . .

As if what?

Alice provided the answer herself. *As if I'd been stabbed.* That's what it had felt like. A blade slicing into her, precise and clean. There had been no pain, just a rush of cold air and a dim horror.

And then?

The luminous light, chill and insubstantial. And hidden within it, a face. A woman's face.

Noubel's voice broke through her surfacing memories, sending them scattering.

"Dr. Tanner?"

Was I hallucinating?

"Dr. Tanner? Shall I fetch someone?"

Alice stared blankly at him for a moment. "No, no thanks. I'm fine. It's just the heat."

"You were saying how you were startled by the noise—"

She forced herself to concentrate. "Yes. The dark was disorientating. I couldn't work out where the sound was coming from, which frightened me. Now, I realize it was only Shelagh and Stephen—"

"Stephen?"

"Stephen Kirkland. K-i-r-k-l-a-n-d."

Noubel turned his notebook round to face her to verify the spelling.

Alice nodded. "Shelagh noticed the boulder and came to find out what was going on. Stephen followed, I suppose." She hesitated again. "I'm not sure quite what happened after that." This time the lie came easily to her lips. "I must have tripped on the steps or something. The next thing I remember is Shelagh calling my name."

"Dr. O'Donnell says that you were unconscious when they found you."

"Only briefly. I don't think I can have been out for more than a minute or two. It didn't feel very long anyhow."

"Do you have a history of blackouts, Dr. Tanner?"

Alice jolted as the terrifying memory of the first time it happened swooped into her mind. "No," she lied.

Noubel didn't notice how pale she'd gone. "You say it was dark," he said, "and that's why you fell. But before you had a light?"

"I had a lighter but I dropped it when I heard the noise. And the ring too."

His reaction was immediate. "A ring?" he said sharply. "You've said nothing about a ring."

"There was a small stone ring lying between the skeletons," she said, alarmed by the look on his face. "I picked it up with my tweezers, to get a better look, but before—"

"What sort of ring?" he interrupted. "What was it made of?"

"I don't know. Some sort of stone, not silver or gold or anything. I didn't really get a proper look."

"Was there anything engraved on it? Letters, a seal, a pattern?"

Alice opened her mouth to answer, then shut it. Suddenly, she didn't want to tell him anything more.

"I'm sorry. It all happened too quickly."

Noubel glared at her for a moment, then clicked his fingers and summoned the young officer standing behind him. Alice thought the boy seemed agitated too.

"*Biau. On a trouvé quelque-chose comme ça?*"

"*Je ne sais pas, Monsieur l'Inspecteur.*"

"*Dépechez-vous, alors. Il faut le chercher . . . Et informez-en Monsieur Authié. Allez! Vite!*"

There was a stubborn band of pain behind Alice's eyes now the painkillers were starting to wear off.

"Did you touch anything else, Dr. Tanner?"

She rubbed her temples with her fingers. "I accidentally knocked one of the skulls out of position with my foot. But apart from that and the ring, nothing. As I've already said."

"What about the piece you found beneath the boulder?"

"The brooch? I gave it to Dr. O'Donnell after we came out of the cave," shifting slightly at the memory. "I've got no idea what she did with it."

Noubel was no longer listening. He kept glancing over his shoulder. Finally, he gave up the pretense and flipped his notebook shut.

"If you would be so kind as to wait, Dr. Tanner. There may be more questions I need to ask you."

"But there's nothing more I can tell you—" she started to protest. "Can't I at least join the others?"

"Later. For now, if you could stay here."

Alice slumped back in her chair, annoyed and exhausted, as Noubel lumbered out of the tent and headed up the mountain to where a group of uniformed officers were examining the boulder.

As Noubel approached, the circle parted, just enough for Alice to catch a glimpse of a tall man in civilian clothes standing in the middle.

She caught her breath.

Dressed in a well-cut pale green summer suit and a crisp white shirt and tie, he was clearly in charge. His authority was obvious, a man used to giving orders and having them obeyed. Noubel looked crumpled and unkempt in comparison. Alice felt a prickling of unease.

It wasn't only the man's clothes and bearing that marked him out. Even from this distance, Alice could feel the force of his personality and charisma. His face was pale and gaunt, accentuated by the way his dark hair was swept back off his high forehead. There was something of the cloister about him. Something familiar.

Don't be stupid. How can you know him?

Alice stood up and walked to the entrance, watching intently as the two men moved away from the group. They were talking. Or rather Noubel was talking, while the other man listened. After another couple of seconds, he turned and climbed up to the entrance to the cave. The officer on duty lifted the tape, he ducked underneath and was gone.

For no reason she could fathom, her palms were wet with apprehension. The hairs on the back of her neck were standing on end, just as they had when she'd heard the sound in the chamber. She could barely breathe.

This is all your fault. You led him here.

Alice pulled herself up short. *What are you talking about?* But the voice in her head would not be quietened.

You led him here.

Her eyes returned again to the entrance to the cave, drawn like a magnet. She couldn't help it. The thought of him in there, after all that had been done to keep the labyrinth hidden.

He'll find it.

"Find what?" she muttered to herself. She wasn't sure.

But she wished she'd taken the ring when she had the chance.

CHAPTER 13

Noubel didn't go into the cave. Instead, he waited outside in the gray shade of the rocky overhang, red-faced.

He knows something's not right, thought Alice. He tossed an occasional comment to the officer on duty and smoked cigarette after cigarette, lighting them from the butt of the last. Alice listened to music to help pass the time. Nickelback blasted into her head, obliterating all other sounds.

After fifteen minutes, the man in the suit reappeared. Noubel and the officer seemed to gain a couple of inches in height. Alice took off her headphones and put the chair back in its original position, before taking up her position at the entrance to the tent.

She watched the two men come down from the cave together.

"I was beginning to think you'd forgotten me, Inspector," she said, when they came within earshot.

Noubel mumbled an apology, but avoided her eye.

"Dr. Tanner, *je vous présente Monsieur Authié.*"

Close up, Alice's first impressions of a man of presence and charisma were reinforced. But his gray eyes were cold and clinical. She felt immediately on guard. Fighting her antipathy, she held out her hand. After a moment's hesitation, Authié took it. His fingers were cool and his touch was insubstantial. It made her flesh creep.

She let go as quickly as she could.

"Shall we go inside?" he said.

"Are you also with the Police Judiciaire, Monsieur Authié?"

A ghost of a reaction flickered in his eyes, but he said nothing. Alice waited, wondering if it was possible he'd not heard her. Noubel shuffled, awkward in the silence. "Monsieur Authié is from the *mairie,* the town hall. In Carcassonne."

"Really?" She found it surprising Carcassonne was under the same jurisdiction as Foix.

Authié took possession of Alice's chair, leaving her with no choice but to sit with her back to the entrance. She felt wary, cautious of him.

He had the practiced smile of a politician, expedient, watchful and noncommittal. It did not reach his eyes.

"I have one or two questions, Dr. Tanner."

"I'm not sure there's anything else I can tell you. I went through everything I could remember with the Inspector."

"Inspector Noubel has given me a thorough summary of your statement, however I need you to go through it once more. There are discrepancies, certain points in your story that need clarification. There might be details you forgot before, things that seemed insignificant at the time."

Alice bit her tongue. "I told the Inspector everything," she repeated stubbornly.

Authié pressed the tips of his fingers together, ignoring her objections. He didn't smile. "Let us start from the moment you first entered the chamber, Dr. Tanner. Step by step."

Alice jolted at his choice of words. *Step by step?* Was he testing her? His face revealed nothing. Her eyes fell to a gold crucifix he wore around his neck, then back to his gray eyes, still staring at her.

Since she felt she had no choice, she began once more. To start with, Authié listened in an intense, concentrated silence. Then the interrogation started. *He's trying to catch me out.*

"Were the words inscribed at the top of the steps legible, Dr. Tanner? Did you take the time to read them?"

"Most of the letters were rubbed away," she said defiantly, challenging him to contradict her. When he did not, Alice felt a burst of satisfaction. "I walked down the steps to the lower level, toward the altar. Then I saw the bodies."

"Did you touch them?"

"No."

He made a slight sound, as if he didn't believe her, then reached into his jacket. "This is yours?" he said, opening his hand to reveal her blue plastic lighter.

Alice went to take it, but he drew his arm back.

"May I have it please?"

"Is it yours, Dr. Tanner?"

"Yes."

He nodded, then slipped it back into his pocket. "You say you did not touch the bodies, however, before, you told Inspector Noubel you had."

Alice flushed. "It was an accident. I knocked one of the skulls with my foot, but I didn't touch them, as such."

"Dr. Tanner, this will go more easily if you just answer my questions." The same cold, hard voice.

"I can't see what—"

"What did they look like?" he said sharply.

Alice felt Noubel flinch at the bullying tone, but he didn't do anything to check it. Her stomach twisting with nerves, she did her best.

"And what did you see between the bodies?"

"A dagger, a knife of some sort. Also a small bag, leather I think." *Don't let him intimidate you.* "I don't know, since I didn't touch it."

Authié narrowed his eyes. "Did you look inside the bag?"

"I've told you, I didn't touch anything—"

"Except for the ring, yes." He suddenly leaned forward, like a snake about to strike. "And this I find mysterious, Dr. Tanner. What I'm asking myself is why you should be interested enough in the ring to pick it up, yet leave everything else undisturbed. You understand my confusion?"

Alice met his gaze. "It caught my eye. That's all."

He gave a sardonic smile. "In the almost pitch black of the cave, you noticed this one, tiny object? How big is it? The size of a, say, one-franc piece? A little larger, smaller?"

Don't tell him anything.

"I would have thought you were capable of assessing its dimensions for yourself," she said coldly.

He smiled. With a sinking feeling, Alice realized she'd somehow played into his hands.

"If only I could, Dr. Tanner," he said mildly. "But now we come to the heart of the matter. There is no ring."

Alice turned cold. "What do you mean?"

"Exactly what I say. The ring is not there. Everything else is, more or less, as you describe it. But no ring."

Alice recoiled as Authié placed his hands of her chair and brought his thin, pale face close to hers. "What have you done with it, Alice?" he whispered.

Don't let him bully you. You've done nothing wrong.

"I have told you *precisely* what happened," she said, struggling to keep the fear from her voice. "The ring slipped out of my hand when I dropped the lighter. If it's not there now, someone else must have taken it. Not me." She darted a glance at Noubel. "If I had taken it, why would I mention it at all in the first place?"

"No one other than you claims to have seen this mysterious ring," he said, ignoring her comments, "which leaves us with one of two options. Either you are mistaken in what you saw. Or else you took it."

Inspector Noubel finally intervened. "Monsieur Authié, really I don't think—"

"You are not paid to think," he snapped, without even looking at the inspector. Noubel colored. Authié continued to stare at Alice. "I'm only stating the facts."

Alice felt she was engaged in a battle, except no one had told her the rules. She was telling the truth, but she could see no way of persuading him.

"Lots of people went into the cave after me," she said doggedly. "The forensic people, police officers, Inspector Noubel, you." She stared defiantly at him. "You were in there a long time." Noubel sucked in his breath. "Shelagh O'Donnell can back me up about the ring. Why don't you ask her?"

He gave the same half-smile. "But I have. She says she knows nothing about the ring."

"But I told her all about it," she cried. "She looked for herself."

"Are you saying Dr. O'Donnell examined the grave?" he said sharply.

Fear was stopping her thinking straight. Her brain had given up. She could no longer remember what she'd said to Noubel and what she'd kept back.

"Was it Dr. O'Donnell who gave you permission to work there in the first place?"

"It wasn't like that," she said, her panic growing.

"Well, did she do anything to *prevent* you from working that part of the mountain?"

"It's not as simple as that."

He sat back in his chair. "In which case, I'm afraid I have no choice."

"No choice but to do what?"

He darted his gaze to her rucksack. Alice dived for it, but she was too slow. Authié got there first and thrust it at Inspector Noubel.

"You've got absolutely no right," she shouted. She turned on the Inspector. "He can't do this, can he? Why don't you do something?"

"Why object if you have nothing to hide?"

"It's a matter of principle! You can't just go through my things."

"Monsieur Authié, je ne suis pas certain—"

"Just do what you're told, Noubel."

Alice tried to grab the bag. Authié's arm shot up and took hold of her wrist. She was so shocked at the physical contact that she froze. Her legs started to shake, whether out of anger or fear she couldn't tell.

She jerked her arm free of Authié's grip and sat back, breathing heavily as Noubel searched through the pockets.

"Continuez. Dépêchez-vous."

Alice watched as he moved on to the main section of the bag, knowing it was only a matter of seconds before he found her sketchpad. The Inspector caught her eye. *He hates this too.* Unfortunately, Authié had also noticed Noubel's slight hesitation.

"What is it, Inspector?"

"Pas de bague."

"What have you found?" said Authié, holding out his hand. Noubel reluctantly handed him the pad. Authié flicked the pages with a patronizing look on his face. Then his look narrowed and, fleetingly, Alice saw genuine surprise in his eyes, before the hooded lids came down again.

He snapped the sketchbook shut.

"*Merci de votre . . . collaboration*, Dr. Tanner," he said.

Alice also stood up. "My drawings, please," she said, trying to keep her voice steady.

"They will be returned to you in due course," he said, slipping the sketchpad inside his pocket. "The bag also. Inspector Noubel will give you a receipt for it and have your statement typed up for you to sign."

Alice was taken by surprise by the sudden and abrupt end to the interview. By the time she'd gathered her wits, Authié had already left the tent, taking her belongings with him.

"Why don't you stop him?" she said, turning on Noubel. "Don't think I'm going to let him get away with that."

His expression hardened. "I'll get your bag back, Dr. Tanner. My advice is to get on with your holiday. Forget all about this."

"There's no way I'm going to let this go," she shouted, but Noubel had already gone, leaving her alone in the middle of the tent, wondering what the hell had just happened.

For a moment, she didn't know what to do. She was furious, as much with herself as Authié, at being so easily intimidated.

But he's different. She'd never reacted so strongly against someone in her life. The shock gradually wore off. She was tempted to report Authié straight away to Dr. Brayling, or even to Shelagh, she wanted to do something. She dismissed the idea. Given her status as persona non grata right now, no one was going to be sympathetic.

Alice was forced to satisfy herself by composing a letter of complaint in her head, as she turned over what had happened and tried to make sense of it. A little later, a different police officer brought the statement for her to sign. Alice read it through thoroughly, but it was an accurate record so far as it went, and she scrawled her signature across the bottom of the page without hesitation.

The Pyrenees were bathed in a soft red light by the time the bones were finally brought out from the cave.

Everybody fell silent as the somber procession made its way down the slopes toward the car park, where the line of white and blue police vehicles stood waiting. One woman crossed herself as they passed by.

Alice joined everybody else on the brow of the hill to watch the police load the mortuary van. No one spoke. The doors were secured, then the vehicle accelerated out of the car park in a shower of gravel and dust. Most of her colleagues went back up to gather their belongings straight away, supervised by two officers who were to secure the site once everyone was ready to leave. Alice lingered a while, unwilling to face anybody, knowing that sympathy would be even harder to deal with than hostility.

From her vantage point on the hill, Alice watched as the solemn convoy zigzagged away down the valley, getting smaller and smaller until it was no more than a smudge on the horizon.

The camp had grown quiet around her. Realizing she couldn't delay any longer, Alice was about to go back up too when she noticed Authié hadn't yet gone. She edged a little closer, watching with interest as he laid his jacket carefully on the back seat of his expensive-looking silver car. He slammed the door, and then took a phone from his pocket. Alice could hear the gentle drumming of his fingers on the roof as he waited for a connection.

When he spoke, the message was brief and to the point.

"*Ce n'est plus là,*" was all he said. It's gone.

CHAPTER 14
Chartres

The great Gothic cathedral of Notre Dame de Chartres towered high above the patchwork of pepper-tiled rooftops and gables, and half-timbered and limestone houses which make up the historic city center. Below the crowded labyrinth of narrow, curving streets, in the shadows of the buildings, the river Eure was still in the dappled light of the late afternoon sun.

Tourists jostled one another at the West Door of the cathedral. Men wielded their video cameras like weapons, recording rather than experiencing the brilliant kaleidoscope of color spilling from the three lancet windows above the Royal Portal.

Until the eighteenth century, the nine entrances leading into the cathedral close could be sealed at times of danger. The gates were long gone now, but the attitude of mind persisted. Chartres was still a city of two halves, the old and the new. The most exclusive streets were those to the north of the Cloister, where the Bishop's Palace once stood. The pale stone edifices looked out imperiously toward the cathedral, shrouded with an air of centuries-old Catholic influence and power.

The house of the de l'Oradore family dominated the rue du Cheval Blanc. It had survived the Revolution and the Occupation and stood now as a testimony to old money. Its brass knocker and letterbox gleamed and the shrubs in the planters on either side of the steps leading up to its double doors were perfectly clipped.

The front door led into an imposing hall. The floor was dark, polished wood and a heavy glass vase of freshly cut white lilies sat on an oval table at its center. Display cases set around the edges—each discreetly alarmed—contained a priceless selection of Egyptian artifacts acquired by the de l'Oradore family after Napoleon's triumphant return from his North African campaigns in the early nineteenth century. It was one of the largest Egyptian collections in private hands.

The current head of the family, Marie-Cécile de l'Oradore, traded in antiques of all periods, although she shared her late grandfather's preference for the medieval past. Two substantial French tapestries hung on the paneled wall opposite the front door, both of which she had acquired since coming into her inheritance five years ago. The family's most valuable pieces—pictures, jewelry, manuscripts—were locked away in the safe, out of sight.

In the master bedroom on the first floor of the house, overlooking the rue du Cheval Blanc, Will Franklin, Marie-Cécile's current lover, lay on his back on the four-poster bed with the sheet pulled up to his waist.

His tanned arms were folded behind his head and his light brown hair, streaked blond by childhood summers spent at Martha's Vineyard, framed an engaging face and little-boy-lost smile.

Marie-Cécile herself was sitting in an ornate Louis XIV armchair beside the fireplace, her long, smooth legs crossed at the knees. The ivory sheen of her silk camisole shimmered against the deep blue velvet upholstery.

She had the distinctive profile of the de l'Oradore family, a pale, aquiline beauty, although her lips were both sensuous and full and her cat-like green eyes were fringed with generous dark lashes. Her perfectly cut black curls skimmed the top of chiseled shoulders.

"This is such a great room," said Will. "The perfect setting for you. Cool, expensive, subtle."

The tiny diamond studs in her ears glinted as she leaned forward to stub out her cigarette.

"It was my grandfather's room originally."

Her English was flawless, with just a shimmer of a French accent that still turned him on. She stood up and walked across the room toward him, her feet making no sound on the thick, pale blue carpet.

Will smiled expectantly as he breathed in the unique smell of her: sex, Chanel and a hint of Gauloise.

"Over," she said, making a twisting movement with her finger in the air. "Turn over."

Will did as he was told. Marie-Cécile began to massage his neck and broad shoulders. He could feel his body stretch and relax under her touch. Neither of them paid any attention to the sound of the front door opening and closing below. He didn't even register the voices in the hall, the footsteps taking the stairs two by two and striding along the corridor.

There were a couple of sharp raps on the bedroom door. *"Maman!"* Will tensed.

"It's only my son," she said. *"Oui? Qu'est-ce que c'est?"*

"Maman! Je veux te parler."

Will lifted his head. "I thought he wasn't due back until tomorrow."

"He isn't."

"Maman!" François-Baptiste repeated. *"C'est important."*

"If I'm in the way . . ." he said awkwardly.

Marie-Cécile continued to massage his shoulders. "He knows not to disturb me. I will talk to him later." She raised her voice. "*Pas maintenant*, François-Baptiste." Then she added in English for Will's benefit, as she ran her hands down his back: "Now is not . . . convenient."

Will rolled onto his back and sat up, feeling embarrassed. In the three months he'd known Marie-Cécile, he'd never met her son. François-Baptiste had been away at university, then on holiday with friends. Only now did it occur to him that Marie-Cécile had engineered it.

"Aren't you going to talk to him?"

"If it makes you happy," she said, slipping off the bed. She opened the door a fraction. There was a muffled exchange that Will couldn't hear, then the sound of feet stomping off down the hall. She turned the key in the lock and turned back to face him.

"Better?" she said softly.

Slowly, she moved back toward him, looking at him from the fringe of her long, dark eyelashes. There was something deliberate about her movements, like a performance, but Will felt his body respond all the same.

She pushed him back on to the bed and straddled him, draping her elegant arms over his shoulders. Her sharp nails left faint scratch marks across his skin. He could feel her knees pressing into his sides. He reached up and ran his fingers down her smooth, toned arms and brushed her breasts with the back of his hands through the silk. The thin silk straps slipped easily from her sculptured shoulders.

The mobile phone lying on the bedside table rang. Will ignored it. He eased the delicate camisole down her lean body to her waist.

"They'll call back if it's important."

Marie-Cécile glanced at the number on the screen. Immediately, her mood changed.

"I must take this," she said.

Will tried to stop her, but she pushed him away impatiently. "Not now."

Covering herself, she walked away to the window. "*Oui. J'écoute.*"

He heard the crackle of a bad line. "*Trouve-le, alors!*" she said and disconnected. Her face flushed with anger, Marie-Cécile reached for a cigarette and lit it. Her hands were shaking.

"Is there a problem?"

To start with, Will thought she hadn't heard him. She looked as if she'd forgotten he was even in the room. Then, she glanced over.

"Something has come up," she said.

Will waited, until he realized it was all the explanation he was going to get and she was expecting him to go.

"I'm sorry," she said, in a conciliatory tone. "I'd much rather stay with you, *mais . . .*"

Annoyed, Will got up and pulled on his jeans.

"Will I see you for dinner?"

She pulled a face. "I have an engagement. Business, if you remember." She shrugged. "Later, *oui*?"

"How late is later? Ten o'clock? Midnight?"

She came over and threaded her fingers through his. "I am sorry."

Will tried to pull away, although she wouldn't let him. "You're always doing this. I never know what's going on."

She moved closer so he could feel her breasts pressing against his chest through the thin silk. Despite his bad temper, he felt his body react.

"It's just business," she murmured. "Nothing to be jealous about."

"I'm not jealous." He'd lost count of the times they'd had this conversation. "It's more that—"

"*Ce soir,*" she said, releasing him. "Now, I must get ready."

Before he had a chance to object, she had disappeared into the bathroom and closed the door behind her.

When Marie-Cécile emerged from her shower she was relieved to find Will had gone. She wouldn't have been surprised to find him still sprawled across the bed with that innocent expression on his face.

His demands were starting to get on her nerves. Increasingly, he wanted more of her time and attention than she was prepared to give. He seemed to be misunderstanding the nature of the relationship. She would have to deal with it.

Marie-Cécile put Will from her mind. She looked around. Her maid had been in and tidied the room. Her things were laid out ready on the bed. Her gold handmade slippers were on the floor beside it.

She lit another cigarette from her case. She was smoking too much, but she was nervous tonight. She tapped the end of the filter against the lid before lighting it. It was another mannerism she'd inherited from her grandfather, like so much else.

Marie-Cécile walked over to the mirror and allowed the white silk bathrobe to slide from her shoulders. It pooled around her feet on the floor. She tilted her head to one side and stared in the mirror with a critical eye. The long lean body, unfashionably pale; the full high breasts, the flawless skin. She ran her hand over her dark nipples then lower, tracing the outline of her hip bones, her flat stomach. There were a few more lines around her eyes and mouth perhaps, but otherwise she was little marked by time.

The ormolu clock on the mantle above the fireplace began to chime the hour, reminding her she should begin her preparations. She reached and took the full length, diaphanous shift from the hanger. Cut high at the back, with a sharp V-neck at the front, it had been tailored for her.

Marie-Cécile hooked the straps, narrow ribbons of gold, over her angular shoulders, and then sat down at the dressing table. She brushed her hair, twisting the curls around her fingers, until it shone like polished jet. She loved this moment of metamorphosis, when she ceased to be herself and became the *Navigatairé*. The process connected back through time to all those who had filled this same role before her.

Marie-Cécile smiled. Only her grandfather would understand how she felt now. Euphoric, exhilarated, invincible. Not tonight, but the next time she did this, it would be in the place where her ancestors once had stood. But not him. It was painful how close the cave was to the site of her grandfather's excavations fifty years ago. He'd been right all along. Just a matter of a few kilometers to the east and it would have been him and not her who stood poised to change history.

She'd inherited the de l'Oradore family business on his death five years ago. It was a role he had been grooming her for, for as long as she could remember. Her father—his only son—was a disappointment to him. Marie-Cécile had been aware of this from a very early age. At six, her grandfather had taken her education in hand—social, academic and philosophical. He had a passion for the finer things of life and an amazing eye for color and craftsmanship. Furniture, tapestries, couture, paintings, books, his taste was immaculate. Everything she valued about herself, she had learned from him.

He had also taught her about power, how to use it and how to keep it. When she was eighteen and he believed her ready, her grandfather had formally disinherited his own son and named her instead as his heir.

There had only been one stumble in their relationship, her unexpected and unwanted pregnancy. Despite his dedication to the Quest for the ancient secret of the Grail, her grandfather's Catholicism was strong and orthodox and he did not approve of children born outside marriage. Abortion was out of the question. Adoption was out of the question. It was only when he saw that motherhood made no difference to her determination—that, if anything, it sharpened her ambition and ruthlessness—that he allowed her back into his life.

She inhaled deeply on her cigarette, welcoming the burning smoke as it curled down her throat and into her lungs, resenting the power of her memories. Even more than twenty years later, the memory of her exile filled her with a cold desperation. Her *excommunication*, he'd called it.

It was a good description. It had felt like being dead.

Marie-Cécile shook her head to shake the maudlin thoughts away. She wanted nothing to disturb her mood tonight. She couldn't allow anything to cast a shadow over tonight. She wanted no mistakes.

She turned back to the mirror. First, she applied a pale foundation and dusted her skin with a gold face powder that reflected the light. Next, she outlined her lids and brows with heavy kohl pencil that accentuated her dark lashes and black pupils, then a green eye shadow, iridescent like a peacock's tail. For her lips, she chose a metallic copper gloss flecked with gold, kissing a tissue to seal the color. Finally, she sprayed a haze of perfume into the air and let it fall, like mist, onto the surface of her skin.

Three boxes were lined up on the dressing table, the red leather and brass clasps polished and gleaming. Each piece of ceremonial jewelry was several hundred years old, but modeled on pieces thousands of years older. In the first, there was a gold headdress, like a tiara, rising to a point in the center; in the second, two gold amulets, shaped like snakes, their glittering eyes made of cut emerald; the third contained a necklace, a solid band of gold with the symbol suspended from the middle. The gleaming surfaces echoed with an imagined memory of the dust, the heat of ancient Egypt.

When she was ready, Marie-Cécile moved over to the window. Below her, the streets of Chartres lay spread out like a picture postcard, the everyday shops and cars and restaurants nestling in the shadows of the great Gothic cathedral. Soon, from these same houses, would come the men and women chosen to take part in tonight's ritual.

She closed her eyes to the familiar skyline and darkening horizon. Now, she no longer saw the spire and the gray cloisters. Instead, in her mind's eye, she saw the whole world, like a glittering map, stretched out before her.

Within her reach at last.

CHAPTER 15

Foix

Alice was jolted awake by a persistent ringing in her ear.

Where the hell am I? The beige phone on the shelf above the bed rang again.

Of course. Her hotel room in Foix. She'd come back from the site, done some packing, then had a shower. The last thing she remembered was lying down on her bed for five minutes.

Alice fumbled for the receiver. *"Oui. Allo?"*

The owner of the hotel, Monsieur Annaud, had a strong local accent, all flat vowels and nasal consonants. Alice had trouble understanding him face to face. On the phone, without the benefit of eyebrows and hand gestures, it was impossible. He sounded like a cartoon character.

"Plus lentement, s'il vous plaît," she said, trying to slow him down. *"Vous parlez trop vite. Je ne comprends pas."*

There was a pause. She heard rapid muttering in the background. Then Madame Annaud came on and explained there was someone waiting for Alice in reception.

"Une femme?" she said hopefully.

Alice had left a note for Shelagh at the site house, as well as a couple of messages on her voicemail, but she'd heard nothing.

"Non, c'est un homme," replied Madame Annaud.

"Okay," she sighed, disappointed. *"J'arrive. Deux minutes."*

She ran a comb through her hair, which was still damp, then pulled on a skirt and T-shirt, pushed her feet into a pair of espadrilles, then headed downstairs, wondering who the hell it could be.

The main team were all staying in a small auberge close to the excavation site. In any case, she'd already said her goodbyes to those who wanted to hear them. Nobody else knew she was here. Since she'd broken up with Oliver, there was no one to tell anyway.

The reception area was deserted. She peered into the gloom, expecting to see Madame Annaud sitting behind the high wooden desk, but there was no one there. Alice took a quick look round the corner at the waiting room. The old wicker chairs, dusty on the underside, were unoccupied, as were the two large leather sofas that stood at right angles to the fireplace, draped with horse brasses and testimonials from grateful past guests. A lopsided spinner of postcards, offering dog-eared views of everything Foix and the Ariège had to offer, was still.

Alice went back to the desk and rang the bell. There was a rattle of beads in the doorway as Monsieur Annaud appeared from the family's private quarters.

"Il y a quelqu'un pour moi?"

"Là," he said, leaning out over the counter to point.

Alice shook her head. *"Personne."*

He came round to look, then shrugged, surprised to find the lounge was deserted. *"Dehors?* Outside?" He mimed a man smoking.

The hotel was on a small side street, which ran between the main thoroughfare—filled with administrative buildings, fast-food restaurants as well as the extraordinary 1930s Art Deco post office—and the more picturesque medieval center of Foix with its cafés and antique shops.

Alice looked to the left, then to the right, but nobody appeared to be waiting. The shops were all closed at this time of day and the road was pretty much empty.

Puzzled, she turned to go back inside, when a man appeared out of a doorway. In his early twenties, he was wearing a pale summer suit that was a little too big for him. His thick black hair was neatly short and his eyes were obscured behind dark glasses. He had a cigarette in his hand.

"Dr. Tanner."

"Oui," she said cautiously. *"Vous me cherchez?"*

He reached into his top pocket. *"Pour vous. Tenez,"* he said, thrusting an envelope at her. He kept darting his eyes about, clearly nervous that someone would see them. Alice suddenly recognized him as the young uniformed officer who'd been with Inspector Noubel.

"Je vous ai déjà rencontré, non? Au Pic de Soularac."

He switched to English. "Please," he said urgently. "Take."

"Vous êtes avec Inspecteur Noubel?" she insisted.

He had tiny beads of sweat on his forehead. He took Alice by surprise by grabbing her hand and forcing the envelope into it.

"Hey!" she objected. "What is this?"

But he'd already disappeared, swallowed up into one of the many alleyways that led up to the castle.

For a moment, Alice stood staring at the empty space in the street, half- minded to follow him. Then she reconsidered. The truth was, he'd scared her. She looked down at the letter in her hand as if it was a bomb about to go off, then took a deep breath and slid her finger under the flap. Inside the envelope was a single sheet of cheap writing paper with

117

APPELEZ scrawled across it in childish capitals. Below that was a telephone number: 02 68 72 31 26.

Alice frowned. It wasn't local. The code for the Ariège was 05.

She turned it over in case there was something on the other side, but it was blank. She was about to throw the note in the bin, then thought better of it. *Might as well keep it for now.* Putting it in her pocket, she dumped the envelope on top of the ice-cream wrappers, then went back in, feeling mystified.

Alice didn't notice the man step out from the doorway of the café opposite. By the time he reached into the bin to retrieve the envelope, she was already back in her room.

Adrenaline pumping through his veins, Yves Biau finally stopped running. He bent over, hands on his knees, to get his breath back.

High above him, the great Château of Foix towered over the town as it had done for more than a thousand years. It was the symbol of the independence of the region, the only significant fortress never to be taken in the crusade against the Languedoc. A refuge for the Cathars and freedom fighters driven from the cities and plains.

Biau knew he was being followed. They—whoever they were—had made no attempt to hide. His hand went to his gun beneath his jacket. At least he'd done what Shelagh asked him. Now, if he could get over the border into Andorra before they realized he'd gone, he might be all right. Biau understood now that it was too late to halt the events he'd helped set in motion. He'd done everything they told him, but she kept coming back. Whatever he did would never be enough.

The package had gone by the last post to his grandmother. She would know what to do with it. It was the only thing he could think of to make up for what he'd done.

Biau looked up and down the street. No one.

He stepped out and started to walk, heading home by a circuitous, illogical route, in case they were waiting for him there. Coming from this direction, he'd have a chance of spotting them before they saw him.

As he crossed through the covered market, his subconscious mind registered the silver Mercedes in the Place Saint-Volusien, but he paid little attention. He didn't hear the soft cough of the engine ticking over, nor the shift of gears as the car started to glide forward, rumbling softly over the cobbled stones of the medieval old town.

As Biau stepped off the pavement to cross the road, the car accelerated violently, catapulting forward like a plane on a runway. He spun round, shock frozen on his face. A dull thud and his legs were taken out from under him as his suddenly weightless body was thrown into and over the windscreen. Biau seemed to float for a fraction of a second before being hurled violently against one of the cast-iron stanchions that supported the sloped roof of the covered market.

He hung there, suspended in midair, like a child in a centrifuge at a fairground. Then gravity claimed him and he dropped straight to the ground, leaving a trail of red blood on the black metal pillar.

The Mercedes did not stop.

The noise brought people in the local bars out on to the streets. A couple of women looked out from windows overlooking the square. The owner of the Café PMU took one look and ran back inside to call the police. A woman started screaming and was quickly hushed as a crowd formed around the body.

At first, Alice took no notice of the noise. But as the wailing of the sirens grew closer, she moved to her hotel window like everyone else and looked out.

It's nothing to do with you.

There was no reason to get involved. And yet, for some reason she couldn't account for, Alice found herself leaving her room and heading for the square.

There was a police car blocking the small road that led from the corner of the square, its lights flashing silently. Just the other side, a group of people had formed a semicircle around something or someone lying on the ground.

"You're not safe anywhere," an American woman was muttering to her husband, "not even in Europe."

Alice's sense of foreboding got stronger the closer she got. She couldn't bear the thought of what she might see, but somehow couldn't stop herself. A second police car emerged from a side street and screeched to a halt beside the first. Faces turned, the thicket of arms and legs and bodies thinning just long enough for Alice to see the body on the ground. A pale suit, black hair; sunglasses with brown lenses and gold arms, lying close by.

It can't be him.

Alice pushed her way through, shoving people out of the way until she reached the front. The boy was lying motionless on the ground. Her hand went automatically to the paper in her pocket. *This can't be a coincidence.*

Struck dumb with shock, Alice blundered back. A car door slammed. She jumped and spun round, in time to see Inspector Noubel levering himself out of the driver's seat. She shrank back into the mass of people. *Don't let him see you.* Instinct sent her across the square, away from Noubel, her head down.

As soon as she rounded the corner, she broke into a run.

.   .   .

"S'il vous plaît," shouted Noubel, clearing a path through the onlookers. *"Police. S'il vous plaît."*

Yves Biau was spreadeagled on the unforgiving ground, his arms flung out at right angles. One leg was doubled under him, clearly broken, a white ankle bone protruding from his trousers. The other leg lay unnaturally flat, flopped sideways. One of his tan loafers had come off.

Noubel crouched down and tried to find a pulse. The boy was still breathing, in short, shallow gasps, but his skin was clammy to the touch and his eyes were closed. In the distance, Noubel heard the welcome wail of an ambulance.

"S'il vous plaît," he shouted again, hauling himself to his feet. *"Poussez-vous."* Stand back.

Two more police cars arrived. Word had gone out over the radio that an officer was down, so there were more police than bystanders. They cordoned off the street and separated witnesses from onlookers. They were efficient and methodical, but the tension showed in their faces.

"It wasn't an accident, Inspector," said the American woman. "The car drove right at him, real fast. He didn't stand a chance."

Noubel looked at her intently. "You saw the incident, Madame?"

"Sure I did."

"Did you see what type of car it was? The make?"

She shook her head. "Silver, that's as much I can say." She turned to her husband.

"Mercedes," he said immediately. "Didn't get a good look myself. Only turned around when I heard the noise."

"Registration number?"

"I think the last number was eleven. It happened too quick."

"The street was quite empty, Officer," the wife repeated, as if she feared he wasn't taking her seriously.

"Did you see how many people were in the car?"

"One for sure in the front. Couldn't say if there were folks in the rear."

Noubel handed her over to an officer to take down her details, then walked round to the back of the ambulance where Biau was being lifted in on a stretcher. His neck and head were supported by a brace, but a steady stream of blood was flowing from beneath the bandage wrapped around the wound, staining his shirt red.

His skin was unnaturally white, the color of wax. There was a tube taped to the corner of his mouth and a mobile drip attached to his hand.

"Il pourra s'en tirer?" Will he make it?

The paramedic pulled a face. "If I were you," he said, slamming the doors shut, "I'd be calling the next of kin."

Noubel banged on the side of the ambulance as it pulled away, then, satisfied his men were doing their job, he wandered back to his car, cursing himself. He lowered himself into the front seat, feeling every one of his fifty years, reflecting on all the wrong decisions he'd taken today that had led to this. He slid a finger under the collar of his shirt and loosened his tie.

He knew he should have talked to the boy earlier. Biau hadn't been himself from the moment he'd arrived at the Pic de Soularac. He was normally enthusiastic, the first to volunteer. Today, he'd been nervous and on edge, then he'd vanished for half the afternoon.

Noubel tapped his fingers nervously on the steering wheel. Authié claimed Biau had never given him the message about the ring. And why would he lie about something like that?

At the thought of Paul Authié, Noubel felt a sharp pain in his abdomen. He popped a peppermint in his mouth to relieve the burning. That was another mistake. He shouldn't have let Authié near Dr. Tanner, although, when he thought about it, he wasn't sure what he could have done to prevent it. When reports of the skeletons at Soularac had come through, orders that Paul Authié should be given access to the site and assistance had accompanied them. So far, Noubel hadn't been able to find out how Authié had heard about the discovery so fast, let alone worm his way onto the site.

Noubel had never met Authié in person before, although he knew him by reputation. Most police officers did. A lawyer, known for his hard-line religious views, Authié was said to have half the judiciaire and gendarmerie of the Midi in his pockets. More specifically, a colleague of Noubel's had been called to give evidence in a case Authié was defending. Two members of a far-right group were accused of the murder of an Algerian taxi driver in Carcassonne. There'd been rumors of intimidation. In the end, both defendants were acquitted and several police officers forced to retire.

Noubel looked down at Biau's sunglasses, which he'd picked up from the ground. He'd been unhappy earlier. Now he liked the situation even less.

The radio crackled into life, belching out the information Noubel needed about Biau's next of kin. He sat for a moment longer, putting off the moment. Then he started to make the calls.

CHAPTER 16

It was eleven o'clock when Alice reached the outskirts of Toulouse. She was too tired to carry on to Carcassonne, so she decided to head for the city center and find somewhere to stay the night.

The journey had passed in a flash. Her head was full of jumbled images of the skeletons and the knife beside them; the white face looming out at her in the dead gray light; the body lying in front of the church in Foix. Was he dead?

And the labyrinth. Always, in the end, she came back to the labyrinth. Alice told herself she was being paranoid, that it was nothing to do with her. *You were just in the wrong place at the wrong time.* But no matter how many times she said it, Alice did not believe it.

She kicked off her shoes and lay down fully clothed on the bed. Everything about the room was cheap. Featureless plastic and hardboard, gray tiles and fake wood. The sheets were overstarched and scratched like paper against her skin.

She took the Bushmills single malt from her rucksack. There were a couple of fingers left in the bottle. Unexpectedly a lump came to her throat. She'd been saving the last couple of inches for her last night at the dig. She tried again, but Shelagh's phone was still on divert. Fighting back her irritation, she left yet another message. She wished Shelagh would quit playing games.

Alice washed down a couple of painkillers with the whisky, then got into bed and turned the light off. She was totally exhausted, but she couldn't get comfortable. Her head was throbbing, her wrist felt hot and swollen and the cut on her arm was hurting like hell. Worse than ever.

The room was stuffy and hot. After tossing and turning, listening to bells strike midnight, then one o'clock, Alice got up to open the window and let some air in. It didn't help. Her mind wouldn't stay still. She tried to think of white sands and clear blue water, Caribbean beaches and Hawaiian sunsets, but her brain kept coming back to the gray rock and chill subterranean air of the mountain.

She was scared to sleep. What if the dream came back again?

The hours crawled by. Her mouth was dry and her heart staggered under the influence of the whisky. Not until the pale white dawn crept under the worn edges of the curtains did her mind finally give in.

This time, a different dream.

She was riding a chestnut horse through the snow. Its winter coat was thick and glossy, and its white mane and tail were plaited with red ribbons. She was dressed for hunting in her best cloak with the squirrel-fur *pelisse* and hood and long leather gloves lined with marten fur that went up as high as her elbows.

A man was riding beside her on a gray gelding, a bigger, more powerful animal with a black mane and tail. He pulled repeatedly on the reins to keep it steady. His brown hair was long for a man, skimming his shoulders. His blue velvet cloak streamed behind him as he drove his mount on. Alice saw he wore a dagger at his waist. Around his neck was a silver chain with a single green stone hanging from it, which banged up and down against his chest to the rhythm of the horse.

He kept glancing over at her with a mixture of pride and ownership. The connection between them was strong, intimate. In her sleep, Alice shifted position and smiled.

Some way off, a horn was blowing sharp and shrill in the crisp December air, proclaiming that the hounds were on the trail of a wolf. She knew it was December, a special month. She knew she was happy.

Then, the light changed.

Now she was alone in a part of the forest she did not recognize. The trees were taller and more dense, their bare branches black and twisted against the white, snow-laden sky, like dead men's fingers. Somewhere behind her, unseen and threatening, the dogs were gaining on her, excited by the promise of blood.

She was no longer the hunter, but the quarry.

The forest reverberated with a thousand thundering hooves, getting closer and closer. She could hear the baying of the huntsmen now. They were shouting to one another in a language she did not understand, but she knew they were looking for her.

Her horse stumbled. Alice was thrown, falling forward out of the saddle and down to the hard, wintry ground. She heard the bone in her shoulder crack, then searing pain. She looked down in horror. A piece of dead wood, frozen solid like the head of an arrow, had pierced her sleeve and impaled her arm.

With numb and desperate fingers, Alice pulled at the fragment until it came loose, closing her eyes against the aching pain. Straight away, the blood started to flow, but she couldn't let that stop her.

Staunching the bleeding with the hem of her cloak, Alice scrambled to her feet and forced herself on through the naked branches and petrified undergrowth. The brittle twigs snapped under her feet and the ice-cold air pinched her cheeks and made her eyes water.

The ringing in her ears was louder now, more insistent, and she felt faint. As insubstantial as a ghost.

Suddenly, the forest was gone and Alice found herself standing on the edge of a cliff. There was nowhere left to go. At her feet was a sheer drop to a wooded precipice below. In front of her were the mountains, capped with snow, stretching as far as the eye could see. They were so close she felt she could almost reach out and touch them.

In her sleep, Alice shifted uneasily.

Let me wake up. Please.

She struggled to wake up, but she couldn't. The dream held her too tightly in its coils.

The dogs burst out of the cover of the trees behind her, barking, snarling. Their breath clouded the air as their jaws snapped, drools of spit and blood hanging from their teeth. In the gathering dusk, the tips of the huntsmen's spears glinted brightly. Their eyes were filled with hate, with excitement. She could hear them whispering, jeering, taunting her.

"Hérétique, hérétique."

In that split second, the decision was made. If it was her time to die, it would not be at the hands of such men. Alice lifted her arms wide and jumped, commending her body to the air.

Straight away, the world fell silent.

Time ceased to have any meaning as she fell, slowly and gently, her green skirts billowing out around her. Now she realized there was something pinned to her back, a piece of material in the shape of a star. No, not a star but a cross. A yellow cross. *Rouelle.* As the unfamiliar word drifted in and then out of her mind, the cross came loose and floated away from her, like a leaf dropping from a tree in autumn.

The ground came no nearer. Alice was no longer afraid. For even as the dream images started to splinter and break apart, her subconscious mind understood what her conscious mind could not. That it was not her—Alice—who fell, but another.

And this was not a dream, but a memory. A fragment from a life lived a long, long time ago.

CHAPTER 17
Carcassona

Twigs and leaves cracked as Alaïs shifted position.

There was a rich smell of moss, lichen and earth in her nose, her mouth. Something sharp pierced the back of her hand, the tiniest jab that immediately began to sting. A mosquito or an ant. She could feel the poison seeping into her blood. Alaïs moved to brush the insect away. The movement made her retch.

Where am I?

The answer, like an echo. *Defòra.* Outside.

She was lying facedown on the ground. Her skin was clammy, slightly chill from the dew. Daybreak or dusk? Her clothes, tangled around her, were damp. Taking it slowly, Alaïs managed to lever herself into a sitting position, leaning against the trunk of a beech tree to keep herself steady.

Doçament. Softly, carefully.

Through the trees at the top of the slope she could see the sky was white, strengthening to pink on the horizon. Flat clouds floated like ships becalmed. She could make out the black outlines of weeping willows. Behind her were pear and cherry trees, drab and naked of color this late in the season.

Dawn, then. Alaïs tried to focus on her surroundings. It seemed very bright, blinding, even though there was no sun. She could hear water not far off, shallow and moving lazily over the stones. In the distance, the distinctive *kveck-kveck* of an eagle owl coming back from his night's hunting.

Alaïs glanced down at her arms, which were marked with small, angry red bites. She examined the scratches and cuts on her legs too. As well as insect bites, her ankles were ringed with dried blood. She held her hands up close to her face. Her knuckles were bruised and sore. Lines of rust-red streaks between the fingers.

A memory. Of being dragged, arms trailing along the ground.

No, before that.

Walking across the courtyard. Lights in the upper windows.

Fear pricked the back of her neck. Footsteps in the dark, the callused hand across her mouth, then the blow.

Perilhòs. Danger.

She raised her hand to her head and then winced as her fingers connected with the sticky mass of blood and hair behind her ear. She screwed her eyes shut, trying to blot out the memory of the hands crawling over her like rats. Two men. A commonplace smell, of horses, ale and straw.

Did they find the merel?

Alaïs struggled to stand. She had to tell her father what had happened. He was going to Montpellier, that much she could remember. She had to speak with him first. She tried to get up, but her legs would not hold her. Her head was spinning again and she was falling, falling, slipping back into a weightless sleep. She tried to fight it and stay conscious, but it was no use. Past and present and future were part of an infinite time now, stretching out white before her. Color and sound and light ceased to have any meaning.

CHAPTER 18

With a final, anxious glance back over his shoulder, Bertrand Pelletier rode out of the Eastern Gate at Viscount Trencavel's side. He could not understand why Alaïs had not come to see them off.

Pelletier rode in silence, lost in his own thoughts, hearing little of the inconsequential chatter going on around him. His spirits were troubled at her absence from the Cour d'Honneur to see them off and wish the expedition well. Surprised, disappointed too, if he could bring himself to admit it. He wished now he had sent François to wake her.

Despite the earliness of the hour, the streets were lined with people waving and cheering. Only the finest horses had been chosen. Palfreys whose resilience and stamina could be relied upon, as well as the strongest geldings and mares from the stables of the Château Comtal picked for speed and endurance. Raymond-Roger Trencavel rode his favorite bay stallion, a horse he'd trained himself from a colt. Its coat was the color of a fox in winter and on its muzzle was a distinctive white blaze, the exact shape, or so it was said, of the Trencavel lands.

Every shield displayed the Trencavel ensign. The crest was embroidered on every flag and the vest each *chevalier* wore over his traveling armor. The rising sun glanced off the shining helmets, swords and bridles. Even the saddlebags of the pack horses had been polished until the grooms could see their faces reflected in the leather.

It had taken some time to decide how large the *envoi* should be. Too small and Trencavel would seem an unworthy and unimpressive ally and they would be easy pickings on the road. Too large and it would look like a declaration of war.

Finally, sixteen *chevaliers* had been chosen, Guilhem du Mas among them, despite Pelletier's objections. With their *écuyers,* a handful of servants and churchmen, Jehan Congost and a smith for working repairs to the horses' shoes en route, the party numbered some thirty in total.

Their destination was Montpellier, the principal city within the domains of the viscount of Nîmes and the birthplace of Raymond-Roger's wife, Dame Agnès. Like Trencavel, Nîmes was a vassal of the king of Aragon, Pedro II, so even though Montpellier was a Catholic city—and

Pedro himself a staunch and energetic persecutor of heresy—there was reason to expect they would have safe passage.

They had allowed three days to ride from Carcassonne. It was anybody's guess as to which of them, Trencavel or the count of Toulouse, would arrive in the city first.

At first they headed east, following the course of the Aude toward the rising sun. At Trèbes, they turned northwest into the lands of the Minervois, following the old Roman road that ran through La Redorte, the fortified hill town of Azille, and on to Olonzac.

The best land was given over to the *canabières*, the hemp fields, which stretched as far as the eye could see. To their right were vines, some pruned, others growing wild and untended at the side of the track behind vigorous hedgerows. To their left was a sea of emerald-green stalks of the barley fields, which would turn to gold by harvest time. Peasants, their wide-brimmed straw hats obscuring their faces, were already hard at work, reaping the last of the season's wheat. The iron curve of their scythes catching the rising sun from time to time.

Beyond the river bank, lined with oak trees and marsh willow, were the deep and silent forests where the wild eagles flew. Stag, lynx and bear were plentiful, wolves and foxes too in the winter. Towering above the lowland woods and coppice were the dark forests of the Montagne Noire where the wild boar was king.

With the resilience and optimism of youth, Viscount Trencavel was in good spirits, exchanging lighthearted anecdotes and listening to tales of past exploits. He argued with his men about the best hunting dogs, greyhounds or mastiffs, about the price of a good brood bitch these days, gossiped about who had wagered what at darts or dice.

Nobody talked of the purpose of the expedition, nor of what would happen if the viscount failed in his petitions to his uncle.

A raucous shout from the back of the line drew Pelletier's attention. He glanced over his shoulder. Guilhem du Mas was riding three abreast with Alzeu de Preixan and Thierry Cazanon, *chevaliers* who'd also trained in Carcassonne and been dubbed the same Passiontide.

Aware of the older man's critical scrutiny, Guilhem raised his head and met his gaze with an insolent stare. For a moment they held each other fixed. Then, the younger man inclined his head slightly, an insincere acknowledgment, and turned away. Pelletier felt his blood grow hot, all the worse for knowing there was nothing he could do.

For hour after hour they rode across the plains. The conversation faltered, then petered out as the excitement that had accompanied their departure from the Cité gave way to apprehension.

The sun climbed ever higher in the sky. The churchmen suffered the most in their black worsted habits. Rivulets of sweat were dripping down the bishop's forehead and Jehan Congost's spongy face had turned an unpleasant blotchy red, the color of foxgloves. Bees, crickets and cicadas rattled and hummed in the brown grass. Mosquitoes pricked at their wrists and hands, and flies tormented the horses, causing them to switch their manes and tails in irritation.

Only when the sun was full overhead did Viscount Trencavel lead them off the road to rest awhile. They settled on a glade beside a slow-flowing stream, having established the grazing was safe. The *écuyers* unsaddled the horses and cooled their coats with willow leaves dipped in the water. Cuts and bites were treated with dock leaves or mustard poultices.

The *chevaliers* removed their traveling armor and boots, washing the dust and sweat from their hands and necks. A small contingent of servants was dispatched to the nearest farm, returning some time later with bread and sausage, white goat's cheese, olives and strong, local wine.

As the news spread that Viscount Trencavel was camped nearby, a steady stream of farmers and peasants, old men and young women, weavers and brewers started to make their way to their humble camp under the trees, carrying gifts for their *seigneur*: baskets of cherries and newly fallen plums, a goose, salt and fish.

Pelletier was uneasy. It would delay them and use up precious time. They had a great deal of ground to cover before the evening shadows lengthened and they pitched camp for the night. But, like his father and mother before him, Raymond-Roger enjoyed meeting his subjects and would have none turned away.

"It is for this that we swallow our pride and go to make peace with my uncle," he said quietly. "To protect all that is good and innocent and true in our way of life, *è*? And, if necessary, we shall fight for it."

Like an ancient warrior king, Viscount Trencavel held court in the shade of the holm oak trees. He accepted all the tributes offered to him with grace and charm and dignity. He knew that this day would become a story to be treasured, woven into the life of the village.

One of the last to approach was a pretty, dark-skinned girl of five or six, with bright eyes the color of blackberries, who gave a brief curtsey and offered a posey of wild orchids, white sneezewort and meadow honeysuckle. Her hands were shaking.

Bending down to the girl's level, Viscount Trencavel pulled a linen handkerchief from his belt and offered it to her. Even Pelletier smiled as the tiny fingers reached out timidly and took the crisp white square of cloth.

"And what is your name, *Madomaisèla*," he asked.

"Ernestine, *Messire*," she whispered.

Trencavel nodded. "Well, Madomaisèla Ernestine," he said, plucking a pink bloom from the bunch of flowers and fixing it to his tunic, "I shall wear this for good luck. And to remind me of the kindness of the people of Puicheric."

Only when the last of the visitors had left the camp, did Raymond-Roger Trencavel unbuckle his sword and sit down to eat. When hunger was satisfied, one by one, man and boy stretched out on the soft grass or leaned back against the trunk of a tree and dozed, their bellies full of wine and their heads thick with the afternoon heat.

Pelletier alone did not settle. Once he was certain Viscount Trencavel had no need of him for the time being, he set off to walk by the stream, desiring solitude.

Waterboatmen skated over the water and brightly colored dragonflies skimmed the surface, shimmering, darting and slipping through the heavy air.

As soon as he was out of sight of the camp, Pelletier sat down on a blackened trunk of a fallen tree and took Harif's letter from his pocket. He didn't read it. He didn't even open it, just held it tight between his forefinger and thumb, like a talisman.

He could not stop thinking of Alaïs. His thoughts rocked backward and forward like a balance. At one moment he regretted confiding in her at all. But if not Alaïs, then who? There was no one else he could trust. The next moment, he feared he had told her too little.

God willing, all would be well. If their petition to the count of Toulouse was favorably received, before the month was out, they would be returning to Carcassonne in triumph without a drop of blood being spilled. For Pelletier's own part, he would find Simeon in Béziers and learn the identity of the "sister" of whom Harif had written.

If destiny willed it so.

Pelletier sighed. He looked out over the tranquil scene spread out before him and saw in his imagination the opposite. Instead of the old world, unchanged and unchanging, he saw chaos and devastation and destruction. The end of all things.

He bowed his head. He could not have done other than he had. If he did not return to Carcassonne, then at least he would die in the knowledge that he had done his best to protect the Trilogy. Alaïs would fulfill his obligations. His vows would become her vows. The secret would not be lost in the pandemonium of battle or left to rot in a French gaol.

The sounds of the camp stirring brought Pelletier back to the present.

It was time to move on. There were many more hours of riding before sunset.

Pelletier returned Harif's letter to his pouch and walked quickly back to the camp, aware that such moments of peace and quiet contemplation might be in short supply in the days ahead.

CHAPTER 19

When Alaïs woke again, she was lying between linen sheets, not on grass. There was a low, dull whistling in her ears, like an autumn wind echoing through the trees. Her body felt curiously heavy and weighted down, as if it didn't belong to her. She had been dreaming that Esclarmonde was there with her, putting her cool hand on her brow to draw the fever out.

Her eyes fluttered open. Above her head was the familiar wooden canopy of her own bed, the dark blue night-curtains tied back. The chamber was suffused with the soft, golden light of dusk. The air, although still hot and heavy, carried in it the promise of night. She caught the faint aroma of freshly burned herbs. Rosemary and the scent of lavender.

She could hear women's voices too, coarse and low, somewhere close by. They were whispering as if trying not to disturb her. Their words hissed like fat dripping from a spit onto a fire. Slowly, Alaïs turned her head on her pillow toward the noise. Alziette, the unpopular wife of the head groom, and Ranier, a sly and spiteful gossip with an uncouth, boorish husband, both troublemakers, were sitting by the empty fireplace like a pair of old crows. Her sister, Oriane, used them often for errands, but Alaïs mistrusted them and could not account for how they came to be in her room. Her father would never have allowed it.

Then she remembered. He was not here. He had gone to Saint-Gilles or Montpellier, she couldn't quite remember. Guilhem too.

"So where were they?" Ranier hissed, her voice greedy for scandal.

"In the orchard, right down by the brook by the willow trees," replied Alziette. "Mazelle's oldest girl saw them go down there. Bitch that she is, she rushed straight back to her mother. Then Mazelle herself came flying into the courtyard, wringing her hands at the shame of it and how she didn't want to be the one to tell me."

"She's always been jealous of your girl, è. Her daughters are all fat as hogs and pockmarked. The whole lot of them, as plain as pikes." Ranier bent her head closer. "So what did you do?"

"What could I do but go and see for myself. I spotted them the moment I got down there. It's not as if they'd made much effort to conceal themselves. I got hold of Raoul by his hair—nasty coarse brown hair he's got—and boxed his ears. All the while he was pulling at his belt with one hand, his face red from the shame of being caught. When I turned on Jeannette, he wriggled out of my grasp and ran off without even so much as a backward glance."

Ranier tutted.

"All the while Jeannette was wailing, carrying on, saying how Raoul loved her and wants to marry her. To hear her talk, you'd think no girl had ever had her head turned by pretty words before."

"Perhaps his intentions are honest?"

Alziette snorted. "He's in no position to marry," she complained. "Five older brothers and only two of them wed. His father's in the tavern day and night. Every last *sol* they've got goes straight into Gaston's pocket."

Alaïs tried to close her ears to the women's mundane gossip. They were like vultures picking over carrion.

"But then again," Alziette said slyly, "it was fortunate, as it turned out. If circumstances had not taken you down there, then you wouldn't have found *her*."

Alaïs tensed, sensing the two heads turn toward the bed.

"That's so," agreed Ranier. "And I dare say I'll be well rewarded when her father returns."

Alaïs listened, but learned nothing more. The shadows lengthened. She drifted in and out of sleep.

By and by, a night nurse came to replace Alziette and Ranier, another of her sister's favored servants. The noise of the woman dragging the cracked wooden pallet out from under the bed woke Alaïs. She heard a soft whump as the nurse lowered herself down on to the lumpy mattress, the weight of her body pushing the air out from between the dry straw stuffing. Within moments, the grunts and labored snoring, wheezing and snuffling from the foot of the bed announced she was asleep.

Alaïs was suddenly wide awake. Her head was full of her father's last instruction to her. To keep safe the labyrinth board. She eased herself up into a sitting position and looked among the fragments of material and candles.

The board was no longer there.

Careful not to wake the nurse, Alaïs tugged open the door of the bedside table. Its hinge was stiff from lack of use and it creaked as she eased it open. Alaïs ran her fingers around the edge of the bed, in case the board had slipped between the mattress and wooden frame of her bed. It was not there either.

Res. Nothing.

She didn't like the way her thoughts were tending. Her father had dismissed her suggestion that his identity had been discovered, but was he right? *Both the* merel *and the board had gone.*

Alaïs swung her legs over the bed and tiptoed across the room to her sewing chair. She needed to be sure. Her cloak was draped over the back. Someone had tried to clean it, but the red embroidered hem was caked with mud, obscuring the stitching in places. It smelled of the yard or the stables, acrid and sour. Her hands came up empty, as she knew they would. Her purse was gone, the *merel* with it.

Events were moving too fast. Suddenly, the old familiar shadows seemed full of menace. She felt threats all around, even in the grunts coming from the foot of the bed.

What if my attackers are still in the château? What if they come back for me?

Alaïs quickly got dressed, picked up the *calèlh* and adjusted the flame. The thought of crossing the dark courtyard alone frightened her, but she couldn't sit in her chamber, just waiting for something to happen.

Coratge. Courage.

Alaïs ran across the Cour d'Honneur to the Tour Pinte, shielding the guttering flame with her hand. She had to find François.

She opened the door a fraction and called his name into the darkness. There was no answer. She slipped inside.

"François," she whispered again.

The lamp cast a pale yellow glow, enough to see that there was someone lying on the pallet at the foot of her father's bed.

Putting the lamp on the ground, Alaïs bent down and touched him lightly on the shoulder. Straight away she snapped her arm back as if her fingers had been burned. It felt wrong.

"François?"

Still no reply. Alaïs grasped the rough edge of the blanket, counted to three, then ripped it back.

Underneath was a pile of old clothes and furs, carefully arranged to look like a sleeping figure. She felt dizzy with relief, although puzzled.

In the corridor outside a noise caught her attention. Alaïs snatched up the lamp and extinguished the flame, then tucked herself in the shadows behind the bed.

She heard the door creak open. The intruder hesitated, perhaps smelling the oil from the lamp, perhaps noticing the disarranged blankets. He drew his knife from its sheath.

"Who's there?" he said. "Show yourself."

"François," said Alaïs with relief, stepping out from behind the curtains. "It's me. You can put your weapon away."

He looked more startled than she felt.

"Dame, forgive me. I didn't realize."

She looked at him with interest. He was breathing heavily, as if he'd been running. "The fault is mine, but where have you been at this hour?" she asked.

"I—"

A woman, she supposed, although why he should be so embarrassed about it, she could not fathom. She took pity on him.

"In fact, François, it is of no matter. I'm here because you are the only person I trust to tell me what happened to me."

The color drained from his face. "I know nothing, Dame," he said quickly in a strangled voice.

"Come, you must have heard rumors, kitchen gossip, surely?"

"Very little."

"Well, let us try to construct the story together," she said, mystified by his attitude. "I remember walking back from my father's chamber, after you had summoned me to him. Then two men came upon me. I woke to find myself in the orchard, near a stream. It was early in the day. When next I woke, it was to find myself in my own chambers."

"Would you know the men again, Dame?"

Alaïs looked sharply at him. "No. It was dark and it all happened too quickly."

"Was anything taken?"

She hesitated. "Nothing of value," she said, uneasy in the lie. "Then I know that Alziette Baichère raised the alarm. I heard her boasting about it earlier, although I cannot for the life of me understand how she came to be sitting with me. Why not Rixende? Or any other of my women?"

"It was on Dame Oriane's orders, Dame. She has taken personal charge of your care."

"Did not people remark upon her concern?" she said. It was entirely out of character. "My sister is not known for such . . . skills."

François nodded. "But she was most insistent, Dame."

Alaïs shook her head. The faintest recollection sparked in her mind. A fleeting memory of being enclosed within a small space, stone not wood, the acrid stench of urine and animals and neglect. The more she tried to chase the memory down, the farther it slipped away from her.

She brought herself back to the matter in hand.

"I presume my father has departed for Montpelhièr, François."

He nodded. "Two days past, Dame."

"It is Wednesday," she murmured, aghast. She had lost two days. She frowned. "When they left, François, did my father not question why I was not there to bid him farewell?"

"He did, Dame, but . . . he forbade me wake you."

This makes no sense. "But what of my husband? Did Guilhem not say I never returned to our chamber that night?"

"I believe Chevalier du Mas spent the early part of the night at the forge, Dame, then attended the service of blessing with Viscount Trencavel in the chapel. He seemed as surprised by your absence as Intendant Pelletier, and besides . . ."

He broke off.

"Go on. Say what is in your mind, François. I will not blame you."

"With your leave, Dame, I think Chevalier du Mas would not wish to appear ignorant of your whereabouts before your father."

The moment the words were out of his mouth, Alaïs knew he was right. At present the ill-feeling between her husband and father was worse than ever. Alaïs tightened her lips, not wishing to betray her agreement.

"But they were taking such a risk," she said, returning to the attack. "To carry out such an assault on me in the heart of the Château Comtal was madness enough. To compound their felony by taking me captive . . . How could they have hoped to get away with it?"

She pulled herself up short, realizing what she had said.

"Everybody was much occupied, Dame. The curfew was not set. So although the Western Gate was closed, the Eastern Gate stood open all night. It would have been easy for two men to transport you between them, provided your face, your clothing, were hidden. There were many ladies . . . women, I mean, of the sort . . ."

Alaïs stifled a grin. "Thank you, François. I quite understand your point."

The smile faded from her face. She needed to think, decide what she should do next. She was more confused than ever. And her ignorance of why things had happened, in the manner they had, compounded her fear. *It is hard to act against a faceless enemy.*

"It would be well to circulate it that I can remember nothing of the attack, François," she said after a while. "That way if my assailants remain within the château, they will have no need to feel threatened."

The thought of making the same journey back across the courtyard chilled her soul. Besides, she would not sleep under the eyes of Oriane's nurse. Alaïs had no doubt she was set to spy on her and report to her sister.

"I will rest here for what remains of the night," she added.

To her surprise, François looked horrified. "But, Dame, it is not seemly for you—"

"I'm sorry to put you from your bed," she said, softening her command with a smile, "but my sleeping companion in my chamber is not to my liking." An impassive, shuttered look descended over his face. "But if you could stay close by, François, in case I have further need of you, I would be grateful."

He did not return her smile. "As you wish, Dame."

Alaïs stared at him for a moment, then decided she was reading too much into his manner. She asked him to light the lamp, then she dismissed him.

As soon as François had gone, Alaïs curled up in the center of her father's bed. Alone again, the pain of Guilhem's absence returned like a dull ache. She tried to summon his face to her mind, his eyes, the line of his jaw, but his features blurred and would not stay fixed. Alaïs knew this inability to find his image in her mind was borne of anger. Over and over, she reminded herself Guilhem had been only fulfilling his responsibilities as a *chevalier*. He had not acted wrongly or falsely. In fact, he had acted appropriately. On the eve of so important a mission, his duty was to his liege lord and to those making the journey with him, not to his wife. Yet, however many times Alaïs told herself this, she could not quieten the voices in her head. Whatever she said made no difference to what she felt. That when she'd had need of Guilhem's protection, he had failed her. Unjust as it was, she blamed Guilhem.

If her absence had been discovered at first light, then the men might have been caught.

And my father would not have left thinking ill of me.

CHAPTER 20

In a deserted farm outside Aniane, in the flat, fertile lands to the west of Montpellier, an elderly Cathar *parfait* and his eight *credentes,* believers, crouched in the corner of a barn, behind a collection of old harnesses for oxen and mules.

One of the men was badly wounded. Gray and pink flesh flopped open around the white splintered bones that had been his face. His eye had been dislodged from its socket by the force of the kick that had shattered his cheek. Blood congealed around the gaping hole. His friends had refused to leave him when the house in which they had gathered to pray had been attacked by a small, renegade group of soldiers that had broken away from the French army.

But he had slowed them down and lost them the advantage of knowing the land. All day the Crusaders had hunted them. Night had not saved them and now they were trapped. The Cathars could hear them shouting in the courtyard, the sound of dry wood catching light. They were preparing a pyre.

The *parfait* knew they were facing the end. There would be no mercy from men such as this, driven by hatred and ignorance and bigotry. There had never been an army the like of it on Christian soil. The *parfait* would not have believed it had he not seen it with his own eyes. He'd been traveling south, on a parallel course with the Host. He had seen the huge and unwieldy barges floating down the River Rhône, carrying equipment and supplies, as well as wooden chests ringed with bands of steel that contained precious holy relics to bless the expedition. The hooves of thousands of animals and men riding alongside created a giant cloud of dust, which floated above the Host.

From the start, townspeople and villagers had shut their gates, watching from behind their walls and praying that the army would pass them by. Stories of increasing violence and horror circulated. There were reports of farms being burned, reprisals for farmers who had refused to allow the soldiers to pillage their land. Cathar believers, denounced as heretics, had been burned at the stake in Puylaroque. The entire Jewish community of Montélimar, men, women and children, had been put to the sword and their bleeding heads mounted on spikes outside the city walls, carrion for the crows.

In Saint-Paul de Trois Châteaux, a *parfait* was crucified by a small band of Gascon *routiers*. They tied him to a makeshift cross made from two pieces of wood lashed together with rope and hammered nails through his hands. The weight of his body dragged him down, but he still would not recant or apostatize his faith. In the end, bored with the slow death, the soldiers disemboweled him and left him to rot.

These and other acts of barbarism were either denied by the abbott of Cîteaux and the French barons or else disclaimed as the work of a few renegades. But as he crouched in the dark, the *parfait* knew that the words of lords, priests and papal legates counted for nothing out here. He could smell the bloodlust on the breath of the men who had hunted them down to this small corner of the Devil's earthly creation.

He recognized Evil.

All he could do now was try to save the souls of his believers so they could look upon the face of God. Their passing from this world into the next would not be gentle.

The wounded man was still conscious. He whimpered softly, but a final stillness had come over him and his skin was tinged with the grayness of death. The *parfait* laid his hands upon the man's head as he administered the last rites of their religion and spoke the words of the *consolament*.

The remaining believers joined hands in a circle and began to pray.

"Holy Father, just God of good spirits, thou who are never deceived, who dost never lie or doubt, grant us to know . . ."

The soldiers were kicking against the door now, laughing, jeering. It would not be long now before they found them. The youngest of the women, no more than fourteen years old, began to cry. The tears ran hopelessly, silently, down her cheeks.

". . . grant us to know what thou knowest, to love what thou dost love; for we are not of this world, and this world is not of us, and we fear lest we meet death in this realm of an alien god."

The *parfait* raised his voice as the horizontal beam holding the door shut fractured in two. Splinters of wood, as sharp as arrowheads, exploded into the barn as the men burst in. Lit by the orange glow of the fire burning in the courtyard, he could see their eyes were glazed and inhuman. He counted ten of them, each with a sword.

His eyes went to the commander who followed them in. A tall man, with a pale thin face and expressionless eyes, as calm and controlled as his men were hot and ill disciplined. He had an air of cruel authority about him, a man used to being obeyed.

On his orders, the fugitives were dragged from their hiding place. He lifted his arm and thrust his blade into the *parfait*'s chest. For an instant, he held his gaze. The Frenchman's flint gray eyes were stiff with contempt. He raised his arm a second time and plunged his sword into the top of the old man's skull, splattering red pulp and gray brains into the straw.

With their priest murdered, panic broke out. The others tried to run, but the ground was already slippery with blood. A soldier grabbed a woman by her hair and thrust his sword into her back. Her father tried to pull him off, but the soldier swung round and sliced him across the belly. His eyes opened wide in shock as the soldier twisted the knife, then pushed the skewered body off the blade with his foot.

The youngest soldier turned away and vomited into the straw.

Within minutes all the men lay dead, their bodies strewn about the barn. The captain ordered his men to take the two older women outside. The girl he kept behind, the puking boy too. He needed to harden up.

She backed away from him, her eyes alive with fear. He smiled. He was in no hurry and there was nowhere for her to run. He paced around her, like a wolf watching its prey, then, without warning, he struck. In a single movement he grabbed her around the throat and smashed her head back against the wall and ripped her dress open. She was screaming louder now, hitting and kicking out wildly. He drove his fist into her face, relishing the splinter of bone beneath his touch.

Her legs buckled. She sank to her knees, leaving a trail of blood down the wood. He bent over and ripped her shift from her body, splitting the material from top to bottom in a single tear. She whimpered as he pulled her skirts up to her waist.

"They must not be allowed to breed and bring others like themselves into the world," he said in a cold voice, drawing his knife from its sheath.

He did not intend to pollute his flesh by touching the heretic. Grasping the blade, he plunged the hilt deep inside the girl's stomach. With all the hate he felt for her kind, he drove the knife into her again and again, until her body lay motionless before him. As a final act of desecration, he rolled her over onto her front and, with two deep sweeps of his knife, carved the sign of the cross on her naked back. Pearls of blood, like rubies, sprang up on her white skin.

"That should serve as a lesson for any others who pass this way," he said calmly. "Now, get rid of it."

Wiping his blade on her torn dress, he straightened up.

The boy was sobbing. His clothes were stained with vomit and blood. He tried to do what his captain commanded, but he was too slow.

He grabbed the boy by the throat. "I said, get rid of it. Quick. If you don't want to join them." He kicked the boy in the small of his back, leaving a footprint of blood, dust and dirt on his tunic. A soldier with a weak stomach was no use to him.

The makeshift pyre in the middle of the farmyard was burning fiercely, fanned by the hot night winds that swept up from the Mediterranean Sea.

The soldiers were standing well back, their hands at their faces to shield themselves from the heat. Their horses, tethered by the gate, were stamping with agitated hooves. The stench of death was in their nostrils, making them nervous.

The women had been stripped and made to kneel on the ground in front of their captors, their feet tied and their hands bound tightly behind their back. Their faces, scratched breasts and bare shoulders showed marks of their ill use, but they were silent. Somebody gasped as the girl's corpse was thrown down in front of them.

The captain walked toward the fire. He was bored now, restless to be gone. Killing heretics was not the reason he had taken the Cross. This brutal expedition was a gift to his men. They needed to be kept occupied, to keep their skills sharp and to stop them turning on each other.

The night sky was filled with white stars around a full moon. He realized it must be past midnight, perhaps later. He'd intended to be back long before now, in case word came.

"Shall we give them to the fire, my lord?"

With a sudden, single stroke, he drew his sword and severed the head of the nearest woman. Blood pumped from a vein in her neck, splashing his legs and feet. The skull fell to the ground with a soft thud. He kicked her still twitching body until it fell forward into the dirt.

"Kill the rest of these heretic bitches, then burn the bodies, the barn too. We've delayed long enough."

CHAPTER 21

Alaïs woke as dawn slipped into the room.

For a moment, she couldn't remember how she came to be in her father's chamber. She sat up and stretched the sleep from her bones, waiting until the memory of the day before came back vivid and strong.

Some time during the long hours between midnight and daybreak she had reached a decision. Despite her broken night, her mind was as clear as a mountain stream. She could not sit by, passively waiting for her father to return. She had no way of judging the consequences of each day's delay. When he had spoken of his sacred duty to the *Noublesso de los Seres* and the secret they guarded, he had left her in no doubt that his honor and pride lay in his ability to fulfill his vows. Her duty was to seek him out, tell him all that had happened, put the matter back in his hands.

Far better to act than do nothing.

Alaïs walked over to the window and opened the shutters to let in the morning air. In the distance the Montagne Noire shimmered purple in the gathering dawn, enduring and timeless. The sight of the mountains strengthened her resolve. The world was calling her to join it.

She was taking a risk, a woman traveling alone. Willful, her father would call it. But she was an excellent rider, quick and instinctive, and she had faith in her ability to outride any group of *routiers* or bandits. Besides, to her knowledge, there had been no attacks on Viscount Trencavel's lands.

Alaïs raised her hand to the bruise at the back of her head, evidence that someone meant her harm. If it was her time to die, then far better to face death with her sword in her hand than sit waiting for her enemies to strike again.

Alaïs picked up her cold lamp from the table, catching her reflection in the black-streaked glass. She was pale, her skin the color of buttermilk, and her eyes glinted with fatigue. But there was a sense of purpose that had not been there before.

Alaïs wished she did not have to return to her chamber, but she had no choice. Carefully stepping over François, she made her way across the courtyard and back into the living quarters. There was no one about.

Oriane's faithful shadow, Guirande, was sleeping on the floor outside her sister's chamber as Alaïs tiptoed past, her pretty, pouting face slack in sleep.

The silence that met her as she entered her room told her that the nurse was no longer there. She had presumably woken to find her gone and taken herself off.

Alaïs set to work, wasting no time. The success of her plan depended on her ability to deceive everyone into believing she was too weak to venture far from home. No one within the household could know that her destination was Montpellier.

She took from her wardrobe her lightest hunting dress, the tawny red of a squirrel's pelt, with pale, stone-colored fitted sleeves, generous under the arm, which tapered to a diamond-shaped point. She tied a thin leather belt around her waist, to which she attached her eating knife and her *borsa*, winter hunting purse.

Alaïs pulled up her hunting boots to just below her knees, tightened the leather laces around the top, to hold a second knife, then adjusted the buckle, and put on a plain brown hooded cloak with no trim.

When she was dressed, Alaïs took a few precious gemstones and jewelry from her casket, including her sunstone necklace and turquoise ring and choker. They might be useful in exchange or to buy safe passage or shelter, particularly once she was beyond the borders of Viscount Trencavel's lands.

Finally, satisfied she had forgotten nothing, she retrieved her sword from its hiding place behind the bed where it had lain, untouched, since her marriage. Alaïs held the sword firmly in her right hand and raised it in front of her face, measuring the blade against the flat of her hand. It was still straight and true, despite lack of use. She carved a figure of eight in the air, reminding herself of its weight and character. She smiled. It felt right in her hand.

Alaïs crept into the kitchen and begged barley bread, figs, salted fish, a tablet of cheese and a flagon of wine from Jacques. He gave her much more than she needed, as he always did. For once, she was grateful for his generosity.

She roused her servant, Rixende, and whispered a message for her to deliver to Dame Agnès that Alaïs was feeling better and would join the ladies of the household in the *Solar* after Tierce. Rixende looked surprised, but made no comment. Alaïs disliked this part of her duties and usually begged to be excused whenever possible. She felt caged in the company of women and was bored by the inconsequential tapestry talk. However, today it would serve as perfect proof that she was intending to return to the château.

Alaïs hoped she would not be missed until later. If her luck held, only when the chapel bell tolled for Vespers would they realize she had not come home and raise the alarm.

And by then I will be long gone.

"Do not go to Dame Agnès until after she has broken fast, Rixende," she said. "Not until the first rays of the sun strike the west wall of the courtyard, is that clear? *Oc?* Before that, if anyone comes searching for me—even my father's manservant—you may tell them that I have gone to ride in the fields beyond Sant-Miquel."

The stables were in the northeastern corner of the courtyard between the Tour des Casernes and the Tour du Major. Horses stamped the ground and pricked up their ears at her approach, whinnying gently, hoping for hay. Alaïs stopped at the first stall and ran her hand over the broad nose of her old gray mare. Her forelock and withers were flecked with coarse white hairs.

"Not today, my old friend," she said. "I couldn't ask so much of you."

Her other horse was in the stall next door. The six-year-old Arab mare, Tatou, had been a surprise wedding gift from her father. A chestnut, the color of winter acorns, with a white tail and mane, flaxen fetlocks and white spots on all four feet. Standing as high as Alaïs' shoulders, Tatou had the distinctive flat face of her breed, dense bones, a firm back and an easy temperament. More important, she had stamina and was very fast.

To her relief, the only person in the stables was Amiel, the eldest of the farrier's sons, dozing in the hay in the far corner of the stalls. He scrambled to his feet when he saw her, embarrassed to be caught sleeping.

Alaïs cut short his apologies.

Amiel checked the mare's hooves and shoes, to be sure she was fit to ride, then lifted down an undercloth and, at Alaïs' request, a riding rather than hunting saddle, then a bridle. Alaïs could feel the tightness in her chest. She jumped at the slightest sound from the courtyard, spinning round when she heard a voice.

Only when he was done did Alaïs produce the sword from beneath her cloak.

"The blade is dull," she said.

Their eyes met. Without a word, Amiel took the sword and carried it to the anvil in the forge. The fire was burning, stoked all night and all day by a succession of boys barely big enough to transport the heavy, spiky bundles of brushwood from one side of the smithy to the other.

Alaïs watched as sparks flew from the stone, seeing the tension in Amiel's shoulders as he brought the hammer down on to the blade, sharpening, flattening and rebalancing.

"It's a good sword, Dame Alaïs," he said levelly. "It will serve you well, although . . . I pray God you will not have need of it."

She smiled. *"Ieu tanben."* Me too.

He helped her mount and led her across the courtyard. Alaïs' heart was in her mouth that she would be seen at this last moment and her plan would ruined.

But there was no one and soon they reached the Eastern Gate.

"God speed, Dame Alaïs," whispered Amiel, as Alaïs pressed a *sol* into his hand. The guards opened the gates and Alaïs urged Tatou forward across the bridge and out into the early morning streets of Carcassonne, her heart thudding. The first challenge was over.

As soon as she was clear of the Porte Narbonnaise, Alaïs gave Tatou her head.

Libertat. Freedom.

As she rode toward the sun rising in the east, Alaïs felt in harmony with the world. Her hair brushed back off her face and the wind brought the color back to her cheeks. As Tatou galloped over the plains, she wondered if this was how the soul felt as it left the body on its four-day journey to heaven. This sense of God's Grace, this transcendence, of all base creation stripping away everything physical, until nothing but spirit remained?

Alaïs smiled. The *parfaits* preached that the time would come when all souls would be saved and all questions answered in heaven. But for now she was prepared to wait. There was too much to accomplish yet on earth for her to think of leaving it.

With her shadow streaming out behind her, all thoughts of Oriane, of the household, all fear faded. She was free. At her back, the sand-colored walls and towers of the Cité grew smaller and smaller, until they disappeared altogether.

CHAPTER 22
Toulouse

At Blagnac airport in Toulouse, the security official paid more attention to Marie-Cécile de l'Oradore's legs than the passports of the other passengers.

She turned heads as she walked across the expanse of austere gray and white tiles. Her symmetrical black curls, her tailored red jacket and skirt, her crisp white shirt. Everything marked her out as someone important, someone who did not expect to stand in line or be kept waiting.

Her usual driver was waiting at the arrivals gate, conspicuous in his dark suit among the crowd of relatives and holidaymakers in T-shirts and shorts. She smiled and inquired after his family as they walked to the car, although her mind was on other things. When she turned on her mobile, there was a message from Will, which she deleted.

As the car moved smoothly into the stream of traffic on the *rocade* that ringed Toulouse, Marie-Cécile allowed herself to relax. Last night's ceremony had been exhilarating as never before. Armed with the knowledge that the cave had been found, she had felt transformed, fulfilled by the ritual and seduced by the power inherited from her grandfather. When she had lifted her hands and spoken the incantation she had felt pure energy flowing through her veins.

Even the business of silencing Tavernier, an initiate who'd proved unreliable, had been accomplished without difficulty. Provided no one else talked—and she was sure now they would not—there was nothing to worry about. Marie-Cécile hadn't wasted time giving him the chance to defend himself. The transcripts provided of the interviews between him and a journalist were evidence enough, so far as she was concerned.

Even so. Marie-Cécile opened her eyes.

There were things about the business that concerned her. The way Tavernier's indiscretion had come to light; the fact that the journalist's notes were surprisingly concise and consistent; the fact that the journalist, herself, was missing.

Most of all she disliked the coincidence of the timing. There was no reason to connect the discovery of the cave at the Pic de Soularac with an execution already planned—and subsequently carried out—in Chartres, yet in her mind they had become linked.

The car slowed. She opened her eyes to see the driver had stopped to take a ticket for the autoroute. She tapped on the glass. "*Pour le péage,*" she said, handing him a fifty-euro note rolled between manicured fingers. She wanted no paper trail.

Marie-Cécile had business to attend to in Avignonet, about thirty kilometers southeast of Toulouse. She'd go on to Carcassonne from there. Her meeting was scheduled for nine o'clock, although she intended to arrive earlier. How long she stayed in Carcassonne depended on the man she was going to meet.

She crossed her long legs and smiled. She was looking forward to seeing if he lived up to his reputation.

CHAPTER 23

Carcassonne

Just after ten o'clock, the man known as Audric Baillard walked out of the SNCF station in Carcassonne and headed toward the town. He was slight and cut a distinguished, if old-fashioned, figure in his pale suit. He walked fast, holding a tall wooden walking stick like a staff between his thin fingers. His Panama hat shielded his eyes from the glare.

Baillard crossed the Canal du Midi and passed the magnificent Hotel du Terminus, with its ostentatious art déco mirrors and swirling decorative iron doors. Carcassonne had changed a great deal. There was evidence of it all around him as he made his way down the pedestrian street that cut through the heart of the Basse Ville. New clothing shops, *pâtisseries*, bookshops and jewelers. There was an air of prosperity. Once more, it was a destination. A city at the center of things.

The white paved tiles of Place Carnot shone in the sun. That was new. The magnificent nineteenth-century fountain had been restored, its water sparklingly clean. The square was dotted with brightly colored café chairs and tables. Baillard glanced toward Bar Félix and smiled at its familiar, shabby awnings under the lime trees. Some things, at least, remained unchanged.

He walked up a narrow, bustling side street that led to the Pont Vieux. The brown heritage signs for the fortified medieval Cité were another indication of how the place had transformed itself from Michelin guide *"vaut le détour"* to international tourist destination and UNESCO world heritage site.

Then he was out into the open and there it was. Baillard felt, as he always did, the sharp pang of homecoming, even though it was no longer the place he had known.

A decorative railing had been set across the entrance to the Pont Vieux to keep out the traffic. Time was that a man had to squash himself against the wall to avoid the stream of camper vans, caravans, trucks and motorbikes that had chugged their way across the narrow bridge. Then, the stonework had borne the scars of decades of pollution. Now, the parapet was clean. Perhaps a little too clean. But the battered stone Jesus was still hanging on his cross like a rag doll, halfway across the bridge, marking the boundary between the Bastide Sant-Louis and the fortified old town.

He pulled a yellow handkerchief from his top pocket and carefully wiped his face and forehead beneath the rim of his hat. The edges of the river far below him were lush and tended, with sand-colored paths winding through the trees and bushes. On the north bank, set among sweeping lawns, there were well-tended flower beds, filled with huge, exotic flowers. Well-dressed ladies sat on the metal benches in the shade of the trees, looking down over the water and talking, while their small dogs panted patiently beside them, or snapped at the heels of the occasional jogger.

The Pont Vieux led straight into the Quartier de la Trivalle, which had been transformed from a drab suburb into the gateway to the medieval Cité. Black wrought-iron railings had been set at intervals along the pavements to stop cars from parking. Fiery orange, purple and crimson pansies trailed out of their containers like hair tumbling down a young girl's back. Chrome tables and chairs glittered outside the cafés and twisted copper-topped lamps had elbowed aside the old, workaday streetlights. Even the old iron and plastic guttering, which leaked and cracked in the heavy rain and heat, had been replaced by sleek, brushed-metal drainpipes with ends shaped like the mouths of angry fish.

The *boulangerie* and *alimentation générale* had survived, as had the Hôtel du Pont Vieux, but the *boucherie* now sold antiques and the haberdashers was a new age emporium, dispensing crystals, tarot cards and books on spiritual enlightenment.

How many years had it been since last he was here? He'd lost count.

Baillard turned right into rue de la Gaffe and saw the signs of creeping gentrification here too. The street was only just wide enough for a single car, more an alleyway than a road. There was an art gallery on the corner—La Maison du Chevalier—with two large arched windows protected by metal bars, like a Hollywood portcullis. There were six painted wooden shields on the wall and a metal ring by the door for people to tie their dogs where once they tethered horses.

Several of the doors were newly painted. He saw white ceramic house numbers with blue and yellow borders and twists of tiny flowers. The occasional backpacker, clutching maps and water bottles, stopped to ask in halting French for directions to the Cité, but there was little other movement.

Jeanne Giraud lived in a small house backing onto the grassy slopes that led steeply up to the medieval ramparts. At her end of the street, fewer of the dwellings had been refurbished. Some were derelict or boarded up. An old woman and a man sat outside on chairs brought out from their kitchen. Baillard raised his hat and wished them good day as he passed. He knew some of Jeanne's neighbors by sight, having built up a nodding acquaintance over the years.

Jeanne was sitting outside her front door in the shade, anticipating his arrival. She looked neat and efficient as always, in a plain long-sleeved shirt and a straight dark skirt. Her hair was drawn back into a bun at the nape of her neck. She looked like the schoolteacher she had been, until her retirement twenty years ago. In the years they'd known each other, he'd never seen her anything less than perfectly and formally turned out.

Audric smiled, remembering how curious she had been in the early days, always asking questions. Where did he live? What did he do in the long months they did not see each other? Where did he go?

Traveling, he'd told her. Researching and gathering material for his books, visiting friends.

Who, she had asked?

Companions, those with whom he'd studied and shared experiences. He had told her of his friendship with Grace.

A while later, he admitted his home was in a village in the Pyrenees, not far from Montségur. But he shared very little else about himself and, as the decades slipped by, she had given up asking.

Jeanne was an intuitive and methodical researcher, diligent, conscientious and unsentimental, all invaluable qualities. For the past thirty years or so, she had worked with him on every one of his books, most particularly his last, unfinished work, a biography of a Cathar family in thirteenth-century Carcassonne.

For Jeanne, it had been a piece of detective work. For Audric, it was a labor of love.

Jeanne raised her hand when she saw him coming. "Audric," she smiled. "It's been a long time."

Her took her hands between his. *"Bonjorn."*

She stood back to look him up and down. "You look well."

"Tè tanben," he answered. You too.

"You've made good time."

He nodded. "The train was punctual."

Jeanne looked scandalized. "You didn't walk from the station?"

"It's not so far," he smiled. "I admit, I wanted to see how Carcassona had changed since last I was here."

Baillard followed her into the cool little house. The brown and beige tiles on the floor and walls gave everything a somber, old-fashioned look. A small oval table stood in the center of the room, its battered legs sticking out from underneath a yellow and blue oilskin cloth. There was a bureau in the corner with an old-fashioned typewriter sitting on it, next to French windows that gave on to a small terrace.

Jeanne came out of the pantry with a tray with a jug of water, a bowl of ice, a plate of crisp, peppered biscuits, a bowl of sour green olives and a saucer for the pits. She put the tray carefully down on the table and then reached up to the narrow wooden ledge that ran, at shoulder height, the length of the room. Her hand found a bottle of Guignolet, a bitter cherry liqueur he knew she kept only for his rare visits.

The ice cracked and chinked against the sides as the bright red alcohol trickled over the cubes. For a while they sat in companionable silence, as they had done many times before. An occasional fragment of guide book commentary, belched out in several languages, filtered down from the Cité as the tourist train completed one of its regular circuits of the walls.

Audric carefully put his glass on the table. "So," he said. "Tell me what happened."

Jeanne pulled her chair closer to the table. "My grandson Yves, as you know, is with the Police Judiciaire, *département de l'Ariège,* stationed in Foix itself. Yesterday, he was called to an archeological dig in the Sabarthès Mountains, close to the Pic de Soularac, where two skeletons had been found. Yves was surprised his superiors seemed to be treating it as a potential murder scene, even though he said it was clear the skeletons had been there for some considerable time." She paused. "Of course, Yves did not interview the woman who found the bodies himself, but he was present. Yves knows a little of the work I've been doing for you, enough certainly to know the discovery of this cave would be of interest."

Audric drew in his breath. For so many years he had tried to imagine how he would feel at this moment. He had never lost faith that, at last, the time would come when he would learn the truth of those final hours.

The decades rolled one into the other. He watched the seasons follow their endless cycle; the green of spring slipping into the gold of summer; the burnished palette of autumn vanishing beneath the austere whiteness of the winter; the first thaw of the mountain streams in spring.

Still, no word had come. *E ara?* And now?

"Yves went inside the cave himself?" he asked.

Jeanne nodded.

"What did he see?"

"There was an altar. Behind it, carved into the rock itself, was the symbol of the labyrinth."

"And the bodies? Where were they?"

"In a grave, no more than a dip in the ground in truth, in front of the altar. There were objects lying between the bodies, although there were too many people for him to get close enough to see properly."

"How many were there?"

"Two. Two skeletons."

"But that—" He stopped. "No matter, Jeanne. Please, go on."

"Underneath the . . . them, he picked up this."

Jeanne pushed a small object across the table.

Audric did not move. After so long, he feared to touch it.

"Yves telephoned from the post office in Foix late yesterday afternoon. The line was bad and it was hard to hear, but he said he took the ring because he didn't trust the people looking for it. He sounded worried." Jeanne paused. "No, he sounded frightened, Audric. Things weren't being done right. Usual procedures were not being followed, there were all sorts of people on site who should not have been there. He was whispering, as if he was frightened of being overheard."

"Who knows he went into the cave?"

"I don't know. The officers on duty? His commanding officer? Probably others."

Baillard looked at the ring on the table, then stretched out and picked it up. Holding it between his thumb and forefinger, he tilted it toward the light. The delicate pattern of the labyrinth carved on the underside was clearly visible.

"Is it his ring?" Jeanne asked.

Audric couldn't trust himself to answer. He was wondering at the chance that had delivered the ring into his hands. Wondering if it *was* chance.

"Did Yves say where the bodies had been taken?"

She shook her head.

"Could you ask him? And, if he could, a list of all those who were at the site yesterday when the cave was opened."

"I'll ask. I'm sure he'll help if he can."

Baillard slipped the ring on to his thumb. "Please convey my gratitude to Yves. It must have cost him dear to take this. He has no idea how important his quick thinking may turn out to be." He smiled. "Did he say what else was discovered with the bodies?"

"A dagger, a small leather bag with nothing inside, a lamp on—"

"*Vuèg?*" he said in disbelief. "Empty? But that cannot be."

"Inspector Noubel, the senior officer, apparently pressed the woman on this point. Yves said she was adamant. She claimed she'd touched nothing but the ring."

"And did your grandson think her truthful?"

"He didn't say."

"If . . . someone else must have taken it," he muttered to himself, his brow furrowed in thought. "What did Yves tell you about this woman?"

"Very little. She is English, in her twenties, a volunteer, not an archeologist. She was staying in Foix at the invitation of a friend, who is the second in charge at the excavation."

"Did he tell you her name?"

"Taylor, I think he said." She frowned. "No, not Taylor. Perhaps it was Tanner. Yes, that's it. Alice Tanner."

Time stood still. *"Es vertat?"* Can it be true? The name echoed inside his head. *"Es vertat?"* he repeated in a whisper.

Had she taken the book? Recognized it? No, no. He stopped himself. That made no sense. If the book, then why not the ring also?

Baillard placed his hands flat on the table to stop them trembling, then met Jeanne's gaze.

"Do you think you could ask Yves if he has an address? If he knows where, *Madomaisèla*—?" He broke off, unable to continue.

"I can ask," she replied, then added: "Are you all right, Audric?"

"Tired." He tried to smile. "Nothing more."

"I had expected you to be more . . . pleased. It is—at least, could be— the culmination of your years of work."

"It is so much to take in."

"You seem to be shocked by the news rather than excited."

Baillard imagined how he must look: eyes too bright, face too pale, hands shaking.

"I am excited," he said. "And most grateful to Yves and, of course, to you too, but . . ." He took a deep breath. "If perhaps you could telephone Yves now? If I could speak with him in person? Perhaps even meet?"

Jeanne got up from the table and walked into the hall, where the telephone stood on a small table at the foot of the stairs.

Baillard looked out of the window to the slopes that led up to the walls of the Cité. An image of her singing while she worked came into his mind, a vision of the light falling in bright slats between the branches of the trees, casting a dappled light on the water. All around her were the sounds and smells of spring; pinpricks of color in the undergrowth, blues, pinks and yellows, the rich deep earth and the heady scent of the box trees either side of the rocky path. The promise of warmth and summer days to come.

He jumped as Jeanne's voice called him back from the gentle colors of the past.

"There's no answer," she said.

CHAPTER 24
Chartres

In the kitchen of the house in rue du Cheval Blanc in Chartres, Will Franklin drank the milk straight from the plastic bottle, trying to kill the taste of stale brandy on his breath.

The housekeeper had laid the breakfast table early that morning before going off duty. The Italian coffee percolator was on the stove. Will assumed it was for Francois-Baptiste's benefit, since the housekeeper didn't usually go to such trouble for him when Marie-Cécile was away. He guessed François-Baptiste was also sleeping late since everything was immaculate, not a spoon or knife out of place. Two bowls, two plates, two cups and saucers. Four different types of jams as well as honey stood next to a large bowl. Will lifted the white linen cloth. Beneath it were peaches, nectarines and melon, as well as apples.

Will had no appetite. The previous night, to pass the time until Marie-Cécile appeared, he'd had first one drink, then a second and a third. It was well after midnight when she put in an appearance, by which stage, he had drunk himself into an alcoholic haze. She'd been in a wild mood, keen to make up for their argument. They hadn't gone to sleep until dawn.

Will's fingers tightened around the piece of paper in his hand. Marie-Cécile hadn't even bothered to write the note herself. Once again, it had been left to the housekeeper to inform him she'd gone out of town on business and hoped to be back before the weekend.

Will and Marie-Cécile had met at a party to launch a new art gallery in Chartres back in the spring, through friends of friends of his parents. Will was at the beginning of a six-month sabbatical traveling around Europe; Marie-Cécile was one of the backers of the gallery. She'd hit on him rather than the other way round. Attracted and flattered by the attention, Will had found himself pouring out his life story over a bottle of champagne. They'd left the gallery together and been together ever since.

Technically together, Will thought sourly. He turned on the tap and splashed cold water on his face. He called her this morning, not sure what he wanted to say, but her phone was switched off. He'd had enough of this constant state of flux, never knowing where he stood.

Will stared out of the window at the little courtyard at the back of the house. Like everything else in the house, it was perfectly designed, and precise. Nothing as nature intended. Light gray pebbles, high terra-cotta planters with lemon trees and orange trees along the back, south-facing wall. In the window box, rows of red geraniums, their petals already swollen by the sun, stood tall. Covering the small wrought-iron gate in the wall was ivy, centuries old. Everything spoke of permanence. It would all be here long after Will was gone.

He felt like a man waking from a dream to discover the real world was not as he'd imagined. The smart thing would be to cut his losses, no hard feelings, and move on. However disillusioned he felt about their relationship, Marie-Cécile had been both generous and kind to him and, if he was honest, had kept to her side of the bargain. It was his unrealistic expectations that had let him down. It wasn't her fault. She'd broken no promises.

Only now could Will see how ironic it was he'd chosen to spend the last three months in precisely the same sort of house he'd grown up in and had fled to Europe to escape. Cultural differences apart, the atmosphere in the house reminded him of his parents' place back home, elegant and stylish, somewhere designed for entertaining and display rather than as a home. Then, as now, Will had spent much of his time alone, rattling from one immaculate room to another.

The trip was Will's opportunity to work out what it was he wanted to do with his life. His original plan had been to work his way down through France to Spain, gathering ideas for his writing, getting inspired, but since he'd been in Chartres, he'd barely written a single sentence. His subjects were rebellion, anger and anxiety, the unholy trinity of American life. Back home, he'd found plenty to rage against. Here, he'd been left with nothing to say. The only subject that occupied his mind was Marie-Cécile and it was the one subject off limits.

He finished the last of the milk and threw the plastic bottle into the rubbish bin. He took another look at the table and decided to go out for breakfast. The thought of making polite conversation with François-Baptiste turned his stomach.

Will emerged out of the pass corridor. The high-ceilinged entrance hall was silent except for the precise ticking of the ornate grandmother clock.

To the right of the stairs, a narrow door led down to the extensive wine cellars beneath the house. Will grabbed his denim jacket from the newel post and was about to cross the hall when he noticed one of the tapestries was crooked. It was only a little out of line, but in the perfect symmetry of the rest of the paneled hall, it stuck out.

Will reached out to straighten it, then hesitated. There was a thin sliver of light running down the wall behind the polished wood. He looked up at the window above the door and stairs, even though he knew the sun wasn't in the hall at this time of day.

The light seemed to be coming from behind the dark wooden paneling. Puzzled, he lifted the tapestry away from the wall. Concealed deep within the pattern of the wood was a small door, cut flush with the paneling. There was a small brass bolt sunk into the dark wood holding it shut and a flat circular pull, like the handle of a door of a squash court. All very discreet.

Will tried the bolt. It was well oiled and slid open easily. A gentle creak, then the door sprang open away from him, releasing a subtle smell of subterranean spaces and hidden basement rooms. His hands on the edge of the door, he peered in and straight away found the source of the light, a single frosted bulb set at the top of a steep flight of stairs descending into the gloom.

He found two switches just inside the door. One operated the single bulb above the door; the other, a line of dim, yellow candle bulbs which hung from metal spikes drilled into the stone wall all the way down the left-hand side of the stairs. On both sides blue braided cord had been threaded through black metal hoops to make handrails.

Will stepped down onto the first step. The ceiling was low, a mixture of old brick, flint and stone, only a couple of inches above Will's head. It was confined but the air was clean and fresh. It didn't have the feel of a place forgotten.

The deeper he went, the colder it got. Twenty steps and counting. It wasn't damp, though, and although he couldn't see any fans or form of ventilation, there seemed to be a flow of fresh air coming from somewhere.

At the bottom, Will found he was standing in a small lobby. There was nothing on the walls, no signs, just the stairs behind him and a door in front, which filled the width and height of the corridor. The electric light cast a sickly yellow glow over everything.

Adrenaline kicked in as Will walked toward the door.

The cumbersome, old-fashioned key in the lock turned easily. Once he was through, the atmosphere changed immediately. Gone was the concrete floor. Instead, there was a thick burgundy carpet that swallowed the sound of his feet. The functional lighting had given way to ornate metal sconces. The walls were made of the same mixture of brick and stone as before, except now they were decorated by tapestries, images of medieval knights, porcelain-skinned women and hooded priests in white robes, their heads bowed and their arms outstretched.

There was the trace of something else in the air too, now. Incense, a sweet heavy scent that reminded him of the long-forgotten Christmases and Easters of his childhood.

Will looked back over his shoulder. The sight of the stairs beyond the open door, leading back up to the house, reassured him. The short corridor came to a dead end, with a heavy velvet curtain hanging from a black iron rail. It was covered with embroidered gold symbols, a mixture of Egyptian hieroglyphs, astrological markings and signs of the zodiac.

He reached out and pulled back the curtain.

Behind it was another door, this one clearly much older. Fashioned from the same dark paneling as the hall upstairs, the edges were decorated with wooden scrolls and motifs. The central panels were entirely plain, punctuated only by woodworm holes no bigger than pinheads. There was no handle he could see, no lock, no way of opening it at all.

The lintel was crowned by ornate carvings, stone rather than wood. Will ran his fingers over the top looking for some sort of catch. There had to be a way through. He worked his way up from the bottom on one side, across the top of the door, and then back down the other until, finally, he found it. A small depression just above floor level.

Crouching down, Will pressed down hard. There was a sharp, hollow click, like a marble bouncing on a tiled floor. The mechanism released and the door sprang open.

Will straightened up, his breathing a little crazy and his palms damp. The short hairs on the back of his neck and the backs of his arms were standing on end. No more than a couple of minutes, he told himself, and he'd be out of here. He just wanted to take a quick look. No big deal. Firmly, he put his hand on the door and pushed.

It was totally black inside, although straight away he could sense he was in a bigger space, perhaps a cellar. The smell of burned incense was much stronger.

Will groped at the wall for a light switch, but he could find nothing. Realizing if he hooked back the curtain it would let in a little light from the corridor, he tied the cumbersome velvet into a huge figure-of-eight knot, then turned back to face whatever lay ahead.

The first thing Will saw was his own shadow, elongated and lanky, silhouetted over the threshold. Then, as his eyes got accustomed to the brown-black gloom, finally he saw what lay beyond in the dark.

He was standing at the end of a long, rectangular chamber. The ceiling was low and vaulted. Ecclesiastical-style wooden benches, like at a refectory table, lined the two longest walls, disappearing farther than his eye could see. Around the top, where the walls met the roof, was a frieze, a repeating pattern of words and symbols. They looked like the same Egyptian symbols he'd seen on the curtain outside.

Will wiped his hands on his jeans. Directly ahead, in the center of the chamber, was an imposing stone chest, like a tomb. He walked all the way round it, running his hand across the surface. It seemed smooth, except for a large circular motif in the middle. He leaned forward to get a better look and followed the lines with his fingers. Some sort of pattern of decreasing circles, like the rings around Saturn.

As his eyes farther adjusted, he could pick out that on each of the four sides a letter was carved into the stone: *E* at the head, *N* and *S* on the two longest sides opposite each other, *O* at the foot. The points of the compass?

Then he noticed the small block of stone, about thirty centimeters high, set at the base of the chest, aligned with the letter *E*. It had a shallow curve in the middle, like an executioner's block.

The ground around it was darker that the rest of the floor. It looked damp, as if it had recently been scrubbed. Will crouched down and rubbed the mark with his fingers. Disinfectant and something else, a sour smell, like rust. There was something caught beneath the corner of the stone. Will scraped it out with his nails.

It was a fragment of cloth, cotton or linen, frayed at the edges as if it had caught on a nail and been ripped. In the corner, there were small brown spots. Like dried blood.

He dropped the material and ran, slamming the door and unhooking the curtain before he knew what he was doing. He charged along the corridor, through both doors and powered his way up the narrow, steep stairs, two at a time, until he was back in the hall.

Will doubled over, hands on his knees, and tried to get his breath back. Then, realizing that whatever else happened, he couldn't risk anyone coming in and guessing he'd been down there, he reached in and killed the lights. With shaking fingers he bolted the door and pulled the tapestry back into place, until nothing was visible from the outside.

For a moment, he just stood there. The grandmother clock told him that no more than twenty minutes had passed.

Will looked down at his hands, turning them over and back as if they didn't belong to him. He rubbed the tips of his forefinger and thumb together, then sniffed. It smelled like blood.

CHAPTER 25
Toulouse

Alice woke with a splitting headache. For a moment, she had no idea where she was. She squinted out of the corner of her eye at the empty bottle standing on the bedside table. *Serves you right.*

She rolled on to her side and grabbled at her watch.

Ten forty-five.

Alice groaned and fell back on the pillow. Her mouth was as stale as a pub ashtray and her tongue was coated with the sour remains of the whisky.

I need aspirin. Water.

Alice staggered to the bathroom and stared at herself in the mirror. She looked as bad as she felt. Her forehead was a mottled kaleidoscope of green, purple and yellow bruises. She had dark rings under her eyes. There was a faint recollection of dreaming of woods, winter branches brittle with frost. The labyrinth reproduced on a piece of yellow material? She couldn't remember.

Her journey from Foix last night was something of a blur too. She couldn't even quite remember what had made her head for Toulouse rather than Carcassonne, which would have been the more obvious choice. Alice groaned. Foix, Carcassonne, Toulouse. There was no way she was going anywhere until she felt better. She lay back on her bed and waited for the painkillers to kick in.

Twenty minutes later, she was still delicate but the thudding behind her eyes had diminished to a dull ache. She stood under the steaming shower until the water ran cold. Her thoughts went back to Shelagh and the rest of the team. She wondered what they were all doing right now. Usually, the team went up to the site at eight o'clock and stayed up there till it got dark. They lived and breathed the excavation. She couldn't imagine how any of them were going to cope without their routine.

Wrapped in the hotel's tiny, threadbare towel, Alice checked her phone for messages. Still nothing. Last night, she'd felt depressed about it, now she was pissed off. More than once during their ten-year friendship, Shelagh had withdrawn into resentful silences that had lasted weeks. Each time, it had been down to Alice to sort things out and she realized she resented it.

Let her make the running this time.

Alice riffled through her makeup bag until she found an old tube of concealer, rarely used, with which she covered up the worst of the bruising. Then she added eyeliner and a touch of lipstick. She finger dried her hair. Finally, she chose her most comfortable skirt and new blue halter top, packed everything else, then went down to check out before she headed off to explore Toulouse.

She still felt bad, but it was nothing that fresh air and a serious shot of caffeine wouldn't fix.

Having put her bags in the car, Alice decided she would simply walk and see where she ended up. The air conditioning in her hire car wasn't great, so her plan was to wait until the temperature dropped before setting off for Carcassonne.

As she passed beneath the dappled shade of the plane trees and looked at the clothes and perfumes displayed in the shop windows, she started to feel more herself. She was embarrassed by the way she'd behaved last night. Totally paranoid, total overreaction. This morning, the idea that someone was after her seemed absurd. Her fingers went to the telephone number in her pocket. *You didn't imagine him though.*

Alice pushed the thought away. She was going to be positive, look forward. Make the most of being in Toulouse.

She meandered through the alleys and passages of the old town, letting her feet guide her. The ornate pink stone and brick facades of the buildings were elegant and discreet. The names on the street signs and fountains and monuments proclaimed Toulouse's long and glorious history. Military leaders, medieval saints, eighteenth-century poets, twentieth-century freedom fighters, the city's noble past from Roman times to the present.

Alice went into the cathedral of Saint-Etienne, partly to get out of the sun. She enjoyed the tranquillity and peace of cathedrals and churches, a legacy of sightseeing with her parents when she was a child, and she spent a pleasant half-hour wandering around, half reading the signs on the walls and looking at the stained glass.

Realizing she was starting to feel hungry, Alice decided to finish with the cloisters, then go and find somewhere to have lunch. She hadn't taken more than a few steps when she heard a child crying. She turned to look, but there was no one there. Feeling vaguely uneasy, she carried on walking. The sobbing seemed to be growing louder. Now she could hear someone whispering. A man's voice, close by, hissing in her ears.

"Hérétique, hérétique . . ."

Alice spun round. "Hello? *Allo? Il y a quelqu'un?*"

There was nobody there. Like a malicious whisper, the word repeated itself over and over inside her head. *Hérétique, hérétique.*

She clasped her hands over her ears. On the pillars and gray stone walls, faces seemed to be appearing. Tortured mouths, twisted hands reaching out for help, oozing from every hidden corner.

Then Alice caught a glimpse of someone ahead, nearly out of sight. A woman in a long green dress and a red cloak, moving in and out of the shadows. In her hand, she carried a wicker basket. Alice called out to attract her attention just as three men, monks, stepped out from behind the pillar. The woman shouted as they grabbed hold of her. The woman was struggling as the monks started to drag her away.

Alice tried to attract their attention, but no sound came from her mouth. Only the woman herself seemed to hear, for she turned round and looked straight into Alice's eyes. Now the monks had encircled the woman. They stretched their voluminous arms out wide above her like black wings.

"Leave her alone," Alice cried, starting to run toward them. But the farther she went, the more distant the figures became, until finally they disappeared altogether. It was as if they had melted into the walls of the cloister itself.

Bewildered, Alice ran her hands over the stone. She turned to the left and right, seeking an explanation, but the space was completely empty. At last, panic took over. She ran toward the exit to the street, expecting to see the black robed men behind her, chasing her, swooping down on her.

Outside, everything was as it had been before.

It's okay. You're okay. Breathing heavily, Alice slumped back against the wall. As she got herself under control, she realized the emotion she was feeling was not terror any more, but grief. She had no need of a history book to tell her something terrible had happened in this place. There was an atmosphere of suffering, scars that could not be hidden by concrete or stone. The ghosts told their own story. When she put a hand up to her face, she found she was crying.

As soon as her legs were strong enough to carry her, she headed back toward the center of town. She was determined to put as much space between herself and Saint-Etienne as she could. She couldn't account for what was happening to her, but she wasn't going to give in.

Reassured by the normal, everyday life going on all around her, Alice found herself in a small, pedestrian square. In the top right-hand corner there was a brasserie with a cyclamen-pink awning and rows of gleaming silver chairs and round tables laid out on the pavement.

Alice got the only remaining table and ordered straight away, making a concerted effort to relax. She knocked back a couple of glasses of water, then leaned back in her chair and tried to enjoy the touch of the sun on her face. She poured herself a glass of rosé, added a few ice cubes, and took a mouthful. It wasn't like her to be so easily freaked out.

But then you're not in such great emotional shape.

All year she'd been living flat out. She'd split up with her long-term boyfriend. The relationship had been dying on its feet for years and it was a relief to be on her own, but it was no less painful for that. Her pride was battered and her heart was bruised. To forget about him, she'd worked too hard and played too hard, anything to not brood about where things had gone wrong. Two weeks in the south of France was supposed to recharge her batteries. Get her back on an even keel.

Alice pulled a face. *Some holiday.*

The arrival of the waiter put paid to any further self-analysis. The omelet was perfect, yellow and runny on the inside, with generous chunks of mushroom and plenty of parsley. Alice ate with a fierce concentration. Only when she was mopping up the last threads of olive oil with her bread, did she start to turn her mind to how she was going to spend the rest of the afternoon.

By the time the coffee came, Alice knew.

The Bibliothèque de Toulouse was a large, square stone building. Alice flashed her British Library Readers' Room pass at a bored and inattentive assistant at the desk, which got her in. After getting lost on the stairs a few times, she found herself in the extensive general history section. On either side of the central aisle were long, polished wooden desks with a spine of reading lamps running along the center of the tables. Few of the seats were occupied at this time on a hot, July afternoon.

At the far end, spanning the width of the room, was what Alice was looking for: a row of computer terminals. Alice registered at the reception desk, was given a password and allocated a workstation.

As soon as she was connected, Alice typed the word "labyrinth" in the box on the search engine. The green loading bar at the bottom of the screen filled up quickly. Rather than relying on her own memory, she was confident she'd find a match for her labyrinth somewhere among all the hundreds of sites. It was so obvious she couldn't believe she hadn't thought of it earlier.

Straight away, the differences between a traditional labyrinth and her memory of the image carved on the cave wall and ring were obvious. A classical labyrinth was made up of intricately connected concentric circles leading in ever-decreasing circles to the center, whereas she was pretty sure the one in the Pic de Soularac had been a combination of dead ends and straight lines which doubled back on themselves, leading nowhere. It was more like a maze.

The true ancient origins of the labyrinth symbol and mythologies associated with it were complex and difficult to trace. The earliest designs were thought to be more than three thousand years old. Labyrinth symbols had been discovered carved in wood, rock, tile or stone, as well as in woven designs or constructed into the natural environment as turf or garden labyrinths.

The first labyrinths in Europe dated from the late Bronze Age and early Iron Age, from 1200 to 500 B.C., and were discovered around the early trading centers of the Mediterranean. Carvings dated between 900 and 500 B.C. had been found at Val Camonica in northern Italy and Pontevedra in Galicia, and in the top northwestern corner of Spain at Cabo Fisterra Finisterre. Alice looked hard at the illustration. It was more reminiscent of what she'd seen in the cave than anything else so far. She tilted her head to one side. Close, but not a match.

It made sense that the symbol would have traveled from the east with the merchants and traders from Egypt and the outer reaches of the Roman Empire, adapted and changed by its interaction with other cultures. It also made sense that the labyrinth, evidently a pre-Christian symbol, should have been hijacked by the Christian church. Both the Byzantine and the Roman Church were guilty of absorbing much older symbols and myths into their religious orthodoxy.

Several sites were dedicated to the most famous labyrinth of them all: Knossos, on the island of Crete where, according to legend, the mythical Minotaur, half-man, half-bull, had been imprisoned. Alice skipped them, instinct telling her that line of research would take her nowhere. The only point worth noting was that Minoan labyrinthine designs had been excavated at the site of the ancient city of Avaris in Egypt, dating back to 1550 B.C., as well as found in temples at Kom Ombo in Egypt and Seville.

Alice filed the information at the back of her mind.

From the twelfth and thirteenth centuries onward, the labyrinth symbol was appearing regularly in hand-copied medieval manuscripts that circulated around the monasteries and courts of Europe, with scribes embellishing and developing illustrations, creating their own trademark designs.

By the early medieval period, a mathematically perfect eleven-circuit, twelve-wall, four-axis labyrinth had become the most popular form of all. She looked at a reproduction of the carving of a labyrinth on the wall of the thirteenth-century church of St. Pantaleon in Arcera, northern Spain and another, slightly earlier, from the cathedral of Lucca in Tuscany. She clicked on a map showing the occurrence of labyrinths in European churches, chapels and cathedrals.

That's extraordinary.

Alice could hardly believe her eyes. There were more labyrinths in France than in the whole of Italy, Belgium, Germany, Spain, England and Ireland put together: Amiens, St. Quentin, Arras, St. Omer, Caen and Bayeux in northern France; Poitiers, Orléans, Sens and Auxerre in the center; Toulouse and Mirepoix in the southwest; the list went on and on.

The most famous pavement labyrinth of all was in northern France, set in the center of the nave of the first—and most impressive—of the Gothic medieval cathedrals, Chartres.

Alice smacked her hand on the table, causing several disapproving heads to pop up around her. Of course. How stupid could she be? Chartres was twinned with her hometown of Chichester, on the English south coast. In fact, her first visit abroad had been on a school trip to Chartres when she was eleven. She had vague memories of it raining all the time and standing huddled in a raincoat, cold and damp, beneath imposing stone pillars and vaults. But she had no recollection of the labyrinth.

There was no labyrinth in Chichester Cathedral, but the city was also twinned with Ravenna in Italy. Alice ran her finger across the screen until she'd found what she was looking for. Laid into the marble floor of the church of San Vitale in Ravenna was a labyrinth. According to the caption it was only a quarter of the size of the labyrinth in Chartres and dated to a much earlier period in history, perhaps as far back as the fifth century A.D., but was there all the same.

Alice finished cutting and pasting the text she wanted into a text document and hit Print. Once it was going, she typed "Cathedral Chartres France" into the search box.

Although there had been some sort of structure on the site as far back as the eighth century, she discovered the current cathedral in Chartres dated from the thirteenth century. Ever since then, esoteric beliefs and theories had attached themselves to the building. There were rumors that within its vaulting roof and elaborate stone pillars was concealed a secret of great significance. Despite the strenuous efforts of the Catholic Church, these legends and myths endured.

No one knew on whose orders the labyrinth had been built or for what purpose.

Alice selected the paragraphs she needed, and then exited.

The last page finished printing and the machine fell silent. All around people were beginning to pack up. The sour-faced receptionist caught her eye and tapped her watch.

Alice nodded and gathered her papers, then joined the line at the counter waiting to check out. The queue moved slowly. Shafts of late-afternoon sunlight fell through the high windows in Jacob's ladders, making the particles of dust dance in the beams.

The woman in front of Alice had an armful of books to check out and seemed to have a query about each one. She let her mind focus on the worry that had been bugging her all afternoon. Was it likely that in all the hundreds of images she'd looked at, in all the hundreds and thousands of words, there hadn't been a single exact match for the stone labyrinth at the Pic de Soularac?

Possible, but not likely.

The man behind her was standing too close, like someone on a tube train trying to read the newspaper over her shoulder. Alice turned and glared at him. He took a step back. His face was vaguely familiar.

"Oui, merci," she said, as she got to the desk and paid for the printing she'd done. Nearly thirty sheets in all.

As she emerged on to the steps of the library the bells of Saint-Etienne were striking seven. She'd been in there longer than she realized.

Keen to be on her way now, Alice hurried back to where she'd parked the car on the far side of the river. She was so caught up in her thoughts that she didn't notice the man from the queue following her along the river walkway, keeping a safe distance. And she didn't notice him take a phone from his pocket and make a call as she pulled out into the slow-moving traffic.

THE GUARDIANS OF
THE BOOKS

CHAPTER 26
Besièrs

JULHET 1209

Dusk was falling as Alaïs reached the plains outside the town of Coursan.

She had made good speed, following the old Roman road through the Minervois toward Capestang, across the sweeping hemp fields, the *canabières*, and the emerald seas of barley.

Each day since setting out from Carcassonne, Alaïs had ridden until the sun became too fierce. Then she and Tatou took shelter and rested, before traveling on until dusk when the air was filled with biting insects and the cries of night jays, owls and bats.

The first night she'd found lodgings in the fortified town of Azille with friends of Esclarmonde. As she traveled farther east, she saw fewer people in the fields and villages and those that she did see were suspicious, wariness showing in their dark eyes. She heard rumors of atrocities committed by renegade bands of French soldiers or by *routiers*, mercenaries, bandits. Each tale was more bloody, more wicked than the last.

Alaïs pulled Tatou to a walk, not sure if she should press on to Coursan or look for shelter close by. The clouds were marching fast across an increasingly angry gray sky and the air was very still. In the distance, there was the occasional rumble of thunder, growling like a bear waking from a winter sleep. Alaïs did not want to risk being caught in the open when the storm hit.

Tatou was nervous. Alaïs could feel her tendons bristling beneath her coat and twice she shied away from sudden movements of hare or fox in hedgerows at the roadside.

Ahead Alaïs could see there was a small copse of oak and ash. It wasn't dense enough to be the natural summer habitat of larger animals, such as wild boar or lynx. But the trees were tall and generous and the tops of their branches looked to be woven tightly together, like entwined fingers, which would provide good cover. The fact there was a clear path, a winding ribbon of dry earth worn away by countless feet, suggested the wood was a popular local shortcut to the town.

Tatou shifted uneasily beneath her as a flicker of lightning momentarily lit the darkening sky. It helped her make up her mind. She would wait until the storm had passed over.

Whispering encouragement, Alaïs persuaded the mare forward into the dark green embrace of the wood.

The men had lost their quarry some time earlier. Only the threat of a storm prevented them doubling back and returning to camp.

After several weeks of riding, their pale French skin was tanned dark by the fierce southern sun. Their traveling armor and surcoats, bearing the arms of their master, lay hidden in the thicket. They hoped yet to retrieve something from their abortive mission.

A sound. The crack of a dried branch, the rolling gait of a bridled horse, the iron of its hooves striking occasional pieces of stone.

A man with a mouthful of jagged, blackened teeth crawled forward to get a better look. Some way off he could see a figure on a small, chestnut Arab threading its way through the woods. He leered. Perhaps their *sortie* was not going to be a waste of time after all. The rider's clothes were plain and worth little, but a horse of that calibre would fetch a good price.

He threw a stone at his companion hidden on the other side of the track.

"*Lève-toi!*" he said, jerking his head toward Alaïs. "*Regarde.*"

"Would you look at that," he muttered. "*Une femme. Et seule.*"

"Are you certain she's alone?"

"I can't hear any others."

The two men picked up the ends of the rope that lay across the path, concealed under the leaves, and waited for her to come to them.

Alaïs' courage ebbed as she rode deeper into the wood.

The topsoil was damp, although the ground beneath was still hard. The leaves at the side of the path rustled beneath Tatou's feet. Alaïs tried to concentrate on the reassuring sounds of the birds in the trees, but the hairs on her arms and on the back of her neck were standing on end. There was threat in the silence, not peace.

It is but your imagination only.

Tatou sensed it too. Without warning, something flew up out of the ground, with the sound of an arrow from a bow.

A woodcock? A snake?

Tatou reared up on her hind legs, slashing wildly at the air with her hooves and whinnying in terror. Alaïs had no time to react. Her hood flew back off her face and her arms came away from the reins as she was thrown backwards out of her saddle. Pain exploded in her shoulder as she hit the ground hard, knocking the breath clean out of her. Panting, she rolled on to her side and tried to stand. She had to try to hold Tatou before she bolted.

"Tatou, *doçament*," she cried, staggering to her feet. "Tatou!"

Alaïs staggered forward, then stopped. There was a man standing in front of her on the path, blocking her way. He was smiling through blackened teeth. In his hand was a knife, its dull blade discolored brown at the tip.

There was a movement to her right. Alaïs' eyes darted sideways. A second man, his face disfigured by a jagged scar running from his left eye to the corner of his mouth, was holding Tatou's bridle and waving a stick.

"No," she heard herself cry out. "Leave her."

Despite the pain in her shoulder, her hand found the hilt of her sword. *Give them what they want and they may yet not harm you.* He took a step toward her. Alaïs drew her blade, slicing through the air in an arc. Keeping her eyes on his face, she fumbled in her purse and threw a handful of coins down on the path.

"Take it. I have nothing else of value."

He looked at the scattering of silver on the ground, then spat contemptuously. Wiping his mouth with the back of his hand, he took another step closer.

Alaïs raised her sword. "I warn you. Do not approach," she shouted, making a figure of eight in the air with the blade so he couldn't get near.

"*Ligote-la,*" he ordered to the other.

Alaïs turned cold. For an instant, her courage faltered. They were French soldiers, not bandits. The stories she'd heard on her journey flashed into her mind.

Then she gathered herself and swung the sword again.

"Come no closer," she shouted, her voice stiff with fear. "I will kill you before I—"

Alaïs spun round and hurled herself at the second man, who had come round behind her. Screaming, Alaïs sent the stick flying from his hand. Pulling a knife from his belt, he roared and dived toward her. Grasping her sword with both hands, Alaïs plunged it down on his hand, stabbing at him like a bear at a baiting. Blood spurted from his arm.

She pulled her arms back for a second strike when stars suddenly exploded in her head, purple and white. She staggered forward at the force of the blow, then pain brought tears to her eyes as she was jerked back to her feet by her hair. She felt the cold point of a blade at her throat.

"Putain," he hissed, striking her across the face with his bleeding hand.
"Laisse-tomber." Drop it.

Cornered, Alaïs let the sword fall from her hand. The second man kicked it away, before producing a coarse linen hood from his belt and forcing it over her head. Alaïs struggled to get free, but the sour smell of the dusty material caught in her mouth and made her cough. Still, she fought it, until a fist hit her in the stomach and she doubled over on the path.

She had no strength left to resist as they wrenched her arms behind her back and bound her wrists.

"Reste-là."

They moved away. Alaïs could hear them going through her saddle-bags, lifting the leather flaps and throwing things out on to the ground. They were talking, arguing perhaps. She found it hard to tell in their harsh language.

Why have they not killed me?

Straight away, the answer crept like an unwelcome ghost into her mind. *They would have some sport first.*

Alaïs struggled desperately to loosen her ties, even though she knew that if she did get her hands free, she wouldn't get far. They'd hunt her down. They were laughing now. Drinking. They were in no hurry.

Tears of desperation sprang into her eyes. Her head fell back, exhausted, on the hard ground.

At first, Alaïs couldn't work out where the rumbling was coming from. Then she realized. Horses. The sound of their iron hooves galloping over the plains. She pressed her ear closer to the ground. Five, maybe six horses, heading toward the wood.

In the distance, there was a growl of thunder. The storm was also getting closer. At last, there was something she could do. If she could get far enough away, then maybe she had a chance.

Slowly, as quietly as possible, she started to edge her way off the path until she felt the sharp brambles against her legs. Struggling to her knees, she moved her head up and down until she managed to work the hood loose. *Are they looking?*

No one shouted. Bending her neck, she shook her head from side to side, gently at first, then more vigorously, until finally the material slid off. Alaïs took a couple of deep gulps of air, then tried to get her bearings.

She was just out of their line of vision, although if they turned round and saw her gone, it would take them no time to find her. Alaïs pressed her ear to the ground once more. The riders were coming from Coursan. A party of hunters? Scouts?

A crack of thunder echoed through the wood, setting birds to flight from the highest nests. Their panicked wings beat the air, swooped and fell, before falling back into the protection of the trees. Tatou whinnied and pawed at the ground.

Praying that the gathering storm would continue to mask the sound of the riders until they were close enough, Alaïs pushed herself back into the undergrowth, crawling over the stones and twigs.

"*Ohé!*"

Alaïs froze. They'd seen her. She swallowed a scream as the men came running back to where she'd been lying. A clap of thunder overhead drew their eyes up, a look of fear in their faces. *They are not accustomed to the violence of our southern storms.* Even from here, she could smell the fear. Their skin was rank with it.

Taking advantage of their hesitation, Alaïs pressed on. She was on her feet now, starting to run.

She was not quick enough. The one with the scar launched himself at her, punching her in the side of the head as he brought her down.

"*Hérétique,*" he yelled as he scrambled on top of her, pinioning her to the ground. Alaïs tried to shake him off, but he was too heavy and her skirts were caught in the thorns of the undergrowth. She could smell the blood from his injured hand as he thrust her face down into the twigs and leaves on the ground.

"I warned you to stay still, *putain.*"

He unbuckled his belt, breathing heavily as he tossed it aside. *Pray he has not yet heard the riders.* She tried to shake him off her, but he was too heavy. She let loose a roar from her throat, anything to mask the approach of the horses.

He hit her again, splitting her lip. She could taste the blood in her mouth.

"*Putain.*"

Suddenly, different voices. "*Ara, ara!*" Now.

Alaïs heard the twang of a bow and the flight of a single arrow through the air, then again and again as a storm of darts flew out of the evergreen shadows, splintering bark and wood where they made contact.

"*Avança! Ara, avança!*"

The Frenchman sprang up just as an arrow thudded into his chest, thick and heavy, spinning him round like a top. For a moment, he seemed to be held in the air, then he started to sway, his eyes frozen like the stone gaze of a statue. A single drop of blood appeared in the corner of his mouth, and then rolled down his chin.

His legs buckled. He dropped to his knees, as if in prayer, then very slowly tipped forward like a tree felled in the wood. Alaïs came to her senses just in time, scrambling out of his way as the body crashed heavily to the ground.

"*Aval!* On!"

The riders rode the other Frenchman down. He had run into the woods for cover, but more arrows flew. One hit his shoulder and he stumbled. The next hit the back of his thigh. The third, in the small of his back, brought him down. His body fell forward to the ground, spasmed, then was still.

The same voice called the halt. "*Arèst.* Hold fire." At last, the hunters broke cover and came into view. "Hold your fire."

Alaïs got to her feet. *Friends or men also to be feared?* The leader was wearing a cobalt-blue hunting tunic under his cloak, both of good quality. His leather boots, belt and quiver were fashioned from pale leather in the local style and his boots heavy, unmarked. He looked a man of moderate means and substance, a man of the Midi.

Her arms were still bound behind her back. She was aware that she had little advantage on her side. Her lip was swollen and bleeding and her clothes were stained.

"*Seigneur,* my gratitude for this service," she said, stiffening her voice with confidence. "Raise your visor and identify yourself, so I may know the face of my liberator."

"Is that all the gratitude I get, Dame?" he said, doing as she asked. Alaïs was relieved to see he was smiling.

He dismounted and drew a knife from his belt. Alaïs stepped back. "To cut your ties," he said lightly.

Alaïs flushed and offered her wrists. "Of course. *Mercé.*"

He gave a brief bow. "Amiel de Coursan. These are my father's woods."

Alaïs gave a sigh of relief. "Forgive me my discourtesy, but I had to be sure you were not . . ."

"Your caution is both wise and understandable in the circumstances. And you are, Dame?"

"Alaïs of Carcassona, daughter to Intendant Pelletier, steward to Viscount Trencavel, and wife to Guilhem du Mas."

"I am honored to make your acquaintance, Dame Alaïs." He kissed her hand. "Are you much hurt?"

"A few cuts and scratches only, although my shoulder pains me a little where I was thrown."

"Where is your escort?"

Alaïs hesitated a moment. "I am traveling alone."

He looked at her with surprise. "These are strange times to venture out without protection, Dame. These plains are overrun with French soldiers."

"I did not intend to ride so late. I was seeking shelter from the storm."

Alaïs glanced up, suddenly realizing that no rain had yet fallen.

"It's just the heavens making complaint," he said, reading her look. "A false tempest, no more."

While Alaïs calmed Tatou, de Coursan's men ordered the corpses to be stripped of weapons and clothing. They found their armor and ensigns hidden deeper in the wood where they had tethered their horses. De Coursan picked up the corner of material with the tip of his sword revealing, beneath a coating of mud, a flash of silver on a green background.

"Chartres," said de Coursan with contempt. "They're the worst. Jackals, the lot of them. We've had more reports of acts—"

He broke off abruptly.

Alaïs looked at him. "Reports of what?"

"It is of no matter," he said quickly. "Shall we return to the town?"

They rode in single file to the far side of the woods and out on to the plains.

"You have some purpose in these parts, Dame Alaïs?"

"I go in search of my father, who is in Montpelhièr with Viscount Trencavel. I have news of great importance that could not wait for his return to Carcassona."

A frown fell across de Coursan's face.

"What? What have you heard?"

"You will stay with us the night, Dame Alaïs. Once your injuries have been tended, my father will tell you what news we have heard. At dawn I will escort you myself to Besièrs."

Alaïs turned to look at him. "To Besièrs, *Messire*?"

"If the rumors are true, it is in Besièrs you will find your father and Viscount Trencavel."

CHAPTER 27

Sweat dripped from his stallion's coat as Viscount Trencavel led his men toward Béziers, thunder rolling at their heels.

Sweat foamed on the horses' bridles and spittle flecked in the corners of their mouths. Their flanks and withers were streaked with blood where the spurs and whip drove them relentlessly on through the night. The silver moon came out from behind the torn, black clouds scudding low on the horizon, lighting up the white blaze on his horse's nose.

Pelletier rode at the viscount's side, his lips pursed shut. It had gone badly at Montpellier. Given the bad blood that existed between the viscount and his uncle, he had not expected the count to be easily persuaded into an alliance, despite the ties of family and seigneurial obligation that bound the two men. He had hoped, however, that the count might intercede on his nephew's account.

In the event, he had refused even to receive him. It was a deliberate and unequivocal insult. Trencavel had been left to kick his heels outside the French camp until word came today that an audience was to be granted.

Permitted to take only Pelletier and two of his *chevaliers,* Viscount Trencavel had been shown to the tent of the abbot of Cîteaux, where they were asked to disarm. This they had done. Once inside, rather than the Abbott, the viscount was received instead by two of the papal legates.

Raymond-Roger had barely been allowed to open his mouth while the legates castigated him for allowing heresy to spread unchecked through his dominions. They criticized his policy of appointing Jews to senior positions in his leading cities. They cited several examples of his turning a blind eye to the perfidious and pernicious behavior of Cathar bishops within his territories.

Finally, when they had finished, the legates had dismissed Viscount Trencavel as if he was some insignificant minor landowner rather than the lord of one of the most powerful dynasties of the Midi. Pelletier's blood boiled even now when he thought of it.

The abbot's spies had briefed the legates well. Each of the charges, while inaccurate and misrepresented in intention, was accurate in fact and supported by testimony and eyewitness account. That, even more than the calculated insult to his honor, left Pelletier in no doubt that Viscount

Trencavel was to be the new enemy. The Host needed someone to fight. With the capitulation of the count of Toulouse, there was no other candidate.

They had left the Crusaders' camp outside Montpellier immediately. Glancing up at the moon, Pelletier calculated that if they held their pace they should reach Béziers by dawn. Viscount Trencavel wished to warn the Biterois in person that the French army was no more than fifteen leagues away and intent on war. The Roman road that ran from Montpellier to Béziers lay wide open and there was no way of blocking it.

He would bid the city fathers prepare for a siege, at the same time as seeking reinforcements to support the garrison at Carcassonne. The longer the Host could be delayed in Béziers, the longer he would have to prepare the fortifications. He also intended to offer refuge in Carcassonne to those who were most at risk from the French—Jews, the few Saracen traders from Spain, as well as the *Bons Homes*. It was not only seigneurial duty that motivated him. Much of the administration and organization of Béziers was in the hands of Jewish diplomats and merchants. Under threat of war or no, he wasn't prepared to be deprived of the services of so many valued and skilled servants.

Trencavel's decision made Pelletier's task easier. He touched his hand against Harif's letter concealed in his pouch. Once they were in Béziers, all he had to do was excuse himself for long enough to find Simeon.

A pale sun was rising over the river Orb as the exhausted men rode across the great arched stone bridge.

Béziers stood proud and high above them, grand and seemingly impregnable behind its ancient stone walls. The spires of the cathedral and the great churches dedicated to Santa-Magdalena, Sant Jude and Santa-Maria glittered in the dawn light.

Despite his fatigue, Raymond-Roger Trencavel had lost nothing of his natural authority and bearing as he urged his horse up through the network of suburbs and steep winding streets that led to the main gates. The fall of the horses' shoes against the cobbles roused people from their sleep in the quiet suburbs that surrounded the fortified walls.

Pelletier dismounted and called to the watch to open the gates and let them enter. They made slow progress, news having spread that Viscount Trencavel was in the city, but eventually they reached the suzerain's residence.

Raymond-Roger greeted the suzerain with genuine affection. He was an old friend and ally, a gifted diplomat and administrator and loyal to the Trencavel dynasty. Pelletier waited while the two men greeted each other in the custom of the Midi and exchanged tokens of esteem. Having completed the formalities with unusual haste, Trencavel moved straight to business. The suzerain listened with deepening concern. As soon as the viscount had finished speaking, he sent messengers to summon the city's consuls to council.

While they were talking, a table had been set in the center of the hall covered with bread, meats, cheese, fruit and wine.

"Messire," said the suzerain. "I would be honored if you would avail yourself of my hospitality while we wait."

Pelletier saw his chance. He slipped forward and spoke quietly into Viscount Trencavel's ear.

"Messire, could you spare me? I would check on our men myself. See that they have all they need. Make sure that their tongues are still and their spirits steady."

Trencavel looked up at him with astonishment. "Now, Bertrand?"

"If you please, *Messire.*"

"I have no doubt our men are being well cared for," he said, smiling at his host. "You should eat, rest a while."

"With my humble apologies, I would still ask to be excused."

Raymond-Roger scanned Pelletier's face for an explanation but found none.

"Very well," he said in the end, still puzzled. "You have one hour."

The streets were noisy and growing ever more crowded as rumors spread. A mass of people was gathering in the main square in front of the cathedral.

Pelletier knew Béziers well, having visited many times with Viscount Trencavel in the past, but he was going against the flow and only his size and authority stopped him from being knocked down in the crush. Holding Harif's letter tight in his fist, as soon as he reached the Jewish quarter he asked passersby if they knew of Simeon. He felt a tug on his sleeve. He looked down to see a pretty dark-haired, dark-eyed child.

"I know where he lives," she said. "Follow me."

The girl led him into the commercial quarter where the moneylenders had their businesses and through a warren of seemingly identical side streets crammed with shops and houses. She came to a halt outside an unremarkable door.

He cast his eyes around until he'd found what he was looking for. The sign of a bookbinder carved above Simeon's initials. Pelletier smiled with relief. It was the right house. Thanking her, he pressed a coin into the girl's hand and sent her away. Then he lifted the heavy brass knocker and struck the door three times.

It had been a long time, more than fifteen years. Would there still be the easy affection between them?

The door opened a fraction, enough to reveal a woman staring suspiciously at him. Her black eyes were hostile. She was wearing a green veil that covered her hair and the lower part of her face, and the traditional wide, pale trousers gathered at the ankle worn by Jewish women in the Holy Land. Her long, yellow jacket reached down to her knees.

"I wish to speak with Simeon," he said.

She shook her head and tried to shut the door, but he wedged it open with his foot.

"Give him this," he said, easing the ring from his thumb and forcing it into the woman's hands. "Tell him Bertrand Pelletier is here."

He heard her gasp. Straight away, she stood back to let him enter. Pelletier followed her through a heavy red curtain, decorated with golden coins stitched top and bottom.

"Attendez," she said, gesturing he should stay where he was.

The bracelets around her wrist and ankles chinked as she scuttled down the long corridor and disappeared.

From the outside, the building looked tall and narrow, but now he was inside, Pelletier could see it was deceptive. Rooms led off the central corridor to both left and right. Despite the urgency of his mission, Pelletier gazed around with delight. The floor was laid with blue and white tiles rather than wood, and beautiful rugs hung from the walls. It reminded him of the elegant, exotic houses of Jerusalem. It had been many years, but the colors, textures and smells of that alien land still spoke to him.

"Bertrand Pelletier, by all that's sacred in this tired old world!"

Pelletier turned toward the sound to see a small figure in a long purple surcoat rushing toward him, his arms outstretched. His heart leaped at the sight of his old friend. His black eyes twinkled as bright as ever. Pelletier was nearly knocked over by the force of Simeon's embrace, even though he was a good head taller.

"Bertrand, Bertrand," Simeon said affectionately, his deep voice booming through the silent corridor. "What took you so long, eh?"

"Simeon, my old friend," he laughed, clasping Simeon's shoulder as he got his breath back. "How it does my spirit good to see you, and so well. Look at you," he said, tugging his friend's long black beard, always Simeon's greatest vanity. "A little gray here and there, but still as fine as ever! Life has treated you well?"

Simeon raised his shoulders. "Could be better, it could be worse," he said, standing back. "And what of you, Bertrand? A few more lines on your face, maybe, but still the same fierce eyes and broad shoulders." He patted him on the chest with the flat of his hand. "Still as strong as an ox."

His arm around Simeon's shoulder, Pelletier was taken to a small room at the rear of the house overlooking a small courtyard. There were two large sofas, covered with silk cushions of red, purple and blue. Several ebony tables were set around the room decorated with delicate vases and large flat bowls filled with sweet almond biscuits.

"Come, take off your boots. Esther will bring us tea." He stood back and looked Pelletier up and down again. "Bertrand Pelletier," he said again, shaking his head. "Can I trust these old eyes? After so many years are you really here? Or are you a ghost? A figment of an old man's imagination?"

Pelletier smiled. "I wish I was here under more auspicious circumstances, Simeon."

He nodded. "Of course. Come, Bertrand, come. Sit."

"I've come with our Lord Trencavel, Simeon, to warn Besièrs of the army approaching from the north. Listen to the bells calling the city fathers to council."

"It's hard to ignore your Christian bells," Simeon replied, raising his eyebrows, "although they do not usually ring for our benefit!"

"This will affect the Jews as much—if not more—than those they call heretics, you know that."

"As it ever does," he said mildly. "Is the Host as large as they are saying?"

"Twenty thousand strong, maybe more. We cannot fight them in open combat, Simeon, the numbers against us are too great. If Besièrs can hold the invaders here for some time, then at least it will give us the chance to raise a fighting force in the west and prepare the defenses of Carcassona. All who wish it will be offered refuge there."

"I have been happy here. This city has treated me—us—well."

"Besièrs is no longer safe. Not for you, not for the books."

"I know it. Still," he sighed, "I will be sorry to go."

"God willing, it will not be for long." Pelletier paused, confused by his friend's unflinching acceptance of the situation. "This is an unjust war, Simeon, preached out of lies and deceit. How can you accept it so easily?"

Simeon spread his hands wide. "Accept it, Bertrand? What would you have me do? What would you have me say? One of your Christian saints, Francis, prayed that God should grant him the strength to accept those things he could not change. What will happen will happen, whether I wish it or no. So, yes, I accept. It does not mean that I like it or wish it were not otherwise."

Pelletier shook his head.

"Anger serves no purpose. You must have faith. To trust in a greater meaning, beyond our lives or knowledge, requires a leap of faith. The great religions each have their own stories—Holy Scripture, the Qur'an, the Torah—to make sense of these insignificant lives of ours." He paused, his eyes sparkling in mischief. "The *Bons Homes*, now they do not seek to make sense of the evil men do. Their faith teaches them that this is not

God's earth, a perfect creation, but instead an imperfect and corrupt realm. They do not expect goodness and love to triumph over adversity. They know that in our temporal lives they will not." He smiled. "And yet here you are, Bertrand, surprised when Evil meets you face to face. It is strange that, no?"

Pelletier's head shot up as if he'd been found out. Did Simeon know? How could he?

Simeon caught his expression, although he made no further reference to it. "Conversely, my faith tells me the world was made by God, that it is perfect in every particular. But whenever men turn away from the words of the prophets, the balance between God and man is disturbed and retribution will follow as sure as night follows the day."

Pelletier opened his mouth to speak, then closed it again.

"This war is not our affair, Bertrand, despite your duty to Viscount Trencavel. You and I have a wider purpose. We are joined by our vows. It is that which must now guide our steps and inform our decisions." He reached out and clasped Pelletier's shoulder. "So, my friend, keep your anger and your sword in readiness for those battles you can win."

"How did you know?" he said. "Have you heard something?"

Simeon chuckled. "That you were a follower of the new church? No, no, I have heard nothing to that effect. It is a discussion we will have some time in the future, God willing, not now. Much as I would dearly love to talk theology with you, Bertrand, we have pressing matters to attend to."

The arrival of the servant with a tray of hot mint tea and sweet biscuits stopped the conversation. She placed it on the table in front of them, before removing herself to a bench in the corner of the room.

"Do not concern yourself," Simeon said, seeing Pelletier's worry that their conversation was to be overheard. "Esther came with me from Chartres. She speaks Hebrew and a few words of French only. She does not understand your tongue at all."

"Very well." Pelletier pulled out Harif's letter and handed it to Simeon.

"I received one such at Shauvot, a month past," he said when he'd finished reading. "It warned me to expect you although, I confess, you have been slower than I expected."

Pelletier folded the letter and returned it to his pouch.

"So the books are still in your possession, Simeon? Here within this house? We must take them—"

A violent hammering at the door shattered the tranquillity of the room. Immediately, Esther was on her feet, her almond eyes alert. At a sign from Simeon, she hurried out into the corridor.

"You do still have the books?" repeated Pelletier, urgent now, the expression on Simeon's face making him suddenly anxious. "They are not lost?"

"Not lost, my friend," he started to say when they were interrupted by Esther.

"Master, there is a lady asking to be admitted." The words in Hebrew rattled off her tongue, too fast for Pelletier's rusty ears to follow.

"What manner of lady?"

Esther shook her head. "I know not, master. She says she must see your guest Intendant Pelletier."

They all turned at the sound of feet in the corridor behind them.

"You left her alone?" Simeon said with concern, struggling to get up.

Pelletier also rose to his feet. He blinked, unwilling to trust the evidence of his eyes. Even thoughts of his mission disappeared from his mind as he looked at Alaïs, who had come to a halt in the doorway. Her face was flushed and her quick brown eyes were flashing with apology and determination.

"Forgive me for this intrusion," she said, looking from her father to Simeon, then back, "but I did not think your servant would admit me." In two strides, Pelletier had crossed the room and thrown his arms around her.

"Do not be angry that I disobeyed you," she said, more timidly. "I had to come."

"And this charming lady is . . ." said Simeon.

Pelletier took Alaïs' hand and led her into the center of the room. "Of course. I am forgetting myself. Simeon, may I present to you my daughter Alaïs, although how or by what means she comes to be here in Besièrs, I cannot tell you!" Alaïs bowed her head. "And this is my dearest, my oldest friend, Simeon of Chartres, formerly of the Holy City of Jerusalem."

Simeon's face was wreathed in smiles. "Bertrand's daughter. Alaïs." He took her hands. "You are most welcome."

CHAPTER 28

"Will you tell me of your friendship?" Alaïs said, as soon as she was seated on the sofa beside her father. She turned to Simeon. "I asked him once before, but he was not minded to confide in me then."

Simeon was older than she had imagined. His shoulders were stooped and his face crisscrossed with lines, a map of a life that had seen grief and loss as well as great happiness and laughter. His eyebrows were thick and bushy and his eyes bright, revealing a sparkling intelligence. His curly hair was mostly gray, but his long beard, perfumed and oiled, was still as black as a raven's wing. She could see why her father might have mistaken the man in the river for his friend.

Discreetly, Alaïs dropped her eyes to his hands and felt a flash of satisfaction. She had supposed right. On his left thumb he wore a ring identical to her father's.

"Come, Bertrand," Simeon was saying. "She has earned the story. After all, she has ridden far enough to hear it!"

Alaïs felt her father grow still beside her. She glanced at him. His mouth was set in a tight line.

He is angry now he realizes what I've done.

"You did not ride from Carcassona without an escort?" he said. "You would not be so foolish to make such a journey alone? You would not take such a risk?"

"I—"

"Answer me."

"It seemed the wisest—"

"Wisest," he erupted. "Of all the—"

Simeon chuckled. "Still the same old temper, Bertrand."

Alaïs swallowed a smile as she put her hand on her father's arm.

"Paire," she said patiently. "You can see I am safe. Nothing happened."

He glanced down at her scratched hands. Alaïs quickly pulled the cloak over them. "Nothing much happened. It's nothing. A slight cut."

"You were armed?"

She nodded. "Of course."

"Then where—?"

"I thought it unwise to walk through the streets of Besièrs so attired."

Alaïs looked at him with innocent eyes.

"Quite," he muttered under his breath. "And no ill befell you? You are not hurt?"

Aware of her bruised shoulder, Alaïs met his gaze. "Nothing," she lied. He frowned, although he looked slightly mollified. "How did you know we were here?"

"I learned of it from Amiel de Coursan, the son of the *seigneur,* who most generously gave me escort."

Simeon was nodding. "He's much admired in these parts."

"You have been very fortunate," Pelletier said, still reluctant to let the matter drop. "Fortunate and very, very foolish. You could have been killed. I still cannot believe you—"

"You were going to tell her how we met, Bertrand," said Simeon lightly. "The bells are no longer ringing, so the Council must now have started. We have a little time."

For a moment, her father continued to scowl. Then his shoulders dropped and resignation filled his features.

"Very well, very well. Since you both wish it."

Alaïs exchanged a glance with Simeon. "He wears the ring like yours, *Paire.*"

Pelletier smiled. "Simeon was recruited by Harif in the Holy Land, as I was, although some time earlier and our paths did not cross. As the threat from Saladin and his armies increased, Harif sent Simeon back to his native city of Chartres. I followed a few months later, taking the three parchments with me. The journey took more than a year, but when I finally reached Chartres, Simeon was waiting for me as Harif had promised." His memories made him smile. "How much I hated the cold and wet after the heat, the light of Jerusalem. It was so bleak, so forsaken a place. But Simeon and I, we understood each other from the start. His task was to bind the parchments into three separate volumes. While he toiled over the books, I came to admire his learning, his wisdom and his good humor."

"Bertrand, really," murmured Simeon, although Alaïs could see he liked the compliments well enough.

"As for Simeon," Pelletier continued, "you will have to ask him yourself what he saw in an uncultured, unlettered soldier. It is not for me to judge."

"You were willing to learn, my friend, to listen," said Simeon softly. "That marked you out from most of your faith."

"I always knew the books were to be separated," Pelletier resumed. "As soon as Simeon's work was completed, I received word from Harif that I was to return to my birthplace, where a position awaited as *Intendant* to the new Viscount Trencavel. Looking back with the hindsight of years, I find it extraordinary that I never asked what was to become of the other two books. I assumed Simeon was to keep one, although I never actually knew that for certain. The other? I didn't even ask. My lack of curiosity shames me now. But, I simply took the book entrusted to me and traveled south."

"It should not shame you," said Simeon softly. "You did what was asked of you in good faith and with a strong heart."

"Before your appearance put all other thoughts from my mind, we were talking of the books, Alaïs."

Simeon cleared his throat. "Book," he said. "I have but one."

"What?" he said sharply. "But Harif's letter . . . I took it to mean that both were still in your possession? Or that, at the very least, you knew where each was to be found?"

Simeon shook his head. "Once, yes, but not for many years now. The *Book of Numbers* is here. As for the other, I confess I was hoping that *you* might have news to share with *me*."

"If you do not have it, then who does?" Pelletier said urgently. "I assumed you had taken both with you when you left Chartres."

"I did."

"But—"

Alaïs put her hand on her father's arm. "Let Simeon explain."

For a moment, it looked as if Pelletier might lose his temper, then he nodded. "Very well," he said gruffly. "Tell your story."

"How like you she is, my friend," Simeon chuckled. "Shortly after your departure from Chartres, I received word from the *Navigatairé* that a guardian would come and take the second book, the *Book of Potions*, although nothing to indicate who that person might be. I held myself ready, waiting always. Time passed, I grew older, but still no one came. Then, in the year of your Lord 1194—shortly before the terrible fire that destroyed the cathedral and much of the city of Chartres—a man did come, a Christian, a knight, calling himself Philippe de Saint-Mauré."

"His name is familiar. He was in the Holy Land at the same time as I was, although we did not meet." Pelletier frowned. "Why had he waited so long?"

"That, my friend, is the question I asked myself. Saint-Mauré passed me a *merel*, in the appropriate manner. He wore the ring that you and I both are honored to wear. I had no reason to doubt him . . . and yet—" Simeon shrugged. "There was something false about him. His eyes were sharp, like a fox. I did not trust him. He did not seem to me the sort of man Harif would have chosen. There was no honor in him. So I decided, despite the tokens of good faith he carried, that I should test him."

The words had slipped out before she could stop them. "How so?"

"Alaïs," her father warned.

"It is all right, Bertrand. I pretended not to understand. I wrung my hands, humble, apologetic, begging his pardon but he must have confused me with someone else. He drew his sword."

"Which confirmed your suspicion he was not who or what he claimed to be."

"He threatened and railed against me, but my servants came and he was outnumbered, so he had no choice but to withdraw." Simeon leaned forward, dropping his voice to a whisper. "As soon as I was sure he had gone, I wrapped the two books inside a bundle of old clothes and took shelter with a Christian family nearby who I trusted not to betray me. I could not decide what to do for the best. I was not certain of what I knew. Was he an impostor? Or was he indeed a guardian, but one whose heart had been blackened by greed or the promise of power and wealth? Had he betrayed us? If the former, then there was yet a chance that the real guardian would come to Chartres and find me gone. If the latter, I felt it my duty to find out what I could. Even now, I do not know if I chose wisely."

"You did what you thought was right," said Alaïs, ignoring the warning look from her father telling her to keep silent. "No man can do more."

"Right or wrong, the fact is I did not go for two days more. Then the mutilated body of a man was found floating in the river Eure. His eyes and tongue had been put out. The rumor spread he was a knight in the service of the eldest son of Charles d'Evreux, whose lands are not far from Chartres."

"Philippe de Saint-Mauré."

Simeon nodded. "The Jews were blamed for the murder. Straight away the reprisals started. I was a convenient scapegoat. Word spread that they were coming for me. There were witnesses, they claimed, who'd seen Saint-Mauré at my door, witnesses who would swear that we argued and blows were exchanged. This decided me. Maybe this Saint-Mauré was who he said he was. Maybe he was an honest man, maybe not. It no longer mattered. He was dead—I believed—because of what he had discovered about the Labyrinth Trilogy. His death and the manner of it persuaded me that there were others involved. That the secret of the Grail had indeed been betrayed."

"How did you escape?" asked Alaïs.

"My servants were already gone, and safe I hoped. I hid until the following morning. As soon as the gates of the city were opened, having shaved my beard, I slipped out in the guise of an elderly woman. Esther came with me."

"So you were not there as they were building the stone labyrinth in the new cathedral?" said Pelletier. Alaïs was mystified to see he was smiling, as if at some private joke. "You have not seen it."

"What is it?" she demanded.

Simeon chuckled, addressing himself only to Pelletier. "No, although I hear it has served its purpose well. Many are drawn there to that ring of dead stone. They look, they search, not understanding that only a false secret lies beneath their feet."

"What is this labyrinth?" repeated Alaïs.

Still they paid her no attention.

"I would have given you shelter in Carcassona. A roof over your head, protection. Why did you not come to me?"

"Believe me, Bertrand, I wanted nothing more. But you forget how different the north was from these more tolerant lands of the Pays d'Oc. I could not travel freely, my friend. Life was hard for Jews at that time. We were under curfew, our businesses were regularly attacked and looted." He paused for breath. "Besides, I never would have forgiven myself if I had led them—whoever *they* might be—to you. When I fled Chartres that night, I had no thought of where I was heading. The safest course of action seemed to be to disappear until the fuss had died down. In the event, the fire drove all other matters out of my mind."

"How did you find yourself in Besièrs?" said Alaïs, determined to rejoin the conversation. "Did Harif send you here?"

Simeon shook his head. "It was chance and good fortune, Alaïs, not design. I journeyed first to Champagne, where I passed the winter. The following spring, as soon as the snows had melted, I headed south. I was lucky enough to fall in with a group of English Jews, fleeing persecution in their own land. They were heading for Besièrs. It seemed as good a destination as any. The city had a reputation for tolerance—Jews were in positions of trust and authority, our learning, our skills were respected. Its proximity to Carcassona meant that I would be on hand if Harif needed me." He turned to Bertrand. "God, in his wisdom, knows how hard it has been knowing that you were but a few days' ride away, but caution and wisdom dictated it had to be thus."

He sat forward, his black eyes alive. "Even then there were verses, lays, circulating in the courts of the north. In Champagne, the troubadours and minstrels were singing of a magical cup, a life-giving elixir, too close to the truth to be ignored." Pelletier nodded. He too had heard such songs. "So weighing all things in the balance, it was safer to keep myself apart. I would never have forgiven myself if I had led them to your door, my friend."

Pelletier gave a long sigh. "I fear, Simeon, that despite our best efforts we have been betrayed, although I have no hard and fast proof of it. There are those who know of the connection between us, I am convinced of it. Whether they also know the nature of our bond, I cannot say."

"Something has happened to make you think this?"

"A week ago or more, Alaïs came across a man floating in the river

Aude, a Jew. His throat had been cut and his left thumb severed from his hand. Nothing else was taken. There was no reason to think so, but I thought of you. I thought he had been mistaken for you." He paused. "Before this there have been other indications. I confided something of my responsibility to Alaïs, in the event that something happened to me and I was unable to return to Carcassona."

This is the moment to tell him why you are come.

"Father, since you—"

He held up a hand to stop her interrupting. "Have there been any indications your whereabouts have been discovered, Simeon? Either by those who sought you in Chartres or others?"

Simeon was shaking his head. "Of late, no. More than fifteen years have passed since I came south and I can tell you that, in all that time, there has not been a single day when I've not expected to feel a knife at my throat. But, as to anything out of the ordinary, no."

Alaïs could keep silent no longer. "Father, what I have to say has bearing on this matter. I must tell you of what has happened since you left Carcassona. Please."

By the time Alaïs had finished, her father's face was scarlet. She feared he would lose his temper. He would allow neither Alaïs nor Simeon to calm him.

"The Trilogy is discovered," he ranted. "There can be no doubt about it."

"Be still, Bertrand," said Simeon firmly. "Your anger serves only to cloud your judgment."

Alaïs turned to the windows, aware of the growing levels of noise in the street. Pelletier, too, after a moment's hesitation, raised his head.

"The bells have started again," he said quickly. "I must return to the suzerain's residence. Viscount Trencavel expects me." He stood up. "I must think further on what you have told me, Alaïs, and consider what should be done. For now, we must concentrate our efforts on departure." He turned to his friend. "You will come with us, Simeon."

While Pelletier had been talking, Simeon had opened an ornately carved wooden chest that stood on the far side of the room. Alaïs edged closer. The lid was lined with deep crimson velvet, gathered in deep folds like the curtains around a bed.

Simeon shook his head. "I will not ride with you. I will follow with my people. So, for safety's sake, you should take this."

Alaïs watched Simeon slide his hand along the bottom of the chest. There was a click, then a small drawer sprung open at the base. When he straightened up, Alaïs saw he was holding an object enclosed in a sheepskin chemise.

The two men exchanged glances, then Pelletier took the book from Simeon's outstretched hand and concealed it beneath his cloak.

"In his letter, Harif mentions a sister in Carcassona," said Simeon.

Pelletier nodded. "A friend to the *Noublesso* is my interpretation of his words. I cannot believe he means more."

"It was a woman who came to take the second book from me, Bertrand," Simeon said mildly. "Like you, at the time I confess I assumed she was no more than a courier, but in the light of your letter . . ."

Pelletier dismissed the suggestion with a wave of his hand. "I cannot believe Harif would appoint a woman guardian, whatever the circumstances. He would not take the risk."

Alaïs almost spoke, but bit her tongue.

Simeon shrugged. "We should consider the possibility."

"Well, what manner of woman was she?" Pelletier said impatiently. "Someone who could reasonably be expected to take custody of so precious an object?"

Simeon shook his head. "Truthfully, she was not. She was neither highborn nor in the lowest station of life. She was past the age of childbearing, although she had a child with her. She was traveling to Carcassona via Servian, her hometown."

Alaïs sat up straight.

"That is a meager amount of information," complained Bertrand. "She did not give you her name?"

"No and nor did I ask it, since she bore a letter from Harif. I gave her bread, cheese, fruit for the journey, then she left."

They were now arrived at the door to the street.

"I do not like to leave you," Alaïs said abruptly, suddenly fearful for Simeon.

Simeon smiled. "I shall be fine, child. Esther will pack those things I wish to take with me to Carcassona. I will travel anonymously in the crowd. It will be safer for us all if I do so."

Pelletier nodded. "The Jewish quarter lies on the river, to the east of Carcassona, not far from the suburb of Sant-Vicens. Send word when you arrive."

"I will."

The two men embraced, then Pelletier stepped out into the now crowded street. Alaïs went to follow, but Simeon put his hand on her arm to hold her back.

"You have great courage, Alaïs. You have been steadfast in your duty to your father. To the *Noublesso* too. But watch over him. His temper can lead him astray and there will be difficult times, difficult choices ahead."

Glancing over her shoulder, Alaïs dropped her voice so her father couldn't hear. "What was the nature of the second book taken by this woman to Carcassona? The book that yet is unfound?"

"The *Book of Potions*," he replied. "A list of herbs and plants. To your father was entrusted the *Book of Words*, to me the *Book of Numbers*."

To each their own skill.

"I think that tells you what you wanted to know?" Simeon said, looking knowingly at her from under his bushy eyebrows. "Or perhaps confirms a thought?"

She smiled. *"Benlèu."* Perhaps.

Alaïs kissed him, and then ran to catch her father up.

Food for the journey. A board too, perhaps.

Alaïs resolved to keep her idea to herself for now, until she was sure, even though she was now all but certain she knew where the book would be found. All the myriad connections that ran through their lives like a spider's web were suddenly clear to her. All the tiny hints and clues missed, because not looked for.

CHAPTER 29

As they hurried back through the town, it was clear that already the exodus had begun.

Jews and Saracens were moving toward the main gates, some on foot, some with carts laden down with belongings, books, maps, furniture; financiers with horses saddled and carrying baskets, chests and scales for weighing, rolls of parchment. Alaïs noticed a few Christian families in the crowd too.

The courtyard of the suzerain's palace was bleached white in the morning sun. As they passed through the gates, Alaïs saw the look of relief on her father's face as he realized the Council was not yet concluded.

"Does anyone else know you are here?"

Alaïs stopped dead in her tracks, horrified to realize she'd not thought of Guilhem at all. "No. I came straight to find you."

She was irritated by the look of pleasure that flashed across her father's face.

He nodded. "Wait here. I will inform Viscount Trencavel of your presence and ask his permission for you to ride with us. Your husband, also, should be told."

Alaïs watched as he disappeared into the shadows of the house. Dismissed, she turned and looked around. Animals stretched out in the shade, their fur flattened against the cool, pale walls, unconcerned by the affairs of men. Despite her experiences and the stories Amiel de Coursan had told her, here, in the tranquillity of the palace, Alaïs found it hard to believe the threat was as imminent as they claimed.

Behind her, the doors were flung open and a tide of men flooded down the steps and across the courtyard. Alaïs pressed herself against a pillar to avoid being caught up in the rush.

The courtyard erupted with the sound of shouting, commands, orders issued and obeyed, *écuyers* running to fetch their masters' horses. In a heartbeat the palace was transformed from the seat of administration to the heart of the garrison.

Through the commotion, Alaïs heard someone calling her name. Guilhem. Her heart leaped into her mouth. She turned, straining to see where his voice was coming from.

"Alaïs," he cried in disbelief. "How? What are you doing here?"

Now she could see him, striding through the crowds, clearing a path, until he was lifting her into his arms, squeezing her so hard that she thought every last breath would be driven out of her body. For an instant, the sight of him, the smell of him, drove everything from her mind. All was forgotten, all was forgiven. She felt shy almost, captivated by his obvious pleasure and delight to see her. Alaïs closed her eyes and imagined them alone, returned miraculously to the Château Comtal, as if the tribulations of the past few days were but the stuff of bad dreams.

"How I've missed you," said Guilhem, kissing her neck, her throat, her hands. Alaïs winced.

"*Mon còr,* what is it?"

"Nothing," she said quickly.

Guilhem lifted her cloak and saw the angry purple bruising across her shoulder. "Nothing, by Sant-Foy. How in the name of—"

"I fell," she said. "My shoulder took the worst of it. It is worse than it looks. Please, do not concern yourself."

Now Guilhem looked uncertain, caught between concern and doubt. "Is this how you fill your hours when I am away?" he said, suspicion forming in his eyes. He took a step back. "Why are you here, Alaïs?"

She faltered. "To bring a message to my father."

The moment the words were out of her mouth, Alaïs realized she had said the wrong thing. Her intense pleasure immediately turned to anxiety. His brow darkened.

"What message?"

Her mind went blank. What might her father have said? What possible excuse could she give?

"I—"

"What message, Alaïs?"

She caught her breath. More than anything, she wanted there to be lightness between them, but she had given her word to her father.

"*Messire,* forgive me, but I cannot say. It was a matter for his ears alone."

"Cannot or will not?"

"Cannot, Guilhem," she said with regret. "I would that it were otherwise."

"Did he send for you?" he said furiously. "Did he send for you without asking my permission?"

"No, no one sent for me," she cried. "I came of my own accord."

"But yet you will not tell me why."

"I beseech you, Guilhem. Do not ask me to break my word to my father. Please. Try to understand."

He grabbed hold of her arms and shook her. "You will not tell me?

No?" He gave a sharp, bitter laugh. "And to think I believed I had first claim on you. What a fool to think so!"

Alaïs tried to stop him leaving, but he was already striding away from her through the crowds. "Guilhem! Wait."

"What's the matter?"

She spun round to see that her father had come up behind her.

"My husband is offended by my unwillingness to confide in him."

"Did you tell him I forbid you to speak of it?"

"I tried, but he was not minded to listen."

Pelletier scowled. "He has no right to ask you to break your word."

Alaïs held her ground, feeling anger well up inside her.

"With respect, *Paire*, he has every right. He is my husband. He deserves my obedience and my loyalty."

"You are not being disloyal," Pelletier said impatiently. "His anger will pass. This is not the time nor the place."

"He feels things deeply. Insults go deep with him."

"As do we all," he replied. "Each of us feels deeply. However, the rest of us do not let our emotions govern our common sense. Come, Alaïs. Put it from your mind. Guilhem is here to serve his *seigneur* not fret over his wife. As soon as we are back in Carcassona, I'm sure all will be quickly resolved between you." He placed a kiss on the top of her head. "Let it lie. Now, fetch Tatou. You must get ready to leave."

Slowly, she turned and followed him to the stables. "You will speak with Oriane about her part in this. I feel sure she knows something of what happened to me."

Pelletier waved his hand. "I'm sure you misjudge your sister. For too long there has been discord between you, which I have allowed to run unchecked, believing it would pass."

"Forgive me, *Paire*, but I do not think you see her true character."

Pelletier ignored her comment. "You are inclined to judge Oriane too harshly, Alaïs. I am certain she undertook your care for the best of motives. Did you even ask her?" Alaïs flushed. "Exactly. I see from your face you did not." He paused again. "She is your sister, Alaïs. You owe her better."

The unfairness of the rebuke ignited the anger simmering inside her chest.

"It is not I—"

"*If* I have the chance, I will talk to Oriane," he said firmly, making it clear the subject was closed.

Alaïs flushed, but held her tongue. She had always known she was her father's favorite and therefore she understood that it was his lack of affection for Oriane that pricked at his conscience and made him blind to her faults. Of her, he had higher expectations.

Frustrated, Alaïs fell into step beside him. "Will you try to seek out those who took the *merel*? Have you—"

"Enough, Alaïs. No more can be accomplished until we return to Carcassona. Now, may God grant us speed and good fortune to carry us swiftly home." Pelletier stopped and looked around. "And pray that Besièrs has the strength to hold them here."

CHAPTER 30

Carcassonne

TUESDAY, 5 JULY 2005

Alice felt her spirits lift as she drove away from Toulouse.

The motorway ran dead straight through a green and brown fertile landscape of crops. Now and then she saw fields of sunflowers, their faces tilted from the late afternoon sun. For much of the journey, the high-speed railway ran alongside the road. After the mountains and undulating valleys of the Ariège, which had been her introduction to this part of France, it appeared a more tamed landscape.

There were clusters of small villages on the hilltops. Isolated houses with windows shuttered and a *clocher-mur*, the bells silhouetted against the pink dusk sky. She read the names of the towns as she passed— Avignonet, Castelnaudary, Saint-Papoul, Bram, Mirepoix—rolling the words over her tongue like wine. In her mind's eye, each promised the secret of cobbled streets and history buried in pale stone walls.

Alice crossed into the *département* of the Aude. A brown heritage sign read: *Vous êtes en Pays Cathare.* She smiled. Cathar country. She was quickly learning that the region defined itself as much by its past as its present. Not just Foix, but also Toulouse, Beziers and Carcassonne itself, all the great cities of the southwest living still in the shadow of events that had taken place nearly eight hundred years ago. Books, souvenirs, post-cards, videos, an entire tourist industry had grown up on the back of it. Like the evening shadows lengthening in the west, the signs seemed to be drawing her toward Carcassonne.

By nine o'clock, Alice was through the *péage* and following the signs for the city center. She felt nervous and excited, strangely apprehensive, as she picked her way through gray industrial suburbs and retail parks. She was close now, she could feel it.

The traffic lights turned green and Alice surged forward, carried along by the flow of traffic, driving over roundabouts and bridges, then suddenly in countryside again. Coarse scrub along the *rocade*, wild grasses and twisted trees blown horizontal by the wind.

Alice cleared the brow of the hill and there it was.

The medieval Cité dominated the landscape. It was so much more imposing than Alice had imagined, more substantial and complete. From this distance, with the purple mountains thrown into sharp relief behind in the distance, it looked like a magical kingdom floating in the sky.

She fell in love immediately.

Alice pulled over and got out of the car. There were two sets of ramparts, an inner and an outer ring. She could pick out the cathedral and the castle. One rectangular, symmetrical tower, very thin, very tall, stood higher than everything else.

The Cité was set on top of a grassy hill. The slopes swept down to streets filled with red-roofed houses. On the flat land at the bottom there were fields of vines, fig and olive trees, wigwams of heavy ripe tomatoes in rows.

Reluctant to venture closer and risk breaking the spell, Alice watched the sun set, stripping the color from everything. She shivered, the evening air suddenly chill on her bare arms.

Her memory provided the words she needed. *To arrive where we started and know the place for the first time.*

For the first time, Alice understood exactly what Eliot had meant.

CHAPTER 31

Paul Authié's legal practice was in the heart of the Basse Ville of Carcassonne.

His business had expanded fast in the last two years and his address reflected his success. A building of glass and steel, designed by a leading architect. An elegant walled courtyard, an atrium garden separating the business spaces and corridors. It was discreet and stylish.

Authié was in his private office on the fourth floor. The huge window faced west overlooking the cathedral of Saint-Michel and the barracks of the parachute regiment. The room was a reflection of the man, neat and with a tightly controlled ambience of affluence and orthodox good taste.

The entire outer wall of the office was glass. At this time of day the blinds were drawn against the late afternoon sun. Framed and mounted photographs covered the other three walls, together with testimonials and certificates. There were several old maps, originals, not reproductions. Some depicted the routes of the Crusades, others were illustrations of the shifting historical boundaries of the Languedoc. The paper was yellow and the reds and greens of the ink had faded in places, giving an uneven, mottled distribution of color.

A long and wide desk, designed for the space, was positioned in front of the window. It was almost empty, except for a large leather-rimmed blotter and a few framed photographs, one a studio portrait of his ex-wife and two children. Clients were reassured by evidence of stability and family values, so he kept it on display.

There were three other photos: the first was a formal portrait of himself, at twenty-one, shortly after his graduation from the École Nationale d'Administration in Paris, shaking hands with Jean-Marie Le Pen, the leader of the Front Nationale; the second was taken at Compostella; the third, taken last year, showed him with the abbot of Cîteaux, among others, on the occasion of Authié's most recent, and most substantial, donation to the Society of Jesus.

Each photograph reminded him of how far he had come.

The phone on his desk buzzed. *"Oui?"* His secretary announced his visitors had arrived. "Send them up."

Javier Domingo and Cyrille Braissart were both ex-police. Braissart had been dismissed in 1999 for excessive use of force when questioning a suspect, Domingo a year later on charges of intimidation and accepting bribes. The fact that neither had served time was thanks to Authié's skillful work. They'd worked for him since then.

"Well?" he said. "If you've got an explanation, this would be the time to share it." They shut the door and stood in silence in front of his desk. "No? Nothing to say?" He jabbed the air with his finger. "You had better start praying Biau doesn't wake up and remember who was driving the car."

"He won't, sir."

"You're suddenly a doctor now, are you Braissart?"

"His condition's deteriorated during the day."

Authié turned his back on them, hands on his hips, and stared through the slats and out of the window toward the cathedral.

"Well, what have you got for me?"

"Biau passed her a note," said Domingo.

"Which has disappeared," he said sarcastically, "along with the girl herself. Why are you here, Domingo, if you've got nothing new to say? Why are you wasting my time?"

Domingo flushed an ugly red. "We know where she is, sir. Santini picked her up in Toulouse earlier today."

"And?"

"She left Toulouse about an hour ago," said Braissart. "She spent the afternoon in the Bibliothèque Nationale. Santini's faxing through a list of the sites she visited."

"You put a trace on the car? Or is that too much to ask?"

"We did. She is heading for Carcassonne."

Authié sat down in his chair and stared at them across the expanse of desk. "So you'll be on your way to wait for her at the hotel, won't you Domingo?"

"Yes, sir. Which h—"

"Montmorency," he snapped. He put his fingers together. "I don't want her to know we're watching her. Search the room, the car, everything, but don't let her know."

"Are we looking for anything other than the ring and the note, sir?"

"A book," he said, "about so high. Board covers, held together with leather ties. It's very valuable and very delicate." He reached into a file on his desk and tossed a photograph across the desk. "Similar to this one." He gave Domingo a few seconds to look, then slid the photo back toward himself. "If there's nothing else . . ."

"We also acquired this from a nurse in the hospital," Braissart said quickly, holding out a slip of paper. "Biau had it in his pocket."

Authié took it. It was a recorded delivery receipt for a package posted from the central post office in Foix late on Monday afternoon to an address in Carcassonne.

"Who's Jeanne Giraud?" he said.

"Biau's grandmother, on his mother's side."

"Is she now," he said softly. He reached forward and pressed the intercom on his desk. "Aurélie, I need information on a Jeanne Giraud. G-i-r-a-u-d. Lives in rue de la Gaffe. Soon as you can." Authié sat back in his chair. "Does she know what's happened to her grandson?"

Braissart's silence answered his question. "Find out," he said sharply. "On second thoughts, while Domingo is paying Dr. Tanner a visit, get over to Madame Giraud's house and look around—discreetly. I'll meet you in the car park opposite the Porte Narbonnaise in"—he glanced at his watch—"thirty minutes."

The intercom buzzed again.

"What are you waiting for?" he said, dismissing them with his hand. He waited until the door had closed before he answered.

"Yes, Aurélie?"

His hand went to the gold crucifix at his neck as he listened.

"Did she say why she wanted the meeting brought forward an hour? Of course it's inconvenient," he said, cutting off his secretary's apologies. He pulled his mobile phone from his jacket pocket. There were no messages. In the past, she'd always made contact direct and in person.

"I'm going to have to go out, Aurélie," he said. "Drop the report on Giraud at my apartment on your way home. Before eight o'clock."

Then Authié snatched his jacket from the back of the chair, took a pair of gloves from his drawer and left.

Audric Baillard was sitting at a small desk in the front bedroom of Jeanne Giraud's house. The shutters were partially closed and the room was dappled with the semi-filtered light of the late afternoon. Behind him was an old-fashioned single bed, with a carved wooden headboard and footboard, freshly made with plain white cotton sheets.

Jeanne had given this room over to his use many years ago, there for him when he needed it. In a gesture that had touched him enormously, she had furnished the room with copies of all his past publications, which sat on a single wooden shelf above the bed.

Baillard had few possessions. All he kept in the room was a change of clothes and writing materials. At the beginning of their long association, Jeanne had teased him about his preference for pen and ink and paper, as thick and heavy as parchment. He'd just smiled, telling her he was too old to change his habits.

Now, he wondered. Now, change was inevitable.

He leaned back in his chair, thinking of Jeanne and how much her friendship had meant to him. In every season of his life, he had found good men and women to aid him, but Jeanne was special. It was through Jeanne that he had located Grace Tanner, although the two women had never met.

The sound of pans clattering in the kitchen drew his thoughts back to the present. Baillard picked up his pen and felt the years falling away, a sudden absence of age and experience. He felt young again.

All at once, the words came easily to his mind and he began to write. The letter was short and to the point. When he was done, Audric blotted the glistening ink and folded the paper neatly in three to make an envelope of it. As soon as he had her address, the letter could be sent.

Then it was in her hands. Only she could decide.

"Si es atal es atal." What will be, will be.

The telephone rang. Baillard opened his eyes. He heard Jeanne answer, then a sharp cry. At first, he thought it must come from the street outside. Then the sound of the receiver hitting the tiled floor.

Without knowing why, he found himself standing up, sensitive to a change in the atmosphere. He turned toward the sound of Jeanne's feet coming up the stairs.

"Qu'es?" he said immediately. What is it? "Jeanne," he said, more urgently. "What has happened? Who telephoned?"

She looked at him blankly. "It's Yves. He's been hurt."

Audric looked at her in horror. *"Quora?"* When?

"Last night. A hit-and-run. They only just managed to get hold of Claudette. That was her calling."

"How badly hurt is he?"

Jeanne didn't seem to hear him. "They are sending someone to take me to the hospital in Foix."

"Who? Claudette is organizing this?"

Jeanne shook her head.

"The police."

"Would you like me to come with you?"

"Yes," she said after a moment's hesitation, then, like a sleepwalker, she went out of the room and across the landing. A moment later, Baillard heard her bedroom door shut.

Powerless, fearful of the news, he turned back to the room. He knew it was no accident of timing. His eyes fell upon the letter he'd written. He took half a step forward, thinking that he could stop the inevitable chain of events while there was still time.

Then Baillard let his hand fall back to his side. To burn the letter would render worthless everything he had fought for, everything he had endured.

He must follow the path to the end.

Baillard fell to his knees and began to pray. The old words were stiff on his lips at first, but soon they were flowing easily again, connecting him to all those who had spoken such words before.

A car horn blaring in the street outside drew him back to the present. Feeling stiff and tired, he struggled to his feet. He slipped the letter into his breast pocket, picked up his jacket from the back of the door, then went to tell Jeanne it was time to go.

Authié parked his car in one of the large and anonymous municipal car parks opposite the Porte Narbonnaise. Hordes of foreigners, armed with guidebooks and cameras, swarmed everywhere. He despised it all, the exploitation of history and the mindless commercialization of his past for the entertainment of the Japanese, the Americans, the English. He loathed the restored walls and inauthentic gray slated towers, the packaging of an imagined past for the stupid and the faithless.

Braissart was waiting for him as arranged and gave his report quickly. The house was empty and there was easy access at the back through the gardens. According to neighbors, a police car had collected Madame Giraud about fifteen minutes ago. There had been an elderly man with her.

"Who?"

"They've seen him around before, but no one knew his name."

Having dismissed Braissart, Authié set off down the hill. The house was about three-quarters of the way down on the left-hand side. The door was locked and the shutters were closed, but an air of recent habitation hung about the place.

He continued to the end of the street, turned left into rue Barbarcane and along to the Place Saint-Gimer. A few residents were sitting outside their houses overlooking the parked cars in the square. A group of boys on bicycles, stripped to the waist and tanned dark by the sun, were hanging about on the steps of the church. Authié paid them no attention. He walked briskly along the tarmacked access road that ran along the backs of the first few houses and gardens of rue de la Gaffe. Then he climbed to the right to follow a narrow dirt path that wound across the grassy slopes below the walls of the Cité.

Soon Authié was overlooking the back of Giraud's property. The walls were painted the same powder yellow as at the front. A small, unlocked wooden gate led to a paved garden. Pendulous figs, almost black with sweetness, hung from a generous tree, which covered most of the terrace from the eyes of her neighbors. The terra-cotta tiles were stained purple where overripe figs had fallen and burst.

The glass back doors were framed beneath a wooden pergola covered with vines. Authié peered through and saw that, although the key was in the lock, the doors were also bolted top and bottom. Since he didn't want to leave evidence, he looked around for another way in.

Alongside the French windows was a small kitchen window that had been left open at the top. Authié slipped on the latex gloves, threaded his arm through the gap and manipulated the old-fashioned clasp until he slipped the catch. It was stiff and the hinges groaned in complaint as he eased it open. When the gap was wide enough, he squeezed in his fingers and released the lower window.

A smell of olives and sour bread greeted him as he climbed in to the chill pantry. A wire guard protected the cheese board. The shelves contained bottles, jars of pickles, jams and mustard. On the table was a wooden chopping board and a white tea towel covering a few crumbs from an old baguette. Apricots sat in a colander in the sink, nearly overripe, waiting to be washed. Two glasses, upended, stood on the draining board.

Authié walked through into the main room. There was a bureau in the corner on which sat an old electric typewriter. He pressed the on/off button and it buzzed into life. He slipped a piece of paper in and struck a couple of keys. The letters appeared in a sharp black row on the page.

Sliding the machine forward, Authié searched the pigeonholes behind. Jeanne Giraud was an orderly woman and everything was clearly labeled and filed: bills in the first section, personal letters in the second, pension and insurance documents in the third, miscellaneous circulars and flyers in the last.

Nothing caught his interest. He turned his attention to the drawers. The first two yielded the usual stationery: pens, paper clips, envelopes, stamps, and stores of white A4 paper. The bottom drawer was locked. Using a paperknife, Authié carefully and efficiently slid the blade into the space between the drawer and the carcass and popped the lock.

There was only one thing inside, a small padded envelope. Big enough to contain a ring but not the book. It was postmarked Ariège: 18:20, 4 July 2005.

Authié slipped his fingers inside. It was empty except for the delivery receipt confirming that Madame Giraud had signed for the package at eight-twenty. It matched the slip Braissart had given him.

Authié slipped it into the inside pocket of his jacket.

Not incontrovertible proof Biau had taken the ring and sent it to his grandmother, but it pointed that way. Authié continued his search for the object itself. Having completed his examination of the ground floor, he went upstairs. The door to the back bedroom was straight ahead. This was clearly Giraud's room, bright and clean and feminine. He searched the wardrobe and chest of drawers, his expert fingers riffling through the small but good quality clothes and underwear. Everything was neatly folded and ordered and smelled faintly of rose water.

A jewelry box sat on the dressing table in front of the mirror. A couple of brooches, a string of yellowed pearls and a gold bracelet were mixed in with several pairs of earrings and a silver crucifix. Her wedding and engagement rings sat stiffly in the worn red felt, as if they were rarely taken out.

The front bedroom was bare and plain in contrast, empty except for a single bed and a desk under the window with a lamp on it. Authié approved. It reminded him of the austere cells of the abbey.

There were signs of recent occupation. A half-empty glass of water stood on the bedside table, next to a volume of Occitan poetry by René Nelli, its paper marked around the edges. Authié moved to the desk. An old-fashioned pen and ink bottle stood on the top, together with several sheets of heavy paper. There was a piece of blotting paper, barely used.

He could hardly believe what he was seeing. Someone had sat at this desk and written a letter to Alice Tanner. The name was perfectly legible.

Authié turned the blotter round and tried to decipher the signature half visible at the bottom. The handwriting was old fashioned and some of the letters merged into others, but he persevered until he had the skeleton of a name.

He folded the coarse paper and slipped it into his breast pocket. As he turned to leave the room, his eye was caught by a scrap of paper on the floor, caught between the door and the doorjamb. Authié picked it up. It was a fragment of a railway ticket, a single, dated today. The destination, Carcassonne, was clear, but the name of the issuing station was missing.

The sound of the bells of Saint-Gimer striking the hour reminded him of how little time he had to get back. With a last look around to check that everything was as he had found it, he left the way he had come.

Twenty minutes later, he was sitting on the balcony of his apartment on the Quai de Paicherou looking back over the river to the medieval Cité. On the table in front of him was a bottle of Château Villerambert Moureau and two glasses. On his lap was a file containing the information his secretary had gathered in the past hour on Jeanne Giraud. The other dossier contained the preliminary report from the forensic anthropologist on the bodies found in the cave.

Authié reflected for a moment, then removed several sheets from Giraud's file. Then he resealed the envelope, poured himself a glass of wine and waited for his visitor to arrive.

CHAPTER 32

All along the high embankment of the Quai de Paicherou, men and women sat on metal benches overlooking the Aude. The sweeping, cultivated lawns of the public gardens were divided up by brightly planted flowerbeds and cultivated paths. The garish purples and yellows and oranges in the children's playground matched the riotous colors of the flowers in the beds—red-hot pokers, huge lilies, delphiniums and geraniums.

Marie-Cécile cast an appraising eye over Paul Authié's building. It was what she had expected, a discreet and understated *quartier* that had no need to shout, a mixture of family homes and private apartments. As she watched, a woman with a purple silk scarf and a bright red shirt cycled past on the towpath.

She became aware someone was watching her. Without turning her head, she glanced up to see a man was standing on the top floor balcony, both hands placed on the wrought-iron railings, looking down at the car. Marie-Cécile smiled. She recognized Paul Authié from his photographs. At this distance, it did not look as if they had done him justice.

Her driver rang the bell. She watched Authié turn, then disappear through the balcony doors. By the time her chauffeur was opening the door of the car, Authié was standing in the entrance, ready to greet her.

She had chosen her clothes carefully, a pale brown sleeveless linen dress and matching jacket, formal but not too official. Very simple, very stylish.

Close up, her first impressions were reinforced. Authié was tall and well toned, wearing a casual but well-cut suit and white shirt. His hair was swept back from his forehead, accentuating the fine bones of his pale face. An unnerving gaze. But beneath the urbane exterior, Marie-Cécile sensed the determination of the bare-knuckle fighter.

Ten minutes later, having accepted a glass of wine, she felt she had a sense of the man she was dealing with. Marie-Cécile smiled as she leaned forward and extinguished her cigarette in the heavy glass ashtray.

"*Bon, aux affaires.* Inside would be better, I think."

Authié stood aside to let her through the glass doors that led into the immaculate but impersonal living room. Pale carpets and lampshades, high-backed chairs around a glass table.

"More wine? Or can I get you something else to drink?"

"Pastis, if you have it."

"Ice? Water?"

"Ice."

Marie-Cécile sat in one of the cream leather armchairs angled on either side of a small glass coffee table and watched him mix the drinks. The subtle scent of aniseed filled the room.

Authié handed her the drink, before sitting in the chair opposite.

"Thank you," she smiled her thanks. "So. Paul. If you don't mind, I'd like you to run through the precise sequence of events."

If he was irritated, he didn't show it. She observed him closely as he talked, but his report was clear and precise, identical in every respect to what he had told her before.

"And the skeletons themselves? They've been taken to Toulouse?"

"To the forensic anthropology department at the university, yes."

"When do you expect to hear anything?"

His response was to pass her the white A4 envelope from the table. Not above a bit of showmanship, she thought.

"Already? That's very quick work."

"I called in a favor."

Marie-Cécile laid it on her lap. "Thank you. I'll read it later," she said smoothly. "For now, why don't you summarize for me. You've read it, I presume?"

"It's only a preliminary report, pending the results of more detailed tests," he cautioned.

"Understood," she said, leaning back in the chair.

"The bones are those of a man and a woman. Estimate, somewhere between seven to nine hundred years old. The male skeleton showed indications of unhealed wounds on his pelvis and top of the femur, suggesting the possibility they were inflicted shortly before death. There was evidence of older, healed fractures on his right arm and collarbone."

"Age?"

"Adult, neither very young nor old. Somewhere between twenty and sixty. They should be able to narrow it down after further tests. The woman the same bracket. The cranial cavity was depressed on one side, which could have been caused either by a blow to the head or by a fall. She had borne at least one child. There was also evidence of a healed fracture in her right foot and an unhealed break in her left ulna, between elbow and wrist."

"Cause of death?"

"He's not prepared to commit himself at this early stage, although his opinion is it will be hard to isolate one clearly identifiable diagnosis. Given the sort of time period we're talking about, it's probable that both died as a combination of their injuries, loss of blood and, possibly, starvation."

"He thinks they were still alive when they were entombed in the cave?"

Authié shrugged, although she registered the flicker of interest in his gray eyes. Marie-Cécile took a cigarette from her case and rolled it between her fingers for a moment, while she thought.

"What about the objects found between the bodies?" she said, leaning forward for him to light her cigarette.

"Again, the same caveat, but his estimate is they date from the late twelfth to mid-thirteenth century. The lamp on the altar might be slightly older and is of Arab design, Spain possibly, more likely farther afield. The knife was an ordinary eating knife, for meat and fruit. There is evidence of blood on the blade. Tests will confirm if it's animal or human. The bag was leather, locally sourced and typical of the Languedoc in that period. No clues as to what, if anything, it contained, although there were particles of metal in the lining and slight traces of sheepskin in the stitching."

Marie-Cécile kept her voice as steady as she could. "What else?"

"The woman who discovered the cave, Dr. Tanner, found a large copper and silver buckle. It was trapped beneath the boulder outside the entrance to the cave. He's also dated this to the same sort of period and believes it to be local or possibly Aragonese. There's a photograph of it in the envelope."

Marie-Cécile waved her hand. "I'm not interested in a buckle, Paul," she said. She breathed a spiral of smoke into the air. "I do, however, want to know why you haven't found the book."

She saw his long fingers wind round the arms of his chair.

"We have no evidence the book was actually there," he said calmly. "Although the leather pouch is certainly big enough to have contained a book of the size you seek."

"And what about the ring? Do you doubt that was there also?"

Again, he did not let her provoke him. "On the contrary, I am certain the ring was there."

"Well?"

"It was there, but some time between the cave being discovered and my arrival with the police, it was taken."

"But you have no evidence of that either," she said, her voice sharp now. "Unless I am mistaken, you do not have the ring either."

Marie-Cécile watched as Authié produced a piece of paper from his pocket. "Dr. Tanner was most insistent, so much so that she drew this," he said, handing it over. "It's crude, I admit, but it's a pretty good match for the description you gave me. Don't you think?"

She took the sketch from his hand. The size, shape and proportion were not identical, but close enough to the diagram of the labyrinth ring

Marie-Cécile had locked in her safe in Chartres. No one outside the de l'Oradore family had seen it for eight hundred years. It had to be genuine.

"Quite the artist," she murmured. "Was this the only drawing she did?"

His gray eyes looked clear into hers without faltering. "There are others, but this was the only one worth bothering about."

"Why don't you let me be the judge of that," she said quietly.

"I'm afraid, Madame de l'Oradore, I took only this. The others seemed irrelevant." Authié shrugged apologetically. "Besides, Inspector Noubel, the investigation officer, was already suspicious of my interest."

"Next time . . ." she started to say, then stopped. She extinguished her cigarette, grinding it so hard that tobacco spilled out in a fan. "You searched Dr. Tanner's belongings, I presume?"

He nodded. "The ring wasn't there."

"It's small. She could easily have hidden it somewhere."

"Technically," he agreed, "although I don't think she did. If she stole it, why would she mention it in the first place? Also"—he leaned over and tapped the paper—"if she had got the original in her possession, why bother to make a record of it?"

Marie-Cécile looked at the drawing. "It's surprisingly accurate for something done from memory."

"I agree."

"Where is she now?"

"Here. In Carcassonne. It appears she has a meeting with a solicitor tomorrow."

"Concerning?"

He shrugged. "A legacy, something of that sort. She's due to fly home on Sunday."

The doubts Marie-Cécile had from the moment she'd heard about the find yesterday were intensifying the more he told her. Something didn't add up.

"How did Dr. Tanner get her place on the team?" she said. "Was she recommended?"

Authié looked surprised. "Dr. Tanner wasn't actually a member of the team," he said lightly. "I'm sure I mentioned this."

Her lips tightened. "You did not."

"I'm sorry," he said smoothly. "I was sure I had. Dr. Tanner's a volunteer. Since most excavations rely on unpaid help, when a request was put in for her to join the team for this week, there seemed no reason to turn it down."

"Who requested it?"

"Shelagh O'Donnell, I believe," he said blandly, "the number two on the site."

"She's a friend of Dr. O'Donnell?" she said, struggling to conceal her surprise.

"Obviously, it crossed my mind therefore that Dr. Tanner might have passed the ring to her. Unfortunately, I didn't have a chance to interview her on Monday and now she appears to have disappeared."

"She's what?" she said sharply. "When? Who knows about this?"

"O'Donnell was at the site house last night. She took a phone call, then went out shortly afterwards. No one's seen her since."

Marie-Cécile lit another cigarette to steady her nerves. "Why was I not told about this before?"

"I didn't realize you would be interested in something so peripheral to your main concerns. I apologize."

"Have the police been informed?"

"Not yet. Dr. Brayling, the site director, has given everyone a few days' leave. He thinks it's possible—probable—that O'Donnell has simply taken off without bothering to let anyone know."

"I do not want the police involved," she said forcefully. "It would be extremely regrettable."

"I quite agree, Madame de l'Oradore. Dr. Brayling is not a fool. If he believes O'Donnell has taken something from the site, then it's hardly in his best interests to involve the authorities."

"Do you think O'Donnell stole the ring?"

Authié evaded the question. "I think we should find her."

"That's not what I asked. And the book? Do you think she might have taken that too?"

Authié met her gaze straight on. "As I said, I remain open-minded about whether or not the book was ever there." He paused. "*If* it was, I'm not convinced she could have got it away from the site without being seen. The ring's a different matter."

"Well, *someone* did," she snapped in frustration.

"As I said, if it was there at all."

Marie-Cécile sprang to her feet, taking him by surprise, and walked round the table until she was standing in front of him. For the first time, she saw a flash of alarm in his gray eyes. She bent down and pressed her hand flat against his chest.

"I can feel your heart beating," she said softly. "Beating very hard. Now why might that be, Paul?" Holding his gaze, she pressed him back against the chair. "I don't tolerate mistakes. And I don't like not being kept informed." Their eyes locked. "You understand me?"

Authié did not answer. She had not intended him to.

"All you had to do was deliver to me the objects you promised. That's what I'm paying you for. So, find the English girl, deal with Noubel if necessary, the rest is your business. I don't want to hear about it."

"If I've done anything to give you the impression that—"

She put her fingers to his lips and felt him flinch at the physical contact.

"I don't want to hear it."

She released the pressure and stepped away from him, back out onto the balcony. The evening had stripped the color from everything, leaving the buildings and bridges silhouetted against the darkening sky.

A moment later, Authié came and stood next to her.

"I don't doubt you are doing your best, Paul," she said quietly. He put his hands next to hers on the railings and, for a second, their fingers touched. "There are other members of the *Noublesso Véritables* in Carcassonne, of course, who would serve just as well. However, given the extent of your involvement so far . . ."

She left the sentence hanging. From the stiffening of his shoulders and back, she knew the warning shot had hit home. She raised her hand to attract her driver, who was waiting below.

"I would like to visit the Pic de Soularac myself."

"You're staying in Carcassonne?"

She hid her smile. "For a few days, yes."

"I was under the impression you didn't wish to enter the chamber until the night of the ceremony—"

"I've changed my mind," she said, turning to face him. "Now I'm here." She smiled. "I have things to attend to, so if you could pick me up at one o'clock, that will give me time to read your report. I'm at the Hôtel de la Cité."

Marie-Cécile walked back inside, picked up the envelope and put it in her handbag.

"*Bien. A demain,* Paul. Sleep well."

Aware of his eyes on her back watching her walk down the stairs, Marie-Cécile could only admire his self-control. But as she got into the car, she had the satisfaction of hearing a glass hit the wall and shatter in Authié's apartment two floors above.

The lounge of the hotel was thick with cigar smoke. After-dinner drinkers in summer suits or evening dresses sat enfolded in the deep leather armchairs and the discreet shadows of the high-backed mahogany settles.

Marie-Cécile walked slowly up the sweeping staircase. Black and white photographs looked down on her, reminders of the hotel's celebrated turn-of-the-century past.

When she reached her room, she changed out of her clothes into her bathrobe. As always, last thing at night, she looked at herself in the mirror, dispassionately, as if scrutinizing a work of art. Translucent skin, high cheekbones, the distinctive de l'Oradore profile.

Marie-Cécile smoothed her fingers over her face and neck. She would not allow her beauty to fade with the passing of the years. If all went well, then she would succeed in doing what her grandfather had dreamed of. She would cheat old age. Cheat death.

She frowned. But only if the book and ring could be found. With a renewed sense of purpose, Marie-Cécile lit a cigarette and wandered over to the window, looking out over the gardens while she waited for her call to be answered. Murmured late-night conversations floated up to her from the terrace. Beyond the battlements of the Cité walls, beyond the river, the lights of the Basse Ville sparkled like cheap white and orange Christmas decorations.

"François-Baptiste? *C'est moi.* Has anyone called in the past twenty-four hours on my private number?" She listened. "No? Has she called you?" She waited. "I've just been told of a problem this end." She drummed her fingers on her arm while he talked. "Have there been any developments with the other matter?"

The reply was not what she wanted to hear. "National or just local?" A pause. "Keep me in touch. Call me if anything else comes up, otherwise I'll be back Thursday night."

After she'd hung up, Marie-Cécile allowed her thoughts to dwell on the other man in her house. Will was sweet enough, keen to please, but the relationship had run its course. He was too demanding and his adolescent jealousies were starting to get on her nerves. He was always asking questions. She needed no complications at the moment.

Besides, they needed the house to themselves.

She turned on the reading light and got out the report Authié had given her on the skeletons, as well as a dossier on Authié himself, which had been compiled when he'd been put forward for election to the *Noublesso Véritable* two years ago, from her suitcase.

She skimmed the document, although she knew it well enough. There were a couple of accusations of sexual assault when he was a student. Both women had been paid off, she assumed, since no charges were ever brought. There had been allegations of an attack on an Algerian woman during a pro-Islamic rally, although again no charge had been made; evidence of involvement in an anti-Semitic publication at university, as well as allegations of sexual and physical abuse from his ex-wife, which had also come to nothing.

More significant were the regular and increasingly substantial donations to the Society of Jesus, the Jesuits. In the past couple of years his involvement with fundamentalist groups opposed to Vatican II and the modernizing of the Catholic Church had also been growing.

To Marie-Cécile's mind, such evidence of hardline religious commitment sat uneasily with membership of the *Noublesso*. Authié had pledged his service to the organization and he had been useful so far. He had arranged the excavation at the Pic de Soularac efficiently and everything appeared to be in hand for wrapping things up just as quickly. The warning of the breach of security in Chartres had come via one of his contacts. His intelligence was always clear and reliable.

Nonetheless, Marie-Cécile didn't trust him. He was too ambitious. Set against his successes were the failures of the past forty-eight hours. She did not believe he'd be so stupid as to take either the ring or the book himself, but Authié did not seem the sort of a man to let things disappear from under his nose.

She hesitated, then made a second call.

"I have a job for you. I am interested in a book, approximately twenty centimeters high by ten centimeters wide, leather over board, held together by leather ties. Also, a man's stone ring, flat face, a thin line around the middle and an engraving on the underside. There might even be a small token, about the size of a ten franc piece, with it." She paused. "Carcassonne. A flat on the Quai de Paicherou and an office in the rue de Verdun. Both belong to Paul Authié."

CHAPTER 33

Alice's hotel was immediately opposite the main gates into the medieval Cité, set in pretty gardens, sunk down out of sight of the road.

She was shown to a comfortable room on the first floor. Alice flung open the windows to let the world in. Smells of meat cooking, garlic and vanilla, cigar smoke floated into the room.

She unpacked quickly and showered, then called Shelagh again, more out of habit than expectation. Still no answer. She shrugged. Nobody could accuse her of not trying.

Armed with the guidebook she'd bought in a service station on the journey from Toulouse, Alice left the hotel and crossed the road toward the Cité. Steep concrete steps led up into a small park bordered on two sides by bushes and tall evergreens and plane trees. A brightly lit nineteenth-century carousel dominated the far end of the gardens, its garish fin-de-siècle ornamentation out of place in the shadow of the sandstone medieval fortifications. Covered with a brown and white striped canopy, with a painted frieze of knights and ladies and white horses around the rim, everything was pink and gold—charging horses, spinning teacups, fairy-tale carriages. Even the ticket kiosk looked like a booth at a fairground. A bell rang and children squealed as the carousel began to turn, slowly belching out its antique mechanical song.

Beyond the carousel, Alice could see the gray heads and shoulders of tombs and gravestones behind the walls of the cemetery, a row of cypress and yew protecting the sleepers from casual glances. To the right of the gates, a group of men played *pétanque*.

For a moment, she stood still, facing the entrance to the Cité head on, preparing herself to go in. To her right was a stone pillar from which an ugly stone gargoyle stared out, its flat face uncompromising and blunt. It looked newly restored.

SUM CARCAS. I am Carcas.

Dame Carcas, the Saracen queen and wife of King Balaack, after whom Carcassonne was said to be named after resisting a five-year siege by Charlemagne.

Alice walked over the covered drawbridge, which was squat and confined and fashioned from stone, chain and wood. The boards creaked and clattered beneath her feet. There was no water in the moat beneath her, only grass speckled with wild flowers.

It led into the *Lices,* a dusty, wide area between the outer and inner ring of fortifications. To left and right, children were climbing on the walls and staging mock battles with plastic swords. Straight ahead was the Porte Narbonnaise. As she passed beneath the high, narrow arch, Alice raised her eyes. A benign stone statue of the Virgin Mary looked down at her.

The moment Alice passed through the gates all sense of space vanished. The rue Cros-Mayrevieille, the cobbled main street, was very narrow and sloped upwards. The buildings were packed so closely together that a person could lean out of the top story of one house and join hands with someone on the opposite side.

The high buildings trapped the noise. Different languages, shouting, laughing, gesturing as a car crawled by with barely a hand's width to spare on either side. Shops leaped out at her, selling postcards, guidebooks, a mannequin in the stocks advertising a museum of inquisitional instruments of torture, soaps and cushions and tableware, everywhere replica swords and shields. Twisted wrought-iron brackets stuck out from the wall with wooden signs attached to them: *l'Éperon Médiéval,* the Medieval Spur, sold replica swords and porcelain dolls; *A Saint Louis* sold soap, souvenirs and tableware.

Alice let her feet guide her to the main square, Place Marcou. It was small and filled with restaurants and clipped plane trees. Their spreading branches, wide like entwined and sheltering hands above the tables and chairs, competed with the brightly colored awnings. The names of the individual cafés were printed on the top—Le Marcou, Le Trouvère, Le Ménestrel.

Alice strolled over the cobbles and out the other side, finding herself back at the junction of the rue Cros-Mayrevieille and the Place du Château, where a triangle of shops, *crêperies* and restaurants surrounded a stone obelisk about two and one-half meters high, topped by a bust of the nineteenth-century historian Jean-Pierre Cros-Mayrevieille. Around the bottom was a bronze frieze of the fortifications.

She walked forward until she was standing in front of a sweeping semicircular wall that protected the Château Comtal. Behind the imposing locked gates were the turrets and battlements of the castle. *A fortress within a fortress.*

Alice stopped, realizing that this had been her destination all along. The Château Comtal, home of the Trencavel family.

She peered through the tall wooden gates. There was something familiar about it all, as if she was returning to a place she'd been once, long ago, and forgotten. There were glass ticket booths on either side of the entrance, blinds drawn, with printed signs advertising the opening hours.

Beyond that was a gray expanse of gravel and dust, not grass, which led to a flat, narrow bridge, about two meters across.

Alice stepped away from the gates, promising herself she'd come back first thing in the morning. She turned to the right and followed signs for the Porte de Rodez. It was set between two distinctive, horseshoe-shaped towers. She climbed down the wide steps, worn away in the middle by countless feet.

The difference in age between the inner and outer walls was most evident here. The outer fortifications, which she read had been built at the end of the thirteenth century and restored during the nineteenth, were gray and the blocks were relatively equal in size. Detractors would claim it was just another indication of how inappropriately the restoration had been carried out. Alice didn't care. The spirit of the place was what moved her. The inner wall, including the western wall of the Château Comtal itself, was composed of a mixture of red tiles of the Gallo-Roman remains and the crumbling sandstone of the twelfth century.

Alice felt a sense of peace after the noise within the Cité, a feeling of belonging here, among such mountains and skies. With her arms resting on the battlements, she stood looking down to the river, imagining the cold touch of the water between her toes.

Only when the remains of the day gave way to dusk, did Alice turn and head back into the Cité.

CHAPTER 34
Carcassona

JULHET 1209

They rode in single file as they approached Carcassonne, Raymond-Roger Trencavel at the head, followed closely by Bertrand Pelletier. The *chevalier* Guilhem du Mas brought up the rear.

Alaïs was at the back with the clergy.

Less than a week had passed since she had left, but it seemed much longer. Spirits were low. Although the Trencavel ensigns fluttered intact in the breeze and the same number of men were returning as had set out, the expression on the viscount's face told the story of the failure of their petition.

The horses slowed to a walk as they approached the gates. Alaïs leaned forward and patted Tatou on the neck. She was tired and she'd thrown a shoe, but the mare's stamina could not be faulted.

The crowds were several deep as they passed under the Trencavel coat of arms hanging between the two towers of the Porte Narbonnaise. Children ran alongside the horses, throwing flowers in their path and cheering. Women waved makeshift pennants and kerchiefs out of top-floor windows, as Trencavel led them up through the streets toward the Château Comtal.

Alaïs felt nothing but relief as they crossed the narrow bridge and through the Eastern Gates. The Cour d'Honneur erupted in sound, everybody waving and calling out. *Écuyers* sprang forward to take their masters' horses, servants ran to make ready the bathhouse, scullions headed for the kitchen with pails of water ready so that a feast could be prepared.

Among the forest of waving arms and smiling faces, Alaïs caught sight of Oriane. Her father's servant, François, was standing close behind. She flushed at the thought of how she had tricked him and slipped away from under his nose.

She saw Oriane scanning the crowd. Her eyes came briefly to rest upon her husband, Jehan Congost. A look of contempt flitted across Oriane's face, before she moved on and to her discomfort, fixed her gaze upon Alaïs. Alaïs pretended not to notice, but she could feel her sister staring at her across the sea of heads. When she looked again, Oriane had gone.

Alaïs dismounted, taking care not to knock her injured shoulder, and handed Tatou's reins to Amiel to take to the stables. Her relief at being home had already passed. Melancholy settled over her like a winter fog. Everyone else seemed to be in someone's arms, a wife, a mother, an aunt, a sister. She searched for Guilhem, but he was nowhere to be seen. *In the bathhouse already.* Even her father had gone.

Alaïs wandered into the smaller courtyard, seeking solitude. She couldn't shake a verse by Raymond de Mirval from her mind, although he made her mood worse. *"Res contr' Amor non es guirens, lai on sos poders s'atura."* There is no protection against love, once it chooses to exert its power.

When Alaïs had first heard the poem the emotions expressed in it were unknown to her. Even so, as she'd sat in the Cour d'Honneur, her thin arms hooped around her child's knees, listening to the *trouvère* as he sang of a heart torn in two, she had understood the sentiment behind the words well enough.

Tears sprang into her eyes. Angrily, she rubbed them away with the back of her hand. She would not give in to self-pity. She sat down on a secluded bench in the shade.

She and Guilhem had often walked in the Cour du Midi in the days before their marriage. Then, the trees had been turning gold and a carpet of autumn leaves, the color of burned copper and ocher, had covered the ground. Alaïs traced a pattern in the dust with the tip of her boot, wondering how she and Guilhem could be reconciled. She lacked the art and he lacked the inclination.

Oriane often stopped talking to her husband for days. Then, as quickly as the silence had fallen, it would lift and Oriane would be sweet and attentive to Jehan, until the next time. What few memories Alaïs had of her parents' marriage were of similar periods of light and dark.

Alaïs had not expected this to be her fate. She had stood before the priest in the chapel in her red veil and spoken her wedding vows. The flames from the flickering red Michelmas candles sending shadows dancing over the altar bedecked with flowering winter hawthorn. She had believed, and did still in her heart, in a love that would last forever.

Her friend and mentor, Esclarmonde, was petitioned by lovers for potions and posies to regain or capture affection. Wine mulled with mint leaves and parsnips, forget-me-knots to keep a lover fruitful, bunches of yellow primrose. For all her respect for Esclarmonde's skills, Alaïs had always dismissed such behavior as superstitious nonsense. She did not want to believe love could be so easily tricked and bought.

There were others, she knew, who offered more dangerous magic, black charms to bewitch or to harm faithless suitors. Esclarmonde warned her against such dark powers, the obvious manifestation of the Devil's dominion over the world. No good could ever come of such ill.

Today, for the first time in her life, Alaïs had a flicker of understanding of what might drive women to such desperate measures.

"Filha."

Alaïs jumped up.

"Where have you been?" said Pelletier, out of breath. "I have searched everywhere for you."

"I did not hear you, *Paire,*" she said.

"Work to prepare the *Ciutat* will begin as soon as Viscount Trencavel has been reunited with his wife and son. There will be little time to draw breath in the days ahead."

"When are you expecting Simeon to arrive?"

"A day or two more yet." He frowned. "I wish I could have persuaded him to travel with us. But, he believes he will be less conspicuous among his own people. He may well be right."

"And once he is here," she pressed on, "you will decide what is to be done? I have an idea about—"

Alaïs stopped, realizing she would rather test her theory first before making a fool of herself in front of her father. *And him.*

"An idea?" he said.

"It's nothing," she said quickly. "I was just going to ask if I could be present when you and Simeon meet to talk."

Consternation flickered across his lined face. She could see him struggling to decide.

"In the light of the service you have performed so far," he said in the end, "you may hear what we have to say. However"—he held up a finger in warning—"on the clear understanding that you are there as an observer only. Any active participation in this matter is at an end. I will not have you putting yourself at risk again."

A bubble of excitement inside her grew. *I will persuade him otherwise when the time comes.*

She lowered her eyes and folded her hands meekly in her lap. "Of course, *Paire.* I will obey your wishes."

Pelletier shot her a look, but did not pursue it. "There is one more ser-

vice I must ask of you, Alaïs. Viscount Trencavel will make a public celebration of his safe return to Carcassona, while the news of our failure to
agree to terms with Toulouse is not yet widely known. Dame Agnès will
observe Vespers in the cathedral church of Sant-Nasari this evening
rather than in the chapel." He paused. "I wish you to attend. Your sister
too."

Alaïs was astounded. Although she attended services in the chapel of
the Château Comtal from time to time, her father had not challenged her
decision to abstain from services in the cathedral.

"I know you must be weary, but Viscount Trencavel believes it important that no just criticism could be made of his conduct—and that of
those closest to him—at this time. If there are spies within the *Ciutat*—
and I have no doubt that there are—we do not wish our spiritual failings,
as they might be interpreted, to reach the ears of our enemies."

"It's not a question of fatigue," she said furiously. "Bishop de Rochefort
and his priests, they're hypocrites. They preach one thing but do another."
Pelletier turned red, whether through anger or embarrassment, she could
not be sure. "By this token, will you be attending also?" she demanded.

Pelletier did not meet her eye. "You will appreciate I will be occupied
with Viscount Trencavel."

Alaïs glared at him. "Very well," she said at last. "I will obey you, *Paire*.
But do not expect me to kneel before the figure of a broken man on a cross
of wood and pray."

For a moment, she thought she had been too outspoken. Then, to her
astonishment, her father began to laugh.

"Quite right," he said. "I would expect nothing less of you. Just be careful, Alaïs. Do not express such views unwisely. They may be watching."

Alaïs passed the next few hours in her chamber. She made a poultice of
fresh wild marjoram for her stiff neck and shoulder. At the same time, she
listened to her servant's good-natured chatter.

According to Rixende, opinion was divided over Alaïs' early morning
flight from the château. Some expressed admiration for Alaïs' fortitude
and bravery. Others, Oriane among them, criticized her. She had made a
fool of her husband by acting in so rash a manner. Worse, she had jeop-
ardized the success of the mission. Alaïs hoped this was not what Guilhem felt, although she feared it was. His thoughts tended to run along
well-trodden paths. More than that, his pride was easily hurt and Alaïs
knew from experience his desire to be admired, to be celebrated within
the household, sometimes led him to say and do things contrary to his
true nature. If he felt himself humiliated, there was no saying how he
would react.

"But they can hardly say so now, Dame Alaïs," Rixende said, as she cleared away the remains of the compress. "All have returned safely. If that doesn't prove God is on our side, then what does!"

Alaïs gave a pale smile. She suspected Rixende would see things in a different light once news of the true state of affairs spread through the Cité.

The bells were clamoring and the sky was flecked pink and white as they walked from the Château Comtal toward Sant-Nasari. At the head of the procession was a priest, decked in white and holding a golden cross high in the air. The other priests, nuns and monks followed.

Behind them, came Dame Agnès, the wives of the consuls, her ladies-in-waiting bringing up the rear. Alaïs was obliged to partner her sister.

Oriane did not address a single word to her, good or ill. As always, she drew the eyes and admiration of the crowd. She was wearing a deep red dress, with a delicate gold and black girdle pulled tight to accentuate her high waist and rounded hips. Her black hair was washed and oiled and her hands were clasped in front of her in an attitude of piety, perfectly displaying the alms purse that dangled from her wrist.

Alaïs assumed the purse was a gift from an admirer, a wealthy one at that judging by the pearls set around the neck and the motto embroidered in gold thread.

Beneath the ceremony and display, Alaïs was aware of an undercurrent of apprehension and suspicion.

She didn't notice François until he tapped her lightly on the arm.

"Esclarmonde has returned," he whispered in her ear. "I have come directly from there."

Alaïs spun round to face him. "Did you speak with her?"

He hesitated. "Not really, Dame."

Immediately, she stepped out of the line. "I will go."

"May I suggest, Dame, you wait until after the service is finished?" he suggested, glancing to the door. Alaïs followed his eyes. Three black-hooded monks were standing guard, clearly noting who was present and who was not. "It would be unfortunate if your absence reflected badly on Dame Agnès or your father. It could be interpreted as a sign of your sympathy for the new church."

"Of course, yes." She thought a moment. "But please tell Esclarmonde I will be with her as soon as I can."

Alaïs dipped her fingers in the *bénitier* and crossed herself with holy water, in case anyone was watching.

She found a space in the tightly packed north transept, as far away as she could get from Oriane without attracting attention. Candles flickered high above the nave from chandeliers suspended from the roof. From below, they looked like huge wheels of steel that might at any time come crashing down upon the sinners below.

Although surprised to find his church full after so long empty, the bishop's voice was thin and insubstantial, barely audible over the mass of people breathing and shuffling in the heat. How different it was from the simplicity of Esclarmonde's church.

Her father's church also.

The *Bons Homes* valued inner faith above outward display. They needed no consecrated buildings, no superstitious rituals, no humiliating obeisance designed to keep ordinary men apart from God. They did not worship images nor prostrate themselves before idols or instruments of torture. For the *Bons Chrétiens*, the power of God lay in the word. They needed only books and prayers, words spoken and read aloud. Salvation was nothing to do with the alms or relics or Sabbath prayers spoken in a language only the priests understood.

In their eyes, all were equal in the Grace of the Holy Father—Jew or Saracen, man and woman, the beast of the fields and the birds of the air. There would be no hell, no final day of judgment, because through God's grace all would be saved, although many would be destined to live life many times over before they regained God's kingdom.

Although Alaïs had not actually attended a worship, because of Esclarmonde she was familiar with the words of their prayers and rituals. What mattered was that in these darkening times, the *Bons Chrétiens* were good men, tolerant men, men of peace who celebrated a God of Light rather than cowering under the wrath of the Catholics' cruel God.

At last, Alaïs heard the words of the *Benedictus*. This was her moment to slip away. She bowed her head. Slowly, her hands clasped, careful not to attract attention, Alaïs edged back toward the door.

A few moments later, and she was free.

CHAPTER 35

Esclarmonde's house lay in the shadow of the Tour du Balthazar.

Alaïs hesitated a moment before tapping on the shutter, watching her friend moving about inside through the large window overlooking the street. She was wearing a plain green dress and her hair, streaked with gray, was tied back.

I know I am right.

Alaïs felt a surge of affection. She was certain her suspicions would prove true. Esclarmonde glanced up. Straight away, she raised her arm and waved, a smile lighting her face.

"Alaïs. You are most welcome. We have missed you, Sajhë and I."

The familiar smell of herbs and spices hit Alaïs the moment she stepped under the lintel into the single downstairs room. A pan of water was boiling over the small fire in the center of the room. A table, a bench and two chairs were set against the wall.

A heavy curtain separated the front from the back of the room. It was in here that Esclarmonde gave consultations. Since she had no visitors, the curtain was pinned back and rows of earthenware containers stood in lines on long shelves. Bunches of herbs and sprigs of dried flowers hung from the ceiling. On the table, there was a lantern and a pestle and mortar, the twin of the one Alaïs had. It had been a wedding gift from Esclarmonde.

A ladder led up to a small platform above the consulting area where Esclarmonde and Sajhë slept. He was up there and gave a shout when he saw who it was, hurling down the rungs and throwing his arms around her waist. Immediately, he launched into a description of all the things he'd done and seen and heard since last they'd met.

Sajhë was a good storyteller, full of description and color, and his amber eyes sparkled with excitement as he spoke.

"I need you to deliver one or two messages for me, *manhac*." Esclarmonde said, after giving him his head for a while. "Dame Alaïs will excuse you." Sajhë was about to object, when the look on his great-grandmother's face stopped him. "It won't take long."

Alaïs ruffled his hair. "You have an observant eye, Sajhë, and a skill with words. Perhaps you'll be a poet when you are older?"

He shook his head. "I want to be a *chevalier*, Dame. I want to fight."

"Sajhë," said Esclarmonde sternly. "Listen to me now."

She spoke the names of the people he was to visit and then gave him the message that two *parfaits* from Albi would be in the copse east of the suburb of Sant-Miquel in three nights' time. "Are you sure of the message?" He nodded. "Good," she smiled, kissing the top of his head, then put her finger to her lip. "Remember. Only to those of whom I have spoken. Now, go. The sooner you leave, the sooner you'll be back and can recite more of your stories to Dame Alaïs."

"Do you not fear he will be overheard?" asked Alaïs as Esclarmonde closed the door.

"Sajhë is a sensible boy. He knows to speak only to those for whom the message is intended." She leaned out of the window and pulled the shutters closed. "Does anyone know you're here?"

"Only François. It was he who told me you were returned."

A strange look appeared in Esclarmonde's eyes, but she said nothing of it. "Best keep it that way, *è*."

She sat down at the table and gestured that Alaïs should join her.

"Now, Alaïs. Was your journey to Besièrs successful?"

Alaïs blushed. "You heard about that."

"All of Carcassona knows of it. The talk has been of little else." Her face grew serious. "I was concerned when I heard, coming so soon after the attack upon you."

"You know about that too? Since you did not send word, I thought perhaps you were away."

"Far from it. I came to the Château the day you were discovered, but this same François would not give me leave to enter. On your sister's orders no one was to be admitted without her permission."

"He did not say so," she said, puzzled at the oversight. "Nor, indeed, did Oriane, although that surprises me less."

"How so?"

"She watched me all the time, with a purpose rather than affection, or so it seemed." Alaïs paused. "Forgive me for not confiding my plans to you, Esclarmonde, but the time between the decision and execution of the plan was too brief to allow it."

Esclarmonde waved her hand. "Let me tell you what happened here while you were gone. Some few days after you had left the château, a man arrived asking after Raoul."

"Raoul?"

"The boy who found you in the orchard." Esclarmonde gave a wry smile. "He has gained some notoriety since the attack on you, aggrandizing his own role to the point that if you heard him speak, you would think he had taken on the armies of Saladin single-handed to save your life."

"I have no memory of him at all," said Alaïs, shaking her head. "Did he see anything, do you think?"

Esclarmonde shrugged. "I doubt it. You had been missing more than a day before the alarm was raised. I cannot believe Raoul witnessed the actual attack otherwise he would have spoken up earlier. Anyway, the stranger approached Raoul and took him to the *taberna Sant Joan dels Evangèlis*. He plied him with ale, flattered him. Raoul is but a boy for all his talk and swagger, and a rather dull-witted one at that, with the result that by the time Gaston was shutting up for the night, Raoul was incapable of putting one foot in front of the other. His companion offered to see him safely to his lodgings."

"Yes?"

"Raoul never arrived home. Nor has he been seen since."

"And the man?"

"Vanished, as if he had never been. In the tavern, he claimed to be from Alzonne. While you were in Besièrs, I traveled there. No one had heard of him."

"So we can learn nothing from that quarter."

Esclarmonde shook her head. "How came it that you were in the courtyard that time of night," she said. Her voice was calm and steady, but there was no mistaking the serious intent behind her words.

Alaïs told her. When she had finished, Esclarmonde was silent for a moment.

"There are two questions," she said in the end. "The first is who knew that you had been summoned to your father's presence, for I do not believe that your assailants were there by chance. The second is, presuming they were not the instigators of the plot, for whom were they acting?"

"I told no one. My father advised me against it."

"François brought the message."

"Yes," admitted Alaïs, "but I cannot believe François would—"

"Any number of servants might have seen him come to your chamber and overheard you talking." She fixed Alaïs with her direct and intelligent stare. "Why did you follow your father to Besièrs?"

The change of subject was so sudden, so unexpected, that it took Alaïs by surprise.

"I was—" she began, somber, but careful. She had come to Esclarmonde to find out answers to her questions. Instead, she found herself the witness. "He gave me a token," she said, not taking her eyes from Esclarmonde's face, "a token, with an engraving of a labyrinth. It was that the thieves took. Because of what my father had told me, I feared that every day that passed in ignorance of what had come to pass, might jeopardize the—" She broke off, not sure how to continue.

Instead of looking alarmed, Esclarmonde was smiling. "Did you tell him about the board too, Alaïs?" she said softly.

"On the eve of his departure, yes, before . . . before the attack. He was much perturbed, especially when I admitted I did not know where it had come from." She paused. "But how do you know that I—"

"Sajhë saw it when he helped you buy cheese in the market and told me of it. As you remarked, he is observant."

"It is a strange thing for a boy of eleven to remark upon."

"He recognized its importance to me," Esclarmonde replied.

"Like the *merel*."

Their eyes met.

Esclarmonde hesitated. "No," she said, choosing her words with care. "No, not exactly."

"You have it?" said Alaïs slowly.

Esclarmonde nodded.

"But why did you simply not ask? I would have given it willingly."

"Sajhë was there the night of your disappearance to make just such a request. He waited and waited and when, finally, you still did not return to your chamber, he took it. In the circumstances, it was good that he did."

"And you have it still?"

Esclarmonde nodded.

Alaïs felt a surge of triumph, proud that she had been right about her friend, the last guardian.

I saw the pattern. It spoke to me.

"Answer me this, Esclarmonde," she said, her excitement making her hurry. "If the board belongs to you, why did my father not know it?"

Esclarmonde smiled. "For the same reason he does not know why I have it. Because Harif wished it. For the safety of the Trilogy."

Alaïs couldn't trust herself to speak.

"Good. So, now we understand each other, you must tell me all you know."

Esclarmonde listened carefully until Alaïs had reached the end of her story.

"And Simeon is making his way to Carcassona?"

"Yes, although he gave the book to my father for safekeeping."

"A wise precaution." She nodded. "I shall be looking forward to making his acquaintance properly. He sounds a fine man."

"I liked him enormously," admitted Alaïs. "In Besièrs, my father was disappointed to discover Simeon had but one of the books. He was expecting both."

Esclarmonde was about to answer when there was a sudden hammering on the shutters and door.

Both women leaped to their feet.

"Atencion! Atencion!"

"What is it? What's going on?" cried Alaïs.

"Soldiers! In your father's absence, there have been a number of searches."

"But what are they looking for?"

"Criminals, they say, but in truth for *Bons Homes.*"

"But on whose authority do they act? The consuls?"

Esclarmonde shook her head. "Bérenger de Rochefort, our noble bishop; the Spanish monk Domingo de Guzman and his friar preachers; legates, who can say? They do not announce themselves."

"That's against our laws to—"

Esclarmonde raised a finger to her lips. "Sssh. They might yet pass us by."

At that moment, a savage kick sent splinters of wood flying into the room. The latch gave and the door smashed back against the stone wall with a hollow thud. Two men-at-arms, their features concealed by helmets worn low over their faces, burst into the room.

"I am Alaïs du Mas, the daughter of Intendant Pelletier. I demand to know on whose authority you act."

They did not lower their weapons nor raise their visors.

"I insist that you—"

There was a flash of red in the doorway and to Alaïs' horror, Oriane appeared in the doorway. "Sister! What brings you here in this manner?"

"I come at our father's request to escort you back to the Château Comtal. Your somewhat hasty departure from Vespers has already reached his ears. Fearing some catastrophe might have overtaken you, he bid me find you."

You are lying.

"He would never think such a thing unless you had planted the idea in his head in the first place," she said immediately. Alaïs glanced at the soldiers. "And was it his idea to bring an armed guard?"

"We all have your best interests at heart," she said, smiling slightly. "They were, I admit, perhaps overzealous."

"There is no need for you to concern yourself. I will return to the Château Comtal when I am ready."

Alaïs suddenly realized Oriane wasn't paying attention. Her eyes were sweeping around the room. Alaïs felt a hard cold feeling in her stomach. Could Oriane have overheard their conversation?

Immediately, she changed tactics. "On second thought, perhaps I will accompany you now. My business here is concluded."

"Business, sister?"

Oriane started to prowl around the room, running her hand over the backs of the chairs and the surface of the table. She opened the lid of the chest standing in the corner, then let it fall shut with a snap. Alaïs watched her anxiously.

She halted on the threshold of Esclarmonde's consulting room. "What is it you do through there, *sorcière*," Oriane said contemptuously, acknowledging Esclarmonde for the first time. "Potions, spells for the weakminded?" She put her head inside, a look of disgust on her face, then withdrew. "There are many who say you are a witch, Esclarmonde de Servian, a *faitilhièr* as the common people say."

"How dare you address her like that!" exclaimed Alaïs.

"You are welcome to look, Dame Oriane, if it pleases you," said Esclarmonde mildly.

Oriane suddenly grabbed Alaïs' arm. "That is enough from you," she said, digging her sharp nails into Alaïs' skin. "You declared yourself ready to return to the château, so let us go."

Before she knew it, Alaïs found herself back in the street. The soldiers were so close behind her that she could feel their breath on the back of her neck. A fleeting memory of the smell of ale, a callused hand over her mouth.

"Quick," said Oriane, poking her in the back.

For Esclarmonde's sake, Alaïs felt she had no choice but to comply with Oriane's wishes. At the corner of the street, Alaïs managed to throw a final glance over her shoulder. Esclarmonde was standing in the doorway, watching. Quickly, she raised her finger to her lips. A clear warning to say nothing.

CHAPTER 36

In the *donjon*, Pelletier rubbed his eyes and stretched his arms to relieve the stiffness in his bones.

For many hours, messengers had been dispatched from the Château Comtal carrying letters to all of Trencavel's sixty vassals not already making their way to Carcassonne. The strongest of his vassals were independent in all but name, so Pelletier was mindful of the need for Raymond-Roger to persuade and appeal rather than command. Each letter laid bare the threat in the clearest terms. The French were massing on their borders preparing for an invasion the like of which the Midi had never seen. The garrison at Carcassonne had to be strengthened. They must fulfill their obligation of allegiance and come with as many good men as they could muster.

"*A la perfin*," said Trencavel, softening the wax over the flame before setting his seal upon it. At last.

Pelletier returned to his viscount's side, nodding to Jehan Congost. He had little time for Oriane's husband usually, but on this occasion he had to admit Congost and his team of scribes had worked tirelessly and efficiently. Now, as the servant took the final missive to the last waiting messenger, Pelletier gave the *escrivans* permission to leave too. Following Congost's lead, one by one they rose, cracking the joints of their stiff fingers, rubbing tired eyes, gathering up their rolls of parchment, quills and inks. Pelletier waited until he and Viscount Trencavel were alone.

"You should rest, *Messire*," he said. "You need to conserve your strength."

Trencavel laughed. "*Força e vertu*," he said, echoing the words he'd spoken in Béziers. Strength and courage. "Do not worry, Bertrand, I am well. Never better." The viscount put his hand on Pelletier's shoulder. "You, my old friend, do look in need of rest."

"I confess the thought is attractive, *Messire*," he admitted. After weeks of broken nights, he felt every one of his fifty-two years.

"Tonight we will all sleep in our own beds, Bertrand, although I'm afraid that hour is still some way off, for us at least." His handsome face grew solemn. "It is essential I meet with the consuls as soon as possible, as many as can be gathered at such notice."

Pelletier nodded. "Do you have a particular request?"

"Even if all of our vassals heed my call, and come bringing a fair contingent of soldiers with them, we need more men." He spread his hands.

"You wish the consuls to raise a war chest?"

"We need enough to buy the services of disciplined, battle-skilled mercenaries, Aragonese or Catalan, the closer to hand the better."

"Have you considered a raise in taxes? On salt, perhaps? Wheat?"

"It's too soon for that. For now, I would rather try to gather the funds we need through gift than obligation." He paused. "If that fails, then I will consider more stringent measures. How progresses the fortification?"

"All masons and sawyers within the *Ciutat*, Sant-Vincens and Sant-Miquel have been summoned, as well as from the villages to the north. Work to dismantle the choir stalls in the cathedral and the priests' refectory has already begun."

Trencavel grinned. "Bérenger de Rochefort will not like that!"

"The bishop will have to accept it," Pelletier growled. "We need all the timber we can get, as quickly as possible, to start work constructing the *ambans* and *cadefalcs*. His palace and the cloisters are the closest source of wood available."

Raymond-Roger held up his hands in mock surrender. "I'm not challenging your decision," he laughed. "The hoards and brattices are more important than the bishop's comfort! Tell me, Bertrand, has Pierre-Roger de Cabaret arrived yet?"

"Not yet, *Messire*, although he is expected at any time."

"Send him straight to me when he comes, Bertrand. If possible, I would delay speaking with the consuls until he is here. They hold him in high esteem. Any word from Termenès or Foix?"

"None yet, *Messire*."

A while later, Pelletier stood looking out over the Cour d'Honneur, his hands on his hips, pleased at how quickly work was progressing. Already, sounds of sawing and hammering, the rumble of cart wheels delivering wood, nails and tar, the roar of the fires in the smithy filled the courtyard.

Out of the corner of his eye, he noticed Alaïs running across the courtyard toward him. He frowned.

"Why did you send Oriane to fetch me?" she demanded as she came level with him.

He looked bewildered. "Oriane? To fetch you from where?"

"I was visiting a friend, Esclarmonde de Servian, in the southern quarter of the *Ciutat*, when Oriane arrived, accompanied by two soldiers, claiming you had sent her to bring me back to the château." She watched her father's face for signs of a reaction, but saw only bafflement. "Is she speaking the truth?"

"I have not seen Oriane."

"Have you spoken to her as you promised, about her behavior in your absence?"

"I have not yet had the chance."

"I beseech you, do not underestimate her. She knows something, something that could harm you, I am convinced of it."

Pelletier's face turned red. "I will not have you accusing your sister. This has got—"

"The labyrinth board belongs to Esclarmonde," she blurted out.

He stopped as if she had struck him. "What? What do you mean?"

"Simeon gave it, remember, to the woman who came for the second book."

"It cannot be," he said, with such force that Alaïs took a step back.

"Esclarmonde is the other guardian," Alaïs persisted, talking faster before he stopped her. "The sister in Carcassona of whom Harif wrote. She knew about the *merel* too."

"And Esclarmonde has told you she is a guardian?" he demanded. "Because if she has, then—"

"I did not ask her directly," Alaïs replied firmly, then added. "It makes sense, *Paire*. She is exactly the nature of person Harif would choose."

She paused. "What do you know of Esclarmonde?"

"I know of her reputation as a wise woman. And have reason to be grateful to her for the love and attention she has shown to you. She has a grandson, you say?"

"Great-grandson, yes. Sajhë. He is eleven. Esclarmonde comes from Servian, *Messire*. She came to Carcassona when Sajhë was a baby. The timings all fit with what Simeon reported."

"Intendant Pelletier."

They both turned as a servant hurried toward them.

"*Messire,* my lord Trencavel requests your presence immediately in his chambers. Pierre-Roger, Lord of Cabaret, has arrived."

"Where is François?"

"I know not, *Messire*."

Pelletier glowered at him in frustration, then back to Alaïs.

"Tell my lord I will attend him immediately," he said brusquely. "Then find François and send him to me. The man's never where he should be."

"At least speak with Esclarmonde. Hear what she has to say. I will take word to her."

He hesitated, then gave in. "When Simeon comes, then I will listen to what your wise woman has to say."

Pelletier strode up the stairs. At the top, he stopped.

"One thing, Alaïs. How did Oriane know where to find you?"

"She must have followed me from Sant-Nasari, although . . ." she stopped, as she realized Oriane wouldn't have had time to enlist the help of the soldiers and return so quickly. "I don't know," she admitted. "But I am sure of—"

But Pelletier was already gone. As she walked across the courtyard, Alaïs was relieved to see that Oriane was no longer anywhere to be seen. Then she stopped.

What if she went back?

Alaïs picked up her skirts and ran.

As soon as she rounded the corner of Esclarmonde's street, Alaïs saw her fears were justified. The shutters hung by a thread and the door had been ripped clean from its frame.

"Esclarmonde," she cried. "Are you here?"

Alaïs went inside. The furniture lay upturned, the arms of the chair snapped like broken bones. The contents of the chest were thrown carelessly on the ground and the remains of the fire had been kicked over, leaving clouds of soft, gray ash smudged on the floor.

She climbed a few steps up the ladder. Straw, bedding and feathers covered the wooden slats of the sleeping area, everything ripped through. The marks of the pikes and swords as they had plunged through the fabric were easy to see.

The mess in Esclarmonde's consulting room was worse. The curtain had been ripped from the ceiling. Smashed earthenware jars and shattered bowls lay all around in pools of spilled liquids and compresses, brown, white and deep red. Bunches of herbs, flowers and leaves lay trampled into the earth floor.

Had Esclarmonde been here when the soldiers returned? Alaïs ran back outside, in the hope of finding someone who could tell her what had happened. The doors all around were shut and the windows latched.

"Dame Alaïs."

At first she thought she'd imagined it. "Dame Alaïs."

"Sajhë?" she whispered. "Sajhë? Where are you?"

"Up here."

Alaïs stepped out of the shadow of the building and looked up. In the gathering dusk, she could just make out a tumbling mass of light brown hair and two amber eyes peering at her from between the sloped eaves of the houses.

"Sajhë, you'll kill yourself!"

"I won't," he grinned. "I've done it lots of times. I can get in and out of the Château Comtal over the roof too!"

"Well, you're making me dizzy. Come down."

Alaïs held her breath as Sajhë swung himself over the edge and dropped on the ground in front of her.

"What happened? Where's Esclarmonde?"

"*Menina* is safe. She told me to wait until you came. She knew you would."

Glancing over her shoulder, Alaïs drew him into the shelter of a doorway. "What happened?" she repeated urgently.

Sajhë looked unhappily at his feet. "The soldiers came back. I heard most of it from the window. *Menina* feared they would, once your sister had taken you back to the château, so as soon as you were gone, we gathered everything of importance and hid in the cellars." He took a deep breath. "They were very quick. We heard them going from door to door asking for us, questioning the neighbors. I could hear them stamping around over our heads, making the floor shake, but they didn't find the trap door. I was frightened." He broke off, all mischief gone from his voice. "They broke *Menina*'s jars. All her medicines."

"I know," she said softly. "I saw."

"They didn't stop shouting. They said they were looking for heretics, but they were lying, I think. They didn't ask the usual questions."

Alaïs put her fingers under his chin and made him look at her.

"This is very important, Sajhë. Were they the same soldiers who came before? Did you see them?"

"I didn't see."

"Never mind," she said quickly, seeing he was close to tears. "It sounds as if you were very brave. You must have been a great comfort to Esclarmonde." She hesitated. "Was anyone with them?"

"I don't think so," he said miserably. "I couldn't stop them."

Alaïs put her arms around him as the first tear rolled down his cheek.

"Ssh, ssh, it will be well. Don't distress yourself. You did your best, Sajhë. That is all any of us can do."

He nodded.

"Where is Esclarmonde now?"

"There's a house in Sant-Miquel," he gulped. "She says we are to wait there until you tell us Intendant Pelletier is coming."

Alaïs stiffened. "Is that what Esclarmonde said, Sajhë?" she said quickly. "That she is waiting for a message from my father?"

Sajhë looked puzzled. "Is she mistaken then?"

"No, no, it's just that I don't see how . . ." Alaïs broke off. "Never mind. It doesn't matter." She wiped his face with her kerchief. "There. That's better. My father does wish to talk with Esclarmonde, however he is waiting on the arrival of another . . . a friend who is traveling from Besièrs."

Sajhë nodded. "Simeon."

Alaïs looked at him in astonishment. "Yes," she said, smiling now. "Simeon. Tell me, Sajhë, is there anything you don't know?"

He managed to raise a grin. "Not much."

"You must tell Esclarmonde I will tell my father of what has happened, but that she—you both—should stay in Sant-Miquel for the time being."

He surprised her by taking her hand. "Tell her yourself," he said. "She will be glad to see you. And you can talk more. *Menina* said you had to go before you had finished talking."

Alaïs looked down at his amber eyes, shining brightly with enthusiasm. "Will you come?"

She laughed. "For you, Sajhë? Of course. But not now. It is too dangerous. They might be watching the house. I will send word."

Sajhë nodded, then disappeared as quickly as he had come.

"Deman al vèspre," he called out.

CHAPTER 37

Jehan Congost had seen little of his wife since returning from Montpellier. Oriane had not welcomed him home as she should, showing no respect for the hardships and indignities he'd suffered. He had also not forgotten her lewd behavior in their chamber shortly before his departure.

He scuttled across the courtyard, muttering to himself, then into the living quarters. Pelletier's manservant, François, was coming toward him. Congost thought him untrustworthy, inclined to think too much of himself, always skulking around and reporting everything back to his master. There was no business for him to be in the living quarters at this time of day.

François bowed his head. "*Escrivan.*"

Congost did not acknowledge him.

By the time he reached his quarters, Congost had worked himself into a frenzy of righteous indignation. The time had come to teach Oriane a lesson. He could not allow such provocative and deliberate disobedience to go unpunished. He flung open the door without knocking.

"Oriane! Where are you? Come here."

The room was empty. In his frustration at finding her absent, he swept everything off the table. Bowls smashed, the candle holder clattered on the ground. He strode over to the wardrobe and pulled everything out and wrenched the covers off the bed, the bedding with her wanton on them.

Furious, Congost threw himself down on a chair and looked at his handiwork. Torn material, broken bowls, candles. It was Oriane's fault. Her ill behavior had caused this.

He went in search of Guirande to clear up the mess, reflecting on the ways he could bring his errant wife to heel.

The air was humid and heavy when Guilhem emerged from the bathhouse to find Guirande waiting for him, her wide mouth upturned in a slight smile.

His mood darkened. "What is it?"

She giggled and looked at him from beneath a fringe of dark lashes. "Well?" he said harshly. "If you have something to say, say it, or leave me in peace."

Guirande leaned forward and whispered in his ear.

He straightened up. "What does she want?"

"I cannot say, *Messire*. My lady does not confide her wishes to me."

"You're a poor liar, Guirande."

"Is there any message?"

He hesitated. "Tell your mistress I will attend her presently." He pressed a coin into her hand. "And keep your mouth shut."

He watched her go, then walked to the center of the courtyard and sat down beneath the elm tree. He didn't have to go. Why put himself in the way of temptation? It was too dangerous. *She* was dangerous.

He had never intended things to go so far. A winter's night, bare skin wrapped in furs, his blood heated by the mulled wine and the exhilaration of the chase. A kind of madness had come over him. He'd been bewitched.

In the morning, he'd woken with regret and vowed that it would never happen again. For the first few months after his marriage, he had kept his word. Then there had been another such night, then a third and a fourth. She overwhelmed him, took his senses captive.

Now, given how things were, he was even more desperate to ensure no whisper of scandal seeped out. But he must be careful. It was important to finish the affair well. He would keep this appointment only to tell her that their meetings must stop.

He stood up and headed for the orchard before his courage failed. At the gate, he stopped, his hand on the latch, reluctant to go farther. Then he saw her standing beneath the willow tree, a shadowed figure in the fading light. His heart leaped in his chest. She looked like a dark angel, her hair shining like jet in the dusk, tumbling unbraided down her back in twists.

Guilhem took a deep breath. He should turn back. But at that moment, as if she could sense his indecision, Oriane turned and he felt the power of her gaze, drawing him to her. He told his *écuyer* to keep watch at the gate, then stepped through on to the soft grass and walked toward her.

"I feared you would not come," she said as he drew level.

"I cannot stay."

He felt the warm tips of her fingers brush against his, then her hands gentle on his wrist.

"Then I beg your pardon for disturbing you," she murmured, pressing herself against him.

"Someone will see us," he hissed, trying to pull away.

Oriane tilted her face and he caught the scent of her perfume. He tried to ignore the stirrings of desire. "Why do you speak so harshly to me?" she pleaded. "There is no one here to see. I have posted a watch at the gate. Besides, everyone is too busy tonight to pay attention to us."

"They are not so immersed in their own business that they don't notice," he said. "Everybody is watching, listening. Hoping for something they can use to their advantage."

"Such ugly thoughts," she murmured, stroking his hair. "Forget everyone else. For now, think only of me." Oriane was so close now he could feel her heart beating through the thin fabric of her dress. "Why are you so cold, *Messire*? Have I said something to offend you?"

He could feel his resolve weakening as his blood grew hotter. "Oriane, we are sinning. You know it. We wrong your husband and my wife by our unholy—"

"Love?" she suggested and she laughed, a pretty, light sound that turned his heart over. "'Love is not a sin, it is a virtue that makes the bad good and the good better.' You have heard the troubadours."

He found himself holding her beautiful face in his hands.

"That is but a song. The reality of our vows is quite another matter. Or are you minded to misconstrue my meaning?" He took a deep breath. "What I am saying is that we must not meet anymore."

He felt her grow still in his arms. "You no longer want me, *Messire*?" she whispered. Her hair, loose and thick, had fallen across her face, concealing her from him.

"Don't," he said, but his resolve was weakening.

"Is there something I can do to prove my love for you?" she said, her voice so broken, so soft, that he could barely hear her. "If I have not pleased you, *Messire,* then tell me."

He entwined his fingers with hers. "You've done nothing wrong. You're beautiful, Oriane, you are—" he broke off, no longer able to think of the right words to say. The clasp on Oriane's cloak came undone. It fell to the ground, the vibrant, shimmering blue material pooling like water at her feet. She looked so vulnerable, so powerless, it was all he could do not to sweep her up in his arms.

"No," he murmured. "I cannot . . ."

Guilhem tried to summon up Alaïs' face, imagined her steady gaze on him, her trusting smile. Unusual for a man of his rank and position, he believed in his wedding vows. He did not want to betray her. Many nights in the early days of their marriage, watching her as she slept in the quiet of their chamber, he understood he was—he *could* be—a better man because he was loved by her.

He attempted to pull himself free. But now all he could hear was Oriane's voice, mixed up with the spiteful chattering of the household saying how Alaïs had made a fool of him by following him to Béziers. The roaring in his head grew louder, drowning out Alaïs' light voice. Her image grew fainter, paler. She was drifting away from him, leaving him to resist temptation alone.

"I adore you," whispered Oriane, sliding her hand between his legs. Despite his resolution, he closed his eyes, helpless to resist the soft whispering of her voice. It was like the wind in the trees. "Since your return from Besièrs, I have barely caught sight of you." Guilhem tried to speak, but his throat was dry. "They are saying Viscount Trencavel favors you most of all his *chevaliers,*" she said.

Guilhem could no longer distinguish one word from another. His blood pulsed too loud, too heavily in his head, swamping every other sound or sensation.

He laid her down on the ground.

"Tell me what happened between the viscount and his uncle," she murmured in his ear. "Tell me what happened in Besièrs." Guilhem gasped as she wrapped her legs around him and drew him to her. "Tell me how your fortunes have changed."

"It is not a story I can share," he breathed, conscious only of the movement of her body beneath his.

Oriane bit his lip. "You can share it with me."

He shouted her name, no longer caring who might be listening or watching. He did not see the look of satisfaction in her green eyes nor the traces of blood—his blood—on her lips.

Pelletier looked around him, displeased to see neither Oriane nor Alaïs at the supper table.

Despite the preparations for war going on around them, there was an element of celebration in the Great Hall that Viscount Trencavel and his retinue had returned safely home.

The meeting with the consuls had passed off well. Pelletier had no doubt they would raise the funds they needed. Messengers were arriving every hour from the châteaux closest to Carcassonne. So far, no vassal had failed to pledge allegiance and or offer men or money.

As soon as Viscount Trencavel and Dame Agnès had withdrawn, Pelletier excused himself and went out for some air. His indecision lay heavy on his shoulders once more.

"Your brother awaits you in Besièrs, your sister in Carcassona."

Fortune had restored Simeon and the second book more quickly than Pelletier had believed possible. Now, if Alaïs' suspicions were right, it seemed the third book might also be close at hand.

Pelletier's hand drifted to his chest, where Simeon's book lay next to his heart.

Alaïs was woken by a loud clatter as the shutter banged against the wall. She sat up with a jolt, her heart thumping. In her dream, she had been back in the woods outside Coursan, hands bound, struggling to escape from the coarse hood.

She picked up one of the pillows, still warm with sleep, and held it to her chest. Guilhem's scent still hung about the bed, even though it had been more than a week since last he had laid his head beside hers.

There was another bang as the shutter smashed against the wall. The storm was whistling around the towers and skimming the surface of the roof. The last thing she remembered was asking Rixende to bring her something to eat.

Rixende knocked at the door and came timidly into the room.

"Forgive me, Dame. I did not want to wake you, but he insisted I should."

"Guilhem?" she said quickly.

Rixende shook her head. "Your father. He bids you join him at the eastern gatehouse."

"Now? But it must be after twelve?"

"The midnight has not yet struck, Dame."

"Why has he sent you rather than François?"

"I don't know, Dame."

Leaving Rixende to keep watch in her chamber, Alaïs threw her cloak over her shoulders, and hurried downstairs. Thunder was still rumbling over the mountains as she rushed across the courtyard to join him.

"Where are we going?" she shouted over the wind, as they hurried through the East Gate.

"To Sant-Nasari," he said. "To where the *Book of Words* is hidden."

Oriane lay stretched out, like a cat, on her bed, listening to the wind. Guirande had done a good job, both at restoring the room to order and describing the damage her husband had done. What had set him in such a rage, Oriane did not know. Nor did she care.

All men—courtiers, scribes, *chevaliers*, priests—were the same under the skin. Their resolve snapped like twigs in winter for all their talk of honor. The first betrayal was the hardest. After that, it never ceased to amaze her how quickly secrets spewed from their faithless lips, how their actions denied all they claimed to hold dear.

She had learned more than she expected. The irony was, Guilhem didn't even understand the significance of what he had told her tonight. She had suspected Alaïs had followed their father to Béziers. Now she knew she was right. She knew, too, something of what had passed between them on the night of his departure.

The sole reason Oriane had concerned herself with Alaïs' recuperation was in the hope of tricking her sister into betraying their father's confidence, but it had not worked. The only thing of note was Alaïs' distress at the loss of a wooden board from her chamber. She'd talked about it in her sleep as she tossed and turned. So far, despite her best efforts, all attempts to retrieve the board had failed.

Oriane stretched her arms above her head. Even in her wildest dreams, she had never imagined her father possessed something of such power and such influence that men would pay a king's ransom to obtain it. All she had to do was be patient.

After what Guilhem had told her tonight, she realized the board was of less significance than she'd thought. If only they'd had more time, she would have coaxed from him the name of the man her father had met in Béziers. *If* he knew it.

Oriane sat up. François would know. She clapped her hands.

"Take this to François," she said to Guirande. "Let no one see you."

CHAPTER 38

Night had fallen over the Crusader camp.

Guy d'Evreux wiped his greasy hands on the cloth a nervous servant was holding out to him. He drained his cup and glanced toward the abbot of Cîteaux at the head of the table to see if he was ready to rise.

He was not.

Smug and self-satisfied in his white robes, the abbot had positioned himself between the duke of Burgundy and the count of Nevers. The constant jockeying for position that went on between the two and their followers had started before the Host had even left Lyon.

From the glazed look on their faces, it was clear that Arnald-Amalric was once more castigating them. Heresy, the fires of hell, the dangers of the vernacular, all subjects about which he was capable of lambasting an audience for hours.

Evreux had no respect for either of them. He thought their ambitions pathetic—a few gold coins, wine and whores, a little fighting, then home in glory having served their forty days. Only de Montfort, seated a little farther down the table, seemed to be listening. His eyes burned with an unpleasant zeal matched only by the abbot's own fanaticism.

Evreux knew de Montfort by reputation only, even though they were near neighbors. Evreux had inherited land to the north of Chartres with good hunting. A combination of strategic marriage and repressive taxation had ensured the family's wealth had grown steadily over the past fifty years. He had no brothers to challenge his title and no significant debts.

De Montfort's lands were outside Paris, less than two days' ride from Evreux's estate. It was known de Montfort had taken the Cross at the personal request of the duke of Burgundy, but his ambition was common knowledge, as were his piety and courage. He was a veteran of the eastern campaigns in Syria and Palestine, one of the few Crusaders who'd refused to take part in the siege of the Christian city of Zara during the Fourth Crusade to the Holy Land.

Although now in his forties, de Montfort was still as strong as an ox. Moody, introspective, he inspired extravagant loyalty in his men, but was distrusted by many of the barons, who thought him devious and ambitious beyond his status. Evreux despised him, as he despised all those who proclaimed their actions as the work of God.

Evreux had taken the Cross for a single reason. As soon as he had accomplished his purpose, he would return to Chartres with the books he had been hunting half his lifetime. He had no intention of dying on the altar of other men's beliefs.

"What is it?" he growled to the servant who'd appeared at his shoulder.

"There's a messenger come for you, my lord."

Evreux glanced up. "Where is he?" he said sharply.

"Waiting just outside the camp. He would not give his name."

"From Carcassonne?"

"He would not say, my lord."

Bowing briefly to the top table, Evreux excused himself and slipped away, his pale face flushed. He walked quickly between the tents and animals to the glade on the eastern boundary of the camp.

At first, he could pick out only indistinct shapes in the dark between the trees. As he got closer, he recognized the man as a servant of an informer in Béziers.

"Well?" he said, disappointment hardening his voice.

The messenger dropped to his knees. "We found their bodies in woods outside Coursan."

His gray eyes narrowed. "Coursan? They were supposed to be tailing Trencavel and his men. What business had they in Coursan?"

"I cannot say, my lord," he stammered.

At his glance, two more of his men appeared from behind the trees, their hands resting lightly on the hilts of their swords.

"What was found at the site?"

"Nothing, my lord. Surcoats, weapons, horses, even the arrows that killed them were . . . were not there. The bodies had been stripped. Everything was taken."

"So their identity is known?"

The servant took a step back. "The talk within the *castellum* is all of Amaury de Coursan's bravery, not so much of who the men were. There was a girl, the daughter of Viscount Trencavel's steward. Alaïs."

"She was traveling alone?"

"I know not, my lord, but de Coursan escorted her personally to Besièrs. She was reunited with her father in the Jewish quarter. They spent some time there. In a private house."

Evreux paused. "Did they indeed," he murmured, a smile forming on his thin lips. "And the name of this Jew?"

"I was not given his name, my lord."

"Was he part of the exodus to Carcassonne?"

"He was."

Evreux was relieved, although he did not show it. He fingered the dagger in his belt. "Who else knows of this?"

"No one, my lord, I swear. I have told no one."

Evreux struck without warning, plunging the knife clean into the man's throat. Eyes alive with shock, he started to choke as his dying gasps hissed from the wound and blood, pumping red, sprayed the earth around him. The messenger dropped to his knees, clawing frantically at his throat to remove the blade, lacerating his hands, then fell forward.

For a moment, his body lay jerking violently on the stained earth, then he gave a final shudder and was still.

Evreux's face expressed no emotion. He held out his hand, palm up, waiting for one of his soldiers to return his dagger. He wiped it on the corner of the dead man's tunic and returned it to its sheath.

"Get rid of him," Evreux said, prodding the body with the toe of his boot. "I want the Jew found. I want to know if he is still here or is already in Carcassonne. You have a physical likeness?"

The soldier nodded.

"Good. Unless there is news from there, do not disturb me again tonight."

CHAPTER 39

Carcassonne

WEDNESDAY, 6 JULY 2005

Alice swam twenty lengths of the hotel pool and then had breakfast on the terrace watching the rays of the sun creep above the trees. By nine-thirty she was waiting in line for the Château Comtal to open. She paid and was given a leaflet in eccentric English about the history of the castle.

Wooden platforms had been constructed on two sections of the battlements to the right of the gate and around the top of the horseshoe-shaped Tour de Casernes, like a crow's nest on a ship.

A stillness descended over her as she walked through the formidable metal and wooden double doors of the Eastern Gatehouse and into the courtyard.

The Cour d'Honneur was mostly in shadow. Already, there were lots of visitors, like her, wandering around, reading and looking. In the time of the Trencavels an elm tree stood in the center of the courtyard under which three generations of viscounts dispensed justice. There was no sign of it now. In its place were two perfectly proportioned plane trees, the shadow of their leaves cast on the western wall of the courtyard as the sun peeked its face above the battlement walls opposite.

The far northern corner of the Cour d'Honneur was already in full sunlight. A few pigeons nested in the empty doorways and cracks in the walls and abandoned arches of the Tour du Major and the Tour du Degré. A flash of memory—of the feel of a rough wooden ladder, the struts lashed with rope, clambering like an urchin from floor to floor.

Alice looked up, trying to distinguish in her mind between what was in front of her eyes and the physical sensation in the tips of her fingers.

There was little to see.

Then a devastating sense of loss swooped down on her. Grief closed around her heart like a fist.

He lay here. She wept for him here.

Alice looked down. Two raised bronze lines on the ground marked out the site of where a building had once stood. There was a row of letters set into the ground. She crouched down and read that this had been the site of the chapel of the Château Comtal, dedicated to Sainte-Marie. *Sant-Maria.*

Nothing remained.

Alice shook her head, unnerved by the strength of her emotions. The world that had existed eight hundred years ago beneath these sweeping southern skies existed here still, beneath the surface. The sense of someone standing at her shoulder was very strong, as if the frontier between her present and another's past was disintegrating.

She closed her eyes, blocking out the modern colors and shapes and sounds, imagining the people who had lived here, allowing their voices to speak to her.

This once had been a good place to live. Red candles flickering on an altar, flowering hawthorn, hands joined in matrimony.

The voices of other visitors drew Alice back to the present and the past faded as she resumed her circuit. Now she was inside the château, she could see that the wooden galleries constructed along the battlements were open to the air at the back. Set deep into the walls were more of the small, square holes she'd noticed on her tour around the *lices* yesterday evening. The leaflet told her they marked the joists where the upper floors would have been.

Alice glanced at the time and was pleased to see she had enough time to visit the museum before her appointment. The twelfth- and thirteenth-century rooms, all that remained of the original buildings, housed a collection of stone chancels, columns, corbels, fountains and tombs, dating from the Roman period to the fifteenth century.

She wandered, not much engaged. The powerful sensations that swamped her in the courtyard had disappeared, leaving her feeling vaguely restless. She followed the arrows through the rooms until she found herself in the Round Room, rectangular in shape despite its name.

The hairs on the back of her neck stood on end. It had a barrel-vaulted ceiling and the remains of a mural of a battle scene on the two long walls. The sign told her Bernard Aton Trencavel, who had taken part in the First Crusade and fought the Moors in Spain, had commissioned the mural at the end of the eleventh century. Among the fabulous creatures and birds decorating the frieze was a leopard, a zebu, a swan, a bull and something that looked like a camel.

Alice looked up in admiration at the cerulean blue ceiling, faded and cracked, but beautiful still. On the panel to her left, two *chevaliers* were fighting, the one dressed in black, holding a round shield, destined to fall forevermore under the other's lance. On the wall opposite, a battle between Saracen and Christian knights was being played out. It was better preserved and more complete and Alice stepped closer to get a better look. In the center, two *chevaliers* confronted each other, one mounted on an ocher horse, the other, the Christian knight, on a white horse, bearing an almond-shaped shield. Without thinking, she reached up to touch. The attendant tutted and shook her head.

The last place she visited before leaving the castle was a small garden off the main courtyard, the Cour du Midi. It was derelict, with only the memory of the high arched windows left standing. Green tendrils of ivy and other plants wound through the empty columns and cracks in the walls. It had an air of faded grandeur.

As she wandered slowly around, then back into the sun, Alice was filled with a sense, not of grief this time, but regret.

The streets of the Cité were even busier by the time Alice emerged from the Château Comtal.

She still had time to kill before her meeting with the solicitor, so she turned in the opposite direction to last night and walked to the Place St. Nazaire, which was dominated by the basilica. It was the fin-de-siècle facade of the Hotel de la Cité, understated but grand all the same, that caught her eye. Covered by ivy, with wrought-iron gates, arched stained-glass windows and deep red awnings the color of ripe cherries, it whispered of money.

As she watched, the doors slid open, revealing the paneled and tapestried walls, and a woman appeared. Tall, with high cheekbones and immaculately cut black hair held off her face with gold-rimmed sunglasses. Her pale brown sleeveless shirt and matching trousers seemed to shimmer and reflect the light as she moved. With a gold bracelet on her wrist and a choker at her neck, she looked like an Egyptian princess.

Alice was sure she'd seen the woman before. In a magazine or in a film, perhaps on television?

The woman got into a car. Alice watched her until she was out of sight, then walked to the door of the basilica. A beggar stood outside, her hand stretched out. Alice fished in her pocket and pressed a coin into the woman's hand, then went to go in.

She froze, her hand on the door. She felt as if she was caught in a tunnel of cold air.

Don't be stupid.

Alice once more tried to make herself go in, determined not to give in to such irrational feelings. The same terror that had overwhelmed her at Saint-Étienne in Toulouse held her back.

Apologizing to the people behind, Alice stepped out of the line and sank down on a shaded stone ledge beside the north door.

What the hell is happening to me?

Her parents had taught her to pray. When she was old enough to question the presence of evil in the world and found that the Church could provide no satisfactory answers, she'd taught herself to stop. But she remembered the sense of meaning that religion can confer. The certainty, the promise of salvation lying somewhere beyond the clouds that had never entirely left her. When she had time, like Larkin, she always stopped. She felt at home in churches. They evoked in her a sense of history and a shared past which spoke to her through the architecture, the windows, the choir stalls.

But not here.

In these Catholic cathedrals of the Midi she felt not peace but threat. The stench of evil seemed to bleed out of the bricks. She looked up at the hideous gargoyles that leered down at her, their twisted mouths distorted and sneering.

Alice got up quickly and left the square. She kept glancing over her shoulder, telling herself she was imagining it, yet not able to shake the feeling there was someone at her heels.

It's just your imagination.

Even when she left the Cité and started to walk down rue Trivalle toward the main town, she felt just as nervous. No matter what she said to herself, she was sure someone was following her.

The offices of Daniel Delagarde were in rue George Brassens. The brass sign on the wall gleamed in the sunlight. She was a little early for her appointment, so she stopped to read the names before going in. Karen Fleury was about halfway up, one of only two women.

Alice went up the gray stone steps, pushed open the glass double doors and found herself in a tiled reception area. She gave her name to the woman at a highly polished mahogany table and was directed to a waiting area. The silence was oppressive. A rather bucolic looking man in his late fifties nodded to her as she walked in. Copies of *Paris Match*, *Immo Média* and several back editions of French *Vogue* were neatly stacked on a large coffee table in the center of the room. There was an ormolu clock on the white marble mantelpiece and a tall, rectangular glass vase filled with sunflowers in the grate.

Alice sat down in a black leather armchair next to the window and pretended to read.

"Ms. Tanner? Karen Fleury. Good to meet you."

Alice stood up, immediately liking the look of her. In her mid-thirties, Ms. Fleury exuded an air of competence in a somber black suit and white blouse. Her neat blonde hair was clipped short. She wore a gold cross at her neck.

"My funeral clothes," she said, noticing Alice's glance. "Very hot in this weather."

"I can imagine."

She held back the door for Alice to pass through. "Shall we?"

"How long have you been working out here?" asked Alice, as they walked down an increasingly shabby network of corridors.

"We moved here a couple of years ago. My husband's French. Loads of English people are moving down here, all needing solicitors to help them, so it's worked our rather well."

Karen led her into a small office at the back of the building.

"It's great you could come in person," she said, gesturing Alice to a chair. "I'd assumed we'd conduct most of our business over the phone."

"Good timing. Just after I received the letter from you, a friend who's working outside Foix invited me to come and visit her. It seemed too much of an opportunity to ignore." She paused. "Besides, given the size and nature of the bequest, it seemed the least I could do to come in person."

Karen smiled. "Well, it makes things easier from my point of view and will also speed things up." She pulled a brown file toward her. "From what you said on the phone, it didn't sound as if you knew much about your aunt."

Alice pulled a face. "Actually, I'd never heard of her at all. I'd no idea Dad had any living relatives, let alone a half sister. I was under the impression my parents were both only children. There certainly weren't any aunts or uncles around at Christmas or birthdays."

Karen glanced down at her notes. "You lost them some time ago."

"They were killed in a car accident when I was seventeen," she said. "May 1993. Just before I was due to sit my A levels."

"Dreadful for you."

Alice nodded. What more was there to say?

"You have no brothers or sisters?"

"I assumed that my parents left it too late. They were both quite old, relatively speaking, when I was born. In their forties."

Karen nodded. "Well, in the circumstances, I think the best thing is for me to simply go through everything I've got in the file about your aunt's estate and the terms of her will. Once we're done here, you can go and have a look at the house if you'd like to. It's in a small town about an hour's drive from here, Sallèles d'Aude."

"That sounds fine."

"So what I've got here," Karen continued, tapping the file, "is pretty basic stuff, names and dates and so forth. I'm sure when you visit the house you'll get a better sense of her personally from her private papers and effects. Once you've had a look, you can decide if you'd like us to have the house cleared or if you'd rather do it yourself. How much longer are you here?"

246

"Technically until Sunday, although I'm thinking about staying on. There's nothing desperately urgent I need to get back for."

Karen nodded as she glanced at her notes.

"Well, let's start and see how we get on. Grace Alice Tanner was your father's half sister. She was born in London in 1912, the youngest and only surviving child of five. Two other girls died in infancy and the two boys were killed in World War I. Her mother passed away in"—she paused, running her finger down the page until she found the date she was looking for—"1928 after a long illness and the family broke up. Grace had left home by then and her father moved away from the area and subsequently married again. There was one child from that marriage, your father, who was born the following year. So far as I can tell from the records, there appears to have been little or no contact between Miss Tanner and her father—your grandfather—from that point onward."

"I didn't know, but do you think it's likely my father knew he had a half sister?"

"I have no idea. My guess would be that he didn't."

"But Grace clearly knew of him?"

"Yes, although how and when she found out, again I don't know. More to the point, she knew about you. She revised her will in 1993, after your parents' deaths, naming you as her sole beneficiary. By that time, she had been living in France for some time."

Alice frowned. "If she knew about me and about what had happened, I don't understand why she didn't get in touch."

Karen shrugged. "It's possible she thought you wouldn't welcome the contact. Since we don't know what caused the rift in the family, she might have thought your father had prejudiced you against her. In cases such as this, it's not uncommon for an assumption to be made—sometimes rightly so—that any overture would be rejected. Once contact is severed it can be hard to repair the damage."

"You didn't draw up the will, I'm assuming?"

Karen smiled. "No, it was well before my time. But I talked to the colleague who did. He's retired now, but he remembers your aunt. She was very matter-of-fact, no fuss or sentimentality. She knew exactly what she wanted, which was for everything to be left to you."

"So you don't know why she came to be living here in the first place?"

"I'm afraid not." She paused. "From our point of view, it's all relatively straightforward. So, as I said, I think your best bet is to go to the house and look around. You might find out more about her that way. Given you're going to be around for a few days more, we can meet later in the week. I'm in court tomorrow and Friday, but I'd be happy to see you on Saturday morning if that is convenient." She stood up and held out her

hand. "Leave a message with my assistant and let me know what you decide."

"I'd like to visit her grave while I'm here."

"Of course. I'll get the details. If I remember rightfully, the circumstances were unusual." Karen stopped at her assistant's desk on their way
out. "Dominique, *tu peux me trouver le numéro du lot de cimetière de
Madame Tanner. Le cimetière de la Cité. Merci.*"

"In what way unusual?" asked Alice.

"Madame Tanner wasn't buried in Sallèles d'Aude but here in Carcassonne, in the cemetery outside the Cité walls, in the family tomb of a
friend." Karen took the printout from her assistant and skimmed the information. "That's right, I remember now. Jeanne Giraud, a local woman,
although there didn't appear to be any evidence the two women even
knew each other. Madame Giraud's address is also here, along with the
plot details."

"Thank you. I'll be in touch."

"Dominique will show you out," she smiled. "Let me know how you get
on."

CHAPTER 40
Ariège

Paul Authié had expected Marie-Cécile to use the journey into the Ariège to continue last night's discussion or else ask him about the report. But apart from the occasional comment, she said nothing.

In the confined space of the car, he was very physically aware of her. Her perfume caught in his nose, the scent of her skin. Today she was wearing a pale brown sleeveless shirt and matching trousers. Sunglasses concealed her eyes and her lips and nails were the same, burnt red.

Authié shot the cuffs on his shirt, glancing discreetly at his watch. Allowing a couple of hours at the site, then the journey back, they were unlikely to be back in Carcassonne much before the end of the afternoon. It was very frustrating.

"Any news of O'Donnell?" she said.

Authié was startled to hear his thoughts voiced aloud. "Not so far."

"And the policeman?" she said, turning to face him.

"There's no longer a problem."

"Since when?"

"Early this morning."

"Did you learn anything more from him?"

Authié shook his head.

"So long as nothing can be traced back to you, Paul."

"It won't be."

She was silent for a moment, then asked: "And the English woman?"

"She arrived in Carcassonne last night. I've got someone tailing her."

"You don't think she went to Toulouse in order to deposit the ring or the book there?"

"Unless she handed it over to someone inside the hotel, then no. She had no visitors. She talked to no one, either in the street or in the library."

They arrived at the Pic de Soularac just after one o'clock. A wooden palisade had been erected around the car park. The gate was padlocked shut. As arranged, there was no one on duty to witness their arrival.

Authié opened the gate and drove through. The site was unnaturally quiet after the activity of Monday afternoon. An air of abandonment hung about everything. The sides of the tents battened down, the pots and pans and rows of tools neatly labeled.

"Where's the entrance?"

Authié pointed up to where the crime scene tape still flapped in the breeze.

He took a torch from the glove compartment. They climbed up the lower slopes in silence, the oppressive afternoon heat weighing down on them. Authié pointed to the boulder, still lying on its side, like the head of a fallen idol, then led her the final few meters to the cave itself.

"I would like to go in alone," she said as they reached the top.

He was irritated, but didn't show it. He was confident there was nothing in the chamber for her to find. He'd combed every last centimeter of the cave himself. He handed her the torch.

"As you wish," he said.

Authié watched as she disappeared into the tunnel, the beam of light getting weaker and more distant until it vanished altogether.

He wandered away from the entrance, until he was out of earshot.

Even being close to the chamber made him angry. His hand went to the crucifix at his neck, like a talisman to ward off the evil of the place.

"In the name of the Father, the Son and the Holy Ghost," he said, crossing himself. Authié waited until his breathing had returned to normal, before calling his office.

"What have you got for me?"

A look of satisfaction spread across his face as he listened. "At the hotel? Did they speak to one another?" He listened to the reply. "Okay. Keep with her and see what she does."

He smiled and disconnected. Something else to add to his list of questions for O'Donnell.

His secretary had found surprisingly little on Baillard. He had no car, no passport, was not listed at the land registry, no phone, nothing was registered within the system. Even his *numéro de securité sociale* was missing. Officially, he didn't seem to exist. He was a man with no past.

It crossed Authié's mind Baillard might be a disaffected ex-member of the *Noublesso Véritable*. His age, his background, his interest in Cathar history and knowledge of hieroglyphics linked him to the Labyrinth Trilogy.

Authié knew there was a connection. It was just a matter of finding it. He would destroy the cave now, without a moment's hesitation, were it not for the fact that he was still not in possession of the books. He was God's instrument by which the four-thousand-year-old heresy would finally be wiped from the face of the earth. Only when the profane parchments were returned to the chamber would he act. Then he would give everyone and everything to the fire.

The thought that he only had two days in which to find the book spurred him back into action. His gray eyes sharp with conviction, Authié made another call.

"Tomorrow morning," he said. "Have her ready."

Audric Baillard was aware of the click of Jeanne's brown shoes on the gray linoleum as they walked in silence through the hospital in Foix.

Everything else was white. His clothes, the color of chalk, the uniforms of the technicians, their rubber-soled footwear, the walls, the charts, clipboards. Inspector Noubel, crumpled and disheveled, stood out in the sterile environment. He looked as if he'd not changed for days.

A trolley was being pushed up the corridor toward them, its wheels creaking painfully in the hushed environment. They stood back to allow it to pass. The nurse acknowledged the courtesy with a slight bob of her head.

Baillard was aware that they were treating Jeanne with particular care. Their sympathy, no doubt genuine, was mixed with concern at how she would cope with the shock. He gave a grim smile. The young always forgot Jeanne's generation had seen and experienced more than they ever had. War, the Occupation, the Resistance. They had fought and killed and seen their friends die. They were tough. Nothing surprised them except, perhaps, for the dogged resilience of the human spirit.

Noubel came to a halt in front of a large white door. He pushed it open and stood back to let them go in first. Cool air and the sharp smell of disinfectant slid out. Baillard removed his hat and held it to his chest.

The machines were silent now. In the center of the room was the bed, underneath the window, the shape beneath covered by a sheet that hung crooked over the sides.

"They did everything they could," Noubel muttered.

"Was my grandson murdered, Inspector?" asked Jeanne. It was the first time she'd spoken since arriving at the hospital and learning they had arrived too late.

Baillard saw the inspector's hands jerk nervously at his side.

"It's too early to say, Madame Giraud, however—"

"Are you treating it as a suspicious death, Inspector, yes or no?"

"Yes."

"Thank you," she said in the same tone of voice. "That is all I wanted to know."

"If there's nothing else," said Noubel, edging toward the door, "I will leave you to pay your respects. I will be with Madame Claudette in the relatives' room if you need me."

The door closed with a sharp click. Jeanne took a step closer to the bed. Her face was gray and her mouth tight, but her back and shoulders were as straight as ever.

She turned down the sheet. The stillness of death slipped into the room. Baillard could see how young Yves looked. His skin was very white and smooth, free of lines. The top of his head was covered by bandages. Strands of his black hair peeked out around the edges. His hands, the knuckles red and scratched, were folded on his chest like a boy pharaoh.

Baillard watched Jeanne as she bent down and kissed her grandson on the forehead. Then, with a steady hand she covered his face and turned away.

"Shall we?" she said, taking Baillard's arm.

They walked back into the empty corridor. Baillard glanced to left and right, then led Jeanne to a row of institutional plastic chairs fixed to the wall. The silence was oppressive. Automatically they dropped their voices, even though there was no one around to overhear.

"I had been concerned about him for some time, Audric," she said. "I had seen a change in him. He became withdrawn, anxious."

"Did you ask him what was wrong?"

She nodded. "He claimed there was nothing. Just stress, overwork."

Audric laid his hand on her arm. "He loved you, Jeanne. Perhaps there was nothing. Perhaps there was." He paused. "*If* Yves was involved in something wrong, it went against his nature. His conscience was troubled. In the end, when most it mattered, he did the right thing. He sent the ring to you, regardless of the consequences."

"Inspector Noubel asked me about the ring. He wanted to know if I had spoken to Yves on Monday."

"What answer did you give?"

"Truthfully, that I had not."

Audric sighed with relief.

"But you think Yves was being paid to pass on information, don't you, Audric?" Her voice was hesitant, but firm. "Tell me. I would rather hear the truth."

He raised his hands. "How can I speak the truth when I do not know it?"

"Then tell me what you *suspect*. Not knowing—" she broke off—"there is nothing worse."

Baillard imagined the moment the boulder fell across the entrance to the cave, trapping them inside. Not knowing what was happening to her. The smell of the box, the roar of the flames, the soldiers shouting as they ran. Half-remembered places and images. Not knowing if she was alive or dead.

"Es vertat," he said softly. "It is the not knowing that is unbearable." He sighed once again. "Very well. I do believe Yves was being paid for providing information, yes—about the Trilogy primarily, but probably other things as well. I imagine it seemed harmless at first—a telephone call here or there, details about where someone might be, who they might talk to—but soon I suspect they started to ask of him more than he wished to give."

"You say 'they'? Do you know who is responsible then?"

"Speculation, no more," he said quickly. "Mankind does not much change, Jeanne. On the surface, we seem different. We evolve, we develop new rules, new standards of living. Each generation asserts modern values and dismisses the old, priding itself on its sophistication, its wisdom. We appear to have little in common with those that have gone before us." He tapped his chest. "But within these tunics of flesh, the human heart beats the same as it ever did. Greed, desire for power, fear of death, these emotions do not change." His voice softened. "The things that are fine in life, too, do not change. Love, courage, willingness to lay down one's life for what one believes in, kindness."

"Will it ever end?"

Baillard hesitated. "I pray that it will."

Above their heads, the clock marked the passing of time. At the far end of the corridor, hushed voices, footsteps, the squeak of rubber soles on the tiled floor, heard briefly, then gone.

"You will not go to the police?" said Jeanne eventually.

"I do not think it wise."

"You don't trust Inspector Noubel?"

"Benlèu." Perhaps. "Did the police return Yves' personal belongings to you? The clothes he was wearing when he was brought in, the contents of his pockets?"

"His clothes were . . . were beyond saving. Inspector Noubel said there was nothing in his pockets except for his wallet and keys."

"Nothing at all? No *carte d'identité,* no papers, no telephone? Did he not think that odd?"

"He said nothing," she replied.

"And his apartment. Did they find anything there? Papers?"

Jeanne shrugged. "I don't know." She paused. "I asked one of his friends to draw me up a list of who was at the site on Monday afternoon." She handed him a piece of paper with names scribbled on it. "It's not complete."

He looked down. "And this?" he queried, pointing at the name of a hotel.

Jeanne looked. "You wanted to know where the English woman was staying." She paused. "Or, at least, that's the information she gave the inspector."

"Dr. Alice Tanner," he murmured under his breath. After so long, she had come to him. "Then that is where I shall send my letter."

"I could deliver it for you when I return home."

"No," he said sharply. Jeanne looked up in surprise. "Forgive me," he said quickly. "You are kind to offer, but . . . I do not think it wise for you to return home. For now, at least."

"Whyever not?"

"It will not take them long to discover Yves sent the ring to you, if they do not know already. Please, stay with friends. Go away somewhere, with Claudette, anywhere. It is not safe."

To his surprise, she did not argue. "Ever since we got here you've been looking over your shoulder."

Baillard smiled. He had thought he'd kept his anxiety hidden.

"What about you, Audric?"

"It is different for me," he said. "I have been waiting for this moment for . . . for longer than I can say, Jeanne. It is how it is meant to be, for good or ill."

For a moment, Jeanne said nothing.

"Who is she, Audric?" she said softly. "This English girl? Why does she matter so much to you?"

He smiled, but he could not answer.

"Where will you go from here?" she asked in the end.

Baillard caught his breath. An image of his village, as it had once been, came to his mind.

"*Oustâou,*" he replied softly. "I will return home. *A la perfin.*" At last.

CHAPTER 41

Shelagh had grown accustomed to the dark.

She was being held in a stable or animal pen of some sort. There was a sharp, acrid smell of droppings, urine, straw and a sweet sickly odor, like rancid meat. A strip of white light showed under the door, but she couldn't tell if it was late afternoon or early morning. She wasn't even sure what day it was.

The rope around her legs chafed, irritating the raw, broken skin on her ankles. Her wrists were tied together and she was tethered to one of several metal rings attached to the wall.

Shelagh shifted position, trying to get comfortable. Insects were crawling across her hands and face. She was covered in bites. Her wrists were sore where the rope was rubbing and her shoulders were stiff where her arms had been pulled back for so long. Mice or rats scuttled in the straw in the corners of the pen, but she'd become accustomed to them in the same way she'd ceased to notice the pain.

If only she'd rung Alice. Another mistake. Shelagh wondered if Alice had kept trying or given up. If she rang the site house and found she was missing, she'd realize something was wrong, wouldn't she? What about Yves? Brayling had called the police . . .

Shelagh felt her eyes well up. More likely they didn't realize she was missing. Several of her colleagues had announced their intention to take off for a few days until the situation was resolved. Maybe they thought she'd done the same.

She had gone beyond hunger some time back, but she was thirsty. She felt as if she'd swallowed a block of sandpaper. The small amount of water they'd given her had gone and her lips were cracked where she'd licked them, over and over. She tried to remember how long a normal, healthy person could survive without water. A day? A week?

Shelagh heard the scrunch of the gravel. Her heart contracted and adrenaline surged through her, as it did every time she heard a sound outside. Until now, nobody had come in.

She pulled herself up into a sitting position as the padlock was unlocked. There was a heavy clunk as the chain fell, folding up on itself, in spirals of dull chatter, then the sound of the door juddering on its hinges.

Shelagh turned her face away as sunlight, aggressively bright, burst into the gloom of the hut and a dark, stocky man ducked under the lintel. He was wearing a jacket, despite the heat, and his eyes were hidden behind sunglasses. Instinctively, Shelagh shrank back against the wall, ashamed of the tight knot of fear in her stomach.

The man crossed the hut in two strides. He grabbed the rope and dragged her to her feet. He produced a knife from his pocket.

Shelagh flinched, tried to pull away. "*Non,*" she whispered. "Please." She despised the pleading tone of her voice, but couldn't help it. Terror had stripped her pride away.

He smiled as he brought the blade close to her throat, revealing rotten teeth stained yellow from smoking. He reached behind her and cut through the rope tethering her to the wall, then jerked on the rope, pulling her forward. Weak and disorientated, Shelagh lost her balance and dropped heavily to her knees.

"I can't walk. You'll have to untie me." She darted a glance at her feet. "*Mes pieds.*"

The man hesitated a moment, then sawed through the thicker bonds on her ankles as if he was carving meat.

"*Lève-toi. Vite!*" He raised his arm as if he was going to hit her, but then jerked on the rope again, dragging her toward him. "*Vite.*" Her legs were stiff, but she was too scared to disobey. Her ankles were ringed with broken skin, which strained with every step she took, sending pain shooting up her calves.

The ground lurched and pitched beneath her as she stumbled out into the light. The sun was fierce. She felt it burning into her retinas. The air was hot and humid. It seemed to squat over the yard and buildings like a malignant Buddha.

As she walked the short distance from her makeshift prison, one of several disused animal pens she could now see, Shelagh forced herself to look around, realizing it might be the only chance she'd get to figure out where they had taken her. And who *they* were, she added. Despite everything, she wasn't sure.

It had started back in March. He'd been charming, flattering, and apologetic almost for bothering her. He was working on someone else's behalf, he'd explained, someone who wished to remain anonymous. All he'd wanted was for her to make one phone call. Information, nothing more. He was prepared to pay a great deal. A little later, the deal changed: half for the information, more on delivery. Looking back, Shelagh wasn't sure when she'd started to have doubts.

The client didn't fit the normal profile of the gullible collector willing to pay over the odds, no questions asked. For a start, he sounded young. Usually they were like medieval relic hunters, superstitious, susceptible, stupid, obsessed. He was none of these things. That alone should have been enough to set alarm bells ringing.

In retrospect, it seemed absurd she'd never stopped to ask herself why, if the ring and the book were indeed only of sentimental value, he was prepared to go to such trouble.

Any moral objections Shelagh had about stealing and selling artifacts had gone years ago. She'd suffered too much at the hands of old-fashioned museums and elitist academic institutions to believe they were more appropriate custodians of the treasures of antiquity than private collectors. She took the money; they got what they wanted. Everybody was happy. It wasn't her business what happened afterward.

Looking back, she realized she had been frightened long before the second phone call, certainly weeks before she had invited Alice to come to the Pic de Soularac. Then when Yves Biau had made contact and they had compared stories . . . The knot in her chest tightened.

If something happened to Alice it was her fault.

They reached the farmhouse, a medium-sized building, ringed by derelict outbuildings, a garage and a wine barn. The paint on the shutters and the front door was peeling and the empty black windows gaped. Two cars were parked out front, otherwise it was completely deserted.

All around were unbroken views of mountains and valleys. At least she was still in the Pyrenees. For some reason, that gave her hope.

The door stood open, as if they were expected. It was cool inside although, at first glance, deserted. A layer of dust covered everything. It looked like it had once been a hotel or *auberge*. There was a reception desk straight ahead, above which was a row of hooks, all empty, that looked as if they once had held keys.

He jerked the rope to keep her moving. This close, he smelled of sweat, cheap aftershave and stale tobacco. Shelagh caught the sound of voices coming from a room to her left. The door was slightly ajar. She swiveled her eyes to try to see something and caught a glimpse of one man standing in front of the window, his back to her. Leather shoes and legs encased in light summer trousers.

She was forced up the stairs to the second floor, then along a corridor and up a confined, narrow staircase leading to an airless attic that occupied nearly the whole top floor of the house. They came to a halt in front of a door built into the eaves.

He shot the bolts and shoved her in the small of her back, sending her flying forward. She landed heavily, hitting her elbow on the ground, as he slammed the door behind him. Despite the pain, Shelagh threw herself at the door, shouting and pummeling the metal casing with her fists, but it had been specially adapted and there was metal flashing around the edges.

In the end, she gave up and turned round to inspect her new home.

There was a mattress pushed against the far wall. A blanket was folded neatly on it. Opposite the door there was a small window. Metal bars had been hammered across the inside. Shelagh walked stiffly across the room and saw she was now at the back of the house. The bars were solid and didn't move at all when she pulled them. It was a sheer drop down anyway.

There was a small hand basin in the corner, with a bucket next to it. She relieved herself and, with difficulty, turned the taps. The pipes spluttered and coughed like a 40-a-day-smoker but, after a couple of false starts, a thin dribble of water appeared. Cupping her filthy hands, Shelagh drank until her insides hurt. Then she washed as best she could, dabbing the rope burns on her wrists and ankles, which were caked in dry blood.

A little later, he brought her something to eat. More than usual.

"Why I am here?"

He put the tray down in the middle of the room.

"Why have you brought me here? *Pourquoi je suis là?*"

"*Il te le dira.*"

"Who wants to talk to me?"

He gestured at the food. "*Mange.*"

"You'll have to untie me." Then she repeated, "Who? Tell me."

He pushed the tray forward with his foot. "Eat."

When he'd gone, Shelagh fell upon the food. She ate every scrap, even the core and pips of the apple, then returned to the window. The first rays of the sun burst over the crest of the mountain, turning the world from gray to white.

In the distance, she heard the sound of a car, driving slowly toward the farmhouse.

CHAPTER 42

Karen's directions were good. An hour after leaving Carcassonne, Alice found herself on the outskirts of Narbonne. She followed signs to Cuxac d'Aude and Capestang along a pretty road bordered on either side by high bamboo and wild grasses leaping in the winds, sheltering fertile green fields. It was very different from the mountains of the Ariège or the garrigue of the Corbières.

It was nearly two o'clock by the time Alice drove into Sallèles d'Aude. She parked under the lime trees and parasol pines that bordered the Canal du Midi, just down from the lock gates, then wound her way through pretty streets until she arrived at the rue des Burgues.

Grace's tiny three-story house was on the corner and gave straight onto the street. A fairy-tale summer rose, its crimson blooms hanging heavily from the bough, framed the old-fashioned wooden door and large brown shutters. The lock was stiff and Alice had to jiggle the heavy brass key around until she managed to make it turn. She gave a good hard shove and a sharp kick. The door creaked open, scraping over the black and white tiles and free newspapers blocking the door from the inside.

It opened straight into a single downstairs room, the kitchen area to her left and a larger living area to her right. The house felt cold and damp, the maudlin smell of a home long abandoned. The chill air crept around her bare legs like a cat. Alice tried the light switch, but the electricity had been turned off. Picking up the junk mail and circulars and putting it out of the way on the table, she leaned over the sink, opened the window and struggled with the ornate latch to pin back the shutters.

A jug kettle and an old-fashioned cooker with a grill pan at eye level were the closest her aunt had come to mod cons. The draining board was empty and the sink was clean, although a couple of sponges, rigid like dry old bones, were wedged behind the taps.

Alice crossed the room and opened the large window in the living room and pushed back the heavy brown shutters. Straightaway, the sun flooded in, transforming the room. Leaning out, she breathed in the scent of the roses, relaxing under the touch of the hot summer air for a moment, letting it chase her feelings of discomfort away. She felt like an intruder, poking around someone else's life without permission.

Two high-backed wooden armchairs were set at an angle to the fireplace. The chimney surround was gray stone, with a few china ornaments arranged on the mantel, coated with dust. The blackened remains of a fire long cold sat in the grate. Alice pushed with her toe and it collapsed, sending a cloud of fine, gray ash billowing over everything.

Hanging on the wall beside the fireplace was an oil painting of a stone house with a sloping, red-tiled roof, set among fields of sunflowers and vines. Alice peered at the signature scrawled across the bottom right hand corner: BAILLARD.

A dining table, four chairs and a sideboard occupied the back of the room. Alice opened the doors and found a set of coasters and mats, decorated with pictures of French cathedrals, a pile of linen napkins and a canteen of silver cutlery, which rattled loudly as she pushed the drawer shut. The best china—serving dishes, cream jug, dessert bowls, and a gravy boat—was tucked away on the shelves underneath.

In the far corner of the room were two doors. The first turned out to be the utility cupboard—ironing board, dustpan and brush, broom, a couple of coat hooks and lots of carrier bags from Géant tucked one inside the other. The second door concealed the stairs.

Her sandals clipped on the wooden treads as she made her way up into the dark. There was a pink-tiled, functional bathroom straight ahead, with a lump of dried-out soap on the basin and a bone-dry flannel hanging on a hook next to the no-nonsense mirror.

Grace's bedroom was to the left. The single bed was made up with sheets and blankets and a heavy feather eiderdown. On a mahogany bedside cupboard was an ancient bottle of Milk of Magnesia with a white crust around its top, and a biography of Eleanor of Aquitaine by Alison Weir.

The sight of an old-fashioned bookmark marking the page tugged at her heartstrings. She could imagine Grace turning off the light to go to sleep, slipping the bookmark in to save the page. But time had run out. She had died before she had the chance to finish. Feeling uncharacteristically sentimental, Alice put the book to one side. She'd take it with her and give it a home.

In the drawer of the bedside table was a lavender bag, the pink ribbon at its neck bleached with age, as well as a prescription and a box of new handkerchiefs. Several other books filled the ledge beneath. Alice crouched down and tilted her head to one side to read the spines, always unable to resist snooping at what other people had on their shelves. It was much as she would expect. A Mary Stewart or two, a couple of Joanna Trollopes, an old book club edition of *Peyton Place* and a slim volume about the Cathars. The author's name was printed in capital letters: A. S. BAILLARD. Alice raised her eyebrows. The same person who had painted

the picture downstairs? The name of the translator was printed underneath: *J. GIRAUD.*

Alice turned the book over and read the blurb. A translation of the
Gospel of St. John into Occitan, as well as several books about Ancient
Egypt and an award-winning biography of Jean-François Champollion,
the nineteenth-century scholar who'd deciphered the secret of hieroglyphs.

Something sparked in Alice's brain. The library in Toulouse with the
maps and charts and illustrations blinking on the screen in front of her
eyes. *Egypt again.*

The front cover illustration of Baillard's book was a photograph of a
ruined castle, shrouded in purple mist, perched perilously at the top of
a sheer rock. Alice recognized it from postcards and guidebooks as
Montségur.

She opened it. The pages fell open of their own accord about two-
thirds of the way through, where a piece of card had been tucked into the
spine. Alice started to read:

> *The fortified citadel of Montségur is set high on the mountaintop, nearly*
> *an hour's climb up from the village of Montségur. Often hidden by clouds,*
> *three sides of the castle are hewn out of the mountainside itself. It is an ex-*
> *traordinary natural fortress. What remains dates not from the thirteenth*
> *century but from more recent wars of occupation. Yet the spirit of place re-*
> *minds the visitor always of its tragic past.*
>
> *The legends associated with Montségur—the safe mountain—are le-*
> *gion. Some believe it is a solar temple, others that it was the inspiration*
> *for Wagner's Munsalvaesche, his Safe or Grail Mountain in his greatest*
> *work,* Parsival. *Others believed it to have been the final resting place of*
> *the Graal. It has been suggested that the Cathars were the guardians of*
> *the Cup of Christ, together with many other treasures from the Temple of*
> *Solomon in Jerusalem, or perhaps Visigoth gold and other riches from un-*
> *specified sources.*
>
> *While it is believed the fabled Cathar treasure was smuggled away*
> *from the besieged citadel in January 1244, shortly before the final defeat,*
> *that treasure has never been found. Rumors that this most precious of ob-*
> *jects was lost are inaccurate.* *

Alice followed the asterisk to the note to the bottom of the page. Rather
than a footnote there was a quotation from the Gospel of St. John, chap-
ter eight, verse thirty-two: *"And ye shall know the truth, and the truth shall*
make you free."

She raised her eyebrows. It didn't seem to have much relevance with
the text at all.

Alice put Baillard's book with the others, ready to take with her, then crossed to the back bedroom.

There was an old-fashioned Singer sewing machine, incongruously English in the thick-walled French house. Her mother had had one exactly like it and sat sewing for hours on end, filling the house with the comforting thud and rat-a-tat of the treadle.

Alice smoothed her hand over the dust-covered surface. It looked to be in good working order. She opened each of the compartments in turn, finding cotton reels, needles, pins, fragments of lace and ribbon, a card of old-fashioned silver press studs and a box of assorted buttons.

She turned to the oak desk by the window which overlooked a small, enclosed courtyard at the back of the house. The first two drawers were lined with wallpaper but completely empty. The third, surprisingly, was locked, although the key had been left in the keyhole.

With a combination of force and jiggling of the tiny silver key, Alice managed to pull it open. Sitting at the bottom of the drawer was a shoe-box. She lifted it out and placed it on top of the desk.

Everything was very neat inside. There was a bundle of photographs tied up with string. A single letter lay loose on the top. It was addressed to *Mme Tanner* in black, spidery script. Postmarked *Carcassonne, 16 Mars 2001*, the word *PRIORITAIRE* was stamped across it in red. There was no return address on the back, simply a name printed in the same italic script: *Expéditeur Audric S. Baillard.*

Alice slid her fingers inside and pulled out a single sheet of thick cream paper. There was no date or address or explanation, just a poem written in the same hand.

> *Bona nuèit, bona nuèit . . .*
> *Braves amics, pica mièja-nuèit*
> *Cal finir velhada*
> *Ejos la flassada*

A faint memory rippled across the surface of her unconscious mind like a song long forgotten. The words scratched at the top of the steps in the cave. It was the same language, she'd swear, her unconscious mind making the connection her conscious mind could not.

Alice leaned back against the bed. March the sixteenth, a couple of days before her aunt's death. Had she put it in the box herself or had that been left to someone else? Baillard himself?

Putting the poem to one side, Alice undid the string.

There were ten photographs in all, all black and white and arranged in chronological order. The month, place and date were printed on the back in capital letters in pencil. The first photograph was a studio portrait of a serious little boy in school uniform, his hair combed flat with a sharp parting. Alice turned it over. FREDERICK WILLIAM TANNER, SEPTEMBER 1937 was written on the back in blue ink. Different handwriting.

Her heart did a somersault. The same photo of her dad had stood on the mantelpiece at home, next to her parents' wedding photograph and a portrait of Alice herself at the age of six in a smocked party dress with puffed sleeves. She traced the lines of his face with her fingers. It proved, if nothing else, that Grace was aware of her little brother's existence, even if they'd never met.

Alice put it to one side and moved to the next, working her way methodically through the pile. The earliest photograph she found of her aunt herself was surprisingly recent, taken at a summer fête in July 1958.

There was a distinct family resemblance. Like Alice, Grace was petite with delicate almost elfin features, although her hair was straight and gray and cut uncompromisingly short. Grace was looking straight at the camera, her handbag held firmly in front of her like a barrier.

The final photograph was another shot of Grace, a few years older, standing with an elderly man. Alice creased her brow. He reminded her of someone. She turned the photo slightly, to change the way the light fell on the image.

They were standing in front of an old stone wall. There was something formal about the pose, as if they didn't know each other well. From their clothes, it was late spring or summer. Grace was wearing a short-sleeved summer dress, gathered at the waist. Her companion was tall and very thin in a pale summer suit. His face was obscured by the shadow of his panama hat but his speckled, creased hands gave his age away.

On the wall behind them a French street sign was partially visible. Alice peered at the tiny sign and managed to make out the words Rue des Trois Degrès. The caption on the back was in Baillard's spidery handwriting: *AB e GT, junh 1993, Chartres.*

Chartres again. Grace and Audric Baillard, it had to be. And 1993, the year her parents had died.

Putting that to one side too, Alice took out the only item left in the box, a small, old-fashioned book. The black leather was cracked and held together with a corroded brass zip and the words HOLY BIBLE were embossed in gold on the front.

After several attempts, Alice managed to get it open. At first glance, it seemed like any other standard King James edition. It was only when she got three-quarters of the way through that she discovered a hole had been cut through the tissue-thin pages to create a shallow, rectangular hiding place, about ten centimeters by eight.

Inside, folded tight, were several sheets of paper, which Alice carefully opened out. A pale stone disc, the size of a one euro piece, fell out and landed in her lap. It was flat and very thin, made of stone, not metal. Surprised, she balanced it between her fingers. There were two letters engraved on it. *NS*. Compass points? Somebody's initials? Some kind of currency?

Alice turned the disc over. Engraved on the other side was the labyrinth, identical in every respect to the markings on the underside of the ring and on the wall of the cave.

Common sense told her there would be a perfectly acceptable explanation for the coincidence, although nothing came immediately to mind. She looked with apprehension at the papers that had contained the disc. She was nervous of what she might discover, but she was too curious to leave them unopened.

You can't stop now.

Alice began to unfold the pages. She had to stop herself sighing with relief. It was only a family tree. The first sheet was headed ARBRE GÉNÉALOGIQUE. The ink was faded and hard to read in places, but certain words stood out. Most names were in black, but on the second line one name, ALAÏS PELLETIER–DU MAS *(1193–)*, was written in red ink. Alice couldn't decipher the name next to it but, on the line below and set slightly to the right, was another name, SAJHË DE SERVIAN, written in green.

Beside both names was a small, delicate motif picked out in gold. Alice reached for the stone disc and laid it next to the symbol on the page, pattern side up. They were identical.

One by one, she turned the sheets over until she got to the last page. There she found an entry for Grace, her date of death added in a different color ink. Below that and to the side, were Alice's parents.

The final entry was hers. ALICE GRACE *(1976–)* picked out in red ink. Next to it, the labyrinth symbol.

With her knees drawn up to her chin and her arms hooped around her legs, Alice lost track of how long she sat in the still, abandoned room. Finally, she understood. The past was reaching out to claim her. Whether she wished it or not.

CHAPTER 43

The journey back from Sallèles d'Aude to Carcassonne passed in a blur. When Alice got back, the hotel lobby was crowded with new arrivals, so she retrieved her key herself from its hook, and then went upstairs without anyone noticing.

As she went to unlock the door, she noticed it was ajar.

Alice hesitated. She put the shoebox and books down on the ground, then carefully pushed the door open wide.

"Allo? Hello?"

She cast her eyes around the room. Everything inside looked as she'd left it. Still feeling apprehensive, Alice stepped over the things on the threshold, and took a cautious step inside. She stopped. There was a smell of vanilla and stale tobacco.

There was a movement behind the door. Her heart leaped into her mouth. She spun round, just in time to register a gray jacket and black hair reflected in the glass, before she was shoved hard in the chest and sent flying back. Her head smashed against the mirrored door of the wardrobe, setting the wire coat hangers on the rail inside rattling like marbles on a tin roof.

The room went fuzzy around the edges. Everything dancing, out of focus. Alice blinked. She could hear him running away down the corridor. *Go. Quick.*

Alice staggered to her feet and went after him. She hurtled down the stairs and into the lobby, where a large party of Italians were blocking her exit. In panic, she cast her eyes around the busy lobby, just in time to see the man disappearing through the side entrance.

She pushed her way through the forest of people and luggage, clambering over suitcases and luggage, then out after him into the gardens. He was already at the top of the drive. Summoning every last ounce of energy, Alice ran, but he was too fast.

By the time she reached the main road, there was no sign of him. He'd disappeared into the crowds of tourists on their way down from the Cité. Alice put her hands on her knees, trying to get her breath back. Then she straightened up and felt the back of her head with her fingers. Already a bruise was forming.

With a last look at the road, Alice turned and walked back to reception. Apologizing, she went straight to the front of the queue.

"Pardon, mais vous l'avez vu?"

The girl on duty looked put out. "I'll be with you as soon as I've finished with this gentleman," she said.

"I'm afraid this can't wait," she said. "There was someone in my room. He just ran out. A couple of minutes ago."

"Really, *Madame,* if you could just wait a moment—"

Alice raised her voice so that everyone could hear. *"Il y avait quelqu'un dans ma chambre. Un voleur."*

The crowded reception fell silent. The girl's eyes widened. She slid from her stool and disappeared. Seconds later, the owner of the hotel appeared and steered Alice away from the main area.

"What seems to be the problem, *Madame?"* he said in a low voice.

Alice explained.

"The door's not been forced," he said, checking the catch, when he accompanied her back upstairs.

With the proprietor watching from the doorway, Alice checked to see if anything was missing. To her confusion, nothing was. Her passport was still at the bottom of the wardrobe, although it had been moved. The same was true of the contents of her rucksack. Nothing was gone, but it was all in slightly the wrong place. Hardly proof.

Alice checked the bathroom. At last, she'd found something.

"Monsieur, s'il vous plaît," she called out. She pointed at the hand basin. *"Regardez."*

There was a strong smell of lavender where her soap had been hacked into pieces. Her toothpaste also had been cut open and the contents squeezed out. *"Voilà. Comme je vous ai dit."* As I told you.

He looked concerned, but doubtful. Did Madame want him to call the police? He would ask the other guests if they had noticed anything, of course, but since nothing seemed to be missing . . . ? He left the sentence hanging.

The shock suddenly kicked in. This wasn't a random burglary. Whoever it was had been looking for something specific, something they believed she had.

Who knew she was here? Noubel, Paul Authié, Karen Fleury and her staff, Shelagh. To her knowledge, no one else.

"No," she said quickly. "No police. Since nothing's gone. But I want to move to another room." He started to protest that the hotel was full, then stopped when he saw the look on her face.

"I'll see what I can do."

.   .   .

Twenty minutes later, Alice was installed in a different part of the hotel.

She was nervous. For the second or third time, she checked the door was locked and the windows fastened. She sat on the bed surrounded by her things, trying to decide what to do. Alice got up, walked around the tiny room, sat down again, got up again. She was still not certain she shouldn't move to a new hotel.

What if he comes back tonight?

An alarm went off. Alice jumped out of her skin, before realizing it was only her phone, ringing in her jacket pocket.

"Allo, oui?"

It was a relief to hear Stephen's voice, one of Shelagh's colleagues from the dig. "Hi, Steve. No, sorry. I only just got in. I haven't had time to check my messages yet. What's up?"

As she listened, the color drained from her face as he told her the dig was being closed down.

"But why? What possible reason did Brayling give?"

"He said it wasn't up to him."

"Just because of the skeletons?"

"The police didn't say."

Her heart started to thump. "They were there when Brayling announced this?" she said.

"They were partly there about Shelagh," he said, then stopped. "I was just wondering, Alice, if you'd heard from her at all since you left."

"Not a thing since Monday. I tried her several times yesterday, but she's not returned any of my calls. Why?"

Alice found herself on her feet as she waited for Stephen to answer.

"She seems to have gone off," he said in the end. "Brayling's inclined to put a sinister interpretation on it. He suspects her of stealing something from the site."

"Shelagh wouldn't do that," she exclaimed. "No way. She's not the sort to . . ."

But as she was speaking, the thought of Shelagh's angry white face came back to her. She felt disloyal, but Alice was suddenly less confident.

"Is this what the police think too?" she demanded.

"I don't know. It's just all a bit odd," he said vaguely. "One of the policemen at the site on Monday has been killed by a hit-and-run driver in Foix," he continued. "It was in the paper. It appears Shelagh and he knew each other."

Alice sank down on to the bed. "Sorry, Steve. I'm finding this hard to take in. Is anybody looking for her? Doing anything at all?"

"There is one thing," he said tentatively. "I'd do it myself, but I'm heading home first thing tomorrow. No point hanging about."

"What is it?"

"Before the excavation started, I know Shelagh was staying with friends in Chartres. It did occur to me that she might have gone there, just forgotten to let anyone know."

It seemed a long shot to Alice, but it was better than nothing.

"I did call the number. A boy answered and claimed not to have heard of Shelagh, but I'm sure it's the number she gave me. I had it stored in my phone."

Alice picked up a pencil and paper. "Give it to me. I'll have a go," she said, poised to write.

Her hand froze.

"I'm sorry, Steven." Her voice sounded hollow, as if she was speaking from a long way away. "Run that by me again."

"It's 02 68 72 31 26," he repeated. "And you'll let me know if you find out anything?"

It was the number Biau had given her.

"Leave it with me," she said, barely aware of what she was saying. "I'll keep in touch."

Alice knew she should call Noubel. Tell him about her non-burglary and her encounter with Biau, but she hesitated. She wasn't sure she could trust Noubel. He'd done nothing to stop Authié.

She reached into her rucksack and pulled out her roadmap of France. *The idea's crazy. It's an eight-hour drive at least.*

Something was niggling at the back of her mind. She went back to the notes she'd made in the library.

In the mountain of words about Chartres Cathedral, there had been a passing reference to the Holy Grail. There, too, was a labyrinth. Alice found the paragraph she was looking for. She read it through twice, to make sure she hadn't misunderstood, then she jerked the chair out from under the desk and sat down with the book by Audric Baillard and opened it at the page marked.

> *Others believed it to have been the final resting place of the Graal. It has been suggested that the Cathars were the guardians of the Cup of Christ . . .*

The Cathar treasure was smuggled away from Montségur. To the Pic de Soularac? Alice turned to the map at the front of the book. Montségur to the Sabarthès Mountains was not far. What if the treasure was hidden there?

What connects Chartres and Carcassonne?

In the distance, she heard the first growls of thunder. The room was now bathed in a strange orange light from the street lamps outside bouncing off the underside of the night clouds. A wind had blown up, rattling the shutters and sending bits of rubbish scuttling across the car parks.

As Alice drew the curtains the first heavy drops of rain started to fall, exploding like spots of black ink on the windowsill. She wanted to leave now. But it was late and she didn't want to risk driving through the storm.

She locked the windows and doors, set her alarm, then climbed fully clothed into bed to wait for the morning.

At first, everything was the same. Familiar, peaceful. She was floating in the white weightless world, transparent and silent. Then, like the trap door clattering open beneath the gallows, there was a sudden lurch and she fell down through the open sky toward the wooded mountainside rushing up to meet her.

She knew where she was. At Montségur, in early summer.

Alice started to run as soon as her feet hit the ground, stumbling along a steep, rough forest track between two columns of high trees. The trees were dense and tall and towered above her. She grabbed at the branches to slow herself, but her hands went straight through and clumps of tiny leaves came away in her fingers, like hair on a brush, staining the tips green.

The path sloped away beneath her feet. Alice was aware of the crunch of stone and rock, which had replaced the soft earth, moss and twigs on the track higher up the mountain. Still, there was no sound. No birds singing, no voices calling, nothing but her own ragged breathing.

The path twisted and coiled back on itself, sending her scuttling this way and that, until she rounded the corner and saw the silent wall of fire blocking the path ahead. She put her hands up to shield her face from the billowing, puffing, red and orange and yellow flames that whipped and swirled in the air, like reeds under the surface of a river.

Now the dream was changing. This time rather than the multitude of faces taking shape in the flames, there was only one, a young woman with a gentle yet forceful expression, reaching out and taking the book from Alice's hand.

She was singing, in a voice of spun silver.

"Bona nuèit, bona nuèit."

This time, no chill fingers grabbed her ankles or shackled her to the earth. The fire no longer claimed her. Now she was spiraling through the air like a wisp of smoke, the woman's thin, strong arms embracing her, holding her tight. She was safe.

"Braves amics, pica mièja-nuèit."

Alice smiled as together they soared higher and higher toward the light, leaving the world far beneath.

CHAPTER 44
Carcassona

JULHET 1209

Alaïs rose early, awoken by the sounds of sawing and banging in the courtyard below. She looked out of the window at the wooden galleries and brattices being constructed over the walls of the Château Comtal.

The impressive wooden skeleton was taking shape quickly. Like a covered walkway in the sky, it provided the perfect vantage point from which the archers could rain down a hail of arrows on the enemy in the unlikely event that the walls of the Cité itself were breached.

She dressed quickly and ran down to the courtyard. In the smithy the fires were roaring. Hammers and anvils rang out as weapons were sharpened and shaped; sappers yelled to one another in short, sharp bursts, as the axles, ropes and counterweights of the *pèireras*, the ballistas, were prepared.

Standing outside the stable, Alaïs saw Guilhem. Her heart turned over. *Notice me.* He did not turn and he did not look up. Alaïs raised her hand to call out, but then cowardice overcame her and she let her arm drop back to her side. She would not humiliate herself by begging for his affection when he was unwilling to give it.

The scenes of industry within the Château Comtal were reproduced in the Cité. Stone from the Corbières was being piled high in the central square, ready for the ballistas and the catapults. There was an acrid stench of urine from the tannery where animal hides were being prepared to protect the galleries from fire. A steady procession of carts was coming in through the Porte Narbonnaise bringing food to support the Cité: salted meat from La Piège and the Lauragais, wine from the Carcassès, barley and wheat from the plains, beans and lentils from the market gardens of Sant-Miquel and Sant-Vicens.

There was a sense of pride and purpose behind the activity. Only the clouds of noxious black smoke over the river and marshes to the north—where Viscount Trencavel had ordered the mills to be burned and the crops destroyed—served as a reminder of how imminent and real was the threat.

Alaïs waited for Sajhë at the agreed meeting place. Her mind was full of questions she wished to ask Esclarmonde, that swooped in and out of her head, first one, then another, like birds at a river. By the time Sajhë did arrive, she was tongue-tied with anticipation.

She followed him through unnamed streets into the suburb of Sant-Miquel, until they arrived at a low doorway set hard by the outer walls. The sound of men digging trenches to prevent the enemy getting close enough to mine the walls was very loud. Sajhë had to shout to make himself heard.

"*Menina* is waiting inside," he said, his face suddenly solemn.

"Are you not coming in?"

"She told me to bring you, then go back to the château to find Intendant Pelletier."

"Seek him in the Cour d'Honneur," she said.

"Okay," he said, his grin back in place. "See you later."

Alaïs pushed open the door and called out, looking forward to seeing Esclarmonde, then checked her step. In the shadows, she could see a second figure sitting on a chair in the corner of the room.

"Come in, come in," said Esclarmonde, the smile showing in her voice. "I believe you already know Simeon."

Alaïs was astonished. "Simeon? Already?" she cried with delight, rushing to him and taking his hands. "What news? When did you arrive in Carcassona? Where are you lodging?"

Simeon gave a deep, rich laugh. "So many questions! Such haste to know everything and so quickly! Bertrand said that, as a child, you never stopped asking questions!"

Alaïs acknowledged the truth of this with a smile. She slid along the bench at the table and accepted the cup of wine Esclarmonde offered, listening as Simeon continued to talk to Esclarmonde. Already there seemed to be a bond, an ease between them.

He was a skillful storyteller, weaving tales of his life in Chartres and Béziers with memories of his life in the Holy Land. The time passed quickly as he talked of the hills of Judea in springtime, told them of the plains of Sephal covered with lilies, yellow and purple irises and pink almond trees, which stretched like a carpet to the ends of the earth. Alaïs was captivated.

The shadows lengthened. As they did so, the atmosphere changed, without Alaïs being aware it was happening. She was conscious of a nervous fluttering in her stomach, an anticipation of what was to come. She wondered if this was how Guilhem or her father felt on the eve of a battle. This sense of time hanging in the balance.

She glanced across at Esclarmonde, her hands folded in her lap and her face serene. She looked composed and poised.

"I'm sure my father will be here soon," she said, feeling responsible for his continued absence. "He gave me his word."

"We know," said Simeon, patting her hand. His skin was as dry as parchment.

"We may not be able to wait much longer," said Esclarmonde, looking to the door that remained firmly shut. "The owners of this house will soon return."

Alaïs intercepted a look between them. Unable to bear the tension any longer, she leaned forward.

"Yesterday, you did not answer my question, Esclarmonde." She was amazed at how steady she sounded. "Are you also a guardian? Is the book my father seeks in your safe-keeping?"

For a moment, her words seemed to hang in the air between them, claimed by no one. Then, to Alaïs' surprise, Simeon chuckled.

"How much did your father tell you about the *Noublesso*?" he said, his black eyes twinkling.

"That there were always five guardians, pledged to protect the books of the Labyrinth Trilogy."

"And did he explain why there were five?"

Alaïs shook her head.

"Always, the *Navigatairé,* the leader, is supported by four initiates. Together, they represent the five points of the human body and the power of the number five. Each guardian is chosen for their fortitude, their determination and their loyalty. Christian, Saracen, Jew, it is our soul, our courage that matters, not blood or birth or race. It also reflects the nature of the secret we are pledged to protect, which belongs to every faith and to none." He smiled. "For more than two thousand years, the *Noublesso de los Seres* has existed—although not always under that name—to watch over and protect the secret. Sometimes our presence has been hidden, other times we have lived openly."

Alaïs turned to Esclarmonde. "My father is unwilling to accept your identity. He cannot believe it."

"It flies in the face of his expectation."

"It was ever thus with Bertrand," chuckled Simeon.

"He would not have anticipated the fifth guardian being a woman," Alaïs said, coming to her father's defense.

"It was less remarkable in times gone past," said Simeon. "Egypt, As-syria, Rome, Babylon, these ancient cultures of which you have heard tell, accorded more respect to the female state than these dark times of ours."

Alaïs thought a moment. "Do you think Harif is right to believe the books will be safer in the mountains?" she asked.

Simeon raised his hands. "It is not for us to seek the truth or to question what will or will not be. Our task is simply to guard the books and to protect them from harm. To make sure that they are ready when they are needed."

"Which is why Harif chose your father to carry the books, rather than either of us," continued Esclarmonde. "His position makes him the most suitable *envoi*. He has access to men and horses, he can travel more freely than either of us."

Alaïs hesitated, not wishing to be disloyal to her father. "He is reluctant to leave the viscount. He is torn between his old and his new loyalties."

"We all feel such conflicts," said Simeon. "We all have found ourselves struggling to choose what path to take for the best. Bertrand is fortunate to have lived so long without having to make his choice." He took her hands between his. "Bertrand cannot delay, Alaïs. You must encourage him to fulfill his responsibilities. That Carcassona has not fallen before does not mean that it cannot."

Alaïs felt their eyes upon her. She stood up and walked over to the hearth. Her heart was racing as an idea took shape in her mind.

"Is it permitted for another to act in his stead?" she said in a level voice.

Esclarmonde understood. "I do not think your father would allow it. You are too precious to him."

Alaïs turned back to face them. "Before he left for Montpelhièr, he believed me equal to the task. In principle, he has already given me leave."

Simeon nodded. "That's true, but the situation changes daily. As the French approach the borders of Viscount Trencavel's lands, the roads every day become more dangerous, as I saw for myself. It will not be long before it is too perilous to travel at all."

Alaïs held her ground. "But I will be going in the opposite direction," she said, looking from one to the other. "And you did not answer my question. If the traditions of the *Noublesso* do not prohibit me taking this burden from my father's shoulders, then I offer my service in his place. I am more than capable of protecting myself. I am an excellent rider, skilled with sword and bow. No one would ever suspect me of—"

Simeon raised his hand. "You misinterpret our hesitation, child. I certainly do not doubt your courage or your resolve."

"Then give me your blessing."

Simeon sighed and turned to Esclarmonde. "Sister, what say you? If Bertrand agrees, of course."

"I beseech you, Esclarmonde," Alaïs pleaded, "give your voice to my request. I know my father."

"I can promise nothing," she said, in the end, "but I will not argue against you." Alaïs let a smile break out on her face. "But you must abide by his decision," Esclarmonde continued. "If he will not give his permission, you must accept it."

He can't say no. I won't let him.

"I will obey him, of course," she said.

The door opened and Sajhë burst into the room, followed by Bertrand Pelletier.

He embraced Alaïs, greeted Simeon with much relief and affection, and then paid more formal respects to Esclarmonde. Alaïs and Sajhë fetched wine and bread while Simeon explained what had so far passed between them.

To Alaïs' surprise, her father listened in silence and without comment. Sajhë was wide-eyed to begin with, but soon grew sleepy and curled up against his grandmother. Alaïs took no part in the conversation, knowing Simeon and Esclarmonde would plead her case better than she, but from time to time she threw a look at her father.

His face was gray and lined and he looked exhausted. She could see he did not know what to do.

Finally, there were no more words to speak. An expectant hush fell over the tiny room. Each of them waiting, none sure of the way the decision would go.

Alaïs cleared her throat. "So, *Paire*. What is your decision? Will you give me leave to go?"

Pelletier sighed. "I do not want you put at risk."

Her spirits sank. "I know that, and I am grateful for your love of me. But I want to help. I am capable of it."

"I have a suggestion that might yet satisfy you both," said Esclarmonde quietly. "Allow Alaïs to travel ahead with the Trilogy, but part of the way only, as far as Limoux, say. I have friends there who can provide safe lodging. When your work here is completed and Viscount Trencavel can spare you, you can join her and make the journey to the mountains together."

Pelletier scowled. "I do not see this helps at all. The madness of undertaking such a voyage during these unsettled times will draw attention, which is the one thing we most wish to avoid. Besides, I cannot say how long my responsibilities will keep me in Carcassona."

Alaïs' eyes flashed. "That's easy. I could publish it that I was fulfilling a private pledge made on the occasion of my marriage," she said, thinking as she went along. "I could say I wished to make a gift to the abbot of Sant-Hilaire. From there, it is no distance to Limoux."

"This sudden display of piety will convince no one," said Pelletier, with a sudden flash of humor, "least of all your husband."

Simeon shook his finger. "It is an excellent idea, Bertrand. No one would challenge such a pilgrimage at this time. Besides, Alaïs is the daughter of the steward of Carcassona. No one would dare challenge her intentions."

Pelletier shifted in his chair, his face stubborn and set. "I am still of the opinion that the Trilogy is best protected here, within the *Ciutat*. Harif cannot be as aware of the current situation as we are. Carcassona will not be taken."

"All cities, however strong, however indomitable, can fall. You know this. The *Navigatairé*'s instructions are to deliver the books to him in the mountains." He fixed Pelletier with his black eyes. "I understand you do not feel you can abandon Viscount Trencavel at this time. You have said so and we accept it. It is your conscience that speaks to you, for good or ill." He paused. "However, if not you, then another must go in your place."

Alaïs saw how painfully her father struggled to reconcile his warring emotions. Moved, she reached out and put her hand over his. He did not speak, but he did acknowledge her gesture by squeezing her fingers.

"Aquò es vòstre," she said softly. Let me do this for you.

Pelletier let a long sigh come from his lips. "You put yourself in great danger, *Filha*." Alaïs nodded. "And yet still you wish to do this?"

"It will be an honor to serve you in this way."

Simeon placed his hand on Pelletier's shoulder. "She is brave, this daughter of yours. Steadfast. Like you, my old friend."

Alaïs hardly dared breathe.

"My heart counsels against this," Pelletier said at last. "My head speaks otherwise, so . . ." He paused, as if dreading what he was about to say. "If your husband and Dame Agnès will release you—and Esclarmonde will go as chaperone—then I give my permission."

Alaïs leaned across the table and kissed her father on the lips.

"You have chosen wisely," said Simeon, beaming.

"How many men can you spare us, Intendant Pelletier?" asked Esclarmonde.

"Four men-at-arms, six at most."

"And how soon can arrangements be made?"

"Inside a week," Pelletier replied. "To act too quickly will attract attention. I must seek permission from Dame Agnès and you from your husband, Alaïs." She opened her mouth to say Guilhem would hardly notice her gone, then thought better of it. "For this plan of yours to work, *Filha*, etiquette must be observed." All indecision gone from his face and manner, he stood to take his leave. "Alaïs, return to the Château Comtal and seek out François. Inform him of your plans, in the barest terms, and tell him to wait upon me presently."

"Are you not coming?"

"Presently."

"Very well. Should I take Esclarmonde's book with me?"

Pelletier gave a wry smile. "Since Esclarmonde is to accompany you, Alaïs, I feel sure the book will be safe with her a while longer."

"I didn't mean to suggest . . ."

Pelletier patted the pouch beneath his cloak. "Simeon's book, however." He reached beneath his cloak and withdrew the sheepskin chemise Alaïs had seen briefly in Besièrs as Simeon handed it over. "Take it to the château. Sew it into your traveling cloak. I will fetch the *Book of Words* by and by."

Alaïs took the book and put it into her purse, then raised her eyes to her father. "Thank you, *Paire,* for putting your faith in me."

Pelletier blushed. Sajhë scrambled to his feet. "I'll make sure Dame Alaïs gets home safely," he said. Everybody laughed.

"Mind you do, *gentilòme*," said Pelletier, slapping him on the back. "All our hopes rest on her shoulders."

"I see your qualities in her," said Simeon as they walked toward the gates that led out of Sant-Miquel to the Jewish suburb beyond. "She's courageous, stubborn, loyal. She does not give in easily. Is your eldest daughter as much like you?"

"Oriane favors her mother," he said shortly. "She has Marguerite's looks and temperament."

"It often happens like that. Sometimes the child is a good match to one parent, sometimes the other." He paused. "She is married to Viscount Trencavel's *escrivan*?"

Pelletier sighed. "It is not a happy marriage. Congost is not young and is intolerant of her ways. But for all that, he is a man of position within the household."

They walked a few steps more in silence. "If she favors Marguerite, she must be beautiful."

"Oriane has charm and a grace that draws the eye. Many men would court her. Some make no secret of it."

"Your daughters must be of great comfort to you."

Pelletier shot a glance at Simeon. "Alaïs, yes." He hesitated. "I dare say I am to blame, but I find Oriane's company less . . . I try to be even-handed, but I fear there is little love lost between them."

"A pity," Simeon murmured.

They had arrived at the gates. Pelletier came to a halt.

"I wish I could persuade you to stay within the *Ciutat*. In Sant-Miquel at the very least. If our enemies are at hand, I will not be able to protect you outside the walls—"

Simeon put his hand on Pelletier's arm. "You worry too much, my friend. My role is over now. I gave you the book entrusted to me. The other two books are also within these walls. You have Esclarmonde and Alaïs to help you. What would anyone have with me now?" He fixed his friend with his dark glittering eyes. "My place is with my own people."

There was something in Simeon's tone that alarmed Pelletier.

"I will not accept there is anything final in this leave-taking," he said fiercely. "We'll be drinking wine together before the month is out, mark my words."

"It's not your words I mistrust, my friend, but the swords of the French."

"By next spring I wager it will all be over. The French will have limped home with their tails between their legs, the count of Toulouse will be seeking a new alliance, and you and I will be sitting reminiscing over our lost youth by the fire."

"Pas a pas, se va luènh," said Simeon, embracing him. "And give my fond regards to Harif. Tell him I'm still waiting for that game of chess he promised me thirty years ago!"

Pelletier raised his hand in farewell as Simeon walked out through the gates. He did not look back.

"Intendant Pelletier!"

Pelletier carried on looking into the crowd of people making their way toward the river, but he could no longer distinguish Simeon.

"Messire!" the messenger, red-faced and breathless, repeated.

"What is it?"

"You are needed at the Porte Narbonnaise, *Messire.*"

CHAPTER 45

Alaïs pushed open the door to her chamber and ran in.

"Guilhem?"

Even though she needed solitude and had no expectation it would be otherwise, she still was disappointed to find the room empty.

Alaïs locked the door, unhooked her purse from her waist, laid it on the table and removed the book from its protective covering. It was the size of a lady's psalter. The outer wooden boards were covered with leather, completely plain and a little worn at the corners.

Alaïs undid the leather ties and let the book fall open in her hands, like a butterfly displaying its wings. The first page was empty apart from a tiny chalice in gold leaf in the center, sparkling like a jewel on the heavy cream parchment. It was no bigger than the pattern that appeared on her father's ring or the *merel* she'd had so briefly in her possession.

She turned the page. Four lines of black script looked up at her, written in an ornate and elegant hand.

Around the edges were pictures and symbols, a repeated pattern like a running stitch around the hem of a cloak. Birds, animals, figures with long arms and sharp fingers. Alaïs caught her breath.

These are the faces and figures of my dreams.

One by one, she turned the pages. Each was covered with lines of black script, with nothing on the reverse side. She recognized words of Simeon's language, although she didn't understand it. Most of the book was written in her own language. The first letter of each new page was illuminated, in red, blue or yellow with gold surrounds, but otherwise they were plain. No illustrations in the margins, no other letters picked out within the body of the text and the words following on one from the other with few gaps or indications to show where one thought ended and another began.

Alaïs reached the parchment concealed in the center of the book. It was thicker and darker than the pages surrounding it, goatskin rather than vellum. Rather than symbols or illustrations, there were only a few words, accompanied by rows of numbers and measurements. It looked like some sort of a map.

She could just pick out tiny arrows pointing in different directions. A few of them were gold, but mostly they were black.

In the beginning of time

In the land of Egypt

The master of secrets

Gave words and script

Alaïs tried reading the page from the top from left to right, but that didn't make sense and she came to a dead end. Next she tried deciphering the page from bottom to top, right to left, like a stained-glass window in a church, but that didn't make sense either. Finally she read alternate lines or picked out words from every third line, but still understood nothing.

Look beyond the visible images to the secrets concealed beneath.

She thought hard. To each guardian according to their skills and knowledge. Esclarmonde had her ability to heal and cure, so to her Harif had entrusted the *Book of Potions*. Simeon was a scholar of an ancient Jewish system of numbers, to him the *Book of Numbers*. *This book.*

What had led Harif to choose her father as the guardian of the *Book of Words*?

Deep in thought, Alaïs lit the lamp and went to her nightstand. She took out some parchment, ink and a quill. Pelletier had been determined his daughters should be taught to read and write, having learned the value of these things in the Holy Land. Oriane cared only for accomplishments appropriate to a lady of the household—dancing, singing, falconry, and embroidery. Writing was, as she never stopped staying, for old men and priests. Alaïs, however, had grasped the opportunity with both hands. She had been quick to learn and, although there were few opportunities for her to use her skills, she held them close to her.

Alaïs spread her writing materials on the table. She didn't understand the parchment, nor could she hope to replicate the exquisite workmanship, colors and style. But she could at least make a copy while she had the chance.

It took her some time, but at last she was finished and laid the parchment copy on the table to dry. Then, aware of how her father might return to the Château Comtal at any moment with the *Book of Words*, Alaïs quickly turned her attention to concealing the book as her father had suggested.

Her favorite red cloak was no good. The material was too delicate and the hem bulged. Instead she picked a heavy brown cloak. It was a winter garment, intended to be worn for hunting, but that couldn't be helped. With expert fingers, Alaïs unpicked the *passementerie* at the front until she had made a gap wide enough to squeeze the book inside. Next, she took the thread Sajhë had brought her from the market, which exactly matched the color of the material, and sewed the book in place at the back, secure.

Alaïs held the cloak up and swung it over her shoulders. It was uneven at present but, once she had her father's book too, it would be better balanced.

She had only one more task to accomplish. Leaving the cloak draped over the chair, Alaïs went back to the table to see if the ink was dry. Mindful she could be interrupted at any moment, she folded the parchment and slipped it inside a lavender posy. She stitched the opening shut, so that no one could come upon it by accident, then placed it back under her pillow.

Alaïs looked around, satisfied with what she had accomplished, and started to clear up her sewing materials.

There was a knock at the door. Alaïs rushed to open it, expecting to see her father. Instead, she found Guilhem standing on the threshold, unsure of his welcome. The familiar half-smile, the little-boy-lost eyes.

"May I come in, Dame?" he asked softly.

Her instinct was to throw her arms about him. Caution held her back. Too much had been said. Too little forgiven.

"May I?"

"It is your chamber also," she said lightly. "I would not deny you admittance."

"So formal," he said, closing the door behind him. "I would that pleasure not duty made you answer thus."

"I am . . ." she hesitated, thrown off balance by the intense longing sweeping through her. "I am happy to see you, *Messire*."

"You look tired," he said, reaching to touch her face.

How easy it would be to give in. To give all of herself to him.

She closed her eyes, almost feeling his fingers moving over her skin. A caress, as light as a whisper and as natural as breathing. Alaïs imagined herself leaning toward him, letting him hold her up. His presence made her dizzy, made her feel weak.

I cannot. Must not.

Alaïs forced open her eyes and took a step back. "Don't," she whispered. "Please don't."

Guilhem took her hand and held it between his. Alaïs could see he was nervous.

"Soon . . . unless God intervenes, we will face them. When the time comes, Alzeu, Thierry, the others, we all will ride out. And might not return."

"Yes," she said softly, wishing some of the life would return to his face.

"Since our return from Besièrs, I have behaved ill toward you, Alaïs, without cause or justification. I'm sorry for it and have come to ask your forgiveness. Too often I am jealous and my jealousy leads me to say things—things—that I regret."

Alaïs held his gaze but, unsure of how she felt, did not trust herself to speak.

Guilhem moved closer. "But you are not displeased to see me."

She smiled. "You have been absent from me so long, Guilhem, I hardly know what to feel."

"Do you wish me to leave you?"

Alaïs felt tears spring into her eyes, which gave her the courage to stand firm. She did not want him to see her cry.

"I think it would be best." She reached into the neck of her dress and pulled out a handkerchief, which she pressed into his hand. "There is yet time for things to be right between us."

"Time is the one thing that we do not have, little Alaïs," he said gently. "But, unless God or the French allow it, I will come again tomorrow."

Alaïs thought of the books and of the responsibility resting on her shoulders. How, soon, she would be leaving. *I might never see him more.* Her heartstrings cracked. She hesitated, and then embraced him fiercely, as if to imprint his outline on hers.

Then, as swiftly as she had taken him, she let him go.

"We are all in God's hands," she said. "Now, please leave, Guilhem."

"Tomorrow?"

"We will see."

Alaïs stood like a statue, hands clasped in front of her to stop them from shaking, until the door had shut and Guilhem was gone. Then, lost in thought, she wandered slowly back to the table, wondering what had driven him to come. Love? Regret? Or something else?

CHAPTER 46

Simeon glanced up at the sky. Gray clouds jostled for position, obscuring the sun. He had journeyed some distance from the Cité already, but wanted to get back to his lodgings before the storm hit.

Once he reached the outskirts of the woods that separated the plains outside Carcassonne from the river, he slowed his pace. He was out of breath, too old to travel so far on foot. He leaned heavily against his staff and loosened the neck of his robe. It was not so far now. Esther would have a meal waiting for him, perhaps a little wine. The thought restored him. Perhaps Bertrand was right? Perhaps it would be over by spring.

Simeon did not notice the two men who stepped out behind him on the path. He was not aware of the raised arm, the club coming down on his head, until he felt the blow and the darkness took him.

By the time Pelletier arrived at the Porte Narbonnaise, a crowd had already formed.

"Let me through," he shouted, pushing everyone out of his way until he reached the front. A man was slumped on all fours on the ground. Blood was flowing from a cut on his forehead.

Two men-at-arms towered above him, their pikes pointed at his neck. The man was evidently a musician. His tabor was punctured and his pipe had been snapped in two and tossed aside, like bones at a feast.

"What in the name of Sant-Foy is going on?" Pelletier demanded. "What is this man's offense?"

"He did not stop when ordered to do so," the older of the soldiers replied. His face was a patchwork of scars and old wounds. "He has no authorization."

Pelletier crouched down beside the musician.

"I am Bertrand Pelletier, intendant to the viscount. What is your business in Carcassona?"

The man's eyes flickered open. "Intendant Pelletier?" he murmured, clutching Pelletier's arm.

"It is I. Speak, friend."

"Besièrs es presa," Béziers is taken.

Close by, a woman stifled a cry and clasped her hand to her mouth.

Shocked to his core, Pelletier found himself on his feet again.

"You," he commanded, "fetch reinforcements to relieve you here and help get this man to the château. If he does not regain his speech through your ill treatment, it will be the worse for you." Pelletier spun to the crowd. "Mind my words well," he shouted. "No citizen is to speak of what you have witnessed here. We will know soon enough the truth of the matter."

When they reached the Château Comtal, Pelletier ordered the musician to be taken to the kitchens to have his wounds dressed, while he went immediately to inform Viscount Trencavel. Some little time later, fortified by sweet wine and honey, the musician was brought to the *donjon*.

He was pale but in command of himself. Fearing the man's legs would not hold him, Pelletier ordered a stool to be fetched so he could give his testimony sitting down.

"Tell us your name, *amic*," he said.

"Pierre de Murviel, *Messire*."

Viscount Trencavel sat in the middle, his allies around him in a semicircle.

"*Benvenguda*, Pierre de Murviel," he said. "You have news for us."

Sitting bolt upright with his hands on his knees, his face as white as milk, he cleared his throat and began to talk. He had been born in Béziers, although he had spent the past few years in the courts of Navarre and Aragon. He was a musician, having learned his trade from Raimon de Mirval himself, the finest troubadour of the Midi. It was on the strength of this that he'd received an invitation from the suzerain of Béziers. Seeing an opportunity to visit his family again, he'd accepted and returned home.

His voice was so quiet that the listeners had to strain to hear what he was saying. "Tell us of Besièrs," said Trencavel. "Leave no detail unspoken."

"The French army arrived at the walls the day before the Feast Day of Santa Maria Magdalena and pitched camp along the left bank of the River Orb. Closest to the river were the pilgrims and mercenaries, beggars and unfortunates, a tattered rabble of men, bare footed and wearing only breeches and shirts. Further away, the colors of the barons and the churchmen flew above their pavilions in a mass of green and gold and red. They built flagpoles and felled trees for enclosures for their animals."

"Who was sent to parley?"

"The Bishop of Besièrs, Renaud de Montpeyroux."

"It is said he is a traitor, *Messire*," said Pelletier, leaning over and whispering in his ear, "that he has already taken the Cross."

"Bishop Montpeyroux returned with a list of supposed heretics drawn up by the papal legates. I don't know how many were set down on the parchment, *Messire*, but hundreds certainly. The names of some of the most influential, most wealthy, most noble citizens of Besièrs were written there, as well as followers of the new church and those who were accused of being *Bons Chrétiens*. If the consuls would hand over the heretics, then Besièrs would be spared. If not . . ." He left the words hanging.

"What answer gave the consuls?" said Pelletier. It was the first indication of whether or not the alliance would hold against the French.

"That they would rather be drowned in the salt sea's brine than surrender or betray their fellow citizens."

Trencavel gave the slightest sigh.

"The bishop withdrew from the city, taking with him a small number of Catholic priests. The commander of our garrison, Bernard de Servian, began to organize the defenses."

He stopped and swallowed hard. Even Congost, bent over his parchment, stopped and looked up.

"The morning of July the twenty-second dawned quietly enough. It was hot, even at first light. A handful of Crusaders, camp followers not even soldiers, went to the river, immediately below the fortifications to the south of the city. They were observed from the walls. Insults were traded. One of the *routiers* walked on to the bridge, swaggering, swearing. It so inflamed our young men on the walls, they armed themselves with spears, clubs, even a makeshift drum and banner. Determined to teach the French a lesson, they threw open the gate and charged down the slope before anyone knew what was happening, shouting at the tops of their voices and attacked the man. It was over in moments. They threw the *routier*'s dead body off the bridge into the river."

Pelletier glanced at Viscount Trencavel. His face was white.

"From the walls, the townspeople screamed at the boys to come back, but they were too dizzied with confidence to listen. The noise of the brawl drew the attention of the captain of the mercenaries, the *roi* as the French call him. Seeing the gate standing open, he gave the order to attack. At last the youths realized the danger, but it was too late. The *routiers* slaughtered them where they stood. The few that made it back tried to secure the gate, but the *routiers* were too quick, too well armed. They forced their way through and held it open.

"Within moments, French soldiers were hammering at the walls, armed with picks and mattocks and scaling ladders. Bernard de Servian did his best to defend the ramparts and hold the keep, but everything happened too quickly. The mercenaries held the gate.

"Once the Crusaders were inside, the massacre began. There were bodies everywhere, dead and mutilated; we were in blood knee deep. Children were cut from their mothers' arms and skewered on the points of pikes and swords. Heads were severed from limbs and mounted on the walls for the crows to pick clean, so it seemed that a line of bloody gargoyles, fashioned from flesh and bone not stone, gaped down on our defeat. They butchered all who they came upon, without regard to age or sex."

Viscount Trencavel could remain silent no longer. "But how came it that the legates or the French barons did not stop this carnage? Did they not know of it?"

Du Murviel raised his head. "They knew, *Messire*."

"But a massacre of innocent people goes against all honor, all convention in war," said Pierre-Roger de Cabaret. "I cannot believe that the abbot of Cîteaux, for all his zeal and hatred of heresy, would sanction the slaughter of Christian women and children, in a state of sin?"

"It is said that the abbot was asked how he should tell the good Catholics from the heretics: '*Tuez-les tous. Dieu reconnâitra les siens,*'" said du Murviel in a hollow voice. "'Kill them all. God will recognize his own.' Or so it is rumored that he spoke."

Trencavel and de Cabaret exchanged glances.

"Go on," ordered Pelletier grimly. "Finish your story."

"The great bells of Besièrs were ringing the alarm. Women and children crowded into the Church of Sant-Jude and the Church of Santa Maria Magdalena in the upper town, thousands of people crammed inside like animals in a pen. The Catholic priests vested themselves and sang the Requiem, but the Crusaders broke down the door and slaughtered them all."

His voice faltered. "In the space of a few brief hours, our entire city had been turned into a charnel house. The looting started. All our fine houses were stripped bare by greed and barbarity. Only now, did the French barons, through greed not conscience, seek to control the *routiers*. They, in turn, were furious to be deprived of the spoils they had earned, so set the town alight so none could benefit. The wooden dwellings of the slums went up like a tinderbox. The roof timbers of the cathedral caught light and collapsed, trapping all those sheltering inside. So fierce were the flames, the cathedral cracked down the middle."

"Tell me this, *amic*. How many survive?" said the viscount.

The musician dropped his head. "None, *Messire*. Save those few of us who escaped the city. Otherwise, all are dead."

"Twenty thousand slaughtered in the space of a single morning," Raymond-Roger muttered in horror. "How can this be?"

Nobody answered. There were no words equal to the task.

Trencavel raised his head and looked down at the musicians.

"You have seen sights that no man should see, Pierre du Murviel. You have shown great bravery and courage in bringing this news to us. Carcassona is in your debt and I will see you are well rewarded." He paused. "Before you take your leave, I would ask you one further question. Did my uncle, Raymond, Count of Toulouse, take part in the sack of the city?"

"I do not believe so, *Messire*. It was rumored he remained in the French camp."

Trencavel glanced at Pelletier. "That, at least, is something."

"And as you traveled to Carcassona, did you pass anyone on the road?" Pelletier asked. "Has the news of this massacre spread?"

"I know not, *Messire*. I stayed away from the main routes, following the old passes through the gorges of Lagrasse. But I saw no soldiers."

Viscount Trencavel looked to his consuls in case they had questions to ask, but no one spoke.

"Very well," he said, turning back to the musician. "You may take your leave. Once more, our thanks."

As soon as du Murviel he'd been led away, Trencavel turned to Pelletier.

"Why have we received no word? It beggars belief we should not have heard whisperings at least. Four days have passed since the massacre."

"If du Murviel's tale is true, then who is left to carry the news?" said de Cabaret grimly.

"Even so," said Trencavel, dismissing the comment with a wave of his hand. "Send out fresh riders immediately, as many as we can spare. We must know if the Host remains yet at Besièrs or already marches east. Their victory will give speed to their progress."

Everyone bowed as he stood up.

"Command the consuls to publish this ill news throughout the *Ciutat*. I go to the *capèla* Sant-Maria. Send my wife to me there."

Pelletier felt as if his legs were encased in armor as he climbed the stairs to the living quarters. There seemed to be something around his chest, a band or a ligature, stopping him from breathing freely.

Alaïs was waiting for him at the door.

"You have brought the book?" she said eagerly. The look on his face stopped her in her tracks. "What is it? Has something happened?"

"I have not been to Sant-Nasari, *Filha*. There has been news." Pelletier sat heavily down in a chair.

"What manner of news?" He heard the dread in her voice.

"Besièrs has fallen," he said. "Three, four days ago. None survive."

Alaïs stumbled to the bench. "All dead?" she said, horror-struck. "Women and children also?"

"We stand now on the very edge of perdition," he said. "If they are capable of visiting such atrocities on innocent . . ."

She sat down opposite him. "What will happen now?" she said.

For the first time he could remember, Pelletier heard fear in his daughter's voice. "We can only wait and see," he said.

He sensed rather than heard her draw breath.

"But this makes no difference to what we agreed," she said carefully. "You will allow me to take the Trilogy to safety."

"The situation has changed."

A look of fierce determination came over her. "With respect, *Paire*, there is even more reason to let us go. If we don't, the books will be trapped within the *Ciutat*. That cannot be what you want." She paused. He made no answer. "After everything you and Simeon and Esclarmonde have sacrificed, all the years of hiding, keeping the books safe, only to fail at the last."

"What happened in Besièrs will not happen here," he said firmly. "Carcassona can withstand siege. It *will* withstand. The books will be safer kept here."

Alaïs stretched across the table and took his hand.

"I beseech you, do not go back on your word."

"*Arèst*, Alaïs," he said sharply. "We do not know where the army is. Already, the tragedy that has befallen Besièrs is old news. Several days have passed since these events took place, even though they are fresh to us. An advance guard might already be within striking distance of the *Ciutat*. If I let you go, I would be signing your death warrant."

"But—"

"I forbid it. It is too dangerous."

"I am prepared to take the risk."

"No, Alaïs," he shouted, fear fueling his temper. "I will not sacrifice you. The duty is mine, not yours."

"Then come with me," she cried. "Tonight. Let's take the books and go, now, while still there is the chance."

"It is too dangerous," he repeated stubbornly.

"Do you think I do not know that? Yes, it may be that our journey will end at the point of a French sword. But surely it is better to die in the trying, than let fear of what may come to pass take our courage from us?"

To her surprise, frustration also, he smiled. "Your spirit does you credit, *Filha*," he said, although he sounded defeated. "But the books stay within the *Ciutat*."

Alaïs stared at him aghast, then turned and ran out of the room.

CHAPTER 47
Besièrs

For three days after their unexpected victory at Béziers, the Crusaders remained in the fertile meadows and abundant countryside surrounding the city. To have taken such a prize with so few casualties was a miracle. God could have given no clearer a sign of the justness of their cause.

Above them were the smoking ruins of the once great city. Fragments of gray ash spiralled up into the incongruous blue of the summer skies and were scattered by the winds over the defeated land. From time to time, the unmistakeable sound of crumpling masonry and brittle, broken timbers could be heard.

The following morning, the Host struck camp and headed south across open country toward the Roman city of Narbonne. At the front of the column of men was the abbot of Cîteaux, flanked by the papal legates, his temporal authority strengthened by the devastating defeat of the city that had dared to harbor heresy. Every cross of white or gold seemed to shimmer like the finest cloth upon the backs of God's warriors. Every crucifix seemed to catch the rays of the brilliant sun.

The conquering army wound its way like a snake through the landscape of saltpans, stagnant pools and extensive tracts of yellow scrub, whipped by the fierce winds that blew off the Golfe du Lion. Vines grew wild along the roadsides, as well as olive and almond trees.

The French soldiers, untried and unused to the extreme climate of the south, had never seen terrain like it. They crossed themselves, seeing it as proof that they had indeed entered a land abandoned by God.

A deputation led by the archbishop of Narbonne and the viscount of the city met the Crusaders at Capestang on 25 July.

Narbonne was a rich trading port on the Mediterranean Sea, although the heart of the city was some distance inland. With rumors of the horrors inflicted upon Béziers fresh in their minds—and hoping to save Narbonne from the same fate—both church and state were prepared to sacrifice their independence and honor. In front of witnesses, the bishop of Narbonne and the viscount of Narbonne knelt before the abbot and made full and complete submission to the Church. They agreed to deliver all known heretics to the legates, to confiscate all property owned by Cathars and Jews, even to pay a tax on their possessions to subsidize the Crusade.

Within hours, terms had been ratified. Narbonne would be spared. Never had a war chest been won so easily.

If the abbot and his legates were surprised at the speed with which the Narbonnais relinquished their birthright, they did not show it. If the men who marched beneath the vermilion colors of the count of Toulouse were embarrassed by the lack of courage of their countrymen, they did not voice it.

The order was given to change course. They would stay outside Narbonne for the night, then head for Olonzac in the morning. After that, it was but a few days' march to Carcassonne itself.

The following day, the fortified hilltop town of Azille surrendered, throwing its gates open wide to the invaders. Several families denounced as heretics were burned on a pyre hastily constructed in the central marketplace. The black smoke wound through the narrow, steep streets and slipped over the thick walls of the town to the flat countryside beyond.

One by one, the small châteaux and villages surrendered without a sword being raised. The neighboring town of La Redorte followed Azille's example, as did most of the hamlets and clusters of tiny dwellings in between. Other *places fortes* they found deserted.

The Host helped themselves to what they wanted from the bursting granaries and well-stocked fruit stores and moved on. What little resistance the army did encounter was met with violent and swift reprisals. Steadily, the savage reputation of the army spread, like a malignant shadow stretching out black before them. Little by little, the ancient bond between the people of the eastern Languedoc and the Trencavel dynasty was broken.

On the eve of the Feast Day of St. Nazaire, five days after their victory at Béziers, the advance guard reached Trèbes, two days ahead of the main army.

During the course of the afternoon, it grew steadily more humid. The hazy afternoon light gave way to a glowering gray. A few rumbles of thunder growled in the sky, followed by a violent crack of lightning. As the Crusaders rode through the gates of the town, left unguarded and open, the first drops of rain began to fall.

The streets were eerily deserted. Everyone had disappeared, stolen away like wraiths or spirits. The sky was an endless expanse of black and purple, as bruised clouds scudded across the horizon. When the storm hit, sweeping across the plains surrounding the town, the thunder cracked and roared overhead as if the heavens themselves were disintegrating.

The horses slithered and slipped on the cobbled stones. Each alleyway, every passage, became a river. The rain pounded ferociously on shield and helmet. Rats scurried to the steps to the church, seeking refuge from the swirling torrents. The tower was hit by lightning, but did not burn.

Soldiers from the north fell to their knees, crossing themselves and praying that God would spare them. The flat lands around Chartres, the fields of Burgundy or the wooded countryside of Champagne offered nothing so extreme.

As quickly as it had struck, like a lumbering beast, the storm passed on. The air became fresh and pleasant. The Crusaders heard the bells in the nearby monastery start to ring out in thanks for their safe deliverance. Taking it as a sign the worst was over, they emerged from the trees and set to work. The squires searched for safe grazing for the horses. Servants began to unpack their masters' belongings and went in search of dry kindling to lay the fires.

Gradually, the camp took shape.

Dusk fell. The sky was a patchwork of pinks and purples. As the final wisps of trailing white cloud drifted away, the northerners got their first glimpse of the towers and turrets of Carcassonne, revealed suddenly on the horizon.

The Cité seemed to rise out of the land itself, a stone fortress in the sky looking down in grandeur upon the world of men. Nothing they had heard had prepared the Crusaders for this first sight of the place they had come to conquer. Words did not begin to do justice to its splendor.

It was magnificent, dominant. Impregnable.

CHAPTER 48

When he came to his senses, Simeon was no longer in the wood, but in some sort of byre. He had a memory of traveling, a long way. His ribs were sore from the motion of the horse.

The smell was terrible, a mixture of sweat, goat, damp straw and something he could not quite identify. A sickliness, like decaying flowers. There were several harnesses hanging from the wall and a pitchfork propped up in the corner closest to the door, which came no higher than a man's shoulder. On the wall opposite the door were five or six metal rings for tethering animals.

Simeon glanced down. The hood they'd put over his head was lying next to him on the ground. His hands were still tied, as were his feet.

Coughing and trying to spit the coarse threads of the material out of his mouth, he levered himself up into a sitting position. Feeling bruised and stiff, Simeon slowly shuffled backward on the ground until he reached the door. It took some time, but the relief of feeling something solid against his shoulders and back was immense. Patiently, he pushed himself to his feet, his head nearly hitting the roof. He banged against the door. The wood groaned and strained, but it was barred from the outside and would not open.

Simeon had no idea where he was, still close to Carcassonne or farther afield. He had half memories of being carried on horseback through the woods, then over flat land. From the little he knew of the terrain, he guessed that meant they were somewhere around Trèbes.

He could see a slither of light under the small gap at the bottom of the door, a dark blue, but not yet the pitch black of night. When he pressed his ear to the ground, he could hear the murmur of his captors close by.

They were waiting for someone to arrive. The thought chilled him, evidence, although he barely needed it, that this was no random ambush.

Simeon shuffled his way back to the far side of the byre. Over time, he dozed, slumping sideways and jerking awake, then sliding into sleep again.

The sound of someone shouting brought him to his senses. Immediately, every nerve in his body was alert. He heard the sound of men scrambling to their feet, then a thud as the heavy wooden bar securing the door was removed.

Three shadowy figures appeared in the doorway, silhouetted against the bright sunlight beyond. Simeon blinked, unable to see much.

"*Où est-il?*" Where is he?

It was an educated northern voice, cold and peremptory. There was a pause. The torch was held higher, picking out Simeon where he stood blinking in the shadows. "Bring him to me."

Simeon barely had time to recognize the leader of the ambush, when he was grabbed by the arms and thrown on his knees in front of the Frenchman.

Slowly, Simeon raised his eyes. The man had a cruel, thin face and expressionless eyes the color of flint. His tunic and trousers were of good quality, cut in the northern style, although they gave no indication of his status or position.

"Where is it?" he demanded.

Simeon raised his head. "I don't understand," he replied in Yiddish.

The kick took him by surprise. He felt a rib snap and he fell backwards, his legs buckling under him. Simeon felt rough hands beneath his armpits propping him back in position.

"I know who you are, Jew," he said. "There is no sense in playing this game with me. I will ask you once again. Where is the book?"

Simeon raised his head once more and said nothing.

This time, the man went for his face. Pain exploded inside his head as his mouth split open and teeth cracked in his jaw. Simeon could taste blood and saliva, stinging, on his tongue and throat.

"I have pursued you like an animal, Jew," he said, "all the way from Chartres, to Béziers, to here. Tracked you down, like an animal. You have wasted a great deal of my time. My patience is growing thin." He took a step closer so that Simeon could see the hate in his gray, dead eyes. "Once more: where is the book? Did you give it to Pelletier? *C'est ça?*"

Two thoughts came simultaneously into Simeon's mind. First, that he could not save himself. Second, that he must protect his friends. He still had that power. His eyes were swollen shut and blood pooled in the torn hollows of his lids.

"I have the right to know the name of my accuser," he said through a mouth too broken for speech. "I would pray for you."

The man's eyes narrowed. "Make no mistake, you will tell me where you have hidden the book."

He jerked his head.

Simeon was hauled to his feet. They ripped the clothes from him and threw him flat over a cart, one man holding his hands, the other his legs to expose his back. Simeon heard the sharp crack of the leather in the air just before the buckle connected with his bare skin. His body jerked in agony. "Where is it?" Simeon closed his eyes as the belt whipped down again through the air. "Is it in Carcassonne already? Or do you still have it with you, Jew?" He was shouting in time with the stroke. "You will tell me. You. Or them."

Blood was flowing from the lacerations on his back. Simeon began to pray in the custom of his fathers, ancient, holy words thrown out into the darkness, keeping his mind from the pain.

"*Où—est—le—livre?*" the man insisted, another strike for every word.

It was the last thing Simeon heard before the darkness reached out and took him.

CHAPTER 49

The Crusade's advance guard arrived within sight of Carcassonne on the Feast Day of Sant-Nasari, following the road from Trèbes. The guards at the Tour Pinte lit the fires. The alarm bells were rung.

By the evening of the next day, the first of August, the French camp on the far side of the river had grown until there was a rival city of tents and pavilions, banners and golden crosses glittering in the sun. Barons from the north, Gascon mercenaries, soldiers from Chartres and Burgundy and Paris, sappers, longbowmen archers, priests, camp followers.

At Vespers, Viscount Trencavel ascended the ramparts, accompanied by Pierre-Roger de Cabaret, Bertrand Pelletier and one or two others. In the distance, trails of smoke spiraled up into the air. The river was a ribbon of silver.

"There are so very many."

"No more than we expected, *Messire*," replied Pelletier.

"How long, think you, before the main army arrives?"

"It's hard to be sure," he replied. "So large a fighting force will travel slowly. The heat will hinder them too."

"Hinder them, yes," said Trencavel. "Stop them, no."

"We're ready for them, *Messire*. The *Ciutat* is well stocked. The *hourds* are completed to protect the walls from their sappers; all broken sections or points of weakness have been repaired and blocked; all the towers are manned." Pelletier waved his hand. "The hawsers holding the mills in place in the river have been cut and the crops burned. The French will find little to sustain them here."

His eyes flashing, Trencavel suddenly turned to de Cabaret.

"Let's saddle our horses and make a *sortie*. Before night arrives and the sun sets, let's take four hundred of our best men, those most skilled with lance, and with sword, and chase the French from our slopes. They will not expect us to take the battle to them. What say you?"

Pelletier sympathized with his desire to strike first. He also knew it would be an act of supreme folly.

"There are battalions on the plains, *Messire*, *routiers*, small contingents from the advance party."

Pierre-Roger de Cabaret added his voice. "Do not sacrifice your men, Raymond."

"But if we could strike the first blow . . ."

"We have prepared for siege, *Messire,* not open battle. The garrison is strong. The bravest, most experienced *chevaliers* are here, waiting for their chance to prove themselves."

"But?" Trencavel sighed.

"You would be sacrificing them for no gain," he said firmly.

"Your people trust you, they love you," Pelletier said. "They will lay down their lives for you if need be. But, we should wait. Let them bring the battle to us."

"I fear it is my pride that has brought us to this place," he said in a low voice. "Somehow, I did not expect it to come to this, so soon." He smiled. "Do you remember how my mother used to fill the château with singing and dancing, Bertrand? All the greatest troubadours and jongleurs came to play for her. Aiméric de Pegulham, Arnaut de Carcassès, even Guilhem Fabre and Bernat Alanham from Narbonne. We were always feasting, celebrating."

"I have heard it was the finest court in the Pays d'Oc." He put his hand on his master's shoulder. "And will be again."

The bells fell silent. All eyes were on Viscount Trencavel.

When he spoke, Pelletier was proud to hear all trace of self-doubt was gone from his lord's voice. He was no longer a boy remembering his childhood, but a captain on the eve of battle.

"Order the posterns to be closed and the gates to be barred, Bertrand, and summon the commander of the garrison to the *donjon*. We will be ready for the French when they come."

"Perhaps also send reinforcements to Sant-Vicens, *Messire,*" suggested de Cabaret. "When the Host attacks, they will start there. And we cannot afford to relinquish our access to the river."

Trencavel nodded.

Pelletier lingered a while after the others had gone, looking out over the land, as if to imprint its image in his mind.

To the north, the walls of Sant-Vicens were low and sparsely defended by towers. If the invaders penetrated the suburbs, they would be able to approach within bowshot of the Cité walls under the cover of the houses. The southern suburb, Sant-Miquel, would hold longer.

It was true that the Carcassonne was ready for siege. There was plenty of food—bread, cheese, beans—and goats for milk. But there were too many people within the walls and Pelletier was concerned about the supply of water. On his word, a guard was set on each of the wells and rationing was in place.

As he walked out of the Tour Pinte into the courtyard, Pelletier found his thoughts once more turning to Simeon. Twice he had sent François to the Jewish *quartier* for news, but both times he had returned empty-handed and Pelletier's anxiety increased with each passing day.

He took a quick look around the courtyard and decided he could be spared for a few hours.

He headed for the stables.

Pelletier followed the most direct route across the plains and through the woods, very aware of the Host camped in the distance.

Although the Jewish quarter was crowded and people were on the streets, it was unnaturally quiet and hushed. There was fear and apprehension on every face, young and old. Soon, they knew, the fighting would begin. As Pelletier rode through the narrow alleys, women and children looked up at him with anxious eyes, looking for hope in his face. He had nothing to offer them.

No one had any news of Simeon. He found his lodgings easily enough, but the door was barred. He dismounted and knocked on the house opposite.

"I seek a man called Simeon," he said, when a woman came fearfully to door. "Do you know of whom I speak?"

She nodded. "He came with the others from Besièrs."

"Can you remember when last you saw him?"

"A few days back, before we heard the news of Besièrs, he went to Carcassona. A man came for him."

Pelletier frowned. "What manner of man?"

"A high-born servant. Orange hair," she said, wrinkling her nose. "Simeon appeared to know him."

Pelletier's bafflement deepened. It sounded like François, except how could it be? He said he had not found Simeon.

"That was the last time I saw him."

"You are saying Simeon did not return from Carcassona?"

"If he's got any sense, he'll have stayed. He will be safer there than here."

"Is it possible Simeon could have come back without you seeing him?" he said desperately. "You might have been sleeping. You might not have noticed him return."

"Look, *Messire*," she replied, pointing to the house across the street. "You can see for yourself. *Vuèg*." Empty.

CHAPTER 50

Oriane tiptoed along the corridor to her sister's chamber.

"Alaïs!" Oriane was sure her sister was once again with their father, but she was cautious. *"Sòrre?"*

When no one answered, Oriane opened the door and stepped inside. With the skill of a thief, she quickly began to search Alaïs' possessions. Bottles, jars and bowls, her wardrobe, drawers filled with cloth and perfumes and sweet-smelling herbs. Oriane patted the pillows and found a lavender posy, which didn't interest her. Then she checked over and beneath the bed. There was nothing but dead insects and cobwebs.

As she turned back to face the room, she noticed a heavy brown hunting cloak lying over the back of Alaïs' sewing chair. Her threads and needles were spread all around. Oriane felt a spark of excitement. Why a winter cloak at this time of year? Why was Alaïs mending her clothes herself?

She picked it up and immediately felt something was wrong. It was lopsided and hung crookedly. Oriane lifted the corner and saw something had been sewn into the hem.

Quickly, she unpicked the stitching, pushed her fingers inside and pulled out a small, rectangular object, wrapped in a piece of linen.

She was about to investigate, when a noise in the corridor outside drew her attention. Quick as a flash, Oriane concealed the parcel beneath her dress and returned the cloak to the back of the chair.

A hand descended heavily on her shoulder. Oriane jumped.

"What the hell do you think you're doing?" he said.

"Guilhem," she gasped, clasping her hand to her chest. "You startled me."

"What are you doing in my wife's chamber, Oriane?"

Oriane raised her chin. "I could ask you the same question."

In the darkening room, she saw his expression harden and knew the dart had hit home.

"I have every right to be here, whereas you do not . . ." He glanced at the cloak, then back to her face.

"What are you doing?"

She met his gaze. "Nothing that concerns you."

Guilhem kicked the door shut with his heel.

"You forget yourself, Dame," he said, grabbing her wrist.

"Don't be a fool, Guilhem," she said in a low voice. "Open the door. It will go ill for both of us if someone comes and finds us together."

"Don't play games with me, Oriane. I'm in no mood for them. I'm not letting you go unless you tell me what you are doing here. Did he send you here?"

Oriane looked at him with genuine confusion. "I don't know what you're talking about, Guilhem, on my word."

His fingers were digging deep into her skin. "Did you think I wouldn't notice, è? I saw you together, Oriane."

Relief flooded through her. Now she understood the reason for his temper. Provided Guilhem had not recognized her companion, she could turn the misunderstanding to her advantage.

"Let me go," she said, trying to twist out of his grasp. "If you remember, *Messire,* you were the one who said we could meet no longer." She tossed her black hair and glared at him, eyes flashing. "So if I choose to seek comfort elsewhere, how can it concern you? You have no right over me."

"Who is he?"

Oriane thought quickly. She needed a name that would satisfy him. "Before I tell you, I want you to promise that you will not do anything unwise," she pleaded, playing for time.

"At this moment, Dame, you are not in a position to set terms."

"Then at least let us go elsewhere, to my chamber, the courtyard, anywhere but here. If Alaïs should come . . ."

From the expression on his face, Oriane knew she had got him. His greatest fear now was that Alaïs would discover his infidelity.

"Very well," he said roughly. He flung open the door with his free hand, then half pushed, half dragged her along the corridor. By the time they reached her chamber, Oriane had gathered her thoughts.

"Speak, Dame," he commanded.

Her eyes fixed on the ground, Oriane confessed she had accepted the attentions of a new suitor, the son of one of the viscount's allies. He had long admired her.

"Is this the truth?" he demanded.

"I swear it is, on my life," she whispered, glancing up at him through tear-stained lashes.

He was still suspicious, but there was a flicker of indecision in his eyes.

"This does not answer why you were in my wife's chamber."

"Safeguarding your reputation only," she said. "Returning to its rightful place something of yours."

"What manner of thing?"

"My husband found a man's buckle in my chamber." She made a shape with her hands. "About so big, fashioned from copper and silver."

"I have lost such a buckle," he admitted.

"Jehan was determined to identify the owner and publish his name. Knowing it to be yours, I decided the safest thing was to return it to your chamber."

Guilhem was frowning. "Why not return the buckle to me?"

"You are avoiding me, *Messire*," she said softly. "I did not know when, even if, I would see you. Besides, if we had been noticed together, it could have been proof of what once was between us. Judge my actions foolish. But do not doubt the intention behind them."

Oriane could see he was not convinced, but dared not push the matter further. His hand went to the blade at his waist.

"If you breathe a word of this to Alaïs," he said, "I will kill you, Oriane, God strike me down if I don't."

"She will not learn of it from me," she said, then smiled. "Unless, of course, I find myself with no choice. I must protect myself. And," she paused. Guilhem drew a deep breath. "And as it happens," she continued, "there is a favor I would ask of you."

His eyes narrowed. "And if I am not so minded?"

"All I want is to know if our father has given Alaïs anything of value to keep, that's all."

"You are asking me to spy upon my own wife," he said, his voice rising in disbelief. "I will do no such thing, Oriane, and you will do nothing to upset her, is that clear?"

"*I* upset her. It's your fear of discovery that brings out this chivalry in you. You're the one who betrayed her all those nights you lay with me, Guilhem. It is only information I seek. I will learn what I want to know, with or without your help. However, if you make it difficult . . ." She left the threat hanging in the air.

"You wouldn't dare."

"It would be nothing to tell Alaïs everything we did together, share with her the things you whispered to me, the gifts you gave me. She would believe me, Guilhem. Too much of your soul shows in your face."

Disgusted by her, by himself, Guilhem threw open the door. "Damn you to hell, Oriane," he said, then stormed away down the corridor.

Oriane smiled. She had snared him.

Alaïs had spent all afternoon trying to find her father. No one had seen him. She had ventured into the Cité, hoping at least to be able to talk to Esclarmonde. But she and Sajhë were no longer in Sant-Miquel and did not appear to have yet returned home.

In the end, exhausted and apprehensive, Alaïs returned to her chamber alone. She could not go to bed. She was too nervous, too anxious, so she lit a lamp and sat at her table.

It was after the bells had struck one that she was woken by footsteps outside the door. She raised her head from her arms and looked blearily in the direction of the sound.

"Rixende?" she whispered into the dark. "Is that you?"

"No, not Rixende," he said.

"Guilhem?"

He came into the light, smiling as if not sure of his welcome. "Forgive me. I promised to leave you, I know, but . . . may I?"

Alaïs sat up.

"I have been in the chapel," he said. "I have prayed, but I do not think my words flew up."

Guilhem sat down on the end of the bed. After a moment's hesitation, she went to him. He seemed to have something on his mind.

"Here," she whispered. "Let me help you."

She unstrapped his boots and helped him with his shoulder harness and belt. The leather and buckle fell with a clunk to the floor.

"What does Viscount Trencavel think will happen?" she asked.

Guilhem lay back on the bed and closed his eyes. "That the Host will attack Sant-Vicens first, then Sant-Miquel, in order to be able to approach close to the walls of the *Ciutat* itself."

Alaïs sat down beside him and smoothed his hair from his face. The feel of his skin under her fingers made her shiver.

"You should sleep, *Messire*. You will need all your strength for the battle to come."

Lazily, he opened his eyes and smiled up at her. "You could help me rest."

Alaïs smiled and reached over for a preparation of rosemary she kept on her bedside table. She knelt beside him and massaged the cool lotion into his temples.

"When I was looking for my father, earlier, I went to my sister's chamber. I think there was someone with her."

"Probably Congost," he said sharply.

"I don't think so. He and the other scribes sleep in the Tour Pinte at present, in case the viscount needs them." She paused. "There was laughter."

Guilhem put his finger on her mouth to stop her. "Enough of Oriane," he whispered, slipping his hands around her waist and drawing her to him. She could taste the wine on his lips. "You have the scent of camomile and honey," he said. He reached up and loosened her hair so it fell like a waterfall around her face.

"*Mon còr.*"

The hairs on the back of her neck stood on end at his touch, his skin against hers, so startling and intimate. Slowly, carefully, not taking his brown eyes from her face, Guilhem eased her dress from her shoulders, then lower to her waist. Alaïs shifted. The material came loose and slithered off the bed to the floor, like a winter skin no longer needed.

Guilhem lifted the bedcover to let her under and laid her down beside him, on pillows that still held the memory of him. For a moment, they lay, arm to arm, side to side, her feet cold against the heat of his skin. He bent over her. Now Alaïs could feel his breath, whispering over the surface of her skin like a summer breeze. His lips dancing, his tongue slipping, sliding over her breasts. Alaïs caught her breath as he took her nipple into his mouth, licking, teasing.

Guilhem raised his head. He gave a half-smile.

Then, still holding her gaze, he lowered his body into the space between her bare legs. Alaïs stared at his brown eyes, unblinking and serious.

"*Mon còr,*" he said again.

Gently, Guilhem eased himself inside her, little by little, until she had taken the whole of him. For a moment he lay still, contained within her, as if resting.

Alaïs felt strong, powerful, as if at this moment she could do anything, be anyone. A hypnotic, heavy warmth was seeping through her limbs, filling her up, devouring her senses. Her head was filled with the sound of her blood beating. She had no sense of time or space. There was only Guilhem and the flickering shadows of the lamp.

Slowly, he began to move.

"Alaïs." The words slipped from between his lips.

She placed her hands on his back, her fingers splayed wide in the shape of stars. She could feel the strength of him, the force in his tanned arms and firm thighs, the soft hair on his chest brushing against her. His tongue was darting between her lips, hot and wet and hungry.

He was breathing faster, harder, driven on by desire, by need. Alaïs held him to her as Guilhem cried out her name. He shuddered, then was still.

Gradually, the roaring in her head faded away until nothing remained but the hushed silence of the room.

Later, after they had talked and whispered promises in the dark, they drifted into sleep. The oil burned away. The flame in the lamp guttered and died. Alaïs and Guilhem did not notice. They were not aware of the silver march of the moon across the sky, nor the purple light of dawn as it came creeping through the window. They knew nothing but each other as they lay sleeping in one another's arms, a wife and her husband, lovers once more.

Reconciled. At peace.

CHAPTER 51

THURSDAY, 7 JULY 2005

Alice woke seconds before the alarm went off to find herself sprawled across the bed, papers strewn all about her.

The family tree was in front of her, together with her notes from the library in Toulouse. She grinned. Quite like her student days, when she was forever falling asleep at her desk.

She didn't feel bad about it, though. Despite the burglary last night, this morning she felt in good spirits. Contented, happy even.

Alice stretched her arms and neck, then got up to open the shutters and window. The sky was cut through with pale slashes of light and flat white clouds. The slopes of the Cité were in shadow and the grassy banks beneath the walls shimmered with early morning dew. Above the turrets and towers, the sky was blue, like a bolt of silk. Wrens and larks sang to one another across the rooftops. Evidence of the aftermath of the storm was everywhere. Debris blown against railings, boxes sodden and upturned at the back of the hotel, newspapers pooled at the foot of the street lamps in the car park.

Alice was uneasy at the idea of leaving Carcassonne, as if the act of departure would precipitate something. But she had to take some action and, at this point, Chartres was her only lead to Shelagh.

It was a good day for a journey.

As she packed her papers away, she admitted she was also being sensible. She didn't want to sit around like a victim, waiting for last night's intruder to come back.

She explained to the receptionist that she was going out of town for a day but to hold her room.

"You have a woman waiting to see you, Madame," the girl said, pointing to the lounge. "I was about to call your room."

"Oh?" Alice turned to look. "Did she say what she wanted?"

The receptionist shook her head.

"Okay. Thank you."

"Also, this came for you this morning," she added, handing over a letter. Alice glanced at the postmark. It came from Foix yesterday. She didn't recognize the handwriting. She was about to open it, when the woman waiting for her approached.

"Dr. Tanner?" she said. She looked nervous.

Alice put the letter in her jacket pocket to read later. "Yes?"

"I have a message for you from Audric Baillard. He wonders if you could meet him in the cemetery?"

The woman was vaguely familiar, although Alice couldn't immediately place her.

"Do I know you from somewhere?" she said.

The woman hesitated. "From Daniel Delargarde," she said in a rush. *"Notaires."*

Alice looked again. She didn't remember seeing her yesterday, but there were a lot of people in the central office.

"Monsieur Baillard is waiting for you at the Giraud-Biau tomb."

"Really?" said Alice. "Why didn't he come himself?"

"I have to go now."

Then the woman turned tail and disappeared, leaving Alice staring after her, baffled. She turned to the receptionist, who shrugged.

Alice glanced at her watch. She was keen to get going. She'd got a long drive ahead of her. On the other hand, ten minutes wasn't going to make any difference.

"A demain," she said to the receptionist, but she'd already gone back to whatever it was she was doing.

Alice detoured via the car to leave her rucksack, then, vaguely irritated, she hurried across the road to the cemetery.

The atmosphere changed the moment Alice walked through the high metal gates. The early morning bustle of the Cité awaking was replaced by stillness.

There was a low, whitewashed building on her right. Outside a row of black and green plastic watering cans hung on hooks. Alice peered in through the window and saw an old jacket slung over the back of a chair and a newspaper open on the table, as if someone had only just left.

Alice walked slowly up the central aisle, feeling suddenly on edge. She found the atmosphere oppressive. Gray sculpted headstones, white porcelain cameos and black granite inscriptions marking birth and death, resting places bought by local families *à perpétuité* to mark their passing. Photographs of those who had died young jostled for space beside the features of the old. At the base of many of the tombs were flowers, some real and dying, others fashioned from silk or plastic or porcelain.

Following the directions Karen Fleury had given her, Alice found the Giraud-Biau grave easily enough. It was a large flat tomb at the top of the central aisle overlooked by a stone angel with open arms and furled wings.

She glanced around. There was no sign of Baillard.

Alice traced her fingers across the surface. Here lay most of Jeanne Giraud's family, a woman she knew nothing about other than she was a link between Audric Baillard and Grace. Only now, as she stood staring at the chiseled names of one family, did Alice realize how very unusual it was that space had been found her for her aunt.

A noise in one of the cross aisles caught her attention. She looked around, expecting to see the elderly man of the photograph making his way toward her.

"Dr. Tanner?"

There were two men, both wearing light summer suits, both dark-haired and with their eyes obscured by sunglasses.

"Yes?"

The shorter of the two flashed a badge at her.

"Police. We have a few questions we need to ask you."

Alice's stomach lurched. "Concerning what?"

"It won't take long, *Madame*."

"I'd like to see some ID."

He reached into his breast pocket and produced a card. She had no idea if it was authentic or not. But the gun in the holster underneath the jacket looked real enough. Her pulse started to race.

Alice pretended to examine it as she cast a look around the graveyard. There was no one about. The aisles stretched away empty in all directions.

"What is this about?" she said again, trying to keep her voice steady.

"If you could just come with us."

They can't do anything in broad daylight.

Too late, Alice realized why the woman who'd delivered the message was familiar. She'd similar characteristics to the man she'd seen briefly in her room last night. *This man.*

Out of the corner of her eye, Alice could see there was a flight of concrete steps leading down to the newest section of the graveyard. Beyond that there was a gate.

He put his hand on her arm. "*Maintenant, Dr. Tan—*"

Alice launched herself forward, like a sprinter out of the blocks, taking them by surprise. They were slow to react. A shout went up, but she was already down the steps and running through the gate, out into the Chemin des Anglais.

A car put-putting up the hill slammed on its brakes. Alice didn't stop. She hurled herself over a rickety wooden farm gate and tore through the rows of vines, stumbling on the furrowed earth. She could feel the men at her back, gaining on her. Blood pounded in her ears, the muscles in her legs were pulled tight as piano strings, but she kept going.

At the bottom of the field was a tight-meshed wire fence, too high to jump. Alice looked round in panic, then spotted a gap in the far corner. Throwing herself to the ground, she crawled along the earth on her belly, feeling the sharp rocks and stones digging into her palms and knees. She slithered under the wire, the frayed edges catching on her jacket, holding her as fast as a fly in a spider's web. She pulled and with a super-human effort, yanked herself free, leaving a scrap of blue denim on the wire.

She found herself in a market garden, filled with long rows of tall bamboo frames supporting aubergines, courgettes and runner beans, which shielded her. Keeping her head down, Alice zigzagged through the allotments, heading for the shelter of the outbuildings. A huge mastiff on a heavy metal chain lunged at her as she rounded the corner, barking ferociously and snapping its vicious jaws. She stifled a scream and jumped back.

The main entrance to the farm led straight out on to the busy main road at the bottom of the hill. Once she was on the pavement, she allowed herself a glance over her shoulder. Empty, silent space stretched behind her. They'd stopped following.

Alice put her hands on her knees and doubled over, panting with exertion and relief, waiting for the shaking in her arms and legs to stop. Already, her mind was starting to click into motion.

What are you going to do? The men would go back to the hotel and wait for her there. She couldn't go back there. She felt in her pocket and was relieved to find she hadn't lost the car keys in her panic to get away. Her rucksack was squashed under the front seat.

You must call Noubel.

She could picture the scrap of paper with Noubel's number in her rucksack under the seat of the car with everything in it. Alice brushed herself down. Her jeans were covered in dirt and ripped on one knee. Her only chance was to go back to the car and pray they weren't waiting for her there.

Alice walked fast along rue Barbarcane, keeping her head down every time a car went past. She passed the church, then took a shortcut down a small road to the right called rue de la Gaffe.

Who'd sent them?

She walked quickly, keeping to the shadows. It was hard to tell where one house ended and the next began. Alice felt a sudden prickling at the back of her neck. She stopped, glanced to her right at the pretty house with yellow walls, expecting to see someone watching her from the doorway. But the door was firmly shut and the shutters locked. After a moment's hesitation, Alice continued.

Should she change her mind about Chartres?

If anything, Alice realized that having confirmation she was in danger—that it wasn't just her imagination—strengthened her resolve. As she thought about it, she became more certain Authié was behind what was going on. He believed she'd stolen the ring. He was clearly determined to get it back.

Call Noubel.

Again, she ignored her own advice. So far, the inspector had done nothing. A policeman was dead, Shelagh was missing. Better to rely on no one but herself.

Alice had arrived at the steps that connected rue Trivalle to the back of the car park, reasoning that if they were waiting for her, they were more likely to be at the main entrance.

The steps were steep and there was a high wall on this side of the area, which stopped her from being able to see in but gave a clear view to anyone looking down from above. If they were there, she wouldn't know it until it was too late.

Only one way to find out.

Alice took a deep breath and ran up the steps, her legs powered by the adrenalin racing through her veins. At the top, she stopped and looked around. There were a couple of coaches and cars, but very few people about.

The car was sitting where she'd left it. She picked her way between the lines of parked cars, keeping low. Her hands were shaking as she slid into the front seat. She was still expecting the men to loom up in front of her. She could still hear their voices, shouting, in her head. The moment she was in, she locked the doors and rammed the key into the ignition.

Her eyes darting in all directions, hands white on the steering wheel, Alice waited until a camper van was pulling away and the attendant raised the barrier. She accelerated and shot across the tarmac, too fast, aiming straight for the exit. The attendant shouted and leaped back, but Alice took no notice.

She kept driving.

CHAPTER 52

Audric Baillard stood on the railway station platform at Foix with Jeanne, waiting for the Andorra train.

"Ten minutes," Jeanne said, glancing at her watch. "It's not too late. You could change your mind and come with me?"

He smiled at her persistence. "You know I cannot."

She waved her hand impatiently. "You've devoted thirty years to telling their story, Audric. Alaïs, her sister, her father, her husband—you have spent your life in their company." Her voice softened. "But what of the living?"

"Their life is my life, Jeanne," he said with a quiet dignity. "Words are our only weapons against the lies of history. We must bear witness to the truth. If we do not, those we love die twice over." He paused. "I will not find peace until I know how it ended."

"After eight hundred years? The truth might be buried too deep." Jeanne hesitated. "And perhaps it is better that way. Some secrets are better for remaining hidden."

Baillard was looking ahead at the mountains. "I regret the sorrow I have brought into your life, you know that."

"That's not what I meant, Audric."

"But to discover the truth and set it down," he continued, as if she had not spoken. "It is that I live for, Jeanne."

"Truth! But what about those you fight, Audric? What are they seeking? The truth? I doubt it."

"No," he admitted in the end. "I do not think that is their purpose."

"Then what?" she said, impatient. "I am going, as you advised me to do. What possible harm can it do to tell me now?"

Still he hesitated.

Jeanne persisted. "Are the *Noublesso Véritable* and the *Noublesso de los Seres* but different names for the same organization?"

"No," the word escaped from his lips more severely than he'd intended. "No."

"Well then?"

Audric sighed. "The *Noublesso de los Seres* were the appointed guardians of the Grail parchments. For thousands of years they fulfilled this role.

Until, indeed, the parchments were separated." He paused, choosing his words with care. "The *Noublesso Véritable*, on the other hand, was formed only one hundred and fifty years ago, when the lost language of the parchments began to be understood once more. The name *Véritable*—meaning true or real guardians—was a deliberate attempt to give validity to the organization."

"So the *Noublesso de los Seres* no longer exists?"

Audric shook his head. "Once the Trilogy was separated the reason for the guardians' existence was gone."

Jeanne frowned. "But did they not attempt to regain the lost parchments?"

"At first, yes," he admitted, "but they failed. In time, it became more foolhardy to continue, for fear of sacrificing the one remaining parchment for the sake of regaining the other two. Since the ability to read the texts was lost by all, the secret could not be revealed. Only one person . . ." Baillard faltered. He felt Jeanne's eyes on him. "The one person with the knowledge to read the parchments chose not to pass on his learning."

"What changed?"

"For hundreds of years, nothing. Then in 1798 the Emperor Napoleon sailed for Egypt, taking savants and scholars with him as well as soldiers. They discovered there the remains of the ancient civilizations that had ruled those lands thousands of years ago. Hundreds of artifacts, sacred tables, stones, were brought back to France. From that moment on, it was only a matter of time before the ancient languages—demotic, cuneiform, hieroglyphs—were deciphered. As you know, Jean-François Champollion was the first to realize that hieroglyphs should be read, not as symbols of ideas or scripts, but as a phonetic script. In 1822, he cracked the code, to use the vulgar expression. To the ancient Egyptians, writing was a gift from the Gods—indeed the word *hieroglyph* means divine speech."

"But if the Grail parchments are written in the language of ancient Egypt . . ." she tailed off. "If you are saying what I think you are, Audric . . ." She shook her head. "That such a society as the *Noublesso* existed, yes. That the Trilogy was believed to contain an ancient secret, then again, yes. But, for the rest? It's inconceivable."

Audric smiled. "But how better to protect a secret than allow it to be concealed beneath another? To appropriate or assimilate the powerful symbols, the ideas of others, is the way civilizations survive."

"What do you mean?"

"People dig for the truth. They think they have found it. They stop, never imagining that something more astounding lies beneath. History is full of religious, ritualistic, social signifiers, stolen from one society to help build up another. For example, the day Christians celebrate the birth of Jesus the Nazarene, December the twenty-fifth, is actually the feast of the

Sol Invictus, as well as the winter Solstice. The Christian cross, just like the Grail, is actually an ancient Egyptian symbol, the *ankh*, appropriated and modified by the Emperor Constantine. *In hoc signo vinces*—by this sign shalt thou conquer—words attributed to him when seeing a symbol in the shape of a cross appear in the sky. More recently, followers of the Third Reich appropriated the swastika to symbolize their order. It is in fact an ancient Hindu symbol of rebirth."

"The labyrinth," she said, understanding.

"L'antica simbol del Miègjorn." The ancient symbol of the Midi.

Jeanne sat in thoughtful silence, hands folded in her lap, her feet crossed at the ankles. "And what of now?" she said at last.

"Once the cave was opened, it was only ever a matter of time, Jeanne," he said. "I am not the only one who knows this."

"But the Sabarthès Mountains were excavated by the Nazis during the war," she said. "The Nazi Grail hunters knew the rumors that the Cathar treasure was buried somewhere in the mountains. They spent years excavating every site of possible esoteric interest. If this cave is of such significance, how was it not discovered sixty years ago?"

"We made sure that they did not."

"You were there?" she said, her voice sharp with surprise.

Baillard smiled. "There are conflicts within the *Noublesso Véritable*," he said, avoiding her question. "The leader of the organization is a woman called Marie-Cécile de l'Oradore. She believes in the Grail and would regain it. She believes in the Quest." He paused. "However, there is another within the organization." His face grew somber. "His motives are different."

"You must speak to Inspector Noubel," she said fiercely.

"But what if, as I said, he is working for them also? It is too great a risk."

The shrill blast of the horn split the quiet of the station. They both turned toward the train drawing into the station with a screech of brakes. The conversation was over.

"I don't want to leave you here alone, Audric."

"I know," he said, taking her hand to help her up into the train. "But this is how it is supposed to end."

"End?"

She slid open the window and reached for his hand. "Please take care. Do not gamble too much of yourself."

All along the platform the heavy doors slammed shut and the train pulled away, slowly at first, then picking up speed until it had disappeared into the folds of the mountains.

CHAPTER 53

Shelagh could sense there was someone in the room with her.

She struggled to lift her head. She felt sick. Her mouth was dry and there was a dull thudding in her head, like the monotonous hum of an air-conditioning unit. She couldn't move. It took a few seconds for her to identify the fact she was sitting on a chair now, her arms pulled tight behind her back and her ankles strapped to the wooden legs.

There was a slight movement, a creak of the bare floorboards as someone shifted position.

"Who's there?"

Her palms were slippery with fear. A trickle of sweat ran down the small of her back. Shelagh forced her eyes open, but she still couldn't see. She panicked, shaking her head, blinking, trying to bring back the light until she realized the hood was back on her head. It smelled of earth and mold.

Was she still in the farmhouse? She remembered the needle, the surprise of the sharp injection. The same man who brought her food. Surely someone would come and save her? Wouldn't they?

"Who's there?" No one answered, although she could feel them close. The air was greasy with the smell of aftershave and cigarettes. "What do you want?"

The door opened. Footsteps. Shelagh felt the change in atmosphere. An instinct for self-preservation kicked in and she struggled wildly for a moment to get free. The rope only tightened, putting more pressure on her shoulders, making them ache.

The door shut with an ominous, heavy thud.

She fell still. For a moment, there was silence, then the sound of someone walking toward her, closer and closer. Shelagh shrank back in her chair. He stopped right in front of her. She felt her entire body contract, as if there were thousands of tiny wires pulling at her skin. Like an animal circling his prey, he walked round the chair a couple of times, and then dropped his hands on her shoulders.

"Who are you? Please, take this blindfold off at least."

"We need to have another talk, Dr. O'Donnell."

A voice she knew, cold and precise, cut through her like a knife. She realized it was him she had been expecting. Him she feared.

He suddenly jerked the chair back.

Shelagh screamed, plummeting backwards, powerless to stop herself falling. She never hit the ground. He stopped her, inches above the floor, so she was lying almost flat, her head tipped back and her feet suspended in the air.

"You're not in a position to ask for anything, Dr. O'Donnell."

He held her in that position for what seemed like hours. Then, without warning, he suddenly righted the chair. Shelagh's neck snapped forward with the force of it. She was becoming disorientated, like a child in a game of blind man's bluff.

"Who are you working for, O'Donnell?"

"I can't breathe," she whispered.

He ignored her. She heard him click his fingers and the sound of a second chair being placed in front of her. He sat down and pulled her toward him so his knees were pressing against her thighs.

"Let's take it back to Monday afternoon. Why did you let your friend go to that part of the site?"

"Alice has got nothing to do with this," she cried. "I didn't let her work there, she just went of her own accord. I didn't even know. It was just a mistake. She doesn't know anything."

"So tell me what you know, Shelagh." Her name in his mouth sounded like a threat.

"I don't know anything," she cried. "I told you everything I knew on Monday, I swear it."

The blow came out of nowhere, striking her right cheek and slamming her head back. Shelagh could taste blood in her mouth, sliding over her tongue and down the back of her throat.

"Did your friend take the ring?" he said in a level voice.

"No, no, I swear she didn't."

He squeezed harder. "Then who? You? You were on your own with the skeletons for long enough. Dr. Tanner told me that."

"Why would I take it? It's worth nothing to me."

"Why are you so sure Dr. Tanner didn't take it?"

"She wouldn't. She just wouldn't," she cried. "Lots of other people went in. Any of them could have taken it. Dr. Brayling, the police—" Shelagh abruptly stopped.

"As you say, the police," he said. She held her breath. "Any one of them could have taken the ring. Yves Biau, for example."

Shelagh froze. She could hear the rise and fall of his breathing, calm and unhurried. He knew.

"The ring wasn't there."

He sighed. "Did Biau give the ring to you? To give to your friend?"

"I don't know what you mean," she managed to say.

He hit her again, this time with his fist, not the flat of his hand. Blood spurted from her nose and poured down her chin.

"What I don't understand," he was saying, as if nothing had happened, "is why he didn't give you the book as well, Dr. O'Donnell."

"He gave me nothing," she choked.

"Dr. Brayling says you left the site house on Monday night carrying a bag."

"He's lying."

"Who are you working for?" he said softly, gently. "This will stop. If your friend isn't involved, there's no reason for her to be harmed."

"She's not," she whimpered. "Alice doesn't know . . ."

Shelagh flinched as he placed his hand on her throat, stroking her at first in a parody of affection. Then he started to squeeze, harder and harder, until it felt like an iron collar tightening around her neck. She thrashed from side to side, trying to get some air, but he was too strong.

"Were you and Biau both working for her?" he said.

Just as she could feel herself starting to lose consciousness, he released her. She felt him fumbling with the buttons on her shirt, undoing them one by one.

"What are you doing?" she whispered, then flinched at his cold, clinical touch on her skin.

"No one's looking for you." There was a click, then Shelagh smelled lighter fuel. "No one's going to come."

"Please don't hurt me . . ."

"You and Biau were working together?"

She nodded.

"For Madame de l'Oradore?"

She nodded again. "Her son," she managed to say. "François-Baptiste. I only talked to him . . ."

She could feel the flame close to her skin.

"And what about the book?"

"I couldn't find it. Yves neither."

She sensed him react, then he pulled his hand back.

"So why did Biau go to Foix? You know he went to Dr. Tanner's hotel?"

Shelagh tried to shake her head, but it sent a new wave of pain shuddering through her body.

"He passed something to her."

"It wasn't the book," she managed to say.

Before she could choke out the rest of the sentence, the door opened and she heard muffled voices in the corridor, then the combination of the smell of aftershave and sweat.

"How were you supposed to get the book to Madame de l'Oradore?"

"François-Baptiste." It hurt to speak. "Meet him at the Pic de—I had

313

a number to ring." She recoiled at the touch of his hand on her breast. "Please don't—"

"You see how much easier it is when you cooperate? Now, in a moment, you're going to make that call for me."

Shelagh tried to shake her head in terror. "If they find out I've told you, they'll kill me."

"And I will kill you and Mademoiselle Tanner if you don't," he said calmly. "It's your choice."

Shelagh had no way of knowing if he had Alice. If she was safe or here too.

"He is expecting you to call when you have the book, yes?"

She no longer had the courage to lie. She nodded. "They are more concerned with a small disc, the size of the ring, than the ring itself."

With horror, Shelagh realized she'd told him the one thing he hadn't known.

"What's the disc for?" he demanded.

"I don't know."

Shelagh heard herself screaming as the flame licked her skin.

"What—is—it—for?" he said. There was no emotion in his voice. She was freezing cold. There was a dreadful smell of burning flesh, sweet and sickly.

She could no longer distinguish one word from another as the pain started to carry her away. She was drifting, falling. She felt her neck giving way.

"We're losing her. Get the hood off."

The material was dragged off, catching on the cuts and split skin.

"Fits inside the ring . . ."

Her voice sounded as if it was coming from underwater. "Like a key. To the labyrinth . . ."

"Who else knows about this?" he was shouting at her, but she knew he couldn't reach her now. Her chin dropped down on to her chest. He jerked her head back. One of her eyes was swollen shut, but the other flickered open. All she could see was a mass of blurred faces, moving in and out of her line of vision. "She doesn't realize . . ."

"Who?" he said. "Madame de l'Oradore? Jeanne Giraud?"

"Alice," she whispered.

CHAPTER 54

Alice arrived in Chartres late in the afternoon. She found a hotel, then bought a map and went straight to the address she'd been given by directory enquiries. Alice looked up in surprise at the elegant town house, with its gleaming brass knocker and letter box and elegant plants in the window boxes, and the tubs framing the steps. Alice couldn't imagine Shelagh staying here.

What the hell are you going to say if someone answers?

Alice took a deep breath, then walked up the steps and rang the bell. There was no answer. She waited, took a pace back and looked up at the windows, then tried again. She dialed the number. Seconds later, she could hear a phone ringing inside.

At least it was the right place.

It was an anticlimax but, if she was honest, a relief also. The confrontation, if that's what was coming, could wait.

The square in front of the cathedral was thronging with tourists, all clutching cameras, and tour guides holding flags or colorful umbrellas held high. Orderly Germans, self-conscious English, glamorous Italians, quiet Japanese, enthusiastic Americans. All the children looked bored.

At some point during the long drive north, she'd stopped thinking she would learn anything from the labyrinth in Chartres. It seemed so obviously connected—the cave at the Pic de Soularac, to Grace, to her personally—*too* obvious. Part of her felt like she'd been set up to follow a false trail.

Still, Alice bought a ticket and joined an English-language tour, scheduled to start outside in five minutes. Their guide was an efficient, middle-aged woman with a superior manner and clipped voice.

"To the modern eye, cathedrals are gray, soaring structures of devotion and faith. However, in medieval times, they were very colorful, rather than like Hindu shrines in India or Thailand. The statues and tympana that adorned the great portals, in Chartres as elsewhere, were tricked out in polychrome." The guide pointed up at the outside with her umbrella. "Look closely and you can still see fragments of pink, blue and yellow clinging to the cracks in the statues."

All around Alice, people were nodding obediently.

"In 1194," the woman continued, "a fire destroyed most of the city of Chartres as well as the cathedral itself. At first it was believed that the cathedral's holiest relic, the *sancta camisia*—the robe supposedly worn by Mary at the birth of Christ—had been destroyed. But after three days the relic was discovered, having been hidden by the monks in the crypt. This was seen as a miracle, a sign that the cathedral should be rebuilt. The current edifice was finished in 1223 and in 1260 consecrated as the Cathedral Church of the Assumption of Our Lady, the first cathedral in France to be dedicated to the Virgin Mary."

Alice listened with half an ear, until they arrived at the northern side of the cathedral. The guide pointed at the eerie stone procession of Old Testament kings and queens carved above the north portal.

Alice felt a flutter of nervous excitement.

"This is the only significant representation of the Old Testament in the cathedral," said the guide, beckoning them closer. "On this pillar is a carving which many people believe shows the Ark of the Covenant being carried away from Jerusalem by Menelik, son of Solomon and the Queen of Sheba, despite the fact that historians claim the story of Menelik was not known in Europe until the fifteenth century. And here"—she lowered her arm a little—"is another mystery. Those of you with good eyesight might just be able to make out the Latin—*HIC AMITITUR ARCHA CEDERIS*." She looked round the group and smiled smugly. "The Latin scholars among you will realize that the inscription does not make sense. Some guidebooks translate *ARCHA CEDERIS* as: 'You are to work through the Ark' and translate the entire inscription as: 'Here things take their course: you are to work through the Ark.' However, if you take *CEDERIS* to be a corruption of *FOEDERIS*, as some commentators have suggested, then the inscription might be translated as: 'Here it is let go, the Ark of the Covenant.'"

She looked around the group. "This door, among other things, is one of the reasons for the number of myths and legends that have grown up around the cathedral. Unusually, the names of the master builders of Chartres Cathedral are not known. It is likely that, for some reason, no records were kept and the names were simply forgotten. However, those with more, shall we say, *lurid* imaginations have interpreted the absence of information differently. The most persistent of the rumors has it that the cathedral was built by descendants of the Poor Knights of Solomon, the Knights Templar, as a codified book in stone, a gigantic puzzle decipherable only by the initiated. Many believed the bones of Mary Magdalene had once been buried beneath the labyrinth. Or even the Holy Grail itself."

"Has anybody looked?" Alice said, regretting the words the second they were out of her mouth. Disapproving eyes swiveled to her like a spotlight.

The guide raised her eyebrows. "Certainly. On more than one occasion. But most of you will not be surprised to hear they found nothing. Another myth." She paused. "Shall we move inside?"

Feeling awkward, Alice followed the group to the West Door and joined the queue to enter the cathedral. Straight away, everybody dropped their voices as the distinctive smell of stone and incense worked their magic. In the side chapels and by the main entrance, flickering rows of devotional candles sparkled in the gloom.

She braced herself for some sort of reaction, visions of the past, as she'd experienced in Toulouse and Carcassonne. She felt nothing and after a while, she relaxed and began to enjoy herself. From her research, she knew Chartres Cathedral was said to have the finest collection of stained glass anywhere in the world, but she was unprepared for the dazzling brilliance of the windows. A kaleidoscope of shimmering color flooded the cathedral, depicting scenes of everyday and biblical life. The Rose Window and the Blue Virgin Window, the Noah Window showing the Flood and the animals marching two by two into the ark. As she wandered around, Alice tried to imagine what it must have been like when the walls were covered with frescos and decked with richly woven tapestries, the Eastern fabrics and silken banners all embroidered with gold. To medieval eyes, the contrast between the splendors of God's temple and the world outside the cloister must have been overwhelming. Proof positive, perhaps, of God's glory on earth.

"And, finally," the guide said, "we come to the famous eleven-circuit pavement labyrinth. Completed in 1200, it is the largest in Europe. The original centerpiece is long gone, but the rest is intact. For medieval Christians, the labyrinth provided an opportunity to undertake a spiritual pilgrimage, in place of an actual journey to Jerusalem. Hence the fact that pavement labyrinths—as opposed to those found on the walls of churches and cathedrals—were often known as the *chemin de Jérusalem*, that is, the road or path to Jerusalem. Pilgrims would walk the circuit toward the center, sometimes many times, symbolic of a growing understanding or closeness to God. Penitents often completed the journey on their knees, sometimes taking many days over it."

Alice edged to the front, her heart racing, only now realizing subconsciously she'd been putting this moment off.

This is the moment.

She took a deep breath. The symmetry was destroyed by the rows of chairs on either side of the nave facing the altar for evensong. Even so, and despite knowing its dimensions from her research, Alice was taken aback by the size of it. It entirely dominated the cathedral.

Slowly, like everyone else, Alice began to walk the labyrinth, round and round in ever decreasing circles, like a halting game of follow-my-leader, until she arrived at the center.

She felt nothing. No shiver up her spine, no moment of enlightenment or transformation. Nothing. She crouched down and touched the ground. The stone was smooth and cool, but it did not speak to her.

Alice gave a wry smile. *What were you expecting?*

She didn't even need to get her drawing of the cave labyrinth from her bag to know that there was nothing for her here. Without a fuss, Alice excused herself from the group, and slipped away.

After the fierce heat of the Midi, the gentle northern sun was a relief and Alice spent the next hour exploring the picturesque historic town center. She was half looking for the corner where Grace and Audric Baillard had posed for the camera.

It didn't seem to exist or else was outside the area covered by the map. Most of the streets had taken their names from the trades practiced there in previous times: clockmakers, tanners, equerries and stationers, testament to Chartres' importance as the great center of paper making and book binding in France in the twelfth and thirteenth centuries. But no rue des Trois Degrès.

Finally, Alice arrived back where she had started, in front of the West Door of the cathedral. She sat down on the wall, leaning against the railings. Immediately, her gaze honed in on the corner of the street directly opposite. She jumped up and ran over to read the sign on the wall: RUE DE L'ÉTROIT DEGRÉ, DITE AUSSI RUE DES TROIS DEGRÉS (DES TROIS MARCHES).

The road had been renamed. Smiling to herself, Alice stepped back to get a better view and knocked into a man buried in a newspaper.

"*Pardon,*" she said, moving sideways.

"No, excuse me," he said, in a pleasant East Coast accent. "It was my fault. I wasn't paying attention to where I was going. Are you okay?"

"I'm fine."

To her surprise, he was staring intently at her.

"Is there . . ."

"It's Alice, right?"

"Yes?" she said cautiously.

"Alice, of course. Hi," he said, pushing his fingers through his mop of shaggy brown hair. "How amazing!"

"I'm sorry, but I—"

"William Franklin," he said, holding out his hand. "Will. We met in London, nineteen-ninety four or five. Big group of us. You were dating a guy . . . what was he called . . . Oliver. Is that right? I'd gone over to visit with my cousin."

Alice had a vague memory of an afternoon in an overcrowded flat filled with Oliver's university friends. She thought she could just about remember an American boy, engaging, good looking, although she'd been head over heels in love at that stage, noticing no one else.

This boy?

"You have a good memory," she said, shaking his hand. "It was a long time ago."

"You haven't changed so much," he said, smiling. "So, how is Oliver anyhow?"

Alice pulled a face. "We're not still together."

"That's too bad," he said. There was a slight pause, then added: "Who's in the photo?"

Alice looked down. She'd forgotten she was still holding it.

"My aunt. I came across this in some of her things and, since I was here, I thought I'd see if I could track down where it was taken." She grinned. "It's been harder than you'd imagine."

Will looked over her shoulder. "And the guy?"

"Just a friend. A writer."

Another a pause, as if both wanted to keep the conversation going, but didn't quite know what to say. Will looked back to the picture.

"She looks nice."

"Nice? She looks rather determined to me, although I don't know that for a fact. I never met her."

"Really? So how come you're carrying her photo around?"

Alice put the photograph back in her bag. "It's complicated."

"I can do complicated," he grinned. "Look . . ." he hesitated. "Do you want to get coffee or something? If you've not got someplace else you've got to be."

Alice was surprised but, actually, she'd been thinking the same thing.

"Do you usually go picking up random women like this?"

"Not usually," he said. "The question is do you usually accept?"

Alice felt as if she was looking down on the scene from above. Watching a man and a woman, who looked like her, walk into the old-fashioned *patisserie* with the cakes and pastries laid out in long glass cabinets.

I can't believe I'm doing this.

Sights, smells, sounds. The waiters dipping in and out of the tables, the burned, bitter aroma of the coffee, the hiss of milk in the machine, the clink of forks on the plate, everything was especially vivid. Most of all Will himself, the way he smiled, the turn of his head, the way his fingers went to the silver chain at his neck when he was talking.

They sat at a table outside. The spire of the cathedral was just visible over the tops of the houses. A slight constraint descended on them when they sat down. They both started talking at once. Alice laughed, Will apologized.

Cautiously, tentatively, they started to fill in the stories of their lives since they'd last met.

"You looked really engrossed," she said, turning his newspaper around so she could read the headline. "You know, when you came hurtling round that corner and we collided."

Will grinned. "Yeah, sorry about that," he apologized. "The local paper's not usually so exciting. A man's been found dead in the river, right in the center of the city. He'd been stabbed in the back, his hands and feet were tied, the local radio station's going crazy. They seem to think it's some kind of ritual killing. Now they're linking it to the disappearance last week of a local journalist, who was writing an *exposé* of secret religious societies."

The smile fell from Alice's face. "Can I see that?" she said, reaching for the paper.

"Sure. Help yourself."

Her sense of uneasiness grew as she read the list of names. The *Noublesso Véritable.* There was something familiar about the name.

"Are you okay?" Alice looked up to see Will gazing at her.

"Sorry," she said. "I was miles away. It's just I've come across something similar recently. The coincidence gave me a shock."

"Coincidence? Sounds intriguing."

"It's a long story."

"I'm in no hurry," said Will, propping his elbows on the table and smiling encouragingly at her.

After being trapped inside her own thoughts for so long, Alice was tempted by the chance of finally talking to someone. And she sort of knew him. *Only tell him what you want.*

"Well, I'm not sure this is going to make much sense," she began. "A couple of months ago I discovered, totally out of the blue, that an aunt I'd never heard of had died and left everything to me, including a house in France."

"The lady in the photo."

She nodded. "She's called Grace Tanner. I was due to come to France anyway, to visit a friend who was working at an archeological dig in the Pyrenees, so I decided to run the two trips together." She hesitated. "Some things happened at the dig—I won't bore you by going into detail—except to say there seemed to be . . . Well, never mind." She took a breath. "Yesterday, after a meeting with the solicitor, I went to my aunt's house and I found some things . . . something, a pattern, which I'd seen at the dig." She stumbled, inarticulate. "There was also a book by an author called Audric Baillard who, I'm almost a hundred percent certain, is the man in the photo."

"He's still alive?"

"So far as I know. I haven't been able to track him down."

"What's his relationship with your aunt?"

"I'm not sure. I'm hoping he'll be able to tell me. He's my only link to her. And other things."

To the labyrinth, the family tree, to my dream.

When she looked up, she saw Will was looking confused, but engaged. "I can't say I'm much the wiser yet," he said with a grin.

"I'm not explaining it very well," she admitted. "Let's talk about something less complicated. You never did tell me what you were doing in Chartres."

"Like every other American in France, trying to write."

Alice smiled. "Isn't Paris more traditional?"

"I started off there, but I guess I found it too, well, impersonal, if you know what I mean. My parents knew folks here. I liked it. Ended up staying a while."

Alice nodded, expecting him to carry on. Instead, he returned to something she'd said earlier. "This pattern you mentioned," he said casually. "That you found at the dig and then at Grace's house, what was special about it?"

She hesitated. "It's a labyrinth."

"Is that why you're here in Chartres then? To go to the cathedral?"

"It's not quite the same . . ." She stopped as caution returned. "Partly, although it's more because I'm hoping to catch up with a friend. Shelagh. There's a . . . a possibility she might be in Chartres." Alice reached in her bag and passed the scrap of paper with the address scribbled on it across the table to Will. "I went there earlier, but there was no one there. So I decided to do my sightseeing, then go back in about an hour or so."

Alice was shocked to see Will had turned white. He looked dumbstruck.

"Are you okay?" she asked.

"Why do you think your friend might be there?" he said in a tight voice.

"I don't, for sure," she said, still puzzled by the change that had come over him.

"This is the friend you went to visit at the dig?"

She nodded.

"And she saw this labyrinth pattern also? Like you?"

"I suppose so, although she didn't mention it. She was more obsessed

321

with something I'd found, which . . ." Alice broke off as Will abruptly stood up.

"What are you doing?" she said, unnerved by the expression on his face as he took her hand.

"Come with me. There's something you ought to see."

"Where are we going?" she asked again, hurrying to keep up with him.

Then they rounded the corner and Alice realized they were at the other end of rue du Cheval Blanc. Will strode toward the house, then ran up the steps to the front door.

"Are you out of your mind? What if someone's come home?"

"There won't be."

"But how do you know?"

Alice watched with astonishment as Will produced a key from his pocket and opened the front door. "Hurry. Before someone sees us."

"You have a key," she said in disbelief. "Suppose you start telling me what the hell's going on."

Will ran back down the steps and grabbed her hand.

"There's a version of your labyrinth here," he hissed. "Okay? *Now*, will you come?"

What if it's another trap?

After everything that had happened, she'd be crazy to follow him. It was too much of a risk. Nobody even knew she was here. Curiosity won out over common sense. Alice looked up at Will's face, eager and anxious at one and the same time.

She decided to give him another chance and trust him.

CHAPTER 55

Alice found herself standing in a grand entrance hall, more like a museum than a private house. Will went straight to a tapestry opposite the front door and pulled it away from the wall.

"What are you doing?"

She ran after him and saw a tiny brass handle set into the paneling. Will rattled and pushed at it, then turned round with frustration.

"Dammit. It's been locked from the other side."

"It's a door?"

"Right."

"And the labyrinth you saw, it's down there?"

Will nodded. "You go down a flight of stairs and along a corridor, which leads into a weird sort of chamber. Egyptian symbols on the wall, a tomb with the symbol of the labyrinth, just like you described, carved on top. Now—" he broke off. "The stuff in the newspaper. The fact your friend had this address . . ."

"You're making a lot of assumptions based on not much," she said.

Will dropped the corner of the tapestry and was striding to a room on the opposite side of the hall. After a moment's hesitation, Alice followed.

"What are you doing?" she hissed as Will opened the door.

Walking into the library was like stepping back in time. It was a formal room with the atmosphere of a men's club. The shutters were partially closed and batons of yellow light lay stretched on the carpet like strips of golden cloth. There was an air of permanence, a smell of antiquity and polish.

Bookshelves ran from floor to ceiling along three sides of the room with sliding book ladders giving access to the highest shelves. Will knew exactly where he was going. There was a section dedicated to books on Chartres, photographic volumes set alongside the more serious examinations of architecture and social history.

Turning anxiously toward the door, her heart racing, Alice watched as Will pulled out a book with a family crest embossed on the front and carried it to the table. Alice looked over his shoulder as he flicked through the pages. Glossy color photographs, old maps of Chartres, line and ink drawings flashed by until Will reached the section he wanted.

"What is it?"

"A book about the de l'Oradore house. *This* house," he said. "The family has lived here for hundreds of years, since it was built. There are architectural floor plans and elevations of each floor of the house."

Will flicked through until he'd found the page he wanted. "There," he said, turning the book round so she could see properly. "Is that it?"

Alice caught her breath. "Oh God," she whispered.

It was a perfect drawing of her labyrinth.

The sound of the front door being slammed shut made them both jump.

"Will, the door! We left it open!"

She could make out muffled voices in the hall, a man and a woman.

"They're coming in here," she hissed.

Will thrust the book into her hands. "Quick," he hissed, pointing at a large three-seater sofa standing beneath the window. "Let me handle this."

Alice scooped up her bag, ran to the sofa and crawled into the gap between it and the wall. There was a pungent smell of cracked leather and old cigar smoke and the dust tickled her nose. She heard Will shut the case with a rattle, then take up position in the middle of the room just as the library door creaked open.

"Qu'est-ce que vous foutez là?"

By tilting her head a little, Alice could just about see the two of them reflected in the glass doors of the cabinets. He was young and tall, about the same size as Will, although more angular. Black curly hair, a high forehead and patrician nose. She frowned. He reminded her of someone.

"François-Baptiste. Hi," said Will. Even to Alice's ears he sounded falsely bright.

"What the fuck are you doing in here?" he repeated in English.

Will flashed the magazine he'd picked up from the table. "Just dropped by to get something to read."

François-Baptiste cast his eye over the title and gave a short laugh.

"Doesn't seem your thing."

"You'd be surprised."

The boy took a step toward Will. "You won't last much longer," he said in a low, bitter voice. "She'll get bored of you and kick you out like all the rest. You didn't even know she was going out of town, did you?"

"What goes on between her and me is none of your business, so if you don't mind—"

François-Baptiste stepped in front of him. "Why the hurry?"

"Don't push me, François-Baptiste, I'm warning you."

François-Baptiste put his hand on Will's chest to stop him passing.

Will pushed the boy's arm away. "Don't touch me."

"What are you going to do about it?"

"*Ça suffit.*"

Both men jerked round. Alice strained to get a better look, but the woman hadn't come far enough into the room.

"What is going on?" she demanded. "Squabbling like children. François-Baptiste? William?"

"*Rien, maman. Je lui demandais—*"

Will was looking stunned as he finally realized who it was who'd come in with François. "Marie-Cécile. I had no idea . . ." He faltered. "I wasn't expecting you back just yet."

The woman moved farther into the room and Alice got a clear look at her face.

It can't be.

Today, she was dressed more formally than the last time Alice had seen her, in a knee-length ocher skirt and matching jacket. Her hair was loose around her face rather than tied back with a scarf.

But there was no mistaking her. It was the same woman Alice had seen outside the Hôtel de la Cité in Carcassonne. This was Marie-Cécile de l'Oradore.

She glanced from mother to son. The family resemblance was strong. The same profile, the same imperious air. The reason for François-Baptiste's jealousy and the antagonism between him and Will now made sense.

"But, actually, my son has a point," Marie-Cécile was saying. "What are you doing in here?"

"I've been . . . I was just looking for something different to read. It's been . . . lonely without you."

Alice winced. He sounded utterly unconvincing.

"Lonely?" she echoed. "Your face tells a different story, Will."

Marie-Cécile leaned forward and kissed Will on the mouth. Alice felt the embarrassment seep into the room. It was uncomfortably intimate. She could see Will's fists were clenched.

He doesn't want me to see this.

The thought, bewildering as it was, came and went from her mind in the blinking of an eye.

Marie-Cécile released him, a glint of satisfaction on her face.

"We'll catch up later, Will. But now, I'm afraid, François-Baptiste and I have a little business to attend to. *Desolée.* So if you'll excuse us."

"In here?"

Too quick. Too obvious.

Marie-Cécile narrowed her eyes. "Why not in here?"

"No reason," he said sharply.

"*Maman. Il est dix-huit heures déjà.*"

"J'arrive," she said, still looking suspiciously at Will.

"Mais, je ne . . ."

"Va le chercher," she snapped. Go and get it.

Alice heard François-Baptiste storm out of the room, then watched Marie-Cécile put her arms around Will's waist and pull him against her. Her nails bright red against the white of his T-shirt. She wanted to look away, but couldn't.

"Tiens," said Marie-Cécile. *"A bientôt."*

"Are you coming now?" said Will. Alice could hear the panic in his voice as he realized he was going to have to leave her trapped.

"Tout à l'heure." Later.

Alice could do nothing. Just listen to the sound of Will's feet walking out.

The two men crossed in the doorway.

"Here," he said, handing his mother a copy of the same paper Will had been reading earlier.

"How did they get hold of the story so quickly?"

"I have no idea." he said sulkily. "Authié, I suspect."

Alice went rigid. *The same Authié?*

"Do you actually know that for a fact, François-Baptiste?" Marie-Cécile was saying.

"Well, someone must have told them. The police sent divers into the Eure on Tuesday, in exactly the right place. They knew what they were looking for. Think about it. Who claimed there was a leak in Chartres in the first place? Authié. Did he ever actually produce any evidence that Tavernier had talked to the journalist?"

"Tavernier?"

"The man in the river," he said acidly.

"Ah, of course." Marie-Cécile lit a cigarette. "The report mentions the *Noublesso Véritable* by name."

"Authié himself could have told them."

"So long as there is nothing to connect Tavernier with this house, there's no problem," she said, sounding bored. "Is there anything?"

"I did everything you told me to do."

"And you have prepared everything for Saturday?"

"Yes," he admitted, "although without the ring or the book, I don't know why we're bothering."

A smile flitted across Marie-Cécile's red lips. "Well, you see, this is why we still need Authié, despite your evident mistrust of him," she said smoothly. "He says he has, *miracle*, retrieved the ring."

"Why the hell didn't you tell me this before?" he said furiously.

"I'm telling you now," she said. "He claims his men took it from the English girl's hotel room in Carcassonne last night."

Alice felt her skin turn cold. *That's impossible.*

"You think he's lying?"

"Don't be idiotic, François-Baptiste," she snapped. "Obviously, he's lying. If Dr. Tanner had taken it, it wouldn't have taken Authié four days to get it. Besides, I had his apartment and his offices searched."

"Then—"

She cut across him. "If—*if*—Authié does have it—which I doubt—then either he got it from Biau's grandmother or else he's had it all along. Possibly he took it from the cave himself."

"But why bother?"

The phone rang, intrusive, loud. Alice's heart leaped into her mouth. François-Baptiste looked to his mother.

"Answer it," she said.

He did what he was told. *"Oui."*

Alice hardly dared breathe for fear she would give herself away.

"Oui, je comprends. Attends." He covered the phone with his hand. "It's O'Donnell. She says she has the book."

"Ask why she's been out of touch."

He nodded. "Where've you been since Monday?" He listened. "Does anybody else know you have it?" He listened. *"Okay. A vingt-deux heures. Demain soir."*

He put the receiver back in its cradle.

"Are you sure it was her?"

"It was her voice. She knew the arrangements."

"He must have been listening in."

"What do you mean?" he said, uncertainly. "Who?"

"For crying out loud, who do you think?" she snapped. "Authié, of course."

"I—"

"Shelagh O'Donnell's been missing for days. As soon as I'm safely out of the way in Chartres, O'Donnell reappears! First the ring, then the book."

François-Baptiste finally lost his temper. "But you were just defending him!" he shouted. "Accusing me of jumping to conclusions. If you know he's working against us, then why didn't you tell me, instead of letting me make a fool of myself? More to the point, why don't you stop him? Have you even ever asked yourself why he wants the books so badly? What he's going to do with them? Auction them to the highest bidder?"

"I am well aware of precisely why he wants the books," she said in a chill voice.

"Why do you always have to do this? You humiliate me all the time!"

327

"The discussion is over," she said. "We'll travel tomorrow. That will get us there in good time for your assignation with O'Donnell and for me to prepare myself. The ceremony will go ahead at midnight as planned."

"You want me to meet her?" he said in disbelief.

"Well, obviously," she said. For the first time, she heard some sort of emotion in her voice. "I want the book, François-Baptiste."

"And if he doesn't have it?"

"I don't think he would go to all this trouble if he didn't."

Alice heard François-Baptiste walk across the room and open the door.

"What about him?" he said, a little of the fire returning to his voice. "You can't leave him here to—"

"Leave Will to me. He, also, is not your concern."

Will was concealed in the cupboard in the kitchen passage.

It was cramped and smelled of leather coats, old boots and waxed jackets, but it was the only place that gave him a clear view of the library and study doors. He saw François-Baptiste come out first and go into the study, followed moments later by Marie-Cécile. Will waited until the heavy door shut, then immediately emerged from the cupboard and ran across the hall to the library.

"Alice," he whispered. "Quick. We've got to get you out of here." There was a slight sound, then she appeared. "I'm so sorry," he said. "This is all my fault. Are you okay?"

She nodded, although she was deathly pale.

Will reached for her hand, but she refused to come with him.

"What is this all about, Will? You live here. You know these people and yet you're prepared to throw it all away helping a stranger. It makes no sense."

He wanted to say she wasn't a stranger, but stopped himself.

"I—"

He didn't know what to say. The room seemed to fade to nothing. All Will saw was Alice's heart-shaped face and her unflinching brown eyes that seemed to be looking into the very heart of him.

"Why didn't you tell me that you . . . that you and she . . . ? That you lived here."

He couldn't meet her gaze. Alice stared at him a moment longer, then moved quickly across the room and out into the hall, leaving him to follow.

"What are you going to do now?" he said desperately.

"Well, I've learned how Shelagh's connected with this house," she said. "She works for them."

"Them?" he said, baffled, opening the front door so they could slip out. "What do you mean?"

"But she's not here. Madame de l'Oradore and her son are looking for her too. From what I heard, I'd guess she's being held somewhere near Foix."

Alice suddenly turned in a panic at the bottom of the steps.

"Will, I've left my bag in the library," she said in horror. "Behind the sofa, with the book."

More than anything, Will wanted to kiss her. The timing couldn't be worse, they were caught up in a situation he didn't understand, Alice didn't even really trust him. And yet it felt right.

Without thinking, Will moved to touch the side of her face. He felt he knew exactly how smooth and cool her skin would feel, as if it was a gesture he'd made a thousand times before. Then the memory of the way she'd withdrawn from him in the café pulled him up short and he stopped, his hand a hair's breadth from her cheek.

"I'm sorry," he started to say, as if Alice could read his mind. She was staring at him, then a brief smile flickered across her taut and anxious face. "I didn't mean to offend you," he stumbled. "It's . . ."

"It doesn't matter," she said, but her voice was soft.

Will gave a sigh of relief. He knew she was wrong. It mattered more than anything in the world, but at least she wasn't angry with him.

"Will," she said, a little sharper this time. "My bag? It's got everything in it. All my notes."

"Sure, yes," he said immediately. "Sorry. I'll get it. Bring it to you." He tried to focus. "Where are you staying?"

"Hôtel Petit Monarque. On the Place des Epars."

"Right," he said, running back up the steps. "Give me thirty minutes."

Will watched her until she was out of sight, then went back inside. There was a sliver of light showing under the study door.

Suddenly the door to the study opened. Will sprang back out of sight between the door and the wall. François-Baptiste came out and walked toward the kitchen. Will heard the pass door swing open and shut, then nothing.

Will pressed his face to the gap so he could see Marie-Cécile. She was sitting at her desk looking at something, something that glinted and caught the light when she moved.

Will forgot what he was supposed to be doing as he watched Marie-Cécile stand up and lift down one of the paintings hanging on the wall behind her. It was her favorite piece of art. She told him all about it once, in the early days. It was a golden canvas with splashes of bright color showing French soldiers gazing upon the toppled pillars and palaces of ancient Egypt. *On Gazing Upon the Sands of Time—1799*, he remembered. That was it.

Behind where the picture had been hanging was a small black metal door cut into the wall with an electronic keypad next to it. She punched in six numbers. There was a sharp click and the combination opened. From out of the safe, she lifted two black packages and carefully put them on the desk. Will adjusted his position, desperate to see what was inside.

He was so caught up that he didn't hear the footsteps coming up behind him.

"Don't move."

"François-Baptiste, I—"

Will felt the cold muzzle of a gun pressing into his side.

"And put your hands where I can see them."

He tried to turn round, but François-Baptiste grabbed his neck and slammed his face flat against the wall.

"Qu'est-ce qui se passe?" Marie-Cécile called out.

François-Baptiste jabbed him again.

"Je m'en occupe," he said. Everything's under control.

Alice looked at her watch again.

He's not coming.

She was standing in the reception of the hotel, staring at the glass doors as if she could conjure Will out of thin air. Nearly an hour had passed since she'd left rue du Cheval Blanc. She didn't know what to do. Her purse, her phone, car keys were all in her jacket pocket. Everything else was in her rucksack.

It doesn't matter. Get away from here.

The longer she waited, the more she started to doubt Will's motives. The fact he'd appeared out of nowhere. Alice went over the sequence of events in her mind.

Was it really just coincidence they'd bumped into each other like that? She'd told no one at all where she was going.

Then why hasn't he come?

At half-past eight, Alice decided she couldn't wait any longer. She explained she wouldn't need the room after all, scribbled a note for Will in case he came, giving her number, then went.

She threw the jacket on the car's front seat and noticed the envelope sticking out of the pocket. The letter she'd been given at the hotel, which she'd forgotten all about. Alice pulled it out and put it on the dashboard to read when she stopped for a break.

Night fell as she drove south. The headlamps of the oncoming cars shone in her eyes, dazzling her. Trees and bushes leaped ghost-like out of the darkness. Orléans, Poitiers, Bordeaux, the signs flashed by.

Cocooned in her own world, for hour after hour, Alice asked herself the same questions over and again. Each time, she came up with a different answer.

Why? For information. She'd certainly handed that to them all right. All her notes, her drawings, the photograph of Grace and Baillard.

He promised to show you the labyrinth chamber.

She'd seen nothing. Just a picture in a book. Alice shook her head. She didn't want to believe it.

Why did he help her get away? Because he'd got what he wanted, rather, what Madame de l'Oradore wanted.

So they can follow you.

CHAPTER 56

Carcassona

AGOST 1209

The French attacked Sant-Vicens at dawn on Monday the third of August.

Alaïs scrambled up the ladders of the Tour du Major to join her father to watch from the battlements. She looked for Guilhem in the crowd, but could not see him.

Now, over the sound of sword and battle cry of the soldiers storming the low defensive walls, she could just make out the sound of singing floating across the plain down from the Gravèta hill.

Veni creator spiritus
Mentes tuorum visita!

"The priests," Alaïs said aghast. "They sing to God as they come to slaughter us."

The suburb began to burn. As smoke spiraled up into the air, behind the low walls, people and animals scattered in panic in all directions.

Grappling hooks were hurled over the parapet quicker than the defenders could cut them down. Dozens of scaling ladders were thrown up to the walls. The garrison kicked them down, set them alight, but some held in place. French foot soldiers swarmed like ants. The more who were cut back, the more there seemed to be.

At the foot of the fortifications on both sides, the injured and dead bodies were stacked one on top of another, like piles of firewood. With every hour that passed, the toll grew greater.

The Crusaders rolled a catapult into place and began their bombardment of the fortifications. The thuds shook Sant-Vicens to its foundations, relentless, implacable in the storm of arrows and missiles thrown from above.

The walls began to crumble.

"They're through," Alaïs shouted. "They've breached the defenses!"

Viscount Trencavel and his men were ready for them. Brandishing sword and ax, two and three abreast they charged the besiegers. The massive hooves of the warhorses trampled all in their path, their heavy steel shoes shattering skulls like husks and crushing limbs in a mass of skin and blood and bone. Street by street, the fighting spread through the suburb, moving ever closer to the walls of the Cité itself. Alaïs could see a mass of terrorized inhabitants flooding through the Porte de Rodez into the Cité to escape the violence of the battle. The old, the infirm, women and children. Every able-bodied man was armed, fighting alongside the soldiers of the garrison. Most were cut down where they stood, clubs no match for the swords of Crusaders.

The defenders fought bravely, but they were outnumbered ten to one. Like an inrushing tide breaking on the shore, the Crusaders stormed through, breaching the fortifications and demolishing sections of the walls.

Trencavel and his *chevaliers* were desperate not to lose control of the river, but it was hopeless. He sounded the retreat.

With the triumphant howls of the French echoing in their ears, the heavy gates of the Porte de Rodez were opened to allow the survivors back into the Cité. As Viscount Trencavel led his defeated band of survivors in single file through the streets back to the Château Comtal, Alaïs looked down in horror at the scene of devastation and destruction below. She had seen death many times, but not on this scale. She felt polluted by the reality of war, the senseless waste of it.

Deceived also. Now she realized how the *chansons à gestes* she had so loved in her childhood had lied. There was no nobility in war. Only suffering.

Alaïs descended the battlements to the courtyard and joined the other women waiting at the gate, praying that Guilhem was among them.

Be safely delivered.

At last, she heard the sound of hooves on the bridge. Alaïs saw him straightaway and her spirit leaped. His face and armor were stained with blood and ash, his eyes reflected the ferocity of the battle, but he was unharmed.

"Your husband fought valiantly, Dame Alaïs," said Viscount Trencavel, noticing her standing there. "He cut down many and saved the lives of many more. We are grateful for both his skill and courage." Alaïs flushed. "Tell me, where is your father?"

She pointed to the northeastern corner of the courtyard. "We witnessed the battle from the *ambans, Messire.*"

Guilhem had dismounted and handed the reins to his *écuyer.*

Alaïs approached him shyly, not sure of her reception. *"Messire."*

He took her pale white hand and raised it to his lips. "Thierry fell," he said in a hollow voice. "They're bringing him back now. He's badly wounded."

"Messire, I am sorry."

"We were as brothers," he continued. "Alzeu too. Barely a month separated us in age. We stood for each other, worked to pay for our hauberks and swords. We were dubbed the same Passiontide."

"I know it," she said softly, drawing his head down to hers. "Come, let me help you, then I will do what I can for Thierry."

She saw his eyes glistened with tears. She hurried on, knowing he would not want her to see him cry.

"Guilhem, come," she said softly. "Take me to him."

Thierry had been taken to the Great Hall with all the others who were badly wounded. The lines of dying and injured men were three deep. Alaïs and the other women did what they could. With her hair wound into a plait over her shoulder, she looked no more than a child.

As the hours passed, the air in the confined chamber grew more putrid and the flies more persistent. For the most part, Alaïs and the other women worked in silence and with steady determination, knowing that there would be little respite before the assault began anew. Priests stepped between the lines of dying and injured soldiers, hearing confession, giving the last rites. Beneath the disguise of their dark robes, two *parfaits* administered the *consolament* to the Cathar believers.

Thierry's injuries were serious. He'd been struck several times. His ankle was broken and a lance had pierced his thigh, shattering the bone inside the leg. Alaïs knew he had lost too much blood, but for Guilhem's sake she did everything she could. She heated a decoction of knitbone root and leaves in hot wax, and then applied it in a compress once it had cooled.

Leaving Guilhem to sit with him, Alaïs turned her attention to those who had the best chance of survival. She dissolved powder of angelica root in carduus water and with the help of scullions from the kitchen carrying the liquid in pails, she spooned the medicine into the mouths of any who could swallow. If she could keep infection at bay and their blood stayed pure, then their wounds had a chance of healing.

Alaïs returned to Thierry whenever she could to refresh the dressings, even though it was clear there was no hope. He was no longer conscious and his skin had taken on the blue-white taint of death. She put her hand on Guilhem's shoulder.

"I'm sorry," she whispered. "It won't be long now."

Guilhem only nodded.

Alaïs worked her way to the far end of the hall. As she passed, a young *chevalier*, little older than she was, cried out. She stopped and knelt down beside him. His child's face was creased with pain and confusion, his lips were cracked and his eyes, which had once been brown, were tortured with fear.

"Hush," she murmured. "Do you have no one?"

He tried to shake his head. Alaïs smoothed his brow with her hand and lifted the cloth that covered his shield arm. Immediately, she let it drop. The boy's shoulder was crushed. Fragments of white bone jutted through torn skin, like a wreck at low tide. There was a gaping hole in his side. Blood was flowing steadily from the wound, creating a pool where he lay.

His right hand was frozen around the hilt of his sword. Alaïs tried to ease it from his grasp, but his rigid fingers would not let it go. Alaïs ripped a piece of material from her skirt and plugged the deep wound. From a vial in her purse, she took a tincture of valerian and dropped two measures onto his lips to ease the pain of his passing. There was nothing else she could do.

Death was unkind. It came slowly. Gradually, the rattling in his chest grew louder as his breathing became labored. As his eyes darkened, his terror grew and he cried out. Alaïs stayed with him, singing to him and stroking his brow until his soul left his body.

"God take your soul," she whispered, closing his eyes. She covered his face, then moved on to the next.

Alaïs worked all day, administering ointment and dressing wounds until her eyes ached and her hands were streaked red with blood. At the end of the day, shafts of evening sunlight broke through the high windows of the Great Hall. The dead had been taken away. The living were as comfortable as their injuries permitted.

She was exhausted, but thoughts of the night before, lying once more in Guilhem's arms, sustained her. Her bones ached and her back was stiff from bending and crouching, but it no longer seemed to matter.

Taking advantage of the frenzy of activity in the rest of the Château Comtal, Oriane slipped away to her chamber to wait for her informer.

"About time," she snapped. "Tell me what you have discovered."

"The Jew died before we learned much, although my lord believes that he had already given his book into your father's safekeeping."

Oriane gave a half-smile, but said nothing. She had confided in no one what she had discovered sewn into Alaïs' cloak.

"What of Esclarmonde de Servian?"

"She was brave, but in the end she told him where the book would be found."

Oriane's green eyes flashed. "And you have it?"

"Not yet."

"But it is within the *Ciutat*? Lord Evreux knows this?"

"He is relying on you, Dame, to provide him with that information."

Oriane thought a moment. "The old woman is dead? The boy too? She cannot interfere in our plans? She cannot get word to my father."

He gave a tight smile. "The woman is dead. The brat eludes us, although I do not believe he can do any damage. When I find him, we will kill him."

Oriane nodded. "And you told Lord Evreux of my . . . interest."

"I did, Dame. He was honored that you should consider being of service in such a way."

"And my terms? He will arrange safe passage out of the *Ciutat*?"

"Provided you deliver the books to him, Dame, he will."

She stood up and started to pace. "Good, this is all good. And you can deal with my husband?"

"If you tell me when and where he will be at the given hour, Dame, then easily." He paused. "It will, however, be more costly than before. The risks are considerably higher, even in such times of unrest. Viscount Trencavel's *escrivan*. He is a man of status."

"I'm well aware of that," she snapped in a cold voice. "How much?"

"Three times what was paid for Raoul," he replied.

"That's impossible!" she said immediately. "I cannot possibly lay my hands on that amount of gold."

"Nevertheless, Dame, that is my price."

"And the book?"

This time, he smiled properly. "That is a matter for separate negotiation, Dame," he said.

CHAPTER 57

The bombardment resumed and continued into the night, a steady thud of missiles, rock and stone, which sent clouds of dust into the air when a strike was made.

From her window, Alaïs could see that the dwellings on the plains had been reduced to smoking rubble. A noxious cloud was hovering above the tops of the trees like a black mist, as if caught in the branches. Some of the inhabitants had made it across the open ground to the rubble of Sant-Vicens and, from there, had sought refuge in the Cité. But most had been cut down as they fled.

In the chapel the candles burned on the altar.

At dawn on Tuesday the fourth of August, Viscount Trencavel and Bertrand Pelletier mounted the ramparts once more.

The French camp was shrouded in the early-morning river mist. Tents, stables, animals, pavilions, an entire city seemed to have taken root. Pelletier looked up. It would be another fiercely hot day. The loss of the river so early in the siege was devastating. Without water, they could not hold out for long. Drought would defeat them, even if the French did not.

Yesterday, Alaïs told him there was rumor of the first case of siege sickness reported in the *quartier* around the Porte de Rodez, which had taken most of the refugees from Sant-Vicens. He had gone to see for himself and although the consul of the quartier had denied it, he feared Alaïs was right.

"You are deep in thought, my friend."

Bertrand turned to face him. "Forgive me, *Messire.*"

Trencavel waved away his apology. "Look at them, Bertrand! They are too many for us to defeat . . . and without water."

"Pedro II of Aragon is said to be only a day's ride away," Pelletier said. "You are his vassal, *Messire.* He is bound to come to your aid."

Pelletier knew an appeal would be difficult—Pedro was a staunch Catholic and also brother-in-law to Raymond VI, Count of Toulouse, even though there was no love lost between the two men, still the historic bond between the House of Trencavel and the House of Aragon was strong.

"The king's diplomatic ambitions are closely tied up with the fate of Carcassona, *Messire*. He has no wish to see the Pays d'Oc controlled by the French." He paused. "Pierre-Roger de Cabaret and your allies support this course of action."

Trencavel placed his hands on the wall in front of him.

"They have said so, yes."

"So you will send word?"

Pedro heeded the call and arrived late in the afternoon of Wednesday the fifth of August.

"Open the gates! Open the gates for *lo Rèi!*"

The gates of the Château Comtal were thrown open. Alaïs was drawn to her window by the noise and ran down to see what was happening. At first, she intended only to ask for news. But when she looked up at the windows of the Great Hall high above her, her curiosity at what was taking place inside got the better of her. Too often she heard news third or fourth hand.

There was a small alcove behind the curtains that separated the Great Hall from the entrance to Viscount Trencavel's private quarters. Alaïs had not tried to get inside the space since she was a girl and would creep down to eavesdrop on her father as he worked. She wasn't sure if she'd even be able to slip into the narrow gap.

Alaïs climbed up on the stone bench and reached for the lowest window of the Tour Pinte that gave on to the Cour du Midi. She hauled herself up, wriggled over the stone ledge and threaded herself in through the narrow gap.

She was in luck. The room was empty. Alaïs jumped down to the ground, taking care to make as little noise as possible, then slowly opened the door and slipped into the space behind the curtain. She shuffled along until she was as close to the gap as she dared be. She was so close to where Viscount Trencavel stood, his hands clasped behind his back, that she could have reached out and touched him.

She was only just in time. At the far end of the Great Hall, the doors were thrown open. She saw her father stride in, followed by the king of Aragon and several of Carcassonne's allies, including the *seigneurs* of Lavaur and Cabaret.

Viscount Trencavel fell to his knees before his liege lord.

"No need for that," said Pedro, bidding him rise.

Physically the two men were strikingly different. The king was Trencavel's senior by many years, of an age with her father. Tall and broad, a bull of a man, his face bore the marks of many military campaigns. His features were heavy, brooding, made more so by his thick, black mustache against his dark skin. His hair, although still black, like her father's was going gray at the temples.

"Bid your men withdraw," he said curtly. "I would talk privately with you, Trencavel."

"With your leave, Sire King, I would ask permission for my steward to remain. I value his counsel."

The king hesitated, and then nodded.

"There are no words that can give adequate expression to our gratitude . . ."

Pedro interrupted. "I've not come to support you, but to help you to see the error of your ways. You have brought this situation upon yourself by your willful refusal to deal with heretics in your dominions. You have had four years—four years—to address the matter, but yet you have done nothing. You allow Cathar bishops to preach openly in your towns and cities. Your vassals openly support the *Bons Homes*—"

"No vassal . . ."

"Do you deny that attacks on holy men and priests have gone unpunished? The humiliation of the men of the church? In your lands, heretics worship openly. Your allies give them protection. It is common knowledge the count of Foix insults the Holy Relics by refusing to bow before them and his sister has slipped so far from grace as to take her vows as a *parfaite*, a ceremony the count saw fit to attend."

"I cannot answer for the count of Foix."

"He is your vassal and your ally," Pedro threw back at him. "Why do you allow this state of affairs to flourish?"

Alaïs felt the viscount draw in his breath. "Sire, you answer your own question. We live side by side with those you call heretics. We grew up together, our closest kinsmen are among them. The *parfaits* lived good and honest lives ministering to an ever-growing flock. I could no more expel them than I could prevent the daily rising of the sun!"

His words did not move Pedro. "Your only hope is to be reconciled with the Holy Mother Church. You are the equal of any of the northern barons the abbot has with him and they will treat you as such if you seek to make amends. But if, for a moment, you give him cause to believe you too hold these heretical thoughts, in your heart if not by your actions, then he will crush you." The king sighed. "Do you really believe you can withstand this, Trencavel? You are outnumbered a hundred to one."

"We have plenty of food."

"Food, yes, but not water. You have lost the river."

Alaïs saw her father dart a glance at the viscount, clearly fearing he would lose his temper.

"I do not wish to defy you or put myself beyond your good offices, but can you not see they come to fight for our land not our souls? This war is not waged for the glory of God but for the greed of men. This is an army of occupation, Sire. *If* I have failed the Church—and so offended you, Sire—I ask your pardon. But I owe no allegiance to the count of Nevers or the abbot of Cîteaux. They have no right, spiritual or temporal, over my lands. I will not betray my people to the French jackals for so base a cause."

Alaïs felt a surge of pride. From the expression on her father's face, she knew he felt it also. For the first time, something of Trencavel's courage and spirit seemed to affect the king.

"These are noble words, Viscount, but they will not help you now. For the sake of your people, whom you love, let me at least tell the abbot of Cîteaux you will hear his terms."

Trencavel walked away to the window and spoke under his breath.

"We do not have enough water to satisfy all those within the *Ciutat*?"

Her father shook his head. "We do not."

Only his hands, white against the stone sill of the window, betrayed how much the words cost him to speak.

"Very well. I will hear what the abbot has to say."

For a while after Pedro had departed, Trencavel said nothing. He stayed where he was, watching the sun sink from the sky. Finally, when the candles were lit, he sat. Pelletier ordered food and drink to be brought from the kitchens.

Alaïs dared not move for fear she would be discovered. She had cramp in her arms and her legs. The walls seemed to be pressing in upon her, but there was nothing she could do.

Beneath the curtains, she could see her father's feet as he paced up and down and heard the low murmurings of conversation from time to time.

It was late when Pedro II returned. From the expression on his face, Alaïs knew straight away the mission had failed. Her spirit sank. It was the last chance to get the Trilogy away from the Cité before the siege began in earnest.

"You have news?" said Trencavel, rising to greet him.

"None that I would give, Viscount," Pedro replied. "It offends me even to deliver his insulting words." He accepted a cup of wine and downed it in one. "The abbot of Cîteaux will allow you and twelve men of your choosing, to leave the château tonight, unmolested, bearing all you can carry."

Alaïs saw the viscount's hands ball into fists. "And Carcassona?"

"The *Ciutat* and everything, everyone else passes to the Host. After Besièrs, the lords will be looking for recompense."

For a moment after he'd spoken, there was silence.

Then, Trencavel finally gave vent to his temper and hurled his cup against the wall. "How dare he offer such an insult!" he roared. "How dare he insult our honor, our pride! I will not abandon a single one of my subjects to these French jackals."

"*Messire,*" murmured Pelletier.

Trencavel stood, hands on his hips, breathing heavily, waiting until his rage had passed.

Then he turned again to the king. "Sire, I am grateful for your intercession and for the offices you have undertaken on our behalf. However, if you will not—or cannot—fight with us, then we must part company. You should withdraw."

Pedro nodded, knowing there was nothing more to be said.

"May God be with you, Trencavel," he said unhappily.

Trencavel met his gaze. "I believe he is," he said defiantly.

As Pelletier accompanied the king from the hall, Alaïs took her chance to slip away.

The Feast of the Transfiguration of the Virgin passed quietly, with little progress made on either side. Trencavel continued to shower down arrows and missiles on the Crusaders, while the mindless thud, thud of the catapult sent rock and stone thundering into the walls. Men fell on both sides, but little ground was gained or lost.

The plains resembled a charnel house. Bodies rotted where they lay, swollen in the heat and feasted on by a plague of black flies. Kites and hawks, circling over the battlefield, picked the bones clean.

On Friday the seventh of August, the Crusaders launched an attack on the southern suburb of Sant-Miquel. For a while, they succeeded in occupying the ditch below the walls, but were repelled by a shower of arrows and stones. After several hours of stalemate, the French withdrew under the continued onslaught, to the jeers and triumph of the Carcassonnais.

At dawn the following day, as the world shimmered silver in the early morning light and a delicate mist floated gently across the slopes where more than a thousand Crusaders stood facing Sant-Miquel, the attack began again.

Helmets and shields, swords and pikes, eyes, glinted in the pale sun. Each man wore a cross pinned to his breast, white against the colors of Nevers, Burgundy, Chartres and Champagne.

Viscount Trencavel had positioned himself on the walls of Sant-Miquel, shoulder to shoulder with his men, ready to repel the attack.

The archers and *dardasiers* held themselves ready, bows set. Below, the foot soldiers were armed with axes, swords and pikes. Behind them, safe within the Cité until they were required, were the *chevaliers*.

In the distance, the French drums began to beat. They banged the hard earth with their pikes, a steady, heavy sound that echoed over the waiting land.

And so it begins.

Alaïs stood on the wall at her father's side, her attention split between looking for her husband, and watching the Crusaders stream down the hill.

When the Host was within range, Viscount Trencavel raised his arm and gave the order. A storm of arrows immediately darkened the sky.

On both sides, men fell. The first scaling ladder was already on the walls. A bolt from a crossbow whizzed through the air and connected with rough, heavy wood and brought it down. The ladder tilted, then overbalanced. It fell slowly at first, then picked up speed, hurling the men to the ground in a splinter of blood, bone and wood.

The Crusaders succeeded in getting a *gata*, a siege engine, up to the walls of the suburb. Sheltered beneath the cover, drenched with water, the sappers began to pull rocks out of the walls and dig a cavity to weaken the fortifications.

Trencavel shouted at the archers to destroy the structure. Another storm of missiles and flaming arrows hurtled through the air on the wooden structure. The sky fizzed with pitch and black smoke until finally it caught alight, sending men, their clothes burning, fleeing from the burning cage, only to be cut down by the arrows.

It was too late. The defenders could only watch as the mine the Crusaders had been preparing for days was fired. Alaïs threw up her hands to protect her face as the explosion threw a violent shower of stone, dust and flame up into the air.

The Crusaders charged through the breach. The roar of the fire drowned out even the screaming of the women and children fleeing the inferno.

The heavy gate between the Cité and Sant-Miquel was dragged open and the *chevaliers* of Carcassonne launched their first attack. *Keep him safe,* she found herself murmuring to herself, as if words could repel arrows.

Now the Crusaders were catapulting the heads of the dead, severed from their bodies, over the walls to engender panic and fear. The shouting and shrieking grew louder as Viscount Trencavel led his men into the fray. He was one of the first to draw blood, driving his sword clean through the neck of a Crusader and kicking the body free of his blade with his boot.

Guilhem was not far behind him in the charge, driving his warhorse through the mass of attackers, trampling all those in his path.

Alaïs caught sight of Alzeu de Preixan at his side. She watched in horror as Alzeu's horse slipped and went down. Straight away, Guilhem pulled his horse round and went to aid his friend. Frenzied by the smell of blood and the clashing steel, Guilhem's mighty horse reared up on its hind legs, crushing a Crusader underfoot, buying Alzeu enough time to scramble back onto his feet and out of danger.

They were heavily outnumbered. Hordes of terrified and injured men, women and children fleeing into the Cité got in their way. The Host advanced relentlessly. Street by street fell under French control.

At last, Alaïs heard the cry go up.

"Repli! Repli!" Pull back.

Under cover of night a handful of defenders stole back into the devastated suburb. They slaughtered the few Crusaders left on guard, set fire to the remaining houses, at least depriving the French of cover from which to resume their bombardment of the Cité.

But the truth was stark.

Both Sant-Vicens and Sant-Miquel had fallen. Carcassonne stood alone.

CHAPTER 58

On Viscount Trencavel's wishes, tables had been set up in the Great Hall. Viscount Trencavel and Dame Agnès were moving between them, thanking the men for the service they had done and yet would do.

Pelletier was feeling increasingly unwell. The room was filled with the smells of burned wax, sweat, cold food and warm ale. He wasn't sure he could stand it much longer. The pains in his stomach were getting worse and more frequent.

He tried to pull himself upright, but without warning, his legs went from under him. Clutching at the table for support, Pelletier pitched forward, sending plates and cups and meat bones flying. He felt as if there was a wild animal gnawing at his belly.

Viscount Trencavel spun round. Someone started shouting. He was aware of servants rushing to help him and someone calling for Alaïs.

He felt hands holding him up and moving him toward the door. François' face swam into focus, then out again. He thought he could hear Alaïs issuing orders, although her voice was coming from a long way away and she seemed to be speaking a language he didn't understand.

"Alaïs," he called out, reaching for her hand in the darkness.

"I'm here. We'll get you to your chamber."

He felt strong arms lift him, the night air on his face as he was carried through the Cour d'Honneur, then up the stairs.

They made slow progress. The spasms in his stomach were getting worse, each more violent than the last. He could feel the pestilence working in him, poisoning his blood and his breath.

"Alaïs . . ." he whispered, this time in fear.

As soon as they reached her father's chamber, Alaïs sent Rixende to find François and collect the medicines she needed from her room. She dispatched two other servants to the kitchens for precious water.

She had her father laid on his bed. She stripped his stained outer robes and put them in a pile to be burned. Pestilence seemed to seep from the pores of his skin. The attacks of diarrhea were getting more frequent and more severe, blood and pus now making up the greater part. Alaïs ordered

344

herbs and flowers to be burned to try to disguise the smell, but no amount of lavender or rosemary could mask the truth of his condition.

Rixende arrived quickly with the ingredients and helped Alaïs to mix the dried red whortleberries with hot water to form a thin paste. Having stripped his stained robes from him and covered him with a clean, thin sheet, Alaïs spooned the liquid between his pallid lips.

The first mouthful he swallowed, then immediately vomited up. She tried again. This time, he managed to swallow, although it cost him much to do so, sending his body into spasms.

Time became meaningless, moving neither fast nor slow, as Alaïs tried to slow the progress of the sickness. At midnight, Viscount Trencavel came to the chamber.

"What news, Dame?"

"He is very sick, *Messire.*"

"Is there anything you need? Physicians, medicines?"

"A little more water, if it can be spared? I sent Rixende to find François, some time ago, but he has not returned."

"It shall be done."

Trencavel glanced over her shoulder to the bed. "How has the affliction taken hold so quickly?"

"It is hard to say why such a disease strikes one so hard and yet passes another by, *Messire.* My father's constitution was much weakened by his time in the Holy Land. He is particularly susceptible to ailments of the stomach." She hesitated. "God willing, it will not spread."

"There is no doubt it is siege sickness?" he said grimly. Alaïs shook her head. "I am sorry to hear it. Send for me if there is any change in his condition."

As the hours slid slowly one into the next, her father's grip on life got weaker. He had moments of lucidity, when he seemed to be aware of what was happening to him. At other times, it seemed he no longer knew where or who he was.

Shortly before dawn, Pelletier's breathing became shallow. Dozing by his side, Alaïs heard the change and was immediately alert.

"Filha . . ."

She felt his hands and his brow and knew there was not long to go. The fever had left him, leaving his skin cold.

His soul struggles to be set free.

"Help me . . .." he managed to say, ". . . to sit."

With Rixende's help, Alaïs managed to prop him up. The sickness had aged him in the course of the one night.

"Don't speak," she whispered. "Guard your strength."

"Alaïs," he admonished her softly. "You know my time has come." His chest was full of splashing, rattling sounds as he struggled for breath. His eyes were hollow and ringed in yellow and pale brown blotches were forming on his hands and neck. "Will you send for a *parfait*?" He forced his sunken eyes open. "I wish to make a good end."

"You wish to be consoled, *Paire*?" she said carefully.

Pelletier managed a thin smile and, for an instant, the man he had been in his life, shone through.

"I have listened well to the words of the *Bons Chrétiens*. I have learned the words of the *melhorer* and the *consolament* . . ." He broke off. "I was born a Christian and I will die one, but not in the corrupt embrace of those who wage war in God's name at our gates. With God's grace, if I have lived well enough, I will join the glorious company of spirits in Heaven."

A fit of coughing overtook him. Alaïs cast her eyes around the room in desperation. She sent a servant to inform Viscount Trencavel her father's condition had worsened. As soon as he had gone, she summoned Rixende.

"I need you to fetch the *parfaits*. They were about the courtyard earlier. Tell them there is one who wishes to receive the *consolament*."

Rixende looked terrified.

"No blame will attach itself to you for carrying a message," she said, trying to reassure the girl. "You do not have to return with them."

A movement from her father drew her attention back to the bed.

"Quick, Rixende. Make haste."

Alaïs bent down. "What is it, *Paire*? I'm here with you."

He was trying to speak, but the words seemed to shrivel in his throat before he could utter them. She tipped a little wine into his mouth and wiped his desiccated lips with a wet cloth.

"The Grail is the word of God, Alaïs. This is what Harif tried to teach me, although I did not understand." His voice stuttered. "But without the *merel* . . . the truth of the labyrinth, it is a false path."

"What about the *merel*?" she whispered urgently, not understanding.

"You were right, Alaïs. I was too stubborn. I should have let you go when there was still a chance."

Alaïs was struggling to make sense of his meandering words. "What path?"

"I have not seen it," he was murmuring, "nor will I now. The cave . . . few have seen it."

Alaïs spun round to the door in despair.

Where is Rixende?

In the corridor outside was the sound of running feet. Rixende appeared, followed by two *parfaits*. Alaïs recognized the elder, a dark-featured man with a thick beard and a gentle expression who she'd met once at Esclarmonde's house. Both were wearing dark blue robes and twisted rope belts with metal buckles in the shape of a fish.

He bowed. "Dame Alaïs." He looked past her to the bed. "It is your father, Intendant Pelletier, who has need of consolation?"

She nodded.

"He has the breath to speak?"

"He will find strength to do so."

There was another disturbance in the corridor as Viscount Trencavel appeared on the threshold.

"*Messire*—" she said in alarm. "He requested the *parfaits* . . . my father wishes to make a good end, *Messire*."

Surprise flickered in his eyes, but he ordered the door to be closed.

"Nevertheless," he said. "I will stay."

Alaïs stared at him for a moment, then turned back to her father as the officiating *parfait* summoned her.

"Intendant Pelletier is in great pain, but his wits are strong still and his courage holds." Alaïs nodded. "He has done nothing to harm our church nor owes us a debt?"

"He is a protector of all friends of God."

Alaïs and Raymond-Roger stood back as the *parfait* walked over to the bed and leaned over the dying man. Bertrand's eyes flickered as he whispered the *melhorer*, the blessing.

"Do you vow to follow the rule of justice and truth and to give yourself to God and to the Church of the *Bons Chrétiens*?"

Pelletier forced the words from his lips. "I—do."

The *parfait* placed the parchment copy of the New Testament on his head. "May God bless you, make a Good Christian of you and lead you to a good end." He recited the *Benedicté*, then the *Adoremus* three times.

Alaïs was moved by the simplicity of the service. Viscount Trencavel looked straight ahead. He seemed to be keeping himself under control with an enormous effort of will.

"Bertrand Pelletier, are you ready to receive the gift of the Lord's Prayer?"

Her father murmured his assent.

In a clear, true voice, the *parfait* spoke the paternoster seven times over, pausing only to allow Pelletier to make his responses.

"This is the prayer that Jesus Christ brought into the world and taught to the *Bons Homes*. Never eat or drink again without repeating this prayer first; and if you fail of this duty, you must need do penance again."

Pelletier tried to nod. The hollow whistling in his chest was louder now, like the wind in autumn trees.

The *parfait* began to read from the Gospel of John.

"In the beginning was the Word, and the Word was with God, and the Word was God. The same was in the beginning with God." Pelletier's hand jerked above the covers as the *parfait* continued to read. ". . . And ye shall know the truth, and the truth shall make you free."

His eyes suddenly flew open. *"Vertat,"* he whispered. "Yes, the truth."

Alaïs grabbed his hand in alarm, but he was slipping away. The light had gone from his eyes. She was aware the *parfait* was speaking faster now, as if he feared there was not enough time to complete the ritual.

"He must speak the final words," he urged Alaïs. "Help him."

"Paire, you must . . ." Grief took her voice from her.

"For every sin . . . I have committed . . . by word or deed," he rasped, "I . . . I ask pardon of God and the Church . . . and all here present."

With evident relief, the *parfait* placed his hands on Pelletier's head and gave him the kiss of peace. Alaïs caught her breath. A look of release had transformed her father's face as the grace of the *consolament* descended to him. It was a moment of transcendence, of understanding. His spirit was ready, now, to leave his sick body and the earth that held him.

"His soul is prepared," said the *parfait.*

Alaïs nodded. She sat on the bed, holding her father's hand. Viscount Trencavel stood on the other side. Pelletier was barely conscious, although he seemed to feel their presence.

"Messire?"

"I'm here, Bertrand."

"Carcassona must not fall."

"I give you my word, in honor of the love and obligation that has been between us these many years, I will do all I can."

Pelletier tried to lift his hand from the blanket. "It has been an honor to serve you."

Alaïs saw the viscount's eyes were filled with tears. "It is I who should thank you, my old friend."

Pelletier tried to raise his head. "Alaïs?"

"I'm here, father," she said quickly. The color had gone from Pelletier's face now. His skin hung in gray folds under his eyes. "No man ever had such a daughter."

He seemed to sigh as the life left his body. Then, silence.

For a moment, Alaïs did not move, breathe, react in any way. Then she felt a wild grief building within her, taking her over, possessing her, until she broke down in an agony of weeping.

CHAPTER 59

A soldier appeared in the doorway. "Lord Trencavel?"

He turned his head. "What is it?"

"A thief, *Messire*. Stealing water from the Place du Plô."

He signaled he would come. "Dame, I must leave you."

Alaïs nodded. She had worn herself out with weeping.

"I will see him buried with the honor and ceremony that befits his status. He was a valiant man, both a loyal counselor and trusted friend."

"His church does not require it, *Messire*. His flesh is nothing. His spirit is already gone. He would wish you to think only of the living."

"Then, see it as an act of selfishness on my part, that I wish to pay my last respects in accordance with the great affection and esteem in which I held your father. I will have his body moved to the *capèla* Sant-Maria."

"He would be honored by such evidence of your love."

"Can I send anyone to sit with you? I cannot spare your husband, but your sister? Women to help you with the laying out?"

Her head darted up, realizing only now that she had not thought of Oriane once. She had even forgotten to inform her their father had been taken sick.

She did not love him.

Alaïs silenced the voice in her head. She had failed in her duty, both to her father and to her sister. She got to her feet.

"I will go to my sister, *Messire*."

She bowed as he left the chamber, then turned back. She could not bring herself to leave her father. She began the process of laying out the body herself. She ordered the bed to be stripped and freshly made, sending the contaminated covers away for burning. Then with Rixende's help, Alaïs prepared the winding sheets and burial oils. She cleaned his body herself and smoothed the hair from his brow so that, in death, he looked like the man he had been in life.

She lingered a while long, looking down at the empty face. *You cannot delay any longer.*

"Inform the viscount his body is ready to be taken to the *capèla*, Rixende. I must inform my sister."

349

Guirande was asleep on the floor outside Oriane's chamber.

Alaïs stepped over her and tried the door. This time, it was unlocked. Oriane lay alone in her bed with the curtains pulled back. Her tousled black curls were spread over the pillow and her skin was milky white in the early morning light. Alaïs marveled that she could sleep at all.

"Sister!"

Oriane opened her green cat-like eyes with a jolt, her face registering alarm, then surprise, before taking on its customary expression of disdain.

"I have ill news," she said. Her voice was dead, cold.

"Could it not wait? The bell for Prime cannot yet have rung."

"It could not. Our father—" she stopped.

How can such words be true?

Alaïs took a deep breath to steady herself. "Our father is dead."

The shock registered on Oriane's face, before her habitual expression returned. "What did you say?" she said, her eyes narrowing.

"Our father passed away this morning. Just before dawn."

"How? How did he die?"

"Is that all you can say?" she cried.

Oriane flew out of bed. "Tell me what he died of?"

"A sickness. It came on very quickly."

"Were you with him at the hour of his passing?"

Alaïs nodded.

"Yet you did not see fit to inform me?" she said furiously.

"I'm sorry," Alaïs whispered. "It all seemed to happen so fast. I know I should have—"

"Who else was there?"

"Our Lord Trencavel, and . . ."

Oriane heard her hesitation. "Our father did confess his sins and receive the last rites?" she demanded. "He died in the Church?"

"Our father did not die unshriven," Alaïs replied, choosing her words with care. "He made his peace with God."

She has guessed.

"What does it matter?" she cried, appalled by Oriane's callous acceptance of the news. "He is dead, sister. Does it mean nothing to you?"

"You have failed in your duty, sister," Oriane jabbed with her finger. "As the elder, I had more right to be there than you. I *should* have been there. And if, in addition to this, I discover you allowed heretics to paw over him as he lay dying, then make no mistake about it, I will make sure you regret it."

"Do you feel no loss, no regret?"

Alaïs could see the answer in Oriane's face. "I feel no more for his passing than I would for a dog in the street. He did not love me. It is many years since I allowed myself to be hurt by the fact. Why, now, would I grieve?" She took a step closer. "It was you he loved. He saw himself in you." She gave an unpleasant smile. "It was you he confided in. Shared his innermost secrets with."

Even in her frozen state, Alaïs felt color fly to her cheeks. "What do you mean?" she said, dreading the answer.

"You know perfectly well what I mean," she hissed. "Do you really think I do not know of your midnight conversations?" She took a step closer. "Your life is going to change, little sister, without him to protect you. You have had things your own way far too long." Oriane darted out a hand and grabbed Alaïs by the wrist.

"Tell me. Where is the third book?"

"I do not know what you mean."

Oriane slapped her with her open hand.

"Where is it?" Oriane hissed. "I know you have it."

"Let me go."

"Don't play games with me, sister. He must have given it to you. Who else would he trust? Tell me where it is. I mean to have it."

A chill ran down Alaïs' spine.

"You can't do this. Someone will come."

"Who?" she demanded. "You forget our father is no longer here to protect you."

"Guilhem."

Oriane laughed. "Of course, I forgot that you are reconciled with your husband. Do you know what your husband really thinks of you?" she continued. "Do you?"

The door flew open and slammed against the wall.

"That is enough!" Guilhem shouted. Oriane immediately dropped her wrist as Alaïs' husband strode across the room and gathered her into his arms. "*Mon còr*, I came as soon as I heard the news of your father's death. I'm so sorry."

"How touching!" Oriane's harsh voice broke the intimacy between them.

"Ask him what brought him back to your bed," she said spitefully, not taking her eyes from Guilhem's face. "Or are you too afraid to hear what he has to say? Ask him, Alaïs. It's not love or desire. This reconciliation is because of the book, nothing more."

"I warn you, hold your tongue!"

"Why? Are you afraid of what I might say?"

Alaïs could feel the tension between them. The knowledge. And immediately she understood.

No. Not that.

"It's not you he wants, Alaïs. He seeks the book. That's what brought him back to your chamber. Can you really be so blind?"

Alaïs took a step away from Guilhem. "Does she speak the truth?"

He swung round to face her, desperation flashing in his eyes.

"She's lying. I swear, on my life, I care nothing for the book. I have told her nothing. How could I?"

"He searched the chamber while you slept. He cannot deny it."

"I did not," he shouted.

Alaïs looked at him. "But you knew there was such a book?"

The alarm that flickered in his eyes gave her the answer she feared.

"She tried to blackmail me to help her, but I refused." His voice cracked, "I refused, Alaïs."

"What hold did she have over you that she would make such a request?" she said softly, almost in a whisper.

Guilhem tried to reach for her, but she backed away from him.

Even now, I would that he denied it.

He dropped his hand. "Once, yes, I . . . Forgive me."

"It's a little late for remorse."

Alaïs ignored Oriane. "Do you love her?"

Guilhem shook his head. "Can't you see what she's doing, Alaïs? She's trying to turn you against me."

Alaïs was dumbstruck that he could believe she would trust him ever again.

He held his hand out. "Please, Alaïs," he pleaded. "I love you."

"Enough of this," said Oriane, stepping into her line of vision. "Where is the book?"

"I do not have it."

"Who does?" said Oriane in a threatening voice.

Alaïs held her ground. "Why do you want it? What is it that is of such importance?"

"Just tell me," she snapped, "and this will all end here."

"And if I will not?"

"It is so easy to sicken," she said. "You nursed our father. Perhaps the illness is already within you." She turned to Guilhem. "You understand what I'm saying, Guilhem? If you go against me."

"I will not allow you to harm her!"

Oriane laughed. "You're hardly in a position to threaten me, Guilhem. I have enough evidence of your treachery to see you hanged."

"Evidence of your own designing," he shouted. "Viscount Trencavel will not believe you."

"You underestimate me, Guilhem, if you think I have left grounds for doubt. Dare you risk it?" She turned back to Alaïs. "Tell me where you have hidden the book or I shall go to the viscount."

Alaïs swallowed hard. What had Guilhem done? She didn't know what to think. Despite her anger, she couldn't bring herself to denounce him.

"François," she said. "Our father gave the book to François."

A look of confusion flickered in Oriane's eyes, then vanished as quickly as it had come.

"Very well. But, I warn you sister, if you are lying you will regret it." She turned and walked to the door.

"Where are you going?"

"To pay my respects to our father, where else? However, before that, I will see you safely to your chamber."

Alaïs raised her head and met her sister's gaze. "That is quite unnecessary."

"Oh, it's entirely necessary. Should François not be able to help me, I would wish to be able to talk with you again."

Guilhem tried to reach for her. "She's lying. I have done nothing wrong."

"What you have or have not done, Guilhem, is no longer any concern of mine," Alaïs said. "You knew what you did when you lay with her. Now, just leave me be."

With her head held high, Alaïs walked along the corridor and into her chamber, with Oriane and Guirande behind her.

"I will return presently. As soon as I have spoken to François."

"As you wish."

Oriane shut the door. Moments later, as Alaïs had feared, the key was turned in the lock. She could hear Guilhem remonstrating with Oriane.

She shut her ears to their voices. She tried to keep the poisonous, jealous images from her mind. Alaïs couldn't stop thinking of Guilhem and Oriane entwined in each other's arms, she couldn't protect herself from the thought of Guilhem whispering to her sister the intimate words he had spoken to her, pearls she'd kept close to her heart.

Alaïs pressed her trembling hand to her chest. She could feel her heart thudding hard against her ribs, bewildered and betrayed. She swallowed hard.

Think not of yourself.

She opened her eyes and dropped her arms to her side, her hands clenched in fists of misery. She could not allow herself to be weak. If she did, then Oriane would have taken everything of worth from her. The time for regret, for recrimination, would come. Now, her promise to her father, keeping the book safe, mattered more than her breaking heart. However difficult, she had to put Guilhem from her mind. She had allowed herself to be imprisoned in her room because of something Oriane had said. *The third book.* Oriane had asked where she'd hidden the third book.

Alaïs ran to the cloak, still hanging over the back of her chair, and snatched it up and patted along the hem where the book had been.

It was no longer there.

Alaïs slumped down on the chair, desperation welling inside her. Oriane had Simeon's book. Soon, she would know she had lied about giving a book to François and return.

And what of Esclarmonde?

Alaïs realized Guilhem was no longer shouting outside the door.

Is he with her?

She didn't know what to think. It didn't matter anyway. He had betrayed her once. He would again. She had to lock her wounded feelings in her battered heart. She had to get out while she had the chance.

Alaïs tore open the lavender bag to retrieve the copy of the parchment in the *Book of Numbers,* then cast a final look around the chamber she'd thought to be her home forever.

She knew she would not be back.

Then, with her heart in her mouth, she went to the window and looked out over the roof. Her only chance was to get out before Oriane came back.

Oriane felt nothing. In the flickering candlelight she stood at the foot of the bier and looked down on her father's body.

Commanding the attendants to withdraw, Oriane bent down as if to kiss her father's head. Her hand closed over his and she slipped the labyrinth ring from his thumb, hardly believing Alaïs had been so stupid as to leave it on his hand.

Oriane straightened up and slipped it into her pocket. She rearranged the sheet, genuflected before the altar and crossed herself and then left in search of François.

CHAPTER 60

Alaïs put her foot on to the ledge and climbed out onto the sill, her head spinning at the thought of what she was about to attempt.

You will fall.

If she did, what did it matter now? Her father was dead. Guilhem was lost to her. In the end, her father's judgment of her husband's character had proved to be true.

What more is there to lose?

Taking a deep breath, Alaïs carefully lowered herself over the sill until her right foot found the tiles. Then, muttering a prayer, she braced her arms and legs and let go. She dropped with a small thump. Her feet slipped from under her. Alaïs hurled herself forward as she skidded down the tiles, desperately trying to gain purchase. Cracks in the tiles, gaps in the wall, anything to stop her plummeting down.

It seemed like she was falling forever. Suddenly, there was a violent jerk and Alaïs came to an abrupt halt. The hem of her dress had snagged on a nail and was holding her fast. She lay quite still, not daring to move. She could feel the tension in the cloth. It was of good quality, but it was stretched as tight as a drum and could tear at any moment.

Alaïs glanced up at the nail. Even if she could reach up that high, it would take both hands to untangle the material, which had wrapped itself several times round the metal spike. She couldn't risk letting go. The only option was to abandon the cloak and try to crawl back up the roof, which joined the outer wall of the Château Comtal on the western side. She should be able to squeeze through the wooden slats of the hourds. The gaps in the defenses were narrow, but she was slight. It was worth trying.

Careful to make no sudden movements, Alaïs reached up and shredded the material until it began to tear. She pulled, first one side, then the other, until she ripped a square from the skirt. Leaving a pocket of material behind, she was free once more.

Alaïs brought up one knee and pushed, then the other. She could feel drops of sweat forming at her temples and between her breasts, where she'd stowed the parchments. Her skin was sore from rubbing against the rough tiles.

Bit by bit, she pulled herself up until the *ambans* were in reach.

Alaïs put her hands out and grasped the wooden struts, which felt reassuringly solid between her fingers. Then she drew her knees up so that she was almost crouching on the roof, wedged into the corner between the battlements and the wall. The gap was smaller than she'd hoped, no deeper than the stretch of a man's hand and perhaps three times as wide. Alaïs extended her right leg, twisted her left leg under to anchor herself firmly, then pulled herself up through the gap. The purse with the copies of the labyrinth parchments was awkward and kept tangling between her legs, but she kept going.

Ignoring her aching limbs, she quickly stood up and picked her way along the barricade. Although she knew the guards would not betray her to Oriane, the sooner she got out of the Château Comtal and to Sant-Nasari, the better.

Peering down to make sure there was no one at the bottom, Alaïs quickly shinned down the ladders to the ground. Her legs buckled under her as she jumped the last few rungs and she cracked down on her back, knocking every last gasp of air out of her.

She glanced toward the chapel. There was no sign of Oriane or François. Keeping close to the walls, Alaïs passed through the stables, pausing at Tatou's stall. She was desperate to drink, to give her suffering mare water, but what little there was went only to the warhorses.

The streets were filled with refugees. Alaïs covered her mouth with her sleeve to keep out the stench of suffering and sickness that hung like a fog over the streets. Wounded men and women, the dispossessed cradling children in their arms, stared blankly up at her with hopeless eyes as she passed.

The square in front of Sant-Nasari was filled with people. With a glance over her shoulder to make sure no one had followed her, Alaïs opened the door and slipped inside. There were people sleeping in the nave. In their misery, they paid little attention.

Candles burned on the main altar. Alaïs hurried up the north transept to a little-visited side chapel with a small plain altar where her father had taken her. Mice ran for cover, their tiny claws scuttling over the flagstones. Kneeling down, Alaïs reached around behind the altar, as he'd shown her. She paddled her fingers over the surface of the wall. A spider, its hiding place disturbed, darted over the exposed skin of her hand, then was gone.

There was a soft click. Alaïs slowly, carefully, eased out the stone and slid it to one side, then stretched her hand into the dusty recess behind. She found the long, thin key, the metal dull with age and disuse, and put it into the lock of the wooden latticed door. The hinges creaked as the wood scraped over the stone floor.

She felt her father's presence strongly now. Alaïs bit her lip to stop herself breaking down.

This is all you can do for him now.

Alaïs reached in and pulled out the box, as she had seen him do. No bigger than a jewelry casket, it was plain and undecorated, with a simple clasp. She lifted the lid. Inside was a sheepskin pouch, as it had been when her father showed her this place. She gave a sigh of relief, only now realizing how much she feared Oriane would somehow have been here before her.

Aware of what little time she had, Alaïs quickly concealed the book beneath her dress and then replaced everything exactly as it had been. If Oriane or Guilhem knew of the hiding place, it would at least delay them if they believed the casket was still in its place.

She ran back through the church, her head covered by her hood, then pushed open the heavy door and was swallowed up in the tide of suffering people milling aimlessly through the square. The sickness that had claimed her father spread quickly. The alleyways were filled with decaying and decomposing carcasses—sheep and goats, even cattle, their swollen bodies releasing foul-smelling gas into the fetid air.

Alaïs found herself heading for Esclarmonde's house. There was no reason to hope she would find her there this time, having failed so many times in the past few days, but she could think of nowhere else to go.

Most of the houses in the southern *quartier* were shuttered and boarded, Esclarmonde's included. Alaïs raised her hand and knocked on the door.

"Esclarmonde?"

Alaïs knocked again. She tried the door, but it was locked. "Sajhë?"

This time she heard something. The sound of feet running and a bolt being shot.

"Dame Alaïs?"

"Sajhë, thank God. Quick, let me in."

The door opened just wide enough to allow her to slip inside.

"Where have you been?" she said, hugging him tight. "What's been happening? Where's Esclarmonde?"

Alaïs felt Sajhë's small hand slip into hers. "Come with me."

He led her through the curtain to the room at the back of the house. A trapdoor was open in the floor. "You've been here all along?" she said. She peered down into the dark and saw a *calèlh* was burning at the bottom of the ladder. "In the cellars? Has my sister been back—"

"It wasn't her," he said in a quavering voice. "Quick, Dame."

Alaïs went down first. Sajhë released the catch and the trap door clattered shut above their heads. He scrambled down after her, jumping the last few rungs to the earth floor.

"This way."

He led her along a damp tunnel into a small hollowed-out area, then held the lamp up so Alaïs could see Esclarmonde, who was lying motionless on a pile of furs and blankets.

"No!" she gasped, running to her side.

Her head was heavily bandaged. Alaïs lifted the corner of the padding and covered her mouth. Esclarmonde's left eye was red, everything covered by a film of blood. There was a clean compress over the wound, but the skin flapped loose around the crushed socket.

"Can you help her?" said Sajhë.

Alaïs lifted the blanket. Her stomach lurched. There was a line of angry red burns across Esclarmonde's chest, the skin yellow and black where the flames had been held.

"Esclarmonde," she whispered, leaning over her. "Can you hear me? It's me, Alaïs. Who did this to you?"

She fancied she saw movement in Esclarmonde's face. Her lips moved slightly. Alaïs turned to Sajhë. "How did you get her down here?"

"Gaston and his brother helped."

Alaïs turned back to the brutalized figure on the bed. "What happened to her, Sajhë?"

He shook his head.

"Has she told you nothing?"

"She . . ." For the first time, his self-possession faltered. "She cannot speak . . . her tongue . . ."

Alaïs turned white. "No," she whispered in horror, then strengthened her voice. "Tell me what you do know then," she said softly.

For Esclarmonde's sake, they both had to be strong.

"After we heard that Besièrs had fallen, *Menina* was worried that Intendant Pelletier would change his mind about letting you take the Trilogy to Harif."

"She was right," she said grimly.

"*Menina* knew you would try to persuade him, but thought Simeon was the only person Intendant Pelletier would heed. I didn't want her to go," he wailed, "but she went anyway to the Jewish *quartier*. I followed, but because I couldn't let her see me, I stayed back, and so I lost sight of her in the woods. I got frightened. I waited until sundown, but then imagining what she would say if she returned home and found I'd disobeyed her, I came home. That's when I . . ." he broke off, his amber eyes burning in his white face.

"Straight away I knew it was her. She had collapsed, outside the gates. Her feet were bleeding as if she had walked a long way." Sajhë looked up at her. "I wanted to fetch you, Dame, but I didn't dare. With Gaston's help, I got her down here. I tried to remember what she would do, which ointments to use." He shrugged. "I did my best."

"You did excellently well," Alaïs said fiercely. "Esclarmonde will be very proud of you."

A movement from the bed drew their attention. They both turned back immediately.

"Esclarmonde," said Alaïs. "Can you hear me? We're both here. You're quite safe."

"She's trying to say something."

Alaïs watched her hands working frantically. "I think she wants parchment and ink," she said.

With Sajhë's help, Esclarmonde managed to write.

"It's François, I think," said Alaïs, frowning.

"What does it mean?"

"I don't know. Maybe he can help," she said. "Listen to me, Sajhë. I have bad news. Simeon is almost certainly dead. My father—my father also has died."

Sajhë took her hand. The gesture was so thoughtful, it brought tears to her eyes. "I am sorry."

Alaïs bit her lip to stop herself from crying. "So for his sake—Simeon and Esclarmonde also—I must keep my word and find my way to Harif. I have . . ." she faltered again. "I regret I have only the *Book of Words*. Simeon's book is gone."

"But Intendant Pelletier gave it to you."

"My sister took it. My husband admitted her to our chamber," she said. "He . . . he has given his heart to my sister. He is no longer to be trusted, Sajhë. It's why I cannot go back to the château. With my father dead, there is nothing to stop them."

Sajhë looked to his grandmother, then back to Alaïs.

"Will she live?" he said in a quiet voice.

"Her injuries are severe, Sajhë. She's lost the sight in her left eye, but . . . there is no infection. Her spirit is strong. She will recover if she chooses to do so."

He nodded, suddenly older than his eleven years.

"But I will take Esclarmonde's book, by your leave, Sajhë."

For a moment, he looked as if his tears were at last going to claim him. "That book, also, is lost," he said in the end.

"No!" said Alaïs. "How?"

"The people who did . . . they took it from her," he said. "*Menina* took it with her when she set out for the Jewish *quartier*. I saw her take it from its hiding place."

"Only one book," Alaïs said, close to tears herself. "Then we are lost. It has all been in vain."

For the next five days, they lived a strange existence.

Alaïs and Sajhë took it in turns to venture up into the streets under cover of darkness. It was immediately clear that there was no way of getting out of Carcassonne unseen. The siege was unbreakable. There was a guard on every postern, every gate, beneath every tower, a solid ring of men and steel around the walls. Day and night, the siege engines bombarded the walls, so the inhabitants of the Cité no longer knew if they heard the sounds of the missiles or but the echo of them in their heads.

It was a relief to return to the cool, damp tunnels where time stood still and there was no night or day.

CHAPTER 61

Guilhem stood beneath the shade of the great elm in the center of the Cour d'Honneur.

On the behalf of the abbot of Cîteaux, the count of Auxerre had ridden up to the Porte Narbonnaise and offered safe conduct to parley. With this surprise proposition Viscount Trencavel's natural optimism had returned. It was evident in his face and his bearing as he addressed the household. His hope and fortitude rubbed off a little on those listening.

The reasons behind the Abbot's sudden change of mind were debatable. The Crusaders were making little progress, but the siege had only lasted a little over a week, which was nothing. Did the abbot's motive matter? Viscount Trencavel claimed not.

Guilhem was barely listening. He was trapped in a web of his own making and could see no way out, neither through words nor the sword. He lived on a knife-edge. Alaïs had been missing for five days. Guilhem had sent discreet search parties out into the Cité and scoured the Château Comtal, but was no nearer to finding where Oriane was keeping her prisoner. He was trapped in a web of his own deceit. Too late had he realized how well Oriane had prepared the ground. If he did not do what she wanted, he would be denounced as a traitor and Alaïs would suffer.

"So, my friends," Trencavel concluded. "Who will accompany me on this journey?"

Guilhem felt Oriane's sharp finger in his back. He found himself stepping forward. He knelt down, his hand on the hilt of his sword, and offered his service. As Raymond-Roger clasped him on the shoulder in gratitude, Guilhem burned with shame.

"You have our great thanks, Guilhem. Who, now, will go with you?"

Six other *chevaliers* joined Guilhem. Oriane slipped between them and bowed before the viscount.

"*Messire*, by your leave."

Congost had not noticed his wife in the mass of men. He flushed red and flapped his hands in embarrassment, as if shooing crows from a field.

"Withdraw, Dame," he stammered in his shrill voice. "This is no place for you."

Oriane ignored him. Trencavel raised his hand and summoned her forward. "What is it that you want to say, Dame?"

"Forgive me, *Messire,* honored *chevaliers,* friends . . . husband. With your leave and God's blessing, I want to offer myself as a member of this party. I have lost a father and now, it appears, a sister too. Such grief is heavy to bear. But if my husband will release me, I would like to redeem my loss and show my love for you, *Messire,* by this act. It is what my father would wish."

Congost looked as if he would like the ground to open up and swallow him. Guilhem stared at the ground. Viscount Trencavel could not hide his surprise.

"With respect, Dame Oriane, this is not a woman's office."

"In which case, I offer myself as a willing hostage, *Messire.* My presence will be proof of your fair intentions, as clear an indication as any that Carcassona will abide by the conventions of the parley."

Trencavel considered for a moment, and then turned to Congost. "She is your wife. Can you spare her in our cause?"

Jehan stuttered and rubbed his sweaty hands on his tunic. He wanted to refuse his permission, but it was clear the proposal had merit in the viscount's eyes.

"My wishes are but the servants to yours," he mumbled.

Trencavel bid her rise. "Your late father, my esteemed friend, would be proud of what you do today."

Oriane looked up at him from under her dark lashes. "And with your leave, may I take François with me? He too, united as we all are in grief for my worthy father, would be glad of the chance to serve."

Guilhem felt the bile rising in his throat, unable to believe any of the listeners would be convinced by Oriane's show of filial affection, but they were. Admiration showed in every face, bar her husband's. Guilhem grimaced. He and Congost alone knew Oriane's true worth. All others were beguiled by her beauty, her gentle words. As once he had been.

Sickened to the bottom of his heart, Guilhem glanced to where François stood impassive, his face a perfect mask, on the outskirts of the group.

"If you believe it will aid our cause, Dame," Viscount Trencavel replied, "then you have my permission."

Oriane curtseyed once more. "Thank you, *Messire.*"

He clapped his hands. "Saddle the horses."

Oriane kept close to Guilhem as they rode across the devastated land to the pavilion of the count of Nevers, where the parley was to take place. From the Cité, those with the strength to climb the walls stood in silence and watched them go.

The moment they entered the camp, Oriane slipped away. Ignoring the lewd and rough calls of the soldiers, she followed François through the sea of tents and colors, until they found themselves in the green and silver of Chartres.

"This way, Dame," murmured François, pointing to a pavilion set a little apart from everyone else. The soldiers stood to attention as they approached and held their pikes across the opening. One of them acknowledged François with a nod.

"Tell your master that Dame Oriane, daughter of the late steward of Carcassona, is here and wishes audience with Lord Evreux."

Oriane was taking a terrible risk coming to him. From François, she knew of his cruelty and quick temper. She was playing for high stakes.

"On what matter?" demanded the soldier.

"My lady will speak to none but Lord Evreux himself."

The man hesitated, then he ducked beneath the opening and disappeared into the tent. Moments, later, he came out and beckoned them to follow.

Her first sight of Guy d'Evreux did nothing to allay her fears. He had his back to her as she entered the tent. He turned and flint gray eyes burned in his pale face. His black hair was oiled back from his forehead in the French style. He had the look of a hawk about to strike.

"Lady, I have heard much about you." His voice was calm and steady, but there was a hint of steel behind it. "I did not expect to have the pleasure of meeting you in person. What can I do for you?"

"I hope it will be a question of what I can do for you, my lord," she said.

Before she knew it, Evreux had taken hold of her wrist.

"I advise you not to bandy words with me, Lady Oriane. Your peasant southern ways will do you no good here." Behind her, she felt François trying not to react. "Do you have news for me, yes or no?" he said. "Speak."

Oriane held her nerve. "This is an ill way to treat one who brings you what most you desire," she said, meeting his gaze.

Evreux raised his arm. "I could beat the information out of you, as soon as be kept waiting and save us both time."

Oriane held her gaze. "Then you will learn only part of what I have to say," she said as steadily as she could. "You have invested much in your quest for the Labyrinth Trilogy. I can give you what you want."

Evreux stared at her a moment, then lowered his arm.

"You have courage, Lady Oriane, I give you that. Whether you also have wisdom remains to be seen."

He clicked his fingers and a servant brought a tray of wine. Oriane's hands were shaking too hard to risk taking a cup.

"No thank you, my lord."

"As you wish," he said, gesturing to her to sit. "What is it you want, my lady?"

"If I deliver to you what you seek, I wish you to take me north when you return home." From the look on his face, Oriane knew she had finally succeeded in surprising him. "As your wife."

"You have a husband," Evreux said, looking over her head to François for confirmation. "Trencavel's scribe, I heard. Is that not the case?"

Oriane held his gaze. "I regret to say my husband was killed. Struck down within the walls whilst doing his duty."

"My condolences for your loss." Evreux pressed his long, thin fingers together, making a church of his hands. "This siege could yet last years. What makes you so sure that I will return north?"

"It is my belief, my Lord Evreux," she said, choosing her words with care, "that your presence here is for one purpose. If, with my assistance, you are able to conclude your business in the south speedily, I can see no reason you would wish to stay beyond your forty days."

Evreux gave a tight smile. "You have no faith in your lord Trencavel's power to persuade?"

"With all due respect to those under whose banner you march, my lord, I do not believe the revered abbot's intention is to conclude this engagement by diplomatic means."

Evreux continued to stare at her. Oriane held her breath.

"You play your hand well, Lady Oriane," he said in the end.

She bowed her head, but did not speak. He got up and walked toward her.

"I accept your proposal," he said, handing her a goblet.

This time, she took it.

"There is one thing more, my lord," she said. "Within Viscount Trencavel's party is a *chevalier*, Guilhem du Mas. He is the husband of my sister. It would be advisable, if this is within your power, to take steps to contain his influence."

"Permanently?"

Oriane shook her head. "He may yet have a part to play in our plans. But it would be advisable to limit his influence. Viscount Trencavel favors him and, with my father gone . . ."

Evreux nodded and dispatched François. "Now, my Lady Oriane," he said, as soon as they were alone. "No more prevarication. Tell me what you have to offer."

CHAPTER 62

"Alaïs! Alaïs! Wake up!"

Someone was shaking her shoulders. That was wrong. She was sitting on the bank of the river, in the peace and dappled light of her private glade. She could feel the cool water trickling between her toes, cold and fresh, and the soft touch of the sun caressing her cheek. She could taste the strong Corbières wine on her tongue and her nose was full of the intoxicating aroma of the warm white bread she lifted to her mouth.

Beside her, Guilhem was lying asleep in the grass.

The world was so green, the sky so blue.

She jolted awake, to find herself still in the dank, semi-gloom of the tunnels. Sajhë was standing over her.

"You must wake up, Dame."

Alaïs scrambled into a sitting position. "What's happened? Is Esclarmonde all right?"

"Viscount Trencavel has been taken."

"Taken," she said in bewilderment. "Taken where? By whom?"

"They are saying by treason. People are saying that the French tricked him into their camp, and then took him by force. Others, that he has given himself to save the *Ciutat.* And . . ."

Sajhë broke off. Even in the half-light, Alaïs could see he was flushing.

"What is it?"

"They are saying Dame Oriane and Chevalier du Mas were of the viscount's party." He hesitated. "They, too, have not returned."

Alaïs got to her feet. She glanced at Esclarmonde, who was sleeping calmly. "She's resting. She will be fine without us for a while. Come. We must find out what is happening."

They ran swiftly along the tunnel and climbed the ladder. Alaïs flung the trap door open and hauled Sajhë up after her.

Outside, the streets were crowded, filled with bewildered people rushing aimlessly backwards and forward.

"Can you tell me what's happening?" she shouted at a man running by. He shook his head and kept running. Sajhë took her hand and dragged her into a small house on the opposite side of the street.

"Gaston will know."

Alaïs followed him in. Gaston and his brother, Pons, rose as she entered.

"Dame."

"Is it true that the viscount has been captured?" she asked.

Gaston nodded. "Yesterday morning the count of Auxerre came to propose a meeting between Viscount Trencavel and the count of Nevers, in the presence of the abbot. He went with a small entourage, your sister among them. As to what happened after that, Dame Alaïs, nobody knows. Either our lord Trencavel gave himself up of his own accord to purchase our freedom or else he was deceived."

"None has returned," added Pons.

"Either way, there will be no fighting," said Gaston quietly. "The garrison has surrendered. The French have already taken possession of the main gates and towers."

"What!" Alaïs exclaimed, looking in disbelief from face to face. "What are the terms of the surrender?"

"That all citizens, Cathar, Jew and Catholic, will be allowed to leave Carcassona without fear of our lives, carrying nothing but the clothes we stand up in."

"There are to be no interrogations? No burnings?"

"It seems not. The entire population is to be exiled, but not harmed."

Alaïs sank down in a chair before her legs gave way from under her.

"What of Dame Agnès?"

"She and the young prince are to be given safe conduct into the custody of the count of Foix, provided she renounces all claims on behalf of her son." Gaston cleared his throat. "I am sorry for the loss of your husband and sister, Dame Alaïs."

"Does anyone know the fate of our men?"

Pons shook his head.

"Is it a trick, think you?" she said fiercely.

"There is no way of knowing, Dame. Only when the exodus begins will we see if the French are as good as their word."

"Everyone is to leave through one gate, the Porte d'Aude to the west of the Cité at the ringing of the bells at dusk."

"It is over then," she said, almost in a whisper. "The *Ciutat* has surrendered."

At least my father did not live to see the viscount in French hands.

"Esclarmonde improves daily, but she is still weak. Can I impose upon you further and ask if you could accompany her from the *Ciutat*?" She paused. "For reasons I dare not confide, for your sake as much as Esclarmonde's, it would be wisest if we traveled separately."

Gaston nodded. "You fear those who inflicted these appalling injuries in the first instance might yet be looking for her?"

Alaïs looked at him in surprise. "Well, yes," she admitted.

"It will be an honor to help you, Dame Alaïs." He flushed red. "Your father . . . He was a fair man."

She nodded. "He was."

As the dying rays of the setting sun painted the outer walls of the Château Comtal with a fierce orange light, the courtyard, the walkways and the Great Hall were silent. Everything was abandoned, empty.

At the Porte d'Aude, a mass of frightened and bewildered people were herded together, desperately trying to keep sight of their loved ones, averting their eyes from the contemptuous faces of the French soldiers, who stared at them as if they were less than human. Their hands rested on the hilts of their swords as if only waiting for an excuse.

Alaïs hoped her disguise would be good enough. She shuffled forward, awkward in men's boots several times too big for her, keeping close to the man in front. She had strapping around her chest to flatten her and to conceal the books and parchments. In breeches, shirt and a nondescript straw hat, she looked like any other boy. She had pebbles in her mouth, which altered the shape of her face, and she'd cut her hair and rubbed mud in it to darken it.

The line moved forward. Alaïs kept looking down, for fear of catching the eye of anyone who might recognize her and give her away. The line thinned to a single file the closer they got to the gate. There were four Crusaders on guard, their expressions dull and resentful. They were stopping people, forcing them to remove their clothes to prove they were smuggling nothing underneath.

Alaïs could see the guards had stopped Esclarmonde's litter. Clutching a kerchief over his mouth, Gaston was explaining his mother was very ill. The guard pulled back the curtain and immediately stepped back. Alaïs hid a smile. She had sewed rotting meat into a pig's bladder and wrapped stained, bloodied bandages around her feet.

The guard waved them through.

Sajhë was several families behind, traveling with Sénher and Na Couza and their six children, who had similar coloring. She had rubbed dirt into his hair to darken it too. The only thing she could not disguise were his eyes, so he was under strict instruction not to look up if he could help it.

The line lurched forward once more. *It's my turn.* They'd agreed she would pretend not to understand if anyone spoke to her.

"Toi! Paysan. Qu'est-ce que tu portes là?"

She kept her head down, resisting the temptation to touch the strapping around her body.

"Eh, toi!"

The pike cut through the air and Alaïs braced herself for a blow that never came. Instead, the girl in front of her was knocked to the ground. She scrambled in the dirt for her hat. She raised her frightened face to her accuser.

"*Canhòt.*"

"What's she say?" the guard muttered. "I can't understand a word they say."

"*Chien.* She's got a puppy."

Before any of them knew what was happening, the soldier had hauled the dog out of her arms and run it through with his spear. Blood splattered over the front of the girl's dress.

"*Allez! Vite.*"

The girl was too shocked to move. Alaïs helped her to her feet and encouraged her to keep moving, steering her through the gate, fighting the impulse to turn around and check on Sajhë.

Now I see them.

On the hill overlooking the gate were the French barons. Not the leaders, who Alaïs presumed were waiting until the evacuation was over before making their entrance into Carcassonne, but knights wearing the colors of Burgundy, Nevers and Chartres.

At the end of the row, closest to the path, a tall, thin man sat astride a powerful gray stallion. Despite the long southern summer, his skin was still as white as milk. Beside him was François. Next to him, Alaïs recognized Oriane's familiar red dress.

But not Guilhem.

Keep walking, keeping your eyes fastened on the ground.

She was so close now that she could smell the leather of the saddles and bridles of the horses. Oriane's eyes seemed to be burning into her.

An old man, with sad eyes full of pain, tapped her on the arm. He needed help on the steep slope. Alaïs gave him her shoulder. It was the luck she needed. Looking to all the world like a grandson and grandfather, she passed directly beneath Oriane's gaze without being recognized.

The path seemed to last forever. Finally, they reached the shaded area at the bottom of the slope where the ground leveled out and the woods and marshes began. Alaïs saw her companion reunited with his son and daughter-in-law, then detached herself from the main crowd and slipped into the trees.

As soon as she was out of sight, Alaïs spat the stones from her mouth. The inside of her cheeks were raw and dry. She rubbed her jaw, trying to ease the discomfort. She took her hat off and ran her fingers through her stubbly hair. It felt like damp straw, prickly and uncomfortable on the back of her neck.

A shout at the gate drew her attention.

No, please. Not him.

A soldier was holding Sajhë by the scruff of the neck. She could see him kicking, trying to get free. He was holding something in his hands. A small box.

Alaïs' heart plummeted. She couldn't risk going back up, so was powerless to do anything. Na Couza was arguing with the soldier, who struck her round the head, sending her sprawling back into the dirt. Sajhë took his chance. He wriggled out of the man's grasp and scrambled down the slope. Sénher Couza helped his wife to her feet.

Alaïs held her breath. For a moment, it seemed as if it was going to be all right. The soldier had lost interest. But then Alaïs heard a woman shouting. Oriane was shouting and pointing at Sajhë, ordering the guards to stop him.

She's recognized him.

Sajhë might not be Alaïs, but he was the next best thing.

There was an immediate outburst of activity. Two of the guards set off down the slopes after Sajhë, but he was a fast runner, sure-footed and confident. Weighted down by their weapons and armor, they were no match for an eleven-year-old boy. Silently, Alaïs urged him on, watching as he darted this way and that, jumping and leaping over the uneven patches of ground, until he reached the cover of the woods.

Realizing she was about to lose him, Oriane sent François to follow. His horse thundered down the track, slipping and skidding on the steep, dry earth, but he covered the ground quickly. Sajhë hurtled into the undergrowth, François hard on his heels.

Alaïs realized Sajhë was heading for the boggy marshland where the Aude split into several tributaries. The ground was green and looked like a meadow in spring, but it was lethal underneath. Local people stayed away.

Alaïs pulled herself up into a tree for a better view. François either didn't realize where Sajhë was going or didn't care, because he spurred his horse on. *He's gaining on him.* Sajhë stumbled and nearly lost his footing, but he managed to keep running, zigzagging through the thicket, leading them through blackberry bushes and thistles.

Suddenly, François let out a howl of anger, which turned immediately to alarm. The sinking mud had wrapped itself around the hind legs of his horse. The terrified animal was baying, flailing its legs. Every desperate attempt only hastened its descent into the treacherous mud.

François threw himself from the saddle and tried to swim to the edges of the bog, but his body sank lower and lower, clawed down into the mud, until only the tips of his fingers could be seen.

Then, there was silence. It seemed to Alaïs as if even the birds had stopped singing. Terrified for Sajhë, she dropped down to the ground, just as he came back into view. He was ashen faced, his bottom lip trembling with exertion, and he was still clutching the wooden box.

"I led him into the marsh," he said.

Alaïs put her hand on his shoulder. "I know. That was clever."

"Was he a traitor too?"

She nodded. "I think that was what Esclarmonde was trying to tell us." Alaïs pursed her lips together, glad her father had not lived to know it was François who had betrayed him. She shook the thought from her mind. "But what were you thinking, Sajhë? Why on earth were you carrying this box? It almost got you killed."

"*Menina* told me to keep it safe."

Sajhë stretched his fingers across the bottom of the box until he was able to press both sides at once. There was a sharp click, then he turned the base, to reveal a flat, concealed drawer. He reached in and pulled out a piece of cloth.

"It's a map. *Menina* said we would need it."

Alaïs understood immediately. "She doesn't mean to come with us," she said heavily, fighting the tears welling up in her eyes.

Sajhë shook his head.

"But why didn't she tell me?" she said, her voice shaking. "Could she not trust me?"

"You would not have let her go."

Alaïs let her head fall back against the tree. She was overwhelmed with the magnitude of her task. Without Esclarmonde she didn't know how she could find the strength to do what was required of her.

As if he could read her mind, Sajhë said: "I'll look after you. And it won't be for long. When we have given the *Book of Words* to Harif, we will come back and find her. *Si es atal es atal.*" Things will be as they will be.

"That we should all be as wise as you."

Sajhë flushed. "This is where we have to go," he said, pointing at the map. "It doesn't appear on any map, but *Menina* calls the village Los Seres."

Of course. Not just the name of the guardians, but also a place.

"You see?" he said. "In the Sabarthès Mountains."

Alaïs nodded. "Yes, yes," she said. "At last, I think I do."

THE RETURN TO
THE MOUNTAINS

CHAPTER 63
Sabarthès Mountains

FRIDAY, 8 JULY 2005

Audric Baillard sat at a table of dark, highly polished wood in his house in the shadow of the mountain.

The ceiling in the main room was low and there were large square tiles on the floor the color of red mountain earth. He had made few changes. This far from civilization, there was no electricity, no running water, no cars or telephones. The only sound was the ticking of the clock marking time.

There was an oil lamp on the table, extinguished now. Next to it was a glass tumbler, filled almost to the brim with Guignolet, filling the room with the subtle scent of alcohol and cherries. On the far side of the table there was a brass tray holding two glasses and a bottle of red wine, unopened, as well as a small wooden platter of savoury biscuits covered with a white linen cloth.

Baillard had opened the shutters so he could see the sunrise. In spring, the trees on the outskirts of the village were dotted with tight silver and white buds and yellow and pink flowers peeped out shyly from the hedgerows and banks. By this late in the year, there was little color left, only the gray and green of the mountain in whose eternal presence he had lived for so long.

A curtain separated his sleeping quarters from the main room. The whole of the back wall was covered with narrow shelves, almost empty now. An old pestle and mortar, a couple of bowls and scoops, a few jars. Also books, both those written by him, and the great voices of Cathar history—Delteil, Duvernoy, Nelli, Marti, Brenon, Rouquette. Works of Arab philosophy sat side by side with translations of ancient Judaic texts, monographs by authors ancient and modern. The rows of paperbacks, incongruous in such a setting, filled the space once occupied by medicines and potions and herbs.

He was prepared to wait.

Baillard raised the glass to his lips and drank deeply.

And if she did not come? If he never learned the truth of those final hours?

He sighed. If she did not come, then he would be forced to take the last steps of his long journey alone. As he had always feared.

CHAPTER 64

By the time dawn broke, Alice was a few kilometers north of Toulouse. She pulled into a service station and drank two cups of hot, sweet coffee to steady her nerves.

Alice read the letter once more. Posted in Foix on Wednesday morning. A letter from Audric Baillard giving directions to his house. She knew it was genuine. She recognized the black spidery writing.

She felt she had no choice but to go.

Alice spread the map on the counter, trying to work out precisely where she was heading. The *hameau* where Baillard lived didn't appear on the map, although he'd mentioned enough landmarks and names of nearby towns for her to work out the general area.

He was confident, he said, that Alice would know the place when she saw it.

As a precaution, and one she realized she should have taken earlier, Alice exchanged her hire car at the airport for one of a different color and make, just in case they were looking for her, then continued her journey south.

She drove past Foix toward Andorra, and then through Tarascon before following Baillard's directions. She turned off the main road at Luzenac and went through Lordat and Bestiac. The landscape changed. It reminded Alice of the slopes of the Alps. Small mountain flowers, long grass, the houses like Swiss chalets.

She passed a sprawling quarry, like a huge white scar gouged into the side of the mountain. Towering electricity pylons and thick black cabling for the winter ski resorts dominated the skyline, black against the summer blue sky.

Alice crossed the river Lauze. She was forced to shift down into second gear as the road got steeper and the bends tighter. She was starting to feel sick from the constant doubling back, when she suddenly found herself in a small village.

There were two shops and a café with a couple of tables and chairs sitting outside on the pavement. Deciding it would be good to check she was still heading the right way, Alice went into the café. The air inside was thick with smoke and hunched, mulish men with weather-beaten faces and blue overalls lined the counter.

Alice ordered coffee and ostentatiously put her map on the counter. Dislike of strangers, particularly women, meant no one spoke to her for a while, but finally she managed to strike up a conversation. No one had heard of Los Seres, but they knew the area and gave what help they could.

She drove higher, gradually getting her bearings. The road became a track, and then finally petered out altogether. Alice parked the car and got out. Only now, standing in the familiar landscape, her nose filled with the smells of the mountain, did she realize that she had in fact doubled back on herself and was actually on the far side of the Pic de Soularac.

Alice climbed to the highest point and shielded her eyes. She identified the *étang* de Tort, a distinctively shaped tarn the men in the bar had told her to look out for. Close by was another expanse of water known locally as the Devil's Lake.

Finally, she orientated herself to the Pic de Saint-Barthélémy, which stood between the Pic de Soularac and Montségur itself.

Straight ahead, a single track wound up through the green scrub and brown earth and bright yellow broom. The dark green leaves of the box were fragrant and sharp. She touched the leaves and rubbed the dew between her fingers.

Alice climbed for ten minutes. Then, the path opened into a clearing, and she was there.

A single-storied house stood alone, surrounded by ruins, the gray stone camouflaged against the mountain behind. And in the doorway stood a man, very thin and very old, with a shock of white hair, wearing the pale suit she remembered from the photograph.

Alice felt her legs were moving of their own accord. The ground leveled out as she walked the last few steps toward him. Baillard watched in silence and was completely still. He did not smile or raise his hand in greeting. Even when she drew close, he did not speak or move. He never took his eyes from her face. They were the most startling color.

Amber mixed with autumn leaves.

Alice stopped in front of him. At last, he smiled. It was like the sun coming out from behind the clouds, transforming the crevices and lines of his face.

"Madomaisèla Tanner," he said. His voice was deep and old, like the wind in the desert. "*Benvenguda.* I knew you would come." He stood back to let her enter. "Please."

Nervous, awkward, Alice ducked under the lintel and stepped through the door into the room, still feeling the intensity of his gaze. It was as if he was trying to commit every feature to memory.

"Monsieur Baillard," she said, then stopped.

She was unable to think of anything to say. His delight, his wonder that she had come—mixed with his faith that she would—made ordinary conversation impossible.

"You resemble her," he said slowly. "There is much of her in your face."

"I've only seen photos, but I thought so too."

He smiled. "I did not mean Grace," he said softly, then turned away, as if he had said too much. "Please, sit down."

Alice glanced surreptiously around the room, noticing the lack of modern equipment. No lights, no heating, nothing electronic. She wondered if there was a kitchen.

"Monsieur Baillard," she started again. "It's a pleasure to meet you. I was wondering . . . how did you know where to find me?"

Again, he smiled. "Does it matter?"

Alice thought about it and realized it did not.

"Madomaisèla Tanner, I know about the Pic de Soularac. I have one question I must ask you before we go any further. Did you find a book?"

More than anything, Alice wanted to say she had. "I'm sorry," she said, shaking her head. "He asked me about it too, but I didn't see it."

"He?"

She frowned. "A man called Paul Authié."

Baillard nodded his head up and down. "Ah, yes," he said, in such a way that Alice felt she didn't need to explain.

"You found this, though, I believe?"

He lifted his left hand and placed it on the table, like a young girl showing off an engagement ring, and she saw to her astonishment he was wearing the stone ring. She smiled. It was so familiar, even though she'd held it for a few seconds at most.

She swallowed hard. "May I?"

Baillard removed it from his thumb. Alice took it and turned it over between her fingers, again discomforted by the intensity of his gaze.

"Does it belong to you?" she heard herself asking, although she feared he would say yes and all that that might mean.

He paused. "No," he said in the end, "although I had one like it once."

"Then who did this belong to?"

"You do not know?" he said.

For a split second, Alice thought she did. Then the spark of understanding disappeared and her mind was clouded once more.

"I'm not sure," she said uncertainly, shaking her head, "but it lacks this, I think." She pulled the labyrinth disc from her pocket. "It was with the family tree at my aunt's house." She handed it to him. "Did you send it to her?"

Baillard did not answer. "Grace was a charming woman, well educated and intelligent. During the course of our first conversation we discovered we had several interests in common, several experiences in common."

"What is it for?" she asked, refusing to be deflected.

"It's called a *merel*. Once there were many. Now, only this one remains."

She watched in amazement as Baillard inserted the disc into the gap in the body of the ring. "*Aquí*. There." He smiled and put the ring back on his thumb.

"Is that decorative only or does it serve some purpose?"

He smiled, as if she had passed some sort of test. "It is the key that is needed," he said softly.

"Needed for what?"

Again, Baillard did not answer. "Alaïs comes to you sometimes when you are sleeping, does she not?"

She was taken aback by the sudden shift in conversation. She didn't know how to react.

"We carry the past within us, in our bones, in our blood," he said. "Alaïs has been with you all of your life, watching over you. You share many qualities with her. She had great courage, a quiet determination, as do you. Alaïs was loyal and steadfast as, I suspect, are you." He stopped and smiled at her again. "She, too, had dreams. Of the old days, of the beginning. Those dreams revealed her destiny to her, although she was reluctant to accept it, as yours now light your way."

Alice felt as if the words were coming at her from a long distance, as if they were nothing to do with her or Baillard or anybody, but had always existed in time and space.

"My dreams have always been about her," she said, not knowing where her words were taking her. "About the fire, the mountain, the book. *This* mountain?" He nodded. "I feel she's trying to tell me something. Her face has grown clearer these past few days, but I still can't hear her speak." She hesitated. "I don't understand what she wants of me."

"Or you of her, perhaps," he said lightly. Baillard poured the wine and handed a glass to Alice.

Despite the earliness of the hour, she took several mouthfuls, feeling the liquid warming her as it slid down her throat.

"Monsieur Baillard, I need to know what happened to Alaïs. Until I do, nothing will make sense. You know, don't you?"

A look of infinite sadness came over him.

"She did survive," she said slowly, fearing to hear the answer. "After Carcassonne . . . they didn't . . . she wasn't captured?"

He placed his hands flat on the table. Thin and speckled brown with age, Alice thought they resembled the claws of a bird.

"Alaïs did not die before her time," he said carefully.

"That doesn't tell me . . ." she started to say.

Baillard held up his hand. "At the Pic de Soularac events were set in motion that will give you—give *us*—the answers we seek. Only through understanding the present, the truth of the past will be known. You seek your friend, *oc*?"

Again, Alice was caught out by the way Baillard jumped from one subject to another.

"How do you know about Shelagh?" she said.

"I know about the excavation and what happened there. Now your friend has disappeared. You are trying to find her."

Deciding there was no point trying to work out how or what he knew, Alice replied.

"She left the site house a couple of days ago. No one's seen her since. I know her disappearance is connected with the discovery of the labyrinth." She hesitated. "In fact, I think I know who might be behind it all. At first, I thought Shelagh might have stolen the ring."

Baillard shook his head. "Yves Biau took it and sent it to his grandmother, Jeanne Giraud."

Alice's eyes widened as another part of the jigsaw slotted into place. "Yves and your friend work for a woman called Madame de l'Oradore." He paused. "Fortunately, Yves had second thoughts. Your friend too, perhaps."

Alice nodded. "Biau passed me a telephone number. Then I discovered Shelagh had called the same number. I found out the address and when I didn't get any answer, I thought I should go and see if she was there. It turned out to be the house of Madame de l'Oradore. In Chartres."

"You went to Chartres?" Baillard said, his eyes bright. "Tell me. Tell me. What did you see?"

He listened in silence until Alice had finished telling him about everything she'd seen and overheard.

"But this young man, Will, he did not show you the chamber?"

Alice shook her head. "After a while, I started to think that maybe it didn't really exist."

"It exists," he said.

"I left my rucksack behind. It had all my notes about the labyrinth in it, the photograph of you with my aunt. It will lead her straight to me." She paused. "That's why Will went back to get it for me."

"And now you fear something has happened to him also?"

"I'm not sure, to tell you the truth. Half the time, I'm frightened for him. The rest of the time, I think he's probably all tied up in it as well."

"Why did you feel you could trust him in the first instance?"

Alice looked up, alerted by the change in his tone. His usually benign gentle expression had vanished.

"Do you feel you owe him something?"

"Owe him something?" Alice repeated, surprised by his choice of words. "No, not that. I barely know him. But, I liked him, I suppose. I felt comfortable in his company. I felt . . ."

"Qué?" What?

"It was more the other way round. It sounds crazy, but it was if *he* felt he owed *me*. Like he was making up to me for something."

Without warning, Baillard pushed his chair back and walked to the window. He was clearly in a state of some confusion.

Alice waited, not understanding what was going on. At last, he turned to face her.

"I will tell you Alaïs' story," he said. "And through the knowing of it, we will perhaps find the courage to face what lies ahead. But know this, Madomaisèla Tanner. Once you have heard it, you will have no choice but to follow the path to its end."

Alice frowned. "It sounds like a warning."

"No," he said quickly. "Far from it. But we must not lose sight of your friend. From what you overheard, we must assume her safety is guaranteed until this evening at least."

"But I don't know where the meeting's supposed to take place," she said. "François-Baptiste didn't say. Only tomorrow night at nine-thirty."

"I can guess," Baillard said calmly. "By dusk we will be there, waiting for them." He glanced out of the open window at the rising sun. "That gives us some time to talk."

"But what if you're wrong?"

Baillard shrugged. "We must hope I am not."

Alice was quiet for a moment. "I just want to know the truth," she said, amazed at how steady her voice sounded.

He smiled. *"Ieu tanben,"* he said. Me too.

CHAPTER 65

Will was aware of being dragged down the flight of narrow stairs to the basement, then along the concrete corridor through the two doors. His head was hanging forward. The smell of incense was less strong, although it still hung, like a memory, in the hushed subterranean gloom.

At first, Will thought they were taking him to the chamber and that they would kill him. A memory of the block of stone at the foot of the tomb, the blood on the floor, flashed into his mind. But, then he was being bumped over a step. He felt the fresh air of early morning on his face and he realized he was outside, in some sort of alley that ran along the back of rue du Cheval Blanc. There were the early morning smells of burned coffee beans and rubbish, the sounds of the garbage truck not far off. Will realized this was how they must have got Tavernier's body away from the house and down to the river.

A spasm of fear went through him and he struggled a little, only to register that his arms and legs were tied. Will heard the sound of a car boot being opened. He was half lifted, half thrown into the back. It wasn't the usual sort of thing. He was in some sort of large box. It smelled of plastic.

As he rolled awkwardly onto his side, his head connected with the back of the container and Will felt the skin around the wound split open. Blood started to trickle down his temple, irritating, stinging. He couldn't move his hands to wipe it away.

Now Will remembered standing outside the door of the study. Then the blinding crack of pain as François-Baptiste brought the gun down on the side of his head; his knees giving way under him; Marie-Cécile's imperious voice once again demanding to know what was going on.

A callused hand grasped his arm. Will felt his sleeve being pushed up and then the sharp point of a needle piercing his skin. Like before. Then, the sound of catches being snapped into place and some sort of covering, a tarpaulin perhaps, being pulled over his prison.

The drug was seeping into his veins, cold, pleasant, anesthetizing the pain. Hazy. Will drifted in and out of consciousness. He felt the car picking up speed. He started to feel queasy as his head rolled from side to side as they took the corners. He thought of Alice. More than anything, he wanted to see her. Tell her he had tried his best. That he had not let her down.

He was hallucinating now. He could picture the swirling, murky green waters of the river Eure flooding into his mouth and nose and lungs. Will tried to keep Alice's face in his mind, her serious brown eyes, her smile. If he could keep her image with him, then perhaps he would be all right.

But the fear of drowning, of dying in this foreign place that meant nothing to him, was more powerful. Will slipped away into the darkness.

In Carcassonne, Paul Authié stood on his balcony looking out over the river Aude, a cup of black coffee in his hand. He had used O'Donnell as bait to get to François-Baptiste de l'Oradore, but instinctively he rejected the idea of a dummy book for her to hand over. The boy would spot it was a fake. Besides, he did want him to see the state she was in and know he'd been set up.

Authié put his cup down on the table and shot the cuffs on his crisp white shirt. The only option was to confront François-Baptiste himself—alone—and tell him he'd bring O'Donnell and the book to Marie-Cécile at the Pic de Soularac in time for the ceremony.

He regretted he'd not retrieved the ring, although he still believed Giraud had passed it to Audric Baillard and that Baillard would come to the Pic de Soularac of his own accord. Authié had no doubt the old man was out there somewhere, watching.

Alice Tanner was more of a problem. The disc O'Donnell had mentioned gave him pause for thought, all the more so because he didn't understand its significance. Tanner was proving surprisingly adept at keeping out of his reach. She'd got away from Domingo and Braissart in the cemetery. They'd lost the car for several hours yesterday and when they did finally pick up the signal this morning, it was only to discover the vehicle was parked at the Hertz depot at Toulouse airport.

Authié closed his thin fingers around his crucifix. By midnight it would all be over. The heretical texts, the heretics themselves, would be destroyed.

In the distance the bell of the cathedral began to call the faithful to Friday mass. Authié glanced at his watch. He would go to confession. With his sins forgiven, in a state of Grace, he would kneel at the altar and receive the Holy Communion. Then he would be ready, body and soul, to fulfill God's purpose.

Will felt the car slow down, then turn off the road on to a farm track.

The driver took it carefully, swerving to avoid the dips and hollows. Will's teeth rattled in his head as the car bumped, jerked, jolted up the hill.

Finally, they stopped. The engine was turned off.

He felt the car rock as both men got out, then the sound of the doors slamming like shots from a gun and the clunk of the central locking. His hands were tied behind his back not in front, which made it harder, but Will twisted his wrists, trying to loosen the straps. He made little progress. The feeling was starting to come back. There was a band of pain across his shoulders from lying awkwardly for so long.

Suddenly, the boot was opened. Will lay completely still, his heart thudding, as the catches on the plastic container were unlocked. One of them took him under the arms, the other behind the knees. He was dragged out of the boot and dropped to the ground.

Even in his drugged state, Will felt they were miles from civilization. The sun was fierce and there was a sharpness, a freshness to the air that spoke of space and lack of human habitation. It was utterly silent, utterly still. No cars, no people. Will blinked. He tried to focus, but it was too bright. The air was too clear. The sun seemed to be burning his eyes, turning everything to white.

He felt the hypodermic stab his arm again and the familiar embrace of the drug in his veins. The men pulled him roughly to his feet and started to drag him up the hill. The ground was steep and he could hear their labored breathing, smell the sweat coming off them as they struggled in the heat.

Will was aware of the scrunch of gravel and stone, then the wooden struts of steps cut into the slope beneath his trailing feet, then the softness of grass.

As he drifted back into semiconsciousness, he realized the whistling sound in his head was the ghostly sighing of the wind.

CHAPTER 66

The Commissioner of the Police Judiciaire of the Haute-Pyrenees strode into Inspector Noubel's office in Foix and slammed the door shut behind him.

"This had better be good, Noubel."

"Thank you for coming, sir. I wouldn't have disturbed your lunch if I thought it could wait."

He grunted. "You've identified Biau's killers?"

"Cyrille Braissart and Javier Domingo," confirmed Noubel, waving a fax that had come through minutes earlier. "Two positive IDs. One shortly before the accident in Foix on Monday night, the second immediately afterwards. The car was found abandoned on the Spanish-Andorra border yesterday." Noubel paused to wipe the sweat from his nose and forehead. "They work for Paul Authié, sir."

The Commissioner lowered his massive frame onto the edge of the desk.

"I'm listening."

"You've heard the allegations against Authié? That he's a member of the *Noublesso Véritable*?" He nodded. "I spoke to the police in Chartres this afternoon—following up the Shelagh O'Donnell link—and they confirmed they're investigating the links between the organization and a murder that took place earlier in the week."

"What's that got to do with Authié?"

"The body was recovered quickly due to an anonymous tip-off."

"Any proof it was Authié?"

"No," Noubel admitted, "but there is evidence he met with a journalist, who's also disappeared. The police in Chartres think there's a link."

Seeing the look of scepticism on his boss' face, Noubel rushed on.

"The excavation at the Pic de Soularac was funded by Madame de l'Oradore. Well hidden, but it's her money behind it. Brayling, the director of the dig, is pushing the idea that O'Donnell has disappeared, having stolen artifacts from the site. But it's not what her friends think." He paused. "I'm sure Authié has her, either on Madame de l'Oradore's orders or on his own account."

The fan in his office was broken and Noubel was perspiring heavily. He could feel rings of sweat mushrooming under his arms.

"It's very thin, Noubel."

"Madame de l'Oradore was in Carcassonne from Tuesday to Thursday, sir. She met twice with Authié. I believe she went with him to the Pic de Soularac."

"There's no crime in that, Noubel."

"When I came in this morning I found this message waiting for me, sir," he said. "That's when I decided we'd got enough to ask for this meeting."

Noubel hit the play button on his voicemail. Jeanne Giraud's voice filled the room. The commissionaire listened, his expression growing grimmer by the second.

"Who is she?" he said when Noubel had played the message a second time.

"Yves Biau's grandmother."

"And Audric Baillard?"

"An author and friend. He accompanied her to the hospital in Foix."

The commissioner put his hands on his hips and dropped his head. Noubel could see he was calculating the potential damage if they went after Authié and failed.

"And you're a hundred percent certain you've got enough to link Domingo and Braissart to both Biau *and* Authié?"

"The descriptions fit, sir."

"They fit half of the Ariège," he growled.

"O'Donnell's been missing for three days, sir."

The commissionaire sighed and heaved himself off the desk.

"What do you want to do, Noubel?"

"I want to pull in Braissart and Domingo, sir."

He nodded.

"Also, I need a search warrant. Authié's got several properties, including a derelict farm in the Sabarthès Mountains, registered in his ex-wife's name. If O'Donnell's being held locally, chances are it's there."

The commissioner was shaking his hand.

"Maybe if you put a personal call through to the prefect . . ."

Noubel waited.

"All right, all right." He pointed a nicotine-stained finger at him. "But I promise you this, Claude, if you fuck up, you're on your own. Authié's an influential man. As for Madame de l'Oradore . . ." He let his arms drop. "If you can't make this stick, they'll rip you to pieces and there won't be a damn thing I can do to stop them."

He turned and walked to the door. Just before he went out, he stopped.

"Remind me who this Baillard is? Do I know him? The name's vaguely familiar."

"Writes about Cathars. An expert on Ancient Egypt too."

"That's not it . . ."

Noubel waited. "No, it's gone," said the commissioner. "But for all we know, Madame Giraud could be making something out of nothing."

"She could, sir, although I have to tell you I've not been able to locate Baillard. No one's seen him since he left the hospital with Madame Giraud on Wednesday night."

The commissioner nodded. "I'll call you when the paperwork's ready. You'll be here?"

"Actually, sir," he said cautiously, "I thought I might have another go at the English woman. She's a friend of O'Donnell. She might know something."

"I'll find you."

As soon as the commissioner had gone, Noubel made a few calls, then grabbed his jacket and headed for his car. By his reckoning, he'd got plenty of time to get to Carcassonne and back before the prefect's signature on the search warrant had dried.

By half-past four, Noubel was sitting with his opposite number in Carcassonne. Arnaud Moureau was an old friend. Noubel knew he could speak freely. He pushed a scrap of paper across the table.

"Dr. Tanner said she would be staying at the Hotel Montmorency."

It took minutes to check she was registered there. "Nice hotel just outside the Cité walls, less than five minutes from rue de la Gaffe. Shall I drive?"

The receptionist was very nervous about being interviewed by two police officers. She was a poor witness, close to tears much of the time. Noubel got more and more impatient until Moureau stepped in. His more avuncular approach yielded better results.

"So, Sylvie," he said gently. "Dr. Tanner left the hotel early yesterday morning, yes?" The girl nodded. "She said she would be back today? I just want to be clear."

"*Oui.*"

"And you haven't heard anything to the contrary. She hasn't telephoned or anything?"

She shook her head.

"Good. Now, is there anything you can tell us? For example, has she had any visitors since she's been staying here?"

The girl hesitated.

"Yesterday a woman came, very early, with a message."

Noubel couldn't help himself jumping in. "What time was this?"

Moureau gestured for him to be quiet. "How early is early, Sylvie?"

"I came on duty at six o'clock. Not long after that."

"Did Dr. Tanner know her? Was she a friend?"

"I don't know. I don't think so. She seemed surprised."

"This is very helpful, Sylvie," said Moureau. "Can you tell us what made you think that?"

"She was asking Dr. Tanner to meet someone in the cemetery. It seemed an odd place to meet."

"Who?" said Noubel. "Did you hear a name?"

Looking even more terrified, Syvlie shook her head. "I don't know if she even went."

"That's okay. You're doing very well. Now, anything else?"

"A letter came for her."

"Post or hand-delivered?"

"There was that business with changing rooms," called a voice from out the back. Sylvie turned and glared at a boy, hidden behind a mound of cardboard boxes. "Pain in the bloody—"

"What business with rooms?" interrupted Noubel.

"I wasn't here," said Sylvie stubbornly.

"But I bet you know about it all the same."

"Dr. Tanner said there was an intruder in her room. Wednesday night. She demanded to be moved."

Noubel stiffened. Immediately, he walked through to the back.

"Causing a lot of extra work for everybody," Moureau was saying mildly, keeping Sylvie occupied.

Noubel followed the smells of cooking and found the boy easily enough.

"Were you here Wednesday night?"

He gave a cocky smile. "On duty in the bar."

"See anything?"

"I saw a woman come charging out of the door and go chasing after some bloke. Didn't know it was Dr. Tanner until after."

"Did you see the man?"

"Not really. It was her I noticed more."

Noubel took the pictures out of his jacket and held them in front of the boy's face. "Recognize either of them?"

"I've seen that one before. Nice suit. Not a tourist. Stuck out a bit. Hanging around. Tuesday, Wednesday maybe. Can't be sure, though."

By the time Noubel got back to the lobby, Moureau had got Sylvie smiling.

"He picked out Domingo. Said he'd seen him around the hotel."

"Doesn't make him the intruder, though," murmured Moureau.

Noubel slid the photo on the counter in front of Sylvie. "Either of these men familiar to you?"

"No," she said, shaking her head, "although . . ." She hesitated, then pointed at the picture of Domingo. "The woman asking for Dr. Tanner looked quite like this."

Noubel exchanged glances with Moureau. "Sister?"

"I'll get it checked out."

"I'm afraid we're going to have to ask you to let us into Dr. Tanner's room," said Noubel.

"I can't do that!"

Moureau overrode her objections. "We'll only be five minutes. It'll be much easier this way, Sylvie. If we have to wait for the manager to give permission, we'll come back with a whole search team. It will be disruptive for everybody."

Sylvie took a key from the hook and took them to Alice's room, looking drawn and nervous.

The windows and curtains were shut and it was stuffy. The bed was neatly made and a quick inspection of the bathroom revealed that there were fresh towels on the rack and the water glasses had been replaced.

"No one's been in here since the chambermaid cleaned yesterday morning," muttered Noubel.

There was nothing personal in the bathroom.

"Anything?" asked Moureau.

Noubel shook his head as he moved on to the wardrobe. There he found Alice's suitcase, packed.

"Looks like she didn't unpack anything when she moved rooms. She's obviously got passport, phone, the basics, with her," he said, running his hands under the edge of the mattress. Holding the handkerchief between his fingers, Noubel pulled open the drawer of the bedside table. It contained a silver strip of headache pills and Audric Baillard's book.

"Moureau," he said sharply. As he passed it over, a small piece of paper fluttered from between the pages to the floor.

"What is it?"

Noubel picked it up, then frowned as he passed it over.

"Problem?" said Moureau.

"This is Yves Biau's writing," he said. "A Chartres number."

He got out his phone to dial, but it rang before he'd finished.

"Noubel," he said abruptly. Moureau's eyes were fixed on him. "That's excellent news, sir. Yes. Right away."

He disconnected.

"We've got the search warrant," he said, heading for the door. "Quicker than I'd expected."

"What do you expect?" said Moureau. "He's a worried man."

CHAPTER 67

"Shall we sit outside?" Audric suggested. "At least until the heat becomes too much."

"That would be lovely," Alice replied, following him out of the little house. She felt like she was in a dream. Everything seemed to be happening in slow motion. The vastness of the mountains, the acres of sky, Baillard's slow and deliberate movements.

Alice felt the strain and confusion of the past few days slipping away from her.

"This will do well," he said in his gentle voice, stopping by a small grassy mound. Baillard sat down with his long, thin legs straight out in front of him like a boy.

Alice hesitated, then sat at his feet. She drew her knees up to her chin and wrapped her arms around her legs, then saw he was smiling again.

"What?" she said, self-conscious suddenly.

Audric just shook his head. *"Los ressons."* The echoes. "Forgive me, Madomaisèla Tanner. Forgive an old man his foolishness."

Alice didn't know what had made him smile so, only that she was happy to see it. "Please, call me Alice. *Madomaisèla* sounds so formal."

He inclined his head. "Very well."

"You speak Occitan rather than French?" she asked.

"Both, yes."

"Others too?"

He smiled self-deprecatingly. "English, Arabic, Spanish, Hebrew. Stories shift their shape, change character, take on different colors depending on the words you use, the language in which you choose to tell them. Sometimes more serious, sometimes more playful, more melodic, say. Here, in this part of what they now call France, the *langue d'Oc* was spoken by the people whose land this was. The *langue d'oïl,* the forerunner of modern-day French, was the language of the invaders. Such choices divided people." He waved his hands. "But, this is not what you came to hear. You want people, not theories, yes?"

It was Alice's turn to smile. "I read one of your books, Monsieur Baillard, which I found at my aunt's house in Sallèles d'Aude."

He nodded. "It's a beautiful place. The Canal de Jonction. Lime trees and *pins parasol* line the banks." He paused. "The leader of the Crusade, Arnald-Amalric, was given a house in Sallèles, you know? Also, in Carcassona and Besièrs."

"No," she said, shaking her head. "Before, when I first arrived, you said Alaïs did not die before her time. She . . . did she survive the fall of Carcassonne?"

Alice was surprised to realize her heart was beating fast.

Baillard nodded. "Alaïs left Carcassona in the company of a boy, Sajhë, the grandson of one of the guardians of the Labyrinth Trilogy." He raised his eyes to see if she was following, then continued when she indicated she was.

"They were heading here," he said. "In the old language *Los Seres* means the mountain crests, the ridges."

"Why here?"

"The *Navigatairé*, the leader of the *Noublesso de los Seres*, the society to which Alaïs' father and Sajhë's grandmother had sworn allegiance, was waiting for them here. Since Alaïs feared she was being pursued, they took an indirect route, first heading west to Fanjeaux, then south to Puivert and Lavelanet, then west again toward the Sabarthès Mountains.

"With the fall of Carcassona, there were soldiers everywhere. They swarmed all over our land like rats. There were also bandits who preyed on the refugees without pity. Alaïs and Sajhë traveled early in the morning and late at night, sheltering from the biting sun in the heat of the day. It was a particularly hot summer, so they slept outdoors when night fell. They survived on nuts, berries, fruit, anything they could forage. Alaïs avoided the towns, except when she was sure of finding a safe house."

"How did they know where to go?" asked Alice, remembering her own journey only hours earlier.

"Sajhë had a map, given to him . . ."

His voice cracked with distress. Alice didn't know why, but she reached out and took his hand. It seemed to give him comfort.

"They made good progress," he continued, "arriving in Los Seres shortly before the Feast Day of Sant-Miquel, at the end of September, just as the land was turning to gold. Already here, in the mountains, was the smell of autumn and wet earth. The smoke hung over the fields as the stubble burned. It was a new world to them, who had been brought up in the shadows and alleyways and overcrowded halls of Carcassona. Such light. Such skies that reached, as it seemed, all the way to heaven." He paused as he looked out over the landscape in front of them. "You understand?"

She nodded, mesmerized by his voice.

"Harif, the *Navigatairé*, was waiting for them." Baillard bowed his head. "When he heard all that had happened, he wept for the soul of

Alaïs' father and for Simeon too. For the loss of the books and for Esclarmonde's generosity in letting Alaïs and Sajhë travel on without her to better secure the safety of the *Book of Words*."

Baillard stopped again and, for a while, was silent. Alice did not want to interrupt or hurry him. The story would tell itself. He would speak when he was ready.

His face softened. "It was a blessed time, both in the mountains and on the plains, or at first so it seemed. Despite the indescribable horror of the defeat of Besièrs, many Carcassonnais believed they would soon be allowed to return home. Many trusted in the Church. They thought that if the heretics were expelled, then their lives would be returned to them."

"But the Crusaders did not leave," she said.

Baillard shook his head. "It was a war for land, not faith," he said. "After the *Ciutat* was defeated in August 1209, Simon de Montfort was elected viscount, despite the fact that Raymond-Roger Trencavel still lived. To modern minds, it is hard to understand how unprecedented, how grave an offense this was. It went against all tradition and honor. War was financed, in part, by the ransoms paid by one noble family to another. Unless convicted of a crime, a *seigneur*'s lands would never be confiscated and given to another. There could have been no clearer indication of the contempt in which the northerners held the Pays d'Oc."

"What happened to Viscount Trencavel?" Alice asked. "I see him remembered everywhere in the Cité."

Baillard nodded. "He is worthy of remembrance. He died—was murdered—after three months of incarceration in the prisons of the Château Comtal, in November 1209. De Montfort published it that he had died of siege sickness, as it was known. Dysentery. No one believed it. There were sporadic uprisings and outbreaks of unrest, until de Montfort was forced to grant Raymond-Roger's two-year-old son and heir an annual allowance of 3,000 sols in return for the legal surrender of the viscounty."

A face suddenly flashed into Alice's mind. A devout, serious woman, pretty, devoted to her husband and son.

"Dame Agnès," she muttered.

Baillard held her in his gaze for a moment. "She too is remembered within the walls of the *Ciutat*," he said quietly. "De Montfort was a devout Catholic. He—perhaps only he—of the Crusaders believed he was doing God's work. He established a tax of house or hearth in favor of the Church, introduced tithes on the first fruits, northern ways.

"The *Ciutat* might have been defeated, but the fortresses of the Minervois, the Montagne Noire, the Pyrenees refused to surrender. The king of Aragon, Pedro, would not accept him as a vassal; Raymond VI, uncle to Viscount Trencavel, withdrew to Toulouse; the counts of Never and

Saint-Pol, others such as Guy d'Evreux, returned north. Simon de Montfort had possession of Carcassona, but he was isolated.

"Merchants, peddlers, weavers brought news of sieges and battles, good and bad. Montréal, Preixan, Saverdun, Pamiers fell, Cabaret was holding out. In the spring of April 1210, after three months of siege, de Montfort took the town of Bram. He ordered his soldiers to round up the defeated garrison and had their eyes put out. Only one man was spared, charged with leading the mutilated procession cross-country to Cabaret, a clear warning to any who resisted that they could expect no mercy.

"The savagery and reprisals escalated. In July 1210, de Montfort besieged the hill fortress of Minerve. The town is protected on two sides by deep rocky gorges cut by rivers over thousands of years. High above the village, de Montfort installed a giant *trébuchet*, known as La Malvoisine — the bad neighbor." He stopped and turned to Alice. "There is a replica there now. Strange to see. For six weeks, de Montfort bombarded the village. When finally Minerve fell, one hundred and forty Cathar *parfaits* refused to recant and were burned on a communal pyre.

"In May 1211, the invaders took Lavaur, after a siege of a month. The Catholics called it 'the very seat of Satan.' In a way, they were right. It was the see of the Cathar bishop of Toulouse and hundreds of *parfaits* and *parfaites* lived peaceably and openly there."

Baillard lifted his glass to his lips and drank.

"Nearly four hundred *credentes* and *parfaits* were burned, including Amaury de Montréal, who had led the resistance, alongside eighty of his knights. The scaffold collapsed under their weight. The French were forced to slit their throats. Fired by bloodlust, invaders rampaged through the town searching for the lady of Lavaur, Guirande, under whose protection the *Bons Homes* had lived. They seized her, misused her. They dragged her through the streets like a common criminal, then threw her into the well and hurled stones down upon her until she was dead. She was buried alive. Or possibly drowned."

"Did they know how bad things were?" she said.

"Alaïs and Sajhë heard some news, but often many months after the event. The war was still concentrated on the plains. They lived simply, but happily, here in Los Seres with Harif. They gathered wood, salted meats for the long dark months of winter, learned how to bake bread and to thatch the roof with straw to protect it against storms."

Baillard's voice had softened.

"Harif taught Sajhë to read, then to write, first the langue d'Oc, then the language of the invaders, as well as a little Arabic and a little Hebrew." He smiled. "Sajhë was an unwilling pupil, preferring activities of the body to those of the mind but, with Alaïs' help, he persevered."

"He probably wanted to prove something to her."

Baillard slid a glance at her, but made no comment.

"Nothing changed until the Passiontide after Sajhë's thirteenth birthday, when Harif told him he was to be apprenticed in the household of Pierre-Roger de Mirepoix to begin his training as a *chevalier*."

"What did Alaïs think of that?"

"She was delighted for him. It was what he always wanted. In Carcassona, he'd watched the *écuyers* polishing their masters' boots and helmets. He had crept into the *lices* to watch them joust. The life of a *chevalier* was beyond his station, but it had not stopped him dreaming of riding out in his own colors. Now it seemed he was to have the chance to prove himself after all."

"So he went?"

Baillard nodded. "Pierre-Roger Mirepoix was a demanding master, although fair, and had a reputation for training his boys well. It was hard work, but Sajhë was clever and quick and worked hard. He learned to tilt his lance at the quintain. He practiced with sword, mace, ball-and-chain, dagger, how to ride straight-backed in a high saddle."

For a while, Alice watched him gazing out over the mountains and thought, not for the first time, how these distant people, in whose company Baillard had spent much of his life, had become flesh and blood to him.

"What of Alaïs during this time?"

"While Sajhë was in Mirepoix, Harif began to instruct Alaïs in the rites and rituals of the *Noublesso*. Already, her skills as a healer and a wise woman had become well known. There were few illnesses, of spirit or body, which she could not treat. Harif taught her much about the stars, about the patterns that make up the world, drawing on the wisdom of the ancient mystics of his land. Alaïs was aware that Harif had a deeper purpose. She knew he was preparing her—preparing Sajhë too, that was why he had sent him away—for their task.

"In the meantime, Sajhë thought little about the village. Morsels of news about Alaïs reached Mirepoix from time to time, brought by shepherds or *parfaits*, but she did not visit. Thanks to her sister Oriane, Alaïs was a fugitive with a price on her head. Harif sent money to purchase Sajhë a hauberk, a palfrey, armor and a sword. He was dubbed when he was only fifteen." He hesitated. "Shortly after that, he went to war. Those who had thrown in their lot with the French, hoping for clemency, switched allegiance, including the count of Toulouse. This time when he called on his liege lord, Pedro II of Aragon, Pedro accepted his responsibilities and in January 1213 rode north. Together with the count of Foix, their combined forces were large enough to inflict significant damage on de Montfort's depleted forces.

"In September 1213, the two armies, north against south, came face to face at Muret. Pedro was a brave leader and a skilled strategist, but the attack was badly mismanaged and, in the heat of battle, Pedro was slain. The south had lost its leader."

Baillard stopped. "Among those fighting for independence was a *chevalier* from Carcassona. Guilhem du Mas." He paused. "He acquitted himself well. He was well liked. Men were drawn to him."

An odd tone had entered his voice, admiration, mixed with something else Alice could not identify. Before she could think more of it, Baillard continued. "On the twenty-fifth day of June, 1218, the wolf was slain."

"The wolf?"

He raised his hands. "Forgive me. In the songs of the time, for example the *Canso de lo Crosada*, de Montfort was known as the wolf. He was killed besieging Tolosa. He was hit on the head by stone from a catapult, it is said, operated by a woman." Alice couldn't help herself smiling. "They carried his body back to Carcassona and saw him buried in the northern manner. His heart, liver and stomach were taken to Sant-Cerni and the bones to Sant-Nasari to be buried beneath a gravestone, which now hangs on the wall of the south transept of the basilica." He paused. "Perhaps you noticed it on your visit to the *Ciutat*?"

Alice blushed. "I . . . I found that I could not enter the Cathedral," she admitted. Baillard looked quickly at her, but said nothing more about the stone.

"Simon de Montfort's son, Amaury, succeeded him, but he was not the commander his father was and, straightaway, he began to lose the lands his father had taken. In 1224, Amaury withdrew. The de Montfort family relinquished their claim to the Trencavel lands. Sajhë was free to return home. Pierre-Roger de Mirepoix was reluctant to allow him to leave, but Sajhë had . . ."

He broke off, then stood up and wandered some way from her down the hill. When he spoke, he did not turn.

"He was twenty-six," he said. "Alaïs was older, but Sajhë . . . he had hopes. He looked on Alaïs with different eyes, no longer the brother to the sister. He knew they could not marry, for Guilhem du Mas still lived, but he dreamed, now he had proved himself, that there could be more between them."

Alice hesitated, then went to stand beside him. When she placed her hand on his arm, Baillard jolted, as if he had forgotten she was there at all.

"What happened?" she said quietly, feeling oddly anxious. She felt as if she was somehow eavesdropping, as if it was too intimate a story to be shared.

"He gathered his courage to speak." He faltered. "Harif knew. If Sajhë had asked his advice, he would have given it. As it was, he kept his counsel."

"Perhaps Sajhë knew he wouldn't wish to hear what Harif had to say."

Baillard gave a half-smile, sad. *"Benlèu."* Perhaps. Alice waited.

"So . . ." she prompted, when it was clear he was not going to continue. "Did Sajhë tell her what he felt?"

"He did."

"Well?" said Alice quickly. "What did she say?"

Baillard turned and looked at her. "Do you not know?" he said, almost in a whisper. "Pray God that you never know what it is like to love, like that, without hope of that love being returned."

Alice sprang to Alaïs' defense, crazy as it was.

"But she did love him," she said firmly. "As a brother. Was that not enough?"

Baillard turned and smiled at her. "It was what he settled for," he replied. "But enough? No. It was not enough."

He turned and started to walk back toward the house. "Shall we?" he said, formal again. "I am a little hot. You, Madomaisèla Tanner, must be tired after your long journey."

Alice noticed how pale, how exhausted he suddenly looked and felt guilty. She glanced at her watch and saw they'd been talking for longer than she'd realized. It was nearly midday.

"Of course," she said quickly, offering him her arm. They walked slowly back to the house together.

"If you will excuse me," he said quietly, once back inside. "I must sleep a while. Perhaps you should rest also?"

"I am tired," she admitted.

"When I awake, I will prepare food, then I will finish the story. Before dusk falls and we turn our mind to other things."

She waited until he had walked to the back of the house and drawn the curtain behind him. Then, feeling strangely bereft, Alice took a blanket for a pillow and went back outside.

She settled herself under the trees. She realized only then that the past had so held her imagination that she'd not thought about Shelagh or Will once.

CHAPTER 68

"What are you doing?" asked François-Baptiste, coming into the room of the small, anonymous chalet not far from the Pic de Soularac.

Marie-Cécile was sitting at the table with the *Book of Numbers* open on a black padded book rest in front of her. She didn't look up.

"Studying the layout of the chamber."

François-Baptiste sat down beside her. "For any particular reason?"

"To remind myself of the points of difference between this diagram and the labyrinth cave itself."

She felt him peering over her shoulder.

"Are there many?" he asked.

"A few. This," she said, her finger hovering above the book, her red nail varnish just visible through her protective cotton gloves. "Our altar is here, as marked. In the actual cave it is closer to the wall."

"Doesn't that mean the labyrinth carving is obscured?"

She turned to look at him, surprised at the intelligence of the comment.

"But if the original guardians used the *Book of Numbers* for their ceremonies, as the *Noublesso Véritable* did, shouldn't they be the same?"

"You would think so, yes," she said. "There is no tomb, that is the most obvious variation, although interestingly the grave where the skeletons were lying was in that exact position."

"Have you heard any more about the bodies?" he asked.

She shook her head.

"So we still don't know who they are?"

She shrugged. "Does it matter?"

"I suppose not," he replied, although she could see her lack of interest bothered him.

"On balance," she continued, "I don't think any of these things matter. It is the *pattern* that is significant, the path walked by the *Navigataíré* as the words are spoken."

"You're confident you'll be able to read the parchment in the *Book of Words*?"

"Provided it dates from the same period as the other parchments, then yes. The hieroglyphs are simple enough."

Anticipation swept through her, so sudden, so swift, that she raised her fingers as if a hand had wrapped itself around her throat. Tonight she would speak the forgotten words. Tonight the power of the Grail would descend to her. Time would be conquered.

"And if O'Donnell's lying?" said François-Baptiste. "If she doesn't have the book? Or if Authié hasn't found it either?"

Marie-Cécile's eyes snapped open, jolted back to the present by her son's abrasive, challenging tone. She looked at him with dislike. "The *Book of Words* is there," she said.

Angry to have her mood spoiled, Marie-Cécile closed the *Book of Numbers* and returned it to its wrapper. She placed the *Book of Potions* on the rest instead.

From the outside, the books looked identical. The same wooden boards covered with leather and held together with thin leather ties.

The first page was empty apart from a tiny gold chalice in the center. The reverse side was blank. On the third page were the words and pictures that also appeared around the top of the walls in the basement chamber in the rue du Cheval Blanc.

The first letter of each of the pages following was illuminated, in red, blue or yellow with gold surrounds, but otherwise the text ran on, one word into the next, with no gaps showing where one thought ended and another began.

Marie-Cécile turned to the parchment in the middle of the book.

Interspersed between the hieroglyphs were tiny pictures of plants and symbols picked out in green. After years of study and research, reading back through the scholarship funded by the de l'Oradore fortune, her grandfather had realized that none of the illustrations were relevant.

Only the hieroglyphs written on the two Grail parchments mattered. All the rest—the words, the pictures, the colors—were there to obscure, to ornament, to hide the truth.

"It's there," she said, fixing François-Baptiste with a fierce look. She could see the doubt in his face, but wisely he decided to say nothing. "Fetch my things," she said sharply. "After that, check where the car's got to."

He returned moments later with her square vanity case.

"Where do you want it?"

"Over there," she said, pointing at the dressing table. Once he'd gone out again, Marie-Cécile walked over and sat down. The outside was soft brown leather, with her initials picked out in gold. It had been a present from her grandfather.

She opened the lid. Inside there was a large mirror and several pockets for brushes, beauty appliances, tissues and a pair of small gold scissors.

The makeup was held in place in the top tray in neat, organized rows. Lipsticks, eye shadows, mascaras, kohl pencil, powder. A deeper compartment underneath contained the three red leather jewelry boxes.

"Where are they?" she said, without turning round.

"Not far away," François-Baptiste replied. She could hear the tension in his voice.

"He's all right?"

He walked toward her and put his hands on her shoulders. "Do you care, *Maman*?"

Marie-Cécile stared at her reflection in the mirror, then at her son, framed in the glass above her head as if posed for a portrait. His voice was casual. His eyes betrayed him.

"No," she replied, and saw his face relax a little. "Just interested."

He squeezed her shoulders, and then took his hands away.

"Alive, to answer your question. Caused trouble when they were getting him out. They had to quieten him down a bit."

She raised her eyebrows. "Not too much so, I hope," she said. "He's no use to me half-conscious."

"Me?" he said sharply.

Marie-Cécile bit her tongue. She needed François-Baptiste in an amenable mood. "To *us*," she said.

CHAPTER 69

Alice was dozing in the shade under the trees when Audric reappeared a couple of hours later.

"I've prepared us a meal," he said.

He looked better for his sleep. His skin had lost its waxy, tight appearance and his eyes shone bright.

Alice gathered her things and followed him back inside. Goat's cheese, olives, tomatoes, peaches, and a jug of wine were laid out on the table.

"Please. Take what you need."

As soon as they were seated, Alice launched into the questions she'd been rehearsing in her head. She noticed he ate little, although he drank some of the wine.

"Did Alaïs try to regain the two books stolen by her sister and husband?"

"To reunite the Labyrinth Trilogy had been Harif's intention as soon as the threat of war first cast its shadow over the Pays d'Oc," he said. "Thanks to her sister, Oriane, there was a price on Alaïs' head. It made it hard for her to travel. On the rare occasions she came down from the village, she went in disguise. To attempt a journey north would have been madness. Sajhë made several plans to get to Chartres. None of them was successful."

"For Alaïs?"

"In part, but also for the sake of his grandmother, Esclarmonde. He felt a responsibility to the *Noublesso de los Seres*, as Alaïs did on behalf of her father."

"What happened to Esclarmonde?"

"Many *Bons Homes* went to northern Italy. Esclarmonde was not well enough to travel so far. Instead, she was taken by Gaston and his brother to a small community in Navarre, where she remained until her death a few years later. Sajhë visited her whenever he could." He paused. "It was a source of great sadness to Alaïs that they never saw one another again."

"And what of Oriane?" asked Alice, after a while. "Did Alaïs receive news of her too?"

"Very little. Of more interest was the labyrinth built in the cathedral church of Notre Dame in Chartres. Nobody knew on whose authority it had been built or what it might mean. It was, in part, why Evreux and Oriane based themselves there, rather than return to his estates farther north."

"And the books themselves had been made in Chartres."

"In truth, it was constructed to draw attention away from the labyrinth cave in the south."

"I saw it yesterday," said Alice.

Was it only yesterday?

"I felt nothing. I mean, it was very beautiful, very impressive, but nothing else."

Audric nodded. "Oriane got what she wanted. Guy d'Evreux took her north as his wife. In exchange, she gave him the *Book of Potions* and the *Book of Numbers* and the pledge to keep searching for the *Book of Words*."

"His wife?" Alice frowned. "But what of—"

"Jehan Congost? He was a good man. Pedantic, jealous, humorless, perhaps, but a loyal servant. François killed him on Oriane's orders." He paused. "François deserved to die. It was a bad end, but he deserved no better."

Alice shook her head. "I was going to say Guilhem," she said.

"He remained in the Midi."

"But did he not have expectations of Oriane?"

"He was tireless in his efforts to drive the Crusaders out. As the years passed, he built up a large following in the mountains. At first, he offered his sword to Pierre-Roger de Mirepoix. Later, when Viscount Trencavel's son attempted to regain the lands stolen from his father, Guilhem fought for him."

"He changed sides?" said Alice, bewildered.

"No, he . . ." Baillard sighed. "No. Guilhem du Mas never betrayed Viscount Trencavel. He was a fool, certainly, but not, in the end, a traitor. Oriane had used him. He was taken prisoner at the same time as Raymond-Roger Trencavel when Carcassona fell. Unlike the viscount, Guilhem managed to escape." Audric took a deep breath, as if it pained him to admit it. "He was not a traitor."

"But Alaïs believed him to be one," she said quietly.

"He was the architect of his own misfortune."

"Yes, I know, but even so . . . to live with such regret, knowing Alaïs thought he was as bad as—"

"Guilhem does not deserve sympathy," Baillard said sharply. "He betrayed Alaïs, he broke his wedding vows, he humiliated her. Yet even so, she . . ." He broke off. "Forgive me. It is sometimes hard to be objective."

Why does it upset him so much?

"He never attempted to see Alaïs?"

"He loved her," Audric said simply. "He would not have risked leading the French to her."

"And she, too, made no attempt to see him?"

Audric slowly shook his head. "Would you have done, in her position?" he asked softly.

Alice thought for a moment. "I don't know. If she loved him, despite what he'd done . . ."

"News of Guilhem's campaigns reached the village from time to time. Alaïs made no comment, but she was proud of the man he had become."

Alice shifted in her chair. Audric seemed to sense her impatience, for he started to talk more briskly.

"For five years after Sajhë returned to the village," he continued, "the uneasy peace reigned. He, Alaïs and Harif lived well. Others from Carcassona lived in the mountains, including Alaïs' former servant, Rixende, who settled in the village. It was a simple life, but a good one." Baillard paused.

"In 1226, everything changed. A new king came to the French throne. Saint-Louis was a zealous man of strong religious conviction. The continuing heresy sickened him. Despite the years of oppression and persecution in the Midi, the Cathar church still rivaled the Catholic Church in authority and influence. The five Cathar bishoprics—Tolosa, Albi, Carcassona, Agen, Razès—were more respected, more influential in many places than their Catholic counterparts.

"At first, none of this affected Alaïs and Sajhë. They carried on much as before. In the winter, Sajhë traveled to Spain to raise money and arms to fund the resistance. Alaïs remained behind. She was a skilled rider, quick with her bow and sword and had great courage, taking messages to the leaders of the resistance in the Ariège and throughout the Sabarthès Mountains. She provided refuge for *parfaits* and *parfaites*, organizing food and shelter and information about where and when services would take place. The *parfaits* were itinerant preachers for the most part, living by their own manual labor. Carding, making bread, spinning wool. They traveled in pairs, a more experienced teacher with a younger initiate. Usually two men, of course, but sometimes women." Audric smiled. "It was much as Esclarmonde, her friend and mentor, had once done in Carcassona.

"Excommunications, indulgences for Crusaders, the new campaign to eradicate the heresy, as they called it, might have continued much as before, were it not for the fact that there was a new pope. Pope Grégoire IX. He was no longer prepared to wait. In 1233, he set up the Holy Inquisition under his direct control. Its task was to seek out and eradicate heretics, wherever and by whatever means. He chose the Dominicans, the Black Friars, as his agents."

"I thought the Inquisition came into being in Spain? You always hear of it in that context."

"A common mistake," he said. "No, the Inquisition was founded to extirpate the Cathars. The terror began. Inquisitors roamed from town to town as they pleased, accusing, denouncing and condemning. There were spies everywhere. There were exhumations, so corpses buried in holy ground could be burned as heretics. By comparing confessions and half confessions, the Inquisitors began to map the path of Catharism from village, to town, to city. The Pay d'Oc began to sink beneath a vicious tide of judicial murder. Good, honest people were condemned. Neighbor turned, in fear, against neighbor. Every major city had an Inquisitional Court, from Tolosa to Carcassona. Once condemned, the Inquisitors turned their victims over to the secular authorities to be imprisoned, beaten, mutilated or burned. They kept their hands clean. Few were acquitted. Even those who were released were forced to wear a yellow cross on their clothing to brand them as heretics."

Alice had a flicker of memory. Of running through the woods to escape the hunters. Of falling. Of a fragment of material, the color of an autumn leaf, floating away from her into the air.

Did I dream it?

Alice looked into Audric's face and saw such distress written there that it turned her heart over.

"In May 1234, the Inquisitors arrived in the town of Limoux. By ill fate, Alaïs had traveled there with Rixende. In the confusion—perhaps they were mistaken for *parfaites,* two women traveling together—they were arrested also and taken to Tolosa."

This is what I have been dreading.

"They did not give their true names, so it was several days before Sajhë heard what had happened. He followed straight away, not caring for his own safety. Even then, luck was not on his side. The Inquisitional hearings were mostly held in the cathedral of Sant-Sernin, so he went there to find her. Alaïs and Rixende, however, had been taken to the cloisters of Sant-Etienne."

Alice caught her breath, remembering the ghost-woman as she was dragged away by the black-robed monks.

"I have been there," she managed to say.

"Conditions were terrible. Dirty, brutal, demeaning. Prisoners were kept without light, without warmth, with only the screams of other prisoners to distinguish night from day. Many died within the walls awaiting trial."

Alice tried to speak, but her mouth was too dry.

"Did she . . ." she stopped, unable to go on.

"The human spirit can withstand much, but once broken, it crumbles like dust. That is what the Inquisitors did. They broke our spirit, as surely as the torturers split skin and bone, until we no longer knew who we were."

"Tell me," she said quickly.

"Sajhë was too late," he said in a level voice. "But Guilhem was not. He had heard that a healer, a mountain woman, had been brought from the mountains for interrogation and, somehow, he guessed it was Alaïs, even though her name did not appear on the register. He bribed the guards to let him through—bribed or threatened, I know not. He found Alaïs. She and Rixende were being held separately from everyone else, which gave him the chance he needed to smuggle her away from Sant-Etienne and out of Tolosa before the Inquisitors realized she had gone."

"But . . ."

"Alaïs always believed that it was Oriane who had ordered her to be imprisoned. Certainly, they did not interrogate her."

Alice felt tears in her eyes. "Did he bring her back to the village?" she said quickly, wiping her face with the back of her hand. "She did come home again?"

Baillard nodded. "She returned in *agost*, shortly before the Feast Day of the Assumption, bringing Rixende with her." The words came out in a rush.

"Guilhem did not travel with them?"

"He did not," he said. "Nor did they meet again until . . ." He paused. Alice sensed, rather than heard, him draw in his breath. "Her daughter was born six months later. Alaïs called her Bertrande, in memory of her father Bertrand Pelletier."

Audric's words seem to hang between them.

Another piece of the jigsaw.

"Guilhem and Alaïs," she whispered to herself. In her mind's eye she could see the Family Tree spread out on Grace's bedroom floor in Sallèles d'Aude. The name ALAÏS PELLETIER–DU MAS (*1193–*) picked out in red ink. When she had looked before she hadn't been able to read the name next to it, only Sajhë's name, written in green ink on the line below and to the side.

"Alaïs and Guilhem," she said again.

A direct line of descent running from them to me.

Alice was desperate to know what had happened in those three months that Guilhem and Alaïs were together. Why had they parted again? She wanted to know why the labyrinth symbol appeared beside Alaïs' name and Sajhë's name.

And my own.

She looked up, excitement building inside her. She was on the verge of letting loose a stream of questions when the look on Audric's face stopped her. Instinctively, she knew he had dwelt long enough on Guilhem.

"What happened after that?" she asked quietly. "Did Alaïs and her daughter stay in Los Seres with Sajhë and Harif?"

From the fleeting smile that appeared briefly on Audric's face, Alice knew he was grateful for the change of subject.

"She was a beautiful child," he said. "Good natured, fair, always laughing, singing. Everybody adored her, Harif in particular. Bertrande sat with him for hours listening to his stories about the Holy Land and about her grandfather, Bertrand Pelletier. As she grew older, she did errands for him. When she was six, he even started to teach her to play chess."

Audric stopped. His face grew somber again. "However, all the time the black hand of the Inquisition was spreading its reach. Having defeated the plains, the Crusaders finally turned their attention to the unconquered strongholds of the Pyrenees and Sabarthès. Trencavel's son, Raymond, returned from exile in 1240 with a contingent of *chevaliers* and was joined by most of the nobility of the Corbières. He had no trouble regaining most of the towns between Limoux and the Montagne Noire. The whole country was mobilized: Saissac, Azille, Laure, the châteaux of Quéribus, Peyrepertuse, Aguilar. But after nearly a month of fighting, he failed to retake Carcassona. In October, he pulled back to Montréal. No one came to his aid. In the end, he was forced to withdraw to Aragon."

Audric paused. "The terror began immediately. Montréal was razed to the ground, Montolieu too. Limoux and Alet surrendered. It was clear to Alaïs, to us all, that the people would pay the price for the failure of the rebellion."

Baillard suddenly stopped and looked up. "Have you been to Montségur, Madomaisèla Alice?" She shook her head. "It is an extraordinary place. A sacred place perhaps. Even now, the spirits linger. It is hewn out of three sides of the mountain. God's temple in the sky."

"The safe mountain," she said without thinking, then blushed to realize she was quoting Baillard's own words back at him.

"Many years earlier, before the beginning of the Crusade, the leaders of the Cathar church had asked the *seigneur* of Montségur, Raymond de Péreille, to rebuild the crumbling *castellum* and strengthen its fortifications. By 1243, Pierre-Roger de Mirepoix, in whose household Sajhë had trained, was in command of the garrison. Fearing for Bertrande and Harif, Alaïs felt they could no longer stay in Los Seres, so Sajhë offered his service and they joined the exodus to Montségur."

Audric nodded. "But they became visible when they traveled. Perhaps they should have separated. Alaïs' name was now on an Inquisitional list."

"Was Alaïs a Cathar?" she asked suddenly, realizing that, even now, she was not sure.

He paused. "The Cathars believed that the world we can see, hear, smell, taste and touch was created by the Devil. They believed the Devil had tricked pure spirits into fleeing God's kingdom and imprisoned them in tunics of flesh here on Earth. They believed if they lived a good enough life and 'made a good end' their souls would be released from bondage and return to God in the glory of Heaven. If not, within four days they would be reincarnated on Earth to start the cycle anew."

Alice remembered the words in Grace's bible.

"That which is born of the flesh is flesh; and that which is born of the Spirit is spirit."

Audric nodded. "What you must understand is that the *Bons Homes* were loved by the people they served. They didn't charge for officiating at marriages, naming children or burying the dead. They extracted no taxes, demanded no tithes. There's a story of a *parfait* coming across a farmer kneeling in the corner of his field: 'What are you doing?' he asked the man. 'Giving thanks to God for bringing forth this fine crop,' the farmer replied. The *parfait* smiled and helped the man to his feet: 'This isn't God's work, but your own. For it was your hand that dug the soil in the spring, who tended it.'" He raised his eyes to Alice. "You understand?"

"I think so," she said tentatively. "They believed individuals had control over their own lives."

"Within the constraints and limitations of the times and place in which we were born, yes."

"But did Alaïs subscribe to this way of thinking?" she persisted.

"Alaïs was like them. She helped people, put the needs of others before her own. She did what she thought was right, regardless of what tradition or custom dictated." He smiled. "Like them she believed there would be no last judgment. She believed that the evil she saw around her could not be of God's making, but, in the end, no. She was not. Alaïs was a woman who believed in the world she could touch and see."

"What about Sajhë?"

Audric did not answer directly. "Although the term *Cathar* is in common usage now, in Alaïs' time believers called themselves *Bons Homes*. The Inquisitional Latin texts refer to them as *albigenses* or *heretici*."

"So where does the term *Cathar* come from?"

"Ah, well, we cannot let the victors write our stories for us," he said. "It is a term that I and others . . ." He stopped, smiling, as if sharing a joke with himself. "There are many different explanations. Perhaps that the word *catar* in Occitan—*cathare* in French—came from the Greek *katharos,* meaning pure. Who can say what was intended?"

Alice frowned, realizing she was missing something, but didn't know what.

"Well, what of the religion itself then? Where did that originate? Not France originally?"

"The origins of European Catharism lie in Bogomilism, a dualist faith that flourished in Bulgaria, Macedonia and Dalmatia from the tenth century onward. It was linked with older religious beliefs—such as Zoroastrianism in Persia or Manicheism. They believed in reincarnation."

An idea started to take shape in her mind. The link between everything Audric was telling her and what she already knew.

Wait and it will find you. Be patient.

"In the Palais des Arts in Lyon," he continued, "there is a manuscript copy of a Cathar text of St. John's Gospel, one of very few documents to escape destruction by the Inquisition. It is written in the *langue d'Oc*, possession of which in those days was considered a heretical, punishable act. Of all the texts sacred to the *Bons Homes*, the Gospel of John was the most important. It is the one which lays most stress on personal, individual enlightenment through knowledge—gnosis. *Bons Homes* refused to worship idols, crosses or altars—carved from the rocks and trees of the Devil's base creation—they held the word of God in the very highest esteem."

In the beginning was the Word, and the Word was with God, and the Word was God.

"Reincarnation," she said slowly, thinking aloud. "How could this possibly be reconciled with orthodox Christian theology?"

"Central to the Christian covenant is the gift of everlasting life to those who believe in Christ and are redeemed through his sacrifice on the Cross. Reincarnation is also a form of eternal life."

The labyrinth. The path to eternal life.

Audric stood up and walked over to the open window. As Alice stared at Baillard's thin, upright back, she sensed a determination in him that had not been there before.

"Tell me, Madomaisèla Tanner," he said, turning to face her. "Do you believe in destiny? Or is it the path we choose to follow that makes us who we are?"

"I—" she started, then stopped. She was no longer sure what she thought. Here in the timeless mountains, high up in the clouds, the everyday world and values did not seem to matter. "I believe in my dreams," she said in the end.

"Do you believe you can change your destiny?" he said, seeking an answer.

Alice found herself nodding. "Otherwise, what's the point? If we are simply walking a path preordained, then all the experiences that make us who we are—love, grief, joy, learning, changing—would count for nothing."

"And you would not stop another from making his own choices?"

"It would depend on the circumstances," she said slowly, nervous now. "Why?"

"I ask you to remember it," he said softly. "That is all. When the time comes, I ask you to remember this. *Si es atal es atal.*"

His words stirred something in her. Alice was sure she had heard them before. She shook her head, but the memory refused to come.

"Things will be as they will be," he said softly.

CHAPTER 70

"Monsieur Baillard, I—"

Audric held up his hand. "*Benlèu*," he said, walking back to the table and picking up the threads of the story as if there had been no interruption. "I will tell you everything you need to know, I give you my word of that."

She opened her mouth, then closed it again.

"It was crowded in the citadel," he said, "but for all that, it was a happy time. For the first time in many years, Alaïs felt safe. Bertrande, now nearly ten years old, was popular with the many children who lived in and around the fortress. Harif, although old and frail, was also in good spirits. He had plenty of company: Bertrande to charm him, *parfaits* to argue with about the nature of God and the world. Sajhë was there at her side for much of the time. Alaïs was happy."

Alice closed her eyes and let the past come to life in her mind.

"It was a good existence and might have continued so but for one reckless act of vengeance. On the twenty-eighth of May 1242, Pierre-Roger de Mirepoix received word that four Inquisitors had arrived in the town of Avignonet. The result would be more *parfaits* and *credentes* imprisoned or sent to the stake. He decided to act. Against the advice of his sergeants, including Sajhë, he assembled a troop of eighty-five knights from the Montségur garrison, their numbers swelled by others who joined en route.

"They walked eight kilometers to Avignonet, arriving the following day. Shortly after the Inquisitor Guillaume Arnaud and his three colleagues had gone to bed, someone within the house opened the locked door and admitted them. The doors to their bedrooms were smashed open and the four Inquisitors and their entourage were hacked to death. Seven different *chevaliers* claimed to have struck the first blows. It is said that Guillaume Arnaud died with the *Te Deum* on his lips. What is certain is that his Inquisitorial records were carried away and destroyed."

"That was a good thing, surely."

"It was the final act of provocation. The massacre brought a swift response. The king decreed that Montségur was to be destroyed, once and for all. An army comprised of northern barons, Catholic inquisitors and mercenaries and collaborators set camp at the foot of the mountain. The siege started, but yet men and women from the citadel still came and went as they pleased. After five months, the garrison had lost only three men and it seemed the siege would fail.

"The Crusaders hired a platoon of Basque mercenaries, who clambered up and pitched camp a stone's throw from the castle walls just as the bitter mountain winter was setting in. There was no imminent danger, but Pierre-Roger decided to withdraw his men from the outworks on the vulnerable eastern side. It was a costly mistake. Armed with information from local collaborators, the mercenaries succeeded in scaling the vertiginous slope on the southeastern side of the mountain. Knifing the sentinels, they took possession of the Roc de la Tour, a spike of stone rising up on the easternmost point of the summit ridge of Montségur. We could only watch, helpless, as the catapults and mangomels were winched up to the Roc. At the same time, on the eastern side of the mountain, a powerful *trébuchet* started to inflict damage on the eastern barbican.

"At Christmas 1243, the French took the barbican. Now they were within only a few dozen yards of the fortress. They installed a new siege engine. The southern and eastern walls of the citadel were both within range."

He was turning the ring round and round on his thumb as he talked.

Alice watched and, as she did so, the memory of another man, turning such a ring as he told her stories, floated into her mind.

"For the first time," Audric continued, "they had to face the possibility that Montségur would fall.

"In the valley below, the standards and banners of the Catholic Church and the fleur-de-lys of the French king—although tattered and faded after ten months of first heat, then rain, then snow—were still flying. The Crusader army, led by the seneschal of Carcassona, Hugues des Arcis, numbered between six and ten thousand. Inside were no more than a hundred fighting men."

"Alaïs wanted to . . ." he stopped. "A meeting was held with the leaders of the Cathar church, Bishop Bertrand Marty and Raymond Aiguilher."

"The Cathar treasure. That's true, then? It existed?"

Baillard nodded. "Two *credentes*, Matheus and Peter Bonnet, were chosen for the task. Wrapped up against the bitter cold of the new year, they strapped the treasure to their backs and stole away out of the castle under cover of night. They avoided the sentries posted on the passable roads that led down from the mountain through the village, and made their way south into the Sabarthès Mountains."

Alice's eyes flared wide. "To the Pic de Soularac."

Again, he nodded. "From there, to be taken on by others. The passes to

Aragon and Navarre were snowbound. Instead they headed for the ports and from there sailed to Lombardy in northern Italy, where there was a thriving, less persecuted community of *Bons Homes*."

"What of the Bonnet brothers?"

"Matheus arrived back alone at the end of *janvièr*. The sentries posted on the road this time were local men, from Camon sur l'Hers, near Mirepoix, and they let him pass. Matheus talked of reinforcements. How there were rumors that the new King of Aragon would come in the spring. But, they were brave words only. By now the siege was too tightly drawn for reinforcements to break through."

Baillard raised his amber eyes and looked at Alice. "We heard rumor too that Oriane was traveling south, accompanied by her son and husband, to provide reinforcements for the siege. This could only mean one thing. That after all the years of running and hiding, finally she had discovered that Alaïs was alive. She wanted the *Book of Words*."

"Surely Alaïs did not have it with her?"

Audric did not answer. "In mid-February, the attackers pushed forward yet again. On the first of March 1244, after a final attempt to dislodge the Basques from the Roc de la Tour, a single horn sounded on the ramparts of the ravaged stronghold." He swallowed hard. "Raymond de Péreille, the *seigneur* of Montségur, and Pierre-Roger of Mirepoix, commander of the garrison, walked out of the Great Gate and surrendered to Hugues des Arcis. The battle was over. Montségur, the final stronghold, had fallen."

Alice leaned back in her chair, wishing it had ended otherwise.

"It had been a harsh and freezing winter on the rocky mountainside and in the valley below. Both sides were exhausted. Negotiations were short. The Act of Surrender was signed the following day by Peter Amiel, the Archbishop of Narbonne.

"The terms were generous. Unprecedented, some would say. The fortress would become the property of the Catholic Church and the French crown, but every inhabitant of the fortress would be pardoned for his past crimes. Even the murderers of the inquisitors at Avignonet were to receive pardon. The men-at-arms would be set free with only light penances, once their crimes had been confessed to the inquisitorial registers. All those who abjured their heretical beliefs would be allowed to walk free, punished only by the obligation to wear a cross on their clothes."

"And those who would not?" said Alice.

"Those who would not recant were to be burned at the stake as heretics."

Baillard took another sip of wine.

"It was usual, at the conclusion of a siege, to seal a bargain by handing over hostages. They included Bishop Bertrand's brother, Raymond, the old *chevalier,* Arnald-Roger de Mirepoix and Raymond de Péreille's young son." Baillard paused. "What was not usual," he said carefully, "was the granting of a period of two weeks' grace. The Cathar leadership asked to be allowed to stay within Montségur for two weeks before they came down from the mountain. The request was granted."

Her heart started to beat faster. "Why?"

Audric smiled. "Historians and theologians have argued for hundreds of years about why the Cathars requested this stay of execution. What needed to be done that had not already been done? The treasure was safe. What was so important as to make the Cathars stay in that damaged and cold mountain fortress a little longer, after all they had suffered already?"

"And why did they?"

"Because Alaïs was with them," he said. "She needed time. Oriane and her men were waiting for her at the foot of the mountain. Harif was within the citadel, Sajhë also, and her daughter. It was too great a risk. If they were captured, the sacrifices made by Simeon and her father and Esclarmonde to safeguard the secret would have been for nothing."

At last, every part of the jigsaw was in place and Alice could see the full picture, clear and vivid and bright, even though she could hardly believe it was true.

Alice looked out of the window at the unchanging, enduring landscape. It was much as it had been in the days when Alaïs lived here. The same sun, the same rain, the same skies.

"Tell me the truth of the Grail," she said quietly.

CHAPTER 71
Montségur

MARÇ 1244

Alaïs stood on the walls of the citadel of Montségur, a slight and solitary figure in her thick winter cloak. Beauty had come with the passing of the years. She was slight, but there was a grace to her face, her neck, her bearing. She looked down at her hands. In the early morning light they looked blue, almost transparent.

The hands of an old woman.

Alaïs smiled. Not old. Younger still than her father when he died.

The light was soft as the rising sun struggled to give the world back its shape and brush away the silhouettes of the night. Alaïs gazed at the ragged snow-covered peaks of the Pyrenees, rising and falling away into the pale horizon, and the purple pine forests on the eastern flank of the mountain. Early morning clouds were scudding over the ragged slopes of the Pic de Sant-Bartélémy. Beyond that, she could almost see the Pic de Soularac.

She imagined her house, plain and welcoming, tucked inside the folds of the hills. She remembered the smoke unfurling from the chimney on cold mornings such as this. Spring came late to the mountains and this had been a hard winter, but it wouldn't be long now. She could see its promise in the pink blush of the sky at dusk. In Los Seres the trees would soon be coming into bud. By April, the mountain pastures would be covered once more with delicate blue, white and yellow flowers.

Down below Alaïs could make out the surviving buildings that made up the village of Montségur, the few huts and dwellings left standing after ten months of siege. The ramshackle cluster of houses was surrounded by the standards and tents of the French army, tattered pinpricks of color and fluttering banners, ragged around the edges. They had suffered the same hard winter as the inhabitants of the citadel.

On the western slopes, at the foot of the mountain, stood a wooden palisade. The besiegers had been building it for days. Yesterday, they hammered a row of stakes up the middle, a crooked wooden spine, each post held in place by a heap of tinder and faggots of straw. At dusk, she had seen them prop ladders around the edges.

A pyre to burn the heretics.

Alaïs shivered. In a few hours it would be over. She was not afraid to die when her time came. But she'd seen too many people burn to be under any illusion that faith would spare them pain. For those that wished it, Alaïs had provided medicines to numb the suffering. Most had chosen to walk unaided from this world to the next.

The purple stones beneath her feet were slippery with frost. Alaïs traced the pattern of the labyrinth on the crisp, white ground with the top of her boot. She was nervous. If her subterfuge worked, the quest for the *Book of Words* would end. If it failed, she had gambled the lives of those who'd given her shelter for all these years—Esclarmonde's people, her father's people—for the sake of the Grail.

The consequences were dreadful to think about.

Alaïs closed her eyes and let herself fly back through the years to the labyrinth cave. Harif, Sajhë, herself. She remembered the smooth caress of the air on her bare arms, the flicker of the candles, the beautiful voices spiraling in the dark. The recollection of the words as she spoke them, so vivid she could almost taste them on her tongue.

Alaïs shivered, thinking of the moment when she finally understood and the incantation came from her lips as if of its own accord. That single moment of ecstasy, of illumination, as everything that had happened before and everything that was yet to come were joined uniquely, as the Grail descended to her.

And through her voice and her hands, to him.

Alaïs gasped. To have lived and had such experiences.

A noise disturbed her. Alaïs opened her eyes and let the past fade. She turned to see Bertrande picking her way along the narrow battlements. Alaïs smiled and raised her hand in greeting.

Her daughter was less serious by nature than Alaïs had been at this age. But in looks, Bertrande was made in her image. The same heart-shaped face, the same direct gaze and long brown hair. But for Alaïs' gray hairs and the lines around her eyes, they could almost be sisters.

The strain of waiting showed on her daughter's face.

"Sajhë says the soldiers are coming," she said in an uncertain voice.

Alaïs shook her head. "They will not come until tomorrow," she said firmly. "And there is still much to occupy our time between now and then." She took Bertrande's cold hands between hers. "I am relying on you to help Sajhë and to care for Rixende. Tonight especially. They need you."

"I don't want to lose you, *Mamà*," she said, her lip trembling.

"You won't," she smiled, praying it was true. "We'll all be together again soon. You must have patience." Bertrande gave her a weak smile. "That's better. Now, come, *Filha*. Let us go down."

CHAPTER 72

At dawn on Wednesday the sixteenth of March, they gathered inside the Great Gate of Montségur.

From the battlements, the members of the garrison watched the Crusaders sent to arrest the *Bons Homes* climb the last section of the rocky path, still slippery with frost this early in the day.

Bertrande was standing with Sajhë and Rixende at the front of the crowd. It was very quiet. After the months of relentless bombardment, she still had not got used to the absence of sound now the mangomels and catapults had fallen silent.

The last two weeks had been a peaceful time. For many, the end of their time. Easter had been celebrated. The *parfaits* and a few *parfaites* had fasted. Despite the promise of pardon for those who abjured their faith, almost half the population of the citadel, Rixende among them, had chosen to receive the *consolament*. They preferred to die as *Bons Chrétiens* rather than live, defeated, under the French crown. Possessions had been bequeathed by those condemned to die for their faith to those condemned to live deprived of their loved ones. Bertrande had helped distribute gifts of wax, pepper, salt, cloth, shoes, a purse, breeches, even a felt hat.

Pierre-Roger de Mirepoix had been presented with a coverlet full of coins. Others had given corn and jerkins for him to distribute among his men. Marquesia de Lanatar had given all her belongings to her granddaughter Philippa, Pierre-Roger's wife.

Bertrande looked around at the silent faces and offered a silent prayer for her mother. Alaïs had chosen Rixende's garments carefully. The dark green dress and a red cloak, the edges and hem embroidered with an intricate pattern of blue and green squares and diamonds and yellow flowers. Her mother had explained it was the image of the cloak she'd worn on her wedding day in the *capèla* Santa-Maria in the Château Comtal. Alaïs was sure her sister Oriane would remember it, despite the passage of years.

As a precaution, Alaïs had also made a small sheepskin bag to be held against the red cloak, a copy of the *chemise* in which each of the books of the Labyrinth Trilogy were stored. Bertrande had helped to fill it with fabric and sheets of parchment so that, from a distance at least, it would deceive. She didn't understand entirely the point of these preparations, only that they mattered. She had been delighted to be allowed to help.

Bertrande reached out and took Sajhë's hand.

The leaders of the Cathar Church, Bishop Bertrand Marty and Raymond Aiguilher, both old men now, stood quietly in their dark blue robes. For years, they had served their ministry from Montségur, traveling from the citadel, preaching the word and delivering comfort to *credentes* in the isolated villages of the mountains and the plains. Now they were ready to lead their people into the fire.

"*Mamà* will be all right," she whispered, trying to reassure herself as much as him. Bertrande felt Rixende's arm on her shoulder.

"I wish you were not . . ."

"I have made my choice," Rixende said quickly. "I choose to die in my faith."

"What if *Mamà* is taken?" whispered Bertrande.

Rixende stroked her hair. "There is nothing we can do but pray."

Bertrande felt tears well up in her eyes when the soldiers reached them. Rixende held out her wrists to be shackled. The boy shook his head. Having not expected so many to choose death, they had not brought enough chains to secure them all.

Bertrande and Sajhë watched in silence as Rixende and the others walked through the Great Gate and began their last descent of the steep, winding mountain path. The red of Alaïs' cloak stood out among the subdued browns and greens, bright against the gray sky.

Led by Bishop Marty, the prisoners began to sing. Montségur had fallen, but they were not defeated. Bertrande wiped the tears from her eyes with the back of her hand. She had promised her mother to be strong. She would do her best to keep her word.

Down below on the meadows of the lower slopes, stands had been erected for the spectators. They were full. The new aristocracy of the Midi, French barons, collaborators, Catholic legates and Inquisitors, invited by Hugues des Arcis, the Seneschal of Carcassonne. All had come to see justice done after more than thirty years of civil war.

Guilhem pulled his cloak hard about him, taking care not to be recognized. His face was known after a lifetime fighting the French. He could not afford to be taken. He glanced around.

If his information was right, somewhere in this crowd was Oriane. He was determined to keep her away from Alaïs. Even after all this time, just the thought of Oriane moved him to anger. He clenched his fists, wishing he could act now. That he did not have to dissemble or wait, just put a knife in her heart as he should have done thirty years before. Guilhem knew he had to be patient. If he tried something now, he'd be cut down before he'd even had the chance to draw his sword.

He ran his eyes along the rows of spectators until he saw the face he was looking for. Oriane was sitting at the middle of the front row. There was nothing of the southern lady left in her. Her clothes were expensive in the more formal and elaborate style of the north. Her blue velvet cloak was trimmed in gold with a thick ermine collar around the neck and hood and matching winter gloves. Although her face was still striking and beautiful, it had grown thin and was spoiled by its hard and bitter expression.

There was a young man with her. The likeness was strong enough for Guilhem to guess he must be one of her sons. Louis, the eldest, he'd heard had joined the Crusade. He had Oriane's coloring and black curls, with his father's aquiline profile.

There was a shout. Guilhem turned round to see the line of prisoners had reached the foot of the mountain and were now being driven toward the pyre. They walked quietly and with dignity. They were singing. Like a choir of angels, Guilhem thought, seeing the look of discomfort the sweetness of the sound brought to the faces of the spectators.

The seneschal of Carcassonne, Hugh des Arcis, stood shoulder to shoulder with the archbishop of Narbonne. On his sign, a gold cross was raised high in the air and the black friars and clergy moved forward to take up their position in front of the palisade.

Behind them, Guilhem could see a row of soldiers holding burning torches. They were struggling to keep the smoke from drifting over to the stands as the flames whipped and cracked in the bitter, gusting north wind.

One by one, the names of the heretics were called out. They stepped forward and climbed the ladders into the pyre. Guilhem felt numb with the horror of it. He hated the fact he could do nothing to stop the executions. Even if he'd enough men with him, he knew they themselves would not wish it. Through force of circumstance rather than belief, Guilhem had spent much time in the company of the *Bons Homes*. He admired and respected them, though he could not claim to understand them.

The mounds of kindling and straw had been soaked in pitch. A few soldiers had climbed inside and were chaining the *parfaits* and *parfaites* to the central posts.

Bishop Marty began to pray.

"Payre sant, Dieu dreiturier dels bons esperits."

Slowly, other voices joined his. The whispering grew and grew, until soon it became a roar. In the stands, the spectators exchanged embarrassed glances with one another and grew restless. This was not what they had come to see.

The archbishop gave a hurried signal and the clergy began to sing, their black robes flapping in the wind, the psalm that had become the anthem of the Crusade. *Veni Spirite Sancti*, the words shouted to drown out the Cathar prayers.

The bishop stepped forward and cast the first torch into the palisade. The soldiers followed his lead. One by one the burning brands were tossed in. The fire was slow to catch, but soon the sparks and crackles became a roar. The flames started to writhe through the straw like snakes, darting this way and that, billowing and puffing, swirling like reeds in the river.

Through the smoke, Guilhem saw something that turned his blood to ice. A red cloak, embroidered with flowers, a deep green dress, the color of moss. He pushed his way to the front.

He couldn't—didn't want—to believe his eyes.

The years fell away and he saw himself, the man he had been, a young *chevalier*, arrogant, proud, confident, kneeling in the *capèla* Sant-Mari. Alaïs was at his side. A Michaelmas wedding, lucky some said. Flowering hawthorn on the altar and the red candles flickering as they exchanged their vows.

Guilhem ran along the back of the stands, desperate to get closer, desperate to prove to himself that it was not her. The fire was hungry. The sickly smell of burning human flesh, surprisingly sweet, was floating over the spectators. The soldiers stood back. Even the clergy were forced to retreat as the furnace burned.

Blood hissed as the soles of feet split open and the bones slid out into the fire, like animals roasting on a spit. The prayers turned to screams.

Guilhem was choking, but he didn't stop. Holding his cloak across his mouth and nose to keep out the foul, pungent, smoke, he tried to get close to the palisade walls, but the swirling cloud of smoke obscured everything.

Suddenly a voice rang out, clear and precise, from within the fire.

"Oriane!"

Was it Alaïs' voice? Guilhem couldn't tell. Shielding his face with his hands, he stumbled toward the noise.

"Oriane!"

This time, there was a shout from the stands. Guilhem spun round and through a gap in the smoke, saw Oriane's face contorted with anger. She was on her feet and gesturing wildly to the guards.

Guilhem imagined he was shouting Alaïs' name too, but he couldn't risk drawing attention to himself. He had come to save her. He had come to help her escape from Oriane, he had helped her once before.

Those three months he had spent with Alaïs after fleeing the Inquisitors in Toulouse had been, quite simply, the happiest time of his life. Alaïs would not stay longer and he could not persuade her to change her mind, nor even to tell him why she had to go. But she had said—and Guilhem had believed it to be true—that one day, when the horror was over, they would once more be together.

"*Mon còr,*" he whispered, almost a sob.

That promise, and the memory of days together, were what had sustained him through the ten long, empty years. Like a light in the dark.

Guilhem felt his heart crack. "Alaïs!"

Against the red cloak, the small white sheepskin package, the size of a book, was burning. The hands that held it were no longer there. They had been reduced to bone and spitting fat and blackened flesh.

There was nothing left, he knew it.

For Guilhem, everything was silent now. There was no more noise, no more pain, nothing but a clear white expanse. The mountain had gone, the sky and the smoke and the screaming had gone. Hope had gone.

Now, his legs could no longer hold him. Guilhem fell to his knees as despair claimed him.

CHAPTER 73
Sabarthès Mountains

FRIDAY, 8 JULY 2005

The stench brought him to his senses. A mixture of ammonia, goat droppings, unwashed bedding and cold, cooked meat. It stuck in his throat and made the inside of his nose burn, like smelling salts held too close.

Will was lying on a rough cot, not much more than a bench, fixed to the wall of the hut. He maneuvered himself into a sitting position and leaned back against the stone wall. The sharp edges stuck into his arms, which were still tied behind his back.

He felt he'd done four rounds in the boxing ring. He was bruised from head to toe where he'd been thrown against the side of the boot on the journey. His temple was throbbing where François-Baptiste had struck him with the gun. He could feel the bruise beneath the skin, hard and angry, and the blood around the wound.

He didn't know what time it was or what day it was. Friday still?

It had been dawn when they left Chartres, maybe as early as five o'clock. When they had got him out of the car it had been afternoon, hot and the sun still bright. He twisted his neck to try to see his watch, but the movement made him feel sick.

Will waited until the nausea had passed. Then he opened his eyes and tried to get his bearings. He appeared to be in some sort of shepherd's hut. There were bars on the small window, no bigger than the size of a book. In the far corner there was a built-in shelf, like some sort of table, and a stool. In the grate alongside there were the remains of a long-dead fire, gray ash and black shavings of wood or paper. A heavy metal cooking pot hung on a stick across the fireplace. Will could see cold fat coagulated around the rim.

Will let himself fall back on the hard mattress, feeling the rough blanket on his battered skin, and wondered where Alice was now.

Outside, there was the sound of footsteps, then a key in a padlock. Will heard the metallic chink of chain being dropped on the ground, then the arthritic creak of the door being pulled open and a voice he half-recognized.

"*C'est l'heure.*" Time to go.

Shelagh was conscious of the air on her bare arms and legs and the sensation of being moved from one place to another.

She identified Paul Authié's voice somewhere in the murmur of sound as she was transported from the farmhouse. Then the distinctive feeling of underground air on her skin, chill and slightly damp, the ground sloping down. Both the men who had held her captive were there. She'd got accustomed to the smell of them. Aftershave, cheap cigarettes, a threatening maleness that made her muscles contract.

They had tied her legs again and her arms behind her back, pulling at the bones in her shoulders. One eye was swollen shut. The combination of lack of food and light and the drugs they gave her to keep her quiet meant that her head was spinning, but she knew where she was.

Authié had brought her back to the cave. She felt the change in atmosphere as they emerged from the tunnel into the chamber, felt the tension in his legs as he carried her down the steps to the sunken area where she'd found Alice unconscious on the ground.

Shelagh registered that there was a light burning somewhere, on the altar perhaps. The man carrying her stopped. They had walked right to the back of the chamber, past the limits she'd gone before. He swung her down off his shoulders, a dead weight, and dropped her. She sensed pain in her side as she hit the ground, but could no longer feel anything.

She didn't understand why he hadn't killed her already.

He had his hands under her arms now and was dragging her along the ground. Grit, stones, sharp fragments of rock, cut into the soles of her feet and her exposed ankles. She was aware of the sensation of her bound hands being tied to something metal and cold, a ring or hoop sunk into the ground.

Assuming she was still unconscious, the men were talking in low voices.

"How many charges have you set?"

"Four."

"To go off at what time?"

"Just after ten. He's going to do it himself." Shelagh could hear the smile in the man's voice. "Get his hands dirty for once. One press of the button and *boom*! The whole lot will go."

"I still can't see why we had to drag her all the way up here," he complained. "Much easier to leave the bitch at the farm."

"He doesn't want her identified. In a few hours' time, half this mountain's going to come down. She'll be buried under half a ton of rock."

Finally, fear gave Shelagh the strength to fight. She pulled against her bonds and tried to stand, but she was too weak and her legs wouldn't hold her. She thought she heard a laugh as she sank back down to the ground, but she couldn't be sure. She wasn't certain now what was real and what was only happening inside her head.

"Aren't we supposed to stay with her?"

The other man laughed. "What's she going to do? Get up and walk out of here? I mean, Christ! Look at her!"

The light started to fade.

Shelagh heard the men's footsteps getting fainter and fainter, until there was nothing but silence and darkness.

CHAPTER 74

"I want to know the truth," Alice repeated. "I want to know how the labyrinth and the Grail are connected. *If* they are connected."

"The truth of the Grail," he said. He fixed her with a look. "Tell me, *Madomaisèla*, what do you know about the Grail?"

"The usual sort of stuff, I suppose," she said, assuming he didn't really want her to answer seriously.

"No, truly. I am interested to hear what you have discovered."

Alice shifted awkwardly in her chair. "I suppose I held to the standard idea that it was a chalice which contained within it an elixir that gave the gift of everlasting life."

Alice broke off and looked self-consciously at Baillard.

"A gift?" he asked, shaking his head. "No, not a gift." He sighed. "And where do you think these stories come from in the first place?"

"The Bible, I suppose. Or possibly the Dead Sea Scrolls. Perhaps from some other early Christian writing, I'm not sure. I've never really thought about it in those terms before."

Audric nodded. "It is a common misconception. In fact, the first versions of the story you talk about originate from the twelfth century, although there are obvious similarities with themes in classical and Celtic literature. And in medieval France in particular."

The memory of the map she'd found at the library in Toulouse suddenly came into her mind.

"Like the labyrinth."

He smiled, but said nothing. "In the last quarter of the twelfth century lived a poet called Chrétien de Troyes. His first patron was Marie, one of the daughters of Eleanor of Aquitaine, who was married to the count of Champagne. After she died in 1181, one of Marie's cousins, Philip of Alsace, Count of Flanders, became his patron.

"Chrétien was immensely popular in his day. He'd made his reputation translating classic stories from Latin and Greek, before he turned his skill to composing a sequence of chivalric stories about the knights you will know as Lancelot, Gawain and Perceval. These allegorical writings gave birth to a tide of stories of King Arthur and his Knights of the Round

Table." He paused. "The Perceval story—*Li contes del graal*—is the earliest extant narrative of the Holy Grail."

"But . . ." Alice started to protest. She frowned. "Surely he can't have made the story up? Not something like that. It can't have appeared out of thin air."

Again, the same half-smile appeared on Audric's face.

"When challenged to name his source, Chrétien claimed that he had acquired the story of the Grail from a book given to him by his patron, Philip. Indeed, it is to Philip that the story of the Grail is dedicated. Sadly, Philip died at the siege of Acre in 1191 during the Third Crusade. As a result, the poem was never finished."

"What happened to Chrétien?"

"There is no record of him after Philip's death. He just disappeared."

"Isn't that odd, if he was so famous?"

"It is possible his death went unrecorded," said Baillard slowly.

Alice looked sharply at him. "But you don't think so?"

Audric did not answer. "Despite Chrétien's decision not to complete his story, all the same, the story of the Holy Grail took on a life of its own. There were direct adaptations from Old French into Middle Dutch and Old Welsh. A few years later, another poet, Wolfram von Eschenbach, wrote a rather burlesque version, *Parzival,* around the year 1200. He claimed he was not following Chrétien's version but another story by an unknown author."

Alice was thinking hard. "How does Chrétien actually describe the Grail?"

"He is vague. He presents it as some sort of dish, rather than a chalice, like the medieval Latin *gradalis,* from which comes the Old French *gradal* or *graal.* Eschenbach is more explicit. His Grail—*grâl*—is a stone."

"So where does the idea come from that the Holy Grail is the cup used by Christ at the Last Supper?"

Audric pressed his fingers together. "Another writer, a man called Robert de Boron. He wrote a verse poem, *Joseph d'Arimathie,* some time between Chrétien's *Perceval* and 1199. De Boron not only has the Grail as a vessel—the chalice of the Last Supper, which he refers to as the *san greal*—but he also fills it with the blood taken from the Cross. In modern French the *sang réal,* the 'true' or 'royal' blood."

He stopped and looked up at Alice.

"For the guardians of the Labyrinth Trilogy, this linguistic confusion—*san greal* and *sang réal*—was a convenient concealment."

"But the Holy Grail is a myth," she said stubbornly. "It cannot be true."

"The *Holy* Grail is a myth, certainly," he said, holding her gaze. "An attractive fable. If you look closely, you will see that all these stories are embellishments of the same theme. The medieval Christian concept of sac-

424

rifice and quest, leading to redemption and salvation. The *Holy* Grail, in Christian terms, was spiritual, a symbolic representation of eternal life rather than something to be taken as a literal truth. That through the sacrifice of Christ and the grace of God, humankind would live forever." He smiled. "But that such a thing as the Grail exists is beyond doubt. That is the truth contained within the pages of the Labyrinth Trilogy. It is this that the Grail guardians, the *Noublesso de los Seres,* gave their lives to keep secret."

Alice was shaking her head in disbelief. "You're saying that the Grail is not a Christian concept at all. That all these myths and legends are built on a . . . a misunderstanding."

"A subterfuge rather than a misunderstanding."

"But for two thousand years the debate has been about the existence of the *Holy* Grail. If now it is revealed not only that such a thing as the Grail legends are true but . . ." Alice broke off. She found it hard to believe what she was saying. "It is not a Christian relic at all, I can't even begin to imagine . . ."

"The Grail is an elixir that has the power both to heal and significantly prolong life. But for a purpose. It was discovered some four thousand years ago in Ancient Egypt. And those who developed it and became aware of its power realized that the secret had to be kept safe from those who would use it for their own benefit as opposed to the benefit of others. The sacred knowledge was recorded in hieroglyphs on three separate sheets of papyrus. One gave the precise layout of the Grail chamber, the labyrinth itself; one listed the ingredients required for the elixir to be prepared; the third the incantation to effect the transformation of the elixir into the Grail. They buried them in the caves outside the ancient city of Avaris."

"Egypt," she said quickly. "When I was doing some research, trying to understand what I had seen here, I noticed how often Egypt came up."

Audric nodded. "The papyri are written in classical hieroglyphs—the word itself means 'God's words' or 'divine speech.' As the great civilization of Egypt fell into dust and decay, the ability to read the hieroglyphs was lost. The knowledge contained in the papyri was preserved, handed down from guardian to guardian, over the generations. The ability to speak the incantation or summon the Grail was lost.

"This turn of events was without design, but it, in turn, added an additional layer of secrecy," he continued. "In the ninth century of the Christian era, an Arab alchemist, Abu Bakr Ahmad Ibn Wahshiyah, decoded the secret of the hieroglyphs. Fortunately, Harif, the *Navigatairé,* became aware of the danger and was able to confound his attempts to share his knowledge. In those days, centers of learning were few and communication between peoples slow and unreliable. After that, the papyri were smuggled to Jerusalem and concealed there within underground chambers on the Plains of Sepal.

"From the 800s to the 1800s, no one made significant progress in deciphering hieroglyphs. No one. Their meaning was only elucidated when Napoleon's scientific and military expedition to North Africa in 1799 uncovered a detailed inscription in the sacred language of hieroglyphs, in everyday demotic Egyptian of the time and Ancient Greek. You have heard of the Rosetta Stone?"

Alice nodded.

"From that point, we feared it was only a matter of time. A Frenchman, Jean-François Champollion, became obsessed with breaking the code. In 1822, he succeeded. The wonders of the ancients, their magic, their spells, everything from funerary inscriptions to the *Book of the Dead,* all suddenly could be read." He paused. "Now, the fact that two books of the Labyrinth Trilogy were in the hands of those who would misuse it became a cause for fear and concern."

His words fell like a warning. Alice shivered. She suddenly realized the day had faded. Outside, the rays of the setting sun had painted the mountains red and gold and orange.

"If the knowledge was so devastating, if used for ill rather than good, then why did Alaïs or the other guardians not destroy the books when they had the chance?" she asked.

She felt Audric grow still. Alice realized she had hit to the heart of his experience, of the story he was telling, even though she didn't understand how.

"If they had not been needed, then yes. Perhaps that might have been a solution."

"Needed? Needed in what way?"

"That the Grail bestows life, the guardians have always known. You called it a gift and," he caught his breath, "I understand that some might see it so. Others might see it with different eyes." Audric stopped. He reached for his glass and took several mouthfuls of wine, before putting it back on the table with a heavy hand. "But it is life given for a purpose."

"What purpose?" she said quickly, fearful he would stop.

"Many times in the past four thousand years, when the need to bear witness has been strong, the power of the Grail has been summoned. The great, long-lived patriarchs of the Christian Bible, the Talmud, the Koran are familiar to us. Adam, Jacob, Moses, Mohammad, Methuselah. Prophets whose work could not be accomplished in the usual span allotted to men. They each lived for hundreds of years."

"But these are parables," protested Alice. "Allegories."

Audric shook his head. "They survived for centuries precisely so that they could speak of what they had witnessed, bear testimony to the truth

of their times. Harif, who persuaded Abu Bakr to conceal his work revealing the language of Ancient Egypt, lived to see the fall of Montségur."

"But that's five hundred years."

"They lived," Audric repeated simply. "Think of the life of a butterfly,
Alice. An entire existence, so brilliant, but lasting just one human day. An
entire lifetime. Time has many meanings."

Alice pushed her chair back and walked away from the table, no longer
knowing what she felt, what she could believe.

She turned. "The labyrinth symbol I saw on the wall of the cave, on the
ring you wear—this is the symbol of the true Grail?"

He nodded.

"And Alaïs? She knew this?"

"At first, like you, she was doubtful. She did not believe in the truth
contained within the pages of the Trilogy, but she fought to protect them
out of love for her father."

"She believed Harif was more than five hundred years old?" she persisted, no longer trying to keep the scepticism out of her voice.

"Not at first, no," he admitted. "But over time, she came to see the
truth. And when her time came, she found she was able to speak the
words, understand the words."

Alice came back to the table and sat down. "But why France? Why
were the papyri brought here at all? Why not leave them where they
were?"

Audric smiled. "Harif took the papyri to the Holy City in the tenth
century of the Christian era and had them hidden near the Plains of
Sepal. For nearly a hundred years, they were safe, until the armies of Sal-
adin advanced on Jerusalem. He chose one of the guardians, a young
Christian *chevalier* called Bertrand Pelletier, to carry the papyri to
France."

Alaïs' father.

Alice realized she was smiling, as if she had just heard news of an old
friend.

"Harif realized two things," Audric continued. "First, that the papyri
would be safer kept within the pages of a book, less vulnerable. Second,
that because rumors of the Grail were starting to circulate through the
courts of Europe, how better to hide the truth than beneath a layer of
myth and fable."

"The stories of the Cathars possessing the Cup of Christ," said Alice,
suddenly understanding.

Baillard nodded. "The followers of Jesus the Nazarene did not expect
him to die on the Cross, yet he did. His death and resurrection helped
give birth to stories of a sacred cup or chalice, a grail that gave everlasting
life. How these were interpreted at the time, I cannot say, but what is cer-

tain is that the crucifixion of the Nazarene gave birth to a wave of persecution. Many fled the Holy Land, including Joseph of Arimathea and Mary Magdalene, who sailed for France. They brought with them, it is said, knowledge of an ancient secret."

"The Grail papyri?"

"Or treasure, jewels taken from the Temple of Solomon. Or the cup that Jesus the Nazarene had drunk from at the Last Supper in which his blood had been gathered as he hung upon the Cross. Or parchments, writings, evidence that Christ had not died crucified but yet lived, hidden in the mountains of the desert for a hundred years and more with a small elect band of believers."

Alice stared dumbstruck at Audric, but his face was a closed book and she could read nothing in it.

"That Christ did not die on the Cross," she repeated, hardly able to believe what she was saying.

"Or other stories," he said slowly. "Some claimed that it was at Narbonne, rather than Marseilles, that Mary Magdalene and Joseph of Arimathea had landed. For centuries it has been common belief that something of great value was hidden somewhere in the Pyrenees."

"So it was not the Cathars who possessed the secret of the Grail," she said, putting the pieces together in her mind, "but Alaïs. They gave her sanctuary."

Alice sat back in her chair, running back over the sequence of events in her mind.

"And now the labyrinth cave has been opened."

"For the first time in nearly eight hundred years, the books can be brought together once more," he said. "And although you, Alice, do not know if you should trust me or dismiss what I say as the delusional ramblings of an old man, there are others who do not doubt."

Alaïs believed in the truth of the Grail.

Deep inside, beyond the limits of her conscious thought, Alice knew he spoke the truth. It was her rational self that found it hard to accept.

"Marie-Cécile," she said heavily.

"Tonight, Madame de l'Oradore will go to the labyrinth cave and attempt to summon the Grail."

Alice felt a wave of apprehension sweep over her.

"But she can't," she said quickly. "She doesn't have the *Book of Words*. She doesn't have the ring."

"I fear she realizes the *Book of Words* must still be within the chamber."

"Is it?"

"I do not know for sure."

"And the ring? She doesn't have that either." She dropped her eyes to his thin hands laid flat on the table.

"She knows I will come."

"But, that's crazy," she exploded. "How can you even contemplate going anywhere near her?"

"Tonight she will attempt to summon the Grail," he said in his low, level voice. "Because of that, they know I will come."

Alice banged her hands on the table. "What about Will? What about Shelagh? Don't you care about them? It won't help them if you are taken as well."

"It is because I care about them—about you, Alice—that I will go. I believe Marie-Cécile intends to force them to participate in the ceremony. There must be five participants, the *Navigataíré* and four others."

"Marie-Cécile, her son, Will, Shelagh and Authié?"

"No, not Authié. Another."

"Then who?"

He avoided the question. "I do not know where Shelagh or Will are now," he said, as if thinking aloud, "but I believe we will find they are taken to the cave at nightfall."

"Who, Audric?" Alice repeated, firmer this time.

Again, he did not answer. He rose to his feet, walked to the window and closed the shutters, before turning to face her.

"We should go."

Alice was frustrated, nervous, bewildered, and most of all frightened. And yet, at the same time, she felt she had no choice.

She thought of Alaïs' name on the Family Tree, separated by eight hundred years from her own. She pictured the symbol of the labyrinth, connecting them across time and space.

Two stories woven into one.

Alice picked up her belongings and followed Audric out into the remains of the fading day.

CHAPTER 75

Montségur

MARÇ 1244

In their hiding place beneath the citadel, Alaïs and her three companions tried to blot out the agonized sound of the torture. But the shouts of pain and the horror penetrated even the thick rock of the mountain. The cries both of the dying and the survivors slid like monsters into her refuge.

Alaïs prayed for Rixende's soul and for its return to God, for all her friends, good men and women, for the pity of it. All she could hope was that her plan had worked.

Only time would tell if Oriane had been deceived into thinking Alaïs and the *Book of Words* had been consumed by the fires.

So great a risk.

Alaïs, Harif and their guides were to remain in their stone tomb until nightfall and the evacuation of the citadel was completed. Then, under cover of darkness, the four fugitives would make their way down the precipitous mountain paths and head for Los Seres. If their luck held, she would be home by dusk tomorrow.

They were in clear breach of the terms of the truce and surrender. If they were caught, retribution would be swift and brutal, Alaïs had no doubt. The cave was barely more than a fold in the rock, shallow and close to the surface. If soldiers searched the citadel thoroughly, they were sure to be discovered.

Alaïs bit her lip at the thought of her daughter. In the darkness, she felt Harif reach for her hand. His skin was dry and dusty, like the desert sands.

"Bertrande is strong," he said, as if he knew what distressed her. "She is like you, *è?* Her courage will hold. Soon, you will be together again. It's not long to wait."

"But she's so young, Harif, too young to witness such things. She must be so frightened . . ."

"She is brave, Alaïs. Sajhë too. They will not fail us."

If I knew you were right . . .

In the dark, her heart wracked with doubt and fear of what was to come, Alaïs sat dry eyed, waiting for the day to pass. The anticipation, not knowing what was happening up above, was almost more than she could bear. The thought of Bertrande's pale, white face continued to haunt her.

And the screaming of the *Bons Homes* as the fire took them went on in her head for a long time after the last victim had fallen silent.

A huge cloud of acrid black smoke was hovering like a storm cloud over the valley, blotting out the day.

Sajhë held Bertrande's hand tightly as they walked through the Great Gate and out of the castle that had been their home for nearly two years. He'd locked his pain deep inside his heart, in a place where the Inquisitors could not reach it. He would not grieve for Rixende now. He could not fear for Alaïs now. He must concentrate on protecting Bertrande and seeing them both safely returned to Los Seres.

The Inquisitors' tables were ready at the bottom of the slopes. The process was to start immediately, in the shadow of the pyre. Sajhë recognized Inquisitor Ferrier, a man loathed throughout the region for his rigid adherence to both the spirit and the letter of ecclesiastical law. He slipped his eyes to the right where Ferrier's partner stood. Inquisitor Duranti was no less feared.

He held Bertrande's hand tighter.

When they got on to the flatter ground, Sajhë realized they were dividing the prisoners up. Old men, members of the garrison and boys were being sent one way, the women and children another. He felt a flash of fear. Bertrande was going to have to face the Inquisitors without him.

She sensed the change in him and looked up, frightened, into his face. "What's happening? What are they going to do to us?"

"*Brava,* they are interrogating the men and the women separately," he said. "Don't worry. Answer their questions. Be brave and stay exactly where you are until I come for you. Don't go anywhere, with anyone else, you understand? No one else at all."

"What will they ask me?" she said in a small voice.

"Your name, your age," Sajhë replied, going over the details she was to hold in her mind one more time. "I'm known as a member of the garrison, but there is no reason for them to associate us together. When they ask you, say you do not know your father. Give Rixende as your mother and tell them you have lived all your life here at Montségur. Whatever happens, do not mention Los Seres. Can you remember all this?"

Bertrande nodded.

"Good girl." Then, trying to reassure her, he added: "My grandmother used to give me messages to take for her when I was no older than you are now. She used to make me repeat them back several times until she was sure I was word perfect."

Bertrande gave a thin smile. "*Mamà* says your memory is terrible. Like a sieve, she says."

"She's right," he said, then grew serious again. "They might also ask you some questions about the *Bons Homes* and what they believe. Answer as honestly as you can. That way, you are less likely to contradict yourself. There's nothing you can tell them they won't already have heard from someone else." He hesitated and added one last reminder. "Remember. Do not mention Alaïs or Harif at all."

Bertrande's eyes filled with tears. "What if the soldiers search the citadel and find her?" she said, her voice rising in panic. "What will they do if they find them?"

"They won't," he replied quickly. "Remember, Bertrande. When the Inquisitors have finished with you, stay exactly where you are. I will come and find you as soon as I can."

Sajhë barely had time to finish his sentence when a guard jabbed him in the back and forced him farther down the hill toward the village. Bertrande was sent in the opposite direction.

He was taken to a wooden pen, where he saw Pierre-Roger de Mirepoix, the commander of the garrison. He had already been interrogated. It was a good sign to Sajhë's mind, a courtesy. It suggested the terms of the surrender were being honored and the garrison were being treated as prisoners of war, not criminals.

As he joined the crowd of soldiers waiting to be called forward, Sajhë slipped his stone ring from his thumb and concealed it beneath his clothes. He felt strangely naked without it. He had rarely removed it since Harif bestowed it upon him twenty years before.

The interrogations were taking place inside two separate tents. The friars were waiting with yellow crosses to attach to the backs of those who'd been found guilty of fraternizing with heretics, and then the prisoners were taken to a secondary holding area beyond, like animals at a market.

It was clear they did not intend to release anyone until everybody, from the oldest to the youngest, had been questioned. The process could take days.

When Sajhë's turn came, he was allowed to walk unaccompanied into the tent. He stopped before Inquisitor Ferrier and waited.

432

Ferrier's waxen face expressed nothing. He demanded Sajhë's name, his age, his rank and his hometown. The goose quill scratched over the parchment.

"Do you believe in Heaven and Hell?" he said abruptly.

"I do."

"Do you believe in Purgatory?"

"I do."

"Do you believe the Son of God was made perfect Man?"

"I'm a soldier, not a monk," he replied, keeping his eyes to the ground.

"Do you believe a human soul has only one body in which, and with which, it will be resurrected?"

"The priests say that it is so."

"Have you ever heard anyone say that swearing oaths is a sin? If so, who?"

This time, Sajhë raised his eyes. "I have not," he said defiantly.

"Come now, sergeant. You've served in the garrison for more than a year and yet do not know that *heretici* refuse to swear oaths?"

"I serve Pierre-Roger de Mirepoix, Inquisitor. I heed not the words of others."

The interrogation continued for some time, but Sajhë stayed faithful to his role as a simple soldier, pleading ignorance of all matters of scripture and belief. He incriminated no one. Claimed to know nothing.

In the end, Inquisitor Ferrier had no choice but to let him go.

It was only late afternoon, but already the sun was setting. Dusk was creeping back into the valley, stealing the shape from things and covering everything with black shadows.

Sajhë was sent to join a group of other soldiers who had already been interrogated. Each of them had been given a blanket, a hunk of stale bread and a cup of wine. He could see such kindness had not been extended to the civilian prisoners.

As the day gathered to a close, Sajhë's spirits fell further.

Not knowing if Bertrande's ordeal was over—or even where in the vast camp she was being held—was eating away at his mind. The thought of Alaïs, waiting, watching the fading of the light, her anxiety growing as the hour of departure approached, filled him with apprehension, all the worse for being unable to do anything to help.

Restless and unable to settle, Sajhë got up to stretch. He could feel the damp and chill seeping into his bones and his legs were stiff from sitting still for so long.

"*Assis,*" growled a guard, tapping him on the shoulder with his pike. He was about to obey, when he noticed movement higher up the mountain. There was a search party making its way toward the rocky outcrop where

Alaïs, Harif and their guides were hidden. The flames from their torches flickered, throwing shadows against the bushes shivering in the wind.

Sajhë's blood turned cold.

They had searched the castle earlier and found nothing. He had thought it was over. But it was clear they were intending to search the undergrowth and the labyrinth of paths that led around the base of the citadel. If they went much farther in that direction, it would bring them to precisely the point where Alaïs would emerge. And it was almost dark.

Sajhë started to run toward the perimeter of the compound.

"Hey!" the guard shouted. "Didn't you hear what I said? *Arrête!*"

Sajhë ignored him. Without thinking about the consequences, he vaulted the wooden fence and pounded up the slope, toward the search party. He could hear the guard calling for reinforcements. His only thought was to draw attention away from Alaïs.

The search party stopped and looked to see what was going on.

Sajhë shouted, needing to turn them from spectators to participants. One by one, they turned. He saw confusion in their faces turn to aggression. They were bored and cold, itching for a fight.

Sajhë had just enough time to realize his plan had worked as a fist was driven into his stomach. He gasped for breath and doubled over. Two of the soldiers held his arms behind him as the punches came at him from all directions. The hilts of their weapons, boots, fists, the onslaught was relentless. He felt the skin beneath his eye split. He could taste blood on his tongue and at the back of his throat as the blows continued to rain down.

Only now did he accept how seriously he'd misjudged the situation. He'd thought only of drawing attention away from Alaïs. An image of Bertrande's pale face, waiting for him to come, slipped into his mind as a fist connected with his jaw and everything went black.

CHAPTER 76

Oriane had devoted her life to her quest to retrieve the *Book of Words*.

Quite soon after returning to Chartres after the defeat of Carcassonne, her husband lost patience with her failure to secure the prize he had paid for. There was never love between them and, when his desire for her faded, his fist and his belt replaced conversation.

She endured the beatings, all the time devising ways in which she would be revenged on him. As his land and wealth increased, and his influence with the French king grew, his attention was drawn to other prizes. He left her alone. Free to resume her quest, Oriane paid informers and employed a network of spies in the Midi, all hunting down information.

Only once had Oriane come close to capturing Alaïs. In May 1234 Oriane had left Chartres and traveled south to Toulouse. When she arrived at the cathedral of Saint-Etienne, it was to discover the guards had been bribed and her sister had disappeared again, as if she had never been.

Oriane was determined not to make the same mistake again. This time, when a rumor had surfaced about a woman, of the right age, the right description, Oriane had come south with one of her sons under cover of the Crusade.

This morning she thought she had seen the book burn in the purple light of dawn. To be so close and yet to fail had sent her into a rage that neither her son Louis nor her servants could assuage. But during the course of the afternoon, Oriane had started to revise her interpretation of the morning's events. If it was Alaïs she had seen—and she was even questioning that—was it likely she would allow the *Book of Words* to burn on an Inquisitional pyre?

Oriane decided not. She sent her servants out into the camp for information and learned that Alaïs had a daughter, a girl of nine or ten, whose father was a soldier serving under Pierre-Roger de Mirepoix. Oriane did not believe her sister would have entrusted so precious an object to a member of the garrison. The soldiers would be searched. But a child?

Oriane waited until it was dark before making her way to the area where the women and children were being held. She bought her passage into the compound. No one questioned or challenged her. She could feel the disapproving looks from the Black Friars as she passed, but their ill judgment did not move her.

Her son, Louis, appeared in front of her, his arrogant face flushed. He was always too desperate for approval, too eager to please.

"*Oui?*" she snapped. "*Qu'est-ce que tu veux?*"

"*Il y a une fille que vous devez voir, Maman.*"

Oriane followed him to the far side of the enclosure, where a girl lay sleeping a little apart from the others.

The physical resemblance to Alaïs was striking. But for the passage of years, Oriane could be looking at her sister's twin. She had the same look of fierce determination, the same coloring as Alaïs at the same age.

"Leave me," she said. "She will not trust me with you standing here."

Louis' face fell, irritating her even more. "Leave me," she repeated, turning her back on him. "Go prepare the horses. I have no need of you here."

When he'd gone, Oriane crouched down and tapped the girl on the arm.

The girl woke immediately and sat up, her eyes bright with fear.

"Who are you?"

"*Una amiga,*" she said, using the language she had abandoned thirty years ago. "A friend."

Bertrande didn't move. "You're French," she said stubbornly, staring at Oriane's clothes and hair. "You weren't in the citadel."

"No," she said, trying to sound patient, "but I was born in Carcassona, just like your mother. We were children together in the Château Comtal. I even knew your grandfather, Intendant Pelletier. I'm sure Alaïs has talked often of him."

"I'm named for him," she said promptly.

Oriane hid a smile. "Well, Bertrande. I've come to get you away from here."

The girl frowned. "But Sajhë told me to stay here until he came for me," she said, a little less cautiously. "He said not to go with anyone else."

"Sajhë said that, did he?" Oriane said, smiling. "Well, he said to me that you were good at looking after yourself, that I should give you something to persuade you to trust me."

Oriane held out the ring she had stolen from her father's cold hand. As she expected, Bertrande recognized it and reached for it.

"Sajhë gave you this?"

"Take it. See for yourself."

Bertrande turned the ring, examining it thoroughly. She stood up. "Where is he?"

"I don't know," she said, frowning furiously. "Unless . . ."

"Yes?" Bertrande looked up at her.

"Do you think he meant you should go home?"

Bertrande thought for a moment. "He might," she said doubtfully.

"Is it far?" asked Oriane casually.

"A day on horseback, perhaps more at this time of year."

"And does this village have a name?" she said lightly.

"Los Seres," Bertrande replied, "although Sajhë told me not to tell the Inquisitors."

The *Noublesso de los Seres*. Not just the name of the Grail guardians but the place where the Grail would be found. Oriane had to bite her tongue to stop herself laughing.

"Let us get rid of this to start with," she said, leaning over and pulling the yellow cross from Bertrande's back. "We don't want anyone to guess that we're runaways. Now, do you have anything to bring with you?"

If the girl had the book with her, there was no need to go any farther. The quest would end here.

Bertrande shook her head. "Nothing."

"Very well, then. Quietly now. We don't want to attract attention."

The girl was still cautious, but as they walked through the sleeping compound, Oriane talked about Alaïs and the Château Comtal. She was charming, persuasive and attentive. Little by little, she won the girl over.

Oriane slipped another coin into the guard's hand at the gate, then led Bertrande to where her son was waiting at the outskirts of the camp with six soldiers on horseback and a covered cart already prepared.

"Are they coming with us?" Bertrande said, suddenly suspicious.

Oriane smiled as she lifted the child into the *calèche*. "We need to be protected from bandits on the journey, don't we? Sajhë would never forgive me if I let anything happen to you."

Once Bertrande was settled, she turned to her son.

"What about me?" he said. "I want to accompany you."

"I need you to stay here," she said, restless now to be gone. "You, if you have not forgotten, are part of the army. You cannot simply disappear. It will be easier and quicker for us all if I go alone."

"But—"

"Do as I say," she said, keeping her voice low so Bertrande could not hear. "Look after our interests here. Deal with the girl's father as discussed. Leave the rest to me."

All Guilhem could think about was finding Oriane. His purpose in coming to Montségur had been to help Alaïs and to keep Oriane from harming her. For nearly thirty years, he'd watched over her from afar.

Now Alaïs was dead, he had nothing to lose. His desire for revenge had grown year by year. He should have killed Oriane when he had the chance. He would not let this opportunity pass by.

With the hood of his cloak pulled down over his face, Guilhem slipped through the Crusaders camp, until he saw the green and silver of Oriane's pavilion.

There were voices inside. French. A young man giving orders. Remembering the youth sitting beside Oriane in the stalls, her son, Guilhem pressed himself against the flapping side of the tent and listened.

"He's a soldier in the garrison," Louis d'Evreux said in his arrogant voice. "Goes by the name of Sajhë de Servian. The one who created the disturbance earlier. Southern peasants," he said with contempt. "Even when they're treated well, they behave like animals." He gave a sharp laugh. "He was taken to the enclosure near the pavilion of Hugues des Arcis, away from the other prisoners in case he incited any more trouble."

Louis dropped his voice so Guilhem could barely hear. "This is for you," he said. Guilhem heard the clinking of coins. "Half now. If the peasant's still alive when you find him, remedy the situation. The rest when the job is done."

Guilhem waited until the soldier came out, then slipped in through the unguarded opening.

"I told you I did not want to be disturbed," Evreux said abruptly, without turning round. Guilhem's knife was at his throat before the man had a chance to call out.

"If you make a sound, I'll kill you," he said.

"Take what you want, take what you want. Don't harm me."

Guilhem cast his eyes around the opulent tent, at the fine carpets and warm blankets. Oriane had achieved the wealth and status she'd always desired. He hoped it had not brought her happiness.

"Tell me your name," he said in a low, savage voice.

"Louis d'Evreux. I don't know who you are, but my mother will—"

Guilhem jerked his head back. "Don't threaten me. You sent your guards away, remember? There's no one to hear you." He pressed the blade harder against the boy's pale northern skin. Evreux went completely still. "That's better. Now. Where is Oriane? If you do not answer, I will cut your throat."

Guilhem felt him react at the use of Oriane's name, but fear loosened his tongue. "She's gone to the women's compound," he gabbled.

"For what purpose?"

"In search of . . . a girl."

"Don't waste my time, *nenon*," he said, jerking his neck back again. "What manner of girl? Why does she matter to Oriane?"

"The child of a heretic. My mother's . . . sister," he said, as if the word was poison in his mouth. "My aunt. My mother wished to see the girl for herself."

"Alaïs," Guilhem whispered in disbelief. "How old is this child?"

He could smell the fear on Evreux's skin. "How do I know? Nine, ten."

"And the father? Did he die too?"

Evreux tried to move. Guilhem increased the pressure around his neck and turned the blade so the tip was pressing beneath Evreux's left ear, ready.

"He's a soldier, one of Pierre-Roger de Mirepoix's men."

Guilhem straight away understood. "And you've sent one of your men to make sure he doesn't live to see the sun rise," he said.

The blade of Guilhem's dagger flashed as it caught the light from the candle.

"Who are you?"

Guilhem ignored him. "Where is Lord Evreux? Why is he not here?"

"My father is dead," he said. There was no grief in his voice, only a sort of boastful pride Guilhem could not understand. "I am master of the Evreux estates now."

Guilhem laughed. "Or, most likely, your mother is."

The boy flinched as if he had been struck.

"Tell me, *Lord* Evreux," he said with contempt, stressing the word, "what does your mother want with the girl?"

"What does it matter? She's the child of heretics. They should've burned them all."

Guilhem felt Evreux's regret at his momentary loss of control the instant the words were spoken, but it was too late. Guilhem flexed his arm and dragged his knife from ear to ear, slitting the youth's throat.

"*Per lo Miègjorn,*" he said. For the Midi.

The blood gushed in spurts on to the fine carpets along the line of the cut. Guilhem released his hold and Evreux fell forward.

"If your servant comes back quickly, you may live. If not, you had better pray your God will forgive your sins."

Guilhem pulled his hood back over his head and ran out. He had to find Sajhë de Servian before Evreux's man did.

The small group jolted its uncomfortable way through the cold night.

Already, Oriane regretted deciding to take the *calèche*. They would have been quicker on horseback. The wooden wheels banged and scraped against the flints and the hard, icy ground.

They avoided the main routes in and out of the valley where roadblocks were still in place, heading south for the first few hours. Then as the winter dusk gave way to the black of night, they turned to the south east.

Bertrande was asleep, her cloak pulled up over her head to keep out the biting wind that whipped under the bottom of the hangings erected over the cart. Oriane had found her endless chatter irritating. She'd plagued her with questions about life in Carcassonne in the old days, before the war.

Oriane fed her biscuits, sugar loaf and spiced wine, with a sleeping draught strong enough to knock a soldier out for days. Finally, the child stopped talking and fell into a deep sleep.

"Wake up!"

Sajhë could hear someone talking. A man. Close by.

He tried to move. Pain shot through every part of his body. Blue flashes sparked behind his eyes.

"Wake up!" The voice was more insistent this time.

Sajhë flinched as something cold was pressed against his bruised face, soothing his skin. Slowly, the memory of the blows beating down on his head, his body, everywhere, came crawling back.

Was he dead?

Then he remembered. Someone shouted, farther down the slope, yelling at the soldiers to stop. His assailants, caught out suddenly, stepping back. Someone, a commander, shouting orders in French. Being dragged down the mountain.

Not dead perhaps.

Sajhë tried to move again. He could feel something hard against his back. He realized his shoulders were pulled tight behind him. He tried to open his eyes, but found one was swollen shut. His other senses were heightened in response. He was aware of the movements of the horses, stamping their hooves on the ground. He could hear the voice of the wind and the cries of nightjars and a solitary owl. These were sounds he understood.

"Can you move your legs?" the man asked.

Sajhë was surprised to find he could, although they ached cruelly. One of the soldiers had stamped on his ankle when he was lying on the ground.

"Can you manage to ride?"

Sajhë watched the man go behind him to cut the ropes binding his arms to the post, and realized there was something familiar about him. Something he recognized in his voice, the turn of his head.

Sajhë staggered to his feet.

"To what do I owe this kindness?" he said, rubbing his wrists. Then, suddenly, he knew. Sajhë saw himself as an eleven year-old boy again, climbing the walls of the Château Comtal and along the battlements, looking for Alaïs. Listening at the window to hear laughter floating on the breeze. A man's voice, talking and teasing.

"Guilhem du Mas," he said slowly.

Guilhem paused and looked with surprise at Sajhë. "Have we met, friend?"

"You would not remember," he said, barely able to look him in the face.

"Tell me, *amic*," he stressed the word. "What do you want with me?"

"I came to . . ." Guilhem was nonplussed by his hostility. "You are Sajhë de Servian?"

"What of it?"

"For the sake of Alaïs, whom we both . . ." Guilhem stopped and composed himself. "Her sister, Oriane, is here, with one of her sons. Part of the Crusader army. Oriane has come for the book."

Sajhë stared. "What book?" he said belligerently.

Guilhem pressed on regardless. "Oriane learned that you had a daughter. She's taken her. I don't know where they're heading, but they left the camp just after dusk. I came to tell you and offer my help." He stood up. "But if you don't want it . . ."

Sajhë felt the color drain from his face. "Wait!" he cried.

"If you want to get your daughter back alive," Guilhem continued steadily, "I suggest you put your grievance against me to one side, whatever its cause."

Guilhem held out his hand to help Sajhë to his feet.

"Do you know where Oriane is likely to have taken her?"

Sajhë stared at the man he had spent a lifetime hating, then, for the sake of Alaïs and her daughter, took the outstretched hand.

"She has a name," he said. "She's called Bertrande."

CHAPTER 77
Pic de Soularac

FRIDAY, 8 JULY 2005

Audric and Alice climbed the mountain in silence.

Too much had been said for any more words to be needed. Audric was breathing heavily, but he kept his eyes trained on the ground at his feet and did not once falter.

"It can't be much farther," she said, as much to herself as to him.

"No."

Five minutes later, Alice realized they had come at the site from the opposite side to the car park. The tents had all gone, but there was evidence of their recent occupancy with the brown, dried-out patches of ground and the odd random piece of rubbish. Alice noticed a trowel and a tent peg, which she picked up and put in her pocket.

They kept climbing, turning up to the left, until they arrived at the boulder Alice had dislodged. It was lying on its side below the entrance to the chamber, exactly where it had fallen. In the ghostly white light of the moon it looked like the head of a fallen idol.

Was it really only Monday?

Baillard stopped and leaned back against the boulder to catch his breath.

"There's not much farther to go," she said, wanting to reassure him. "I'm sorry. I should have warned you it was so steep."

Audric smiled. "I remember," he said. He took her hand. His skin felt tissue-thin. "When we get to the cave, you will wait until I say it is safe to come after me. You must promise me you will stay hidden."

"I still don't think it's a good idea for you to go in alone," she said stubbornly. "Even if you're right and they don't come until after dark, you could get trapped. I wish you'd let me help you, Audric. If I come in with you, I can help you find the book. It will be quicker with two, easier. We can be in and out in minutes. Then we can both hide out here and see what happens."

"Forgive me, but it is better for us to separate."

"I really don't see why, Audric. Nobody knows we're here. We should be quite safe," she said, even though she felt far from it.

"You are very brave, *Madomaisèla*," he said softly. "As she was. Alaïs always put the safety of others before her own. She sacrificed much for those she loved."

"No one's sacrificing anything," Alice said sharply. Fear was making her nervous. "And I still don't understand why you wouldn't let me come earlier. We could have come to the chamber when it was still light and not run the risk of being caught."

Baillard behaved as if she had not spoken.

"You telephoned Inspector Noubel?" he asked.

There is no point arguing. Not now.

"Yes," she sighed heavily. "I said what you told me to say."

"*Ben*," he said softly. "I understand you think I am being unwise, *Madomaisèla*, but you will see. All must happen at the right time, in the right order. There will be no truth else."

"Truth?" she repeated. "You've told me all there is to know, Audric. Everything. Now my only concern is to get Shelagh—and Will—out of here in one piece."

"Everything?" he said softly. "Is such a thing possible?"

Audric turned and looked up at the entrance, a small black opening in the expanse of rock. "One truth may contradict another," he murmured. "Now is not then." He took her arm. "Shall we complete the last stage of our journey?" he said.

Alice glanced quizzically at him, wondering at the mood that had overtaken him. He was calm, thoughtful. A kind of passive acceptance had descended over him, while she was very nervous, frightened at all the things that could go wrong, terrified Noubel would be too late, scared that Audric would turn out to be mistaken.

What if they're already dead?

Alice pushed the thought from her mind. She couldn't afford to think like that. She had to keep believing that everything was going to be all right.

At the entrance, Audric turned and smiled at her, his speckled amber eyes sparkling in anticipation.

"What is it, Audric?" she said quickly. "There's something," she broke off, unable to find the word she wanted. "Something . . ."

"I have been waiting a long time," he said softly.

"Waiting? To find the book?"

He shook his head. "For redemption," he said.

"Redemption? But for what?" Alice was astonished to realize she had tears in her eyes. She bit her lip to stop herself breaking down. "I don't understand, Audric," she said, her voice cracking.

"*Pas a pas se va luènh,*" he said. "You saw these words in the chamber carved at the top of the steps?"

Alice looked at him surprise. "Yes, but how did—"

He held out his hand for the torch. "I must go in."

Battling her conflicting emotions, Alice handed it to him without another word. She watched him walk down the tunnel, waiting until the last pinprick of light had disappeared, before turning away.

The cry of an owl nearby made her jump. The slightest sound seemed magnified a hundred times over. There was malignancy in the darkness. The trees looming around her, the awesome shadow of the mountain itself, the way the rocks seemed to be taking on unfamiliar, threatening shapes. In the distance she thought she heard the sound of a car on a road somewhere down in the valley.

Then the silence came surging back.

Alice glanced at her watch. It was nine-forty.

At a quarter to ten, two powerful car headlights swept into the car park at the foot of the Pic de Soularac.

Paul Authié killed the engine and got out. He was surprised to find François-Baptiste wasn't there waiting for him. Authié glanced up in the direction of the cave with a sudden flash of alarm that they might already be in the chamber.

He dismissed the thought. His nerves were starting to get to him. Braissart and Domingo had been there until an hour ago. If Marie-Cécile or her son had turned up, he'd have heard about it.

His hand went to the control box in his pocket, set to detonate the explosives and already counting down. There was nothing he had to do. Just wait. And watch.

Authié felt for the cross around his neck and started to pray.

A sound in the woods that bordered the car park caught his attention. Authié opened his eyes. He could see nothing. He went back to the car and turned the headlights on full beam. The trees leaped out of the darkness at him, stripped of color.

He shielded his eyes and looked again. This time, he detected movement in the dense undergrowth.

"François-Baptiste?"

No one answered. Authié could feel the short hairs on the back of his neck standing on end. "We haven't got the time for this," he shouted into the darkness, injecting a tone of irritation into his voice. "If you want the book and the ring, come out here where I can see you."

Authié started to wonder if he'd misjudged the situation.

"I'm waiting," he called out.

This time, he heard something. He suppressed a smile as a figure started to take shape among the trees.

"Where's O'Donnell?"

Authié nearly laughed at the sight of François-Baptiste walking toward him, wearing a jacket several sizes too large for him. He looked pathetic.

"You're alone?" he said.

"None of your fucking business," he said, coming to a halt on the edge of the woods. "Where's Shelagh O'Donnell?"

Authié jerked his head in the direction of the cave. "She's already up there waiting for you, François-Baptiste. Thought I'd save you the bother." He gave a short laugh. "I don't think she'll give you any trouble."

"What about the book?"

"In there too." He shot the cuffs on his shirt. "The ring as well. All delivered as promised. On time."

François-Baptiste gave a sharp laugh. "Gift-wrapped too, I suppose," he said sarcastically. "You don't expect me to believe you've just left them up there?"

Authié looked at him with contempt. "My task was to retrieve the book and the ring, which is what I've done. I've also returned your—what shall we call her—your *spy*, at the same time. Call it philanthropy on my part." He narrowed his eyes. "What Madame de l'Oradore chooses to do with her is her business."

Doubt flickered across the boy's face.

"All out of the goodness of your heart?"

"For the *Noublesso Véritable*," Authié said mildly. "Or have you not yet been invited to join? I imagine being merely her son makes no difference. Go and have a look. Or is your mother already up there getting ready?"

François-Baptiste darted a glance at him.

"Did you think she hadn't told me?" Authié took a step toward him. "Do you think I don't know what she does?" He could feel the anger rising in him. "Have you see her, François-Baptiste? Have you seen the ecstasy on her face when she speaks those obscene words, those blasphemous words? It's an offense against God what she is doing!"

"Don't you dare talk about her like that!" he said, his hand moving to his pocket.

Authié laughed. "That's right. Ring her. She'll tell you what to do. What to think. Don't do anything without asking her first."

He turned away and started to walk back to the car. He heard the release of the safety catch seconds before it registered what it was. In disbelief, Authié spun round. He was too slow. He heard the snap of the bullets, one, two in quick succession.

The first went wide. The second hit him in the thigh. The bullet went straight through, shattering the bone, and out the other side. Authié went down, screaming, as the shock of the pain went through him.

François-Baptiste was walking toward him, the gun held straight in front of him with both hands. Authié tried to crawl away, leaving a trail of blood behind him on the gravel, but the boy was upon him now.

For a moment, their eyes met. Then François-Baptiste fired again.

Alice jumped.

The sound of the shots cut through the still mountain air. It bounced off the rock and reverberated around her.

Her heart started to race. She couldn't work out where the shots had come from. At home, she'd know it was only a farmer shooting rabbits or crows.

It didn't sound like a shotgun.

She jumped down to the ground, as quietly as she could, and peered out into the darkness to where she thought the car park was. She heard a car door slam shut. Now, she could pick out the sound of human voices, words carried on the air.

What's Audric doing in there?

They were a long way off, but she could sense their presence on the mountain. Alice heard the occasional sound of a pebble as their feet dislodged gravel and stones from the path. The crack of a twig.

Alice edged closer to the entrance, sending desperate glances toward the cave as if, by sheer force of will, she could conjure Audric out of the darkness.

Why doesn't he come?

"Audric?" she hissed. "There's someone coming. Audric?"

Nothing but silence. Alice peered into the darkness of the tunnel stretching out before her and felt her courage waver.

But you have to warn him.

Praying she'd not left it too late, Alice turned and ran down toward the labyrinth chamber.

CHAPTER 78
Los Seres

MARÇ 1244

Despite Sajhë's injuries, they made good time, following the line of the river south from Montségur. They traveled light and rode hard, stopping only to rest and water the horses, using their swords to break the ice. Guilhem saw immediately that Sajhë's skills exceeded his own.

Guilhem knew a little of Sajhë's past, how he had carried messages from the *parfaits* to the isolated and far-flung villages of the Pyrenees and delivered intelligence to the rebel fighters. It was clear the younger man knew every passable valley and ridge, and every concealed track in the woods, gorges and the plains.

At the same time, Guilhem was aware of Sajhë's fierce dislike, although he said nothing. It was like the burning sun beating down on the back of his neck. Guilhem knew Sajhë's reputation as a loyal, brave and honorable man, ready to die fighting for what he believed in. Despite his animosity, Guilhem could see why Alaïs would love this man and have a child with him, even though the thought was like a knife through his heart.

Luck was with them. There was no new snowfall during the night. The following day, the nineteenth of March, was bright and clear, with few clouds and little wind.

Sajhë and Guilhem arrived in Los Seres at dusk. The village was nestled in a small, secluded valley and, despite the cold, there was the soft smell of spring in the air. The trees on the outskirts of the village were dotted with light green and white. The earliest spring flowers peeped out shyly from the hedgerows and banks as they rode up the track that led to the small cluster of houses. The village seemed deserted, abandoned.

The two men dismounted and led their horses the final distance into the center of the village. The sound of their iron shoes striking against the flint and stone of the hard earth echoed loudly in the silence. A few wisps of smoke floated carefully from one or two of the houses. Eyes peered suspiciously out through the slits and cracks of the shutters, then darted quickly away. French deserters were uncommon this high in the mountains, but not unheard of. Usually, they brought trouble.

Sajhë tethered his horse beside the well. Guilhem did likewise, then followed him as he walked through the center of the village to a small dwelling. There were tiles missing from the roof and the shutters were in need of repair, but the walls were strong. Guilhem thought it wouldn't take much to bring the house back to life.

Guilhem waited while Sajhë pushed the door. The wood, swollen by the damp and stiff from disuse, juddered on its hinges, then creaked open enough for Sajhë to get in.

Guilhem followed, feeling the damp, tomb-like air on his face, numbing his fingers. A mound of leaves and mulch was piled up against the wall opposite the door, clearly blown in by the winter winds. There were fingers of ice on the inside of the shutters and, like a ragged fringe, at the bottom of the sill.

The remains of a meal sat on the table. An old jug, plates, cups and a knife. There was a film of mold on the surface of the wine, like green weed on the surface of a pond. The benches were neatly tucked against the wall.

"This is your home?" Guilhem asked softly.

Sajhë nodded.

"When did you leave?"

"A year ago."

In the center of the room, a rusted cooking pot hung suspended over a pile of ash and charred wood that had long since burned itself out. Guilhem watched with pity as Sajhë leaned over and straightened the lid.

At the back of the house, there was a tattered curtain. He lifted it to reveal another table with two chairs set on either side. The wall was covered with rows of narrow, almost empty shelves. An old pestle and mortar, a couple of bowls and scoops, a few jars, covered in dust, were all that had been left behind. Above the shelf small hooks had been set into the low ceiling from which a few dusty bunches of herbs still hung. A petrified sprig of fleabane and another of blackberry leaves.

"For her medicines," he said, taking Guilhem by surprise. Guilhem stood still, his hands folded in front of him, not wanting to interrupt Sajhë's recollections.

"Everybody came to her, men as well as women. When they were sick or their spirits were troubled, to keep their children healthy through the winter. Bertrande . . . Alaïs let her help with the preparations and deliver packages to the houses."

Sajhë faltered, then fell silent. Guilhem was aware of the lump in his own throat. He too remembered the bottles and jars with which Alaïs had filled their chamber in the Château Comtal, the silent concentration with which she had worked.

Sajhë let the curtain drop from his hand. He tested the rungs of the ladder, then cautiously climbed to the upper platform. Here, rotten with mildew and soiled by animals, was a pile of old blankets and rotten straw, all that remained of where the family had slept. A single candlestick, with the remains of wax, stood beside the bedding, the telltale smoke marks spread like a stain up the wall behind it.

Guilhem couldn't bear to witness Sajhë's grief any longer and went outside to wait. He had no right to intrude.

Some time later, Sajhë reappeared. His eyes were red, but his hands were steady and he walked purposefully toward Guilhem, who was standing at the highest point of the village, looking to the west.

"When does it grow light in the morning?" he said as Sajhë drew level.

The two men were a similar height, although the lines on Guilhem's face and the flecks of gray in his hair betrayed he was fifteen years closer to the grave.

"The sun rises late in the mountains at this time of year."

Guilhem was silent for a moment. "What do you want to do?" he said, respecting Sajhë's right to dictate things from here.

"We must stable the horses, then find somewhere for ourselves to sleep. I doubt they will be here before morning."

"You don't want . . ." Guilhem started, looking toward the house.

"No," he said quickly. "Not there. There's a woman who will give us food and shelter for the night. Tomorrow, we should move farther up the mountain and set up camp somewhere near the cave itself to wait for them."

"You think Oriane will bypass the village?"

"She will guess where Alaïs has concealed the *Book of Words*. She's had time enough to study the other two books over these past thirty years."

Guilhem glanced sideways at him. "Is she right? Is it still there in the cave?"

Sajhë ignored him. "I don't understand how Oriane persuaded Bertrande to go with her," he said. "I told her not to leave without me. To wait until I came."

Guilhem said nothing. There was nothing he could say to allay Sajhë's fears. The younger man's anger quickly burned itself out.

"Do you think Oriane has brought the other two books with her?" he said suddenly.

Guilhem shook his head. "I imagine the books are safe in her vaults somewhere in Evreux or Chartres. Why would she risk bringing them here?"

"Did you love her?"

The question took Guilhem by surprise. "I desired her," he said slowly. "I was bewitched, flushed with my own importance, I . . ."

"Not Oriane," Sajhë said abruptly, "Alaïs."

Guilhem felt as if an iron band had fixed itself round his throat.

"Alaïs," he whispered. For a moment, he stood locked in his memories, until the force of Sajhë's intense gaze brought him back to the cold present.

"After . . ." he faltered. "After Carcassona fell, I saw her only once. For three months, she stayed with me. She had been taken by the Inquisitors, and—"

"I know," Sajhë shouted, then his voice seemed to collapse. "I know of it."

Mystified by Sajhë's reaction, Guilhem kept his eyes straight ahead. To his own surprise, he realized he was smiling.

"Yes." The word slipped from between his lips. "I loved her more than the world. I just did not understand how precious a thing love is, how fragile until I had crushed it in my hands."

"It's why you let her be. After Tolosa, and she returned here?"

Guilhem nodded. "After those weeks together, God knows it was hard to stay away. To see her, just once more . . . I had hoped, when this was all over, we might be . . . But, obviously, she found you. And now today . . ."

Guilhem's voice cracked. Tears welled in his eyes, making them smart in the cold. Beside him, he felt Sajhë shift. For a moment, there was a different quality to the atmosphere between them.

"Forgive me. That I should break down before you." Guilhem took a deep breath. "The bounty Oriane put on Alaïs' head was substantial, tempting even for those who had no reason to wish her harm. I paid Oriane's spies to pass false information. For nigh on thirty years it helped keep her safe."

Guilhem stopped again, the image of the burning book against the blackened red cloak slipping, like an unwelcome guest, into his mind.

"I did not know her faith was so strong," he said. "Or that her desire to keep the *Book of Words* from Oriane would drive her to such steps."

He looked at Sajhë, trying to read the truth written in his eyes.

"I would that she had not chosen to die," he said simply. "For you, as the man she chose, and me, as the fool who had her love and lost it." He stumbled. "But most for the sake of your daughter. To know Alaïs—"

450

"Why are you helping us?" Sajhë interrupted. "Why did you come?"

"To Montségur?"

Sajhë shook his head, impatient. "Not Montségur. Here. Now."

"Revenge," he said.

CHAPTER 79

Alaïs woke with a jolt, stiff and cold. A delicate purple light swept across the gray and green landscape at dawn. A gentle white mist tiptoed through the gulleys and crevices of the mountainside, silent and still.

She looked to Harif. He was sleeping peacefully, his fur-lined cloak drawn up to his ears. He'd found the day and night they had spent traveling hard.

The silence was heavy over the mountain. Despite the cold in her bones and her discomfort, Alaïs relished the solitude after the months of desperate overcrowding and confinement within Montségur. Careful not to disturb Harif, she stood up and stretched, then reached into one of the saddlebags to break off a piece of bread. It was as hard as wood. She poured herself a cup of thick red mountain wine, which was almost too cold to taste. She dipped the bread to soften it, then ate quickly, before preparing food for the others.

She hardly dared think about Bertrande and Sajhë and where they might be at this moment. Still in the camp? Together or apart?

The call of a screech owl returning from his night's hunting split the air. She smiled, soothed by the familiar sounds. Animals rustled in the undergrowth, sudden flurries of claws and teeth. In the woodlands of the valleys lower down, wolves howled their presence. It served to remind her that the world went on the same, its cycles changing with the seasons, without her.

She roused the two guides and told them food was ready, then led the horses to the stream and broke the ice with the hilt of her sword so they could drink.

Then, when the light strengthened, she went to wake Harif. She whispered to him in his own language and put her hand gently on his arm. He often woke in distress these days.

Harif opened his hooded brown eyes, faded now with age.

"Bertrande?"

"It's Alaïs," she said softly.

Harif blinked, confused to find himself on this gray mountainside. Alaïs imagined he had been dreaming of Jerusalem again, the curve and sweep of the mosques and the call to prayer of the Saracen faithful, his travels across the endless sea of the desert.

In the years they had spent in each other's company, Harif had told her of the aromatic spices, the vivid colors and the peppery taste of the food, the terrible brilliance of the blood-red sun. He had told her stories of how he had used the long years of his life. He had talked of the Prophet and the ancient city of Avaris, his first home. He had told her stories about her father in his youth, and the *Noublesso*.

As she looked down at him, his olive skin gray with age, his once black hair white, her heart ached. He was too old for this struggle. He had seen too much, witnessed too much, for it to finish so harshly.

Harif had left his last journey too late. And Alaïs knew, although he had never said so, that only thoughts of Los Seres and Bertrande gave him the strength to keep going.

"Alaïs," he said quietly, adjusting to his surroundings. "Yes."

"It won't be much longer," she said, helping him to his feet. "We're nearly home."

Guilhem and Sajhë talked little as they sat huddled in the shelter of the mountain out of reach of the vicious claws of the wind.

Several times, Guilhem tried to initiate conversation, but Sajhë's taciturn responses defeated him. In the end he gave up trying and withdrew into his own private world, as Sajhë had intended.

He was sick in conscience. He'd spent a lifetime first envying Guilhem, then hating him, and finally learning to forget about him. He had taken Guilhem's place at Alaïs' side, but never in her heart. She had remained constant to her first love. It had endured, despite absence and silence.

Sajhë knew of Guilhem's courage, his fearless and long struggle to drive the Crusaders from the Pays d'Oc, but he did not want to find himself liking Guilhem, admiring him. Nor did he want to feel pity for him. He could see how he grieved for Alaïs. His face spoke of deep loss, regret. Sajhë could not bring himself to speak. But he hated himself for not doing so.

They waited all day, taking it in turns to sleep. Close to dusk a sudden flurry of crows took flight lower down the slopes, flying up into the air like ash from a dying fire. They wheeled and hovered and cawed, beating the chill air with their wings.

"Someone's coming," said Sajhë, immediately alert.

He peered out from behind the boulder, which was perched on the narrow ledge above the entrance to the cave, as if placed there by some giant hand.

He could see nothing, no movement lower down. Cautiously, Sajhë came out of his hiding place. Everything ached, everything was stiff, a combination of the after-effects of the beating and inactivity. His hands were numb, the raw knuckles red and cracked. His face was a mass of bruises and ragged skin.

Sajhë lowered himself over the rocky ledge and dropped to the ground. He landed badly. Pain shot up from his injured ankle.

"Pass me my sword," he said, holding up his arm.

Guilhem handed him the weapon, then came down and joined him as he stood looking out over the valley.

There was a burst of distant voices. Then, faintly in the fading light, Sajhë saw a thin wraith of smoke winding up through the sparse cover of the trees.

Sajhë looked to the horizon, where the purple land and the darkening sky met.

"They're on the southeastern path," he said, "which means Oriane's avoided the village altogether. From that direction, they won't be able to come any farther with the horses. The terrain is too rough. There are gulleys with sheer drops on both sides. They'll have to continue on foot."

The thought of Bertrande, so close by, was suddenly too much to bear.

"I'm going down."

"No!" Guilhem said quickly, then more quietly. "No. The risk is too great. If they see you, you'll put Bertrande's life in danger. We know Oriane will come to the cave. Here, we have the element of surprise. We must wait for her to come to us." He paused. "You must not blame yourself, friend. You could not have prevented this. You serve your daughter by holding fast to our plan."

Sajhë shook Guilhem's hand from his arm.

"You don't have any idea what I'm feeling," he said, his voice shaking with fury. "How dare you presume to know me?"

Guilhem put up his hands in mock surrender. "I'm sorry."

"She's only a child."

"How old is she?"

"Nine," he replied abruptly.

Guilhem frowned. "So old enough to understand," he said, thinking aloud. "So even if Oriane did *persuade* her, rather than force her, to leave the camp, it's likely by now Bertrande will realize something's wrong. Did she know Oriane was in the camp? Does she even know she has an aunt?"

Sajhë nodded. "She knows Oriane is no friend to Alaïs. She would not have gone with her."

"Not if she knew who she was," agreed Guilhem. "But if she didn't?"

Sajhë thought for a moment, then shook his head. "Even then, I can't believe she would go with a stranger. We were clear that she had to wait for us—"

He broke off, realizing he had nearly given himself away, but Guilhem was following his own train of thought. Sajhë gave a sigh of relief.

"I think we will be able to deal with the soldiers after we have rescued Bertrande," Guilhem said. "The more I think about it, the more likely I think it is that Oriane will leave her men in the camp and continue on alone with your daughter."

Sajhë started to listen. "Go on."

"Oriane has waited more than thirty years for this. Concealment is as natural to her as breathing. I don't think she'll risk anybody else knowing the precise location of the cave. She would not want to share the secret and since she believes no one, except her son, knows she is here, she will not be expecting any opposition."

Guilhem paused. "Oriane is—" He broke off. "To gain possession of the Labyrinth Trilogy Oriane has lied, murdered, betrayed her father and her sister. She has damned herself for the books."

"Murdered?"

"Her first husband, Jehan Congost, certainly, although it was not her hand that wielded the knife."

"François," murmured Sajhë, too soft for Guilhem to hear. A shaft of memory, the screaming, the desperate thrashing of the horse's hooves as man and beast were sucked down into the boggy marsh.

"And I've always believed she was responsible for the death of a woman very dear to Alaïs," Guilhem continued. "Her name is lost to me this far after the event, but she was a wise woman who lived in the *Ciutat*. She taught Alaïs everything, about medicines, healing, how to use nature's gifts for good." He paused. "Alaïs loved her."

It was obstinacy that had stopped Sajhë revealing his identity. It was obstinacy and jealousy that prevented him confiding anything of his life with Alaïs.

"Esclarmonde did not die," he said, no longer able to dissemble. Guilhem went very still.

"What?" he said. "Does Alaïs know this?"

Sajhë nodded. "When she fled from the Château Comtal, it was to Esclarmonde—and her grandson—that Alaïs turned for help. She left—"

The sound of Oriane's sharp voice, authoritative and cold, interrupted the conversation. The two men, mountain fighters both, dropped down to the ground. Without a sound, they drew their swords and took up their positions close to the entrance of the cave. Sajhë concealed himself behind a section of rock slightly below the entrance, Guilhem behind a ring of hawthorn bushes, their spiked branches sharp and menacing in the dusk.

The voices were getting nearer. They could hear the soldiers' boots, armor and buckles, as they clambered over the flint and stone of the rocky path.

Sajhë felt as if he was taking every step with Bertrande. Every moment stretched an eternity. The sound of the footsteps, the echo of the voices, repeating over and over again yet never appearing to get any closer.

Finally, two figures emerged from the cover of the trees. Oriane and Bertrande. As Guilhem had thought, they were alone. He could see Guilhem staring at him, warning him not to move yet, to wait until Oriane was in striking distance and they could get Bertrande safely away.

As they got closer, Sajhë clenched his fists to stop himself roaring out in anger. There was a cut on Bertrande's cheek, red against her white frozen face. Oriane had tied a rope around Bertrande's neck, which ran down her back to her hands, bound at the wrists behind her waist. The other end was in Oriane's left hand. In her right, she had a dagger, which she used to jab Bertrande in the back to keep her moving.

Bertrande was walking awkwardly and stumbled often. He narrowed his eyes and saw that, beneath her skirts, her ankles were tied together. The loose measure of rope between them allowed no more than a stride.

Sajhë forced himself to remain still, waiting, watching until they reached the clearing that lay directly beneath the cave.

"You said it was beyond the trees."

Bertrande murmured something too quiet for Sajhë to hear.

"For your sake, I hope you're telling the truth," Oriane said.

"It's in there," Bertrande said. Her voice was steady, but Sajhë could hear the terror behind it and his heart contracted.

The plan was to ambush Oriane at the mouth of the cave. He was to concentrate on getting Bertrande out of Oriane's reach, Guilhem on disarming Oriane before she had the chance to use the knife.

Sajhë looked at Guilhem, who nodded, to let him know he was ready.

"But you mustn't go in," Bertrande was saying. "It's a sacred place. No one but the Guardians can enter."

"Is that so," she jeered. "And who is going to stop me? You?" A look of bitterness came down over her face. "You are so like her, it disgusts me," she said, jerking the rope around her neck so Bertrande cried out in pain. "Alaïs was always telling everyone what to do. Always thought herself better than everyone else."

"That's not true," shouted Bertrande, brave despite the hopelessness of her situation. Sajhë willed her to stop. At the same time, he knew Alaïs would be proud of her courage. *He* was proud of her courage. She was so much her parents' child.

Bertrande had started to cry. "It's wrong. You mustn't go in. It will not allow you to enter. The labyrinth will protect its secret, from you or anyone who seeks it wrongly."

Oriane gave a short laugh. "They are just stories to frighten stupid little children like you."

Bertrande held her ground. "I will not take you any farther."

Oriane raised her hand and struck her, sending her flying back against the rock. A red mist filled Sajhë's head. In three or four strides he threw himself down upon Oriane, a visceral roar issuing from deep inside his chest.

Oriane reacted too quickly, pulling Bertrande to her feet and holding the knife to her throat.

"How disappointing. I thought my son might have coped with so simple a matter. You were already captive—or so I was told—but no matter."

Sajhë smiled at Bertrande, trying to reassure her despite the hopelessness of their situation.

"Drop your sword," Oriane said calmly, "or I will kill her."

"I'm sorry I disobeyed you, Sajhë," Bertrande cried, "but she had your ring. She told me you'd sent her to fetch me."

"Not my ring, *brava*," Sajhë said. He let his sword fall. It fell with a heavy clatter on the hard ground.

"That's better. Now come out here where I can see you. That will do. Stop." She smiled. "All on your own?"

Sajhë said nothing. Oriane flattened the blade against Bertrande's throat, and then nicked her skin beneath her ear. Bertrande cried out as a trail of blood trickled down her neck, like a red ribbon against her pale skin.

"Let her go, Oriane. It's not her you want, but me."

At the sound of Alaïs' voice, the mountain itself seemed to draw breath.

A spirit? Guilhem couldn't tell.

He felt his breath had been sucked from his body, leaving him hollow and weightless. He did not dare move from his hiding place for fear of setting the apparition to flight. He looked at Bertrande, so like her mother, then down the slope to where Alaïs, if it was she, was standing.

A fur hood framed her face and her riding cloak, dirty from the journey, skimmed the white, hoary ground. Her hands, warm within leather gloves, were folded in front of her.

"Let her go, Oriane."

Her words broke the spell.

"Mamà," cried Bertrande, desperately reaching out her arms.

"It cannot be . . ." Oriane said, narrowing her eyes. "You died. I saw you die."

Sajhë lunged toward Oriane and tried to grab Bertrande, but he wasn't quick enough.

"Don't come closer," she shouted, recovering herself. She dragged Bertrande back toward the mouth of the cave. "I swear, I'll kill her."

"Mamà!"

"It cannot be . . . I saw you die."

Alaïs took another step forward. "Let her go, Oriane. Your quarrel is with me."

"There is no quarrel, sister. You have the *Book of Words*. I want it. *C'est pas difficile.*"

"And once you have it?"

Guilhem was transfixed. He still dared not believe the evidence of his eyes, that this was Alaïs, as he had dreamed her in his imagination so often, in his waking hours and when he lay down to sleep.

A movement caught his attention, the glint of steel, of helmets. Guilhem peered. Two soldiers were creeping up behind Alaïs through the heavy scrub. Guilhem glanced to his left at the sound of a boot against the rock.

"Seize them!"

The soldier nearest to Sajhë grabbed his arms and held him fast, as the others broke cover. Quick as lightning, Alaïs drew her sword and spun round, slicing the blade into the closest soldier's side. He fell. The other soldier lunged at her. Sparks flew as the blades clashed, right, left.

Alaïs had the advantage of the higher ground, but she was smaller and weaker.

Guilhem leaped from his hiding place and ran toward her, just as she stumbled and lost her footing. The soldier lunged, stabbing the inside of her arm. Alaïs screamed and dropped the sword, clutching at the wound with her glove to staunch the blood.

"Mamà!"

Guilhem launched himself the last few steps and thrust his sword into the soldier's stomach. Blood vomited from his mouth. His eyes bulged with shock, then he fell.

He did not have time to draw breath.

"Guilhem!" Alaïs shouted. "At the rear."

He spun round to see two more soldiers running up the slopes. With a roar, he withdrew his sword and charged at them. The blade sliced down through the air as he drove them back, striking randomly, mercilessly, first one, then the other.

He was the better swordsman, but he was outnumbered.

Sajhë was now bound and on his knees. One of the soldiers stayed guard, the point of his knife at Sajhë's neck, as the other came to help subdue Guilhem. He came within striking distance of Alaïs. Although she was losing blood fast, she managed to draw a knife from her belt and with her remaining strength, drove it with force between her assailant's legs. He screamed as the blade sank into the top of his thigh.

Blindsided with pain, he lashed out. Guilhem saw Alaïs fly back and hit her head against the rock. She tried to stand, but she was disorientated, and staggering, and her legs gave out. She sank to the ground, blood flowing from the cut on her head.

The dagger still embedded in his leg, the soldier lumbered toward Guilhem, like a bear in a baiting pit. Guilhem stepped back to get out of his way and skidded on the slippery ground, sending stones skeetering down the hillside. It gave the two others the opportunity they needed to jump him and pin him, face down, on the ground.

He felt his ribs snap as a boot connected with his side. He jerked in agony as they kicked him again. He could taste blood in his mouth.

There was no sound from Alaïs. She didn't appear to be moving at all.

Then he heard Sajhë shout. Guilhem lifted his head just as the soldier struck Sajhë sideways with the flat of his sword, knocking him senseless.

Oriane had disappeared into the cave, taking Bertrande with her.

With a roar, Guilhem summoned every last bit of strength left in him, and hurled himself to his feet, sending one of the soldiers flying backwards down the hill. He grasped his sword and drove it into the throat of the one man left standing, as Alaïs staggered to her knees and stuck the other in the back of the leg with his own knife. The howl of pain died in his throat.

Guilhem realized everything had fallen silent.

For a moment, he just stared at Alaïs. Even now, Guilhem was terrified to believe the evidence of his eyes for fear she would be taken away from him again. Then he held out his hand.

Guilhem felt her fingers entwine with his. He felt her skin, torn and battered, like his, cold like he was. Real.

"I thought—"

"I know," she said quickly.

Guilhem didn't want to let her go, but the thought of Bertrande called him back.

"Sajhë's hurt," he said, striding up the slope toward the entrance. "You help him. I'm going after Oriane."

Alaïs bent down to check Sajhë, then immediately ran to catch him up.

"He's unconscious only," she said. "You stay. Tell him what's happened. I have to find Bertrande."

"No, it's what she wants. She'll force you to reveal where you've concealed the book, then she'll kill you both. I've a better chance of bringing your daughter out alive without you, can't you see?"

"*Our* daughter," she said.

Guilhem heard the words, although he could make no sense of them. His heart started to race.

"Alaïs, what—?" he started to say, but she had ducked under his arm and was already running down the tunnel into the darkness.

CHAPTER 80
Ariège

"They've gone to the cave," shouted Noubel, slamming down the receiver, "of all the stupid—"

"Who?"

"Audric Baillard and Alice Tanner. They've taken it into their heads that Shelagh O'Donnell is being held at the Pic de Soularac and are on their way there. She said someone else was there too. An American, William Franklin."

"Who's he?"

"No idea," said Noubel, grabbing his jacket from the back of the door and lumbering out into the corridor.

Moureau followed him. "Who was it on the phone?"

"The front desk. They took the message from Dr. Tanner at nine o'clock, apparently, but 'didn't think I'd want to be disturbed in the middle of an interrogation!' *N'importe quoi!*" Noubel mimicked the nasal voice of the night sergeant.

Both men automatically glanced up at the clock on the wall. It was ten-fifteen.

"What about Braissart and Domingo?" said Moureau, with a glance down the corridor to the interview rooms. Noubel's hunch had been right. The two men had been arrested not far from Authié's ex-wife's farmhouse. They'd been heading south toward Andorra.

"They can wait."

Noubel threw open the door to the car park, sending it flying back against the fire escape. They hurried down the metal stairs to the tarmac.

"Did you get anything out of them?"

"Nothing," said Noubel, jerking open the car door, slinging his jacket on the backseat. He forced himself in behind the steering wheel. "Silent as the grave, the pair of them."

"More frightened of their boss than you," said Moureau, slamming his door. "Any word on Authié?"

"Nothing. He went to Mass earlier in Carcassonne. No sign of him since then."

"The farmhouse?" suggested Moureau, as the car jumped forward toward the main road. "Has the search team reported in yet?"

"No."

Noubel's phone started to ring. Keeping his right hand on the wheel, he stretched into the backseat, releasing a smell of stale sweat from under his arms. He dropped the jacket in Moureau's lap and made frantic gestures while Moureau fished through his pockets.

"Noubel, *oui*?"

His foot slammed down on the brake, sending Moureau flying forward in his seat. "*Putain!* Why in the name of Christ am I only hearing about this now! Is anybody inside?" He listened. "When did it start?" The line was bad and Moureau could hear the signal breaking. "No, no! Stay there. Keep me in touch."

Noubel tossed his phone on the dashboard, turned the siren on and accelerated toward the motorway.

"The farm's on fire," he said, putting his foot to the floor.

"Arson?"

"The nearest neighbor's half a kilometer away. He claims to have heard a couple of loud explosions, then saw the flames and called the firefighters. By the time they'd arrived, the fire had already taken hold."

"Is there anybody in there?" said Moureau anxiously.

"They don't know," he said grimly.

Shelagh was drifting in and out of consciousness.

She had no idea how long it had been since the men had gone. One by one her senses were shutting down. She was no longer aware of her physical surroundings. Arms, legs, body, head, she felt as if she was floating, weightless. She wasn't aware of heat or of cold, nor the stones and dirt beneath her. She was cocooned in her own world. Safe. Free.

She wasn't alone. Faces floated into her mind, people from the past and present, a procession of silent images.

The light seemed to be growing stronger again. Somewhere, just out of her line of vision, there was a juddering white beam of light, sending dancing shadows running up the walls and across the rocky roof of the cave. Like a kaleidoscope, the colors were shifting and changing shape before her eyes.

She thought she could see a man. Very old. She felt his cold, dry hands on her brow, skin as dry as tracing paper. His voice telling her it was going to be all right. That she was safe now.

Now Shelagh could hear other voices, whispering in her head, murmuring, speaking softly, caressing her.

She felt black wings at her shoulder, cradling her tenderly, like a child. Calling her home.

Then, spoiling it, another voice.

"Turn round."

Will realized the roaring was inside his head, the sound of his own blood pumping in his ears, thick and heavy. The sound of the bullets reverberating again and again in his memory.

He swallowed hard and tried to catch his breath. The pungent smell of the leather in his nose and mouth was too strong. It turned his stomach.

How many shots had he heard? Two? Three?

His two bodyguards got out. Will could hear them talking, arguing with François-Baptiste perhaps. Slowly, careful not to draw attention, he levered himself up a little on the backseat of the car. In the light of the headlights, he could see François-Baptiste standing over Authié's dead body, arm hanging by his side, the gun still in his hand. It looked as if someone had thrown a can of red paint over the door and bonnet of Authié's car. Blood, tissue and shards of bone. What remained of Authié's skull.

The nausea rose in his throat. Will swallowed again. Forced himself to keep looking. François-Baptiste started to bend down, hesitated, then quickly turned back instead.

Even though the repeated doses of the drug had left his arms and legs unresponsive, Will felt his body stiffen. He dropped back on the seat, grateful at least they hadn't put him back in the claustrophobic box in the boot of the car.

The door closest to his head was jerked open and Will felt the familiar callused hands on his arms and neck, dragging him across the seat and dropping him on to the ground.

The night air was cool on his face and bare legs. The robe they'd dressed him in was long and wide, although tied at the waist. Will felt self-conscious, vulnerable. And terrified.

He could see Authié's body lying motionless on the gravel. Next to it, tucked behind the front wheel of the car, he could see a tiny red light blinking on and off.

"*Portez-le jusqu'à la grotte.*" François-Baptiste's voice drew Will back. "*Vous nous attendez dehors. En face de l'ouverture.*" He paused. "*Il est dix-heures moins cinq maintenant. Nous allons rentrer dans quarante, peut-être cinquante minutes.*"

Nearly ten o'clock. He let his head hang as the man took hold beneath his arms. As they started to drag him up the slope toward the cave, he wondered if he'd still be alive at eleven.

.   .   .

"Turn round," Marie-Cécile repeated.

A harsh, arrogant voice, Audric thought. He stroked his hand once more across Shelagh's head, and then slowly he drew himself to his full height. His relief at finding her alive had been short-lived. She was in a very bad condition. Without medical help soon, Audric feared she would die.

"Leave the torch there," Marie-Cécile ordered him. "Come down here where I can see you."

Slowly, Audric turned round and stepped down from behind the altar.

She was holding an oil lamp in one hand, a pistol in the other. His first thought was how alike they were. The same green eyes, the black hair curling around the beautiful, austere face. With the gold headdress and necklace, the amulets circling her upper arms and her lean, tall body encased in the white robe, she looked like an Egyptian princess.

"You have come alone, Dame?"

"I hardly think it necessary to be accompanied everywhere I go, *Monsieur*, besides . . ."

He dropped his eyes to the gun. "You do not think I will trouble you," he nodded. "I am old, after all, *oc*?" Then he added: "But also you do not want anyone else to hear."

A suggestion of a smile crossed her lips. "Strength lies in secrecy."

"The man who taught you that is dead, Dame."

Pain sparked in her eyes. "You knew my grandfather?"

"I knew of him," he replied.

"He taught me well. Never confide in anyone. Never trust anyone."

"A lonely way to live, Dame."

"I do not find it so."

She had moved round, circling him like an animal stalking its prey, until she had her back to the altar and he was standing in the center of the chamber, near a dip in the ground.

The grave, he thought. The grave where the bodies were found.

"Where is she?" Marie-Cécile demanded.

He did not answer. "You are much like your grandfather. In character, your features, your persistence. Also, like him, you are misguided."

Anger flickered across her face. "My grandfather was a great man. He honored the Grail. He devoted his life to the quest to find the *Book of Words*, the better to understand."

"Understand, Dame? Or exploit?"

"You don't know anything about him."

"Ah, but I do," he said softly. "People do not change so very much." He hesitated. "And he was so close, was he not?" he continued, dropping his voice even further. "A few kilometers farther to the west and it would have been him who found the cave. Not you."

"It makes no difference now," she said fiercely. "It belongs to us."

"The Grail belongs to no one. It is not something that can be owned or manipulated or bargained with."

Audric stopped. In the light of the oil lamp burning on the altar he looked straight into her eyes.

"It would not have saved him," he said.

From across the chamber, he heard her draw breath.

"The elixir heals and extends life. It would have kept him alive."

"It would have done nothing to save him from the illness stripping the flesh from his bones, Dame, any more than it will give you what you desire." He paused. "The Grail will not come for you."

She took a step toward him. "You *hope* it will not, Baillard, but you're not sure. For all your knowledge, all your research, you do not know what will happen."

"You are mistaken."

"This is your chance, Baillard. After all your years of writing, studying, wondering. Like me, you have devoted your lifetime to this. You want to see this done as much as I do."

"And if I refuse to cooperate?"

She gave a sharp laugh. "Come now. You hardly need to ask. My son will kill her, you know that. How he does so—and how long it takes—is up to you."

Despite the precautions he'd taken, a shiver ran down his spine. Provided Alice stayed where she was, as she had promised, there was no need for alarm. She was safe. It would be over before she realized what was happening.

Memories of Alaïs—Bertrande too—rushed unbidden into his mind. Their impetuous nature, their reluctance to ever obey an order, their foolhardy courage.

Was Alice made of the same metal?

"Everything is ready," she said. "The *Book of Potions* and the *Book of Numbers* are here. So if you will just give me the ring and tell me where the *Book of Words* is concealed . . ."

Audric forced himself to concentrate on Marie-Cécile, not Alice.

"Why are you certain it is still in the chamber?"

She smiled. "Because *you* are here, Baillard. Why else would you come? You want to see the ceremony performed, just once before you die. You will put on the robe," she shouted, suddenly impatient. She gestured with the gun to the piece of white material sitting at the top of the steps. He shook his head and, for a fraction of a second, he saw doubt in her face. "Then you will get me the book."

He noticed that three small, metal rings had been sunk into the floor of the lower section of the chamber. And he remembered that it was Alice who discovered the skeletons in the shallow grave.

He smiled. Soon, he would have the answers he sought.

"Audric," Alice whispered, feeling her way down the tunnel.

Why doesn't he answer?

She felt the ground sloping down beneath her feet as before. It seemed farther this time.

Ahead, in the chamber, she could see a faint glow of yellow light.

"Audric," she called again, her fears growing.

She walked faster, covering the last few meters at a run, until she burst into the chamber and then stopped dead.

This cannot be happening.

Audric was standing at the foot of the steps. He was wearing a long white robe.

I remember this.

Alice shook the memory from her head. Audric's hands were tied in front of him and he was tethered to the ground, like an animal. On the far side of the chamber, lit by an oil lamp flickering on the altar, was Marie-Cécile de l'Oradore.

"That's far enough, I think," she said.

Audric turned, regret and sorrow in his eyes.

"I'm so sorry," she whispered, realizing she had ruined everything. "But I had to warn you . . ."

Before Alice had realized what was happening, someone had grabbed her from behind. She screamed and kicked out, but there were two of them.

It happened like this before.

Then someone called her name. Not Audric.

A wave of nausea swept over her and she started to fall.

"Catch her, you idiots," Marie-Cécile shouted.

CHAPTER 81

Pic de Soularac

MARÇ 1244

Guilhem couldn't catch Alaïs. She was already too far ahead.

He staggered down the tunnel in the dark. Pain pierced his side where his ribs were cracked, stopping him breathing easily. Alaïs' words reeling in his head and fear hardening in his chest kept him going.

The air seemed to be getting colder, chill, as if the life was being sucked out of the cave. He didn't understand. If this was a sacred place, the labyrinth cave, why did he feel in the presence of such malevolence?

Guilhem found himself standing on a natural stone platform. A couple of wide, shallow steps directly in front led down to an area where the ground was flat and smooth. A *calèlh* was burning on a stone altar, giving a little light.

The two sisters were standing facing each other, Oriane still holding the knife to Bertrande's throat. Alaïs was completely still.

Guilhem ducked down, praying Oriane had not seen him. As quietly as he could, he started to edge around the wall, hidden in the shadows, until he was close enough to hear and see what was happening.

Oriane tossed something down on the ground in front of Alaïs.

"Take it," she shouted. "Open the labyrinth. I know the *Book of Words* is concealed here."

Guilhem saw Alaïs' eyes widen in surprise. With shame, he recognized Oriane's supercilious expression.

"Did you never read the *Book of Numbers*? You astound me, sister. The explanation is there for the key."

Alaïs hesitated.

"The ring, with the *merel* inserted in it, unlocks the chamber within the heart of the labyrinth."

Oriane jerked Bertrande's head back, so the skin on her neck was pulled tight. The blade glinted in the light.

"Do it now, sister."

Bertrande cried out. The noise seemed to run right through Guilhem's head like a knife. He looked at Alaïs, frowning, her bad arm hanging uselessly at her side.

"Let her go first," she said.

Oriane shook her head. Her hair had come unbound and her eyes were wild, obsessive. Holding Alaïs' gaze, slowly, with deliberation, she made a small incision on Bertrande's neck.

Bertrande cried again as blood began to trickle down her neck.

"The next cut will be deeper," Oriane said, her voice shaking with hatred. "Get the book."

Alaïs bent down and picked up the ring, then walked to the labyrinth. Oriane followed, dragging Bertrande with her. Alaïs could hear her daughter's breath coming faster and faster and she was losing consciousness, staggering with her feet still tied.

For a moment, she stood, her thoughts spiraling back in time to the moment when first she had seen Harif perform the same task.

Alaïs pressed her left hand on the rough stone labyrinth. Pain shot up her damaged arm. She needed no candle to see the outline of the Egyptian symbol of life, the ankh, as Harif had taught her to call it. Then, shielding her actions from Oriane with her back, she inserted the ring into a small opening at the base of the central circle of the labyrinth, directly in front of her face. For Bertrande's sake, she prayed it would work. Nothing had been spoken; nothing had been prepared as it should have been. The circumstances could not be more different from the only other time she had stood as a supplicant before the labyrinth of stone.

"Di ankh djet," she murmured. The ancient words felt as ashes in her mouth. There was a sharp click, like a key in a lock. For a moment, nothing seemed to happen. Then, from deep in the wall, there was the noise of something shifting, stone against stone. Then Alaïs moved and, in the half-light, Guilhem saw that a compartment had been revealed at the very center of the labyrinth.

"Pass it to me," ordered Oriane. "Put it there, on the altar."

Alaïs did as she was told, never taking her eyes from her sister's face.

"Let her go now. You don't need her anymore."

"Open it," shouted Oriane. "I want to make sure you're not deceiving me."

Guilhem edged closer. Shimmering in gold on the first page was a symbol he had never seen before. An oval, more like a tear in shape, set atop a kind of cross, like a shepherd's crook.

"Keep going," said Oriane. "I want to see it all."

Alaïs' hands were shaking as she turned the pages. Guilhem could see a mixture of strange drawings and lines, row after row of tightly drawn symbols covering the entire sheet.

"Take it, Oriane," said Alaïs, struggling to keep her voice steady. "Take the book and give me back my daughter."

Guilhem saw the blade glint. He realized what was going to happen the instant before it did, that Oriane's jealousy and bitterness would lead her to destroy everything Alaïs loved or valued.

He threw himself at Oriane, knocking her sideways. He felt his cracked ribs give and he nearly passed out with the pain, but he'd done enough to force her to loosen her hold on Bertrande.

The knife dropped from her hand and skidded away out of sight, in the shadows behind the altar. Bertrande was thrown forward in the collision. She screamed, and banged her head on the corner of the altar. Then, she was still.

"Guilhem, take Bertrande," Alaïs screamed at him. "She's hurt, Sajhë's hurt. Help them. There's a man called Harif waiting in the village. He will help you."

Guilhem hesitated.

"Please, Guilhem. Save her!"

Her last words were lost as Oriane staggered to her feet, the knife in her hand, and launched herself at Alaïs. The blade sliced into her already damaged arm.

Guilhem felt as if his heart was being ripped in two. He didn't want to leave Alaïs to face Oriane alone, but he could see Bertrande lying white and still on the ground.

"Please, Guilhem. Go!"

With a last backward glance at Alaïs, he picked up their daughter in his wounded arms, and ran, trying not to see the blood pouring from the cut. He realized it was what Alaïs wanted him to do.

As he staggered clumsily across the chamber, Guilhem heard a rumbling sound, like thunder trapped in the hills. He stumbled, assumed it was his legs unable to hold him. He moved forward again, clearing the top of the steps and going back into the tunnel. He slipped on the loose stones, his legs and arms burning with pain. Then he realized the ground was moving, shaking. The earth beneath his feet was trembling.

His strength was almost gone. Bertrande was motionless in his arms and seemed heavier with every step he took. The noise was getting louder as he plunged on. Chunks of rock and dust began to fall from the roof, plummeting down around him.

Now he could feel the cold air coming to meet him. A few more steps and he had emerged into the gray dusk.

Guilhem ran to where Sajhë lay unconscious, but breathing steadily.

Bertrande was deathly white, but she was starting to whimper and stir in his arms. He laid her down on the ground beside Sajhë, then ran to each of the dead soldiers in turn and ripped their cloaks from their backs to make a covering. Then he tore his own cloak from his neck, sending his silver and copper buckle flying into the dirt. He folded it beneath Bertrande's head for a pillow.

He paused to kiss his daughter on the forehead.

"Filha," he murmured. It was the first, and the last, kiss he would ever give her.

There was an enormous crack from within the cave, like lightning after thunder. Guilhem ran back into the tunnel. The noise was overwhelming in the confined space.

He realized there was something hurtling out of the darkness toward him.

"A spirit . . . a face," Oriane was gibbering, her eyes crazed with fear. "A face in the center of the labyrinth."

"Where is she?" he shouted, grabbing her arm. "What have you done to Alaïs?"

Oriane was covered in blood, her hands, her clothes.

"Faces in the . . . the labyrinth."

Oriane screamed again. Guilhem spun round to see what was behind him, but could see nothing. In that moment, Oriane plunged the knife into his chest.

He knew she had dealt him a mortal blow. Instantly, he felt death taking possession of his limbs. He watched her running from him through clouds, his eyes darkening. He felt revenge die in him too. It no longer mattered.

Oriane ran out into the gray light of the passing day, while Guilhem stumbled blind down into the chamber, desperate to find Alaïs in the chaos of rock and stone and dust.

He found her lying in a small depression in the ground, her fingers wound round the bag that had held the *Book of Words,* the ring clutched in her hand.

"Mon còr," he whispered.

Her eyes flickered open at the sound of his voice. She smiled and Guilhem felt his heart turn over.

"Bertrande?"

"She's safe."

"Sajhë?"

"He will live too."

She caught her breath. "Oriane . . ."

"I let her go. She's badly hurt. She will not get far."

The final flame in the lamp, still burning on the altar, guttered and died. Alaïs and Guilhem did not notice as they lay in each other's arms. They were not aware of the darkness or the peace that descended over the chamber. They knew nothing but each other.

CHAPTER 82

Pic de Soularac

The thin robe provided little protection from the damp chill of the chamber. Alice shivered as she slowly turned her head.

To her right was the altar. The only light came from an old-fashioned oil lamp, standing in its center, sending shadows running up the sloping walls. It was enough to see the symbol of the labyrinth on the rock behind, large and imposing in the confined space.

She sensed there were other people nearby. Alice looked down to her right and nearly cried out loud as she caught her first sight of Shelagh. She was lying curled up on the stone floor like an animal, thin, lifeless, defeated, the evidence of her mistreatment on her skin. Alice couldn't see whether or not she was breathing.

Please God let her still be alive.

Alice slowly became accustomed to the flickering light. She turned her head slightly and saw Audric in the same place as before. He was still tethered by the rope to a ring set in the floor. His white hair formed a kind of halo around his head. He was as still as a statue carved on a tomb.

As if he could sense her eyes on him, he caught her eye, and smiled.

Forgetting for a moment that he must be angry with her for charging in when she'd promised to stay outside, she gave a weak smile.

Just like Shelagh said.

Then she realized something was different about him. She lowered her eyes to Audric's hands, fanned out against the white of the robe.

The ring is missing.

"Shelagh's here," she whispered under her breath. "You were right."

He nodded.

"We have to do something," she hissed.

He gave an almost imperceptible shake of his head and glanced to the far side of the chamber. She followed his gaze.

"Will!" she whispered in disbelief. Relief rushed through her, and something else, followed by pity for the state of him. His hair was matted with dried blood, one of his eyes was swollen and she could see cuts on his face, his hands.

But he's here. With me.

At the sound of her voice, Will opened his eyes. He peered into the darkness. Then, as he saw her, recognized her, a half-smile came to his battered lips.

For a moment, they stared at each other, holding each other's gaze.

My love. The realization gave her courage.

The mournful howl of the wind in the tunnel intensified, mixed now with the murmur of a voice. A monotonous chant, not quite singing. Alice couldn't work out where it was coming from. Fragments of oddly familiar words and phrases echoed through the cave until the air was saturated with the sound: *montanhas,* mountains; *Noblesa,* nobility; *libres,* books; *graal,* grail. Alice started to feel dizzy, intoxicated by the words that clamored like the bells of a cathedral in her head.

Just as she thought she could take no more, the chanting stopped. Quickly, quietly, the melody faded away, leaving nothing but a memory.

A single voice floated into the watchful silence. A woman's voice, clear and precise.

> *In the beginning of time,*
> *In the land of Egypt,*
> *The master of secrets,*
> *Gave words and scripts.*

Alice tore her eyes from Will's face and turned toward the sound. Marie-Cécile appeared from the shadows behind the altar like an apparition. As she stood before the labyrinth, her green eyes, painted with black and gold, sparkled like emeralds in the flickering lamp. Her hair, held back from her face by a golden band with a diamond motif on the forehead, shone like jet. Her elegant arms were bare, except for matching amulets of twisted metal.

She was carrying the three books, one on top of the other, in her hands. She placed them in a row on the altar, beside a plain earthenware bowl. As she reached out to adjust the position of the oil lamp on the altar, Alice registered, almost without realizing it, that Marie-Cécile was wearing Audric's ring on her left thumb.

It looks wrong on her hand.

Alice found herself immersed deep in a past she did not remember. The vellum should be dry and brittle to the touch, like dying leaves on the tree in autumn. But she could almost feel the leather ties between her own fingers, soft and flexible, even though they ought to be stiff through the long years of disuse, as if the memory was written in her bones and blood.

She remembered how the covers shimmered, shifted color under the light.

She could see the image of a tiny gold chalice, no bigger than a ten-pence piece, shining like a jewel on the heavy cream parchment. On the following pages, lines of ornate script. She heard Marie-Cécile speaking into the gloom and, at the same time, behind her eyes she saw the red and blue and yellow and gold letters. The *Book of Potions*.

Images of two-dimensional figures, animals and birds flooded into her head. She could picture a sheet of parchment, thicker than the other pages but different—translucent, yellow. It was papyrus, the weave of the leaves apparent. It was covered with identical symbols as at the beginning of the book, except this time tiny drawings of plants, numbers and measurements were interspersed between them.

She was thinking of the second book now, the *Book of Numbers*. On the first page was a picture of the labyrinth itself, rather than a chalice. Without realizing she was doing so, Alice looked around the chamber once more, this time seeing the space through different eyes, unconsciously verifying its shape and proportions.

She looked back to the altar. Her memory of the third book was the strongest. Shimmering in gold on the first page was the ankh, the ancient Egyptian symbol of life, familiar now the world over. Between the leather-covered wooden boards of the *Book of Words* were blank pages, like a white guard surrounding the papyrus buried in the center of the book. The hieroglyphs were dense and unyielding. Row after row of tightly drawn symbols covered the entire sheet. There were no splashes of color, no indication of where one word ended and the next began.

Concealed within this, was the incantation.

Alice opened her eyes and sensed Audric looking at her.

A look of understanding flashed between them. The words were coming back to her, slipping quietly from the dusty corners of her mind. She was momentarily transported out of herself, for a fraction of a second, looking down on the scene from above.

Eight hundred years ago Alaïs had said these words. And Audric had heard them.

The truth will make us free.

Nothing had changed, yet she was suddenly no longer afraid.

A sound from the altar drew her attention. The stillness passed and the world of the present came rushing back. And, with it, fear.

Marie-Cécile took up the earthenware bowl, small enough to cup between her hands. From beside it she took a small knife with a dull worn blade. She raised her long, white arms above her head.

"Dintrar," she called. Enter.

François-Baptiste stepped from the darkness of the tunnel. His eyes swept around his surroundings like a searchlight, skimming over Audric, then Alice, then coming to rest on Will. Alice saw the triumph on the boy's face and knew that François-Baptiste had inflicted the injuries on Will.

I'll not let you hurt him this time.

Then his gaze moved on. He paused a moment at the sight of the three books laid out in a row on the altar, surprised or relieved, Alice couldn't tell, then his eyes came to rest on the face of his mother.

Despite the distance, Alice could feel the tension between them.

A flicker of a smile played across Marie-Cécile's face as she stepped down from the altar, the knife and the bowl in her hands. Her robe shimmered like spun moonshine in the flickering light of the candles as she moved through the chamber. Alice could smell the subtle trace of her perfume in the air, light beneath the heavy aroma of burning oil in the lamp.

François-Baptiste too started to move. He came down the steps until he was standing behind Will.

Marie-Cécile stopped in front of him and whispered something to Will, too quiet for Alice to hear. Although François-Baptiste's smile stayed in place, she saw the anger in his face as he leaned forward, lifted Will's bound hands and offered his arm to Marie-Cécile.

Alice flinched as Marie-Cécile made a single incision between Will's wrist and elbow. He winced and she could see the shock in his eyes, but he made no sound.

Marie-Cécile held the bowl to catch five drops of blood.

She repeated the process with Audric, then came to a halt in front of Alice. She could see the excitement in Marie-Cécile's face as she traced the point of the blade along the white underside of Alice's arm, along the line of the old wound. Then with the precision of a surgeon with a scalpel, she inserted the knife into the skin and pressed the tip down, slowly, until her scar split open again.

The pain took her by surprise, an ache, not a sharp sensation. Alice felt warm at first, then quickly cold and numb. She stared mesmerized by the drops of blood falling, one by one, into the oddly pale mixture in the bowl.

Then it was over. François-Baptiste released her and followed his mother toward the altar. Marie-Cécile repeated the procedure with her son, then positioned herself between the altar and the labyrinth.

She placed the bowl in the center and drew the knife across her own skin, watching as her own blood trickled down her arm.

The mingling of bloods.

A flash of understanding went through Alice. The Grail belonged to all faiths and none. Christian, Jew, Muslim. Five guardians, chosen for their character, their deeds, not their bloodline. All were equal.

Alice watched Marie-Cécile reach forward and slip something out from between the pages of each of the books in turn. She held up the third one. A sheet of paper. No, not paper, papyrus. As Marie-Cécile held it up to the light, the weave of the reeds was clear. The symbol was clear.

The ankh, the symbol of life.

Marie-Cécile lifted the bowl to her lips and drank. When it was empty, she replaced the bowl with both hands and looked out over the chamber until she had fixed Audric with her gaze. It seemed to Alice she was challenging him to make her stop.

Now she pulled the ring from her thumb and turned to the stone labyrinth, disturbing the hushed air. As the lamplight flickered behind her, sending shadows leaping up the walls, Alice saw, in the shadows in the carved rock, two shapes that she had never before noticed.

Hidden within the outline of the labyrinth, the shadow of the shape of the ankh and the outline of a cup were clearly identifiable.

Alice heard a sharp click, as if a key was being inserted into a lock. For a moment, nothing seemed to happen. Then, from deep in the wall, there was the noise of something shifting, stone against stone.

Marie-Cécile stepped back. Alice saw that a small opening a little bigger than the books had been revealed at the center of the labyrinth. A compartment.

Words and phrases sprang into her mind, Audric's explanation and her own investigations all mixed up together.

At the center of the labyrinth is enlightenment, at the center lies understanding. Alice thought about the Christian pilgrims walking the *Chemin de Jérusalem* in the nave of Chartres Cathedral, walking the ever-decreasing spirals of the labyrinth in search of illumination.

Here, in the Grail labyrinth, the light—literally—was at the heart of things.

Alice watched as Marie-Cécile took the lantern from the altar and hung it in the alcove. It was a perfect fit. Straightaway it brightened and the chamber was flooded with light.

Marie-Cécile lifted a papyrus from one of the books on the altar and slid it into a slot at the front of the alcove. A little of the lamplight was lost and the cave darkened.

She spun round and stared at Audric, her words breaking the spell.

"You said I would see something," she shouted.

He raised his amber eyes to hers. Alice willed him to remain silent, but she knew he would not. For reasons she did not understand, Audric was determined to let the ceremony run its course.

"The true incantation is revealed only when the three papyri are laid one on top of the other. Only then, in the play of light and shadow, will the words that must be spoken, rather than the words that must be silent, be revealed."

Alice was shivering. She understood the cold was inside her, as if her body warmth was bleeding out of her, but she couldn't control herself. Marie-Cécile turned the three parchments around in her fingers.

"Which way round?"

"Release me," Audric said in his calm, quiet voice. "Release me, then take up your position in the center of the chamber. I will show you."

She hesitated, then nodded to François-Baptiste.

"Maman, je ne pense—"

"Do what you're told," she snapped.

In silence, François-Baptiste sliced through the rope holding Audric to the floor, then stepped back.

Marie-Cécile reached behind her and picked up the knife.

"If you do anything," Marie-Cécile said, pointing it at Alice, as Audric walked slowly up the chamber, "I'll kill her. Understand?" She gestured to where François-Baptiste was standing by Will. "Or he will."

"I understand."

He darted a glance at Shelagh lying motionless on the floor, then whispered to Alice. "I am right?" he whispered, suddenly doubtful. "The Grail will not come to her?"

Although Audric was looking at her, Alice felt he was asking his question of somebody else. Someone with whom he had already shared this experience.

Despite herself, Alice found she knew the answer. She was certain. She smiled, giving him the reassurance he needed.

"It will not come," she said under her breath.

"What are you waiting for?" Marie-Cécile shouted.

Audric stepped forward.

"You must take each of the three papyri," he said, "then place them in front of the flame."

"You do it."

Alice watched him take the three translucent sheets and arrange them in his hands, then carefully insert the papyri. For a moment the flame burning in the alcove guttered and seemed to fade. The cave became very dark, as if the lights had been dimmed.

Then, as her eyes adjusted to the increased gloom, Alice saw that now only a handful of hieroglyphs remained, illuminated in a pattern of light and dark that followed the lines of the labyrinth. All unnecessary words had been veiled. *"Di ankh djet . . ."* The words were clear in her mind. *"Di ankh djet,"* she said out loud, then the rest of the phrase, translating in her mind the ancient words she spoke.

"In the beginning of time, in the land of Egypt, the master of secrets, gave words and scripts. Gave life."

Marie-Cécile turned on Alice.

"You read the words," she said, striding toward her and grabbing her arm. "How do you know what they mean?"

"I don't. I don't know."

Alice tried to pull away, but Marie-Cécile jerked her forward toward the point of the knife, so close that Alice could see the brown stains on the worn blade. Her eyes closed and she repeated the phrase.

"Di ankh djet . . ."

Everything seemed to happen at once.

Audric launched himself at Marie-Cécile.

"Maman!"

Will took advantage of François-Baptiste's lapse in concentration. He pulled his leg back and kicked him in the small of the back. Taken by surprise, the boy fired his pistol into the roof of the cave as he fell, deafeningly loud in the confined space. Instantaneously, Alice heard the bullet smash into the solid rock of the mountain and ricochet across the space.

Marie-Cécile's hand flew to her temple. Alice saw the blood pouring between her fingers. She swayed on her feet a moment, then collapsed.

"Maman!" François-Baptiste was already on his feet and running. The gun skidded away across the ground toward the altar.

Audric snatched up Marie-Cecile's knife and cut through Will's bonds with surprising strength, then placed the knife in his hand.

"Release Alice."

Ignoring him, Will dashed across the chamber to where François-Baptiste was on his knees cradling Marie-Cécile in his arms.

"Non, maman. Ne t'en vas pas. Ecoute-moi, maman, réveille-toi."

Will took hold of the shoulders of the boy's oversized jacket and slammed his head down on to the rough stone floor. Then he ran to Alice and started to hack at the rope binding her.

"Is she dead?"

"I don't know."

"What about—"

He kissed her, quickly, on the lips, and then shook her hands free of the rope.

"François-Baptiste will be out long enough for us to get the hell out," he said.

"Get Shelagh, Will," she said, pointing urgently. "I'll help Audric."

Will lifted Shelagh's depleted frame in his arms and started to walk toward the tunnel. Alice ran to Audric.

"The books," she said urgently. "We've got to take them before they come round."

He was standing looking down on the inert bodies of Marie-Cécile and her son.

"Audric, quick," Alice repeated. "We have to get out of here."

"I was wrong to involve you in this," he said softly. "My desire to know, to fulfill a promise I once made and failed to keep, has left me blind to other considerations. Selfish. I thought too much of myself."

Audric put his hand on one of the books.

"You asked why she did not destroy it," he said suddenly. "The answer is, I wouldn't let her. So we devised a plan to deceive Oriane. Because of that, we came back to the chamber. The cycle of dying, of sacrifice, continued. If had not been for that, then perhaps . . ."

He walked round to where Alice was trying to get the papyri from the lamp. "She would not have wanted this. Too many lives lost."

"Audric," she said desperately, "we can talk about this later. Now, we must get them out. This is what you have been waiting for, Audric. The chance to see the Trilogy reunited again. We can't leave them for her."

"I still don't know," he said, his voice dropping to a whisper. "What happened to her at the end."

The oil in the lamp was nearly out, but the gloom was lifted little by little as Alice pulled out the first, then the second, then finally the last of the papyri.

"I have them," she said, spinning round. She scooped up the books from the altar and thrust them at Audric.

"Bring the books. Come on."

Almost dragging Audric with her, Alice picked their way across the gloom of the chamber toward the tunnel. They had stumbled over the dip in the ground where the skeletons had been found, when, from the darkness behind them, there was a loud crack, then the sound of rock shifting, then another two muffled bangs, in quick succession.

Alice threw herself to the ground. It wasn't the sound of the gun again, but a different sort of noise altogether. A rumbling from deep within the earth.

Adrenaline kicked in. Desperately, she crawled forward, holding the papyri in her teeth and praying that Audric was behind her. The material of the robe caught between her legs, slowing her down. Her arm was bleeding profusely and she couldn't put any weight on it, but she managed to get to the bottom of the steps.

Alice was aware of a rumbling sound now, but she couldn't afford to turn round. Her fingers had just found the letters carved at the top, when a voice rang out.

"Stop right there. Or I will shoot him."

Alice froze.

It cannot be her. She was shot. I saw her fall.

"Turn round. Slowly."

Slowly, Alice pulled herself to her feet. Marie-Cécile was standing in front of the altar, unsteady on her feet. Her robe was splattered with blood and her headdress had come off, leaving her hair wild and untamed around her face. In her hand she had François-Baptiste's gun. It was pointed straight at Audric.

"Walk slowly back toward me, Dr. Tanner."

Alice realized that the ground was shifting. She felt the tremor vibrating up through her feet and legs, a low rumbling deep in the ground, getting stronger and more insistent every second.

Marie-Cécile suddenly seemed to hear it too. Confusion momentarily clouded her face. Another thump shook the chamber. This time there was no doubt it was an explosion. A blast of cold air swept through the cave. Behind Marie-Cécile, the lantern started to shake as the stone labyrinth cracked open and started to fragment.

Alice ran back to Audric. The ground was fracturing in two, crumbling beneath her as solid stone and ages-old earth started to split apart. Debris rained down on her from every corner as she jumped to avoid the holes that were opening up all around.

"Give them to me!" Marie-Cécile shouted, turning the gun toward Alice. "Do you really think I'm going to let her take these from me?"

Her words were swallowed by the sounds of falling rock and stone as the chamber collapsed in on itself.

Audric got to his feet and spoke for the first time.

"Her?" he said. "No, not Alice."

Marie-Cécile spun round to see what Audric was looking at.

She screamed.

In the darkness Alice could see something. A glow, a white glow, almost like a face. In terror, Marie-Cécile swung the gun back to Alice. She hesitated, then pulled the trigger. Long enough for Audric to move between them.

Everything seemed to be moving in slow motion.

Alice screamed. Audric sank to his knees. The force of the shot propelled Marie-Cécile backwards and she lost her balance. Her fingers clawed at the air, grasping, desperate, as she slipped into the vast chasm that had opened up in the ground.

Audric was lying on the ground, blood spreading out from the bullet hole in the middle of his chest. His face was the color of paper and she could see the blue veins beneath the thin veneer of skin.

"We've got to get out of here," she cried. "There might be another explosion. It could come down at any moment."

He smiled. "It is over, Alice," he said softly. "*A la perfin*. The Grail has protected its secrets, as it did before. It would not let her take what she wanted."

Alice was shaking her head. "No, the cave was mined, Audric," she said. "There might be another bomb. We have to get out."

"There will be no more," he said. There was no doubt in his voice. "It was the echo of the past."

Alice could see it hurt him to speak. She lowered her head to his. There was a gentle rattling in his chest and his breathing was shallow and faint. She tried to stanch the bleeding, but she could see it was hopeless.

"I wanted to know how she spent her final moments. You understand? I couldn't save her. She was trapped inside and I couldn't get to her." He gasped in pain. Took another gulp of air.

"But this time . . ."

Finally, Alice accepted what she had instinctively known from the moment she had walked into Los Seres and seen him standing in the doorway of the little stone house in the folds of the mountain.

This is his story. These are his memories.

She thought of the family tree, so lovingly and painstakingly compiled. "Sajhë," she said.

For a moment, life flicked in his amber eyes. A look of intense pleasure flooded his dying face.

"When I woke, Bertrande was beside me. Someone had covered us with cloaks to keep the cold out—"

"Guilhem," said Alice, knowing it was true.

"There was a terrible thundering. I saw the stone ledge above the entrance collapse. The boulder was sent crashing to the ground in a welter of stone and flint and dirt, trapping her inside. I couldn't get to her," he said, his voice trembling. "To them."

Then it stopped. Everything was suddenly quiet, still.

"I didn't know," he said again in anguish. "I had given my word to Alaïs if anything happened to her I would ensure the *Book of Words* was safe, but I didn't know. I didn't know if Oriane had the book or where she was." His voice faded to a whisper. "Nothing."

"So the bodies I found were Guilhem and Alaïs," she said, a statement, not a question.

Sajhë nodded. "We found Oriane's body a little way down the hillside. The book was not with her. Only then did I know."

"They died together saving the book. Alaïs wanted you to live, Sajhë. To live and care for Bertrande, your daughter in every way but one."

He smiled. "I knew you would understand," he said. The words slipped

481

from between his lips like a sigh. "I have lived too long without her. Every day I felt her absence. Every day I wished I had not been cursed, to be forced to live my life, while all those whom I love grow old and die. Alaïs, Bertrande . . ."

He broke off. Her heart ached for him.

"You must not feel guilty any longer, Sajhë. Now you know what happened, you must forgive yourself."

Alice could feel him slipping from her.

Keep him talking. Don't let him go to sleep.

"There was a prophecy," he said, "that in the lands of the Pays d'Oc, in our times, one would be born whose destiny was to bear witness to the tragedy that overtook these lands. Like those before me—like Abraham, Methuselah, Harif—I did not wish it. But I accepted it."

Sajhë gasped for breath. Alice drew him closer, cradling his head in her arms. "When?" she tried to say. "Tell me."

"Alaïs summoned the Grail. Here. In this very chamber. I was twenty-five years old. I had returned to Los Seres, believing my life was about to change. I believed I could woo Alaïs and be loved by her."

"She did love you," Alice said fiercely.

"Harif taught her to understand the ancient language of the Egyptians," he continued, smiling. "It seems that some trace of that knowledge lives yet in you. Using the skills Harif had taught her and from her knowledge of the parchments, we came here. Like you, when the time came, Alaïs knew what to say. The Grail worked through her."

"How . . ." Alice stumbled. "What happened?"

"I remember the smooth touch of the air on my skin, the flicker of the candles, the beautiful voices spiraling in the dark. The words seemed to flow from her lips, hardly spoken. Alaïs stood before the altar, Harif with her."

"There must have been others."

"There were, but . . . you will think it strange, but I can hardly remember. All I could see was Alaïs. Her face, rapt in concentration, a slight line between her eyes where she frowned. Her hair flowed down her back like a sheet of water. I saw nothing but her, was aware of nothing but her. She held the cup in her hands and spoke the words. Her eyes flew open in a single moment of illumination. She gave the cup to me and I drank."

His eyelids were fluttering open and shut rapidly, like the beating of a butterfly's wings.

"If your life was such a burden to you, why did you carry on without her?"

"*Perqué?*" he said with surprise. "Why? Because it was what Alaïs wanted. I had to live to tell the story of what happened to the people of these lands, here within these mountains and the plains. To make sure that their story did not die. That is the purpose of the Grail. To help those chosen to bear witness. History is written by the victorious, the liars, the strongest, the most determined. Truth is found most often in the silence, in the quiet places."

Alice nodded. "You did this, Sajhë. You made a difference."

"Guilhem de Tudèla wrote a false record of the Crusade against us for the French. *La Chanson de la Croisade,* he called it. When he died, an anonymous poet, one who was sympathetic to the Pays d'Oc instead, completed it. *La Canso.* Our story."

Despite everything, Alice found herself smiling.

"Los mots, vivents," he whispered. Living words. "It was the beginning. I vowed to Alaïs I would speak the truth, write the truth, so that future generations would know of the horror that once was done in the lands in their name. That they were remembered."

Alice nodded.

"Harif understood. He had walked the lonely path before me. He had traveled the world and seen how words were twisted and broken and turned into lies. He too lived to bear witness." Sajhë drew in his breath. "He lived for only a short time after Alaïs, although he was more than eight hundred years old when he died. Here, in Los Seres, with Bertrande and me at his side."

"But where have you lived, all these years? *How* have you lived?"

"I watched the green of spring give way to the gold of summer, the copper of autumn give way to the white of winter as I have sat and waited for the fading of the light. Over and over again I have asked myself why? If I had known how it would feel to live with such loneliness, to stand, the sole witness to the endless cycle of birth and life and death, what would I have done? I have survived this long life with emptiness in my heart, an emptiness that over the years has spread and spread until it became bigger than my heart itself."

"She loved you, Sajhë," she said, softly. "Not in the way you loved her, but truly and deeply."

A look of peace had come over his face. *"Es vertat.* Now I know it."

"If . . ."

Another flurry of coughing overtook him. This time, specks of blood bubbled at the corner of his mouth. Alice wiped them away with the hem of her robe.

He struggled to sit. "I have written it all down for you, Alice. My last testament. It is waiting for you in Los Seres. In Alaïs' house, where we lived, which now I pass to you."

In the distance, Alice thought she heard the sound of sirens piercing the still night of the mountain.

"They're nearly here," she said, keeping her grief in check. "I said they'd come. Stay with me. Please don't give up."

Sajhë shook his head. "It is done. My journey is ended. Yours is just beginning."

Alice smoothed his white hair away from his face.

"I am not her," she said softly. "I am not Alaïs."

He gave a long, soft sigh. "I know. But she lives on in you . . . and you in her." He stopped. Alice could see how much it hurt him to talk. "I wish we could have had longer, Alice. But to have met you, to have shared these hours with you. It is more than ever I hoped."

Sajhë fell silent. The last vestiges of color drained from his face, from his hands, until there was nothing left.

A prayer, one spoken a long time ago, came to her mind.

"Payre sant, Dieu dreyturier de bons esperits." The once familiar words fell easily from her lips. "Holy Father, legitimate God of good spirits, grant us to know what Thou knowest, and to love what Thou lovest."

Biting back her tears, Alice held him in her arms while his breathing became lighter, softer. Finally, it stopped altogether.

Los Seres

It is eight o'clock in the evening. The end of another perfect summer's day.

Alice walks over to the wide, casement window and opens the shutters to let in the slanting orange light. A slight breeze skims her bare arms. Her skin is the color of hazelnuts and her hair is tied in a single plait down her back.

The sun is low now, a perfect red circle in the pink and white sky. It casts huge black shadows across the neighboring peaks of the Sabarthès Mountains, like swathes of material laid out to dry. From the window she can see the Col des Sept Frères and behind it the Pic de St. Bartélémy.

It is two years to the day that Sajhë died.

At first, Alice found it hard to live with the memories. The sound of the gun in the claustrophobic chamber; the trembling of the earth; the white face in the darkness; the look on Will's face as he burst into the chamber with Inspector Noubel.

Most of all, she was haunted by the memory of the light fading in Audric's eyes—Sajhë, as she learned to think of him. It was peace she saw in them at the end, not sorrow, but it has not made her pain any the less.

The more Alice learned, the more the terrors that held her locked in those final moments began to fade. The past lost its power to hurt her.

She knows Marie-Cécile and her son were killed by the falling rock, both lost to the mountain itself in the earthquake. Paul Authié was found where François-Baptiste had shot him, the timer detonating the four charges ticking relentlessly down to zero beside his dead body. An Armageddon of his own making.

As that summer turned into autumn, autumn to winter, Alice began to recover, with Will's help. Time is doing its work. Time and the promise of a new life. Gradually, the painful memories are fading. Like old photographs, half remembered and indistinct, they gather dust in her mind.

Alice sold her flat in England and together with the proceeds from the sale of her aunt's house in Sallèles d'Aude, she and Will came to Los Seres.

The house where Alaïs once lived with Sajhë, Bertrande and Harif is now their home. They have added to it, made it suitable for modern living, but the spirit of the place is unaltered.

The secret of the Grail is safe, as Alaïs had intended it should be, hidden here in the timeless mountains. The three papyri, torn from their medieval books, lie buried under the rock and stone.

Alice understands that she was destined to finish what had been left unfinished eight hundred years before. She also understands, as Alaïs did, that the real Grail lies in the love handed down from generation to generation, the words spoken by father to son, mother to daughter. The truth lies all about us. In the stones, in the rocks, in the changing pattern of the mountain seasons.

Through the shared stories of our past, we do not die.

Alice does not believe she can put it into words. Unlike Sajhë, she is not a spinner of tales, a writer. She wonders if perhaps it is beyond words. Call it God, call it faith. Perhaps the Grail is too great a truth to be spoken or tied down in time and space and context by so slippery a thing as language.

Alice puts her hands on the ledge and breathes in the subtle smells of evening. Wild thyme, broom, the shimmering memory of heat on the stones, mountain parsley and mint, sage, the scents of her herb garden.

Her reputation is growing. What started as a sequence of private favors, supplying herbs to the restaurants and neighbors in the villages, has become a profitable business. Now, most of the hotels and shops in the area, even as far away as Foix and Mirepoix, carry a range of their products, with the distinctive *Epices Pelletier et Fille* label. The name of her ancestors, reclaimed now as her own.

The *hameau*, Los Seres, is not yet on the map. It is too small. But soon it will be. *Benlèu*.

In the study below, the keyboard has fallen silent. Alice can hear Will moving about in the kitchen, getting plates from the dresser and bread from the pantry. Soon, she will go down. He will open a bottle of wine and she will drink while he cooks.

Tomorrow, Jeanne Giraud will come, a dignified, charming woman who has become part of their lives. In the afternoon, they will go to the nearest village and lay flowers at a monument in the square that commemorates the celebrated Cathar historian and Resistance fighter, Audric S. Baillard. On the plaque, there is an Occitan proverb, chosen by Alice.

"Pas a pas se va luènh."

Later, Alice will walk alone into the mountains where a different plaque marks the spot where he lies beneath the hills, as he always wanted. The stone simply reads SAJHË.

It is enough that he is remembered.

The Family Tree, Sajhë's first gift to Alice, hangs on the wall in the study. Alice has made three changes. She has added the date of Alaïs' and Sajhë's deaths, separated by eight hundred years.

She added Will's name to hers and the date of their marriage.

At the very end, where the story is continuing still, she's added a line: SAJHËSSE GRACE FARMER PELLETIER, b. 28 February 2007.

Alice smiles and walks over to the cot where their daughter is stirring. Her pale, sleepy toes twitch as she starts to wake. Alice catches her breath as her daughter opens her eyes.

She plants a murmuring kiss on the top of her daughter's head and begins a lullaby in the old language, handed down from generation to generation.

> *Bona nuèit, bona nuèit . . .*
> *Braves amics, pica mièja-nuèit*
> *Cal finir velhada*
> *E jos la flassada*

One day, Alice thinks, Sajhësse might sing it to a child of her own.

Holding her daughter in her arms, Alice walks back to the window, thinking of all the things she will teach her. The stories she will tell her of the past and of how things came to be.

Alaïs no longer comes to her in her dreams. But as Alice stands in the fading light looking out over the ancient peaks and crests of the mountains and valleys that stretch farther than her eye can see, she feels the presence of the past all around her, embracing her. Spirits, friends, ghosts who hold out their hands and whisper of their lives, share their secrets with her. They connect her to all those who have stood here before—and all those yet to come—dreaming of what life might hold.

In the distance, a white moon is rising in the speckled sky, promising another fine day tomorrow.

NOTE ON LANGUAGE

In the medieval period, the *langue d'Oc*—from which the region of Languedoc takes its name—was the language of the Midi from Provence to Aquitaine. It was also the language of Christian Jerusalem and the lands occupied by the Crusaders from 1099, and spoken in some parts of northern Spain and northern Italy. It is closely related to Provençal and Catalan.

In the thirteenth century, the *langue d'oil*—the forerunner of modern-day French—was spoken in the northern parts of what is now France.

During the course of the invasions of the south by the north, which began in 1209, the French barons imposed their language on the region they conquered. From the middle of the twentieth century, there has been an Occitan language revival, led by authors, poets and historians such as René Nelli, Jean Duvernoy, Déodat Roché, Michel Roquebert, Anne Brenon, Claude Marti and others. At the time of this writing, there is a bilingual Oc/French school in La Cité in the heart of the medieval citadel of Carcassonne and the Occitan spellings of towns and regions appear alongside the French spellings on road signs.

In *Labyrinth,* to distinguish between the inhabitants of the Pays d'Oc and the French invaders, I have used Occitan or French accordingly. As a result, certain names and places appear in both French and Oc—for example, Carcassonne and Carcassona, Toulouse and Tolosa, Béziers and Besièrs.

Extracts of poetry and sayings are taken from *Proverbs & Dictons de la langue d'Oc* collected by Abbé Pierre Trinquier and from *33 Chants Populaires du Languedoc.*

Inevitably there are differences between medieval Occitan spellings and contemporary usage. For the sake of consistency, I have for the most part used *La Planqueta* by André Lagarde—an Occitan-French dictionary—as my guide.

SELECTED GLOSSARY OF OCCITAN WORDS

Agost August
ambans wooden galleries built for defense around battlements
ben good
benvenguda welcome
bonjorn hello
cadefalcs brattices
calèche an open carriage
calèlh oil lamp
coratge courage
defòra outside
deman tomorrow
dintrar enter
doçament softly
faitilhièr a witch
faratjals pastures
filha daughter
gata a cat (type of siege engine)
graal grail
Janvièr January
Julhet July
libres books
Lo Ciutat the Cité
Lo Miègjorn the Midi
Març March
menina grandmother
meravelhós miraculous
mercé thank you
molin blatier a wheat mill
montanhas mountains
Na Madame/Mrs.
nenon baby
noblessa nobility
oc yes
oustâou home

paire father
pan de blat wheat bread
panièr basket
Payre Sant Holy Father
payrola cauldron
pec idiot
perfin at last
perilhòs danger
res nothing
sénher sir
sirjan d'arms sergeant at arms
sòrre sister
trouvère troubadour
vuèg empty

SELECTED GLOSSARY OF TERMS

Guignolet a Languedocien homebrewed alcoholic aperitif
Mangomel, cat, trebuchet, catapult all forms of medieval siege engines
Michelmas Christmas
Passiontide Easter
Prime the first religious office of the day (about dawn/five o'clock in the
    morning)
Rocade the ring road in Toulouse
Tierce mid-afternoon
Toussaint All Saints' Day, 1 November
Vesprè final religious office of the day (about seven o'clock)

SELECTED BIBLIOGRAPHY

A History of the Crusades—S. Runciman
Bélibaste—Henri Gougaud
Carcassonne in My Heart—Claude Marti
Cathars—Yves Rouquette
Chòlera—Joseph Delteil
Crusader: By Horse to Jerusalem—Tim Severin
Eleanor of Aquitaine—Alison Weir
La Canso: 1209–1219 Les Croisades Contre le Sud—edited by Claude Marti
La Religion Cathare—Michel Roquebert
La Religion des Cathares—Jean Duvernoy
La Vie Quotidienne des Cathares au XIIIe Siècle—René Nelli
La Vrai Visage du Catharisme—Anne Brenon
Les Cathares—Georges Serrus
Les Cathares—René Nelli
Les Femmes Cathares—Anne Brenon
Massacre at Montségur—Zoe Oldenburg
Montaillou: Cathars and Catholics in a French Village—Emmanuel Le Roy Ladurie
Parzival—Wolfram von Eschenbach
The Albigensian Crusade—Jonathan Sumption
The Crusades 1095–1197—J. P. Phillips
The Fourth Crusade—J. P. Phillips
The Gospel of John—Claus Westermann, translated by Siegfried S. Schatzmann
The Keys of Egypt: The Race to Read the Hieroglyphs—Lesley and Roy Adkins
The Story of the Grail (Perceval)—Chrétien de Troyes
The Yellow Cross: The Story of the Last Cathars 1290–1329—René Weis

For a comprehensive list of titles and source material—or to add your own recommended reading—please visit *www.mosselabyrinth.co.uk*